Captain Cobbler

Captain Cobbler:
The Lincolnshire Uprising
1536

by

Keith M. Melton

iUniverse LLC
Bloomington

CAPTAIN COBBLER
THE LINCOLNSHIRE UPRISING, 1536

iUniverse books may be ordered through booksellers or by contacting:

iUniverse
1663 Liberty Drive
Bloomington, IN 47403
www.iuniverse.com
1-800-Authors (1-800-288-4677)

ISBN: 978-1-4759-9778-1 (sc)
ISBN: 978-1-4759-9779-8 (hc)
ISBN: 978-1-4759-9780-4 (e)

Library of Congress Control Number: 2013912945

Printed in the United States of America.

iUniverse rev. date: 8/14/2013

For Tricia and Fatima:

"...without Tricia I would not have started; without Fatima I would not have finished..."

Keith Melton, 2013

I love and shall until I die...

...Henry VIII, 'Pastime with Good Company' 1509

Acknowledgements

I have read a great deal about the Tudor period and medieval times altogether to try and get the lifestyle as clear as possible and the facts of the uprising and their context as accurate as possible, so I am generally indebted to historians of the period for their researches.

In particular my 'guiding light' as far as the happenings in Lincolnshire are concerned was the pamphlet researched and written by the late Anne Ward, who named names and reported what they said in 1536 by delving into the transcriptions of the investigating 'commission' Henry VIII set up. The pamphlet was called "The Lincolnshire Rising 1536" and it was an invaluable source.

Other useful works included Alison Weir's book about Henry's wives "The Six Wives of Henry VIII", "The Pilgrimage of Grace" by Geoffrey Moorhouse and "The Pilgrimage of Grace" by Richard Hoyle. For what happened at the Battle of Bosworth Field I owe a debt to Michael D Miller and his Wars of the Roses site on the internet. Also a general thank you to Wikipedia for background on various of the characters involved.

Many thanks to Tricia Taylor for her painstaking editorial assistance; any remaining grammatical or typographical errors are mine!

Many thanks too to Fernanda Lima Sant Anna da Motta for the design of my book covers, both hardback and softback.

Finally, 'thank you' to the team at iUniverse, who have been very helpful all along the road to publication.

Keith Melton

June 2013

Contents

Dramatis Personae
In Groups

For much of the information about the key local players in the uprising I am indebted to the details in the booklet about "The Lincolnshire Rising 1536" written by **Anne Ward**, whose well researched work, published by the Workers Educational Association, East Midlands District, contains a detailed description of the events of that fateful week, precursor to the much better known Pilgrimage of Grace, which followed when the events in Lincolnshire had been brought to an abrupt end.

The booklet was published in 1986; Anne Ward died, before her time, only a couple of years later in July 1988. I have marked, with an asterisk * all the characters where the primary source was Anne Ward's publication. For the information on Elizabeth Blount, Sir Richard Rich, and on many other real life characters, **Wikipedia** has been a very useful source of information. Details of the lives of other major characters were also drawn from publications named in the acknowledgements.

I have listed the characters in appropriate groups, in alphabetical order using *first names or titles* to sort. So **Lord** Kingston will come before **Thomas** Cromwell for example. A very small number of the characters have been placed in more than one group to help make it easier to find them.

I have marked fictional characters with **(F)** and where I have used my family tree to devise names for them they are marked **(F – fam)**. Mostly, such names will be created from a Christian name of one member of the family tree with a surname of a different family, although there are exceptions.

Beginnings of the Tudor dynasty; end of the Plantagenets

Anne – wife of Richard, Duke of Gloucester, died young (poisoned by her husband?)
Arthur – first-born son of Henry VII and Elizabeth of York, Prince of Wales.
Baron Stanley – Henry Tudor's stepfather, married to Lady Margaret Beaufort.
Catesby – administrator for King Richard III.
Cousin Edward – sickly son of Richard, Duke of Gloucester.
Duke of Buckingham (1483) – Henry Stafford, 2nd Duke of Buckingham, helped Richard III become King, then led rebellion against him; executed 1483.
Edward IV – King of England in 1483, member of the House of York.

Edward and Richard – sons of Edward IV (Princes in the Tower, believed murdered by their Uncle Richard).

Elizabeth of York – daughter of Edward IV, became wife of Henry VII and mother of Henry VIII.

Elizabeth's Mother – Elizabeth Woodville, widow of Edward IV, Queen and mother of Elizabeth of York.

George, Lord Strange – Baron Stanley's nephew, son of Sir William Stanley.

Henry Tudor – became **Henry VII**, and father of Henry VIII, married Elizabeth of York.

John Cheney – died defending Henry Tudor's life.

John de Vere – Earl of Oxford, Henry Tudor's "general", and master strategist.

John Wickham (F) – recent archaeological discovery of Richard III's body found evidence of an arrow in his back; somebody fired it...

Lady Margaret Beaufort – mother of Henry Tudor.

Richard, Duke of Gloucester – Edward IV's younger brother, probably murdered Edward's sons (Princes in the Tower) after Edward died, then succeeded as King Richard III.

Sir William Stanley – Baron Stanley's brother.

Sir William Brandon – Henry Tudor's standard bearer, died saving Henry Tudor's life, father of Charles Brandon (see below).

Spanish Court and Household

Brother Alessandro Geraldini – Catherine's tutor, then priest for her journey to England.

Catalina: Catherine of Aragon – daughter of Isabella and Ferdinand – eventually Queen of England as Henry VIII's first wife.

Count de Cabra – the chief aristocrat of Catherine's sizeable retinue.

Donna Elvira Manuel – Catherine's "governess" and then guardian/companion when she left for England.

Ferdinand of Aragon – Isabella's cousin and husband and Catherine's father. King of Aragon and joint ruler of all Spain with Isabella.

Isabella – Queen of Castile (Catherine's mother).

Maria de Salinas – faithful companion and friend of Catherine. Later married to Lord Willoughby from Lincolnshire (see below) and, as such, was great (x17) grandmother of Princess Diana – a modern Princess of Wales; therefore also 18XGG of current Princes William and Henry Windsor and 19XGG of Prince George.

Louth based group, including Captain Cobbler

Arthur Graye* – known to have had the heretical book by Frith, written as a reply to Sir Thomas More, which contained a denial of the doctrine of transubstantiation. He was a 'singing man'.

Bennett Waterland (F – fam) – recently buried member of the Plough Light.

Bill Cole (F) – accompanies Nicholas on his second journey down towards London and provides perspective on Henry's early French excursions by way of "story-telling".

Bobby Medwell (F) – the name is fictional but someone *did say* the words I put in his mouth about making the king a "breakfast he never had", a strange phrase open to all sorts of interpretation!

Captain Cobbler – Louth shoemaker, Nicholas Melton, see below.

Edward Smithill (F) – just a man in church; no doubt there were pompous people then, as now.

Eleanor (F) – Nicholas needed a religious relative to explain some of the background religious turmoil of Henry VIII's "Great Matter" – which led to the Reformation and the closure of religious houses; in particular the closure of nearby Legbourne Abbey was a significant event.

Eliza Jane Foster (F) – introduced as Nicholas's life-long love interest. Nicholas is understood to have been married, but we know nothing of his real wife.

George Smith (F) – just a man in the Louth host.

George Tuxworth (F- fam) – and **daughter Rebecca** – help the 'back-story' of **Guy Kyme** (see below) – Tuxworth is an ancestral name of mine, but not closely involved in these events.

Guy Kyme* - he really did report the fact about Hull getting new paving but I have given him a much wider role than is recorded as the uprising develops.

Henry Plummer and Great James (Long?)* – they really did block the way for the monk, William Morland, from getting into the church on the Monday morning but all we really know are their names and that Great James was actually a tailor by profession. Fictional surname for Great James.

(Jack?) Bawnus* –his first name is fictional but, it was the case that a "Bawnus" did "pour his heart out" to Mr Heneage and Heneage did offer to go to King Henry personally to ask whether the threats of confiscation of church treasures was likely. The location for this was the Choir of St James.

(Jack?) Page* –his Christian name is fictional but a man by the name of Page did take the book of reckonings from Monk Morland after he came out of Mr Collingwood's house. After the uprising was over the book was found in the possession of Nicholas Melton, passed to him by Mr Page.

Jane Mussenden* (Sister Mary?) – Jane Mussenden was mother superior at Legbourne Abbey at the time of the rebellion. I have introduced her at the time of Eleanor joining the Abbey (see Eleanor above) but do not know how old she was at the time. Also I do not know what she may have called herself so "Sister/Mother Mary" is fictional.

John and Pat ('Ma') Baker (F) – there must also have been nice, well-organised people, then, as well as now, who would know how to plan and organise the catering for a large group of people.

John Taylor* - it is known that when the people assembled on the Tuesday morning they were addressed near the church by Nicholas Melton and John Taylor, so he must have had a significant involvement, but beyond that little is known of him.

Joseph Waterland (F- fam) – 'cousin and friend', The description of him getting the 'giggles' is a family trait I inherited, more from my maternal ancestors than from the

Meltons. My mother's brother, Joe, was a fellow sufferer. Family and friends know I am helpless once I get started!

Ma and Pa Melton – they must have been real otherwise Nicholas would not have existed but I do not know anything historical about them

Mr Goldsmith, Mr Elwood* – were the churchwardens who had to hand over the keys of the church to Nicholas Melton and his friends.

Mrs Hempsall (F) – and husband – I enjoy food and I am sure that there were *always* people who could cook better than average and would be assets to a good household!

Nicholas Melton* – Captain Cobbler. He had a horse and two servants and he wore a 'Coat of Motley'.

Old Uncle Tom (F) – I had to get Nicholas down to London for the coronation somehow.

Richard Foster (F) - fictional son of Thomas Foster senior; and brother of Tom Foster, both of whom were real people.

Richard Nethercotts*, John Wilson* and Robert Norman* – all names known to have been involved in the Louth uprising, saying or doing at least some of the things I have them saying or doing... **Robert Norman*** was a rope-maker in Louth and he was known to have paid... **John Wilson***, who was a sawyer, the princely sum of one penny to spread the words of Thomas Foster (see below) who believed it may have been the last time the congregation could have "followed the crosses" in Louth. Thomas's father, (fictional first name **Thomas?) Foster*** was also known to be a chorister. **Richard Nethercotts*** is known to have rung the common bell with John Wilson on the Monday morning.

Robert Bailey* – was a mercer and a friend of the monk, William Morland (see below). He had been a churchwarden the previous year.

Robert Brown* – did imprison commissioners **Bellow and Millisent** for the duration of the Rising.

(Robert) Collingwood* – we know that Morland 'disappeared' into the house of one Collingwood nearby, possibly Robert Collingwood, who had been a churchwarden in 1531-32.

Robert Melton (F –fam) – Nicholas's older brother.

Robert Proctor* – was the unfortunate former churchwarden whose house was damaged by the mob on that Monday morning.

Robert Sleight (F - fam) – a Louth character (but also see 'Other Lincolnshire persons' below).

Thomas Kendall* – Louth Parish Priest, well educated, had earlier in his career been involved in heresy trials for the Bishop of Lincoln, did not like the 'new learning' that was being required of priests. Known to object to the 'erroneous books' in English, as misleading the common people.

Thomas and John (Jack) Spencer; Robert Bailey; William King* – all as described, were the instigators of the idea of "bringing in" the commissioners going to Caistor.

(Tom) Thomas Foster* – 'singing man' in Louth, I have given him a broader 'family' role here. His father is also called **(Thomas?) Foster** and sang in the choir too.

Tommy Musgrove (F) – a neighbour, and his dogs, **Patch** and **Sir Lancelot** – Wolfhound – not real (then) but a real wolfhound with these characteristics lived near us in my home village and was just like this, soft as a brush – he just wasn't called Sir Lancelot.

Uncle Henry (F) – fictional uncle for Nicholas.

Vicar Sudbury* – previous Vicar of Saint James' Church, Louth.

Walter & Robert Fishwyke* – brothers and amongst the town's elite. They claimed to the commission of inquiry after the uprising, that, together with William Ashby, below, they wanted to stop the rebels going any further than they already had by taking the keys from the churchwardens.

Widow Foster (F) – fictional mother of Thomas Foster senior and grandmother of Tom Foster should really be in the real people list since such a person *must have existed*. But we don't know whether she was widowed or kept chickens.

William Ashby* – Chief Constable of the town of Louth.

William Bonner (F – fam) – fictional neighbour of William Morland – see below.

William Corbett and Jack Bligh (F) – introduced to account for the beating up and murder of Lord Burgh's servant (Nicholas) Weeks. There must have been *real* hot-blooded bullies present to account for the violence and, for me, that did not seem to fit the profiles of any of the main players as I envisaged them.

William Hert* – town butcher and brother of **Sir Robert Hert***, a former monk from Louth Abbey.

William Morland* – monk from the nearby, dissolved, Louth Park Abbey - involved in the up-rising early on the Monday morning. Played a key role in stirring things up as the week went by.

Horncastle Group and other Lincolnshire persons involved in Uprising

Eleazor Swain (F –fam) – just a character.

Davy Bennett (F) – just a character.

John Chapman (F –fam) –the Langworth butcher was real and did fetch a bible to swear the gentry in, but his name here was a family name I used for the novel – but I really did have an ancestor, John Chapman who was a butcher in Langworth... except that was in the 19th century rather than the 16th.

John of Hawmby* – little known of him except he was a rich man in Horncastle.

Leach brothers and cousin, William, Nicholas, Robert and Parson Robert* – All active in setting the rebellion going in nearby Horncastle. William seems to have been the key instigator.

Parson of Snelland (Robert Albright?)* – the 'Parson of Snelland' was the man who told the rebels in the chapter House that Moigne was giving a "false read" - his *name* here, however, is fictional.

Phillip Trotter* – was actively engaged in the Horncastle events. A 'mercer', he saved Dr Raynes (see above) on the Tuesday by accepting a bribe to keep him from harm. Was known to bring information to Louth during that week. It is also thought he may have "borrowed", and used, the suit of armour the Dymocke family left in Horncastle church to 'guard' their family memorial.

Robert Sleight (F – fam) – his cousin **Jack** (and Jack's wife **Jane**) – there possibly *were* Sleights living in Normanby by Spital because I have ancestors by that name (including a Jane Sleight) who lived there in the 19th Century.

Sir John Thimbleby* – did bring a group of men up to join the uprising, from Irnham near Stamford, a long way from Lincoln.

Sir Simon Maltby* – priest, did say the words attributed to him.

The Parson of Conisholme* - name unknown, but did say the things attributed to him.

Thomas Dixon* – a labourer called upon by William Leach to round up other 'poor men' to come and listen to what he had to say about the happenings in Louth.

Thomas Youll* – priest, did say the words attributed to him.

William Blake and John a' Bardney* – involved with 'capturing and bringing in' Thomas Moigne and the sons of Sir William Ayscough from Metheringham.

Yellowbellies – seems an insulting term but for Lincolnshire born people to be a 'yellowbelly' (or yeller belly) is to be proudly from the county. See Wikipedia for possible derivations!

Lincolnshire Gentry, religious leaders and other officials in the county

Bishop Longland of Lincoln – one of five senior clerics who were deemed "heretics" by the protesters during the Lincolnshire uprising and the Pilgrimage of Grace which immediately followed it. Bishop Longland had taken over in Lincoln from Bishop Wolsey (later Cardinal Wolsey) when the latter was elevated by Henry VIII to Archbishop. Longland had supported Henry in his divorce attempts.

Bishop Mackrell* – Abbot of Barlings Abbey, known to be a fine speaker and widely known outside Lincolnshire and associated with Captain Cobbler as a leader of the rebellion – but the official inquiry was told he was 'dragged into it unwillingly'.

Dr Raynes* - chancellor to the Bishop of Lincoln, was at Bolingbroke to examine the priests from that area and was obviously not well during and after that day for he was still there and unwell on the Tuesday following, when a crowd from Horncastle, including Phillip Trotter (see above), threatened him.

Edward Maddison – amongst the group of commissioners (see below, Lord Burgh etc.) – he was chosen to ride down to London with the letter for the king. No actual time is given for the ride but it is written of in terms of it being remarkably quick.

John Bellow and (Roger?) Millisent* – were servants of Thomas Cromwell and commissioners whose task was to oversee the dissolution of Legbourne Abbey. 'Roger' is a fictional Christian name.

John Frankish* - John Frankish was the registrar to the Bishop of Lincoln and was in Louth to conduct the Visitation of the local priests.

John Heneage* – was one of three brothers (one was Dean of Lincoln, the other, **Thomas**, was an associate of Thomas Cromwell, as stated) and **John** acted for the Bishop of Lincoln as administrator for Louth. He *was* there for the town meeting as indicated.

Lord Burgh, Sir Robert Tyrwhitt, Sir William Ayscough, Thomas Moigne, Thomas Portington, Edward Maddison, Thomas Dalyson, John Booth, Thomas Mussenden* – were all commissioners going to Caistor on Tuesday, 3rd October 1536 to assess the subsidy. Do not know if Thomas Mussenden was really related to Jane Mussenden, Abbess of Legbourne, but have taken author's licence to assume he was.

Lord Hussey* – tried to stay aloof from the Lincolnshire rebellion, but there was a strong attempt by the Commonwealth to involve him. He was the most senior aristocrat in Lincolnshire at the time. The county had had no major players, Dukes and so on (or, rather, the arrival of the Duke of Suffolk to Lincolnshire was so very recent, that it had not become the "norm"), so the noble Lord who had served Queen Catherine **(as Sir Robert Hussey)** in the way described was probably a man with torn loyalties.

Lord Willoughby, Baron d'Eresby* – had served the Royal family in various roles for a long time by the time of his death in 1526. He married Maria de Salinas, Catherine's lifelong friend.

Nicholas Sanderson* – a commissioner staying with the Dymockes and **Sir William Sandon***, his father in law.

Nicholas (Weeks?), servant to Lord Burgh* - a man of caution, not wanting the action to upset the status quo but too loyal to Lord Burgh for his own good. (The surname Weeks is fictional).

Prioress of Orford* - really did provide Monk Morland with a horse after his walk from Louth to Orford near Binbrook. Made me wonder what sort of relationship they may have had.

Robert Applewhite (F) – we know the commissioners sent '*a servant*' in to reconnoitre Caistor town before the group moved in... but we do not know his name or whose servant he was?

Robert Sutton* – Mayor of Lincoln.

Sir Robert Dymocke* – elderly, still carried the title of King's Champion, an honorary position held by the family. Formerly a servant of Catherine of Aragon.

Edward Dymocke* – Sir Robert's eldest son and Sheriff of Lincolnshire in 1536.

Arthur Dymocke* - second son of Sir Robert.

Tom Bailey (F) – a 'servant of Maddison's' **was** the person who brought the King's reply into the Cathedral accompanied by a very large group of rebels. Fictional name/position, however.

English Court and Household

Anne Boleyn – second wife of Henry VIII. Her championing of Reformation and her execution in 1536 may have contributed considerably to the instability amongst ordinary folk at the time.

Catherine Willoughby – daughter of Maria de Salinas and Lord Willoughby (see below). She was a ward of the Duke of Suffolk and was betrothed to his son Henry Brandon, 1st Earl of Lincoln.

Duke of Buckingham (1509) – Edward Stafford, 3rd Duke, son of 2nd Duke (see above) High Steward for Henry VIII's Coronation, cousin to Elizabeth of York.

Duke of Norfolk – out of favour with Henry VIII at the time of the uprising, Henry needed his services as his most experienced 'warrior noble'.

Duke of Suffolk – Charles Brandon, son of Sir William Brandon (see above) and great friend of Henry, said to look a lot like him, married Henry's sister Mary after she had been widowed from her marriage to French King Louis IV. Then when Mary died he married his ward, Catherine, (see above) daughter of Maria de Salinas and Lord Willoughby (the marriage brought the Duke lands in Lincolnshire).

Elizabeth (Bessie) Blount[#] – well known to be the "lover" of the King, she produced a healthy bastard son in June 1519 … see her in '**Other Characters**' for longer entry.

Henry VIII – succeeded to the throne in 1509 as a young, handsome, prince. Died, a tyrant, in 1547.

John Walshe – King's Champion for Henry VIII's Coronation – a position which should, by right, have belonged to Sir Robert Dymocke (see below), according to tradition.

Lancaster Herald – Herald of Arms in Ordinary – an officer of the court. Thomas Milner in 1536.

Lord Willoughby, Baron d' Eresby – had served the Royal family in various roles for a long time and died in 1526. He married Maria de Salinas, Catherine's lifelong friend.

Maria, Baroness d'Eresby (Maria de Salinas) – faithful companion and friend of Catherine. Later married to Lord Willoughby from Lincolnshire.

Sir Robert Dymocke* – elderly by 1536, still carried the title of King's Champion, an honorary position held by the family. Formerly a servant of Catherine of Aragon.

Thomas Cromwell – King Henry VIII's Chancellor (see also below for more detail)

English Officials, not part of the Court

John Partington (F) –Lord Kingston (see below) was the real Constable of the Tower and will have had assistance, but I do not know his name.

Legh and Layton – Cromwell's commissioners who had acquired a bad name amongst the people.

Lord Derby – Edward Stanley, 3rd Earl of Derby, great grandson of Baron Stanley, who became 1st Earl of Derby, see above.

Lord Kingston – constable of the Tower of London.

Sir Richard Rich – at the time of this action Rich was Solicitor General. The historian Lord Dacre has said of him that he was a man "of whom nobody has ever said a good word". Under Cromwell he was Chancellor of Augmentations, the "lesser hammer" in the destruction of the monasteries.

Thomas Cromwell – King Henry VIII's Chancellor at this time and (since earlier in 1536) had become the Vicar General of the church in England, architect of the Dissolution of the Monasteries which was providing a rich source of cash for the Crown. Became Baron Cromwell in July 1536.

Other Characters

Alan Barham and **Johann Kirkkgarde (F)** – more fictional people to get Nicholas down to London again and get his Coat of Motley – he really did wear a multi-coloured coat!

Brothers Luke, Mark, Peter and Ignatius and helper "Madge" (F) – trying to give a view of the sort of role monks and monasteries played in a local community.

Charles, King of the Burgundian Netherlands – lived in Ghent, where he inherited the title from his father, **Philip the Handsome** who was married to **Joanna the Mad**, sister to **Catherine of Aragon, Queen of England** – adding colour to Nicholas' acquisition of his Coat of Motley

Elizabeth (Bessie) Blount[#] – well known to be the "lover" of the King, she produced a healthy bastard son in June 1519, when she may have been as young as 16. She was a lady in waiting of the Queen, but was she placed there after the King had taken a fancy to her, or was she there before? Certainly it seems Henry's interest in her began when she was a very young teenager – she may even have been as young as 12. She went on to be married off to **Lord Tailboys** of Lincolnshire when he turned 21 and then when he died she married, in 1536, the younger **Lord Clinton** in Lincoln. Her son **Henry Fitzroy** died, aged 17 in 1536.

Eustace Chapuys – Imperial Ambassador to the English court, notorious schemer and letter writer, but the degree to which this may have been known to Henry at the time is not clear? His letters were in cipher.

Fitzroy, Henry, Duke of Richmond – was the bastard son of **King Henry VIII** and **Bessie Blount**, see above.

Hans de Groot (F) – tailor cousin of **van Planck** who produced the "Coat of Motley".

Jake Hoskyns (F) – just a man in the hostelry. The **hostelry** building is, however, real and now houses the Newark branch of the Nottingham Building Society - it is a delightful building. The walls were, around the time of the story, painted with murals and the renovation of this building revealed faint traces of the wall paintings, which can still be seen near the new plate-glass entrance door.

John Fuller (F) – butt of the tale, "Falling from Grace". He is fictional – although the punishment was real enough in Calais at the time.

Jonno, Jezza and Tommo (F) – London urchins.

Lord Berners, the 'Master of Ordnance')   all these people and the story of the
Lord Essex and Sir Rees ap Thomas   }   lost gun "St John the Evangelist" is
Master Carpenter George Buckemer   )   a true tale (embellished of course!)

Marieke Molenaar(F) – a means of getting Nicholas to the Netherlands to pick up his Coat.

Perkin Warbeck – a stunningly successful con artist or may really have been Richard Plantagenet, one of the nephews of Richard III, (seems quite unlikely?) the second son of Edward IV, who was thought to have been murdered in the Tower with his brother prior to the reign of Henry VII.

Sister Mary; Margaret; the Prioress; and girls of the unnamed priory (F) – a company of bit part players to accompany the introduction of Bessie Blount,. Not known whether Henry ever attended such a place of ill repute but it might explain his apparent disgust later at the 'goings on' of some smaller religious houses – 'methinks he protesteth too much'!

Tom Butcher (F) – an apprentice acquaintance at the moment he is introduced, but will play a significant role later as a fictionalised persona for a real person... just wait and see!

Willum van Planck and family [including Gypsy the dog] (F) –there was a significant Dutch colony in England involved in both the cloth and leather trades, with links to cobbling.

Glossary

Church Ales – Would today probably be called 'Fêtes' designed to have a good time, as a local event, but with the same intention of raising funds for the local church.

Commons/Commonwealth/Commonalty
Interchangeable terms used to mean all of the people of the community other than the gentry. Most people seemed to accept the overall structure of society as necessary and right and that their place in it was fixed by birth.

Devotio Moderna – Was a movement for religious reform, calling for 'apostolic renewal' through the rediscovery of genuine pious practices such as humility, obedience and simplicity of life. It seemed also to work as a charitable group within the church around this time, aimed to provide support to the impoverished or sick in a community. Some historians suggest it may have been involved in encouraging protest against the 'new' reforms of the church in Henry VIII's reign.

Ploughlight (& other '-lights') – Poorer members of a church community would get together to raise money to buy candles for devotionary purposes to help their members get through their period of purgatory after death. The money not only bought candles (the 'lights') but paid for the cost of priests to say prayers for the more recently departed, so the ploughmen of a community, for example, would get together to raise money for departed ploughmen through a group called the Ploughlight.

Subsidy – The 'subsidy' was what the local tax was called. Householders above a certain level of wealth had to pay the 'subsidy' to support all the necessary 'government' expenditure. It was first devised in the 13th century as a tax on the value of 'moveable' goods (rather than just 'land') and was originally set at different levels at different times but in 1334 was standardised so that in rural areas those who were taxed had to pay one fifteenth of the value of their 'moveable' goods and in towns they paid one tenth of the value – so it was also known as the *'fifteenth and tenth'*. Senior gentry would meet to 'assess the subsidy' and this was the reason for the gentry meeting in Caistor in October 1536.

Transubstantiation – Transubstantiation is the doctrine that the consecrated elements of the communion only seem still to be bread and wine, for they have 'really' been converted into the whole substance of the body and blood of Christ. John Frith claimed it was not real but allegorical and was imprisoned and tried for heresy following his continued writings. He was offered a pardon if he would answer yes to two questions. Did he believe in Purgatory and did he believe in Transubstantiation? He said that neither could be proven by the Holy Scriptures and was condemned and burned at the stake on 4th July 1533.

Wapentakes – A wapentake is an old Viking term used for an administrative area equivalent to the Saxon "hundred" – which was an area which would support about one hundred households. Commonly used in Lincolnshire and other strongly Viking settled areas to refer to an administrative and tax area, it is thought the origins of the word may have come from a meeting or assembly to discuss contentious issues. Citizens would put their weapons down to talk an issue through in peace - and when the meeting was over they would be allowed to "take up their weapons" again – "vapnatak" (Old Norse)

The small icon of the pointing hand is a copy of a drawing King Henry VIII used frequently when he was making notes on a document he was reading or writing. I thought it would be fun to use at the start of sections of the novel.

Prologue 1: A Dynasty born of blood
The last Plantagenets: February 1483 – August 1485

Sing a song of sixpence,
A pocket full of rye.
Four and twenty blackbirds,
Baked in a pie.

Elizabeth of York turned seventeen in February 1483 and it was the best birthday she could remember. For one thing, her father, King Edward IV, was at home, not away fighting the French, or even fighting his own countrymen somewhere, as he seemed to be doing much of the time.

Nor was he carousing with one of his "pretty women", for once, and this made her mother at once calmer and somewhat coquettish, rather to Elizabeth's distaste, it has to be said, but better that than shrewish, her normal *'mood of the day'*.

But what made it *really* good was that her favourite uncle, Richard, the Duke of Gloucester, had arranged a surprise birthday party for her. He had invited all her favourite people – including her father and mother, of course – as well as many people she really did not like very much. But then, *"you can't have everything…"* can you? – as her mother was always fond of saying.

By far the best surprise had been that Richard arranged with his kitchen staff to bring out a huge pie for her which, when they cut into the crust and opened it up, released a couple of dozen live birds that flew out causing much mayhem and merriment as they tried to escape!

Uncle Richard was quite a bit younger than her father and was only fourteen when she was born, so she had always got on with him very well. People said he looked a bit odd with his bent shoulder, but he made light of it himself and he always managed to make her laugh if she was feeling in low spirits.

Her two younger brothers, Edward and Richard were both at the party, of course, eating more than was good for them and dancing with the girls. Elizabeth's cousin Edward, Uncle Richard's son, always rather a sickly boy, now ten, sat watching from the side of the room.

At twelve and nine, her brothers had energy to spare and Elizabeth was pleased to countenance the boys taking centre stage for much of the evening, even though it was *her* party, as that allowed her to sit talking animatedly with her favourite Uncle.

Richard's wife, Anne, had pleaded a bad headache, soon after the music had started and had retired to her rooms, so Elizabeth had his full attention – and he was clearly enjoying her company. He seemed to be in particularly good form this evening and was making everyone laugh telling racy tales of his time in exile in the Low Countries, giving excellent impressions of their strangely-accented English and their odd customs.

ೞೞೞೞೞ

When the pie was opened,
The birds began to sing;
Wasn't that a dainty dish,
To set before the king?

Elizabeth's buoyant birthday mood lasted well into March, despite the cold weather. But when her father started to suffer periods of ill health, she was affected by the mood at court which had become very dour. This was especially so when it seemed the leeches were to be put to work, bleeding the king, and the doctors were walking around with long faces most of the time.

Her father succumbed to his illness soon after Easter 1483. Clearly, he knew he was dying because he took the precaution of naming his brother Richard as Lord Protector for the boys who, as minors, would no doubt be in grave danger after his death.

What he could not have known, however, was that the gravest of danger would be from the dastardly Protector himself, their uncle!

Young Edward succeeded his father, as Edward V, on 9th April 1483 and the Coronation was arranged for June. Elizabeth's Uncle Richard took young Edward to the Royal lodgings in the magnificent White Tower of London and told her mother to send Edward's brother Richard to stay there as well, so he could "...*better protect them both...*"

Elizabeth's mother, of course, agreed to this, as she must. Sadly, however, she was never to see either of them again.

Uncle Richard persuaded enough of his friends at court to agree to pass a new law purporting to make the marriage of her father to her mother illegal. This meant that, along with her two brothers, and several sisters, she was thus declared a bastard.

It was a horrible thing to do and for a long time she decided she would never forgive him. Indeed, her mother was incandescent about the whole thing, especially when 'brother-in-law Richard' had himself declared the legal heir to the throne of England in Edward's place.

Richard was duly crowned and there were occasional reports of Elizabeth's brothers at play, or at their leisure, in the Tower through until August. That was when everything seemed to go quiet and nobody saw them in or near the royal lodgings again. Rumours that they had been brutally murdered quickly spread through the capital city and further abroad. But King Richard III denied such a terrible calumny and said they had merely been sent away secretly, to stay with family in France "...*for their safety...*!"

Elizabeth's mother, together with Elizabeth and her five sisters, took sanctuary in Westminster Abbey, where they stayed in safety for nearly a year. They came out of the abbey only after King Richard had promised in public – sworn on the bible, too – that none of them would ever be imprisoned in the Tower, or anywhere else for that matter.

What her uncle never knew, even though he may always have suspected something was afoot, was that Elizabeth's mother was in secret contact with Lady Margaret Beaufort (through the Duke of Buckingham, supposedly one of his best friends as well!)

The very day they arranged to leave the sanctuary of the abbey, Mother took her to one side – literally in a side-chapel – for a "...*quiet word...*"

"When we get back to court, my sweeting, you must act to your Uncle as you have always done, even flirting with him if need be! He must never know Buckingham has been here. And Richard must certainly never know what we have talked about with him, otherwise your head will part company from your body – and mine will too. And his sworn promises will be for naught! If he ever knows that I have promised you in marriage to Henry Tudor, Margaret's son, you will certainly not reach your twentieth year, nor ever bring me grandchildren to dandle on my knee!"

And so, life went on at court, much as it had done before she was seventeen. She missed her brothers' sweet laughter, however, as they played rude pranks on their sisters. Richard's wife Anne died soon afterwards, from a mysterious illness, and the rumour-mill started again.

This time, the rumours were that he had poisoned his wife so he could marry his lovely niece, Elizabeth. The part of her that remembered her favourite uncle with affection almost wanted this rumour to be true, perverse though it was.

And so, for just over a year life continued on this way, until they heard, privily, that Henry Tudor had landed in Wales, travelling through Brittany, from exile in France, and was headed eventually for London. He was apparently picking up rebels on the way, as he travelled, first, up into the English Midlands. This was easier than Henry had expected, because the third Richard of England was not a well-loved king amongst the people.

Nevertheless, the king rounded up his barons, and lords, and their retainers and by the time he arrived in Leicestershire he had 10,000 men with him, to the 5,000 Henry was commanding.

Henry was no man of war – he was fascinated more by finance and the world of commerce – but he was astute and had surrounded himself with warriors. His army was led by John de Vere, the Earl of

Oxford. Oxford had been fighting the Lancastrian cause as long as he could remember.

In addition to the main forces on either side, Henry Tudor's stepfather, Baron Stanley (notionally one of Richard's barons!), and yet another 6,000 men of arms, decided to watch which way the battle would go, ready to step in and join the winning side in time to receive the grateful thanks of the eventual winner for tipping the balance! Stanley's nephew George, Lord Strange, had been made hostage by Richard III, but the baron, and Sir William Stanley, George's father, had promised they would fight with Henry Tudor anyway.

Thus far, at least, they had been retreating gracefully ahead of Tudor's army, marching from Wales, without confronting the rebels. However, even Henry was not yet sure if they would join him as they had promised.

అ అ అ అ అ

Battle of Bosworth Field
August 1485

The early morning sun of 22nd August 1485 picked out the silvery column of Richard's soldiery moving into position on Ambion Hill, south of the town of Market Bosworth in Leicestershire. His men had been instructed to ensure that every bit of armour and weaponry, that could be polished, *was* polished to the highest shine.

Richard had hardly slept a wink and looked dreadful, come the sunrise, but harangued his men into battle readiness, nonetheless. He had been worrying about betrayal – would Northumberland fight when he was needed? Would the Stanleys come to him as he had bid them do?

And what of his own betrayal, of his brother's trust, and his betrayal of his nephews too? Their ghosts had mocked him in his dreams during an all-too-short night *"We'll see you in Hell before we can rest easy!"* – this from a child of twelve, and a child of nine, dressed in black velvet, curling blond ringlets framing their sweet faces. Richard woke in a cold sweat, long before dawn, sleep forgotten, heart pounding!

The two Stanley brothers and their troops had met up late in the evening before, and were already set in lines about half a mile from the royal lines, and perpendicular to them. As soon as Richard saw them he sent the Royal Herald to instruct them, once more, to settle in behind his lines and fight for the safety of England, against a treacherous mixture of Welsh and English opportunists, and Scottish and German mercenaries.

The Baron Stanley slowly sent back an ambiguous message to say he was best placed where he was so that he could outflank Henry Tudor's forces if they began to look effective. So they would stay put for the moment, thank you.

His brother, Sir William, did not bother to send back any message at all, as he had been branded a traitor the week previously, anyway, and his son was taken hostage. In a rage at this news, Richard declared that George, Lord Strange, should be "...*executed forthwith*..." but it appeared that by this time everyone was too busy to carry out the order.

Almost by the time he had finished talking to the returning Herald, and looked back down the hill, Tudor's three troops, normally a centre and two flanks, had performed a tight wheeling movement and formed a trapezoid with the narrow end pointed up the hill. It was like a truncated triangle – much puzzling Richard and his generals and captains, none of whom could explain the tactic. But they could not afford to puzzle for long – the battle would commence very soon.

Nor was there any hesitation from Henry Tudor's forces. They started marching confidently uphill, cannonballs flying over their heads, from their own gunners, towards Richard's troops at the hilltop. Richard's own cannon had been set at the side of Ambion Hill to enfilade the Tudor foot-soldiers.

Once they were within bowshot range of each other, men began to fall on both sides.

Soon afterwards, Richard sounded the charge and his men went flying down the hill at the Tudor army.

Richard and his generals soon discovered what the unusual formation was for, when his men found it difficult to get at the enemy in enough numbers to make an impact. This was especially so, since

Oxford's orders to the rebels had been to stay firm in formation, continually closing ranks "... *if men either side of you should fall!*" It made them a small and difficult target and Richard decided his forces must withdraw and regroup.

It was at this point that he must have had a rush of blood to the head, and decided on an all-or-nothing move. If it went on like this without the Stanleys or Northumberland choosing to intervene on the King's side in a decisive move, the Tudor army could wear his men down and they would soon start suffering defections from the ranks at the very least, possibly even a rout?

Richard had already seen where Henry Tudor himself was, surrounded by a horse-borne troop of no more than one hundred men, if that, and able to move quickly wherever they may be needed in the heat of battle. The red dragon of Cadwallader was fluttering in the breeze above them. They were, in fact starting to move now, towards Stanley's troops, presumably to get them to engage in the battle on their side. If that happened, it was clear to Richard that the day would be lost.

And so Richard decided that he and his knights – a troop of about eighty men – could take them in a surprise move, attacking downhill. It would be the stuff of troubadours and songsters, through the ages, come true!

He turned, and looked into the eyes of his men with a silent, understood, question... *"Do we go, will you follow me?"* To their credit, not one of the soldiers wavered, even though, if the move failed, it would be almost certain death for all of them.

But, if they killed the upstart Henry Tudor, the battle would be finished in time for an early lunch and England would be at peace at last. The only person to call for a withdrawal so they could regroup and fight another day was not a soldier but one of Richard's administrators, Catesby. As a lawyer, he could probably *define* the word GLORY but could not live by the concept, it was so alien to his being. No-one took the slightest bit of notice of him, however, and Richard himself pushed the man away.

So, within seconds they were committed!

And, thus, in a lull in the clashing sounds of battle, all eyes turned to the top of Ambion Hill as the slight figure of the hunchbacked King Richard III spurred his glorious white charger to a canter. He was surrounded by, and followed by, eighty silvery armoured knights of the realm in full battle array. It was a sight to behold!

Most of the foot soldiers on both sides stopped what they were doing (unless actually fending off an enemy soldier!) so the lull turned to almost silence until what seemed like an almighty animal ROAR came from somewhere on the hillside. It was a frightening, alien, noise that everyone *eventually* realised came from Richard's slender, almost feminine, throat. This roar was followed by huge bellows from the following knights as they saw the same red mist as their King.

They were halfway down the hill before anyone on the Tudor side reacted to, or even realised, what was happening. The troop around Henry tightened ranks and made sure their leader was protected by at least two ranks of horsemen. The huge knight Sir John Cheney spurred his horse ahead of the Tudor troop, the intention of the giant soldier being, of course, to block and kill the oncoming wild man.

But size was not a factor today! Cheney o'towered Richard by nearly a foot when standing on the ground and he had a much longer reach but he stood no chance against the berserker king – before he could even raise his sword he was flung from his horse by Richard's gleaming pole-axe.

Richard laid about him with the pole-axe, each blow taking another Tudor defender. Some blows were returned but he felt nothing, cared nothing for anything but Henry Tudor's head, to which he was getting nearer by the second.

Henry, himself, was saved twice.

The first time by his standard bearer, Sir William Brandon, who launched himself between the attacking king and his master. A huge man himself, Brandon was killed by a blow that would have been mighty close to Henry's head if he had not intervened. He left a young wife at home with a one-year-old boy, Charles, who was destined to have a different life altogether from that of his father...

Henry was saved, secondly, by the quick thinking of his stepfather's brother, Sir William Stanley. Stanley spurred *his* horse into action and yelled at his men to follow him downhill at the rear of Richard's charging cavalry group. Perhaps they should be able to stop at least some of the attackers getting to Henry.

And, if they saved the day for the Tudor cause, he would be hailed as a hero rather than scorned as a traitor. But, just before he set off with his own cavalry he turned to his best bowman, standing close by, and told him to "...*slow Richard down, kill him if you can!...*"

Most men would have blanched at the order, knowing they must fail, but John Wickham practised his bowmanship by targeting hares in their mad month of March, when they leapt unpredictably around the fields playing up to potential mates. So, before Stanley reached the rear of Richard's troop and got in his way, Wickham had already managed to let off three arrows at his target.

The first glanced off the coronet that the King wore over his helmet. The second punctured the rear flank of Richard's glorious white charger. The horse did not feel it, he was probably seeing a similar red mist as his rider but it did make him stumble a little. And, as he stumbled, Wickham's third arrow found a gap between two pieces of armour and lodged in the hunched back of King Richard III, the last Plantagenet King of England, and knocked him from his horse.

To be fair, Richard did not feel the arrow, any more than the horse had felt the one that hit its backside, and he simply rolled once and leapt lithely to his feet.

His squire offered him the use of his horse but Richard waved him away, laying about him like a whirling Dervish with his silver pole-axe, fetching blood with nearly every strike, shouting "*Treason,....traitors,... treachery!*" but it was to no avail. There were too many enemy foot-soldiers about him by now and one Welsh soldier thrust his halberd so hard into Richard's helmet that halberd, helmet *and* hair penetrated more than an inch into his brain through his skull.

Despite this fatal blow, he kept moving and thrashing about him with the pole-axe. But more and more sharp-pointed daggers, sharp-edged broadswords, and halberds cut or gouged bloody pieces from his head and torso. Stout oak staffs and Welsh or English boots broke a few bones, too, as he lay there.

Eventually, one man even used Richard's own pole-axe to scalp the wretch on the floor – they truly hated him for what he was reputed to have done to the little princes – until Henry Tudor's voice cut through the skirl, and shouted... "*Enough! He may be the enemy – but the man died a hero's death! Leave him be!*"

The panting men pulled back into a circle surrounding the body of their enemy, and the silence was then broken by a single shout, possibly from Sir William Stanley himself..."*The King is dead! Long live the King!*"

So saying, he took the coronet that Richard had been wearing over his helmet, dented slightly from his bowman's first arrow, and placed it on Henry Tudor's head, to lusty cheers all around. For his part, Henry Tudor smiled a tight-lipped smile – his teeth were in a terrible state and he rarely showed them if he could help it.

For the most part, the fighting stopped almost immediately and Henry in 'kingly magnanimity' held no desire to punish common working folk for simply doing what they had been told to do by their masters. He simply sent them home.

A few diehard Yorkists who could expect little from the new regime tried to regroup to carry on the fight but were chased down and became trapped by the lie of the land and were mercilessly put to death.

Henry Tudor, now King Henry VII of England and Wales, by right of conquest, ordered that Richard's body be taken to Greyfriars' Abbey in Leicester, there to lie openly so it may be seen that the former King was now, indeed, dead.

The men responsible for this last transfer of the body were none too gentle and for some odd reason known only to themselves – *for he was dead and posed no threat* – they tied his hands together before they draped his body over his, now limping, white charger (someone had retrieved the arrow from the horse's rump!)

On the way in to Leicester they passed by the same stone bridge Richard had ridden across earlier, on his way to battle, sending sparks from the stone when he struck the bridge with a spur. This time, draped as he was over the horse it was his head that struck the stone in the same spot in the narrow centre of the bridge, an event one of the local seers claimed to have seen in a vision. It was fortunate he was dead, too, otherwise the blow may have killed him.

The last Plantagenet was exhibited for viewing by his former subjects for two days in the abbey, so they should know he was truly gone. And then the body was unceremoniously dumped in a hastily dug grave, slightly too small for his five foot eight inch height. They did not bother with a coffin since no-one was paying for the funeral and it would have been a waste of good oak.

ଔଔଔଔଔଔ

Happy ever after...
January – September, 1486

Less than six months later, Henry Tudor married Elizabeth of York as had been planned by their mothers in conspiracy; and a little less than nine months later they celebrated the birth of their firstborn son whom they chose to call Arthur, descended, as they both were, of course, from King Arthur of Camelot.

Happy times were ahead...

The king was in his counting house,
Counting out his money;
The queen was in the parlour,
Eating bread and honey.

ଔଔଔଔଔଔ

Prologue 2: Young Catherine
1497 – Alhambra, Spain

The two girls knelt on a cool marble bench peering out through the lattice work window overlooking a small orange grove in the palace grounds. It was pleasant to feel the cooling stone on their knees, for the day was hot and they were furtively watching one of the young kitchen servants picking ripe fruit to place before the English Ambassador they knew to be visiting later.

It was the most unladylike thing Catalina had done for as long as she could remember as she and her friend Maria peeped at the young man's lithe, perspiration-coated, muscles glistening in the shafts of September sun piercing the courtyard.

They stifled a giggle as the youth over-reached himself trying for one of the choicest fruits he could see and nearly overbalanced into his half-full collecting basket. He must have heard something of their smothered laughter but not enough to be sure there was anyone around; and they *were* very well hidden in their dark cool corridor, behind the heavily latticed windows.

Discretion and a delicious fear of being found out prompted them to abandon their shady hiding place to explore more, normally forbidden, territory of their home whilst they were free to do so. These moments of freedom were relatively rare and it was only because Catalina's fearsome duenna, Dona Elvira Manuel, was indisposed today and her tutor, Alessandro Geraldini, was busy helping to organise the welcome for the English Ambassador, that they had more or less been told to make themselves scarce. So they were simply doing as they were told.

They scampered quietly away and paused to peer out through airy vaulted windows overlooking the township below in the still blistering sun. The magnificent red palace of the Alhambra had been Catalina's home for less than half her short life since Moorish Granada had fallen to her parents and their Christian armies, the final victory in their long internal Spanish Crusade. That was the very year their daring explorer Cristofor Colom discovered land across the broad Atlantic Ocean.

Catalina, now eleven, was just six when she and her sisters and brother moved into their new home.

The scene below them was very colourful with peasants' black shawls, contrasting with a few white Moorish robes and keffiyehs moving about past striped awnings and between baskets containing oranges, vegetables of various shapes and hues and even some with brightly coloured spices in golds, reds and greens.

Unexpectedly Catalina sighed so deeply that Maria turned and drew her attention from the colours and scents below to ask her friend what could be the matter.

"Oh ...nothing... (sigh) .... everything! I suddenly felt a deep wish to be somebody other than me – anybody – somebody 'ordinary'. Instead I have to travel next year to cold, wet England and be on my best behaviour always. At least you'll be coming with me."

Maria shivered at the thought of the horrible creeping cold they had heard so much about from Catalina's tutor, in a land where everyone reputedly wore thick animal skins to keep them warm, and where it rained every day.

"But you are the Princess of Wales – or so we have always been instructed to refer to you – promised these many years to Arthur, the next king of England and betrothed to him only last month. It's your duty!" ...But secretly Maria was wishing it was not, either. They had both had to learn to like drinking wine because the water was not fit to drink in England. But even that treat had been spoilt recently by Dona Elvira telling them not to expect the warmth of delightful Spanish wine. "They drink Rhenish wine over there" she had said with a shudder – "they drink it cold and it tastes of stones!"

"Duty...." The word was barely whispered – more of a sigh. Then, as soon as it appeared, her despondent mood disappeared. "Duty can wait for another day – let's go and say hello to the lions". So saying she scuttled through a couple of cool, shady, rooms followed closely by Maria de Salinas until they emerged in the bright sunshine on the Patio de los Leones.

They each sat on a lion's back, riding them as if through the green lushness of Nubia. Fortunately for them the lions were marble so they could neither complain, nor eat them. The fountain of cooling water at their back splashed the girls occasionally, just keeping them cool.

Maria was the one, being the elder by a couple of years, who brought them back into the line of duty...

"...we mustn't sit here for too long in the hot sun, otherwise we'll be as red as those baskets of spice in the market down below and Dona Elvira will oblige us with one of her withering looks!"

Catalina looked down her nose at Maria and treated her to a glorious impression of the old lady's scowl until they both broke into a fit of the giggles and retreated with shaking shoulders into the shade of one of the pillared pavilions.

Sitting inelegantly on another cool marble bench Catalina became serious again but without the despondency of a few minutes earlier.

"You are going to have to call me Catherine when we are in England, like my English great-grandmother, so Mother said last week"

'Mother' – clever, warm and humorous Isabella – was Queen of Castile in her own right and had been married off to her cousin Ferdinand of Aragon, thus bringing two squabbling regions of Spain into peaceful union. So she knew a thing or two of the healing possibilities of marrying the right person.

The fact that her grandmother was of the family of Lancaster in England would give her daughter, Catherine, a source of binding strength to offer the Tudors in a country where the Yorkists and the Lancastrians had been at loggerheads for much of the last hundred years. And Henry VII, the Tudor usurper, needed as much help as he could get to establish the credibility of his dynasty if it were to last. Catalina was most like her mother amongst her siblings and looked up to her as a woman of great wisdom, aspiring to follow her example.

Like all eleven year olds Catalina's mind flitted from one thing to another rather quickly, so Maria was not surprised when the next thing she said was...

"I'm hungry – let's go and see what we can find to eat!"

Before they actually arrived anywhere near the kitchens, however, they were espied by tutor Geraldini who bowed low and informed them with steel in his voice and a twinkle in his eye that the English Ambassador was expected "in less than an hour, and shouldn't the princess be preparing her wardrobe to greet the distinguished visitor!?"

With a somewhat haughty flounce and a little sigh Catalina responded, "Thank you Brother Geraldini. That is exactly where we were headed. Come Maria!" and rather emphasised the fib by turning nearly 180 degrees about before disappearing along the corridor towards her quarters, with a stiffly formal Maria de Salinas trailing self-importantly behind.

The transformation, sometime later when the Princess of Wales entered the ornately decorated Hall of the Ambassadors was remarkable, as, indeed, was the hall itself. The walls were decorated with Mohammedan inscriptions and poems for the Moorish Caliphs who had unwillingly vacated it so recently. And the marble floor reflected filigree rays of sunshine onto the double thrones where Ferdinand and Isabella would normally be seated. They were not present today, however, as they were 'progressing' through the northerly reaches of their Kingdom for the next month and the English Ambassador was actually here to visit the princess in her own right.

A wooden stool, covered in gold leaf and heavily cushioned, had been placed just below the two thrones on a platform of marble to which Catherine now glided under a long green silken dress. She was supported by Maria and another maid of honour. Over the dress was a black lace collar, worked by Catherine herself with a skilled hand, and over the collar fell locks of her red-gold waves of hair, shining in the sun as much as did the silk of her dress.

She seated herself gracefully and bid the Ambassador be called. The reds and golds of the filigreed Moorish decoration in the high-ceilinged room provided a warm, glowing light over the assembled faces of the many, mostly junior, courtiers who were not following the progression of the king and queen.

In the absence of the duenna, Dona Elvira, Brother Geraldini stood by as counsellor to the young princess should she require one. However, the stated purpose of the visit was simply to deliver a letter from her betrothed, Arthur, the Prince of Wales, so no great issues of State were anticipated today.

The Ambassador, a thin grey, rather tired looking man, entered, bowed deeply and was bid *"Welcome"* by Catherine – one of the few words of English she had yet mastered, before she asked him in a passable French how his journey had been. It had been fine, of course, since it was but a short step across the city from his residence. But the letter he brought with him had had a much longer journey across the Golfo de Viscaya and through Spain, before arriving at his door the previous day.

The letter, in Latin, was not long, but well penned and full of flowery phrases of promised love and good wishes, perhaps quietly suggested by supportive adults, for the boy was a year younger than Catherine. It briefly described the betrothal ceremony that had taken place a month before at Woodstock, in England. They had been promised to one another for years, since Catalina was three and Arthur was but two years old

The surprise, accompanying the letter, was a wonderful ring sent by Henry Vll as a "...*blessed token of fatherly affection*", in the short note accompanying it. Although small in size it was still too loose for Catherine to wear safely on her slim fingers without losing it but she treasured it and, placing it on a chain round her neck, she shared her pleasure in it with Maria once the formalities were over.

Perhaps it would not be too bad going to England next year after all...

ର ର ର ର ର ର

The Blackbird Sings... Remembering
Tower of London, 1537 – 6.15am: 29th March

Today was the day he was to die – yet he had slept as well as on any night in the last four months despite the permanent aching he suffered in both shoulders, for which a painful 'wracking', months before, was to blame. He had slept better, indeed, than most nights, all of which had been spent in the tight confines of the white Tower of London. Thankfully the weather had warmed a little recently after one of the coldest winters he had known – cold enough to freeze the Thames for a few weeks and add the pain of chilblains to the aches of his tortures.

He passed from sleeping to waking, utterly, without moving and without even opening his eyes. But he knew that a shaft of early spring sunshine lit a small square of the wall opposite the stone bench upon which he slept in the otherwise gloomy cell. He could hear the crystal notes of his friend, the blackbird, perched in the branches of a tree outside the tower which imprisoned his person, though not his soul, declaring the morning to be fine and bright.

Embedded in the dusty comfort of a grubby, straw-filled mattress and pillow and covered with his multi-coloured coat of motley, he allowed his eyelids slowly to open and take in the early morning light. Motes of dust danced in the sunbeams, rising and falling to mimic the sharp notes of the bird telling the story of his last day on earth.

As his eyes opened more he was surprised by a wavering light on the whitewashed ceiling of the cell he had never noticed before. The early morning sun was clearly playing on the water of the River Thames and the reflected light must have been shining on the blackbird because there was a projected shadow on the ceiling of the bird in full voice, beak wide open. Quite magical.

Today was the day he was to die - yet his mind sheared away from the manner of his death, for the image of being hung, drawn and quartered still brought him to the edge of fear. He had, last evening, however, made peace with his maker and he *knew* a place awaited him in the next life. He also knew from his close friend and cousin, Joseph Waterland, who had been allowed a brief visit to him a few days since, that his wife and young sons were now safe from harm in the northern marshes of faraway Lincolnshire, something he had allowed himself to hope for, yet had not been certain of until Joe's recent visit.

Nicholas quietly but firmly resisted the urging of the normal morning call of nature, so that he could take full advantage of this tranquil moment of relative comfort and peace, for he knew it would certainly be his last in this mortal world. Only when the reflected image of his friend, the blackbird, faded from the ceiling did he sigh and prepare to move.

The sunshine and the birdsong took him back twenty seven years to the first of his three visits to England's capital - or, at least, to the early morning of his departure for the long journey south. He reflected, too, that birdsong had often accompanied key moments in his life. Indeed, family tradition had it that he was delivered into this world as the dawn chorus was at its height, one late May morning at the turn of the century.

So he would be just three months short of his thirty-seventh birthday when he entered the next world – only about half of the three score years and ten promised in the good book.

But he remembered with total clarity the morning he turned nine years old, the sun shining dustily on his excited form - trying so hard not to waken everyone in his excitement. *That* morning he had wanted to leap from the enveloping comfort of the feathers in his truckle bed in the family home in rural Lincolnshire.

Cousin Eleanor, seven years his senior, had stayed the night before and would soon be on her way to join the priory at Legbourne, just the other side of Louth, as a novice nun. Nicholas was to accompany her and his older brother Robert on the road into Louth. Robert was to act as Eleanor's chaperone and bodyguard for this last short stage of her journey from Lincoln. He was still only sixteen, yet often won wrestling contests amongst the young men of the area. And, anyway, there was little real danger in the few miles from their home to Legbourne

Once they arrived there Nicholas would join a favourite friend of the family - a man he knew as 'Old Uncle Tom', even though he was not a blood relation. Tom was droving twenty or more head of cattle to London, in time for the festivities at the coronation of young King

Harry – or, rather, King Henry VIII of England, as he was to become at the end of June. Nicholas had helped Uncle Tom with his droving before, but only ever as far as Lincoln just over twenty miles away, never so far as this journey was to be. This was a special occasion in so many ways.

He knew well enough not to wake his older brother before the dawn chorus had finished, otherwise he would feel Robert's sharp displeasure a'rattling the side of his head, so he kept as still as possible and contemplated what the next few days may bring. So, full of thoughts about the coming trip, he tried to contain his excitement and stayed curled up in his luxurious feather bed, listening to a lone blackbird who had just woken up and who, in turn, would waken the others.

Not that the feather bed indicated his family was rich, they were simply lucky in their neighbours. They lived next to an elderly widow, Widow Foster, her son William (who had also been widowed) and *his* two sons, Thomas and Richard, who were similar in age to Nicholas himself and his brother Robert – as well as his pretty little daughter, Eliza Jane. Very much a tomboy, trying to keep pace with her elder brothers, Eliza Jane was just eighteen months younger than Nicholas.

Widow Foster was known to all and sundry in Louth and for miles around as 'the egg lady' because she had such a way with chickens and seemed to be able to coax them into laying more eggs than could any two other people in the locality.

So, when the stonemasons, who were employed to build the new bell-tower and spire for Louth church, needed eggs, by the score, on a daily basis to help bind their cement, it was to Widow Foster they were sent. She clearly saw the potential market for her eggs – since they were going to be building the tower for several years yet – so she quickly reared nearly five times the number of chickens as she had had previously. As a consequence of this, Robert and Nicholas got roped in to feeding them and helping to clean out the hen coops, a somewhat noisome task!

Finally, when the birds had reached the end of their laying life, the four boys would help kill them and pluck them ready for the pot – often hindered, rather than helped, by an ever willing but frequently troublesome Eliza Jane.

Inevitably there were feathers by the barrow-full. So, as well as the occasional pot-roast for the Melton family, the boys were paid for their help in feathers, which ended up as mattresses, bed-covers, pillows and cushions, first for Pa and Ma Melton, of course, and then as hand-me-downs to the boys as the feathers kept coming and new mattresses and such were made.

Despite the comfort of his bed, however, on this, his ninth birthday, the anticipation of the discoveries that lay in store on this fine spring day was making Nicholas fidget and fret under the warm covers.

His pent-up excitement had to wait only a few minutes more, though, as his father, one of Louth's eight cobblers, was soon stirring in the morning light and readying the household for the bustling day ahead. And when Pa Melton was up and about, woe betide anyone who thought they could lie-a-bed, feathers or not.

Seizing his chance, Nicholas flew out of bed, relieved himself out in the back yard, ducked his head in the rain barrel, gasping at the sharp coldness of the water in the early morning air, and rubbed himself reasonably dry and clean on the rough cloth Mother kept by the kitchen door for just this purpose.

Ready for his great adventure, he then helped his father chop wood for the fire, wanting breakfast to be over and done so he could set off and be gone. Though he'd been to market in Lincoln before, he'd never yet set foot out of the County and was looking forward to his adventure.

"Happy Birthday, young 'un", mumbled his brother, Robert, as he eventually rolled out of bed, tempted by the smell of frying bacon wafting round the house. Not only were they having bacon for breakfast, but several thick rashers were being wrapped up with fresh bread for them all to take with them for lunch later – and maybe supper, too, if he could make it last that long!

Robert reached under his pillow and fetched out a stick with a rather squashed bow fashioned from dried grass tied round the end of it.

"Here you are", he said to Nicholas, "a gift on your birthday – I only hope it don't make you too much of a nuisance to everyone!" Then he gave Nicholas a friendly clout on the back of his head, and took himself outside to complete his own ablutions.

The 'stick' turned out to have a small number of holes whittled in it along its hollowed out length and as he turned it over in his hands and removed the strands of dried grass he realised it was, of course, a whistle. Robert was obviously fed up with Nicholas borrowing *his* whistle, so had decided to make him one of his own.

He couldn't wait to try it out and, without further ado, the birthday lad regaled the household with a short dancing jig he had heard in the market place recently. And, although played entirely from memory, it was mostly right too. Mind you, his father screwed his face up a couple of times when the boy missed a note as he tried to master the brand new instrument.

It amused him for a short time, but his impatience to be gone kept getting the better of him as time dragged slowly by. Nicholas had imagined, vainly as it turned out, that their departure that morning would be early and swift. Now the day had arrived he wanted to be on his way.

The extra delay was caused, however, by the arrival of an uncle, aunt and their two daughters who had not been able to get to the impromptu family gathering held on Eleanor's arrival in Louth the previous day. They wanted to say hello and wish her God-speed for her journey today. The uncle and aunt were over half a generation older than his parents; and, thus, the cousins, too, were more than half a generation older than Nicholas. So, he found himself surrounded by adults clucking, fussing, and generally mithering him and Eleanor with good wishes and gossip.

What was worse, however, indeed *much* worse from Nicholas' point of view, was the hair tousling and '*my, hasn't he grown*' comments, which he had to put up with from them all. His uncle Henry was quite a rotund man, who tended to lean backwards slightly to counterbalance his abundant belly. He sported bushy and wiry mutton-chop side whiskers, and was also beginning to go deaf, so he now tended to bellow whenever he spoke.

"What a fine old time you'll have my lad" he boomed, his hands clasped pudgily over his ampleness. "Mind you behave like a gentleman of course – (Nicholas could sense another episode of hair tousling coming up!) – "we don't want the family name dragged into disrepute....ha, ha, ha!"

The chuckle rumbled across the grass and dislodged a group of twittering sparrows from the thorn hedge, much as if a sparrow hawk had flashed across the grass and swooped over the hedge, sending them into a panic.

Nicholas was pleased and relieved to find amongst the busy throng his contemporary and friend Tom Foster – at least he wouldn't attempt to tousle his hair – and Tom's sister Eliza Jane. Tom, rather less outgoing and adventurous than Nicholas, would not have changed places with his friend for a mess of potage, but little Eliza Jane thought him something of a hero, going out into the unknown world beyond the lane end.

In fact, rather to Nicholas' surprise, she suddenly reached up on her tippy-toes and kissed his cheek, quickly scuttling off to hide behind one of the myriad skirts in the vicinity. Nicholas, startled, but strangely pleased at this turn of events, blushed to the roots of his hair and hoped nobody had noticed the bussing!

Of course, pretty well everyone had, though they all kindly refrained from mentioning it in his hearing. Nevertheless, it would become the stuff of family legend, much amplified and embellished as the years passed by.

He quickly found something inconsequential to busy himself with, making sure his parcel of food rations was securely tied to his stout hazel stick. Of course it was, it had been checked several times already by prudent family adults and he had probably checked it at least six times, himself, in his fretfulness to be gone.

As if he needed yet more to divert attention from his exquisite moment of embarrassment, he also made a point of greeting two of his other friends who were caught up in the general excitement. These were, however, *non-human* friends and took the form of two dogs which belonged to old Tommy Musgrove who lived a little further down the lane in an ancient ramshackle croft.

Patch was a dog who had seen many years of service when Tommy had been able to work as a shepherd but now both man and dog were slow and very doddery on their elderly legs. But Nicholas' *very special* friend was a huge Irish wolf-hound who rejoiced in the name Sir Lancelot, because of his assumed high-born origin.

Sir Lancelot had turned up at the Musgrove croft around six years previously and just adopted it as his own. He caused a lot of anxiety at first since old Tommy and others assumed he must have come from a nearby aristocratic household and they would get into trouble for 'stealing' the dog if they were found sheltering him as theirs. After much enquiry round and about, however, it appeared no-one knew of any households which owned such large dogs and no-one wanted to take any responsibility for it, either, so there he stayed.

His coat was ragged when he arrived and he had welts on his back, so had clearly escaped from a place, maybe many leagues away, where he had been seriously maltreated and beaten. He had, perhaps, been wandering the country lanes for weeks looking for somewhere to call his own, and he was welcomed like a long lost brother by the already ageing Patch, and gradually learned to thrive in the locality.

Everyone treated him warily at first; he was, after all, such a *big* dog, but he was so placid and friendly that he had probably been beaten for *not* being a good guard dog. Nicholas had been about three when Sir Lancelot arrived and did not even reach to the giant's shoulder but they formed an immediate bond. And the only time anyone heard him bark was when Nicholas was seemingly threatened by something or someone.

Otherwise, the dog's favourite habit was to come up close to you, sit more or less on your foot and then lean against you, panting gently, waiting for a scrap if there was one to be had, but just appreciating your company if there wasn't. If, however, you were too busy to grant him your time, all you needed to do was to say "go home Sir Lancelot" in the gentlest voice and he would look up at you, his moist eyes hooded, sigh plaintively and leave you to whatever you were doing.

Many was the time over those six years, however, that Nicholas had ended up unceremoniously dumped onto his backside just by a friendly wag of the tail or nudge of the big head, though he was now, of course, big enough, and fast enough, to dodge the dog's enthusiasm, or at least survive its consequences!

Gradually the time came when everyone was ready to move off and, indeed everyone did move off at once. Firstly, the travelling party, Nicholas, Eleanor and Robert, who were accompanied by Uncle Henry and *his* family entourage in their Sunday best, even though it was not Sunday.

Close behind ambled Ma and Pa Melton, Nicholas' mother and father; and then many of the neighbours too. Everyone walked with them, along the lane, until it split, the more significant branch going on into town, towards the church, and beyond. This was the path Nicholas took with his cousin and brother.

The lesser pathway, somewhat overgrown from less frequent usage, was the route lumbering Uncle Henry and family took to their home in a nearby village.

Mother and Father and the neighbours lingered at the fork in the roads, gossiping and waving, and waving and gossiping, until the travellers were all out of sight and then they straggled back to their homes, all of which were now being gently warmed by the hazy spring sunshine.

Sir Lancelot was a little puzzled at the fuss going on today and looked rather forlorn when Nicholas told him to "go home Sir Lancelot" at the fork in the road, but he sat for a while on an uncomplaining adult's foot as the party waved and gossiped, and gossiped and waved, and then sauntered back to find a gulp or two of water at Musgrove croft and sit companionably with the arthritic Patch.

ଔଔଔଔଔ

Now that the journey was actually starting, Nicholas was relishing in full the prospect of his adventure, hugging it to himself, as his brother Robert and Cousin Eleanor were talking about *her* pending adventure. All this while, they progressed by stages into the market town of Louth, over the river Lud and past the fine church with its extended tower and new spire which was beginning to emerge through the wooden scaffolding.

"The spire's growing slowly..." Robert was saying to Eleanor..."I saw a drawing of it the other day in church; it will be magnificent when it's finished. It'll be the tallest church spire in Lincolnshire, so they say, and you'll be able to see it from miles around. It will help the fieldsmen find their way home at the end of the day."

"When will they finish it?" Eleanor asked.

"I was only listening in to his conversation with one of the guildsmen, but I think the priest was saying it may be another eight to ten years yet. There is a lot of detailed carving to be done at the top of the tower itself and then there's more to do for the spire. You'll probably be Mother Superior by then!"

"If I can just find my way to do God's work..." Eleanor's voice trailed off, she was obviously feeling rather nervous about her future now that it was nearly upon her, and she was clearly not yet comfortable with the clichés of the calling she had chosen to follow.

"I am surprised you sound so unsure. You've always seemed so set in your wish to be a religious."

"I have..." she paused, "and I still am..." she affirmed, as much to herself as to her cousin, "...but it all seems a bit strange now it is nearly upon me". They walked on in a nervy sort of silence for a while, Robert unsure what to say to boost Eleanor's confidence.

Nicholas was walking with them, but was also trying to 'seem' to be on his own, especially as they walked through the town, where he knew he may be seen by the town lads. This was truly a big adventure for him, going to London! Even if he would be walking all the way, slowly, behind about 20 head of beef cattle as they rolled, and inevitably *splattered*, their way through the country lanes. Previous outings with old Uncle Tom to market in Lincoln, with fewer beasts, had left Nicholas with the sure and certain knowledge that he would not smell too good by the end of the journey. And he would need to watch his footing all the way.

It was close to noon when their little party approached the gated entrance of the Legbourne Priory where they had arranged to meet Uncle Tom and his herd of beef on the hoof. They could see the cattle near the gate quietly munching grass while Tom leaned on the wall talking with Sister Mary, who was there waiting to welcome Eleanor.

'Sister Mary', whose 'real' name had been Jane Mussenden, was a girl barely three years older than Eleanor, whose current job in the priory was to tend the animals and fowls they kept on the premises. She was ruddy faced under her wimple and was immediately at ease talking to Tom about the cattle in his charge. Indeed, they were so engrossed in their conversation that the three newcomers were nearly upon them before they were noticed.

Sister Mary's smile – despite a couple of broken teeth – was warmly welcoming and she gave the girl an enveloping hug which dispelled many of Eleanor's nerves.

"I expect you are somewhat weary after your walk this morning, my dear. Come and sit yourself in the bench over here while these boys have a bite to eat – then we'll take you in and get you settled before we take a little soup with the sisters."

"Here, boys, have some fresh milk with your snap." So saying, she fetched a small churn from the shade of the wall and poured beakers of creamy milk for all the modest party including herself and old Tom.

Nicholas untied his food parcel from the hazel stick and opened his store, swapping a fat rasher of cold bacon for one of Uncles Tom's pickled onions. He tucked in to his lunch with relish, his stomach had been rumbling for the last twenty minutes of their journey and he knew they would have a good few miles to go before they stopped again for the night.

Uncle Tom was normally quite a taciturn man but his discourse with Sister Mary on the ins and outs of tending cattle had loosened his tongue somewhat, so Robert was quite surprised when Tom turned to him, while young Nicholas was quietly stuffing his face, and asked him if he had made his first pair of shoes yet?

"No, not yet Uncle Tom. Father says I need to be able to cut the leather without wasting any before he'll let me use any for new shoes, but at least I am getting the hang of all the various tools he has pegged on the wall of his workshop now. He clips my ear each time I pass him the wrong awl, so I am smarting a bit from my mistakes. But it's over a week now since he last clouted me, so perhaps I will make a cobbler yet!"

The exchange made Nicholas wonder if he too were destined to become a cobbler or what other destiny his future may hold...

Nearly thirty years later Nicholas could, even now, feel the thrill he felt then about his journey to the capital, but heavy steps in the distance presaged the arrival of his gaoler and a priest to start the formalities of his doom-laden day.

The priest, who was formerly a favourite of Ann Boleyn's, had somewhat come down in the world since her beheading the previous year, and he was someone Nicholas had never taken to since being incarcerated; the reverend father being a radical reformer of the church and all.

The gaoler on the other hand, John Partington by name, and chief assistant to the Constable of the Tower, Lord Kingston, had been much more friendly and comforting than Nicholas might have expected after the stretching on the wrack which he had had to endure.

Indeed, he had helped Nicholas replace, *with no little pain, however,* his dislocated shoulder joints afterwards. It did cross his mind, however, to wonder whether it was a real friendliness, or whether it may not be a little too 'put on' to be real. Still, it had been easy to accept the proffered friendship at face value in this, otherwise, forbidding place.

ଔଔଔଔଔଔ

December 1536

☞ John Partington (Assistant Constable of Tower of London) Missive to Lord Kingston, Constable. Reporting upon the state and status of prisoners delivered to the Tower in late November

My good Lord Kingston,

As you instructed me I have secured the dozen ringleaders of the Lincolnshire rebellion brought to me of late for indefinite incarceration in the Tower. My Lord Hussey of Sleaford, being an elderly man and of some former renown, I have placed in the rooms that were used for mistress Bullen last year before her execution - since his money and credit are sound. I see that he is fed well but it is apparent that he is unmanned by the terror of his position. He tells me little, directly, but sits in a corner of the room, wringing his hands and muttering that he has been wronged. Indeed his continual muttering is tiresome, but of no value as to information.
Nine other gentlemen of various lesser ranks, and the priest Kendall, have been locked, two and three to a cell in adjoining rooms in the tower and have been fed according to their rank and credit. All have settled to their fate in different degrees and most have accepted the likely outcome of their imprisonment as inevitable and beyond their capacity to change. All take great care, when speaking to me, not to implicate others in their statements and I have, as yet, no new information to impart as to their motivations for being involved in the course of events in Lincolnshire in October. Please advise me as to whether you need me to apply more physical pressure to extract their stories more fully. As you know I do not relish using the wrack unbidden, but if needs must...?
The twelfth person brought to me, the shoemaker, Nicholas Melton,

known generally and widely as "Captain Cobbler", I have placed by himself in a small cell towards the top of the Tower as you required and I have made every effort to befriend him as you suggested in the hope of learning something new about his activity and contacts with other people in October and in the months leading up to the rebellion. Thus far I have to tell you that nothing new has been forthcoming, other than the information he provided at the court of inquisition set up by my Lord Cromwell. When asked direct questions, he seemeth to answer and to have answered in honest vein.

Unlike some of the gentlemen already referred to, who are cautious to be sure not to implicate others, the Cobbler Melton is most earnest in his openness when he talks to me. And he seemeth willing to share his story openly as if no fault could be attached to him for his actions. So far, however, I have made little progress in expanding the list of conspirators beyond those already known.

I remain your faithful servant
John Partington

(Personal notes for my own better recollection – not sent with letter...)

As requested by the Constable of the Tower, Lord Kingston, I have established a friendly relationship with a man in my custody and care, commonly known as Captain Cobbler, Nicholas Melton - from Louth in the County of Lincolnshire - with a view to extracting further "secret" information from him. I spend at least a little time with him on most days of the week and he talks with me freely concerning many topics. And I have, strange to relate, begun to take pleasure in the time in his company for its own sake as well as in the performance of my duty to the Constable in reporting on "Captain Cobbler's" motivation in setting off the rebellion against our beloved King Henry VIII of England.

Cobbler Melton was brought into my custody in November 1536 along with other ringleaders of the plot. My official letters to the Constable go on a weekly basis to Lord Kingston and these notes are, merely, for my own better recollection of our converse over time – or in case I fall ill and am replaced in my duties, so a successor may be properly briefed.

He (Melton) is a man of medium height, medium build and aged in the middle years of his fourth decade as, of course, the century is in the middle years of its fourth decade too – he was apparently born as the century turned, so, at 36, he is just a little younger than myself, therefore, who has just this week achieved the milestone of two score years on this earth.

We thus have much in common in being trained, in both archery and hand-to-hand fighting, in musters of the commonality over the years. In truth he seems to be as "good" as me at hitting an archery target at distance – perhaps thrice out of every five arrows despatched, if we are lucky – although we can both claim that the other two arrows would come to ground near the target at least (which skill should ensure an enemy Frenchman would have trouble walking with an arrow in his boot – making us nearly as safe, perhaps, as if he was pierced through the heart)

Melton is apparently a good horseman, however, and was ill-pleased that his horse had to be sold to pay for his keep in the Tower whilst he shares our company here – especially since it did not, of course, achieve its full value in the market place as a forced sale. He appears to have had more than moderate success at his trade of making shoes, for, as well as keeping a good horse, he also had the assistance of two servants in his business, both unusual benefits of status for a normal cobbler.

He also seemeth to be something of a lynchpin in his local community; acting as secretary of the cobbler's guild and providing his secretarial services to various of the "Lights" in the Church, set up for the support of candles to be lit and prayers to be proffered to help common folk on their

33

journey through purgatory – those who could not afford to buy the services of the priests for themselves or their loved ones individually.

He can read well and apparently understands numbers well so his services were used by the Plough-Light and by the Shepherd-Light at least, probably the sawyer's guild too and perhaps more. He therefore had many dealings with the Church Wardens but seemeth not to trust them entirely.

He said to me once that "…they were often too concerned for their own pockets rather than for the general good of the Church which should have been their true task, for the benefit of the people of the town of Louth." Indeed, he seemeth to be of high moral principle for one of relatively lowly estate.

Because he was involved in the presentation of the Corpus Christi plays and pageants each year he was also well known and seemingly well-liked in Louth (he sometimes took the role of Saint John the Baptist and can project his voice to a marked degree without seeming to shout – a skill he has demonstrated for me here in the tower)

And the town's vicar-priest, Father Kendall, also in custody in the Tower for his involvement in the plot, was both a lifelong friend and working colleague on the production of the plays. They had met long ago when the young Melton joined the Corpus Christi players in Louth when he was about ten and Kendall, a young singer then, was a couple of years older. Kendall's voice had just broken and he had been replaced in the choir by another of Melton's friends, one Thomas Foster, who, according to Melton had had a lovely voice as a child and a "wonderful strong voice" as an adult.

Foster had been singing in the Louth Church choir for over 25 years when the rebellion broke out, and his father Thomas Foster senior, also still sang in Church on Saint's days but not Sundays. So, despite being over 65, Foster senior had retained his capability with harmony.

I mention the Fosters in these notes because it was something Tom Foster said on that fateful Sunday, last October 1st, that may have actually sparked off the rebellion if Melton is telling me the truth!

There had been much talk in the town of the King closing monasteries and churches – much exaggerated, of course. And Tom Foster, who had just visited Grimsby on business and heard some gossip there about the Hull townspeople's reaction to the King's visitation, by selling off their silver plate – chose to repeat it loudly in church. He apparently said as the choir was setting off in procession through the church . . .

"Go we to follow the crosses, for if they be taken from us, we be like to follow them no more".

I gathered from Melton that another of their close acquaintances, Robert Norman, who is a Roper in Louth, made sure he paid someone (I think it was John, or Jack, Wilson – anyway, he was a sawyer and lived locally) to spread Foster's words around the town. I understand Norman gave Wilson a penny for the task to be done.

Melton then told me that he and his friends thought the churchwardens would give up the town's treasures to the visitation without a murmur, so they chose to do something about it themselves to ensure their protection.

છ છ છ છ છ છ

Protest: Save our silver
1536 – Sunday 1ˢᵗ October

The black headscarves of the three elderly widows, scurrying ahead of him through the sudden squall to evening mass, put Nicholas in mind of the rooks that had flown overhead as he was homeward bound the day before. Lifting and twisting in the autumnal gusts they were chattering to each other busily, as were the widows this afternoon.

Who knew what the chatter was about (*in either case*) but it was as busy and sharp as it had been all day amongst everyone Nicholas had encountered since morning mass.

Perhaps, as far as the widows were concerned, it was simply about the magnetism of the Louth priest, Father Thomas Kendall, who they would be seeing presently. A good looking and well-educated man of middle years with a gentle sense of humour; he had a sympathetic ear, always, for his parishioners' tales of woe. He would usually be surrounded by a band of mainly mature women who would help with the cleaning and decoration of the church with willing hands!

Earlier today, though, he had seemed very much out of sorts. Anger, it appeared, had replaced his normal good humour and it had clearly been brewing over night. He had been down the road to Bolingbroke the previous day, Saturday, with many fellow priests from the Louth and Louthesk deanery, to listen to Dr Raynes.

Raynes, the Chancellor to Bishop Longland of Lincoln, was 'examining' the priests in the neighbouring areas of Hill and Bolingbroke, on their views of the king's dreaded 'Ten Articles'. That was soon due to happen here, directly, too, when they would face an inquisition from the Deacon, John Frankish. And Frankish was due in Louth the following day, Monday.

Father Kendall and his fellows had got very hot under the collar about the manner of the questioning. And this had, no doubt, all got jumbled up with the many rumours going the rounds locally. And on top of this there was all the pent up anger about the dissolution of more than fifty religious houses in the County of Lincolnshire over the spring and summer.

In his sermon in the morning service he had chosen to start by dealing with the recently contentious issue of purgatory...

"We all know..." he had intoned "...that we must endure a time in purgatory before we can take our allotted room in the Kingdom of Heaven. This has been a key tenet of our faith from the very beginnings of the church on the rock of Peter...", he held his arms wide to encompass the congregation, the silver threads in his apparel coruscating in the candlelight ... "And we all pray for our dead loved ones that their time in purgatory should be short, as, indeed, we hope and trust others will pray for us when we are gone from this earth.

"The idea of purgatory is at the heart of the community of this very church. It affects the richest parishioners, who can pay for a priest to pray every day of the year for their souls once they are dead, to the very meekest amongst you who spend hours of your time each month raising money for candles.

Candles for the Ploughlight chapel just to take one example – so that the light of the candle, yea the very light of God's goodness..."

His voice lifted and boomed in the vaulted ceiling of the church as he said this, then he almost whispered the line again,"...yea, the very light of God's goodness... can help to speed the passing of a soul. The soul of our friend, Bennett Waterland for example, who died this last six-month, towards his room in our Father's House"

Several voices murmured "Yea, Amen" at this reference to their dearly loved neighbour who had brightened so many lives with his rich laughter at such social events as Father Kendall mentioned. He had also helped many local people to plough their family strips on the town lands.

A large candle for Bennett Waterland was burning brightly all the while as Father Kendall spoke. It took pride of place just now in the side chapel, which also contained the silver gilt candle holders of the Plough-light and Maiden-lights, as well as the more sumptuous silverware of the Assumption Guild of the Blessed Virgin Mary.

Indeed the light of the many candles which had been lit that day twinkled brightly on the polished silver. The eyes of many members of the congregation glistened in the reflected lights, with a sweet melancholy of memories at the mention of their old friend.

"And yet," continued Father Kendall "some bishops…(he carefully did *not* name them, but more than a few townsfolk knew the list would include their own Bishop Longland of Lincoln, for their vicar was sometimes quite indiscreet in his daily conversations!) "Some bishops seem to think such prayers for our departed souls may not work…or why would they support the casting down of our religious houses? More than fifty houses have closed around us in this county alone since springtime!"

Some parishioners swore later that they had seen fire in his eyes as he said this and crashed his heavy hand down on the lectern to punctuate his words.

"Some bishops" he said again with heavy irony "have argued that they can find no mention of purgatory in the bible. But the bible needs to be studied long to read the Word of God truly. You know, for I have told you this before, that I have studied with great masters of learning at Oxford University over many years. And when I was there, I learned that one of the passages which reveals the nature of purgatory is Matthew chapter five verses twenty five and twenty six …"

He read them out slowly in Latin then translated them into English and then, without further reference to his bible, repeated verse twenty six… in English

"Verily I say unto thee, Thou shalt by no means come out thence, until thou hast paid the uttermost farthing."

He let the words hang then in the silence until one or two of the congregation felt uncomfortable and shifted in their seats.

"…*the uttermost farthing*" his voice boomed out again, and the flat of his hand slapped the lectern, making many of his parishioners jump.

"It is, indeed, the prayers of our family and friends that help, farthing by farthing, to repay our past sins and indiscretions. And also, indeed, the prayers of our brethren and sisters in holy life help this process. And now, many of them have been casten-out of their houses in our County of Lincoln of late, and many more besides, across the Wash in Norfolk and across the Humber in Yorkshire."

Another susurration of murmuring welled up in the full church. Nearly everyone present had one or more members of their extended family who had been affected by the wholesale closure of religious houses in Lincolnshire alone, or they knew of a neighbour whose family had been thus affected.

Nicholas, taking precedence at the end of the two rows containing over half of the cobblers of Louth and members of their families, thought of his cousin Eleanor who had recently been thrown out of nearby Legbourne Priory after more than 25 years. The King's Chancellor's men were due there early on the morrow to decide the final fate of the house, its occupants and their accumulated treasures. Barring a miracle, however, or maybe just the intervention of Thomas Cromwell, who had previously acted as sponsor for this fair priory, there was little hope for them. And all the sisters had been required to leave before the Chancellor's men arrived

Nicholas' mind was brought back to the present as his close friend, the priest, Thomas Kendall, continued in a different vein.

"It seems" he was saying, "that the King's Chancellor, that villein Thomas Cromwell, has chosen to interpret this passage in a more literal way. He wants the 'uttermost farthing' from our religious houses to fall into the coffers of his master, the Good King Harry; coffers which have been emptied over the years, and spent on luxuries and Cloth of Gold to drape over wooden frames to impress the French; or spent on armaments to fight the French!"

He was, of course, careful not to imply any criticism of the policy for no doubt that might have been seen to be an act of treason. His words were simply factual. He was simply suggesting that such money should not be replaced at the expense of the church.

"And mark my words" Father Kendall went on, "after the smaller religious houses are finished with, Cromwell will tackle the larger religious houses like Barlings, beyond Wragby..." he raised his right hand and gestured westwards, past the seated congregation... "and Kirkstead, near Horncastle, as well as the big abbeys in Yorkshire and beyond which comfort the poor and benighted."

He paused theatrically...

"Nor will he stop there! He will next be tapping into the rich vein of silver and gold, with which our beautiful church is garnished, and for which you and your families have worked so hard over the years. 'Tis rumoured abroad that the visitation of the bishop's commissioners here in Louth tomorrow will secretly, or, maybe, not so secretly, seek to value the silver plate in our wonderful Church of Saint James, for forward transmission to Cromwell's coffers, too."

At this Kendall raised his eyes, not to his God, as some of his parishioners thought at first, but to the roof of the rood screen which extended over the choir and which sometimes creaked and groaned a little with the weight of solid silver and silver plate resting thereon. Just one small doorway in the wall facing his pulpit led up a spiral stone stairway to the rood screen roof, so it could easily be sealed.

"My predecessor, Vicar Sudbury, provided a glorious silver cross we shall be using later as we process around the church to celebrate Dedication Day, today. And now we have been instructed to celebrate, at the same time, the lives of saints who had their own Saints' days until this year."

A few groans could be heard throughout the church at this move to cut their Holy Days and holidays.

"Your fathers, and their fathers before them, worked tirelessly with their families to add to the wonderful and great treasures we all cherish. They brighten our church at Easter, at the nativity and when we celebrate Corpus Christi and all the other festivals which add to our joys each year."

"You yourselves have scrimped and saved to add to this our treasure and **the uttermost farthing** of that may soon disappear into the treasure chests of Chancellor Cromwell unless we look to protect it."

His face glowered as he went on...

"The very vestments which adorn the statues of Saint James and the Blessed Virgin Mary yonder..." as he spoke, candlelight glistened on the gold thread which ran through these wonderful garments.

"These very vestments may be used in the same profane way that the odious Commissioners Legh and Layton have used vestments from religious houses they visited in Yorkshire. They put them on their sweat stained horses to sit beneath the saddles they perch on."

Some of the more sensitive souls blanched at this reported blasphemy – though many knew it to be true, as stories they heard in Lincoln market place confirmed.

"And today, this very day, the first of October in the year of our Lord 1536, we are enjoined to celebrate, Oh Joyous Day, our Saint Mary Magdelene, the good Saints Swithin, Augustine, Alban, Ethelreda, and Catherine as well as Saints Thomas Becket and Edward the Confessor...What? A murmurration in our church...?" Father Kendall paused quizzically as if he had not expected the congregation to start muttering at his listing of the saints to be celebrated today, for many heads were turned to neighbours and the noise level was rising.

"Shame upon you", he said with heavy irony, "our bishop, at Baron Cromwell's behest, bids us celebrate these worthies of heroic virtue, these martyrs, these workers of miracles all on this very day!"

Another pause...

"What?" he cupped his ear, as if to hear better what his congregants muttered, "you say each of them had his, or her, **own** Holy Day until now? Fie upon you for lazy whelps! How can you get in the harvest, or plant your fields, or do your master's bidding if you are enjoying the pleasures of some Holy Day at every touch and turn. How will the Chancellor's business get done in the courts if they are interrupted during the law terms by random Holy Days in the middle of the week!?"

By now the murmuring had turned to amusement, as everyone realised their Vicar had planted his tongue firmly in his cheek in saying all this. It was a truly sore point for the community this Sunday, accepting the loss of so many days of rest. Father Kendall had clearly tuned in to the feelings of betrayal as people mourned the loss of joy, rest and community-building that went with the holy day celebrations associated with these saints, spread as they had been, formerly, throughout the year.

The amusement had softened the Vicar's anger but, as he had intended, of course, had succeeded in embedding that anger in the hearts and minds of the congregation. And his ploy ensured there would be much talk and reinterpretation of his sermon as the day wore on.

He finished his sermon with two robust, if rather sombre, instructions...

"Look to your church and its treasures...

... and look to your commonwealth for they are all, this day, at risk"

So saying, he blessed the assembled townsfolk and bid them make procession with him around the perimeter of the church in celebration of the church itself; and, of course, in celebration of the aforesaid saints. Stepping carefully down from the pulpit he took hold of the very fine (and very heavy!) silver cross that the town's former Vicar Sudbury had donated to the church for such special occasions. It was a silver cross that was also for use at his own obits, aimed at speeding the passage of his own soul through purgatory.

The deep booming voice of the leader of the choir, Tom Foster, another of Nicholas' friends, then rang out through the church as people readied themselves for the procession to begin...

"Masters all" he shouted, his voice echoing and resonating in the body of the church, "step forth and let us follow the crosses this day: for God knows whether ever we shall follow them again!"

So saying, he and his fellow choristers started the musical chant to which the procession would step out. It was as if everyone had taken in an extra half a lung full of air. The very walls of the church sang out too with the spirit-lifting melody of the *Alleluia, Dies Sanctificus*; the stones resounding to the booming male voices; incense drifting in the cool air, making atmospheric patterns in the sunlight slanting through the high windows. Hearts were stirred and passions roused.

Following the service and the procession everyone had split up into small clusters, the stirred hearts not yet quieted. Some wandered homewards but most, as if afraid to let it out of their sight, stayed close to the church, exchanging gossip and chewing over the priest's words; wondering what was to be done about it all.

Quite a group had gathered round Nicholas Melton and Tom Foster as they all tried to make sense of the crisis brewing in their lives. There were several side conversations going on as various individuals added to the gossip or tried to catch up with bits they had missed and there were frequent exclamations and expostulations...

"Nooo never!..."

"...Did they really!?"

"...'Od's Teeth!",

"Bloomin' 'Eck!"

"People in Hull have sold all the church silver and spent the money on paving slabs so Cromwell cannot steal it all!"

"Get away with you!"

"You remember that obnoxious Clerk of Cromwell's who was here the week before last, said he'd been auditing Tupholme Priory or summat, and said all hoity-toity like '... that silver dish there was meeter for the king than for the likes of us'...? Old Bobby Medwell was all for pulling out his dagger and disembowelling the guy! But Tom here managed to stop him, said it would end up in tears! Bobby said something about making 'the king and the clerk's master' a '...breakfast as they've never had', we took him to mean with the clerk's liver and kidneys!!" So saying the speaker jabbed his hand forward as if with a knife and twisted it round in the air...

"Good grief!"

Eventually, most of the group began to focus on the main conversation, which chiefly featured Nicholas and Tom, odd comments being chipped in by others in the know.

"I don't think that our current crop of churchwardens would make any kind of stand if the bishop's commissioner wanted to walk away with the church plate and them fine silver crosses stacked up on the Rood screen roof." Tom remarked acidly, "They're mealy-mouthed and too afraid of their own shadows, if you ask me."

"And the town centre is too well paved to need to sell the plate and buy tons of York stone like Hull burghers seem to have done" said John Wilson, who had heard it from Guy Kyme, who had recently been over the Humber into Yorkshire.

"There are plenty of towns and villages where it is well known that the people are ready to take a stand in Yorkshire and further north. Now that we are past Michaelmas and the harvest is safely in, all that's needed is for someone to take the lead. It's not been a good harvest though, just a little higher than last year, but we can manage to get through the winter so we should stand firm."

"I am always up for a good fight", said Bobby Medwell from the edge of the group, to general laughter! A few cups of ale and Bobby would plant a punch on anyone's nose as soon as look at them!

"Well, something needs to be done" said Nicholas firmly. "That silver represents too much of the heart of our community and the work of our forefathers, for us to let it be taken away without a struggle!"

"The first thing to do is to make sure everyone knows what the situation is so that everybody shares in what action follows. Everyone knows we have spoken about the problems many times during the summer, as things have been getting worse. But there were a lot of people in Louth who were absent from mass this morning and, perhaps, do not know how urgent it has become for us to act..."

"Not surprised..." chipped in a voice from the edge of the group "nearly didn't come myself this morning when it was raining so hard..."

"At least the sun's out now" said another.

"...be that as it may", Nicholas sighed at the interruptions, "we need to get round and speak to folk who weren't here and let them know what's happening. Tom, why don't you and James here, "indicating one of his fellow Louth cobblers, "make a list of all those you can remember not being in their seats this morning. Then we need to get Father Kendall to delve into his privy purse to pay for ..." he paused here, looking at the people around him...

"...to pay for John, here, Robert and Richard, to dash round this afternoon and let people know what's happening – like we do when we need folk to turn out for Corpus Christi rehearsals."

Nicholas had picked on John Wilson, Robert Norman and Richard Nethercotts as being the most reliable trio to get word passed round quickly and without fuss.

"Don't bother the Vicar" Robert said, "Richard and I will gladly do it for nothing and I will make sure John here is not out of pocket for his time either."

"...'ou needn't worrit nothing about me, neither" chirruped John, " I won't be chargin' my normal fees for sawing tree branches off to make 'em safe".

Quite a few people in the crowd chuckled at this, knowing John was usually wont to make a few pennies from the public purse if his sawyer services were needed for public safety. John continued,

"...as long as I have enough to get myself a glass or two of ale after speaking to everybody and using my voice to its limits, I shall be well satisfied to do my fair share. In fact..."

"Shut up, John!" intervened Richard Nethercotts and Robert Norman, with matching theatrical exclamations.

Robert Norman rolled his eyes! "Let's just get the job done between us! I will make sure you get at least a penny to pay for the ale." So saying, the five men set to their allotted tasks with fervour.

"The rest of us," continued Nicholas, "must stand ready after evensong to spend a watchful night in church. Indeed, not only for tonight, but we must keep watch for as long as it takes to be sure everything is secure and safe against the predations of the Chancellor's wolves."

They spent another good few minutes making detailed plans of who would be needed, for how long, and when. And then, the group gradually split up and went their separate ways for the middle part of the day, most of them homewards to lunch. Nicholas had instructed several of the single men present to try and get some sleep during the latter part of the morning and early afternoon so that they would be able to stay awake when others amongst the group would be falling asleep in the dark hours of the night.

☾☙☾☙☾☙☾☙☾☙

Thus it was that Nicholas later found himself following the three swirling black headscarves through the breezy darkening afternoon to his church for the evening mass.

He had persuaded his wife Eliza Jane to keep the children at home this afternoon so that he would be able to focus clearly on the unfolding events without the possible distraction of any familial responsibilities, so he was walking alone as he came in clear sight of the church ahead. Just at that very moment Tom Foster's father, Thomas senior, appeared at the end of Schoolhouse Lane and nearly bumped into Nicholas, preoccupied as they both were.

They both chuckled at their near collision and then they both dropped their lower jaws as they did a double-take looking down the lane towards the church. Despite the spotting rain and the swirling breeze there were crowds of people greeting each other and chattering outside the building as they waited to get through the doors into shelter. It was the sort of crowd they would only normally see on a fine Easter Sunday, or perhaps on a crisp Christmas morning.

"I know young Tom was busying about this morning" said the older man, referring to his son Tom Foster, "but Robert and John have clearly been even busier through the day!"

"Are you not singing this evening, Pop?" Nicholas had taken to calling him 'Pop' after Thomas had been so kind when Nicholas' own father had died those many years before. It started as a small jest, but it suited them both well, especially as, soon afterwards, Nicholas had married Eliza Jane, Thomas' daughter.

"Nay, lad. This damp weather don't do my throat any favours these

46

days and I was struggling to keep a tune this morning, through a sniffle I seem to have picked up in the last couple of days. They'll just have to manage without me! Ha!"

"I thought you choristers were always much earlier to church than the rest of us! That's why I was surprised to bump into you just now!" By the time Nicholas had said these last words some of the people queuing at the church door had seen them coming along the lane and stood aside to let the two clearly-recognised men through into the building.

It was clear there was some expectation in the air of, well... *something* about to happen, even if everyone was unsure *what* it was they might be expecting.

The expectation seemed to increase as Nicholas entered the fine doors on the south side of the church. Rather than his usual Sunday fustian he had put on his Coat of Motley, the brightly coloured one most people recognised from his involvement in the Corpus Christi plays. His entry, therefore, had some of the drama everyone expected of him when he '*wore*' his charismatic personality which he seemed to 'put on' with this fine multi-coloured coat. It was bright red on the shoulders and lapels, with blues, greens and yellows below!

For most of the year he was a quiet soul – rather shy and retiring in his leather cobbler's apron, in point of fact! But once he donned his colourful coat people knew to pay him extra attention. Indeed, the buzz of chatter in the church stilled as his entrance was noticed and only resumed once he had taken his place at the end of the row where sat the majority of the town's cobblers.

He wondered briefly whether he had been right to suggest Eliza Jane stop at home with the two boys as they would probably have lapped this up if they had realised their father was going to be so much the centre of attention.

The evening mass itself passed in something of a blur for Nicholas, his mind wandering over the possible consequences of his planned action at the close of the service. His nerves were steadied, however, when Thomas Kendall repeated some of the warnings he had given that morning and finished his sermon with the same injunction to the people to...

"Look to your church and its treasures...

... and look to your commonwealth for they are this day at risk"

As he said these words again he was looking directly at Nicholas, who felt uplifted by his friend and spiritual mentor very strongly at that moment. The priest appeared to be speaking directly *just* to him. He probably was, too, after the many conversations they had had over the summer months about just these issues.

"God bless you all," added Father Kendall; words he used at every service to act as dismissal to his flock, but somehow more meaningful than ever this evening. "And God bless the sanctity of the church".

It appeared that the light rain must have stopped whilst the service was going on. Now, a few late rays of bright sunshine shone through the upper windows and played fire onto the gold leaf of the helmet of Saint George; and on his golden sword, which seemed forever about to swoop on the hapless dragon below.

Nicholas took strength from this glint of gold as he looked up to the rood loft wherein lay the church treasures. He looked towards the altar and crossed himself, bowed his head briefly, took a deep breath and in his most actorly voice boomed ...

"NOW, gentlemen"

As he said these words he stepped into the middle aisle of the fine, large and very full church – there were probably at least eight hundred people present. It was clear that the word of something being afoot had spread like wildfire. Then he walked steadily forward from his seat, just a little behind the very centre of the building.

He made a fine figure in his multi-coloured Coat of Motley.

He was followed into the centre aisle, as planned, by at least half a dozen of his fellow cobblers and artisans (the larger ones!) – who walked a step or two behind him. At the same time, more of his neighbours left their seats and ensured the central aisle was well blocked.

This in itself was contrary to what normally happened, but then today was not a normal day, nor even a normal Sunday. Long standing habit, ingrained in the community, was for the church to empty in an orderly way, starting from the front. Here sat the higher echelons of local society in and around the town.

It was not quite as if everyone had only one allotted seat for there was always a little movement to be expected but the higher you were in Louth society the nearer the front you usually sat and as a matter of *'normal respect'* everyone bided their turn to exit the church. And the better dressed, richer ladies and gentlemen usually took some pride in sweeping down the centre aisle nodding to their peers as they left and simply looking as graceful as possible to everyone else – especially when the church was most crowded.

Sometimes those who sat at the outer ends of the pews and benches would leave along the outer side aisles. That, however, brought to light another contrary factor on this day. Several of the menfolk to whom Nicholas had addressed his loud, projected order, were walking in parallel with Nicholas down each of the side aisles, thus blocking the exits for *everyone* at the front of the church.

Some of these gentlefolk had already started to leave their seats as normal and walk towards the doors at the back of the church but found their way blocked in these side aisles before Nicholas had reached his goal of the first three rows which is where the churchwardens were to be found.

Clearly, despite all the gossip, not everyone knew what was happening or what was due to happen. A large and distinctly burly farmer, one Edward Smithill, was *not* amongst those who had clear expectations this evening and he found his way barred by five or six rather stony faced men as he and his wife and four daughters sought to leave.

Normally such a blockage, if accidental, would cleave into two and let the family smoothly through, with forelocks tugged if needful. Today, however, this did not happen and Mr Smithill, who had actually walked into two of these men, assuming they would part as normal, quickly became somewhat red in the face with irritation at this seemingly calculated insult ...

"Stand aside, sir ...***Stand ASIDE, I say!***"

There was some scuffling on the opposite side of the church, too, as two more of the town's minor gentlemen also found their way blocked. Nicholas had been quite clear in giving his instructions earlier on in the day and although no-one moved out of the way they were all very polite in their refusal to move, several of them holding their hands out palm upwards in apology at their 'rudeness' in not moving. Nor did they respond with rough words when told by these gentlemen that it "...would be the worse for them if they did not move themselves *now*". A little scuffling did ensue but it was less unseemly than might have been the case if Nicholas had not been as firm as he had about how everyone should behave.

The atmosphere in the church was, nevertheless, beginning to get a little tense by the time Nicholas reached his targets.

"Mr Goldsmith, Mr Elwood." Nicholas inclined his head politely to the two leading churchwardens. "Gentlemen, we need to relieve you of your sets of keys to the church and the rood screen loft."

His voice was controlled, quite soft in fact, but so distinct and clearly projected that it carried to every corner of the building, as he had, of course, intended. There was a little murmuring as people affirmed to their neighbours that *that was what **they** were expecting!*"... "oh yes..." of course! Even Farmer Smithill went quiet for a few moments seeking to discern why he had been blocked in!

Mr Elwood, the quieter of the two key-bearing churchwardens, looked a little sheepish, but reached deeply into his coat pocket and drew out a heavy bunch of keys, hesitating a little but handing the bunch over to the motley-coated man in front of him with no further fuss. Nicholas relaxed a little, but his relaxation was short-lived.

Mr Goldsmith, a man of very short stature, drew himself up to his full height (not a terribly difficult task of course!) and blurted out...

"This is preposterous, Cobbler Melton! What right do you arrogate to yourself and your bunch of rowdies!? *We* are rightfully the wardens of the treasures of this fine church." He was either unaware of the rumours circulating during the day, or was determined to stand on his dignity.

"I do understand, Mr Goldsmith..." was Nicholas' patient reply in the silence that followed this challenge, "...but are you and your friends prepared to gather in the church tonight and every night for the foreseeable future, as guards, to deny entry to the representatives of Chancellor Cromwell, should he come looking for these wonderful crosses to melt down for his treasure trove"? His voice was all reasonableness but underlying the tone was a ring of steel as he put the lily-livered churchwarden on the spot.

Goldsmith, easily one of the richest men in town – his name itself declaring his occupation – started to bluster as if he was about to defend himself and his fine colleagues against such a slanderous accusation of potential cowardice but Goodman Elwood, also well-off but a much more likeable man, laid a hand on his colleague's sleeve and shook his head slightly. Goldsmith's bluster died away as fast as it had erupted, as he realised the inevitability of events running their course!

After a moment or two of silence he reached for his own bunch of keys and handed them over somewhat meekly to a rousing cheer from the congregation which brought an extra flush to his cheek. Nicholas drew to one side and motioned with his right hand that the churchwardens were free to go and a gap appeared as if by magic in all three exit pathways. The Goldsmith and Elwood families were followed by others from the front four or five rows in a largely well-mannered retreat from the church.

At the side, however, Mr Smithill was none too careful as he harrumphed and barged his way to the back of the church, his womenfolk trailing after him with much better grace, even with a "*Thank you*" from one of his pretty daughters to a young man who had previously blocked her way. He blushed delightfully and started thinking thoughts that would never come true.

The overall noise level escalated quickly as people milled around. But Nicholas chose not to speak again until he had made sure that everyone who was not party to their earlier discussions about protecting the commonwealth treasures had left the church; and he and his colleagues, remaining inside, had shut and locked the main doors against all-comers.

As this was going on, some of the other churchwardens, Robert Bailey and the Fishwyke brothers, Walter and Robert, had called upon William Ashby, Louth's Constable in Chief, to try and stop this mutinous behaviour. However these few men found themselves outnumbered and although voices were raised and some threats levelled against the Cobbler and his group, the planned takeover of the church and its treasures went ahead quite smoothly.

All of a sudden, once the main doors were closed, about twenty men found themselves in almost complete silence. The thick doors shut out the last vestiges of noise and chatter. Nicholas himself broke the silence after he had put the batten in place and locked the doors with the huge iron key on one of the bunches in his possession. Turning towards Robert Norman, he said...

"Robert, take this other bunch of keys that Mr Elwood gave me and go round all the outer doors and make sure each is locked and secure. Take John and a couple of other men and ensure there is something heavy and immovable in front of each of the weaker doors in the building, where there is no batten. Then at least we can just concentrate on these front doors for our main movements in and out."

"Oh – and don't forget to block off that double trapdoor into the crypt, which John normally uses to bring firewood into the church in the winter. We wouldn't want anyone to sneak in under our feet. The rest of you split into two groups and make sure the lower windows on each side of the church are blocked off if there is the least chance they could be broken to gain entry. There is timber and whatever you might need in the crypt, stored where we keep the Corpus Christi materials, if you need to use it."

"I think Harry here knows where the toolboxes are if you need them?" – Harry confirmed this assumption with a nod.

"I will check the rood loft with Tom and then we'll lock the loft access door in the front pillar. When we are all done let us get together under the tower to have a bite of supper and talk about how we go on from here."

"Aye Cap'n Cobbler", joked John Wilson, saluting Nicholas with his right hand clenched across his chest, and each of them set off to do his duty with a smile.

The church was secure by the time the light had faded and Nicholas made sure all the men were present before calling for quiet. The atmosphere was rather brittle and there was a sense of gallows humour in the air. Despite their bravado it was clear that, for some of them, the prospect of a long night in a quiet church was fraught with the possibility of facing the unknown. Nicholas sensed this and started his talk with them by making light of these unstated fears.

"At least being in a sacred house we'll face no ghosts tonight – Father Kendall blessed the church today for all saints and we are safe in the very heart of our community here. The worst we'll have to face is getting sprayed with bat's piss if we sit under the belfry too long. But I think most of them have gone out hunting now it is getting dark."

"We have talked about possibly having to do this most of the summer since the commissioners started closing down the religious houses and stripping them of their treasures for the royal coffers. So now is the time for us to protect our own."

His voice was calm and firm and he could feel the atmosphere lightening as he spoke.

"It is going to be a long night so I suggest we tuck in to our supper now and then some of us might try and sleep a little so we can stay awake in the small hours. So John, what provisions do we have in our larder?"

John Baker, true to his family name, was a bread-maker in the town so at least everyone knew they would not want for tasty fresh bread. John and his goodwife, Pat, known to all locally as 'Mother Baker' (or, more often, Ma Baker) had been in charge of catering for most of the church 'ales' for as long as anyone could remember. She acquired the epithet for her care of three orphan children, as well as her own brood of five strapping sons and three buxom girls. Nicholas and Father Kendall knew they could rely on the Bakers' judgement as to provisioning this unusual event, without anyone starving or wanting for flavour.

John opened the door to a small room leading off from the tower normally used as a store room for trestles, benches and other stuff used for the church ales. In other words it was part of John's 'territory' in normal times and he had thought nothing of making himself at home there on this unusual day. He and his younger brother Jeb, a gaunt shadow of his brother's robust build and something of a simpleton from birth, but always a willing helper, had set up two of the long tables on trestles with benches either side.

The benches would just about cope with all the men at the same time if they cosied up together with no room for their elbows to stick out, but Nicholas had decided to leave a couple of men on guard at the South door and another couple on the vestry door at the nave end of the church in case anyone had thoughts of breaking in this early in the evening. This meant that everyone at least had elbow room to raise a mug of small ale to his lips when he wanted to wash down the food they all felt so ready for.

The four men who had drawn the short straws of duty had been allotted a small hand-bell per pair in case they needed to summon help quickly and a thick slice of bread and dripping to stop their stomachs rumbling until it was their turn to dine. The rest eyed the selection of cold meats, pasties, pickles and cheeses, set out on a third trestle-table against the wall, with pleasure, before setting about the platters with gusto.

As always, John seemed quietly proud of his table of provender.

"Don't stint lads – we've more than enough for tonight, with some left for morning too and my Pat has the women organised to keep replacing the food baskets as we need them if we have to be here a long time. I have kept some vittals aside for them lads as are still doing their duty."

"Thank 'ee John for organising this for us" said Nicholas "and let us all thank the Lord for the food we are about to eat."

"Amen to that" added John and a soft chorus of "Amen" was soon followed by sounds of hungry men tucking in to good fare.

In an aside to John Baker, Nicholas asked, "...did you check with Father Kendall about paying for this out of church funds?"

"I didn't bother him yet, Nicholas, since Pat and I are still holding a small float from the last church ale. We thought we would use that up before we needed to tap into savings. Quite a few of our regulars are giving us their pies, and so on, for free at the moment as well, seein' as 'ow 'tis a commonwealth concern. I dare say that could change if it looks like being a drawn out affair, though!"

"Well, let's hope the commissioners back away soon then – but let me know if your money is running short. Father Kendall and I have warned some of the church's key money men that we might need to call in some favours if we are going to do this properly and make the problems go away for good and all!"

This was said with some asperity and feeling, since Nicholas knew that the church wardens whom he had challenged this evening were in the wider money circle of the church, too. They may not see, or *feel*, the same perspective as some of the less well-off members of the church, for whom this stand of principle was somehow very 'personal' to them and their families.

Nicholas, as secretary to several of the small funding groups or 'lights' of Louth, such as the 'Plough-light', was very conscious of the, often huge, personal efforts put in by many unassuming church members to keep their modest coffers full. Full enough, at least, to keep prayers being said for their former friends and colleagues to ease their way through purgatory. He was also very aware of the huge pride they felt when their work resulted in spare cash. And such funds could be used to the general benefit of the whole church, contributing to one of the best collections of silver plate in the county, and diocese, of Lincoln, so it was said.

When most of the men had had their fill of mouth-watering pasties and other delights from the table and were leaning back to let their stomachs have a little freedom to work more comfortably, Nicholas spoke up...

"All right, then..." In a voice that cut through the several conversations taking place round the benches, "...it is time we made sure we are all clear what we have to do through the rest of the night and into tomorrow..." And, with that, he went over, again, the rota of who would be doing what, and at what hours they would change shifts. He made sure he gave himself the most difficult hours in the depths of the night. His mind was whirling with all the implications of what they were doing, so he knew he would not sleep anyway!

Hardly had they finished sorting the rota out for the next ten hours or so, when there was a slight rustling, and a movement of the shadows at the further end of the church. There were still a few lighted candles dotted strategically through the body of the church but the level of light was very low. The noise suggested that someone was walking towards them along the northern side aisle. A few hearts missed a beat or two because they knew the guards in the vestry should not be leaving their posts. Nicholas, however, knew the gait of his friend, Thomas Kendall, vicar of this parish, in any level of lighting you could name.

He was just about to ease the minds about him with this information, when the shadows spoke to them all in a deeply sonorous, and friendly, voice.

"Good evening one and all – I trust you are comfortable in God's work", there was a chuckle just below the surface of the words, and he was greeted with several murmurs of assent.

"Thomas, good evening to you – will you eat a little now you are here?"

"No thank you, Nicholas, not just at the moment – I have eaten too much cake at the ladies evening meeting, from which I have only just escaped. They were anxious to know just what all you ruffians were doing barricading the church tonight."

At this a real chuckle escaped his lips.

"Why they insist on providing such sweet concoctions for their monthly meetings escapes me – I would much rather have a savoury morsel or two to be honest. I have said as much, too, but I think they compete to let each other know who can afford the most sugar each month. It was Mistress Blanchard's turn this time and she outdid herself."

55

A couple of groans from behind Nicholas indicated Mistress Blanchard's best efforts were well known amongst the assembled group.

"She always can be relied upon to provide a cake for the church ales", John Baker's voice chimed in from behind a door, where he was clearing leftovers "...and 'tis no untruth to say it is always the last to be sold. And I have it on goodly authority (meaning his wife's gossip) that she has been known to send her sister to buy it up on more than one occasion, to make sure it is not left unsold!"

By this time Father Kendall had reached the group under the bell-tower, where the bell ropes were neatly coiled over hooks in the wall ready for use as and when appropriate.

"Your men were well briefed, Nicholas. I had to use my password twice to get in the door tonight, as well as telling them who I was. I deliberately used it quietly first time, too, so they would have had a job hearing me clearly. And I feel sure they had recognised my voice even before that."

"Well, we cannot afford to slip at this point", Nicholas told his friend. "What if the commissioners had you held by force, to trick us into opening the door!?"

"I will bolster them with a little praise when I talk to them later," he added quietly just for Thomas Kendall's ear.

"Now, let us go and sit at the end of yon pews," Nicholas said, louder again now, "and you can tell us in more detail what happened at yesterday's meeting. You might just go over the basic topics again for Tom Foster here, and Robert Norman and John Wilson. I have tried to relay everything you told me yesterday, but it would help us all to understand what we are about if you tell us all about it in your own words, rather than them relying on my second hand version."

He knew they would hear nothing different from what he had already told them but he wanted, perhaps even 'needed', them to know the reliability of his judgement as events unfolded. No doubt there would be a crisis, somewhere along the way, and he didn't want his judgement called into question at a critical moment!

Thomas Kendall lifted an eyebrow just a touch as he looked over at Nicholas, who pretended he hadn't seen the movement, so with an almost invisible shrug of one shoulder the priest led the way to pews, just a little way down the centre aisle of the church.

John Baker briefly made sure his brother, Jeb, had plenty of things to do to keep him well-occupied for the time being, so that they would not be interrupted by Jeb's always preternaturally loud voice asking him "...*what next, John?*"

"So, let's see...", Father Kendall said when they were all five seated – he had picked up a small stool for himself, as the others sat themselves, two on one pew and the other two on the pew in front, slightly twisted so they could all see and hear the vicar as he told his tale.

"...As I think you know" he said, "I went to the Hall in the castle at Old Bolingbroke yesterday where Dr Raynes, the Bishop of Lincoln's Chancellor, had set up his Commission of Inquisition into the Parish clergy."

"It was a meeting called for the clergy of the Deaneries of Hill and Bolingbroke really, so neither I nor my colleagues from the Louth and Louthesk deaneries need have gone but since he'll be coming here soon we thought it would be a good idea to find out how it would work out for us later."

"Dr Raynes welcomed us with a smile, of course, but it was that smile of his which could send butter rancid, so I don't think he really wanted us there! The priests of Hill and Bolingbroke are generally a bit old and doddery so I think he was hoping for a quiet time of it for the first round of his inquiry. I don't think he expected us, more belligerent and, to be frank, better-educated Priests, to turn up and spoil his quiet day."

"The Parson of Conisholme – angry and intense young man, cannot remember his name, he hasn't been there long – was particularly angry at the mid-morning break. He was shouting the odds, about Chancellor Cromwell wanting to relieve most of the priests of their benefices, so that he can start all over again, and charge another round of 'First Fruits' which would go to the crown coffers, now the king is head of the church in England, rather than to the pope as before."

"But that would only happen if the priests cannot show they have understood the 'New Learning' of the Church of England?" interjected Nicholas questioningly.

"That's right", said Father Kendall with a humourless smile, "but during the first session some of the less learned priests were very shaky on what that 'New Learning' was, and Dr Raynes was very unsympathetic when they strayed from the approved text! Also, anytime it happened he was very quick to ask the value of the benefice for his notes, so it was something he clearly had in mind, whether or not they might eventually insist on putting it into practice?!"

"So, our angry young Parson from Conisholme had a point?" queried John Baker.

"Up to a point he had a point" Thomas Kendall agreed, hesitating a little "but I really don't know how many colleagues would be affected. He said he would rather lose his benefice than pay first fruits again – but he is young, and could probably find many other jobs to apply his angry and, no doubt, able mind to. But if it happened to some of my more mature brethren, they would certainly struggle to find another acceptable living."

"What about you?" asked Tom Foster bluntly.

"Well, I know enough about the new learning to pass any test they might devise and, if self-interest were to drive me, I am sure I could protect myself by giving the answers they want to hear. But that is not the point..." his obvious passion about the issue was beginning to show rather clearly now.

"When I was a young man, just out of theological learning in Oxford, I helped the Bishop of Lincoln – Cardinal Wolsey, of course, as he became – in some heresy trials. From that experience I know the fiery stake is the end of the line for obstinate men of learning (as I am now!) who cannot bear to adapt to a new 'truth' imposed by the 'powers that be'. I felt sure, then, that I was on the side of both right and might. And I feel sure, now, that I am on the side of right – but I fear I am NOT on the side of 'might' – and high and mighty they are these days!" referring, of course, to the king's counsellors.

"Dr Raynes was just a sub-dean then, also helping Wolsey, as I was, and he was like a ferret with the issues of the day. Once he got his teeth into a victim he never let go and I cannot see that he has changed a jot since then. If anything he has probably got worse, because he expected a bishopric was his right and it has never happened for him. Perhaps he thinks now that his time has come to be raised up."

"I do not know to what extent he actually agrees with the new 'truths' regarding Our Lady and purgatory, but I think he may be bending with the wind this time round in the hope that he will be promoted. I think it may be too late for him, though, for he seemed definitely not to be a well man yesterday, and was looking ashen before the day had finished."

"Mind you – he had to bear a lot of comments that must have been hard to put up with. Just as we broke for lunch, Thomas Youll, the parson from Sotby said in that heavy 'Stage Whisper' he uses for his sermons sometimes, that the King's Council were '...*false harlots, for devising false laws to spoil the spirituality, at the procurement of the Lord Cromwell*'." Father Kendall was a good mimic, and the men around him smiled at his rasping whisper.

"He clearly meant for Dr Raynes to hear it and I am sure Raynes did, but he chose to pretend not to. Otherwise, I reckon, Tom Youll would be festering in Old Bolingbroke's musty dungeon today".

"He wasn't the only one either. Sir Simon Maltby was there too – sitting just across the aisle from me and he was muttering to himself all afternoon. He was very red in the face and talked of 'raising the commons' when he got home to Farforth. He was totally convinced that Dr Raynes' Commission was going to replace the silver chalices with tin ones and said after the meeting that he '...and other priests had determined to strike down the Chancellor' and trusted in the support of his neighbours."

"I am not sure who he was talking about because I don't think anyone else had spoken of violence – at least not in my hearing – but you never know what secret words he had had, nor with whom!"

"And for my part, I came away from the meeting feeling very angry, too, but for the most part my anger was to do with the changes in spiritual life we shall expect if all these changes in doctrine are firmly put into place. I know you and the other working men of Louth begrudge the loss of holidays from the merging of Saints' days. But I also know that everyone takes a lot of comfort from the prayers we say to help those that have passed away, to make their journey through purgatory more bearable, and swifter if possible – and for me that carries more weight."

"I know the women of the Parish also take great comfort from the special prayers we offer up to Our Lady, for troubles they have in birthing, and in the other difficulties of life that the weaker sex have to bear. They were incensed – when we were speaking of it this evening – that Our Lady has somehow been deemed less venerable than hitherto by the new rulings of the Vicar-General."

"And, as for the so-called English translations of learned matters for the common folk..." He ran out of steam at this point, whether deliberately or not, Nicholas was not quite sure, since he knew there were others who rather liked the idea of accessible biblical teachings they could read themselves.

His friend, Thomas Kendall, was rather in favour of keeping some of the 'magic' in religion for the priesthood; it was something they had discussed many times when preparing for the Corpus Christi plays each year. Nicholas tended to wish for more open-ness but it was something on which they tolerated each other's view. The key issue they *did* agree on was that all the changes taken together would tear the heart out of the community – not least if the church treasures were confiscated as was widely rumoured.

Father Kendall raised his rather weary frame from the stool and placed his hand on Nicholas' shoulder but his eyes took in all the four men there.

"God bless you all for what you are about, this night, in His name, my friends. I hope the men of violence do not use this as an excuse for any blood-letting, though I fear there were some heated words yesterday – and that from men of the cloth, too!" a humourless smile crossed his lips – and then a sigh. "I hope your bold action will stop further ills banging on the doors of our church." And with that he walked with purpose down the central aisle – bowed his head to the altar, crossed himself, and stood for a few seconds before walking purposefully over to the door which would take him into the vestry and outside to his home.

ରାରାରାରାରା

A mere six cold months after these words of Kendall, Nicholas sighed as he awaited his fate and the forthcoming violence to *his* person, of being Hung, Drawn and Quartered. He realised it had been a false hope of Father Kendall's but he did not, indeed, he could not, see, what else they could have done in the face of the wrongs being perpetrated upon the commonwealth by Chancellor Cromwell. For some reason the king was blinded to the consequences of Cromwell's actions – maybe willingly, maybe not?

ରାରାରାରାରା

Heading for England: From Bride to Widow
At sea - 1501

The well-meaning advice Catherine's father, the King of Aragon, had given her just before she left on her long journey to her future in England was, sadly, worthless. Much as the wry look from her mother had suggested may be the case.

"If it gets a little rough at sea" King Ferdinand had said, "...the thing to do is to watch the horizon – it keeps your sense of balance, so you won't feel sea-sick".

It was said quietly when the three of them were standing together in the shaded gardens of the Alhambra Palace watching the last few boxes of provisions being loaded into the carts that would take them to Corunna, on the northern tip of western Spain, Catherine's port of departure by sea to faraway England.

Catherine's mother, standing just behind Ferdinand, held an expression which said, '*...such wisdom from someone who has only ever been on a ship in the calmest of conditions...*' but she prudently said nothing out loud.

Up to a point, the king's advice *had* actually worked when they set sail and Catherine had kept her balance well, as the sea grew bolder beyond the sheltering headland. Her companions had gradually made their excuses and staggered below with faces either pale or already shading to green. But it had stopped working, simply because there was no longer any horizon to watch – the sea was so rough.

The ship was still supposedly in sight of land but the sea was a sort of muddy grey-green and the sky was a sort of muddy grey-blue, both almost as dark as night, though a land-locked clock would have shown only a little after noon. The biggest problem, however, was that the dividing line between the two kinds of grey, not to put too fine a point on it, was not straight like Catherine thought a horizon should be. It had been growing less straight for the last eighteen hours, as a notorious Golfo de Viscaya storm whirled around the ship, tossing it hither and yon. The waves were sometimes as tall as the tallest of the masts – so that, large as the ship had seemed in port, its stature now was diminished and frail.

At first, Catherine had been frightened, terrified even, but her faith was strong and her sense of destiny stronger, so she *knew* in her mind that they would be safe, though Maria and her other companions were much less sure than she. She had eventually given way to the motion and had been rather sick for a while, too, and had felt at death's door. But her strength of will was beginning to prevail.

She had been up on the poop deck now for over two hours, however, in part because she actually felt better in the fresh air than inhaling the unpleasant stench of yesterday's partly digested food, moving unpredictably around the lower deck on a film of seawater. Also, being on deck, listening to the storm, was better than hearing the unproductive retching of so many now-empty stomachs.

She had two strong, wiry, sailors, one on either side of her, to stop her falling from the ship. And she was now starting to feel remarkably alive in the elemental world of the moiling sea. The admiral had gently advised his important passenger that she would " *...probably be safer below...*" but when she insisted on staying on deck, he had marked off two of his most experienced crew members, to ensure she came to no harm.

Her only other company at this moment was Brother Geraldini. Four years earlier, he had been her tutor. Now that the journey was, at last, started, he had been appointed as her Chaplain, and was the only member of her large party who was weathering the storm without succumbing to malady. They were both thoroughly wet through, however.

Conversing was difficult, almost impossible, against the backdrop of storm force winds, creaking timbers and lashing canvas – just one small sail was deployed to maintain steerage, the rest had been safely furled – and the occasional crash of thunder. So their words were intermittent, and shouted.

... ... CRASH ... ...

"Is God punishing us?" Catherine shouted, after one cymbal crash immediately overhead made them all jump. She had been feeling a strong sense of personal guilt for many months now, since she first found out that a pretender to the English throne, one Perkin Warbeck, had just been put to death. He was, supposedly, the lowborn son of a Flemish boatman, but he had vaunted himself as Richard Plantagenet,

Duke of York. He had been executed, along with the real Earl of Warwick (who was just an innocent simpleton, but with true blood-royal).

Her father-in-law-to-be, Henry Vll, had had them put to death after succumbing to pressure from her parents. These men apparently posed a clear threat to the stability of the kingdom into which their daughter Catherine had been contracted to marry. She had a feeling – one that just wouldn't go away – that her marriage to Arthur, so soon to take place, was, therefore, "born of blood". And, that it was all her fault somehow...

... ... CRASH ... ...

"No...He may be testing us, though" Brother Geraldini banged his thigh painfully hard against the ship's rail as he hung tightly onto a rope. He was very much aware that there were no sailors standing by to stop *him* falling overboard!

The ship fell off a particularly high wave at this point and slid down a sharply banking trough at the bottom of which seawater splashed over them, before they climbed another mountainous wave. As they reached the top, all the noises seemed to cancel each other out, and for one tiny moment it was preternaturally quiet.

In that very moment, they met an albatross at the top of the same wave. Blown thousands of miles from his normal hunting grounds by the heavy storms this was, however, just another day at work for him, searching for his food – yet the bird seemed to look deep into Catherine's blue eyes for a split second before the ship plunged down one steep sided valley and he swooped down another, their eyes never to meet again.

The tumult had resumed, but in that one moment's peace Catherine suddenly felt at ease with the world in a way that, at fifteen, she had never felt before. It seemed, however, that the strong August storms were going to go on forever, so the Admiral made a decision to get back to the safety of port. They hove to, at Laredo, on the Castilian coast, where they were destined to stay until the sea calmed enough for them to try once more to continue their journey.

After three weeks of enforced land-based inactivity, but continually buffeted by gales and rocked by squalls, they set out again at the end of September. And, with still-brisk south-westerlies behind them, they made landfall in Plymouth just five days later.

The welcome from the good people of Plymouth, when Catherine eventually arrived, was nearly as tumultuous as the sea had been some weeks earlier – for the young, petite, princess who would one day be their queen.

The whole Spanish party went to mass to thank the good Lord for delivering them safely from the elements and afterwards there was a great feast, served to them by the citizens of Plymouth. Arrangements were then made for the huge party to be transported across the south of England; and in every town and village through which they travelled, local people came to peer at the Princess of Wales and her retinue; and to cheer her onwards.

They had only progressed as far as central Hampshire by the time her husband-to-be, Arthur, Prince of Wales and his father Henry VII, forewarned of their arrival, came upon them residing temporarily at the Bishop's Palace at an inauspicious place called Dogmersfield. And, as well as the name of the place being rather odd, there was an element of farce in this first meeting.

Catherine had retired early to her bed-chamber by the time the English Royal party had arrived and were met by Dona Elvira and Count de Cabra, the chief aristocrat of her sizeable retinue.

Dona Elvira, protective of her charge's privacy, told Henry, politely but firmly, that Catherine had retired to bed and was not to be disturbed until the morning. At this Catherine began to hear raised voices when Henry suspected he had possibly been misled about her beauty – "... *perhaps a pox-ridden cripple lurked behind the closed door?*" She did not understand these words but they did not sound pleasant.

Maria de Salinas and the other ladies of the bedchamber scurried back and forth in the room, Maria saying as much with her expressive brown eyes and hands as with her voice, which was quiet, but firm and controlled; "open that...", "pick that...", "unfasten this...", "tidy that away...", "fold this neatly... over there", "NO – wait – *this first...*" and they had very quickly dressed their mistress in a heavier gown and a thick black lace veil, worried that Henry may soon burst through the door.

They were none too soon, as it happened, for the tall and wiry monarch genuinely supposed that Dona Elvira was hiding some kind of monster and, with the duenna and Count de Cabra still protesting and leaning in to each other to try and prevent his passage, he pushed his way past them into Catherine's bedchamber, strode over to the girl and lifted her veil without any by-your-leave.

Catherine said not a word during the whole performance, trusting Maria's judgement and organisational skills to get the costume exactly right, nor did she speak as her father-in-law-to-be peered closely into her face. But she did hold her ground and boldly looked him in the eye without flinching, yet without malice or anger at the unwarranted intrusion.

It was no laughing matter at the time but Maria and Catherine later shared their amusement at the quite open and evident relief that suffused Henry's face when he discovered a pretty round face with somewhat bemused greenish blue eyes rather than the monstrous deformities he feared. With a "hmmph" and a hasty – maybe even slightly chastened – "Welcome, daughter" the ungracious king withdrew from the chamber, to be followed by a very huffy Dona Elvira, with the Count and Countess de Cabra bringing up the rear. Thus, Maria de Salinas and her company were left to unruffle the princess' feathers and get her back to bed.

Catherine did not see Arthur – he had discretely stayed in the background, either shy or embarrassed, with his father rampaging around – until the following evening. Then, they shared a pleasant round of dancing, first in the English style and then in the Spanish style. Shy though Catherine was, she noted Arthur's tall wiry build, taking after his father, and his easy and charming manner – though she also noticed he was inclined to a chesty cough after a round of dancing of the more energetic type.

Arthur's younger brother Henry was also there; a robust boy of ten with golden ringlets framing his face, now serious, now singing and clapping to the music, now flinging himself round the room with one of the young Spanish maids, now scoffing sweetmeats between dances to replenish his energy, his bright eyes taking everything in avidly.

After this brief social sojourn, the English royal party took themselves off in some haste to London to prepare for the wedding day, planned for just over a week away. Although King Henry was really rather a miserly soul, he recognised the significance of this match for securing the future of his still new dynasty and was unstinting on plans for the wedding itself. The capital city was, thus, bedecked with flags; and feasting preparations were well in place for the celebrations, as his eldest son took Catherine as his bride.

The last few miles of the Spanish party's leisurely journey to the very heart of their new home-to-be was through the area of Southwark, past the bear-baiting pits and pens, which lay to the south of the great river Thames. The young Prince Henry met them at the southern end of London Bridge as a courtesy to escort them onwards.

Henry was covered against the cold in luxurious heavy furs, reputedly brought over to England from the barbaric wilds of Russia. Most boys of ten would have been swamped in such garb, but young Henry was already as tall as Catherine who was five years his senior and he was heavy set with it. He carried himself with arrogant elegance, for, though surrounded by a party of adults, he was certain of himself as the leader of the official welcoming party on behalf of his older brother.

In a high clear voice he welcomed them *"Right merrily"* to the greatest city of the land *"...which is to be your new home"*, stood tall in his saddle and bowed with elegant charm to the Princess of Wales. For her part, now free of heavy veils and with her long red-gold hair free flowing – as became a young bride-to-be – she smiled and inclined her head to her future brother-in-law.

An excellent horsewoman, Catherine was seated on a gloriously caparisoned white charger, gifted to her just days earlier by her future father-in-law – her broadly hooped skirt making her look as wide as she was tall, for she was a diminutive figure. Her obvious charisma, however, made her a memorable sight for onlookers that day. And her mount clearly knew his rider was the centre of everyone's attention and was happily lending his magnificence to the proceedings.

Young Henry turned his own horse, very showily, to ride beside the princess. And he charmingly lent his forearm for Catherine to hold, as he led the party across the narrow passage between the little shops and houses perched on the bridge itself.

The leading citizens and their expensively dressed ladies pressed close to see and be seen by the pretty girl-who-would-be-queen. And behind them were their liveried servants in *their* bright new garb and behind *them* were gentlemen and ladies in less fine – but nevertheless new – day clothes and *their* servants in *their* new outfits. And behind them were ordinary citizens making as good a fist as they could of their more limited wardrobes. And so it went on in layers of decreasingly fashionable, decreasingly clean, increasingly-foul-smelling, massed humanity.

Catherine was momentarily overwhelmed by the seething mass and its pungent aroma and took a brief gasping breath to calm herself. Henry, with solicitous charm well beyond his years, paused slightly and in quiet Latin asked if the princess was unwell. Catherine paused, shook her head almost imperceptibly, took a deep breath and gently pressed Henry's forearm to let him know everything was alright and under control and no-one would ever know otherwise.

Once across the river with many more, well mounted – though, to English eyes, strangely dressed, compatriots behind her – the party clip-clopped its slow way through the streets of the capital, confronted on many corners by plays and pageants for their entertainment. These pageants included one which was enacted in a painted wooden 'castle' and, for reasons beyond Catherine's immediate comprehension, the castle contained a huge red dragon breathing fire. Someone explained later it represented the fierce King Henry, of Welsh ancestry, defeating the foes of his kingdom for the safety of the subjects – the red, fire-breathing dragon of St Cadwallader.

Catherine never really understood the various hidden meanings there were supposed to be in the piece but she did think it was wonderfully theatrical and always thereafter had a soft spot for the red dragon of Wales, of which she was soon to become its princess by marriage.

Her wedding to Prince Arthur – a few days later – was no less theatrical but, considering it had been so long in coming for the young couple and so long in the planning, it all passed in something of a blur. Catherine could recall brief snippets of conversation, some even in English which, by now, she was beginning to understand little by little. It was, however, all a bit more overwhelming than she had anticipated, not least because the bedding of the princess with her new husband took place, of course, in public to show the world it was official and properly done.

Once the couple were actually in the bed the curtains were tactfully drawn around them but they both knew they were surrounded by ladies and gentlemen in waiting and would be throughout the night – many of them staying awake for a long time in case they were needed, of course.

All nearby sets of ears would be attuned to the least indication of need – which also meant that everyone would be able to hear all the exchanges between them too, except, perhaps, the softest of whispers. Both parties could barely understand a word of the other's language though – so soft whispers proved to be of no use whatsoever – and on more than one occasion the mechanical logistics of lovemaking proved to be beyond them, unpractised and embarrassed as they both were.

ଔଔଔଔଔଔ

The morning after......

☞ They both woke early the following morning and Arthur, giving his new bride a quick buss on the cheek, leapt out of bed through the curtains before he could appear too embarrassed and speechless (as he knew himself to be).

Catherine heard him call his menservants to him loudly and imperiously (as only a fourteen-year-old could) and heard a huge laugh when he said, "So, gentlemen, I have been in Spain for the night". Even after she had managed to work out what the individual words actually meant she had no idea why this could have caused such uproarious laughter as it did, and it took some considerable explaining from the slightly more worldly-wise Maria de Salinas to fix in her mind the 'double-entendre' of being *"in Spain"* all night.

When the penny finally did drop for her, she blushed beetroot and Maria had to work very hard not to upset her mistress further by breaking into the laughter she felt bubbling up. As it was, Catherine was cross with Maria for a full twenty-four hours before she began to see the funny side if it herself and let Maria talk to her again.

Indeed, it would be yet another full day before Catherine brought herself to make light of her first night of matrimony and confide to Maria that "not only had Arthur not been *"in Spain"* at all but had found himself quite a long way from the Spanish border before he let loose his cannon". She "...hoped for a more intimate military encounter in due course!"

Nevertheless, on the morning of the first day of the marriage itself, as soon as Catherine had vacated the heavily curtained bed three learned doctors had been sent by the king and the Count de Cabra jointly (two English doctors and one Spanish man of medicine) to inspect the bed.

As they hoped, they found some signs of semen on the bed and since Arthur's signet ring, set with garnets, had severely scratched Catherine's inner thigh during their fumblings, they found several small drops of blood, again as they hoped, although they clearly thought it was from somewhere other than Catherine's thigh. The good doctors, after some mumbling discussions between them, felt able to go back to their respective masters and report, on the basis of their forensic evidence, that the princely marriage was off to an appropriate start. It was, however, a conclusion with which, had Catherine been privy to it, she would not have concurred.

The next few weeks consisted of much to-ing and fro-ing of the child bride and her child groom, getting ready to move their extended household to Wales as the king had ordered, with only an occasional foray into the recesses of the four-poster bed. Outside of the bed's curtains Arthur was much given to noisy shows of boyhood bravado, heavy with innuendo and braggadocio, but behind the darkened screen, Catherine (and depending upon the timing of said episodes of melodrama, minutes or hours later, Maria de Salinas too) knew the story to be rather different. Arthur was either too quick or too soft, or as yet, too inept to conquer his maiden's true virtue.

Catherine's quiet requests for Maria's help fell on stony ground too, since she could only provide theoretically sound advice, being unpractised herself – and Catherine forbade her friend to seek more mature advice. Indeed, probably the only sound counsel Maria felt seriously able to give was to "be patient – it will sort itself out".

In fact it became a problem of diminished importance, anyway, since Arthur busied himself with plans to move to 'take charge' of the Welsh Marches at the behest of his father the king. And so the newlyweds only shared a bed every ten days or so.

Arthur hid his embarrassments behind a farrago of hinted claims, so was in no position to seek real help or counselling even if he had wished to. And, thus it went, that his personal courtiers, many of them only a little older than the prince himself, though, no doubt well versed in matters of lust as some of them were, allowed themselves to assume everything was rosy in the prince's bed.

Sadly the issues never did get sorted out satisfactorily. Only a few weeks afterwards they moved to a different – but damp – household, which made the prince's breathing much worse. And his sickly state became more worrisome to both his doctors and to his young bride.

To the great shock of his parents they received the unwelcome news of his untimely death, delivered by fast courier, only just a few hours after they had read, with amusement, of his rather grandiose plans for the enhancement of his household, in a letter whose journey had been started at a more normal speed some days earlier. The boy-prince was embalmed and rushed by chariot to the Abbey of St Wolfstan's in Worcester where he was buried with but modest ceremony.

Arthur's brother, the young Prince Henry, was genuinely distressed for his sister-in-law and it was quite a while before he realised the personal implications for himself and the change of direction that his life would take. It was a change of direction which would eventually displace the notions of chivalry he felt for Catherine in her young life. Nevertheless he had always felt a close personal connection between them –rather more so than his father, the king, felt towards his Spanish daughter-in-law.

The lean, and parsimonious, seventh Henry had always been primarily a strategist and politician, and he saw Catherine as a bargaining chip rather than as a person in her own right. So when his son Arthur died and his own grief had run its course, Catherine became something of a nuisance in his mind, a responsibility for which he had not planned beyond the marriage itself.

And then there was the matter of the dowry which her parents had sent with her! Henry was very reluctant to lose that from his coffers. Despite his showiness for the marriage ceremonials Henry was very much a miser at heart. And so it was left to his queen, the now matronly Elizabeth of York, to offer Catherine the comfort of shared grief to her daughter-in-law.

As the months of girlish widowhood passed by, Catherine and her household had to tighten their belts as the king kept putting off a resolution of the '*Princess of Wales problem*' and failed to find the will to do anything constructive, or even kind, for her.

Catherine herself retained her dignity but felt herself to be in a very lonely place, with little consolation. Her mother-in-law continued to be kind and thoughtful to her when they met and talked but such meetings became so infrequent she felt isolated and low for much of the time. To some extent she found consolation in her frequent talks with Brother Geraldini – he was a kind counsellor and his strong and handsome looks somehow made it easier to seek out his obvious concern and counselling skills.

This counselling did not pass unnoticed by Henry's spies and he concluded *'the nuisance'* would be less troublesome if her good-looking advisor, Geraldini, was sent packing. So Catherine's miseries were soon added to by the loss of her favourite advisor. She wrote to her father in Spain, of course, but there was little he could do from such a distance, except sympathise and pass on her mother's messages of love and support.

Barely a year after Arthur passed away, however, his mother, Elizabeth of York, died whilst bearing her eighth child. The whole English court grieved the loss of a cornerstone of the royal household. The king's loss of his wife, and love, touched him greatly; unexpected as it was.

For Prince Henry, now the twelve year old Duke of York, the loss of his mother at such a tender age was a cruel blow. And for Arthur's young widow, Catherine of Aragon, it was yet another loss, the effect of which was to isolate her even more in a strange, alien land.

Prince Henry's and Catherine's parents respectively, by the time of Elizabeth's death, had been on the point of betrothing them to one another. Indeed, perhaps the only reason it had not already happened was that there were those at court, like Bishop Warham who believed it was *"not lawful"* in the eyes of God, and an *"unclean thing"*.

King Henry didn't trouble himself with such niceties on his son's behalf and, anyway, wondered whether he shouldn't take Catherine for himself, now he was a widower – an idea insinuated into his mind by the horrible little man who acted as Spain's ambassador, Dr Rodriguez de Pueblar. Catherine really did not like de Pueblar at all, and Maria de Salinas liked him even less.

Catherine's mother, Queen Isabella was, *thankfully from Catherine's viewpoint*, also horrified at this suggestion, however. It was, thus, a short-lived idea, once Catherine had let her own horror be known.

Catherine's parents, Isabella and Ferdinand, following further discreet inquiries, (*based upon a plea from Catherine herself*) now believed their daughter's claim, still to be a virgin. So, they expected that the Pope would therefore provide appropriate dispensation, especially if there was a bribe attached to the request.

And so it proved, less than six months after Queen Elizabeth's death, when the three remaining royal parents signed a betrothal treaty. Not that it made much difference to King Henry's rather uncaring behaviour towards his widowed daughter-in-law – for him, she was *still* rather an encumbrance to be endured and a drain on his purse.

જાજાજાજાજા

Left to her own devices...

The maid was in the garden,
Hanging out the clothes;
When down came a blackbird
And pecked off her nose

The months dragged into years. Catherine's mother died soon afterwards in far-away Spain, and her loneliness and isolation, either of which could have crushed her, finally added to the steel in her personality. She learned how to cope with a situation she had no power to change.

She found that her young brother-in-law, five years her junior, was always chivalrous and solicitous on their occasional meetings when she was invited to court. Young Henry was, whether consciously or not, always at pains to be kind where his father was often thoughtless, or downright mean, and Catherine warmed to him as time drifted by for her in her curious limbo state.

Although his father would never allow them much time together, young Henry would always find time to tell her about some new experience in his life, often making her laugh with tales of tricks he played on his many tutors. He was now, of course, being seriously groomed for kingship in his brother's place – and they *were* betrothed after all!

He would always find, in her, a good listener for his thoughts on religious and moral questions faced by princes, too. Before his brother's untimely death, of course, he had always been encouraged to see himself (*as the second son*) becoming a serious churchman. He had felt destined to be the Archbishop of Canterbury for Arthur, his brother, as king. Therefore, as such, he was wont to listen to and debate with his religious counsellors with a degree of earnestness belying his years.

For her part, Catherine would talk to the young Henry – perhaps unconsciously taking on a motherly role to the boy so much her junior – about the many tales she heard about her father and mother as they had driven out the Moors from their Spanish realms.

Despite her odd accent she told a good story. And although she was too young to have been present at the many battles they fought, Catherine had always been a good listener. And her mother, Queen Isabella, had always been able to relate the excitement of the war years to her children. So, Catherine was able to pass on the excitement and chivalry to young Henry, who lapped up these tales.

Isabella had always been close to the action herself, and was often on, or near, the battlefield, watching the outcome of strategies to which she had frequently contributed ideas of significance, as an astute leader in her own right. Catherine was proud of her mother, and her mother's achievements, and carried her strength as a keen example of how to be a Queen.

Young Henry was always a ready audience for tales of chivalry and princely action, anyway. So both Henry and Catherine came away from these encounters with a more cheerful demeanour and real enjoyment of time shared; shared, too, as equals – when so much of their time required them not to be their true selves. They were, so often, putting on a face and having to be as others seemed to need them to be!

Neither of them could say when their meetings turned into love. There was never a moment for either of them which they could look back on and identify as the point at which Cupid pricked them with his arrow. They just "...*grew into it*".

It was there as if it had always been present. And, as Henry grew into a fit and handsome young prince, the age gap seemed to matter less and less. He had always loved playing the chivalrous knight and with her long glowing red hair and her need to be rescued from a mean tyrant (albeit Henry's own father!) he saw himself as her hero and knight errant - a role in which she quietly encouraged him.

ଔଔଔଔଔଔ

Catherine and her childhood friend, now her chief lady in waiting, Maria de Salinas were taking a break from their needlework one spring morning when the weather was unseasonably warm for this bleak adoptive land of theirs. Wandering the corridors of the castle, as they had once wandered the corridors of the Alhambra Palace, they settled for a while on a broad window seat overlooking an inner courtyard, talking of their childhood memories.

Below them, all of a sudden, the courtyard became a hive of activity. Servants fetched a large square canvas sailcloth and stretched it over the dusty ground, placing a hefty stone at each corner to keep it taught. A trestle table was set up in one corner with a large platter of fresh fruit and pitchers of drink of various kinds. There were jugs of freshly squeezed oranges, reminding the girls once more of their childish memories, as well as ale and jugs of wine.

The provender was quickly followed by a small group of noisy young courtiers who poured drinks for themselves, surprising for Catherine who had only ever seen courtiers handed drinks by bowing servants. Then two very large athletic young men came through the door, one courteously bowing deep to the other as he waved him through first, the two dressed (if you could call it that!) in tight hose and singlets.

The two young men, both large in their own right, were followed by a man of huge proportion, in calf-length soft leather boots and flowing cape. He had a large grizzled beard, a severely pock marked face, deep set eyes and long wavy hair, greying at the sides. His hair was still thick for his apparent years.

Catherine realised, with a start, that the deeply-bowing young man was her brother-in-law, young Henry. The other young man, who was slightly older, and was as tall as Henry, with muscles even more defined on his upper body, must be Charles Brandon, Henry's closest friend.

He was, indeed, more like an older brother than a friend, or a

74

courtier. It dawned on Catherine that, though Henry had spoken of him many times, she had only ever seen him at a distance in all her years of being at or around the court. The few times she *had* seen him he was dressed in flowing robes and she had not realised how powerfully built he was, merely that he was a tall, sturdy fellow.

The two young men acknowledged, with a brief nod, the courtiers present, who playfully bowed back and doffed their caps. One amongst them led a ripple of applause for the two as they shaped up, as opponents of a wrestling match would, in the centre of the stretched sail-cloth. The large, older man stood a little back from the edge of the cloth and folded his arms.

"Gentlemen, you may begin".

Each straightened up and gave a formal bow of the head, hardly more than a nod and then the bout began. At first they circled each other warily. It was obviously not the first time they had wrestled each other and neither was taking a risk of the other grabbing an early advantage from a hasty, ill-planned move on their own part.

Brandon was first to make a move, but it seemed like a feint, of a grab at the prince's left wrist, which was swiftly brushed away. The other young men around the courtyard were beginning to shout encouragement and, bizarrely, given their relative puny stature compared to the main protagonists, were also offering advice as to how to proceed. The support for each young man was quite evenly balanced, and Catherine commented to Maria …

"It seemeth as though half of those present must be fearful of Brandon and his ill-will! Or why would they support him so?"

Maria smiled in recognition of the truth.

"I have to say he's quite the handsomest young man I have seen since we have been in England!" A pause, then she gasped at her ability to find her mouth with her foot without trying, "…apart from your dearly-betrothed prince, of course!"

She checked Catherine's eyes to make sure she had been forgiven her lapse of politesse and then she sighed deeply. The truth was that, until her mistress's position here was sorted out and settled properly, the chances of Maria finding her own happiness languished to the point of disappearance. Moreover, she was now getting to an unmarriageable age – unless her fortune changed markedly soon.

But she could look at and enjoy the two handsome young fellows! Indeed, they both could. So they both did...

By the time the two young women had completed their small exchange of words the combat proper had started and the two young men were now locked in holds that looked none too secure. Charles Brandon had his left arm locked on the prince's right shoulder and under his elbow applying a twisting backward pressure but the prince showed little concern and no indication of pain. The prince had his right leg wrapped around Brandon's left leg trying to unbalance him, but the latter remained upright and stable.

They each twisted, trying to gain better purchase but simply succeeded in unlocking both holds and there was a flurry of slapping and reaching moves as they tried to re-establish secure holds on each other's anatomy.

The large pock-marked, bearded giant stood shaking his head, clearly a little disappointed in the performance of both his charges. Now they stood facing each other with matching holds – each man securely holding the other's right wrist with his own left hand. Both clearly had strong grips and would not easily let go. Bent slightly at the waist, they were each attempting to use their upper body strength to twist the other off balance but they were so closely matched in weight and strength, the interlocked arms were straining but unmoving, each muscle showing huge effort but little effect.

Then suddenly, things changed as Brandon twisted inwards and downwards getting under the prince's body, making a back and flinging him in a quarter circle to land on the floor, on his back, following him down and pinning him to the ground – trying to get his knees onto the prince's shoulders, the better to hold him secure underneath his weight.

Henry, apart from emitting a slight *"OOooff!"* as the wind was knocked out of him when he hit the floor, was not going to settle for a quick loss. He twisted himself so that he was able to bring his well-muscled legs to bear as weapons, scissoring them round his friend's neck and twisting as hard as he could, at the same time writhing his back and shoulders on the ground to try and unbalance his opponent and loosen his hand grip.

Brandon eventually had to let his body follow the twisting of his neck and loosened his downward pressure on the torso of the prince.

But, then he made a positive opportunity from the negative situation, and, whilst his head was still trapped between his opponent's legs, he scuttled sideways in a swift semi-circle with his feet until he was almost standing. This action moved his body weight, and leaning down on Henry's legs forced the knees open enough to extract his head. At the same time he also kept hold of Prince Henry's feet and applied further heavy downward pressure until Henry was almost squashed in half.

Henry wriggled and squirmed but he was not able to shift his courtier opponent and Charles Brandon's young cronies were risking the prince's displeasure by crowing a little too much.

"Enough", the grizzled, caped, giant snapped sharply. Brandon and the prince obeyed instantly – a paradox the Princess Catherine and her friend Maria were surprised about. Clearly it was as much a training session as a real bout!

The giant asked his pupils to step apart which they did willingly enough, a slight smirk on Brandon's face as he thought he had bested his royal opponent. But he found himself the focus of the caped one's attention first.

"You were far too slow getting Henry on the floor in the first place. You had hold of his right wrist seconds before he mirrored your hold – and then it was a struggle for superiority of strength, instead of swift surprise. Let me show you"

So saying he unhooked his cape and folded it neatly on a nearby stool, revealing a torso that was all muscle, not an ounce of fat and each muscle independently defined. He took, without asking, a dagger from one of Henry's retinue and gave it to his trainee.

"Right, young man, now stab me!"

Brandon looked at his mentor and then at the prince and raised his eyebrows as if to say "I'll try not to hurt him – but he told me to stab him!"

They stepped onto the stretched canvas, the courtier looking a little concerned at the possibility of killing the prince's favourite tutor, unarmed as the man was. He should have had no cause for concern, however, as no harm was destined to come to the older man.

The aristocratic 'apprentice' adjusted his hold on the dagger, his right arm downwards, the dagger pointing slightly upwards. His intention was clearly to stab upwards – carefully *not* aiming at the heart, just intending a flesh wound – but he got nowhere near delivering a damaging blow.

The bearded man was completely relaxed, not even adopting a fighting stance, but he must have been watching his attacker's eyes. As soon as the courtier's hand started its upwards swing the master had an iron grip on his wrist, jerked downwards slightly to unbalance his opponent. Tightening his grip, he ducked under Brandon's arm, keeping his grip firm and inevitably twisting as he went. By the time he emerged behind the young man's back the dagger was on the floor, and his arm twisted and folded uncomfortably half way up his back.

The tutor's left arm was snaked around the young courtier's neck and if he had chosen to he could have broken that well-muscled neck as easily as if he had been killing a chicken for the kitchen stew-pot.

As it was he flicked a foot between the feet of the youth and unceremoniously dumped him on the floor, to general laughter all round. Then, to ease the pain of defeat, he put his hands under the young man's arms and lifted him to his feet again, slapping him on the shoulder.

Then he turned his attention to the prince. A brief bow and... "Now, Your Highness..." The words polite, the tone critical.

He invited the prince onto the canvas with a brief gesture of the hand (politely, of course!) – then laid down and raised his legs so the prince could place him in the hold he himself had suffered at the hands of his friend Brandon. Wordlessly the prince obliged and it looked as hopeless for the older man, as it had before for the prince. The prince's strength and weight were prodigious and he was clearly beginning to enjoy having his tutor in a hold which seemed secure. And then...

For Catherine and Maria de Salinas it just seemed a blur but, in seconds, the wrestling master was free and the prince was on the floor! This time, however, it was clear he had been watching the older man carefully as he escaped from his hold moments earlier. Instead of being immobilised, as he had been by his friend, he flexed his shoulder muscles and neck, arched his back slightly, and then twisted inwards towards his tutor's legs, this time using his opponent's weight *against* him.

Henry grabbed an ankle and carried on twisting so that his movement and momentum unbalanced the tutor. So, within seconds Henry was yet again standing with the wrestling master securely pinned down.

After half a minute he stepped back and helped the older man up from the floor, bowed his head slightly in acknowledgement of the lesson learned and then took a theatrical bow for the plaudits of his courtiers. Some of them whispered between themselves wondering if the tutor had been diplomatic in letting the prince "win" the contest but we shall never know!

The slight look of chagrin on the face of the tutor suggested he HAD been genuinely bested – but he was also known around the court for taking part in *masques* so it was possible he was acting and was simply faking the chagrin too?!

Prince Henry was magnanimous in his victory, pulling his tutor to his feet. He cuffed one of the courtiers who had been calling out for Brandon to throw him to the floor and in good humour he took some ale and a thick chunk of ham from the trestle to replace some of the energy lost in his exertions.

As he was draining his cup, his head angled back, he caught sight of Princess Catherine and her lady-in-waiting looking down into the courtyard, and with theatrical excess he bowed to them graciously for watching him at play. Catherine blushed a little at being caught watching vicariously but smiled and kept eye contact with her betrothed.

ରେ ରେ ରେ ରେ ରେ

Not long after this wrestling match, the atmosphere at court changed, as Henry's father, the king, became ill and took to his bed. His doctors were seen walking the corridors with long faces, knowing in their hearts that they were not going to be able to change the course of events for their charge.

Nevertheless they kept bleeding him with leeches, giving the impression such treatment may work for the good. The leeches surely would have said, if they could speak, that it felt good to them, of course! – but the Royal Personage of Henry VII seemed not to improve. And the court simply waited for events to run their course as normally happened in life or, in this case, in death.

When Prince Henry was advised by the doctors that he and the rest of the family should gather round the bedside because the end was very near he was determined not to break down as he had done when his mother died. He had been preparing for this event mentally for several years now – really since his brother Arthur had died, at which point the reality that he would become the centre of attention at his father's deathbed had imposed itself upon his mind – and he had decided how he must be seen: -

...sad but not devastated,
in control but not too cold,
a loving son but not mawkish –
but above all, regal ...

ଔଔଔଔଔଔ

A last breakfast: Remembering more
Tower of London, 1537 – 7.15am: 29ᵗʰ March

The Gaoler, priest and guards spent quite a few minutes in the rooms below Nicholas, gathering together others of the small flock of twelve doomed men who would share a last breakfast with him. For that breakfast, they would be seated on rough benches either side of a trestle table set on the cobbles of a courtyard within the encircling curtain walls of the Tower.

It was a deep and gloomy chasm which the weak sun had yet to penetrate. In those few minutes while the guards were busy below, Nicholas had the time to relieve himself in a rusty pale in the corner of his eyrie and complete his ablutions. Such ablutions consisted of splashing a couple of handfuls of cold water over his face from a jug and much-dented bowl, both of which had seen better days, which had been brought up for him the previous night.

He whispered a gentle 'goodbye' to his friend the blackbird, still perched in the branches of the tree outside. "Thank you for your company".

He also said a silent, heartfelt, prayer before his visitors arrived, commending his soul to the care of Jesus. He was curious to notice that the sense of time in part of his mind had changed dramatically and he was remembering with wonderful clarity of detail all sorts of things that had been part of his thirty-six years on this earth.

At the same time he was still functioning - in all outward appearance - as a normal human being, but moving in a way that felt very slow. And there was no real sense of being any part of the activity going on around him. He still heard voices around him as people spoke, but they seemed muffled and distant.

He was shriven by the priest and offered his last confession but his mind was away in a past world of sunshine peopled with good friends and relations, many of whom had already left this reality he himself was to depart later in the day. He felt sure he would see them all again soon in a better place – a thought that brought a sense of peace and comfort to him, protecting his mind from the fears of the day's true nature.

As he sat with the others at the wobbly trestle tables in the deep shade of the courtyard a wooden trencher was placed in front of each of them with some cold meat and a noggin of bread. The smell of the bread (though drier and with much less wholesome flavour than the bread which assailed the senses in his memory) took his mind back again to that first trip to London he had made at the age of nine. His eyes glazed a little as his memories took on a life of their own in his head...

෪෪෪෪෪

Droving the cattle to London...
May 1509

After saying their various goodbyes at the gates of Legbourne Priory and wishing his cousin Eleanor well in her new religious calling, young Nicholas, Old Tom and Tom's dog Gypsy had rounded up Tom's small herd of beef cattle and moved off slowly on their long journey south.

Their pace was inevitably that of the slowest beast – not that any of them were dashing towards their eventual doom, of course – so there was plenty of time for Nicholas to listen to Tom's occasional tales of times long gone by. These were interspersed by much pleasurable silence and then occasional bursts of activity as Nicholas and Gypsy would run to block a lane to keep the beasts on the right track, or chase after a couple of animals who chose to assert their independence of spirit.

Sometimes they might have to 'hurry' the group along with a well-chosen "Yip, Yip, Haaar!" and a poke with a sharp stick, in order to get to their destined stop for the night, before they lost the daylight. Tom's view was that it was much easier to pen the animals in a village's pen-fold than to waste an hour in the morning collecting sleepy beasts who may have wandered a little during the night. It had the extra benefit that they (the people in the party) would be able to relax over a pot or two of ale (well-watered down for Nicholas, of course) and a bit of good company, usually found with ease in each village along the way.

Tom had done this long journey more than once before and knew pretty well which villages offered the best hospitality, and it was these early breakfasts of fresh-cooked bread – usually accompanied by a chunk of cheese or cold meat – that were replaying in Nicholas' mind now, many years later. One breakfast in particular stood out in his head this morning. They had been travelling a few days and Tom said they would reach their destination of Smithfield market sometime the next day... "the big city of London is just over those hills yonder", pointing south to some meagre undulations in the dusk.

There was a slight breeze at their backs as he said this but when they woke the next morning the wind had freshened a little and was now blowing from the south, from the city itself. So, along with his memorable breakfast, Nicholas had also had his first experience of London – a strong and somewhat sickly smell of humanity in large numbers.

Perhaps, on second thoughts, 'freshened' was not the word to use about what had happened to the wind – it was rather the opposite, and lacking in freshness! And he had thought that following cattle would give him an unwelcome whiffiness in the noses of others! It seemed, now, that no-one would be able to notice his smell of country ordure in the big city, which smelled worse to him than a hundredfold cattle.

It turned out, however, that he was wrong about that too – after three hours of slowly rolling, and splattering, through villages that got closer and closer to one another, they came to Finsbury. From there, right through Clerkenwell and through to Smithfield market itself, there was hardly a field between the outer hamlets of London. Along much of this distance, they were accompanied by small groups of dirty, skinny urchins running alongside and all round them, hurling insults about the 'country stink' that Tom and Nicholas and their charges carried with them. The urban lads were obviously so well-used to their own noisome odour that they lacked any awareness of it as it struck other beings; though it certainly smelt strange, and pungent, to Nicholas.

The *actual* urchins changed by the mile but the insults were broadly the same and it was at this moment in his young life that

Nicholas found a skill that he carried forward into later life that always served him so well. He found he was able to find the right words to deflect the mockery to become a general laughter *with him* rather than scornful laughter *at him* – as it inevitably started out. It was clear that the little buggers thought he was just a dull country bumpkin, since he was walking alongside slow-witted cattle.

Even Tom, who normally used his strong power of silence as a buffer for this type of goading was smiling broadly by the time they reached their journey's end. "You should join the Corpus Christi players in Louth when you get back home young Nick," said Tom after they had penned the beasts and slaked their thirst, "they're always in need of a quick wit like yours for helping to tell their stories each year".

ଔଔଔଔଔଔ

Thinking of that comment now, many years later, Nicholas wondered whether Tom's lightly offered advice had, perhaps, helped to get him into the predicament he presently found himself in. Not that he would ever blame Tom for such well-meant advice – advice that had brought much richness to his life. It led him to reflect that upon such a small thing as a casual word, the whole direction of a person's life might rest.

Tom's suggestion of a thespian life became deeply embedded in his mind during the remainder of his visit to the capital city of his land. Much entertainment, play acting and street theatre of all kinds, would accompany the celebration of the coronation of England's new king, the young Harry – Henry the Eighth – all playing over and again in his young mind.

Once the business of passing responsibility of the beef cattle to the butchers of Smithfield had been sorted out and Old Tom had money chinking in his pockets, he put his hand on Nicholas' shoulder, whistled for his dog Gypsy to follow them close at heel and said...

"Let's get some food inside us, my fellow cattleman!....and see if we can't organise somewhere comfortable to stay and see the city folk partying a bit before we have to go home again. It's not often we get chance to learn our manners from our city cousins at close hand".

Nicholas recognised all these years later a certain irony of expression that had not consciously struck him at the time but must have registered in his young brain, nevertheless, from the old man's tone.

Nicholas realised he had not been overly impressed up to now with big city manners. The houses were close together, and overstuffed with people who were both noisy and noisome. They seemed to be shouting at each other over nothing; there were smelly fluids and solids flowing slowly down each road, sometimes in properly dug channels, sometimes just where they would.

Nicholas' practical experience over the past few days of avoiding the worst splatters of cow dung, helped him enormously in this new fly-ridden environment, but there were many distractions which resulted in small footfall errors. So by the time they reached the destination Tom already had clearly in his mind, Nicholas' left foot was squelching in his shoe rather more than he would have wished.

Nicholas was just looking for some grass where he could wipe his shoe – realising that one thing the city seemed to lack was a clean patch of grass – when it struck him that Tom had recently stopped walking. Moreover, he had just banged on a rickety wooden door that suddenly opened a little, revealing a large round white face which to his surprise appeared to be upside down.

"Tom you old bugger – I wondered if we'd see you this week! Come in, come in do – and your young friend here", noticing Nicholas hovering nearby.

Gypsy's tail was now wagging so wildly that the dog was in danger of falling over with each wag and 'upside-down-face' was almost as excited as the dog, pushing him over and mock fighting as the dog began barking furiously.

"Enough!" shouted Tom but it was not clear whether he was speaking to the dog or the dog's old friend, who was now barking back at the dog. They were obviously well known to each other.

"Willum, this is my young friend and helper, Nicholas Melton – Nicholas, this is my old friend and fellow drinker Willum van Planck"

"Hello, sir" Nicholas said dutifully holding out his hand, which was enveloped in a bear-like paw.

"'T'aint often anybody calls me 'sir' these days" chuckled Willum, "just call me Willum like everybody else and be done with it" he added, in a strange up and down musical accent Nicholas had never heard before, finishing the sentence on an up note, all the while laughing loud and deep.

By this time, of course, Nicholas had worked out that Willum's face was *not* upside down, merely that the man was bald as a coot but had luxuriant sideburns and a rounded bushy beard. He had creases in his forehead that looked for all the world like a smiling mouth the wrong way up, and bushy eyebrows that looked like an upended moustache.

Once he got the hang of it, Willum's face was very friendly, but every now and again Nicholas would see, again, the upside down version and would have to stop himself smiling.

Moments later they were embraced within Willum's family bosom with Mistress van Planck finding a bowl of water for Nicholas to clean his squelching feet, at the same time giving clear instructions to her four very large sons to set about preparing decent hospitality for the visitors. Three of the boys were head and shoulders above Willum and Tom, and had to duck in several places around the family home, but they were a boon to the family and many neighbours when things needed moving, for they each had the strength of an ox and knew well how to use it to good effect.

They were also, for large men, surprisingly dextrous and light on their feet; and within moments it seemed the main room in the house had become a feeding station for the town muster! A large trestle table creaked with heavy platters of various kinds of meat, bread and cold vegetables, and pickles. Judging by the size of the four, this was just a normal portion for them during a day but Nicholas could not believe he and Tom would do anything like justice to this table of fayre. Not that he need have worried, for when the time came to start tucking in the four boys helped quickly to reduce the task to manageably human proportions again!

Both Willum and his wife Hetti – and, indeed, three of the four boys, were talkative sorts, and Nicholas, after several days on the road with Old Tom, who was, by and large, a quiet soul, had his work cut out to follow the threads of their conversations. Nor was Nicholas used to such voluble chatter at home, his father being a somewhat taciturn man.

The thing that made most impact upon his young person, however,

86

was the fact that they all treated him as being grown up beyond his years. And they asked him for his views on things; and what *he* thought of such and such; or so and so.

The only quiet van Planck was the oldest boy Joop (*"pronounced 'Yope', like 'rope'"*, his father said helpfully on introduction *"…but spelt 'Joop', like 'hoop'"*.) It turned out that Joop had been just five when the family moved to England, beginning to speak his native Dutch well, but becoming confused when confronted with a strange new language. His two younger brothers who came with him and, of course, the fourth brother, Marc, who was born here had no problem adjusting. Joop, however, developed a slight stutter which he concealed by the simple device of not saying very much, a habit which had stayed with him, even though his stutter had disappeared once he had mastered his new language.

When he did speak it was usually in short sentences and they tended to appear more profound and significant as a result, earning him a reputation for wisdom in his family and amongst his friends.

The words "Joop has spoken" uttered by one of his siblings, often with an added chuckle, usually concluded a discussion on the merits of something or another, though it did occasionally signal a new round of conversation but with new avenues of debate. And their debates were often lively affairs since none of the four boys would ever (or hardly ever!) admit to being wrong. About anything. Yet, when they did disagree, they managed to do so without any animosity or arrogance.

Nicholas quickly formed a strong bond with the youngest boy, Marc, who was only a couple of years older than him, but with a good deal more bulk. So when Marc offered to show Nicholas round the streets of London in the company of Marc's older brother Joop, Old Tom entertained no fears for his safety.

"Take Gypsy with you young masters – she'll enjoy the outing too" and, indeed, it truly looked that way, the dog's tail flying to and fro as if about to take off on its own. So the foursome hurried out. For Nicholas, it was good to be without responsibility again; he had felt nervous of letting cattle get away from him on the journey down, even though they had been well behaved and mostly under the control of Tom and Gypsy anyway. It seemed as though Gypsy was enjoying freedom from responsibility too, skipping between the boys, then running ahead, then sniffing all the strange smells of the capital city and lagging far behind – only to race back to them on a quick whistle from Nicholas.

The noise and bustle reminded Nicholas of 'Fair days' at home when everyone was out and about – but this was just another ordinary day as far as the city was concerned. Despite their size, the two Van Plancks threaded their way through the streets as if they were nimble footed urchins. In fact, their very size probably helped since anyone quick enough to see them coming tended to step aside and make room for them rather than get bustled into the slime running through the middle of most streets.

Nicholas was trying hard to pick his footing carefully, *as well as* look around him, since he would rather avoid having to bathe his feet again but wanted to take in all the sights around him. Sights, and smells too, in fact. Not far away from the Van Planck's home he smelled the harsh scents of chemicals used in tanning hides, familiar to him from visits he'd made with his father to suppliers of the leather Pa Melton used in his business.

Nicholas knew too that the hides of the cattle he and his 'Uncle Tom' had driven to the City would soon be dunked in the same vats to become shoes eventually, walking these same streets as was Nicholas this day. The meat was to be butchered and preserved for the three weeks now left until the planned coronation of the new king.

As they turned the corner, the smells became more noxious as they were faced with six thigh-high vats, each about four feet across. Four of them were in use, filled with water and lime and pigeon droppings by the bucketful; the whole area was white over and teenage boys were stirring and prodding at skins in the vats, making sure they all got covered and dunked in the foul mixture.

Just beyond these six white-smeared vats were four more with dark brown dye in them and another four beyond that contained light brown dyes. All the vats had yet more boys, either standing on the edge with stirring rods or, in a couple of cases, standing *in* the vats, squishing the hides around to get them evenly coloured. Nicholas had seen all these activities before but not on such a scale. It seemed the whole of London would be getting new shoes for the coronation – and the wedding it was rumoured would go with it.

Many other preparations were under way for the great day too. The boys were suddenly stopped in their tracks by just one small aspect of these preparations when they came upon an untidy little square not far from where the Van Plancks lived. Three large properties had only recently been completed along the longer northern boundary of the square – bigger and more sumptuous than the ten or so properties they had replaced – and the new owners, as befitted their status, had agreed to replace the Square's battered horse trough with a sculpted fountain.

This fountain had only just been completed when the old king died and now the workmen who built it had been instructed to dismantle part of it so that a mechanism could be inserted in the fountain to make it run with wine, for the coronation, rather than water. It took about half an hour for the boys to piece together this information from the crowd of onlookers who had gathered around to watch the goings on – all of which made for good street entertainment for them of course.

The entertainment became just that little bit more exciting when Gypsy managed to get entangled in the legs of one of the workmen who was moving a long piece of marble which had been taken off the fountain temporarily to gain access to the inner workings. The man stumbled and managed to regain his balance momentarily, before the marble took on a life of its own and started to slip from his grasp.

To give the man his credit, he *very nearly* managed to stop the marble reaching the ground but, sadly, not quite! A great shout of *"Hurrah!"* arose from those in the crowd who had seen the whole thing happening as if in slow motion. It was at this point, however, that Joop, Marc and Nicholas thought it would be wise to take off in another direction altogether with Gypsy following on after them, tail wagging excitedly at the strangeness of her human friends. The marble was almost all right – well, apart from now being two bits of marble, when previously it had been one.

A little further along the road they came across a group of boys playing a game in the road that Nicholas had never seen before. One of the lads clearly knew Marc and shouted a greeting, so boys and dog went over and watched them play a game they had just started. John, known to all his friends, including Marc, as Jonno, was apparently getting beaten handsomely by an older boy Marc didn't know, as Marc tried to explain the game to Nicholas.

"They played it in Jerusalem when Jesus was a lad," said Marc "... don't know what they called it then, we just call it 'Stones'."

"So, how..." Nicholas began...

"Well, each player starts with three stones in each of his scoops", there was a line of six small scoops in the dirt of the roadway in front of each lad, "...and each player has a 'home pot' on his right". They had two little wooden bowls, one at either end of the scoops.

"You pick the stones out of one of your scoops and drop them one at a time in the scoops to the right, including your home pot if the right number of stones is there. Then your opponent does the same and so on. If your last stone you drop goes in an empty scoop you win the stones in your opponents opposite scoop and can put them in your home pot. Look... Jonno has just lost those four stones in his end scoop. But watch out. If your opponent has the right number of stones in the right scoop and he can finish in your home pot, he can 'steal' all the stones you have collected there..."

YEA! A great whoop went up, as Jonno did just that and boosted his meagre supply of stones with his opponent's home-potful changing the balance of the game in his favour again. For such an apparently simple game there seemed to be quite a bit of skill involved (or was it luck?) The game went back and forth quite a bit before Jonno eventually lost to the older boy Jezza (Jeremiah or Gerald, Nicholas never did find out?)

"Have you got the idea Nicholas?" Marc asked

"I think so..." somewhat hesitantly came the reply

"Hey Jezza... want to give our country cousin a game?" Marc called over, putting Nicholas in a bit of a spot

"No thanks", came the reply, since it was below the dignity of such a skilled proponent of the game to lower himself for a newcomer, "but I am sure Tommo wouldn't mind playing", thus putting his friend on the spot!

Thus it was that Nicholas played his first game of 'Stones' in London, sitting opposite Tommo and getting off to a bad start by choosing the wrong starting scoop. There was much tutting, and sucking of breath through the teeth, in his camp at this. Also there were superior smiles from Tommo and his mates, as Tommo immediately picked up three of Nicholas' stones for his home pot. But with Marc whispering in one ear and Jonno in the other, the game swung back and forth for a bit until, in a series of three devastating moves he chose for himself, Nicholas suddenly took all of Tommo's stones and won the game. Jezza "hummphed" at the winning moves and Nicholas tried to make light of his win.

"Beginner's luck" he chuckled.

"Natural talent" said Marc.

"Good advice" said Jonno proudly.

Jezza clearly thought he had to correct the balance of superiority for his lads and said he'd better give Nicholas a game after all – and peremptorily ousted Tommo from his seat and started to lay the stones out for a new game.

"I bet he's played before" said Tommo in his own defence.

"No, honestly, I never even knew about the game before" Nicholas replied earnestly.

"OK, step back" Jezza instructed Jonno and Marc, "let him play by himself!"

And so Nicholas' second-game-ever started. Much pausing and frowning as the game took its twists and turns. And even when one of the players was up for a while there was a tension in the air in case the opponent had a sweeping strategy in mind to turn the tables.

After about ten minutes of this cat and mouse play, Nicholas saw quite clearly that he could take Jezza in three moves almost exactly similar to the three he had perpetrated on Tommo earlier. Something stayed his hand, however, and he chose not to dish out the punishment and played a more cautious move next. This gradually led to Jezza taking a winning position and he gave no quarter at this point and took Nicholas' stones in four swooping moves – much to his delight and that of his pals.

As they were walking away from the 'gaming arena' Joop said quietly to Nicholas... "Did you realise you could have won that game earlier?" to which Nicholas replied, also quietly out of Marc's earshot... "Yes, but I shall be leaving town again soon, and Marc will still be here, I didn't want him to lose his friends!"

When the boys and dog got back home, they were full of it – even Joop was joining in and laughing at the antics of Gypsy, whilst still trying to retain the authority of a responsible older brother. This he didn't quite manage to achieve as, rather like the man with the heavy marble slab, he kept tumbling into laughter.

It appeared the adults had been having their fun too – both old Tom and Willum had noses that appeared redder than when the boys had gone out. They seemed to enjoy the tales of the dog's misbehaviour too and, although Tom appeared to scold the dog there was no malice in it. Gypsy's tail never stopped wagging, as if she knew she was the centre of everyone's attention. Once the excitement died down to a dull roar, Tom spoke directly to Nicholas…

"Now then, young Nicholas, I wonder if your Ma and Pa would mind so very much if we stayed here in London a little while longer than planned."

Nicholas actually thought they probably would but he wasn't about to say so.

"Willum here", continued old Tom slowly, "is going to be very busy for the next couple of weeks or so up to the coronation of the new King Harry. He is contracted to put up some of the seating scaffolds for the ladies and gentlemen along the Strand" – Nicholas recalled that he had been told Willum was a Master Carpenter – "and could do with some extra help for the time being, even from an old 'un like me and a young 'un like you! What do you say, young mester Nicholas?"

Nicholas tried to put on a bit of a show of giving the matter some weighty thinking time – indeed he did think his mother might worry just a little – but the opportunity was just too exciting to refuse and he felt safe and secure with Old Tom (actually Tom was only just above 60 and very fit from his active outdoor life!) …and his new London 'family'.

"I think that sounds great, Uncle Tom! Ma and Pa will know I am safe with you! When do we start?"

Willum gave his friend Tom a broad grin and a wink and said; "Tomorrow is when the hard work starts, lad. But Marc, here, and Joop will give you a quick lesson in recognising all my woodworking tools so you will know what to look for when one of us sends you off chasing for something. You'll mostly be fetching and carrying to save me from scurrying everywhere, when a younger pair of legs will be quicker to fetch and carry!"

Marc gave Nicholas a cheery grin, too, not least for the fact that it meant he, Marc, would probably be promoted from the most menial fetching and carrying now that his dad had a new "runner" at his beck and call! Why, he might even get to wield a hammer now and then.

CR CR CR CR CR

They were all up before the crack of dawn next day and there was a lot of yawning going on for quite a while. Nicholas tried hard to keep out of the way for, at this moment, there was really very little for him to do. His mind was still full of hammers, saws, adzes, spoke-shaves and awls from the instructions the previous evening. Indeed there were some tools whose names and purposes he recognised from his father's selection, but this was a mostly new array of items, many rather larger than Pa Melton's tools as well. He was a little afraid he would not remember the names of the tools, or, if he remembered the names, he might not remember the shapes, when asked to pass this or that... at least he felt sure Marc would help if he got stuck.

The two middle boys, Henri and Dirk had helped their father load his heavy waggon during the evening, so the main task before they set off was to feed the two big dray horses and settle them into their harnesses. Henri, who was sixteen and, if anything, slightly taller and heavier than older brother Joop, was "master of horse" in the Van Planck family and the two black and white drays snickered to him in a friendly fashion as he worked with them and got them fixed into position. For his part Henri continually chunnered back to the animals as he and his brother Dirk got the collars into place and tightened the buckles. And Henri's hands were patting and stroking all the time.

At last everything seemed ready and Willum called to Marc... "Open the doors!"

For Nicholas, the Waggon and horses emerging from the big barn doors seemed larger than life. His father had a small horse to visit his better off customers outside the town but standing close to the doors as these snorting beasts took the strain of the waggon – full to the brim with wooden beams and struts and planks of various sizes and hues – and accompanied by a smiling Willum and four very big lads, made him feel very small indeed.

Several other people were standing around to watch the procession too – the horses seemed very popular with the locals and they knew it too, tossing their heads and snuffling magnificently as they pulled their heavy load out and away. Tom and Gypsy dipped into the party, now, from the front door of the house and Tom put his arm round the boy's shoulders as he came by his side.

"Well, it's a fine morning, Nicholas, for our first day with our new employer."

Gypsy barked in agreement "...*a fine day indeed*"! Whereas yesterday she had scampered all over the place when she was out with the boys, this morning she was very careful to stay at her master's heel. It seemed to Nicholas, however, that Gypsy was aching to follow her nose and this was a very tough assignment for her, having to be so disciplined. Or, perhaps that was just what Nicholas was feeling about himself?

Old Tom, Nicholas and Gypsy were following the waggon and Marc was walking with them now he had closed the barn doors behind them. Henri was sitting on the waggon, reins in hand and Dirk was walking alongside the horses, his hands lightly on their harness. Willum and Joop walked in front, occasionally calling "...*make way there*" if anyone had not yet noticed this behemoth bearing down on them.

Willum's house and barn were in Clerkenwell, just north of Smithfield Market where Tom and Nicholas had delivered their small herd of cattle the other day. Willum was heading for the Strand where the seating scaffolding was to be erected. In order to avoid one of the steeper hills on the way, they went along Clerkenwell Road past Gray's Inn before turning left down towards the River Thames and the Strand. It was a slightly longer journey than the more direct route but with tons of wood on board the waggon, the slight risk of something spooking the horses as they were going down through Holborn was worth the detour.

It was as nice a day as you could wish for in early June, bright blue sky, a few fluffy clouds, trees with their spring leaves filling out and beginning to darken, but still fresh and it seemed that everyone around was in good humour.

People were busying about even though the hour was still early and most of the streets were still shaded from the rising sun, once they had turned south towards the Strand. They had to take care a couple of times, avoiding large pot-holes created by a heavy rainstorm last week – the weight of their load would have made it difficult if one of the waggon wheels had dropped into a ten inch deep hole. Otherwise the journey was calm and almost leisurely, the two drays pacing themselves as usual – '*hastening slowly*' as Willum said more than once along the way.

Once they had arrived on the Strand, Willum and Joop went to announce their arrival at the house wherein lived the person who had contracted to have the scaffolding erected. It was planned for his family and courtier friends to watch the young king processing through the London streets and would provide excellent views of the event.

It seemed that all was still as had been agreed with the client. And Nicholas saw a well-dressed young man come out of the house and accompany Willum and Joop back to the roadway, where he confirmed the area which was to be used for laying out the wood in preparation for the job to begin.

Willum was duly mannerly in receiving his instructions, and the young man courteous in delivering them. Nicholas had anticipated seeing a more florid man with a peremptory manner, typical of those he had often seen dealing with traders in his home town of Louth and smiled a little at the comparison.

Once the business had been formalised, the three older boys and Willum began unloading the wood from the waggon and Marc signalled to Nicholas that he should help him in straightening the piles as they were plonked down by his father and brothers. Old Tom was helping to unload too but the Van Plancks were twice the speed and took off bigger armfuls each time. So it was a job quite quickly and smoothly done. And Gypsy managed to keep well out of the way this morning.

Once the waggon was empty they got the horses to pull it through the gate into the man's garden and Henri and Dirk quickly unharnessed the animals, put a loose halter on each of them, fastened to a post, and they were left to munch at the grass around them contentedly.

Willum and Joop set about sorting the wood so that the main framework could be started and for quite a while Nicholas felt he was a bit of a spare part, although he and Marc stood ready to lift, carry or hold bits of wood as required and as instructed.

It appeared as though quite a bit of the preparatory work had been done back at Willum's workshop for, after what seemed a slow start, there were bits of wood that looked, even to his untutored eye, as though they would fit together niftily. Then, suddenly, the sorting process stopped and the hammering started and a framework began to take shape. Nicholas and Marc were now becoming useful

95

again and Nicholas was enjoying the satisfaction of contributing to a constructive process, albeit on a temporary structure – much as he had seen workmen doing back in his hometown as they had started building the new tower and spire for the church.

At one point things seemed to go a bit quiet again until Joop called him over and said... "I am just at a delicate stage of this frame – can you fetch me one of the soft hammers please? Marc should know where it is."

Nicholas dutifully went off and asked Marc, who had a quick look and said he thought his brother Henri had picked it up and he probably had it, so that was where Nicholas headed next. Henri, however, said he hadn't seen it all morning and perhaps his father was using it.

Willum said he thought the boys must have forgotten to pack the soft hammers last night, and sent him across the road to another team working on another scaffolding of seats for one of the houses on the south side of the Strand, and ask if he could borrow one. The same thing happened there, and he got sent from pillar to post but he began noticing that some of the men could not resist smiling – perhaps they thought his accent was amusing? The boss across the road sent him a quarter of a mile along the Strand where there was one more team at work, making yet another set of banked seats in front of an even bigger house.

Here, he was given the run around for yet another quarter of an hour until the Master Carpenter burst out laughing and, to Nicholas' blushes, explained that "...they were having you on young master! There ain't no such thing as a soft hammer! I was going to send you down to the Fleet and suggest you asked there, but I couldn't keep a straight face!"

Nicholas was so cross with himself for getting taken in and close to tears of frustration and anguish but the kindly man who had laughed at him put a hand on his shoulder and explained that it happens to all the young lads on their first day and he remembered he had been sent to look for "Those bendy nails we use on the corners of the frame – 'cos we've run out! And it took me an hour to find I was being bamboozled. How long have you been looking for the 'soft hammers'?"

"About half an hour..." Nicholas hesitatingly admitted to his chagrin.

"Well, you've done well lad – or, should I say I have not done so well, since I couldn't keep a straight face?" and he guffawed yet again, but laughing *with* Nicholas this time rather than at him, since Nicholas was beginning to see the funny side of it. The man cuffed him gently at the side of his head and sent him back "to do some proper work!"

He started walking back the quarter of a mile to where the Van Plancks were working but on his way picked several handfuls of long grasses and in the way that his old Uncle Tom had shown him on the way down to London, he weaved and plaited a short grass rope and then tied it in a tight knot, so when he arrived back he went up to Joop and offered him the bundle, saying "They didn't have any soft hammers left, but I made you this soft rock, will it do instead?"

He felt rather foolish but found them all laughing with him rather than at him and agreed he was "...*ready for some snap*" as Willum called a temporary halt to the work to eat something to replace their energy used during the morning. The rest of the day passed pretty quickly for Nicholas as he watched the seating scaffold take shape and did his share of fetching and carrying.

By the end of the day he was occasionally quick enough to anticipate the needs of one or other of the more skilled workers and several times he was rewarded with a smile as he held out the correct tool before it was requested. It was, however, a long day since it was close to midsummer and there was daylight until late evening. Willum and his family team decided it was much better to work through and get the job finished, rather than leave a few bits and pieces to be completed the next day.

Willum did take a little pity on Nicholas and his old Uncle Tom, who had shown signs of tiredness around seven of the clock! When it was time to get the waggon and horses back to the big barn where they lived he suggested Nicholas and Tom '*help*' Henri with the task. In fact Henri really needed very little help but it meant the new workers got back home in the '*comfort*' of a horse drawn '*carriage*'.

Hetti knew, of course, roughly when to expect her men-folk home, so they arrived in the house to a delicious waft of savoury smells from the stockpot. In fact, Willum and the rest of the family were only a few minutes later than the horse-drawn group because they chose the slightly shorter route and did not have to bed the horses down for the night – watering and feeding them and so on. So Nicholas did not have to wait very long before he could feed the grumbles in his stomach – he was *hungry*!

He was also very tired and was in bed asleep fewer than ten minutes after his meal, sleeping like a log until he was awakened for the next day's work. This pattern of sleep, wake, eat, work, eat, sleep continued for just over a week, with a break on Sunday for church and rest. During all of this time Nicholas could feel the build-up of excitement to the great day approaching and felt proud to be part of the teams preparing the capital city, even though most of his contribution was simply carrying and fetching, and fetching and carrying.

The day itself arrived with a beautiful dawn. A quick shower of rain the previous evening had settled the dust, freshened the air, and greened the leaves all around. But on this day there was hardly a cloud to be seen and any that were there, were little fluffy white clouds, seemingly set in position to set off the lovely blue of the sky.

ଔ ଔ ଔ ଔ ଔ

Back to reality – briefly ... 1537

The blue of the sky then, when he was a boy, exactly matched the blue of the sky on this, the day of his execution. And Nicholas' mind flipped back to the present as the guards harried, and pushed, all the dozen prisoners into the back of two open wagons.

The air was much colder than on that far off day he had been remembering, but it was clear, and the light breeze made them all shiver a little, this early in the morning. The prisoners had all been deprived of their normal clothing, and were wearing rough cloth smocks to see them from the prison to the scaffolds at Tyburn, a little more than three miles away.

Their wrists had been bound behind them, and the bindings tied to the extensions to the sides of the waggons more usually used to keep loads of straw from spilling onto the streets. The waggons had been 'borrowed', for a small fee, from a small-scale haulier who made a few extra pennies each time there was a multiple execution party from the white Tower of London.

The occasional snorting breath of the heavy horses pulling the

98

wagons steamed a little in the cool air, and one of the animals would occasionally stamp a hoof on the cobbles to signify he would like to get on with the business-at-hand. Then he could get back to his usual task pulling tasty sweet-smelling straw, rather than this abnormal load, which gave off the stench of fearful humans.

Nicholas could feel the roughness of the cart chafing his wrists and the contrast between this transport and the wonderful carriages used for Henry's coronation all those years ago could not have been greater ...

CR CR CR CR CR

...The fact that he had such a good memory of what the coronation was like had been down to the ingenuity of Willum and his ability to do some forward planning.

Willum had gained contracts from two different property owners in the Strand for banked seating which they could use to impress all their friends, with front row views of the coronation processions. These two properties were situated either side of a narrow passage and at the very corner of the passage was a small shop tenanted by a good friend of Willum's.

Neither this friend nor the owner of the small shop could afford to splash out on banked seating but Willum talked one of the owners into getting permission from the town authorities to allow the passage to be closed for a few days either side of the coronation so that the "...banked seating outside his property could be built to a high standard of safety with strong and secure woodwork..."

Then in his drawings for each of the two property owners he showed a narrow joining section containing "...strong wooden supports, so their guests would be very safe..." In fact, because of the little corner shop, the joining section was slightly wider than the drawings showed and allowed Willum to build a small enclosed "room". It was more like a shed really! It was wedged between the public seating and entirely covered-in. Apart, that is, from suitably sited peepholes at three levels, one for small children and one for most adults and another for middle sized kids and short adults!

Since the passageway was going to be closed off anyway he was

99

able to create an extension to his secret 'room' by enclosing about four yards of the passage beyond the side door of the little shop. All this took was a little ingenuity and a few extra planks of wood. There was space inside this secret room for about twenty five people if they all scrunched up together but, of course, they would be able to use the whole of the shop property as well. In this way, people could move around quite freely most of the time – it would just be a squash when *everyone* wanted to watch the king and his bride passing by at the same time through the peepholes!

The shop owner, his tenants and the next door neighbours were all in on the secret of course, so they and their close families would be there, but they had all been abjured to keep the secret as quiet as possible. It was going to be very crowded on the streets and everyone would be scrambling for a good view so the idea of the secret room was simply to keep a good view from the bustling, noisome crowds – and, in the Strand, it would be one of the best views available in all of London for ordinary folk.

In fact, with all the van Plancks, the above mentioned shop owner and his tenant and the neighbours and all their families, Nicholas and his Uncle Tom too, there should have been about thirty people all told but a friend of the neighbours had spoken out of turn and so about forty people had turned up and were crowded into this space and the little shop!

Mrs van Planck, and the wife of the shopkeeper, the wife of the shop's owner, and the wife of the neighbour, had spent most of Friday, the twenty-second day of June, preparing food for the Saturday and putting it all, carefully wrapped, into wicker baskets. These had all been smuggled into the shop late in the evening so as not to alert everyone that a secret party was being planned in case of gate-crashers. It was going to be crowded enough just with those "in the know"

Willum van Planck's contribution had been the construction itself, so he had been "let off" any party planning by his good lady! But the shop owner had been prevailed upon to buy a couple of casks of ale which had also been set up and 'tapped' on the Friday night. Mrs van Planck had had a few sharp words with the menfolk to make sure they did not drink all the ale on the Friday night, but they claimed simply to be tasting the ale to make sure it was drinkable on the big day!

It was midsummer, of course. So, being the longest day of the year, and therefore light until very late, it was, naturally, also very late when all these secret activities were being undertaken. And nobody got to bed until after midnight, even young Nicholas, still just nine years old. Yet, despite the lateness of their bedtimes, Nicholas, his Uncle Tom and their hosts, the van Planck family, had all risen very early. They had set off in three separate groups to the location, still trying to disguise their secret. It was a glorious sunny morning, the sun just beginning to reach into some of the darker streets, leaving long shadows of people and things.

Even at this early hour there were a lot of people milling about as it had been declared a holiday, even though it was a Saturday. Thus, they made their way to the secret location, full of excitement for the unfolding day. As they entered the little passageway where Willum had built the "room" they turned left into a gate at the end. Then they walked round to the back of that house and slipped through a small wooden swinging gate in the hedge and into the yard of Willum's friend's shop. Once into the back of the shop, they squeezed past boxes of stock to the side door in the passage and from there into the secret "room".

ଔଔଔଔଔଔ

New beginnings...
The Royal View

It was Saturday morning and King Henry VIII of England, and his new wife, had travelled by Royal Barge from Greenwich on the Friday, so as to be at the Tower of London, as custom demanded, at the start of the day of the coronation.

They had been married little more than a week, and Catherine's cheeks were still glowing with pride and pleasure. All the years she had suffered at the hands of courtiers who had chosen to follow the example of old King Henry VII, in his miserable treatment of the Spanish princess, were being erased in her mind as she was now

101

able, quietly, to rub their noses in it. She would be Queen of England this day.

It was not in her nature to be vengeful, but she would not have been human if she did not occasionally take pleasure at the expense of miserable wretches who had had it in their power to be nice to her; and, yet, had chosen NOT to be!

Not everyone had been horrible, of course, and she had grown to appreciate the kindness of one of her English advisors, Sir John Hussey, and his wife, in difficult circumstances. Sir John had fought alongside Henry Tudor at East Stoke in Nottinghamshire, soon after he became King Henry VII and Sir John had eventually risen to become Comptroller of the King's Household.

So he had had to obey Henry's instructions when the old king was being miserly with Catherine, but he had always given her quiet words of advice about how she might make the best use of her, then limited, resources. Sometimes, he had even helped, from his own means, when she appeared particularly stretched. Hussey had taken her under his wing, as the daughter he had never had. He was proud of his sons, of course, but had always wanted a daughter to spoil. In return, Catherine had a soft spot for him, as if he was a favoured uncle.

So much so, that she had asked her new husband, King Henry VIII, to appoint Hussey as her Chancellor, now she was to be Queen. In his early forties, Hussey was a worldly wise man, and although he dithered a bit now and then, Catherine was always pleased to have his advice, and his wife's empathy. She enjoyed, too, his stories of his home in Lincolnshire, a part of the country she had yet to visit. It sounded so different from her memories of Spain – but in a nice way.

Young Henry had replied, "I will, of course, keep him on as Comptroller of the Royal Household and you may think of him as your 'Chancellor', but I will not rename his job as such, otherwise he may stop doing all the other things he now appears to do so well! I am sure he will give you good advice as my Queen. Indeed, I will require him to do so!" and laughed heartily, a laugh that made Catherine's heart melt.

He had then appointed Lord Mountjoy as her Chamberlain but Catherine would always take Sir John's advice over that of Lord Mountjoy, especially in matters of finance.

This Saturday morning in the Tower of London, however, Sir John

Hussey was really quite in a flap because so many of the details of this day were his responsibility as Comptroller of the royal household. And, if things went wrong...'*my goodness, I don't want to think about what might happen if anything goes wrong!*'

So he was actually dithering more than usual. His closest helpers had come to realise over the years that his first instincts were usually correct and, if he was dithering to the point of indecisiveness, they carried on working on the basis of the FIRST order he had given them. They felt reasonably secure that he would come back to that order, however much he dithered over two or three other possible orders in the meantime.

On this day, however, there were many more people taking orders from him than just his closest helpers. So there were quite a few people around the Tower of London, unused to his manner of working, who were tearing their hair out trying to keep up with his '*dithers*'. First of all putting ten yards of red carpet '*here*', and then moving it to put it '*there*', moving it again, to put it in '*that other place*' before finally moving it back to '*here*' again, where it had started.

One of the other people feeling much more strained than usual was Catherine's oldest friend, and chief lady-in-waiting, Maria De Salinas. She had actually been feeling very guilty for weeks now, since Old King Henry had first become so ill. She knew she should be in a sombre frame of mind, setting an example to the younger ladies in her princess's retinue, about how to behave at a time of courtly sadness and sorrow. But the truth was she had not felt so happy since she left the land of her birth many years before.

She had never really taken to the old King Henry, father of her mistress Catherine's husband-to-be. He was really an old curmudgeon, and had behaved abysmally to her mistress after the death of the Prince of Wales, Catherine's first husband.

She knew it was uncharitable of her – and probably unworthy – but she was actually relieved the old man had shuffled off his earthly coil. She tried telling herself that it was simply a sound strategy, to keep herself strong in order to be able to comfort her mistress at this sad time. And, in so doing, it would keep her own sadness at bay whilst she provided support for Catherine, her friend.

But she knew in her heart that she was dissembling to herself, for she could feel no sadness at his passing, only a great lightening of spirit and a fine sense of optimism for the future; optimism for the future of her princess, but also for her own future too. She might now, at last, be able to find *herself* a husband, a desire and aspiration she had had to batten down hard in the recesses of her mind for so long. She was a little older than Catherine, of course, and even Catherine, at the age of twenty four, was getting somewhat long in the tooth to become married.

Maria's one chance of marital happiness up to now, two or three years previously, had been dashed when Catherine had had no dowry to offer, because Old King Henry had cut off her money supply – miserable wretch.

So, with the old king very ill in bed and not expected to last, she had felt 'elated'; it was the only English word that suited her mood. She felt two inches taller, and had a spring in her step which she tried very hard to suppress around the court. With many years of training and practice she thought she may have hidden it from most of her colleagues in the princess's retinue but she was fairly sure that Catherine herself must have noticed the extra spark in her eye and the hidden smile lurking in her every word during the old king's last days.

She was going to be very busy, of course, over the next few weeks and months with preparations for the marriage and the coronation, so perhaps she would be able to smother the more extreme outward manifestations of her new state of happiness and just seem modestly pleased for her mistress. But there were moments when she felt like skipping down the dark corridors and whistling, two things she had not done since she was a mere child.

Her father had taken great delight in being able to teach his little girl to whistle, bless him and his memory. Maria thought he had really wanted a boy to carry on the family name, but had not been so fortunate. But she knew she had been greatly loved and her father had been very sad when she had had to depart to the cold North with her Princess Catalina.

And now, on this Saturday, the twenty-third day of June, 1509, she had to get everything absolutely right for her mistress. Catherine's actual marriage to young Henry had been carried out almost in secret a couple of weeks before so it had not been a large burden of organisation for Maria. Today, however, this was another story! It was far and away the biggest public event in which Maria had participated, let alone for which she had had any responsibility.

After they were married, Henry insisted that Catherine enlarge her retinue of ladies to include many of the English wives, or daughters, of key courtiers and, somehow, it was Maria's task to make sure they all worked well alongside each other to the benefit of their joint mistress, Catherine herself. Some of the original Spanish ladies, especially the older married ladies, had never bothered to learn any English, so Maria often found herself as interpreter, and referee, in arguments about who should take precedence in seating, walking, riding or even sowing, heaven help her.

There was a lot of this kind of silly argument going on in the run up to the 'Big Day' of the Coronation and Maria tried so very hard to keep such arguments away from her Queen, but sometimes, some of the English 'ladies' took their complaints to their husbands, who took them to their senior 'family' connections in court. They, in turn, might take them to the Duke of Suffolk, who would generally try and sort it out to avoid telling Henry, of course. But then that would come back to the Queen, who would then end up showing her irritation with Maria, for not getting it sorted out in the first place!

Maria de Salinas had broad shoulders and a good organisational mind, however, and she was feeling elated after all, so most of these tensions were defused before becoming dangerously impassioned. But by Saturday morning she was rather feeling the strain and was definitely drained.

She was tired, too, because there had been celebrations the previous evening in the Tower, after the Royal Party had arrived from Greenwich. This was her own fault however, as she could have chosen to go to bed a little earlier, just after Catherine retired. But several glasses of the Spanish wine, sent especially for the occasion by Catherine's father, had made that decision seem *difficult* for some reason.

She had been up since dawn, which was early of course since it was mid-summer and the night had been short, but the birds *had* sung prettily for her during the dawn chorus! She had got her ladies to lay out Catherine's clothes and make sure there would be some delightfully warm water for her mistress to bathe in.

She had sent down to the kitchen for the fresh bread she knew would be ready and the flagon of ale that would accompany it for their breakfast. They would be using beautiful new clear glass tumblers, sent as a present from a duke in the Low Countries; some cousin, it seemed, several times removed from Catherine. Whether they would make the ale taste better she was not sure yet.

Suddenly, she found herself on her own in the Queen's chambers in a rare moment of peaceful silence and she was able to let her shoulders drop for a short time. She had nothing to do and no-one to chase, at least until Catherine came to get dressed for her procession to Westminster Palace, through the City of London, first, and then across Holborn and along the Strand.

She allowed herself to flop down in a chair in the Queen's Chamber, feet splayed out, knees apart, looking as unlike a lady as she had all those years before, sitting on the lions in the Alhambra Palace.

Catherine's dress lay on the bed, beautiful virginal white satin at Catherine's insistence, since she had "...*not known the touch of man*". Even during her short marriage to Henry's brother Arthur, although she might have touched the English prince's "*cannon*", he had never "...*been in Spain*", as he claimed with his boyish arrogance. She would be wearing her long red hair down today, too, as befitted a virgin bride, topped off with a golden coronet studded with precious gems from the Orient.

Maria de Salinas suddenly sat bolt upright in her chair, her mind at attention...

"Dios en cielo! The coronet! I must have it sent up from the vault... do I talk to Lord Mountjoy for that or Sir John Hussey? Oh mi Dios!"

CR CR CR CR CR

Coronation Street-Party...
June 1509

Willum van Planck was last of the forty people to arrive at their 'secret room' on the north side of the Strand. His wife told him he could "...*lie abed this morning ...you did your share of all this before today...*" and much to her surprise he took her at her word and did just that.

Actually, that was not true. Gypsy, the dog, was the last of the *forty-one* to arrive as she walked in on the heels of her master's friend, barking madly as everyone shouted congratulations to Willum, *the architect*, on a job well done. Those with ale-filled tankards, ...or mugs, ...or goblets raised them high in the air and shouted "*Hoorah!*" and those without shouted "*Hoorah!*" anyway.

Willum raised his hands palm down and then put his right forefinger to his lips to "*SShh!*" everyone and pointed upwards to the seats either side of them where the gentlemen and lords and ladies were seated on the banks of seats he had been contracted to provide.

It was actually Nicholas' Uncle Tom who put a hand on Willum's shoulder and smilingly said...

"Don't worry Willum, no-one can hear us! There is already so much noise going on in the Strand that you can only hear a muffled roar from in here, so I don't think we'll be bothering anyone today! The young lords on the seats to our right are already so far gone in drink that they are making much more noise than the vagabonds in the street selling cheap trinkets in loud competition with each other. My guess is that they were drinking last night and never actually managed to get to bed! The young lords, that is, not the vagabonds!!"

"Anyway," Joop added for his father's benefit, "What if they can hear us – nobody can get in – we built this place without a door from the street or a door from the passageway and nobody will think you'd be able to get in through the neighbour's yard and the back door of the shop, through the shop and out of the side entrance!!"

At this, all the van Plancks, and Tom and Nicholas too, chimed in "*Joop has spoken!*" and everyone fell about laughing, including, eventually, Willum himself! There was already plenty of ale going the rounds, even Nicholas had been pressed to have some. He normally had a little watered ale but this was the real stuff, although, to be honest, he was none too keen. To refuse it would have seemed churlish, but he made it last, and thereafter stuck to water.

It wasn't long before the menfolk started to feel the effects of the ale and began to take little trips out into the shop's yard. Mrs van Planck had put her foot down about "*...NOT pissing in the viewing parlour, thank you very much, it'll stink before the king and queen pass us by!*"

She had also arranged for three piss-pots to be placed, genteelly, in a room in the shop for the use of the ladies present and "...*Marc and Nicholas will empty them for us at intervals into the yard.*" ...And woe betide anyone who crossed Mrs van Planck in this mood...

So Nicholas had a job he had not planned on; and he and Marc tried to keep well out of the way, mainly seated on the low bench built for them at the lowest of the peepholes, watching the progress of the day out on the Strand. To be honest, however, Marc was already too tall, really, to comfortably fit this low!

For a while it was just ordinary folk wandering about until a troop of mounted soldiers, followed by soldiers on foot began to clear the street of people, posting sentries along the route, to keep the people off the main thoroughfare. The soldiers had been provided with new uniforms and all looked very splendid, with polished metal shining in the bright sunshine flooding the Strand, and white belts gleaming, too.

Most of the banked seating across on the south side was now beginning to fill up with ladies and gentlemen in their finery, again many of them seeming to have new clothes for the occasion. None of the seating on the south side of the Strand was van Planck seating – Willum had only dealt with contracts on the north side of the wide street.

Heavy footsteps told them that the van Planck seating on either side of them, on this side of the street, was getting pretty full too!

Nicholas and Marc were now having a lengthy discussion about how many soldiers it would take to line the whole of the route from the Tower right along to the Palace of Westminster.

"We don't know that there *are* soldiers all the way."

"I know we don't KNOW there are soldiers all the way, after all we can only see three now and we don't know if there are three spaced the same on this side of the street... but what I am saying is '*IF there were soldiers*' all the w..."

"...and we don't know really how far it is either..."

"...well it is certainly a goodly step. I have not walked the route all the way but I have walked the length of the Strand a good few times and the Palace must be at least as far again... it seemed so when I once went on an errand nearby..."

"...and how far is the Tower in the other direction?..."

"...I haven't walked to it from *here*... but I have, of course, been to see the Tower and it was a long way from home which is where we started out from ..."

"...well, OK, then, we will have to make some guesses. Let us assume it is the same distance from here to the Tower as it is from the house to the Tower. If there was a soldier every five steps, say, how many soldiers would you see between the house and the Tower..."

At this point Mrs van Planck intervened in the discussion, for which intervention most of the adults nearby were rather thankful.

"Let us assume there were a LOT!" – she said with an air of finality – "I thought you boys were sitting there with a purpose, to let us all know what was going on in the street so we don't miss anything..."

"Well, that's just it Ma," said Marc, "...not a thing happening just yet, not since the soldiers marched past, apart from the seats over the way filling up with ladies in fancy dresses..."

At which news Mrs van Planck and several other womenfolk rushed forward, to peer through the adult-height, peeping-windows, to cast their judgement on the fashionability of said ladies. Marc simply rolled his eyes towards Nicholas, who then banged the heel of his hand on his forehead and said...

"...we've been missing the obvious, Marc. How many soldiers were in the troops which just marched past? There's a good chance that they will be counting off, between here and the Palace..."

"Nooo....," said Marc with some exasperation, "There will be loads of soldiers based in the Palace coming out towards us as well!" It was clear this discussion could go on for quite some time...

"I can hear drums," said Joop.

Everybody listened closely and fell silent for a moment to try and hear them as well but it was a few heartbeats before anyone else heard them... "*I can too!*", then they all heard the drums getting closer. Old Uncle Tom was sat looking through the middle height 'window' which had the additional benefit of a slight angle looking back, eastwards along the Strand, towards the direction of the Tower, so he saw the drummers before anyone else.

"There are four of them and they are walking slowly because, behind them, there's a group of tumblers doing acrobatic feats as they progress along the street. There must be about ten of them doing somersaults and such, leaping over each other and flying through the air."

At this point several more of those present thought they should get a look in and Uncle Tom found his view blocked – so he took a good swig of his ale and quietly resolved not to say again what he could see until he had had his fill of seeing it!

"Oh look, men on stilts too!" somebody else got elbowed out of the way after revealing *that* information!

လ လ လ လ လ လ

Just as the men on stilts were approaching the van Planck's secret room on the Strand, Maria de Salinas was helping Catherine, her Princess Catalina, shortly to be Queen of all England and Wales, into the litter in which she was to be carried all the way to the Palace. It had been made by the master-carpenter at the Palace and was a thing of beauty in its own right.

Maria had been somewhat concerned when she learned that a litter was to be the coronation mode of transport from the Tower for her mistress. She had, herself, recently travelled in a two man litter across the city and it was a most uncomfortable ride, joggling and jiggling along rutted roads at trotting speed – the trotting speed of young men that is. On reflection, however, she thought that, since they were both not young men, that might have accounted for at least some of the joggling!?

She was relieved to see that this was a '*transport of delight*' by comparison and had been crafted in such a way that six good men and true would spread the burden between them. There were yokes at front and back between the handles and a padded, curved shoulder arch for each of four more men, one for each handle. The six men chosen were all strong and all the same height, so it should be a very even ride – they would be walking too, which ought to minimise any joggling. Two more men would walk nearby in case one of the six fainted or tripped.

The carriage section of the litter was beautiful too. Larger, by a long way, than normal litters one might see, every day somewhere in the city; the window spaces were wide and high so the Queen-to-be could be seen clearly by her people. They were curtained, of course, if she needed privacy, or if it had been raining, but it was a gorgeous day and the sun would shine delightfully on the wonderful gilt worked into the doors, window frames and roof.

Maria fretted getting the virginal white dress into the litter as neatly as possible, while Catherine smiled benignly as everyone was fussing around her today. She settled back into the softly cushioned leather seat and adjusted her coronet which had shifted slightly when she knocked it as she was leaning forward to lower herself back into the carriage.

Maria just got her to lean a little forward again so she could make sure Catherine's long wavy red hair was set off to look perfect, pulling most of it forward over her shoulders. '*Mi deus en cielo!*' she thought '*I am so glad Catherine did not know how last minute the coronet was!*'

"Maria! Stop bustling, and relax!" Catherine said with a twinkle in her eye. "I arranged with Sir John Hussey last night about delivering the coronet this morning – so you needn't have worried him that it was late this morning. We decided not to get it out of the vault until the last minute, the longer it was out, and not safely attached to my head, the higher the risk of something going wrong!"

'*Oh mi dios! She can read my mind!*' she thought, but she actually stayed very calm and said...

"I shall be walking along just behind you all the way, so if you need me you only need to call out quietly and I shall be there. There will be six of us close by so if you are in need of anything we will be able to sort it out very quickly."

"The Queen shall want for nothing!" boomed a young voice from over Maria's shoulder, "for, of course, I shall be at her side...and the Duke here too!"

Henry had just appeared around the corner from the stables, clearly now ready to set off on the ride of his life so far. His voice seemed a little too high for his six foot three inch stature, yet he made a fine figure on his huge white courser.

The horse was especially groomed for the occasion too, silken bows in his mane and at the top of his tail and golden tassels on his leather halter. His neck was arched finely and his steps, somewhat prancing... he KNEW he was the centre of attention. And his half-brother, another fine white stallion six months his junior, carried the Duke of Buckingham, cousin to Henry's Mother, Elizabeth of York and Lord High Steward for the Coronation, just over a dozen years older than his king.

The queen was wonderfully elegant in her simple flowing white satin dress and the coronet, the duke just wonderful in his jewel-bedecked finery. Above all in elegance and wonder was the eighteen year old King of England. And *he* knew it too! His shoulders were pulled back, his magnificent chest thrust forward, white tights showing off the "...*finest calves in the land*," – his own words!

His shoes, of the softest leather with gold and silver thread laced throughout, rested in stirrups made from solid silver – he was, after all, the richest monarch in Europe. More gold and silver threaded through his doublet, which was slit to allow the soft silken undershirt to show through. There were gold chains round his neck, gold rings on fingers and his thumb, bedecked with the "...*finest jewels in the land*..." Henry's words again!

Over all this he wore a coat of raised gold, itself embroidered with diamonds, rubies, great pearls and other rich stones. And over that he had a robe of crimson velvet, trimmed with ermine. It was a good job it was so early in the morning otherwise he would have been much too hot! He looked magnificent!

His cousin, the Duke of Buckingham, a little older but almost as much of a peacock and only a few inches shorter and a few inches stouter, hardly begrudged Henry his claim about the calves, although he thought his own to be wonderfully fine specimens. And, for today, he wore a little less gold and a lot less silver and fewer rings with fewer jewels. His robe was much duller, dark blue with just a little less ermine! But his look still marked him out as one of the richest, most influential magnates in the land.

Henry's arrival in the courtyard was clearly an indication that it was time to start moving, so there was a considerable amount of shuffling around, making sure everyone was in the position that had been allotted to them according to their rank and status. This alone had cost Sir John Hussey quite a few grey hairs, to make sure no-one suffered any indignity or slight by ending up behind someone they thought they should be in front of!

Henry's magnificent courser was getting impatient and had started counting the seconds with his right foreleg, striking the cobbled courtyard, as if saying *"Time to go! Time to go!"*

Sir John Hussey, Comptroller of the Royal household, decided all the household staff should be party to the setting off of this wonderful pageant. Thus, the edges of the courtyard were crowded with all manner of persons, from serving staff in smart new uniforms, to rosy cheeked cooks, to scullery maids with raw knuckles from all the washing up they had been doing recently, and back to Sir John himself and his elegant wife, proud of her husband's part in all of this.

Judging that everything was all set and no further delay could be tolerated, Sir John gave a sign to the gate guard that they should now begin to raise the portcullis and then shouted his signal for the party to start moving...

"Long Live the King!"

The shout was taken up by everyone in the courtyard...

"Long Live the King!"

"Long Live the King!"

And the trumpeters sounded a fanfare to start the procession and the eight drummers at the head of the procession who had been silently marking time made sure everyone could now hear the procession start and headed for the open portcullis.

The shout inside the courtyard had been taken up by those waiting outside the walls...

"Long Live the King!"

The procession stomped and stamped, and rattled, and trundled, over the wooden drawbridge over the moat. There were already great crowds of people sitting on the grass sward surrounding the moat hoping to get just a glimpse of the king and queen on this lovely day. Gradually, as the procession moved out into Cheapside the shout progressed a little but then stayed about a quarter of a mile ahead of the drummers...

"Long Live the King!"

The Queen's litter moved forward steadily, Maria was pleased to observe, no joggling or jiggling at all, "protected" on the right by the king and on the left by the Duke of Buckingham. Both were riding just a little ahead of the litter so as not to block the view for, or of, the lovely Catherine of Aragon, Princess Catalina, now Queen of all England and Wales, looking beautiful and glowing in her white satin gown, the precious coronet glinting in the sun. She waved, occasionally, quite naturally and graciously, and many were the people that day who claimed afterwards...

"*The Queen actually waved to me...to ME...!!...ohhh 'twas a sight to behold!*"

She was, of course, already well loved by the people of England, who had known her previously, for a short time, as the Princess of Wales and had lined the streets before, for her, when she married Prince Arthur.

They were delighted now, that she had at last found happiness after being widowed at such a young age. She was attractive, there was no doubt, and she looked well and happy, and with such a young, handsome, rich husband! Most people did not know, of course, much of the detail of her relationship with her parsimonious father-in-law and his odious treatment of her, but the fact she was unhappy was quite widely known and rumoured. Good luck to her now and …

"Long Live the King!"

Just a few yards outside the Tower a troop of twenty soldiers on horseback inserted themselves neatly into the front of the procession – there would not have been room for all of them inside the tower's courtyard – and then another troop inserted themselves at the back of the procession once all the Lords and ladies of court had passed them by. Both troops rode horses as black as night.

No-one was expecting any trouble, naturally, but Buckingham had felt it was his responsibility to pre-empt any chance, however slight and far-fetched the threat may have seemed, of any such trouble, by protecting the procession of monarch and nobility. The temporary title of Lord High Steward at Coronations had to mean *something*!

Also riding with the troop at the front was the King's Champion who would have an important role later in the day. He, too, was seated on a magnificent white stallion, a full brother to the courser ridden by the king, just one year younger.

Tradition had it that the second best horse in the King's Mews was loaned to the King's Champion for the day and as long as he did not fail the king he got to keep the horse! (The *best* horse in the King's Mews was, of course, the horse the king himself would ride!) Nobody could actually tell who the King's Champion was because he was in full armour carrying a lance, face mask closed, but Maria knew and quietly disapproved.

The traditional role of King's Champion since 1066 was an honorary role of the title holder of Scrivelsby Manor in Lincolnshire. Originally it was the Marmion family but when that male line died out it went to the Dymocke family, by marriage to Johanna Marmion.

By rights the King's Champion today should have been Sir Robert Dymocke, a man of fifty years of age, but earlier in the week he had suffered a short bout of dysentery.

Henry, with the naivety of youth had, on a whim, offered the role of King's Champion to one of his young friends, John Walshe, with whom he often wrestled. In traditional terms, of course, he was of no importance, but he had one great advantage – he made Henry laugh! And old Sir Robert had one great *dis*advantage – Henry thought him an old stuffed shirt.

Sir Robert Dymocke was another of the older English retainers who had always been kind to Catherine, even in her darker hours after Arthur died, and Maria liked him very well. He was a quietly-spoken man, religiously very devout and was able with uncommon, common-sense, to find ways of easing the burdens of Catherine (and, thereby, Maria) when they were facing difficult times because of old King Henry VII.

When young Henry had made his gauche decision to favour his young friend at the expense of old Sir Robert and hundreds of years of tradition, Catherine had been put out for Sir Robert but there was so much going on in the last week that she quickly put it out of her mind and got on with important and urgent matters. For Maria it had been so much more difficult, for it was she to whom Sir Robert had poured his heart out!

For one thing he was still feeling unwell, constantly having to run to the privy and then he had had to suffer the indignity of having his family tradition trampled on so casually.

After Henry VII had taken the throne all those years before, Sir Robert had acted his role of King's Champion and, in fact, this had worked in his disfavour. When Maria had stood up for him against Henry's callous decision he simply replied, "...*there you are then, he has already had one go at the job, let it be someone else's turn!*" So saying, he quaffed the rest of his goblet of Rhenish wine and walked out of the room, leaving Maria speechless with her mouth hanging open.

And Sir Robert had almost been in tears telling Maria all his family history and the honours that went with the fine stallions the family had acquired over the years! He had made her laugh, as well, because one of the other perquisites of the job was that the King's Champion was able to keep the suit of armour made especially for him for the coronation so "...*we've got suits of armour to cobble dogs with, all over the house at Scrivelsby. Pity the poor fellow who has to keep 'em all clean and shiny!"* He had laughed along with Maria at this point, but his eyes were glistening and she suspected it was not tears of laughter that were shining in the candle light. Then the mood changed anyway, as he had to quickly shuffle off to the privy again!

She kept thinking about this conversation she had had with Sir Robert the other evening because, from her position in the procession, she could see very clearly the armour of the King's Champion – *"Upstart!"* – shining in the June sun just a little way ahead of her.

Catherine had chosen to leave Sir Robert at Greenwich the previous day – he had pleaded recurring bouts of dysentery but Maria thought it was more to do with an aching heart than a sore behind! She thought he would not be able to bear seeing his family role acted out by an obscure nonentity.

છ છ છ છ છ

Following a little way behind the men on stilts, was a large black phalanx of robed priests all swinging censors of smoking incense. At each street corner one of the priests at the front would swing away from the phalanx in a well-choreographed way to take up position in front of the crowds jostling to get a better view.

Nicholas, who at this point was sitting next to his Old Uncle Tom and looking through the angled 'window' facing back towards Holborn and the Tower, decided to try and count the priests on the basis that it might give them a better estimate of the number of soldiers posted on foot by the route of the procession. He could tell that there were 'a lot' but, as for counting them, he gave up after a few attempts. From this distance it just looked like one big black robe with a lot of heads poking through and jumbling up and down!

As far as he could tell, they were not spaced equally on the street, as the soldiers were... (he suddenly realised, too, that he could see four, no...five, SIX more soldiers from this vantage point than before and, yes, they *were* spaced equally apart!) No, the priests were concentrating on street-corners where the crowds were thickest. In other places, there was simply no room for a lot of people to stand... so there was no need for a priest with a swinging censor?

116

'*Oh my word!*' he thought. '*The priests are trying to make London SMELL better for the king and queen as they pass by!*' They seemed to be concentrating the incense where there was most body odour! '*Who on earth spends their time thinking about such things for a coronation!?*' Perhaps the Duke of Buckingham, he had heard so much gossip about recently, appointed to be Lord High Steward for the Coronation who, by all accounts, walked round the city with a sweet-smelling nosegay pressed to his face all the time, waving ordinary folk out of his way as much as he could!? As though people didn't have a bath at least once a month!

Then, thinking about it, not everyone *did* have a bath every month; Marc's brother Henri, for instance; and he did sometimes whiff of horses quite a lot! Perhaps the Duke of Buckingham had a point... certainly London smelt a lot worse than Louth. Just wait until he got home – what a lot of strange tales he would have to tell. His little friend next door, Eliza Jane, would be open mouthed with wonder!

Suddenly, he felt rather homesick... after all, it would soon be nearly a month since he left home, perhaps he should have a word with his old Uncle Tom at the end of the day about them setting off for home again...?

He could not explain just why, but he felt close to tears and he had to take a deep breath so that he would not embarrass himself by sobbing and having all the ladies fussing round him asking if he was all right! He needed something other than '*home*' to think about... and, there it was... a man breathing fire! He blinked... he had heard of fire-breathing dragons of course – but a fire-breathing MAN?

Behind the priests he could see a group of jugglers throwing balls and hoops and clubs into the air in great numbers, either individually or in pairs. And, at the front of this group there was a man with a long stick, like a torch, with fire at one end which he was tossing and twirling in the air. Every now and then, after he had moved a few yards, presumably so that he was in front of a different audience, he would take a small swig of something from a leather drinking bottle at his side, twirl the fire-stick and blow onto the flame as he caught the stick and his breath lit up with the frightening flames of a dragon. Yes, he would have *many* strange tales to tell when he got home!

And behind the jugglers there were more men on stilts, loping long-leggedly forward. And more drummers. And then a small band of musicians, two lutes, two recorders, one of which was huge and very deep sounding, and a tambour keeping time and two fiddlers dressed in very brightly coloured outfits. They were playing some very jaunty tunes and the crowd was cheering them on, stamping and applauding to the beat of the tambour. He liked the multi-coloured shirts of the fiddlers... *'I would like an outfit like that one day!'*

ଔ ଔ ଔ ଔ ଔ ଔ

Maria de Salinas gradually let her mind slow down. Her immediate responsibilities had been successfully concluded and she had nothing to do for at least the next hour, except walk sedately behind the litter which carried her best friend, Catherine, Queen of England, towards her husband's Coronation.

'How strange...' she thought. So many women would think it must be the most wonderful thing in the world to be where she was, doing what she was doing and would have given their right hand to be there in her place. *But...* all she could think about, in her heart of hearts, was how soon she could get away from this awe-full role and try and have a family of her own. Time was passing her by, she was going to end up an old maid, wizened and childless, unless...? Unless 'what' exactly, she did not quite know!

'STOP it!' she thought, *'...it's not YOUR day today... concentrate on your job today!'*

Then, all of a sudden she was giggling behind her hand as the Queen's litter swung awkwardly to the right. And she and her ladies all had to swing to the right as well, to avoid a great pile of steaming horse-shit deposited in the road by one of the black stallions of the troop in front of them.

Twenty horses...she wondered just how many of them would feel the need to relieve themselves of steaming, half-digested hay in the next hour. Then she glanced behind her and nearly broke out giggling again as she saw a man with a bucket hop out from the crowd, scoop up the still-steaming pile and scuttle back into the crowd again before one of the soldiers could react and grab him.

'Now, that was intriguing,' she thought. Was he an official shit collector acting under orders from the Duke of Buckingham, or simply an opportunist horticulturalist seeking to make his vegetables grow better and following alongside the procession hoping for more excellent compost material?

And, if he *was* an official shit collector would he sell his stock of manure for a good price, and what share would the good Duke of Buckingham demand? Would he take his share in money or 'goods in kind'? With these thoughts Maria found herself stifling the giggles again. She must tell *this* story to Catherine later, she would be amused. Indeed, they might have to question the good Duke closely, later on, too!

Maria was now quite content to let her mind wander over all sorts of things she normally did not have time to think about. Not that she was truly 'thinking' now – her casual considerations and 'thinking' were two different things. It was all rather relaxing… she realised that she spent most of her time thinking about her position and about her responsibilities to Catherine… and spent very little time thinking about herself and now '…*wasn't that odd*…' her thoughts were now in ENGLISH…when had THAT happened? When did she stop thinking in her native Spanish? She really had no idea when it had happened but she guessed it must have been quite some time ago.

Her rambling thought patterns were taking her along through cheering crowds without really hearing them and she found herself at the top of a small incline which took them all down to the bridge over the little River Fleet. No doubt it had once been a fast flowing river, else why had it been called 'Fleet' – but now it was gurgling slowly under the bridge, smelling very foul, and she would be so pleased to be over the bridge and up the other side.

She held a perfumed handkerchief over her nose as they crossed the river, not that it did much more than divert her senses briefly from the noxious fumes that hovered over the water. Lining the road on both sides for a hundred yards each side of the River Fleet were many monks in black robes from the Priory of 'Blackfriars', just down a side street from the road the procession was on.

As the procession was approaching to cross the bridge a very elderly man with a ring of silver hair circling his wizened scalp stepped carefully in front of the king's courser and held up a book, perhaps a bible, as a present for the young boy-king.

The Prior of Blackfriars took the king's right hand and patted the back of it gently in a paternal gesture, smiled, bowed his head and walked away again without a word. As far as Maria knew, this little scene was unscripted but clearly Henry was touched by the gesture. Leaning down from his horse, he handed the good book off to a servant with whom he had a few words. Then he looked over to the prior, touched his forehead with his gauntleted hand and mouthed a brief *'thank you'*, before they all moved off again, over the bridge, up the narrow Fleet Street, and on into the broad thoroughfare of the Strand.

ଔଔଔଔଔଔ

☞   The van Planck party had been enjoying the spectacle as the various entertainers had passed by their secret hideout. Not everyone wanted to watch at the same time so there had been a steady flow of bodies from and to the little observation windows. Marc and Nicholas were in most luck because there was not much demand for the lowest of the windows, they more or less had it to themselves – except when Joop and Henri had come to squat down on the floor and rather elbowed them aside! Even then there was room for them both to see if they just leant their heads inwards to the gap!

Once Joop heard the cheering for the king, however...

"Long live the King!"...

...there was a general move towards the windows, since it was clear the Royal Party could not be far behind the cheers. As before, it was old Uncle Tom who first saw the King's Champion and the troop of mounted soldiers who surrounded him. This time, however, he chose to say nothing and was able to keep his view for a couple of minutes before other folk started squeezing in to the space and blocking his view!

Then Joop let out a shout to say he had seen the King's Champion and everyone, literally everyone, was crouching or reaching, craning or peering to try and get a view out of the windows.

"I hear tell," said Joop, "that the King's Champion is always a Dymocke, so that must be Sir Robert Dymocke," he said very knowledgeably. "He was also the King's Champion at the coronation of the late King Henry VII."

"Well, well," said Mrs van Planck proudly, "fancy that!"

"Joop has spoken!" said the rest of the van Planck family and laughed!

"Well, it looks like a much younger man than that riding that there courser," chimed in Uncle Tom, who still had a view of the procession. "Old Sir Robert must be in his fifties, I reckon, and I know I couldn't ride a horse like that when I was fifty. I am sure that's a YOUNG man!"

"You couldn't ride a horse AT ALL when you were fifty, Tom!" shouted Willum van Planck, laughing. "I have never seen you on a horse in all your life!?"

To general laughter around the secret room Tom's riposte was quiet and dignified...

"Well, say what you will, 'tis my view that that is a YOUNG man and that's all I am saying!" This set off a general debate amongst all those, now looking closer at the King's Champion on his fine horse until someone said, "There's the king... just behind the troop of mounted soldiers!"

"Long live the King!"

The shout started echoing along the Strand, accompanied by much stamping of feet from the young, rather tipsy, gentlemen on the banked seats to the right of the van Planck secret room. So much so, that nobody could hear a word anybody else said in the enclosed space. Gypsy the dog barked twice and then slunk out of the room with her tail between her legs – it was clearly TOO noisy for her, perhaps she thought the whole world was being cross with her for some reason?!

Soon the king and the Duke of Buckingham were drawing near and a few moments before they came level with the van Planck's viewing room a black-robed priest swinging his censor moved to block the middle 'window'. The shop-owner was about to prod him with a sharp stick and shout at him when Mrs van Planck reached through their viewing peephole and tapped him gently on the shoulder; and said in the sweetest of her voices...

"Excuse me, Father, I wonder if you could move a couple of steps to your right so we can continue to see the wonderful spectacle his Highness has provided us with?"

The question was accompanied by one of her most vivacious and charming smiles and with an "*Of course, mistress!*" the priest moved out of the way. By this time they had a view of the king's back covered with the wonderful crimson robe; ...and the back end of his magnificent courser, with a silken ribbon at the top of its tail. But they also had a wonderful view of the queen's litter and she was looking directly at them peering through their peek holes.

Forever afterwards, Nicholas told everyone who would listen to his story, that he had been there in London for the king's coronation and saw Queen Catherine as she passed by in her gorgeous gold leaf litter. She looked out of her window and "...*looked directly at me and waved, oooh, 'twas a magnificent sight!*" Eliza Jane always believed him, although not everyone else was quite so sure. They put it down to the exuberance of youth!

Once the king and queen had passed by, the pressure for window space dropped significantly in the secret room and thoughts went to eating the picnic that everyone had contributed to. Nicholas and Marc, however, stuck to their posts in case anything else of significance should happen which they would draw to the attention of the room. Mostly, though they were trying to keep a low profile so that they did not get called upon for their 'other' role... of piss-pot emptiers!

Marc, in particular had been keeping a watch on the number of times the ladies had perhaps left the viewing room. Not that they would have paid a visit to the piss-pots every time they left the room, of course. That was a most unlikely scenario in the general experience he had of life. His experience of ladies was that they could hold their water rather like the mythical beast called a 'camel', which was widely known not to piss or drink for weeks on end!

ଔଔଔଔଔ

Bonfire: The Morning After
Monday 2nd October – 1536

Just outside Louth, in a nondescript cottage, in the little village of Kedington, a burly man woke early in a bad mood with an aching back and a headache. The backache and the headache were both caused by several hours on horseback the day before. The bad mood had no particular cause; that was just how he was ...always!

William Morland was a monk until a few short months before when his abbey, Louth Park, had been closed down by King Henry's commissioners. He had spent but little time in his cottage – inherited from his father a mere five years previously – and most of his time in the abbey across the little bridge over the River Lud. He was close to fifty, and, as one of the senior brothers at the abbey, he had been responsible for the pastoral care of his brethren there. It was a continuation of that role that had had him out on horseback all day on the Sunday.

He had been delivering charitable alms – the so-called 'capacities' – to his former brethren who were now living 'virtuously and honestly' a goodly number of miles away at another of the Order's Houses at Hagnaby near Alford.

Only last night, after he had returned home, had he re-read that part of the 'Act for the Dissolution of Lesser Monasteries' which had been passed by Parliament in February of that year, 1536. Something the abbot had said about the nature of these 'capacities' had disturbed his mind and he wanted to get it straight whilst it was fresh in his thoughts. He took his responsibilities seriously, in line with his dour personality.

He was, however, not really feeling inclined to tolerate the hateful legislation and it had, therefore, rekindled his anger at the dissolution of Louth Park – his home and workplace for so many years. He was angry because it was NOT, in his view, a place where '...manifest sin, vicious, carnal and abominable living...' was '... daily used and committed...' as was explicit in the Act. Nor was it any different in that regard from the House at Hagnaby which had not, not yet anyway, suffered closure and dissolution.

But the last part of the Act did go on to say in more tolerant language '...*and also His Majesty will ordain and provide that the convents of every such religious house shall have their capacities, if they will, to live honestly and virtuously abroad, and some convenient charity disposed to them towards their living, or else shall be committed to such honourable great monasteries of this realm wherein good religion is observed, as shall be limited by his highness, there to live religiously during their lives;*

and it is ordained by the authority aforesaid, that the chief governors and convents of such honourable great monasteries shall take and accept into their houses, from time to time, such number of the persons of the said convents as shall be assigned and appointed by the king's highness, and keep them religiously, during their lives, within their said monasteries, in like manner and form as the convents of such great monasteries be ordered and kept...'

And *that* was Monk Morland's current role, to collect appropriate monies from the remaining sources associated with Louth Park and take them to Hagnaby every so often to ensure his brothers could be '*kept religiously*'.

He had taken a hurried meal of cold meat and dry bread when he got in, tired and aching from his long ride, and was on the point of retiring to bed when his neighbour, also called William – *William Bonner* – one of the former lay-workers from the abbey across the river, stuck his head round the door.

"As you've been out since very early morning you won't have heard of the ruffling in Louth today. There was a big 'to-do' in church this evening and a bunch of townsmen took the church keys from the church wardens and locked the treasures away, keeping guard all night!

...You look dreadful – been a long day?

...I won't keep you from your bed then!"

And, with that – as quick as he had arrived and without waiting for any response – he left again, leaving William Morland speechless and puzzled, as well as tired out. The fact that this intriguing new information kept him from going straight to sleep probably contributed to his morning headache, too.

Since he naturally woke early, he went through his morning prayers – habit dies hard in one trained in the offices of religion – and took a long drink of cold water with the remains of the dry bread left from last night. Into the last inch of water left in his cup he stirred a powdered philtre of special herbs that had been given to him by the infirmarian at Louth Park, Brother Joseph, when the abbey closed. It was said to cure headaches and soothe many other aches and pains. It tasted awful, but was supposed to do you good! He swirled the dregs and drank them down, shuddering slightly at the aftertaste.

After such a long day on horseback yesterday, he weighed up whether he should walk into town or saddle up his horse to take him in. The time it would take to get his horse ready meant that he could nearly have walked into the centre of Louth by the time the saddle was on and tightly girthed...

But... if the 'ruffling' was significant, he thought he might have to visit a few people and talk to them about the events. On balance, he decided it might be worth the time taken to prepare his horse, to save him time again later in the day. So, that is what he did.

Once horsed, he headed straight for the church of Saint James to find out first-hand what was what, and was surprised, straight away, at how crowded the streets were, even though the hour was still early. On the way, he would be passing the shop of a mercer friend of his, Robert Bailey, and decided to have a quiet word with him first to find out what had been happening.

When Monk Morland came upon Robert Bailey's shop he realised there was no way he was going to have a **quiet** word with his friend. The shop was full to overflowing and as well as Bailey standing at the door, Morland recognised Robert Goldsmith beside him and standing behind him was William Ashby, Louth's Constable.

They were all anxious to tell their tale to someone 'new' and he had to slow them down because, as they each told their versions of events, they were falling over each other's tongues. Robert Goldsmith was full of bluster mainly because he felt demeaned by what had happened in church the previous day, when Cobbler Melton relieved him of his set of keys. He vacillated between claiming the treasures would have been safe with the keys in his care – he "*wouldn't have given them up to any commissioner's*" – to being outraged that he had been made to look weak amongst his peers. Then he would charge the common folk with being reckless and liable to get them ALL into trouble with the 'authorities' – presumably the very same commissioners he wouldn't have given the keys to either!?

Morland stayed on horseback through these jumbled stories, and then declared that he would "*...betake myself to church to say my morning mass*", and dug his heels none too gently into his horse's ribs to get the beast walking westwards again, covering the last couple of hundred yards to the church door.

There was a huge crowd gathered outside the doors, much hubbub and barracking with no sign of anyone going in. The monk had a job to get close on horseback, shouting "*Make way there*" a few times with very little result. At last he got within hailing range of the door and, since most of those present were on foot, he was able to project his voice over the heads of the crowd in front of him. He was, of course, recognised from his many years living next to the townspeople at Louth Park and being seen in the town in his robes and roped belt and tonsured head.

"Why are the doors blocked to we who would pray this morning, brothers?" – a civil enough question but asked with a sharp edge and in a booming voice. He had asked the question of the small group of men actually at the barred church door but his answer came from closer at hand. He had been stopped from taking his horse through into the grassy area just outside the south doorway of the church by two very large men, Henry Plummer and a man known to everyone in Louth as Great James, who was the champion wrestler in the whole district, standing at least six foot and six inches tall in his bare feet – not that he was unshod today, he was wearing very heavy boots, made especially for his large feet by Cobbler Melton himself.

For such a big man he spoke very quietly but with the air of one who brooked no disagreement. He was a tailor by profession and spoke as meticulously as he sewed – a delicate task for a man with prodigiously large hands!

"We're keeping the church well and truly locked today because there are many commissioners in town and they shall not get their hands on our treasure. So, sadly, Brother Morland, we would ask you not to trouble us today by seeking entry to the church."

Polite, all the while, but a definite 'NO ENTRY' message

The monk knew better than to pick a fight with this giant of a man, even on horseback he would probably lose, so he pulled his mount away and went round to the main doorway in the centre of the west facing wall under the tower and its fine spire, the tallest and, arguably, the finest in Lincolnshire apart from those on the cathedral church in Lincoln itself.

There were fewer people gathered there, not least because there was a sharp autumn wind blowing round the north–west corner of the church and the south door was shielded from the biting breeze. This door was also firmly closed, with another knot of men standing robustly with their backs to the door, several of them carrying long handled bill-hooks.

He carried on down the lane that led to the River Lud and carried on around the church, now overlooking the river, which was running quite fast at the moment following the heavy rains over the previous few days. There were a few people here as well, all wrapped up against the wind – he acknowledged a couple of hands raised in recognition and greeting. Then, having done a full circuit of the church, he made his way back into the town, dismounting when he got to the house of one of the town's butchers, William Hert, whose brother, Sir Robert, was an old and good friend of Morland's, being another ex-monk from Louth Park.

There were another half dozen men in Hert's kitchen, nearly all of them known to Brother Morland.

"Hello William", hailed the monk, louder than absolutely necessary.

"Hello William", replied the butcher, also louder than necessary.

The two men laughed and, hugging, slapped each other on the back, clearly the best of friends; this apparently being how they normally greeted one another – always louder than necessary! The echoing smiles on the faces of the others gathered in the kitchen reflected the passing humour, and the warmth in the kitchen from the oven brought rosiness to the cheeks of the visitor, as he came in from the cool air outside.

It was a colour which had already garnished the faces of the others there. William the butcher was particularly rosy-faced, in fact he was rather a florid man with broad spatulate fingers and the heavy forearm muscles of a busy purveyor of meats. It was often the case that butchers were amongst the strongest people in a village, a result of all the lifting of sides of beef and whole sheep they had to do in a normal day's work.

"Have you eaten yet, William?" asked the butcher

"I broke a little bread when I first heaved myself out of bed, this morning, but I confess to feeling rather peckish now, my friend." He suddenly realised his headache had disappeared – *'must be the fresh air'*, he thought – *'or maybe the herbs!?'*

"I was just on the point of offering my guests a little breakfast, some cold pork and succulent ham and some fresh beef puddings I am experimenting with this week for the shop. And...", he paused to emphasise the importance of the next few words, "... and I have a pot of pickled walnuts that I have been wanting to break open and try. What do you all say," – his look encompassed all his guests, lighting finally on his brother's best friend, with a smile, " – to joining me in tasting this delicacy with some fresh bread?"

"With a will, William, with a will!" So saying, they all shuffled round taking seats where they could find them. The monk was clearly well-regarded by the rest and ended up sitting in the best chair in the kitchen – a fine high-backed oak chair with a capacious seat and sturdy arms.

"So – tell me what's afoot" – William Morland asked his neighbours once their plates and, indeed, some of their mouths, were full of choice cuts of cold meat, beef puddings still warm from the oven and delightful pickled walnuts, apparently the best the French could supply.

Two men started to speak at once, but full mouths garbled their words and fetched a burst of laughter from the room, so a more abstemious voice set about relating the goings on from the previous day.

The voice was that of an austere man called Nicholas Weeks, who was a body servant of Lord Burgh, come all this long way from near Gainsborough, to buy meats and puddings for his master's kitchen. He had arrived on the Sunday evening as was his wont and boarded with William Hert the butcher, ready to do business with him on the Monday morning.

He had a dry way of telling the story and it was apparent he disapproved of the actions of Nicholas Melton, or *"Cobbler Melton and his band of ruffians"* as he called them. Before they had finished their repast, but after Weeks had told the bulk of his tale of Sunday's happening, the common bell of the church started to ring and carried on ringing insistently less than a hundred yards from where they sat. That was the well-recognised and practised signal for 'Alarm' – but quite what was alarming the men in the church, no-one knew at this moment.

"What the devil...?" began more than one voice and then Week's voice, full of foreboding, chilled them to the bone:-

"At this rate", he pontificated, "there will be those amongst our neighbours who will hang if this behaviour continues".

"Hold your peace, Weeks" snapped William Hert whose mood had been broken by the closeness and urgency of the bells. But, although he snapped, it was not entirely clear that he disagreed with Week's sentiments, just that he thought it ill-advised to voice them at this moment. He was, in fact, much concerned that if any of Cobbler Melton's 'band of ruffians' heard what Weeks said, it might be Hert and his friends who ended swinging from the gibbet for disloyalty to the town's commonality.

"We'd better go and see what the tumult is about", decided William Morland, sighing at his disturbed breakfast – he did rather like his food! His most frequent confessions were about his tendency to the sin of gluttony – a sin he gave way to again as he was leaving – by picking up a choice morsel of succulent ham and rolling a spoonful of walnut pickle up in the slice, munching satisfyingly as he left the butcher's kitchen.

He wiped his hands under his habit before taking the reins of his horse from the boy he had left holding them and mounted, using a nearby step – his knees were not as springy as once they were and, anyway, they were stiff from all the riding he had done the day before. One or two of the other men were mounted as well and they made a little party, surrounded as they were by men, boys and older women making their way towards the church, some running, some walking quickly, others walking more slowly.

The knot of people formerly gathered round the south door, out of the wind, had now moved round in front of the bigger west door, where the land dropped away and where there was more room to accommodate a large and growing gathering of townsfolk.

When the two Williams, butcher Hert and Monk Morland, and their little band turned the corner they saw that the big church doors were now opened wide and they could see John Wilson and Richard Nethercotts, two of Cobbler Melton's band, inside the bell tower. They were pulling on the bell rope, which was lit by a low shaft of morning sunlight glancing through one of the far windows high in the south wall.

The sun was hazy at best, after an overnight shower, but picked out the men's practiced handling of the bell rope. Most of the crowd were in the shadows cast by the church itself but Morland and his colleagues were in the sun's rays because they could not get any closer to the church for the crowds already gathered. And more people were on their way.

Quite a few were trying to make themselves heard by their friends and neighbours, mostly asking each other unanswerable questions – but the Common Bell was uncommonly loud at these close quarters to the church, especially with the west door wide open.

Great James and some of the other bigger men were still there, on guard, with their bill hooks at the ready. And, to Morland's surprise, there was even a small group of men on horseback in their full harness, some with chain mail leggings, and others with metal breastplates. Strangely, he recognised none of them so he assumed they had arrived from one of the nearby villages already accoutred for conflict – presumably having got up very early to be here at this hour. What news had they brought, or were they just anticipating trouble he hadn't yet reckoned with?

There was a good deal of milling around as people gathered and edged closer to the church so they could hear what was going to be said soon. People of all ages, some with makeshift weapons, picks, mallets, more bill hooks or whatever came to hand in a hurry that could be used to break bones or cut, or both.

But there were many still unweaponed and curious to know what the panic was about. The only group hardly represented was that of younger women. They were mostly at home looking after young children who had been told in no uncertain terms by husbands, fathers and uncles and other men folk to "...*stay put and be safe at home*".

On the other hand, there were quite a few older women present, matrons whose children had flown the nest, come to assess the dangers for their extended families, perhaps.

The idea was clearly to bring out all the able bodied townsfolk within half an hour or so as they would have practised in drills for the muster intermittently. Against what precise threat, however, no-one outside the church knew, but since the general subject had been discussed all summer long, no-one was really surprised that something was afoot, especially after the previous day's excitement.

John Wilson could be seen inside the tower having just steadied the bell rope and almost immediately the bell stopped its full-blown donging. The clapper was now, just occasionally, making quieter dongs as it settled. An air of expectation grew and some who had been shouting against the bell's loud noise found their words carrying to all and sundry now, causing a few sporadic bursts of slightly nervous laughter.

Cobbler Melton came out of the church door with three or four others at each shoulder and he held both arms raised a little to quell the noise. As he would do when introducing the Corpus Christi dramas, he waited until there was perfect quiet and then just half a minute longer, as the tension began to build. He knew his voice could grasp and hold an audience – it was always stronger and clearer than people expected from his relatively slight stature. Great James who was standing nearby towered over him by a whole head – mind you he towered over pretty well everybody else there too!

"It seems", started Nicholas, in deceptively stentorian tones, "that we have more visitations of officialdom in this one day than we would normally expect in a month or more ... and there are those amongst us who are suspicious about this." He did not say he was one of them but he left the issue hanging as though he could be persuaded to be suspicious.

"The bishop's chancellor, Dr Raynes, is nearby to begin the inquisition, the Visitation of Parish Clergy hereabouts, and there are serious worries that it will change our lives for the worse. More than two dozen priests from surrounding village churches are here for all those questions they must face."

"Thomas Cromwell's commissioners are nearby, too, closing yet another house of religion and stripping it of its possessions. They are at this very minute at Legbourne Priory just along the road where our Sisters of Mercy have served our community so well. Who knows when these men will finish that misbegotten act and turn their attention to our church and its treasures?"

"And finally the bishop's administrator for the town, Goodman

John Heneage, is here on the pretext of presiding over a meeting to elect this next year's officials for the town. This is a meeting which would normally happen next month and we wonder why it has been changed. Let us say it seems suspicious!"

"We know the religious houses have been stripped of silverware that is precious and some of them have been sold, as if they were simple chattels, to the *wealthy* men of the county". With only a little emphasis he imbued the word 'wealthy' with considerable venom as if they might be parasites on the body of the commonwealth.

"Some of these men have stripped the roofs of lead, stolen fireplaces and panelling for their dwellings and used the remaining shells as sheep shelters against the wind and rain."

Nicholas was winding up the passion and the passion was winding up his audience. His voice boomed again...

"We think it is time to stop these destructive powers in their tracks before they dismantle the whole commonwealth and spirituality of our town and nearby villages, which seems to be their goal. At the very least we need to be asking them questions which make them think more than once about the depths to which they seem to be stooping. Some would have us co-opt the town's administrator to the comfort of the townspeople rather than to the comforts of his heretic bishop – for heretic bishop is what I am informed he is."

At this bold statement there was an audible gasp from some in the crowd, for such strong words were not associated with the normally mild mannered shoe-maker. It certainly got people talking, each with their immediate neighbours, creating a susurration which competed with the noise of the wind in the nearby trees, a wind which was beginning to dislodge some autumn leaves from their twigs and branches.

"Those of you who would have something done about protecting our birthright should come with me and see what mischief Master Heneage is about today..." and with a final shout of "Who is with me?" the Cobbler stalked off quickly into the centre of town, keeping close to the wall of the church until he was clear of the crowd and pulling that crowd with him by his natural magnetism.

Great James, and another hefty fellow, marched one at each shoulder, immediately behind Nicholas; and the others who had been guarding the church followed on behind. John Wilson and several others had been told to shut all the church doors again and keep people out. Nicholas still had the rood loft keys with him, so the people's treasure stayed safe.

William Morland, the monk on horseback, and the group of men with him, appended themselves thereto. In their wake was the group of mounted strangers who were already in harness, ready for action. The whole exploit was beginning to take shape and look a little warlike, a factor which rather concerned Monk Morland and his fellows.

The large crowd of men and boys on foot, together with some of the womenfolk, who had been summoned by the common bell, followed raggedly along behind, some shouting encouragement to others along the way to...

"Join us brothers all, for we go to save our treasure!"

Several laggards, who had heard the common bell but had taken the time to put on harness or sharpen their weapons, or simply decided to finish their breakfasts before venturing out, were now only just coming into the main street from their cottages further away from the church.

"What goes on brothers?"

"Join us brothers all, for we go to save our treasure!"

"What's the fuss?"

"Join us brothers all, for we go to save our treasure!"

What started as a casual statement, turned into a marching call. In fact, a couple of twelve year old boys soon joined the rag-taggle march, each with a drum they had been given to practise on for muster days. They squeezed into the crowd at the back of the first group of men who'd been in the church all night with Nicholas, taking their main tempo from the steps of Great James, and then syncopating little drum rolls into the steady 'rump-tump' of the marching feet.

"Join us brothers all, for we go to save our treasure!"

The rhythm broke as the leading group stopped, suddenly catching sight of Administrator Heneage. He didn't look terribly suspicious, it has to be said, and he was going about his business seemingly unaware that there was any problem. He was slightly other-worldly, his head always stuck in figures and amounts and books and probably not paying much attention to the way others saw him or the world about themselves. Nor had he paid any attention to the church bell being rung this morning – it was said he was a little deaf at times.

His two brothers were, as he said himself, much more 'men-of-the-world' than was he. His brother, Thomas Heneage, was an associate of the famed Thomas Cromwell, the Lord Privy Seal and now – since Henry VIII had recently declared himself head of the church – also Vicar General of the Church in England. Another Heneage brother was now Dean of Lincoln, but, in comparison, John Heneage was a rather dull figure and just seemed to plod along, administering whatever his master the Bishop of Lincoln asked him to administer.

He had been rather enjoying the cool crisp air and the autumn sunshine of this October morning, as he walked along towards his meeting. He had, of course, eventually *heard* the drums and the shouting but was not at all aware that the noise might have anything to do with him. He just found the noise, and general *'skyre'*, a troubling disturbance to the quiet of his morning stroll.

John Heneage had risen very early that morning to ride over to Louth, with just a few pertinent papers in his saddle bag. He had left his horse at the inn round the corner where the stable lad had promised to water and feed the animal, and give him a good rub down. So the bishop's administrator was making his way, on foot, towards the Town Hall where the meeting was to be held. He had just reached the gate of his friend Robert Proctor, one of the eminent men of Louth and a one-time churchwarden, when he became aware that the noise had, in the last minute or two, grown much louder as it got closer. Then, all of a sudden, it died away.

Here again, he did not seem to realise it had gone quiet *because* he had been sighted by the crowd!

Still unconcerned, therefore, and still unaware that he was the centre of attention at that moment, he opened the latch gate and was about to walk the short path to the house when Proctor's front door opened and a worried face glanced between him and the crowds in an agitated fashion. Robert Proctor's hand appeared and quickly beckoned him forward.

"Come in John, do... quickly now!"

"Good morning Robert, well... er ...yes, of course, certainly... indeed" He moved forward a few steps. But, by now, something was impinging onto his conscious mind that, perhaps, not everything was in order this bright morning.

"What... er... what's the ...?" his hesitant query got no further as the sound magnified again.

Nicholas and his immediate contingent had stayed stationary near the gate but the men with pitchforks and bill hooks had surged from the very back of the column to the very front – and very noisy they were too.

... "You've come to steal our silver"

"What are you doing here today?"

"It doesn't belong to Cromwell and your brother..."

... "Don't you two go inside into a huddle-muddle, telling tales we're not privy to"...

Cobbler Melton and his immediate entourage continued to stay still, as the noise grew and the threats flew from behind, and all around them. Some of the men with bill hooks had broken through a young hedge and were closing in on Heneage and Proctor. John Heneage just looked genuinely puzzled, but real concern was showing on Robert Proctor's face which had gone very, very pale.

One group of men had gone round the back of the house and the sound of breaking glass was clearly audible making Nicholas wince as the glass tinkled to the floor. Proctor had two glass windows at the back of the house looking over his garden area; they were his pride and joy and were made of quite flat glass. There was hardly any distortion at all when you looked through them and they were much finer than the glass windows at the Inn, where Heneage had left his horse.

There was shouting, and banging of fists on doors, and then more tinkling as another glass pane broke. Nicholas almost felt sorry for Goodman Proctor – almost!

Proctor was torn between protecting his esteemed visitor, and chasing round the back of the cottage to see what damage had been done to his prized windows.

The monk, William Morland, had grown restive by now and was trying to exert some authority from the saddle but was struggling to keep the horse still – the noise had been rather too much for an old horse, used to a quiet life. Morland tried addressing Nicholas, but was cut short by Cobbler Melton's raised hand.

Indeed the raising of the hand coincided with a quietening of the shouting and general hubbub – but whether it was his perceptive reading of the mood, or whether his raised hand had stilled the voices of his men wasn't entirely clear, even to Nicholas.

Nevertheless, the modest action *had* caught everyone's attention, not least the attention of Heneage and Proctor on the doorstep, one outside, one inside. There was still some noise coming from round the back but most people heard Cobbler Melton's voice, not overly loud, but quietly self-assured...

"Goodman Proctor, Goodman Heneage..." they both gave the town's best known shoe-maker their full attention!

"...it seems that some of my fellow townspeople have been over-zealous in expressing their concerns, for which I apologise. But you may know that we are all very worried that our town treasure is under threat of being confiscated and as you can see everyone is agitated as a result."

"Cobbler Melton," Robert Proctor's voice was quavering somewhat as he spoke, clearly unnerved by the multitude surrounding him. "Mr Heneage here is in Louth for the regular town meeting..."

Shouts of *"No, he's not!"* and *"He's here for the treasure!"* came from various quarters of the assembled throng together with other, less clear, shouts.

"...and he and I need to go over the meeting's agenda." continued Proctor, visibly trembling now, but clearly making a move to get both himself and his visitor inside.

The shouting grew and became just noise again, as men banged sticks against the wall and yet another window-pane broke into shards around the back of the house. Nicholas held his hand aloft again, but the next voice to speak was, in fact, William Morland's who had, by now, got his horse under control and felt able to intervene.

"Mr Proctor, I think there may be more windows broken if the pair of you try to go inside."

Nicholas, with a slight frown at the monk's intervention, took over the sentence deftly, as if on stage, "...so if you would both come with us back to the church, we would be obliged".

He instructed Great James and Eleazor Swain, another very tall broad-shouldered Viking of a man, to escort the two men to the church – probably as much for their own protection from the rather unruly gathering behind them, as for escorting them as 'reluctant guests'.

As it was, some of the rowdier elements of the townsfolk kept jostling the administrator and the former churchwarden 'accidentally' as they walked along – feelings were clearly running high.

The leading party was quite soon back at the big west door of the church and Nicholas had sent a runner along ahead to get the door opened before they arrived so that there would not be an unbearable crush, which might lead to someone getting injured. Even with both doors open there was still a lot of barging. Somehow the monk had moved ahead of everyone else and managed to dismount and secure his horse to a railing near the church *and* get to the west door just a step behind Nicholas and his group of followers.

The press of bodies behind them pushed the leading party a long way into the church and there was still an unseemly racket, many people shouting the odds and quite a lot of waving of poles and bill hooks – it was a wonder no-one had an eye whipped out of its socket.

Monk Morland carried on pushing the leading group so that they decanted from the body of the church into the choir, and Goodman Proctor and Goodman Heneage were pushed hard up against the lectern. It was from this lectern that the choirmaster normally conducted rehearsals and performances of what many thought were the finest singers in the whole County of Lincolnshire, when it came to religious music. There was a tradition of fine singing at Saint James Church in Louth, but the voices in the choir today were much less than musical.

Though it was crowded, there was a calmer atmosphere prevailing, overall, once the choir door was shut against the rowdiest elements. *They* were still making threatening noises from the nave of the church, because they were worried that, even with Cobbler Melton and several of his closest supporters present, something may be amiss.

Strangely, the rich colours of the fine wooden choir stalls and the skilled carvings made people realise they were in a special place, and this calmed frayed nerves quite a lot. The atmosphere quietened measurably. Nicholas was about to start speaking when the monk cleared his throat and spoke over him. This man was beginning to irritate the shoe-maker more than a little.

"So, Mr Heneage, tell us what you are doing here in Louth today", the monk's tone was accusatory.

"Well, ermm, I was... er so to speak, ...I came early to... err..." the administrator was clearly disorientated by his recent experience, and needed some thinking time to place his thoughts in order before speaking. He was rescued by Goodman Proctor, who had recovered his equanimity somewhat, since the focus of the townsfolk's ire seemed to be Mr Heneage and not himself even though it was his house that had suffered the consequences.

"Mr Heneage here," his voice much stronger than before, "has come to preside over the town meeting, which was brought forward a few weeks because we have lost two members of the council who died in recent months. It was considered urgent to ensure that all the main administrative tasks were to be undertaken fully by responsible citizens with the appropriate time and expertise. As you may know, one of the churchwardens – Goodman Ellwood – has been taking on most of the responsibilities of the two deceased counsellors recently, but he has become increasingly pressed by these responsibilities at a time when his wife, Mistress Ellwood, has become unwell of late. Rather than carry on with these temporary arrangements we were seeking to ensure that things were sorted out to everyone's convenience."

"Err, quite so Mr Proctor; quite aptly, and succinctly, put, if I may say so." Mr Heneage had suddenly reacquired his fluency of speech, and thought, in delivering his agreement with Proctor's statement of fact, so much so that Nicholas began to wonder if his 'other worldly' persona was simply an act?.

"So you see, gentlemen, it appears you have been labouring under a misapprehension of my role here this day." Indeed, he seemed to be trying to assume a mantle of authority with his smoother manner of delivery – but it did not quite come off.

With a quick 'daggers-drawn' look at the monk for his earlier intervention, Nicholas made sure the next words were his own.

"Be that as it may, Mr Heneage and, indeed, Mr Proctor," Nicholas included the erstwhile churchwarden with his eyes as well, "we are greatly troubled by the change of date, and its coincidence with other factors at play in the town this week, as you may have gathered by our activity this morning. You will both be aware of the many rumours that have been circulating of late about the threats to our treasure and it is important we manage to get to the bottom of this and find out what is really happening."

"Jack Bawnus here has been making close notes of the rumours, and we have asked him to try and make sense of them all. He will put them to you now, Mr Heneage, and ask you of your opinion as to their veracity."

Jack Bawnus was a young school master at the Louth church choir school. As Louth had a church with a wonderful singing tradition, a fine choir school had gradually been established, funded by the richer townsmen for the benefit of local children with excellent voices. The school then helped the community by providing excellent choirs, which then profited the rich townsmen by affirming their reputations as generous patrons, and fine upstanding gentle-folk, living in a cultured community. So everyone benefitted.

Jack Bawnus had had a fine singing voice as a child but – unlike Tom Foster, whose voice went on to be a fine mature voice – when *Jack* became an adult, his voice broke into pieces which grated painfully upon the ear. His speaking voice was fine but his singing voice... well; let us simply say it did not blend with the rest of the choir. His brain was better put together than his adult voice, however, and, although he was from a poor family in the town, he had won a charitable scholarship to Oxford, and had come back to his school as an assistant teacher, where he tried to teach the boys the rudiments of mathematics.

Jack was not an extrovert like Nicholas, but he was a good organiser and liked to be involved in the backstage area of the Corpus Christi plays, which is how he had become a firm friend of both Nicholas and Vicar Kendall, both considerably older than he was.

Needless to say, they had time to talk a lot about all sorts of things other than the plays themselves during the annual production and presentation cycle and found they had similar views about community, morality and life. So, when the Act to dissolve the monasteries had been brought into law and the church had started changing, they found themselves at the centre of a web of upset and dissatisfaction and grumbling throughout the town of Louth and, indeed, across the County of Lincolnshire and beyond. Between them, they created a formidable melting pot of ideas, talking about them, and teasing things out, until they made sense.

Also, as a mathematician, Jack had a very analytical mind, and he had an ability to put into words what others had been thinking but could not quite say properly. He was also able to ask just the right question at times to get positive answers and action from other people when support was needed for a play's production.

All these were reasons why Nicholas called on him to lay out the concerns of the people of Louth for Administrator Heneage – who now seemed well in control of his wits again. If Heneage *was* involved in some activity which would deprive the people of Louth of their church treasures, Nicholas felt it would emerge in the course of the next few minutes in the way he responded.

Jack Bawnus started a little nervously for this was, after all, rather different from the audience of young boys who were his usual listeners. However, there had been a lot of talking about these things for the last few weeks in one way or another and his capacity for mental organisation meant he had sorted out the strong rumours from the weak; the likely courses of action from the less likely; and the probable implications of the most likely courses of action. Indeed, he and Nicholas and Vicar Kendall had talked for several hours about these issues on Friday night, over a few glasses of ale, and he and Nicholas had talked again that very morning.

He had arrived at the church early, not having been part of the overnight church guard – he had an invalid mother he had to look after – and Nicholas had brought him up to date with what Thomas Kendall had revealed about the meeting he attended on Saturday.

So, thus prompted by Nicholas, he set about laying out the rumours, which had been on everyone's lips, for the Town Administrator, the actions of the townspeople of Hull selling their silver and paving the town with York stone, the comments of men in Grimsby about having their silver confiscated by the commissions going around, and so on. He laid out all the stories they had heard about what happened to the silver, lead roofing and oak panelling from dissolved monasteries and abbeys. And asked what would happen to the fine solid gold cockerel weather-vane, on top of Saint James church spire, donated by the previous Vicar, Vicar Sudbury?

He related the facts, noted by Vicar Kendall at the meeting of the bishop's commission in Old Bolingbroke as recently as Saturday, when Heneage's colleague, Dr Raynes, was clearly taking notes about the richness of the local churches during his questioning of priests about their learning. Why would he make such notes, if not to plan the confiscation of that treasure for Vicar General Cromwell?!

He told Heneage of the Commission which had just started sitting in the priory at Legbourne just outside Louth, in order to dissolve the

House, the dissolution of which had spread the sisters there to the four winds. This diaspora included Nicholas' cousin Eleanor, who was now the main assistant of the prioress there, Jane Mussenden, Mother Maria. Or, at least she had been, until the dissolution.

He made much of the fact that the commissioner there, John Bellow, was a man heartily disliked in Louth and was known to 'ride roughshod' over the sensitivities of others. He had, after all, been taken to the Star Chamber in London by some Louth citizens he had defrauded but had escaped punishment because he was so well connected at court.

"The priory at Legbourne is a small religious house but we all know it to be temperate, well run and it serves the community of Louth in many small ways, too innumerable to count. This man Bellow loves money too much and he has made no secret of the fact that he thinks Saint James Church to be too big, and too rich, for its own good. What are we to make of that, but that it sounds like a direct threat to our treasures?"

It was a tour de force. He hardly seemed to draw breath, and the stutter, which sometimes troubled him, was not present today. Virtually everyone in the crowded room was nodding emphatically in agreement as he covered the points they all knew, without once hesitating, or mumbling, or repeating himself, or wandering off the point. Even the former churchwarden, Robert Proctor, found himself being convinced and nodding along with the others, until he caught himself, and realised he should probably be taking a more neutral viewpoint, a more cautious viewpoint.

John Heneage was listening carefully and, though he had surely heard at least some of the more general rumours before, he was showing interest in the story unfolding, as if for the first time – perhaps it *was* the first time he had heard them in such a coherent form and in such an intense juxtaposition.

Bawnus finished his tale of anguish and summed up in austere and unembellished form with a series of points, each one emphasised by the raising of one of his bony fingers, erect and accusing.

"First, the rumours are widely bruited and consistent over the last few weeks, so it seems probable that they are well based in fact, even if not every single rumour be true."

"Second, we have the evidence of our own eyes, and other senses, that the commissioners hereabouts are making clear notes of valuation of churches, seemingly for purposes other than just the re-charging of 'first fruits' for Thomas Cromwell, on setting new priests in place."

"Third, we have the concurrence of two commissions taking place in Louth at this time, plus your advanced visit to the town, earlier than expected. What are we to make of it and how can you explain all these things happening right now"

He took a deep breath, shut his lips in a tight line and exhaled slowly, folding his arms in expectation. Heneage paused, as if about to speak, but seemed to pause a second or two longer than necessary.

Nicholas, sensing, or perhaps simply imagining, that the monk, William Morland was about to try and take charge of the meeting again, chose to intervene with a summary of his own.

"Well, Mr Heneage, you have heard what concerns we have in great detail and in well-ordered fashion, thank you Jack...", he half-turned to direct his thanks, then turned back to the administrator, "what have you to say?"

"Well," said Heneage in his turn, "Let me take your last point first, since it is the easiest to deal with," he smiled a humourless smile.

"Let me assure you all that my being here is nothing to do with the treasures of your fine church and is a coincidence only of timing. As Mr Proctor here asseverated earlier, we brought the town meeting forward because of the decease of two of its leading members. Current members of the council were struggling with the many things that needed doing and we thought it best if we made the new appointments sooner rather than later so that the work could begin anew and nothing would be lost. "

"I have the agenda here to which we will be working..."

He hesitated, not sure whether to assume that there was someone in the room who could read, other than the monk – and he had noticed the tension when Morland had intervened previously. The decision to make such an assumption was pre-empted by Nicholas who reached his hand out and spoke up.

"Hand the documents over here – let me see what you have" (In fact it was probable that only he and the monk had known that 'asseverated' was just a large word for 'stated'...but, nevertheless...)

Heneage just passed over the agenda, but Nicholas, with merely a peremptory flick of his hand, indicated he wanted to see *all* the papers

Heneage was carrying. Nicholas quickly read the page on which the administrator had written the list of subjects to be spoken about, and decided about, and then, also briefly, riffled through the other pages – thankfully there were not many to look at – and then handed them back.

"It looks, Mr Heneage, as though you speak the truth about the meeting. However, we would be anxious to know what have you to say about the wider matters we have talked about this morning with you?"

"Well, Mr Melton, and gentlemen" he said, returning the civility of address, "I have certainly heard some, at least, of the rumours you have referred to, but, upon my soul, I have never given them any credence. Your rendition of them was remarkable..." he turned here to face Jack Bawnus briefly, "...but, nevertheless, the truth is that many of the rumours are just that – baseless rumours".

"As for the observations on how Dr Raynes was handling the situation of his visitation concerning the Ten Articles and other matters of a religious nature, I fear you will have to take those questions up with Dr Raynes. He and I meet very infrequently..." several pairs of eyes in the room met briefly, and with some disbelief at this, "...and it is not something we have talked about at all, nor am I privy to his directions contained in the papers instructing him on his Commission. For what it is worth, my general understanding is that it is just about what it is *said to be* about, and the visitation really is to test the learning of the priests in the new teachings of the church!"

He appeared a little vexed that the details he and Proctor had been given this morning sounded very persuasive, and it may even be possible that he was trying to convey the view that the assumptions that he was making were perhaps wrong. His brother, the Dean, and other officers of the church in Lincoln did sometimes seem to treat him as rather unworldly and perhaps did not include him in their discussions on weighty matters of religious doctrine and so on. He was, perhaps, thinking to himself, '...*could I actually be wrong?*'

"Now, relating to the Dissolution Commission at Legbourne I am afraid I can be of little help there..." This last comment was accompanied by an almost unconscious shrug of the shoulder. "I am aware that Goodman Bellow has not always been regarded as a friend of the town, or of at least some of its inhabitants..."

There was some muttering at this. Well, to be truthful, it was rather more than muttering,

"Damn villain ...!"

"Rapscallion and bully!"

"......hung by the neck 'til his eyes pop out"

And much more of like kind – so much so there was a danger that Heneage would not be allowed to continue. So Nicholas calmed the crowded room with a masterful understatement, delivered scathingly...

"Let us just say that most of us believe he should not warrant the honorific *'Goodman Bellow'*... Please continue Mr Heneage."

Slightly rattled again at the loathing this man engendered amongst the crowd of Louth citizens pressing against him, and occasionally jostling him, as he spoke, Administrator Heneage said, somewhat tremulously...

"...to the best of my knowledge, the Commission is there just to dissolve the Legbourne Priory – I am sure it has no brief to look into the affairs of the church here in Louth itself. Indeed the priory was formally dissolved just before Michaelmas, which as you know was on the twenty-ninth of September – just last week. No doubt they are sorting out the details of what to do with all the property therein ..." His voice trailed off.

Then, suddenly, his manner changed and he appeared to take it upon himself to *properly* represent the Bishop of Lincoln who was, after all his benefactor and superior, as had been Cardinal Wolsey before that, when *Wolsey* had been Bishop of Lincoln. And, *through* the bishop, of course, he represented the law of the land. It was an overt attempt to exert authority which he believed he should possess but did not feel he actually had at the moment!

Indeed, his authority came not only through the bishop! He was, after all, a Member of Parliament for Grimsby and had been representing Lincolnshire interests (some would say his *family's* interests!) as an MP on and off since 1523, when he was just thirty eight. Why shouldn't he exert his authority? So his next words were delivered with more emphasis, perhaps one might say 'bravado'...

"The Act of Dissolution was not aimed at churches at all" he said with some exasperation and in the tone of a man who knew whereof he spoke as, no doubt, an MP should. "It was aimed to close many small religious houses - '*whereby the governors of such religious houses, and their convent, spoil, destroy, consume, and utterly waste to the great infamy of the king's highness*' "....choosing finally to quote from the Act itself, quite an impressive feat of memory!

Feeling the tension build as the administrator took the official line as his own, Nicholas decided to stop him in his tracks before the irritation of his audience boiled over into action they all might regret!

"Small it may be," said Nicholas in high dudgeon on behalf of everyone present, but not least on behalf of his cousin Eleanor who was not there to defend herself and her sisters in religion, "but to speak of Legbourne as a place of '*utter waste*' is a mockery."

"There were only ten nuns there it is true – one of them is my cousin and she is of the highest moral standing, as are her sisters. Until they were cast out last week with barely enough money to buy 'secular apparel' they looked after half a dozen elderly men and women from the town who had lost their wits and had no immediate family to care for them. They are now left with no money to live on and their charges have been scattered to the four winds. My cousin is now living with us and is distraught at the fate of her 'family', the people she calls her 'uncles and aunts' though they are in truth no relation of mine, simply elderly folk who need special care at the end of their lives!"

Another voice chimed in now and it was no less fierce in its contemptuousness than that of Nicholas. William Morland, who had suffered a similar fate when the equally small Louth Park Abbey had been closed earlier in the year, had managed to keep quiet for some time now, but his ire had finally got the better of him.

"There were only a couple of handfuls of us monks at Louth Park, too," he agreed, "but we were guilty of no sins as grievous as the Act wantonly suggested. We farmed some land and spare produce was brought to Louth's market for the benefit of people here and to contribute to our running costs. We maintained the bridges over the Lud to the east of the town and the roads leading to and from the bridges and now all of that will go to waste – or perhaps the town's counsellors will take on that responsibility?"

"Aye, and you pretend to know so little but some of these men in this room – and probably most of those outside..."

His reference to the crowd of men in the body of the church was timely, for there was now a banging on the door and many loud queries as to "...*what is happening in there, skulduggery we'll be bound!*" The atmosphere outside was clearly getting edgy. The monk paused and then continued.

"Some of the men in this room... and probably most of those outside this door will not know that you yourself were on the first five Commissions of Dissolution in the County of Lincolnshire at the very beginning of the year's progress to '*ransack the religious houses*', were you not?" His voice hardened as he got angrier.

"And what has happened to the land associated with those five houses? We know that most of the land now belongs to the Heneage family, probably bought for a pittance from the king's Vicar General. And will you be buying the gold cockerel that adorns this fine spire, to make a punch bowl perhaps?"

There was some scornful laughter here from the press of local men who knew that before it became such a glorious weathervane, the 'fine cockerel' had actually once been a battered punch bowl! "Rich gold but well-worn with some holes in it" is how it had once been described in the church records. Some of them even referred to it as the Holy Punchbowl, now it sat atop the spire pointing with the wind.

Despite the laughter, it was tense in the choir when Heneage spoke again. There was even a sense that he was trying to mollify the angry souls in the room, and he clearly felt under serious pressure again.

"Look gentlemen..." his tone was almost apologetic and the word 'gentlemen' lengthened as he addressed them, "... I am sure you are wrong in your presumption that the Vicar General and his commissioners have ever thought to include the town and village churches in the Act of Dissolution, only those chapels and churches within the bounds of some of the religious houses. Indeed I would stake my life on it."

An unidentified voice growled "You may already have done that since we have you here in our midst!" He pretended not to notice the threatening words and he carried on speaking although his voice now had a quaver in it as he spoke.

"Gladly, I will take myself down to the His Majesty's Court in London on your behalf and speak to the king personally to ask his views on these matters – get it settled once and for all that way." Some assenting murmurs were heard as he said this and he was relieved that the mood began to change a little.

There was also some talk and some debate about what he had said, almost as if he was not there, present, in the room with them.

"It's an idea..."

"But can we trust the bugger?"

"... just looking to save his skin!"

Several voices suggested the same thing at virtually the same time to the extent that nobody afterwards could actually say whose idea it had been – "*Let's swear him in to our cause!*"

This idea was affirmed almost by acclamation and someone opened the doors to the choir and shouted to the men out in the nave of the church – "Go and fetch the Chief Constable, Constable Ashby, quick as you can."

No-one out there knew what had been going on so there were some shouted questions...

"What's he done...?

"Are we arresting him...?

"String him up..."

Nicholas, who was standing slightly higher than most present, on a step at the eastern end of the choir, called over the top of the heads of the men there to John Wilson who was in the nave, but close by the door.

"John, go with Great James as quickly as you can and find the Chief Constable, William Ashby. We need him here to administer an oath to these men. Go!"

Hearing these instructions directly from Cobbler Melton, the crowd parted like the red sea and a path quickly opened up in front of Wilson and Great James to let them get out of the melee to carry out their task. After that there was a general hubbub as the men in the closed room now all spoke at once to their friends in the nave who hadn't made it inside the choir.

It was not very long before those inside the church knew that the '*search and fetch*' task had been successfully completed – the noise of the accompanying crowd told them John Wilson and Great James had indeed found their man. Ashby had been near the town hall talking to the other senior men of the town who were all waiting for John Heneage to arrive and did not know why he was so late, so the Constable had not been that difficult to find.

Constable Ashby was a tall and well-built fellow but even he seemed somewhat diminished beside Great James. He wore a dark coat of fustian and a floppy hat to mark his status. He carried himself well and carried his years even better. Several men in the crowd surrounding him had felt the back of his hand in their youth when he had been a young upcoming Constable in the town.

Now he felt his responsibility as the chief man of the law in this busy market town and was still not sure what was afoot – something to do with swearing an oath? He had been in church the day before, of course, so he knew St James was the centre of whatever activity had caused the bells to be sounded – but why an oath?

Once inside, of course, his puzzlement was short lived and he was swept to the centre of the goings-on there by the crowd – and by the presence of the giant of a man directly behind him. He looked to Administrator Heneage for an explanation of the event but with a brief gesture of his eyes Heneage indicated that Nicholas was now, for the time being at least, the main character here, and it was he who would explain the reason for calling for the law-officer.

Nicholas explained briefly what had happened, and what was now happening, and finished his briefing of the Constable by saying...

"... and so we need you to administer an oath to Mr Heneage, here, so that we are all clear where we stand. And there can be no going back on the reliance we place on our esteemed Administrator..." was there irony in his voice? "...to act on our behalf in pursuing certain questions with the king and his advisors about the veracity of rumours being bruited about. The oath will prevent him from betraying our interests once he is out of our sight. The same oath will also be administered to Mr Proctor and others, such as we shall decide."

His voice was firm and authoritative, above his station in life maybe, but the authority was, nevertheless, real and felt clearly by all present.

Nicholas observed that the rest of the chief men of the town had been swept along in the Chief Constable's wake. Clearly they also wanted to know exactly what was going on in their town today. So Robert Bailey and the Fishwyke brothers were there, and others who were happy to style themselves as councillors of the town. And all were to be sworn in by the authority of Captain Cobbler!

"Let us go to the altar and let the oaths be made." Nicholas was using his firm, projected, voice so that everyone could hear clearly how things would go. There was quite a bit of jostling as everyone moved further into the church. The huge bible that normally sat on the lectern was brought reverently to the altar and with a few quiet words in the Constable's ear Nicholas explained the desired wording of the oath. Then, more loudly, he made clear that everyone understood what was going on.

"Gentlemen, citizens of Louth", Nicholas was using his diaphragm significantly now and his voice carried to the furthest walls of the church, resonating from the sturdy stones, "we are not sure how all of our actions may be perceived and understood outside the town. We are, however, embarking on a course of action that is of high morality and genuine concern for the common wealth of the citizens of Louth, ourselves, one and all. We shall now include these men in our endeavours, and it is for the best for everyone that they will swear to do their utmost for us and for the mother church. They, and we, will do this whilst staying true to God and the king and doing no harm whatsoever to the commonwealth here in Louth, and beyond."

A sort of ragged cheer came at these words, although many there were not sure whether they were really supposed to cheer in such a place of worship, so the noise fell away somewhat after the first burst of bravado!

The Constable recognised that he had no option but to do as the crowd was asking – so he decided to do it boldly and well.

"Mr Heneage. Please place your left hand on the bible here and raise your right hand to God – and say after me these following words – *'I swear upon this bible that I will be true to God, the king and the commonality.'*"

Mr Heneage did as he was bidden. Then Nicholas called upon the Town Administrator to take on the role of swearing in his fellows and, in their turn, all the chief men stepped up to the altar and placed their hands on the bible.

"I swear upon this bible that I will be true to God, the king and the commonality."

"Constable Ashby – please take your turn and swear the same oath; followed by Brother Morland, and then Mr Hert and the other men in your party too, please". Nicholas added, exerting his new authority calmly but firmly. Mr Hert's 'party' included virtually everyone who had tried to stop the unofficial guarding of the church treasures the previous evening.

The monk looked a little displeased at his inclusion in this category and that he was required to take the oath too but recognised that, to many of these men, he was something of an outsider. This was so, even though he had spent many, many years living within the sounds of the St James Church bells, just to the east of town in Louth Park Abbey. So he did not protest out loud, but coughed a couple of times and then declaimed…

"I swear upon this bible that I will be true to God, the king and the commonality."

And so it began in earnest.

ରେ ରେ ରେ ରେ ରେ

≋⌒ But then, for a few minutes, there was a sense of anti-climax as the town's councillors and others involved in the meeting with Mr Heneage, betook themselves to the Town Hall for their meeting. There was also some general talk about how Mr Heneage would get on with his visit to the king on their behalf, since there was a general feeling that "maybe it would be good to have the king's ear directly".

Events promised to move on faster than anybody might have predicted, however, when yet another visitor was, soon afterwards, seen crossing the bridge near the church. He was making his way on horseback into the centre of the town, unharried at first. But he had been recognised by three of the priests who had just walked out of the church grounds in the wake of the town's councillors and were due to face him later. He was none other than John Frankish, the bishop's registrar.

ରେ ରେ ରେ ରେ ରେ

≋⌒ Because Dr Raynes, the Bishop of Lincoln's chancellor, was feeling unwell, he had sent his colleague John Frankish, the bishop's registrar to stand in for him in Louth to conduct the Visitation on the local priests. Meanwhile, he stayed tucked up in bed, at the Castle in Old Bolingbroke, where he had been on the Saturday. The Chancellor had been in the chair for the Inquisition on the clergy of the Deaneries of Hill and Bolingbroke, whilst John Frankish sat taking notes for him.

Frankish was a small skinny man with a rather rat-like face and wore a wispy beard, covering a face pock-marked from some illness he had suffered as a child. He was very learned, and loved to use long words, and little-used words, when he was speaking, to show off his cleverness. Sadly, this habit did not endear him to his less well-educated colleagues and the Vicar of Harrington and the parsons of Belleau and Biscathorpe had all felt the sharp edge of his tongue on several previous occasions over the years. These were the three who recognised him.

These black-frocked men-of-the-church had started grumbling loudly about the visitor as soon as they saw him and quickly drew a little crowd of townsfolk near to them who were already roused following the recent events within the church. And they proved susceptible to being moved by such grumbling priests.

The crowd grew rapidly and newcomers took up the mood of unease from friends and from the three priests. The tension built up quickly and there was anger in the air by the time Frankish drew to a halt, opposite the Saracen's Head, at Guy Kyme's house (though Kyme himself was away at the coast on business for the Town). He was planning to stay there overnight, after the day's Inquisition.

Several of the townsmen had got between Frankish, and Kyme's front door, to prevent him scuttling inside. The three priests rather carefully stayed away from direct confrontation with their superior. They could, however, be heard clearly, towards the rear of the crowd, egging on the general anger with well-placed comments about *"the little weasel"* and other equally defamatory remarks!

Nicholas and some of his inner circle, who had still been in the church administering the oaths as the Registrar was being harried along the town's streets on his way to his host's house, had now been alerted to the new arrival. They were now working their way towards him, through the growing crowds, as the mood escalated unfavourably for Frankish.

A man who generally found he got his way amongst his colleagues and brethren by using words cleverly, the poor fellow was out of his depth facing a mob of what he would later refer to, demeaningly, as 'peasants'. In truth many of them were tradesmen of one kind

151

or another, and some of them very skilled craftsmen, contributing what they knew to the local economy of this bustling market town. Whatever their daily work, however, craftsmen, peasants or parsons, the disposition of the crowd was angry and getting pretty unpleasant by the time Nicholas worked his way to the front of the knot of milling people.

The scene was not helped by the truculence of Frankish himself.

"I am here on the king's business", he said rather imperiously, waving his commission papers with the Royal Seal dangling for all to see. Indeed, several of the menfolk nearby had doffed their caps as they recognised the Royal Seal and muttered "God save the King!"

However, the general tone did not improve when Frankish said, arrogantly...

"The king shall hear of this, and woe-betide you then!" He was not good at sensing the feelings of the townspeople, to say the least, and his words made matters much worse rather than better.

"Burn the lot of them!" became the general cry, referring to the books he carried. Louth folk believed these were the 'Ten Articles' and 'Injunctions', upon which he was due to examine the priests later that day, along with valuations of the local churches and parishes. The general feeling was that he was set to find a way of extracting money from the commonwealth of the people, and these books were his weapons of war.

Monk Morland was not very far behind Nicholas and really didn't endear himself to the crowd by getting 'hot under his habit' about their idea of burning a few books:-

"Masters, for the Passion of Christ", he exploded, "take heed what ye do, for by this mischief ye are about, we shall all be casten away!"

Great James, the giant of a man who had assumed the role of protector of Nicholas, his 'Captain Cobbler', and was sticking tight by his side, broke his normal silence at this outburst of concern by the monk.

"A turncoat already master monk? Ye just took an oath in the church to be '*true to the commonwealth*' and yet ye now seek to stop that commonwealth looking after its own immediate interests! Have a care!"

Nicholas put a calming hand on Great James' forearm, noting the taut muscles of a man under stress. Normally taciturn by nature, Great

James appeared quite surprised by his own outburst, and lapsed into silence again, a frown furrowing his heavy brow.

"What would you have us do, Monk Morland?" Nicholas asked, as one of the local weavers, John Taylor, came out of his house across the road, just behind the Saracen's Head. He was carrying a large flaming firebrand, ready to set the book bonfire alight. By this time a portion of the crowd had hustled Frankish and his books along the Corn Hill towards the High Cross – a central gathering area in Louth. So Nicholas and the others followed along.

"At least let us take the time to read what is proposed to be burnt, so we do not commit treason unwittingly, to the detriment and danger of us all!" Morland was truly fearful of offending the King's Highness, and yet he knew the cause was just.

Ever wanting to take care that their efforts should not slide into chaos, Nicholas conceded... "*You have a point, master monk*" ...and set about catching up with the burning torch of the weaver.

೮೪೮೪೮೪೮೪೮೪

Someone had fetched some kindling sticks and someone else a ladder, from inside the corn-market. One of the local farmers had a pitchfork he usually used to move hay and straw around his farmyard. But with a leery smile (*he was clearly enjoying the opportunity to get his own back on the churchman for a real or imagined slight, somewhere in their past*) he was using the sharp prongs to '*coax*' the reluctant registrar up the steps of the ladder, so that he could throw his own books on the already brightly burning bonfire of kindling sticks and assorted rubbish brought from the market.

Even the most enthusiastic pyromaniac in the mob knew not to touch the King's Commission, so that scroll was the first document passed to Nicholas and the monk to read. Nicholas glanced at it but it was in Latin and his classical skills were very modest to say the least, so he handed the commission scroll to the monk to read. It was, however, quite a substantial document, so Morland was slow in getting the details sorted out as he read the scroll of script.

Frankish, the registrar, had a large leather satchel filled with papers and small books and pamphlets, and was also carrying some

153

under his arm when he had got off his horse, back in the Corn-market. Some in the mob had already confiscated some of those papers and began tossing them into the quickly expanding flames.

Nicholas took what he could quickly lay hands on and spread them around between himself, Morland and four or five others nearby whom he knew could read well enough. The main thing was to be able to tell if they were likely to be important enough to engage the wrath of their king and liege lord, Henry VIII, if they were destroyed.

Frankish obviously thought the flames were destined to consume him as well, for he was now showing great fear of the mob around him and addressed a plea to the monk – recognising that the monk was probably the most likely person to intervene on his behalf...

"For the Passion of Christ, priest, save my life!"

Morland looked decidedly uncomfortable. He was being asked to put his own life at risk, and for a man with whom he disagreed. But he was also a fellow man-of-the-cloth, so he felt some obligation, in common humanity at least.

Frankish must have realised the monk's dilemma and, perhaps by now, he had got hold of his feelings of overwhelming panic '...*perhaps these peasants do not mean to put me to the fire after all?...*' so he had the presence of mind to become more pragmatic in his speech.

"At least stop them burning the Commission, or they will be casten down for treason!" he shouted, now, above the mob's noise, not knowing whether the monk could hear him over the shouts and cries.

"Try and stop them burning that little book, there, too. It is my book of reckonings and it is where I have recorded all my recent expenses which the Bishop of Lincoln has said he will reimburse for me!" His latest plea referred to a little book, hardly noticeable amongst the mess that had been his satchel.

"If I were to die here, at least my family would be able to claim the money due to them from the mother church as their inheritance." Never more than a small man, Frankish now looked yet further diminished by his fear.

"Stop snivelling Mr Frankish!" Nicholas' charismatic voice declaimed from just behind the weaselly man. For some reason Nicholas failed to identify, Frankish set the hairs on the back of his neck a'bristling...

"No-one here is going to burn your sorry form!"

Captain Cobbler had spoken, and even Frankish could feel the sudden sense of acceptance that ruffled through the bustling mob! He might never know whether they had been intent on committing themselves to such acts of barbarity, but calm now seemed to prevail.

"We are peace-loving people, just protecting our church's treasures from thieving hands – nobody here is capable of murder!"

Nicholas was scathing. Perhaps he was incorrect in his comments on the implied incapability of his neighbours, but scathing, nonetheless.

The monk, too, looked doubtful about this last claim – he knew that any mob could be aroused, even to taking a life, if they lost control of their collective reason.

Indeed Monk Morland was beginning to be concerned for his own skin after being so outspoken earlier and was starting to shrink away from the place with a view to escaping the further notice of the mob. The people making up the mob were now fetching English translations of the New Testament from their own houses if they happened to live nearby. The word had gone around that it would be good if these new-fangled ways were stopped by fire today!

The formidable figure of Great James was holding the ladder, and the farmer with the pitchfork, prodding his behind, kept the registrar up there as people passed items up to him from his satchel. He was then required to send the books flying into the bonfire, or to suffer the sharp consequences of the pitchfork. Monk Morland seemed to be edging away from this action...

"So, where would you be thinking of going, Master Monk?" Nicholas asked sharply.

The Monk's quickness of mind supplied a response which seemed to quieten Captain Cobbler's concerns.

"I was merely intent on taking this commission to Mr Heneage... so that, errm ... So that he could take it as evidence to the king that no real harm had been done here today! ...when he goes on our behalf to visit the king and seeks an audience for our concerns."

Nicholas was about to question Morland further, but was distracted at this point, as a group of men from the choir came along holding armfuls of books to be added to the flames. Arthur Graye, one of the finest bass voices in the choir, held up a book he had at home. He told

155

Nicholas, and the others, it had been written by a man called Frith, who had been burned at the stake, as a heretic, for his views.

"Master Frith was burned at the stake – so 'tis fitting we burn his book at the Cross!" said the singer with an accompanying deep bass chuckle as he flung the offending book onto the flames.

"Frith didn't believe in tran-sub-stan-tiation. But I have a much easier time believing in that notion than I did in reading the word – far too many letters in it!" He chuckled again, stretching the word transubstantiation out as if reading it syllable by syllable.

With a really booming voice, Arthur Graye, although never seeking the visual recognition that would have come if he had appeared on stage during the Corpus Christi plays, was well known in the town as the "voice of God", barrelling out loudly from behind the scenery. In fact, mothers in the town were known to say to their children that they should behave "...otherwise I shall fetch Arthur Graye to tell you off with the Voice of God!"

Whether it really had a positive effect on how the children behaved may never be known however.

When Nicholas turned again to speak with the monk, he was no longer there.

Great James was still holding the step-ladder, at the top of which Frankish perched precariously. James told Nicholas that Robert Collingwood, a former churchwarden, had appeared at the door of his house nearby, and waved the monk inside for some respite. And he had probably offered him a tankard of ale to calm his nerves.

"Keep an eye out for him, then, will you? I don't think I trust the monk entirely, to be honest!" Nicholas confided to Great James and Jack Page who was standing nearby.

Then, after a short pause, Nicholas spoke again...

"I think this bonfire is nearly done with, so I am going to go back to the church and make sure John and Ma Baker know how many mouths they are due to feed this lunchtime. Most people are going to have to go back to their houses and shift for themselves but all the church 'guardians' will, of course, be fed as before. We need to talk about keeping everything under guard for a while yet I think, after today's visits by the High and Mighty of the county."

He nodded with his head in the direction of the trembling Registrar, at this last remark.

"Once the fire is mostly burnt out and safe again, you can send this wretch packing out of town – but make sure you get his book of reckonings from Morland and keep it for us. At a quick glance it seemed to contain more than just his expenses. It may actually prove to be useful information to have, to pursue the charges of greed against the Vicar General, Cromwell." With that, Nicholas headed off along the market place towards the church.

Great James was torn between holding onto the steps to keep Frankish there and following Nicholas to keep him safe. Nicholas had given him a specific instruction, however. He noted, too, that his fellow 'giant', Henry Plummer, was now also shadowing Nicholas closely. So James decided he should stay put, and follow instructions.

෬෬෬෬෬෬

The number of men milling around in the square reduced a little as people began to feel hunger. It was coming up to their usual time for eating lunch. Also, the bonfire had dwindled down to mainly smouldering ashes as Brother Morland dared to come out of Robert Collingwood's house again. Collingwood had a high fence round the back of his garden otherwise the Monk might have taken the back way out...

By this time, too, Frankish had been allowed down from the top of his ladder. He was looking pale and still trembling.

Several men saw Morland at the same time including Great James, who was now holding Frankish by the sleeve of his coat. Jack Page, too, had just returned from taking the ladder back into the Corn Exchange, whence it came.

All of them converged on the hapless Monk and then others, who had not seen him emerge, but had seen the change in movement of their fellows, quickly followed on. It was not long before Morland was surrounded and there was a general hustle and bustle about the group that was fairly menacing.

Aware of his instructions from Captain Cobbler, which had included an injunction to let the monk alone physically, Jack Page was first to speak directly to the man. To give Morland his due, he had drawn his shoulders back and looked prepared to face the crowd down.

"You can keep the King's Commission, Brother Morland," said Page, "...'tis not what we want, but you will give me the book of reckonings of Master Registrar Frankish, here. And then you can kindly escort him from the town, and require him never to return."

The monk cleared his throat as if to speak – he really didn't like being given orders by a man with torn breeches and a worn jerkin. But, then, he clearly thought better of it, correctly judging the mood of the crowd to be still rather angry with him, as well as with Frankish.

Instead, he said quietly to Registrar Frankish that Robert Collingwood had told him that another churchwarden, William Goldsmith, would provide a meal for them all, after which it would be wise for the Registrar to go back to Lincoln. He and Goldsmith would escort him to the town boundary, later, as Captain Cobbler had instructed.

"Gentlemen, if you would excuse us?" The Monk tried for politeness, but achieved only curtness, and although a gap was left for them to pass through it was left deliberately narrow and there was a considerable amount of 'accidental' barging as they passed by towards the Goldsmith's large house, a couple of streets away.

When they got there, the Registrar insisted that he reimburse Goldsmith for the victuals they were given and promised Morland he would be pleased to receive him in Lincoln "...*at any time, to receive any favour he could oblige him with!*" It was an expression of desperate relief, because he was certain in his own mind that he had avoided death only narrowly. And the Monk had tipped the balance in his favour by his intervention.

They ate in relative silence after Frankish said a heartfelt grace, "...for the meal they were about to be blessed with - and the peace in which to eat it."

After eating their fill, and sitting a while to let the food settle, Brother Morland and Churchwarden Goldsmith sent a boy to fetch the registrar's horse from the inn. Then they walked with him across the bridge over the river Lud, and watched him trot off towards Lincoln at a brisk pace.

As the diminutive figure trotted up the rise on the far side of the river, and then round to the left on the Lincoln road, Goldsmith turned to his guest. He told him that whilst the three of them had been eating, one of the Brother Morland's good friends in the town, the butcher William Hert, had left him a message. Hert thought it would be wisest for the monk to stay quietly out of the way during the rest of the afternoon, for he was clearly still in trouble with the mob for favouring Frankish earlier.

"You are welcome to come back to my house again and we can take another glass of wine whilst you keep your head down, William!"

"Many thanks, Master Goldsmith, I think I will do as you suggest!"

As they walked back over the bridge and up towards the church passing its north-east corner back into town everything seemed strangely quiet, after the noisy events of the morning. There were relatively few souls about.

"Where is everybody?"

"I think we should not ask, William, simply be thankful it is so quiet!"

In fact the majority of the book-burning crowd were, by now, walking to Legbourne Priory, just a few miles away, where Commissioners Bellow and Millisent were in the process of dissolving the priory, as instructed by Thomas Cromwell.

ରଃ ରଃ ରଃ ରଃ ରଃ

Falling from Grace:
Understanding truth
Remembering... a Hostelry in Newark, April 1516

Being sentenced, in early 1537, to be '*...hung, drawn and quartered*', had seemed, to Nicholas, a severe punishment when his intention had been simply to help his community. He was not a traitor, nor a rebel, it was all just a misunderstanding.

For the most part, he managed to keep the reality of the punishment out of his mind, but sometimes it came back to fret and worry him. It was threatening to do that right now, but a chance remark the tower's gaoler made to one of the condemned prisoners in his charge, just as they were all climbing into the back of the straw wagon which was to transport them to their place of death, gave his mind an 'escape route'...

The remark, made cynically, was something about the fact that the man was clearly "*...falling from grace...*" It took Nicholas' mind away from his own gruesome fate, later that morning, and his thoughts went back, just over twenty years, to the occasion of his *second* visit to the capital.

That had been in 1516, when he was on his way to be apprenticed to a cobbler in London. He was travelling down to the capital with a family friend as company and protector.

The voice the two of them had heard, all those years before, came to him as if it were today. He found himself suddenly reliving that moment from his youth...

ര‍ളര‍ളര‍ള

"....and it were so wet and muddy that big St. John the Evangelist slipped and slithered in t' mud, overbalanced completely and ended up, face down in t' ditch, in two foot of water. We pushed and pulled for nigh on a quarter of an hour, but we couldn't move him an inch."

Young Nicholas – soon to be turning 16 years old – was just coming into the colourful tavern in the south-west corner of Newark market place, from the pelting rain outside and was both unnerved and puzzled by this overheard tale. He quickly cast his mind back over the biblical learning he had imbibed as a child but could find no recollection of such a story about the extraordinary demise of one of the Apostles, for surely he must have drowned, face-down, in that depth of water?

Nor could he readily grasp why the teller of this tale, a rough-hewn and stocky man, stubbly of countenance and with but three fingers to his right hand, was telling it as if it happened only the day before. Clearly, it must have happened a millennium and a half ago - if, of course, it had happened at all! Very strange!

Despite a great and sudden urge to deny the truth of such an outrageous story, as any hot-blooded, well-schooled youth of fifteen would naturally be tempted to do, he was minded to keep his counsel. Indeed, he was kept quiet, not least, by the efforts he and his companion needed to expend to get comfortable and dry in the crowded hostelry, for it was truly foul weather outside that day.

Firstly, they had to divest themselves of their sodden hats and riding capes without incurring the wrath of the other occupants of the room, most of whom had been indoors long enough to be thoroughly dried out from the persistent downpour. Then, they had to find space to be seated - a task made so much easier by Nicholas' robust, not to say rumbustious, and well-acquainted fellow traveller, William Cole. Cole was not of Newark town itself, but he was well known there, not least in ye Olde White Hart Inn, in the southern-most corner of Newark market-place, where they now found themselves.

"Move along that bench now, Jake Hoskyns, otherwise you'll be joining yon fine pig on the spit, agen the fire!"

"I'm warm enough now, thank'ee, Bill", Jake said, laughing, but moving nonetheless.

"As for you, young David" - here, Bill Cole was addressing a skinny youth of about Nicholas' age - "you're taking up far more than your fair share of room in that big chair. Landlord! Bring us a stool from the kitchen!"

The stool appeared, David moved (with much better grace than Nicholas thought he, Nicholas, might have managed in similar circumstances) and William Cole eased himself into a well-warmed, substantial oaken chair by the blazing log fire, opposite the three fingered yarn-spinner. Nicholas perched himself, damply, on the end of the bench trying hard not to disturb the current occupants of the bench who were already dry and warm.

By the time everyone had settled down again, and a copious platter of well-roasted pork and steaming pease pudding, fresh baked bread and a large mug of ale had appeared in front of the new arrivals, it had become clear to young Nicholas that '...*big St John the Evangelist...*' was no-one of human form.

In fact, it was a large brass siege cannon, lost in a ditch no more than a few miles out of the English stronghold of Calais. And that the time of the tale was less than three years earlier, during the summer of 1513, at the start of King Henry's French campaign.

Nicholas flushed up to the hairline at the potential for embarrassment if he'd have spoken up scornfully when they first entered the room, as he might so easily have done. Fortunately no-one noticed his discomfort, or, if they did, merely put it down to the heat of the fire bringing rosiness to his cheeks.

Gradually, the warmth and good food brought him greater physical comfort as he recovered from the long day's ride he'd had through the surging spring storm.

His spirits, too, were lifted by the convivial company in the busy inn. Bill Cole had thought to send word ahead to the innkeeper early that week, so that they were assured of a room and a bed for the night, despite the lateness of the hour and the impending market on the morrow.

Indeed, notwithstanding the heavy rain, the cobbled town square had still been bustling with men struggling with the elements to put up the stalls for the morning trade. Men cursing the rain, cursing the blustering wind which kept whipping awnings from their slippery-fingered grip and cursing each other for fools and knaves when shouted instructions were misunderstood, or misheard, in the howling weather.

As Nicholas now learned, it was the state of the weather which had brought on the recollection of big St John's fall from grace, from the old soldier seated near the fire grate. Although he answered to the epithet 'Three-fingered Jack', his given name was John Fuller and he spoke with the friendly intonation of a Yorkshire accent.

"I 'ad a full 'and of fingers at the time", he was saying, "...'appen I'll tell you 'ow I lost 'un before the evening's out though, if the ale keeps a'coming in!"

He smiled, disarmingly.

He'd obviously been through the saga before and now had it down to a fine art, knowing just how many jugs of ale and platters of victuals his stories were worth, given a ready audience and a warm fire.

"I'll tell you straight", he went on, leaning forward confidentially, "the weather were as bad as today, if not worse. 'Twas about three years since ...1513 as I recall. In fact, when we set off from Calais three days before, it were so bad that we got nobbut three miles down the road an' we 'ad to pack in fer the day. Most of the fancy tents for the noble lords was nigh on impossible to put up. Those we got up, mostly didn't stay up and I hazard that not a soul got a wink of sleep that night, not even young King Henry hisself."

"Fine figure of a man he is, too, six foot four they say, and sturdy as an oak. The king rode all round that night and, near as I can tell, spoke to everyone in sight. '*Well comrades*' he sez to us, '*now that we have suffered in the beginning, fortune promises us better things, God willing.*' An' we all believed him, a' course, - he looked you straight in the eye and meant it true, as sure as I sit here with you this e'en."

There was something about John Fuller at that point, with his voice quiet and his sense of complete conviction that, when he stopped speaking, there was a hush of affirmation over the room, with just the crackle of the log fire and the occasional spit of fat from the nearly eaten porker, to disturb the silence.

Fuller sat back, took a long pull from his jug of ale, expelled an equally long breath and spoke again in normal tones but with a touch of irony in his voice.

" 'Course, like a'most everything else I knows of, it got worse afore it got better. Aye, and for some," he added with faded sadness, "it ne'er did get any better."

"We didn't move the next day, being Sunday, but on the Monday we marched another five or six miles to a town called Ardres, which were in enemy territory. The townsfolk had promised to provide us wi' vittals as long as we let 'em alone."

"Well! No-one had thought to tell this to the Germans, - or, if they did, they only told 'em in English! So these Almain mercenaries, together wi' a few of our lads went on the rampage, looking for loot.

They was told to quit in the hour and no messin'. But they didn't take a deal of notice of that message either and, in the end, our King Henry went in hisself, with some of 'is own guards, an' sorted 'em out."

"They say he strung at least three Almains up in the town square by the neck to set the matter to rights."

"Whether the looting upset the Frenchies I can't rightly say, or mebbe they thought to test our nerve, but some of their light cavalry kept having a go at us from behind. Then, them of ours as were at the front, decided to get a bit of a move on," ...he spoke confidentially, directly to Nicholas, or so it seemed, "...shoulder to shoulder they was at this stage, for protection like, wi' weapons drawn."

"We was trying to keep up at the back... and that were when big St John went to baptise hisself."

"As I said afore, we pulled an' pushed, pushed an' pulled and got oursens nowhere, e'en wi' a full team of Flanders mares. Then t' 'igh and mighty Master Carpenter from Calais, mester George Buckemer, came farting around and took it upon hisself to get Saint John high and dry wi' a '...carefully crafted block and tackle...' or so he said, all 'oity toity, like."

"None o' the officers or nobles liked 'im too well, so they left 'im to get on wi'it. Aye, and us, too. I'd say there were nigh on a 'undred of us to 'elp lift and 'ammer and pull an' all."

There was another pause for a theatrically timed gulp of ale by the narrator, who then leaned forward and dropped his voice, taking the whole room into his confidence again.

"We was at this game for just over an hour when the bad fish I'd eaten the night before got t' better of me an' I 'ad to dive away into the bushes as quick as you like."

He leaned back again in his chair and shook his head slowly from side to side, as if not even believing, himself, what he was now about to say.

"Masters, one and all," he paused, looking round at the attentive throng, '...that bad fish surely saved my life."

"There I were, groaning my innards out, behind a large laurel bush, when the whole French army descended from t' nearby hills and laid into 'igh an' mighty mester Buckemer and my comrades, wi'out mercy. Only about ten of our lot was fightin' men, the rest just workmen, joiners, blacksmiths – like me – carters, an' coopers and the like."

165

"Well - they did t' best they could. But it were a bloodbath, and over in nobbut a few minutes. Them as weren't killed... Aye, an' that were precious few... was trussed up an' carted off, goodness knows where. I 'aven't seen 'em since, anyroad."

"And there were nowt I could do. I were 'elpless behind a shrub wi' my leggin's round my ankles, daring not even to breathe, let alone groan anymore."

"I got the most terrible cramps in my legs, but I nivver moved a muscle 'til 'alf an hour after the last Frenchman 'ad left. By the time I'd got meself moving again and caught up wi' the rest of the lads who had left us to it earlier, it were just about dark. The truth 'ad somehow got back to camp afore I did and everyone were talking about it. One of our little four man scouting groups on 'orseback 'ad been sent to find out what t'delay were all about - but they must've taken a different road from me, 'cos I saw nowt of 'em, goin' or comin'."

John Fuller lapsed into silence at this point and if, afterwards, you'd asked any man then present in the room, he would have said there was a '...*tear in the eye of Three-fingered Jack...*' as he leaned his head back on the old oak settle.

Someone called for more ale all round and, by turns, the noise level in the bar rose to a convivial hubbub once more.

Nicholas, who had listened to the tale as avidly as the next man, was now ready for his bed, if the truth were told. He had, after all, been up since four o'clock that morning and the food, drink and warm fire were all conspiring to close his eyes, but his companion, big Bill Cole, with a strange edge to his voice, had just asked John Fuller what happened next. Nicholas decided it would be unseemly to leave before the tale was finished.

"What 'appened next, you say sir?"

"Aye, sir, I do."

"Well, sir, for several days, nowt much at all. We all waited round, dryin' out in t' summer sun, repairing tents and the like. We was just past the town of Tournehem, on the river Hem, '...*wherein lay as fair a castle as you might wish to see...*' as I heared one o' our fine lords say to another, '...*set, exquisite, in rolling wooded countryside...*' Fine words or not, it were a pretty sight, I'll grant."

"Young King Henry were in a right fine temper about losing one of 'is twelve Apostles. We all heard 'im a'shoutin' at my good Lord Essex,

166

for such a carry on - specially when 'e found out that the Frenchies 'ad walked away with one of our bombards, we called the 'Red Gun'."

One of the younger voices in the room piped up to ask "Why was that, sir?"

"Why - because of the colour it were painted, sir!"

The possibility of such an obvious answer had eluded the young man and the assembled throng guffawed in kindly mocking of his innocence. He wisely played no further part in the conversation.

Three fingered Jack took up again with his tale.

"To cut the long of it short, sirs, my lord Essex and Sir Rees ap Thomas was sent back wi' my lord Berners, the 'Mester of Ordnance' and 'is pioneers and a great troop of archers and swordsmen to see if they could recover Saint John; 'e were still in t' ditch, yer see!"

"An' it were dry now, so the job were a lot easier. It were a great blessin', too, that I'd 'aten no bad fish the night before, much to the benefit of big St John and meself - for it weren't needed to save my life this day, 'cos we wasn't attacked again, until we'd got the Evangelist out of the river."

"The Frenchies tried a skirmish or two, but me an' my comrades got the better of them this time an' soon sent 'em packing."

"Aye, an' no doubt you played a hero's role this time", Bill Cole's voice boomed into the temporary quiet.

Nicholas was startled into wakefulness by the ferocity of his friend's jibe. Puzzled by the animosity of the tone, as was everyone in the room, Nicholas waited to hear more.

The tendons in Bill Cole's neck stood out with apoplectic fury and his eyes bulged. Everyone had been so intent on Fuller's story that Cole's deepening anger had gone unnoticed.

"The tale you tell is accurate in every detail except one, my friend."

No-one in the room could have heard so much venom crammed into the word 'friend' as they heard just then.

"The minor detail you have wrong is that you weren't even there. I know, because I was! Oh, I have no doubt you were in France. And I have a good idea how you lost your finger, too, which I shall relate in a moment, but you were certainly not with big St John the Evangelist that day!"

Fuller now began to look very uncomfortable, his eyes darting round looking for a quick way out of the crowded room.

There wasn't one! In becoming the centre of attention for his story telling, he had also become totally encircled by his audience. The focus was now on William Cole, his deep anger seeming more under control as he spoke again. This time he addressed his remarks to the room at large, taking over the role of story teller.

"We *did* lose big St John in a ditch and those of us as were left with George Buckemer to pull the Evangelist out *were* attacked with little mercy by the French army. I got a broken rib and a six inch scar on my back to prove it. There were sixteen of us alive after the attack but my young brother Jeb and a goodly number of my friends lost their lives, hacked to death in the space of but a few minutes. We had no chance. Totally surrounded and outnumbered."

"I was bundled into a cart with three other men who couldn't walk and we were taken back to the coast at Boulogne, where we were held until after King Henry's army returned to England. We were treated civilly enough and once my rib had mended we were free to wander round the town during the day, for the gates were well guarded and we couldn't get to the boats."

Bill Cole now even smiled a little at a prompted recollection.

"I managed to learn some of the French tongue from a pretty serving wench in one of Boulogne's taverns; at least enough to ask for wine, butter and eggs."

"And where the nearest bed was!" Jake Hoskyns added to much laughter all round.

"How did this'un lose his finger, then, Bill?" another voice asked from the crowd.

"I don't know for sure", said Bill with great honesty, "but before we set out from Calais I heard tell of a man who was caught asleep on guard duty three times in one night by the watch sergeant."

"The punishment for this crime is special to Calais, although I do hear tell they do something similar in Berwick, up north, for dozy watchmen who drink too much for their own good – aye, and for all they're watching over too!"

"If someone on watch is caught asleep twice, and the sergeant of the watch finds him asleep again and is able to twist his nose for him, without him waking up first, then he'll be put under lock and key until morning, when the whole town will be called out to watch him pay the penalty."

All the time he was relating this tale, Bill Cole was watching John

Fuller as close as could be. Fuller, meanwhile, kept his eyes glued to the ground.

"They have a special large basket, hanging out from the town wall over the sea. It's a bit like a crab catching basket, but big enough to hold a man. In the basket he goes and in with him goes a loaf of bread and a bottle of wine and a knife."

"The bread is to stop him starving, the wine to give him Dutch courage to face the long drop, and the knife to cut the rope that holds the basket to the wall. The art is to get the timing right."

"They say that time and tide wait for no man!"

"If the tide is out, the drop to the rocks is enough to break a few bones at the very least if it doesn't break your skull open! But, of course, if the tide is right in and the **basket** doesn't break open straight away, then you'll probably drown instead!"

"If you time it right though – so that the water is deep enough to break your fall, but shallow enough to let your basket break on the rocks without drowning you in the process – you have a chance of staying alive!"

"I wasn't in Calais at the time - I arrived a week after it had happened - but I heard tell of a man being caught asleep three times in one night. He apparently survived."

Bill Cole paused dramatically.

"But he did lose one of the fingers from his right hand when he bounced on the rocks!"

At this point, Three-fingered Jack looked up from the floor and he had about him the haughty yet frightened look of a stag at bay. His breathing was fast and shallow, his cheeks flushed, his eyes darting about searching for a desperate route for escape.

There was nowhere to go!

He took a deep breath and spoke in a defiant tone.

"So, what if it were me? So ...what?" His voice cracked, and the tears that formed in his eyes were real this time – tears of self-pity. It was the first time he had been found out in nearly two years of story-telling.

Into the silence that followed big William Cole spoke briefly once more.

"In Calais they call this punishment the '*Fall from Grace*'."

ଔଔଔଔଔଔ

On the Road: Rites of Passage
The next day, April 1516

The tension in the room was palpable and Nicholas was beginning to wonder what would happen next. But the unbearable moment was broken by the breaking of wind! One of the market stall holders, who had just come in from the foul weather outside, and knowing nothing of the unfolding story, lifted his right foot a couple of inches from the floor and let out a deep rasping fart, exclaiming to one and all... *"Phawww – that's better out than in! ...which is more than you can say for this bloody weather."*

Several ribald comments were made and great guffaws of laughter filled the room, along with a strong whiff of decomposing cabbage. Speakers and listeners alike were immediately released from the thrall of silence and movement rippled through the room. Several present, including Nicholas, used the opportunity to betake themselves to bed in readiness for an early start the following morning – market day.

Bill Coles signalled to his young friend that he would be along shortly. Nicholas' head was reeling with novel thoughts and new experiences he wanted to mull over with his mentor, but it had been a long day in the saddle and promised to be another long day again on the morrow.

The reflections on the tales he had heard this evening would have to wait until they were travelling again because the lad was asleep before his head touched the straw-filled sacking pillow. The next he knew was when a shaft of early morning sun woke him betimes, and he awoke to a day that could hardly be more different from the day just past. The storm had not only abated, it had disappeared entirely, leaving barely a cloud in the sky, and the daylight was ringing with the clang and clamour of the preparations for the market – a lively din which spoke of a lively day ahead.

Breakfasting on a thick slice of cold succulent pork and a large tankard of small ale, there was no time to spend in gossip. So the chance to revisit Calais or the recent French wars would have to wait as the pair of them had much ground to cover if they were to reach Stamford before nightfall, which was their goal. They needed to get moving.

The innkeeper's bill was settled and they were a good three miles along the London Road 'ere the church bells were ringing out seven of the clock. Delightful day though it was, there were still puddles of mud and water from the great storm the previous day. The dampness made the going slippery underfoot and curls of steam were rising in the air from the wet grasses at the roadside.

Dew-pearled spiders' webs were glistening brightly in the hedgerows, and the sun warmed the left sides of their faces and the right shoulders of locals passing them in the road as they took their wares into Newark market, whence Bill Cole and Nicholas had just departed.

Bill seemed somewhat quieter today than hitherto so Nicholas was rather wary of breaking into his quietude at this juncture to ask more about his experiences in France – he was sure there would be time later.

଼ ଼ ଼ ଼ ଼ ଼

One of life's lessons he learned that day, however, was that 'later' sometimes took an unexpected turn!

They were making good time during the morning whilst both they and their horses were fresh, and it was not too long before they sighted the church towers in and around the rolling countryside of Grantham.

Not far from the town itself they were intending to cross a small bridge over the normally meandering River Witham but the heavy rain had brought the quiet river into spate and had washed away part of the bridge overnight.

No doubt the river had subsided a little from its highest point but it was still a noisy torrent ahead of them. The storm had been a very heavy one!

"There's nowt for it lad but we'll have to wade across", shouted Bill above the noise and grinning at his companion.

With a somewhat nervous grin back, Nicholas said "After you sir!"

and took tighter hold of his mount's reins. It was a good job that he did take a strong grip, too.

Just as Bill was coaxing his horse into the fast moving water a large wooden strut from the already broken bridge broke away from the spars attached to the bank. The sharp crack this made, spooked both the horses. Nicholas was lucky that he was still on solid ground and was quickly able to calm his mount down.

Bill's horse, though, was just testing his footing under water when the sound caught his attention and in that split second his left foreleg slipped between two stones and he plunged forward. The weight of the water rushing by unbalanced him and there was a sickening second crack as a bone splintered under the pressure. The horse rolled his eyes madly and let out an unearthly scream of pain and tried desperately to regain his balance, succeeding only in unceremoniously dumping his rider into the river.

The effect of this for the horse was to unbalance him yet again but by this time he had all four legs in the water and he tried to twist and regain the bank but the first leg to touch solid ground was the broken left foreleg which collapsed under him sending him toppling back into the water, this time landing awkwardly on top of his ex-rider.

Nicholas watched helplessly from the bank as the struggle carried on below him; by now both horse and former rider were being carried downstream at an accelerating rate. They were rushing along more or less in mid-stream, the horse keeping his head well clear of the water whilst Bill seemed to be unconscious. Fortunately he was on his back so he wasn't in immediate danger of drowning – but nor was he making any move to get towards the bank again to get out of the river.

Nicholas, his heart thumping with dread, was able to follow them downstream only with care because on his side of the river it was mainly wooded and there was no well-trodden pathway to follow. Fairly quickly, therefore, a gap opened up between him and his water-borne companion.

He urged his mount onwards as fast as he dared, dodging under low hanging branches and weaving in and out of trees, hoping madly that his haste would not bring more trouble amongst the fallen trunks and soft ground. Gradually the woodland thinned out and he was able to speed forward along a wet meadow, cutting left to take a short cut as the river looped round in a semi-circle.

As he came back towards the bank he could see that the river was now wider and probably deeper in the middle, because the swirling water had slowed right down and his friend Bill and the still-frightened horse were moving at a more moderate speed. Also he realised that the extra width was partly caused by the river over-topping a narrow shelf of the low bank at that point.

Nicholas leapt off his horse and made sure he tied it securely to a nearby tree – it would be all he needed for his horse to wander off and leave him stranded!

He had a length of rope with him, one end of which he quickly tied round the same tree that his horse was tethered to, the other end of which he tied as securely as possible round his waist and he cautiously ventured into the flowing water.

It was colder than he expected and he needed to get deeper if he was going to have a chance of grabbing Bill as he passed. His foot slipped on wet stones and he fell banging his knees and turning his ankle...

"Careful!" he muttered to himself...

...he MUST reach out as far as possible. He managed to stand again and pulled tightly with his right hand against the rope which was now at almost full stretch...

Leaning as far as possible he could almost touch Bill's coat... but not quite...

He stumbled again, his ankle burning with pain, thankfully dulled by the cold water but – looking back to make sure his rope was secure – he let go the rope, trusting the knot around his waist. Then he was able to stretch out with both arms just far enough for his fingertips to touch the coat but not hold it.

The water was carrying Bill past him now and he was beginning to think he might fail, when an eddy in the water just turned Bill's inert shape an inch or two so that his foot came within Nicholas' reach.

Nicholas managed to get three fingers and his thumb onto the toe of Bill's boot and he clamped on as hard as he could. With the water supporting Bill's weight it was just enough for him to use the leverage of the rope to turn his friend and catch hold of his left leg as well as the toe of his right boot. The rope was now nearly cutting him in two but he steadied himself and gradually – *oh, so slowly* – inched his way to the bank, each moment improving his precarious hold on his friend.

The weight of the water was pushing Bill downstream – to Nicholas' left – but he could now let the water do most of the work of bringing them to safety as he gradually shuffled, crablike, towards the security of solid ground – just as long as he didn't let go... Gradually, he was able to get more purchase and managed to drag Bill clear of the water. The rope had held well and he was able to use it now to pull himself back up the bank and steady Bill's weight into a safe position.

One final exertion and Bill's inert body landed heavily on the wet grass of the bank. The impact must have squashed his lungs in a positive way and he spluttered and expelled a spray of water, coming back to consciousness more or less at the same time.

"Wha..what happened...?" Bill asked groggily.

"You fell in the river and I think you probably broke your leg and knocked yourself out". The pained exclamation from Bill as Nicholas tried to move him higher onto the bank gave emphasis to Nicholas' obviously correct guess.

As they were exchanging these few words, Bill's horse had also gained a purchase on the shallow shelf Nicholas had used to reach Bill and was struggling to pull itself from the river. The horse's eyes rolled wildly from fear, and from the pain in his own right foreleg, which was bent at an odd angle as he staggered onto the bank, barely missing his former rider's head as he stumbled upwards to relative safety. Once on dry land again – and balanced on three legs – the horse tried shaking its head to shake off the water, but the rapid movement made his injured leg move too – and that was not good.

Nicholas, momentarily distracted from his task by the whinnied pain of the horse, realised that another unpleasant task would soon be his when he would have to put the poor thing down with a sharp knife to its jugular.

He was then struck by the un-nerving thought that Bill's pain probably at least matched that of his horse but that he would, of course, be making every effort to *save* Bill – no question of slitting Bill's throat! He quickly came to realise that he was going to have to seek a lot of help before that could be guaranteed, too, given his friend's immobility. It seemed there were possibly two separate fractures in his lower leg, after all.

He made Bill as comfortable as possible on the grassy bank while he went to search for two strong sticks to act as splints. He found a coppiced ash nearby and hacked two stout young branches off and trimmed them to approximate length as quick as he could. By the time he got back, Bill was more or less fully conscious again.

"If you're going to tie those sticks to me you'd better look in my saddle bag and get me that flask of spirit before you start..."

This was said as if he thought Nicholas knew about a flask in the saddle bag, which wasn't the case, but it didn't take a deal of finding. As it was, the horse flinched when Nicholas came near as though he thought the human was going to force him to move. He was so good with horses, however, that he was able to gentle the poor beast into accepting his efforts without panicking. Nicholas stroked the horse's neck as he began to move away and it gave a relieved snicker of gratitude at being left in peace to bear its pain. He unstoppered the top and handed the flask to Bill's outstretched hand.

"I will try to hurt as little as possible" Nicholas said as his friend took the amber nectar from him and gulped heavily three times. Normally a very modest drinker Bill had, nevertheless, been in enough battle conditions in his soldiering days to know that only a very good slug of spirits would get anywhere near dulling the inevitable pain which he was now anticipating, as his young friend set about straightening and splinting his leg.

Despite his nervousness at the possibility of hurting Bill with poorly executed work, Nicholas used strips torn from one of his shirts to secure the splints. He surprised himself with the neat a job he managed to do on the splints without causing any more groans or expletives. Indeed at one point Bill started giggling for no apparent reason.

"Sh'alright!" he giggled, "take no notish of me – no idea why am laughing – musht be the drink – hehehe... ...oww!" A hiccup made him jar his leg and he suddenly turned pale again. He was probably entirely sober again, too.

All the time he was doing this, there were accompanying small sounds coming from the injured horse which had more or less stabilised itself on three legs, the fourth badly out of shape and dangling uncomfortably.

Nicholas made sure Bill was comfortable after tying the last knot required to support his splints safely and then faced the task he had been dreading more. He had seen the farrier once in Louth who had

had to deal with a badly injured horse, and had been impressed with his gentleness and then the speed with which he wielded his knife, which he had kept hidden from the horse until the last minute.

Using this memory to guide him he moved cautiously over to the stricken horse – his knife ready to use but shielded by his body from the horse's view.

"Steady big fella; I know ...it hurts" he breathed out through his nose, pretending to be a horse approaching, and the horse gave a brief answering whuffle through his nostrils too.

"Steady boy, you'll feel better soon", the lie comforting Nicholas, probably rather more than it did the horse. He walked as soft and slow as he could so the horse did not take fright. As it was, its eyes were open too wide and rolling a little; the pain must have been quite intense! Nicholas breathed out noisily through his nose again as he eased round the horse's head and took gentle hold of his mane.

"Steady boy." This last comment was as much meant for himself now the deed was close and in one smooth movement he lifted the knife and cut deep into the horse's neck. Thankfully the knife was sharp and only one movement was needed. Nicholas had been worried he might fail his nerve at the last minute and be too tentative.

The horse rolled his eyes as his head jerked up away from the new pain and seemed to look Nicholas in the eye accusingly at this betrayal – but the cut had been a deep one and the quick blood loss from the horse's brain made the beast stagger and begin to topple very soon.

Nicholas had to be careful not to get in the way of the dying animal's fall since there was no one nearby who could extricate him if he got trapped under half a ton of horse flesh – but he kept hold of its mane to provide a comforting - indeed almost a loving – contact at the end.

"Sorry fella" he kept whispering as he patted the fallen animal on the shoulder but it probably was beyond feeling the contact by now. "I am going to have to leave you here, too – at least it's a decent spot for your last resting place".

In a sombre mood he went back to his travelling companion who had sobered up again quickly as he watched the drama of his horse's last moments alive. In a calm, quiet voice Bill gave his friend encouragement and support.

"Well done lad – you handled him well and kindly at the end. There was nothing more to be done than you did."

A pause.

"I know" sighed a sad Nicholas, "I dare say I will remember his accusing look 'til my dying day though."

"But we couldn't leave him here in that state" Bill continued.

"No – I know. I know." Nicholas sighed again "It's just..." and the rest of the sentence trailed away into silence.

Then the needs of the moment brought Nicholas back from his rumination on '*life...*' as he realised his tasks were nowhere near completed. He had a man with a badly broken leg laid out on the ground and somehow had to get him up and onto his own horse before they could move any further.

There was a fair bit of 'hemming' and 'hawing' between them as one or the other would say "*can we...hmmm ... no, that's not going to work*"

In the end they decided between them that there was no way they were going to get Bill sat astride Nicholas' horse, and hanging him over the horse's back like a long bag of sticks would not be practicable, nor comfortable. It seemed that the most likely success would come from putting together a sort of litter to drag behind the horse. The bumps would be uncomfortable, but getting the litter underneath Bill and then hauling him up a few inches so a make-shift harness could be put over the horse's rump, would probably be easier than trying to lift a heavy man nearly six feet up into the air.

"Cut me a good length of that rope", Bill said, "...and I will strip it apart into string which we can use to tie the wood together for the litter, while you go and find the wood."

Nicholas saw there was a coppiced willow tree nearby which looked as though it had branches long enough and straight enough for the main stems of the litter. His sharp knife, now cleaned of the horse's blood, made relatively short work of cutting and trimming sticks of the right length. Hopefully the willow would also be flexible enough to absorb some of the bumps along the way.

He worked as quickly as he could but by the time he was ready to lift Bill onto the makeshift litter and then hoist the litter up to secure its supporting rope onto his saddle, at least a couple of hours must have passed since Bill first got his ducking. Bill Cole was now getting thoroughly cold and was shivering with both the cold and the pain. The spirit was helping him a little with both, but there was now not much left and Nicholas felt a sense of urgency which he was not sure he could meet. But he knew he must try.

He was able to remove the saddle from the deceased horse. He had to cut the girth to do so, however, and then tie it over the top of his own saddle as the only sensible way of carrying it, and Bill's small sack of belongings, securely. So he would need to walk along, leading his horse rather than riding it. With the litter to consider as well, their progress would have been slow in any event.

He was worried about trying to get the litter through the woodland area he had crossed so it meant continuing to walk along the bank downstream, but that meant they were walking away from Grantham rather than towards it. Bill might have known the distance to the next bridge, but by now his teeth were chattering and his eyes had a distant look in them as the shock of his injuries began to take hold, so Nicholas was reluctant to ask the question. And so they set off downstream.

As it was, little more than an hour's walk brought them to a small stone bridge which had withstood the ravages of the river. Although the river had risen far enough to overflow its boundaries so that it was very wet underfoot, it was safe and easy to cross. Better yet, there were people about on the other side of the river – a group of five men, two of them in the distinctive cloaks of Greyfriars. Nicholas guessed there must be an abbey nearby.

The men were busy with something at the side of the road, although Nicholas could not see what it was from the centre of the bridge as he hailed them. As he got closer and they started moving towards him to help, he saw that they had apparently been filling in, and levelling, some bad ruts and holes in the roadway on the other side of the bridge which had clearly got worse than usual in the heavy rains the previous day. The smaller of the two Greyfriars, a brisk little man, clearly in charge of the group, hurried over to see how they might help.

Nicholas explained as quickly as he could what had happened and the busy fellow immediately instructed the youngest member of his party, a wiry lad of a similar age to Nicholas: "......run quickly to find Brother Peter and get him to make a bed up in our infirmary. Tell him we look like having a guest for a while who will need his ministrations. We will not be far behind you all being well."

He introduced himself as Brother Mark and rattled off brief instructions to the remaining two laymen with him to pick up the end of the litter, "to afford our friend here a more comfortable last mile of his journey to bed". With a flashed smile to his religious brother he told Nicholas that "Brother Luke here will tidy the road-mending and follow on behind with our bag of tools, whilst I guide you along the roadway. You just keep walking the horse gently along and we'll get your friend to assistance very soon."

Nicholas looked quickly over to where Brother Luke was beginning his task of tidying and thought it was a good job the Brother was a big fellow as there were several stout handled tools to gather up once they had all left him to it. Nevertheless, he was mightily relieved to have someone take charge of the situation, although he still felt the heavy responsibility of ensuring Bill Coles was finally safe and sound resting on his young shoulders. He was pleased that they would soon be in the company of someone who should know what to do for Bill's leg.

He also permitted himself a small smile at the thought they may soon be in the presence of Brothers Matthew and John if the nearby monastery was consistent in its naming policy of its religious brethren. Then he had to pull his shoulders back for the final stretch of the journey as he realised he was now feeling very tired, as much from the responsibility as from the physical efforts he had exerted, though these were significant over the last few hours.

After less than another half hour had passed they were in sight of a fine looking building in the soft grey weathered stone of his native Lincolnshire. A warm honey coloured stone when new, time and rain left older buildings with a still warm look but in soft grey hues mainly, often with the light greens and greys of various lichens to soften it still further.

As they entered the gates there was a sense of bustle in the place but also a sense of peace and cheerfulness as the brothers and their lay helpers were bringing their working day to a close – making sure animals were in their pens. Making sure, too, that wood for the fires was handy as the fires were built up for the evening. And all the other tasks that needed to be done before late afternoon darkness fell.

Brother Mark guided them to a honey coloured building (Nicholas really loved the colour of the local stone!) which was obviously a newer building used to house the infirmary of a busy community. By now Bill Coles was twitching and muttering on his litter, clearly not fully conscious and making no sense at all. Brother Mark seemed quite concerned at his state and was quick to get the litter unfastened from the horse and have the injured man carried into the infirmary where Brother Peter was waiting.

Brother Peter did not trouble to introduce himself or the motherly looking woman at his side but with the most casual of hand movements he shooed the laymen away who had been taking the weight of the litter on their shoulders for the last mile. That they took no offence at this gave Nicholas pause, and he knew intuitively that they held Brother Peter in high regard, and so were not at all put out at his casually brusque behaviour. It was also clear that Brother Mark and Nicholas were not included in the shooing signal – so they stayed close at hand.

Brother Peter examined Bill's leg quickly and closely without moving it, or even hardly touching it, murmuring softly, almost as if to himself. It was, however, apparent that the real audience for his continuing remarks was the motherly woman at his side, who occasionally nodded and murmured back to him. He noted the broken flesh where the shard of bone had torn through after the break, checked the alignment of the lower leg and foot, nodded briefly and then looked appraisingly at Nicholas.

"You did a good job with the splints young man, I think we may be able to save your friend's leg with care and patience – though I don't doubt he will be subject to a pronounced limp for the rest of his days. Now go and rest whilst we work".

Nicholas managed a muted *"Thank you"*, feeling for a moment that he should stay and then realised he would, probably, simply be in the way. He had been impressed with the note of care in Brother Peter's voice, and had been equally taken with both the brief praise, and the fact that he had been referred to as 'young man' rather than 'boy'. A little glow of pride struck him as Brother Mark lightly touched his elbow and indicated, with the gentlest of pressures, that Nicholas might now accompany him out of the room.

The two laymen had already gone, and as Nicholas looked back into the room from the doorway he noted the motherly woman giving Bill a few drops of something from a vial, soon after which Bill clearly dropped into an unconscious state, his neck and shoulders relaxing visibly. His last glimpse was of Brother Peter wielding a large and obviously very sharp knife to cut the bindings from the splints as carefully as possible so that he did not disturb the alignment of the leg.

At this stage his own shoulders also dropped as he realised that his friend was in capable hands and his own responsibility was now done, for the moment, at least. He could afford to relax a little, but with that relaxation came an overwhelming sense of weariness. Brother Mark guided him to the kitchens.

ଓଓଓଓଓଓ

"It is not yet time for the community to eat supper but from what you have said, you missed out on eating any food since you broke fast this morning and, by the look of you, you probably need a little sustenance!"

Nicholas had not noticed any pangs of hunger up to this point but as they came closer to the kitchens, and cooking smells drifted across his path, his stomach started growling and gurgling. "*I think you may be right!*" He managed a weak smile.

The kitchen was governed by a round brother with a ruddy glow to his face – Brother Ignatius. Perhaps there was not going to be either a Brother Matthew or a Brother Luke after all. Brother Ignatius' shape suggested that he clearly enjoyed cooking and tasting the food he cooked. Quickly apprised of their visitor's hunger problem by Brother Mark, Brother Ignatius lifted the lid of a large cauldron near the kitchen fire and drew two large ladles of soup, decanting them into a thick wooden bowl. Then he beckoned Nicholas to sit at the trestle under a high-level window and placed the bowl in front of him. He then picked up a large loaf which was still warm from the oven and hacked off a thick slab of warm crusty bread. Simple fare indeed but oh, so tasty!

As Nicholas ate, Brother Mark sat with him.

"You will stay with us tonight young sir". It was a statement rather than a question. "And, after making sure your friend is comfortable in the morning, you will no doubt resume your journey onwards later in the day tomorrow." This seemed a good idea to Nicholas, but since his mouth was now full of soup and bread he simply nodded his agreement with head and eyes.

He managed to get through three bowls of soup, each with an accompanying slab of warm bread. Brother Ignatius took it as a compliment to his cooking, as was justified, and beamed delightedly as Nicholas proffered kind words on the taste, comparing it well with his mother's high standards of craft in the kitchen. Clearly Brother Mark was pleased to have an audience, too, and Nicholas soon realised that Brother Mark was essentially the 'master of works' at the monastery and wanted to regale Nicholas with the breadth of his responsibilities and those of the monastery in the wider community, the remit for which also fell to him.

He was busy explaining that there were several bridges which fell within his charge, but he expressed some relief that the bridge that had collapsed should have been maintained by someone else and to know that he therefore bore no responsibility for the incident.

Sir Montagu Thyme was an absentee landlord who had acquired rights over some 200 acres of land along both banks of the River Witham through his marriage to a young ward of the Percy family – quite a catch for him, since the family was important in the northern reaches of England, especially when the Scots rampaged over the borders.

"The land is, in reality, managed by a neighbouring farmer who takes a fee for his service, but spends far too much of his time drinking ale rather than getting on with his work. Now we know what has happened to that wooden bridge, I will make sure we can offer to help him. At least we will be able to improve the lot of the nearby villages which use it most," commented Brother Mark, whose enthusiasm for his responsibilities knew no bounds.

ଔଔଔଔଔଔ

Onward to London – and beyond: Becoming a man
Seeing the world through new eyes – 1516

Early the next morning Nicholas was awoken by the distant strains of melodious chanting coming from the nearby abbey chapel. It was a sound he recognised from the choir practising in the great church of Saint James, back in Louth. For a little while he felt a strong sense of homesickness as the sounds ebbed and flowed, with the light morning breezes pulling and pushing them to him, and from him.

He quickly refreshed himself with a splash or two of water from the bowl he had been left with the evening previously in his cell. Then he made his way to the kitchen where Brother Ignatius was preparing to help break the fast of his brothers who were still singing away in the chapel. He greeted Nicholas cheerily and bade him sit at the large trestle table set against the wall of the kitchen, cutting him some of yet another freshly baked loaf which he set before him on a wooden platter. This was accompanied by a pottery beaker of creamy milk, provided earlier that morning by a gentle, if rather bony, cow, the Brothers called 'Jess'. She lived in a somewhat muddy byre, just beyond the kitchens, with her three month old calf.

As he broke his fast he enquired of Brother Ignatius if he knew how his friend Bill was faring in the infirmary.

"Brother Peter tells me that your friend had a quiet night and slept well enough. I took him a little bread and a beaker of milk a while ago and, although he looked rather pale, his appetite was good enough, always a good sign!" The accompanying chuckle from Brother Ignatius boosted Nicholas' spirits as he realised how worried he had felt when he woke this morning.

He quickly finished his own modest repast and, excusing himself from the company of the ruddy-complexioned Brother, he made his way to the infirmary to check on his friend's well-being. Brother Peter was not in attendance himself but his motherly assistant, whom Nicholas now discovered went by the name of Madge, was busy cleansing Bill with a cloth well dampened with warm water from a nearby bowl.

She smiled at Nicholas as he entered the infirmary and before he could ask, she told him that Bill had had a good night so she felt she could "*...get rid of the smell of the river this morning!*" They had left him to rest last evening after putting him in new tighter splints and cleaning his torn flesh and sewing him back together.

Bill looked very pale still but he managed a wan smile for his young friend and life-saver. His eyes looked a little out of focus this morning so perhaps he was still under the influence of whatever magical potion Brother Peter had plied him with to make him more comfortable. He joked a little with Madge as she continued her work and Nicholas smiled to see him in apparently good spirits.

As he approached the bedside Bill stopped joshing with Madge to grasp Nicholas by the hand and offer his sincere thanks for the young man's fine efforts at rescue yesterday. Despite Bill's weakened condition the grip was strong and Nicholas was moved by Bill's sincerity and appreciation.

"I don't think I am exaggerating to say that I owe you my life!" Bill said, still grasping Nicholas' hand with both of his.

Nicholas felt somewhat embarrassed at such an assessment and tried to minimise his role but Bill persisted. "I have known men die on a battlefield for want of immediate attention with wounds of lesser proportion than mine," he said with feeling. "And Brother Peter was very sure that your care was crucial to me once you had dragged me from the water. And, of course, if you had not been so quick-witted I might not even have made it out of the river! I certainly would not have made it by myself, and may not have made it if I had been with a lesser companion! So, I thank you heartily my young friend!"

"I am just sorry that you will have to make your way onwards without my company after I promised your parents I would '*look after you*'! It seems I was the one who needed looking after," he added with a broad smile. "So, thank you again!"

They talked a little while longer but it quickly became apparent to Nicholas that Bill was flagging, even after only a short while talking. It was also clear that Madge was beginning to get concerned that her charge was over-exerting himself after such a recent shock to his system and she started to hint, subtly at first, but with increasing anxiety, that it was time to let the patient rest again!

As they were saying their final goodbyes Brother Peter came by to check on his charge – Nicholas had noted the chanting had stopped – and so Nicholas was pleased he was also able to say 'goodbye' and 'thank you' to Brother Peter, whom he felt earned far more approbation as Bill's 'saviour' than had just been given to himself, by both Bill and the medical monk.

ଔଔଔଔଔଔ

Once he was mounted up again, the remainder of the journey Nicholas made to London, he made on his own. The journey was without further incident, thankfully, and he was delighted at the ease with which he found his way back to the welcoming home of Willum and Hetti van Planck and their 'boys'.

Having sent word ahead, a few weeks previously, his visit was anticipated. So, everyone was pleased to see him, and listen to his tales of the journey. They then proceeded to feed him – too much, as before. They were naturally concerned at the fate of his friend Bill Coles, of course, but there was much praise for him for his fortitude and calm actions in the face of adversity, even though he had tried to play down his role in rescuing Bill from probable death.

He spent a pleasant couple of days with the van Plancks, until it was time for his appointment with Johann Kirkkgarde, a close friend of Willum's, also originally from the Low Countries. He was to serve the last four years of his apprenticeship with Kirkkgarde. It was an unusual arrangement which followed from unusual circumstances at home.

A run of deaths from the sleeping sickness in Louth had hit Pa Melton's customers more than usual, and business had slowed up. Nicholas' brother Robert had joined his father in business after finishing his own apprenticeship. Then they had taken on an apprentice, Alan Barham, a cousin of Nicholas, when business was good. This was three years before Nicholas was due to start his apprenticeship.

The family was now struggling to do enough business to warrant two apprentices, however, following the downturn of business. So, they looked for other opportunities for Nicholas to learn his trade. They thought this might be fairer than throwing Alan out in the cold with nothing to show for it, so near the end of his training – a view Nicholas shared.

Everything was tight in Louth from the effects of the illness, so most of the other town cobblers were little better off than Pa Melton. A chance remark about the situation by old Uncle Tom to Willum van Planck on one of his trips to London, led to the offer of help from Willum's old friend and neighbour, Johann, who was struggling with a different problem. He had *too much* business to cope with after his only apprentice had ended up drowned in the Thames, after drinking much more one night than was good for him.

Nicholas was looking forward to the new challenge, not least because he and Robert had been snapping at each other for a while now. The cause was probably nothing other than sibling rivalry, certainly nothing that warranted the sort of big argument that occurred most days. Except...

Nicholas vaguely wondered if Robert was jealous of his friendship with Eliza Jane Foster, the girl next door, who was now growing into a very comely girl. Yet their friendship remained akin to that of a "brother and sister", as it had been most of their lives. So why Robert was often so grumpy, Nicholas wasn't sure.

Mind you, now he was thinking about it, he would have liked Eliza Jane to have been there in London to hear his stories of derring-do on the journey! He found he missed her more than he had realised he would, even after only a few days absence.

As it was, once he arrived at the Kirkkgarde workshop, his daily life became very busy. Johann Kirkkgarde quickly appreciated that his new apprentice already knew much about his trade, so he put him to work catching up with a backlog of simple, but tiresome, tasks he himself had been struggling to cope with as well as his normal load of work.

For his part, Nicholas found he had decent enough lodging above the workshop although he quickly missed the comfort of the feather mattress and pillow he had grown so used to all his life. The straw made his bed dustier than felt comfortable and was rather itchy to his skin! Still, he determined he would not complain!

The Cobbler Kirkkgarde lived with his wife, a couple of streets away to the west of the workshop, fairly close-by the van Plancks. Goodwife Kirkkgarde was a quiet, thin, mouse-like woman, who made Nicholas welcome enough for an evening meal with the couple. He was, however, expected to take himself to his lodgings above the workshop at night and fend for himself to break his fast in the morning. He also had to find his own food during the day, so the lack of homeliness contrasted significantly with the hearty van Planck household, where he had always felt he was one of the family. This was not least true because Goodwife Kirkkgarde provided meals that were, let us say, sparing in nature. This was, perhaps, of little surprise, since she was so spare herself! Though, which was cause and which effect, no-one could say.

The workshop was only a step or two away from the leather tanning and dyeing manufactories Nicholas remembered seeing (and smelling!) when he had visited the city a few short years before. Since he was often sent on errands to this area he quickly made himself a new set of acquaintances amongst the apprentices in the area. They were rather a rough bunch of lads but jovial enough with the stranger from the country.

They were often playing pranks on each other or some unwitting victim. Nicholas remembered his search for a 'soft hammer' on his previous visit so was always on the lookout for being fooled. For their part, his new colleagues saw him as a rather quiet type, for he was, in truth, somewhat reserved when not involved in acting a role for the Corpus Christi cycle of plays, in which he enjoyed participating, back at home in Louth, as old Uncle Tom thought he might.

Nevertheless, after he had been there a few weeks, he was pleased to be asked to join the group for an *'entertaining afternoon'* on their regular weekly half-day holiday. Nobody bothered to explain what the entertainment was going to be, and he didn't bother to ask how he might be entertained. It was, apparently, not going to cost them anything apart from the exercise associated with a longish walk through the City, through streets he had heard of but never been along. So, he was happy enough to go along with the flow.

He tried, so far as he could, to note a number of landmarks along the way in case he got separated from the group and he had to find his own way home. Then he suddenly realised he was close to the city's river, the great swirl of the Thames.

He decided that if he *did* get lost he could soon find the river again by asking and work his way up-river towards where the River Fleet emptied itself into the main river. Once he was *there* he knew he could find his way home from that point, having delivered two pairs of riding boots to a gentleman customer of Cobbler Kirkkgarde.

Fairly soon the rag-taggle group of apprentices came in view of a fine white stone tower, the famed Tower of London, where Nicholas knew they kept traitors and other prisoners of the king. It was a fine early summer day and there was a lot of activity on the river banks. There were large sailing vessels of various kinds being loaded, or unloaded, amongst a skirl of noise, alongside fishing vessels selling their fresh-caught harvest of fishes to customers of all manner of rank and dress.

At one spot there was a stall selling cockles and jellied eels, so the apprentices paused for a spot of sustenance and banter with the stall-holder. It was while they were eating, that Nicholas discovered what the 'entertainment' was going to be for the afternoon.

There had been a few weeks of celebration since February, anyway, when the Queen Catherine had produced a girl child, Mary Tudor, and he thought it might have been something to do with that, even though several months were now passed. But it turned out that it was to be a much more gruesome afternoon altogether!

The gossip was that Chancellor Wolsey had uncovered a cell of traitors who were stirring up trouble in the West Country. He was not sure what it was all about but the outcome was to be the public execution of three men that afternoon – they were going to be hung, drawn and quartered.

Of course, Nicholas had heard about the process – it was just the sort of thing schoolboys all over the country told each other in the most bloodthirsty way, but he had never seen it for himself. Actually he wasn't sure he wanted to see it if he was honest with himself, but he could not back out now – he would have made himself look foolish amongst his new apprentice friends!

So he finished his last few cockles – not a delicacy he had been familiar with in Louth! – and tagged along with the rest of them as they made their way noisily to the execution site, three or four miles west of the Tower in the village of Tyburn. Punishments such as these were usually conducted in the morning but, as it was a half day,

Chancellor Wolsey had decided to stage it in the afternoon to make sure there was a good crowd to see it who would thus be *'educated'* in the consequences of treason.

Nicholas trailed a little behind the group hoping he might get a chance to slip away, unnoticed, but such an opportunity did not present itself. One of the older apprentices, Tom Butcher, was regaling one of the youngest with the details, since he appeared to be one of the few boys of his age who did not know how it was all carried out. Nicholas was also rather hazy on several of these details but wisely chose to keep quiet. He was not at all sure whether he believed everything Tom Butcher was saying...

"They usually fetch 'em out in a wagon in smocks, having sold off their clothes near the Tower before they set off. Then they get 'em to take off the smocks when they get to the scaffold, so they can be used again for the next lot." Tom said knowledgeably.

"Naahhh!" said John, one of the leather-tanner apprentices, with legs stained dark brown up to about mid-thigh from trampling in the dyestuff, and wearing a very tatty smock himself. "They just like to show the old girls a bit of male flesh to get 'em excited!"

"That's true", chipped in someone else, "there's always a good few spinster women in the front row watching with eyes a-goggling! And some of 'em sometimes get more than they bargain for!"

That comment brought a burst of laughter from the noisy lads which Nicholas didn't understand. Tom continued to tell his story in serious tones...

"Then, for the first part – the *'hanging'* – they put a noose round their necks and throw the rope over the scaffold. Sometimes they will use a horse to pull the rope or sometimes two or three blokes will haul on the rope until the traitor is hanging by his neck, with his feet just a few inches off the ground."

"Does that kill them?" the younger boy asked.

A chorus of "no", and another burst of laughter from the group, puzzled both the younger listener, a grocer's apprentice called Jack, and Nicholas as well. Neither wanted to embarrass themselves by asking what the lads meant but the older youth, Tom, merely smiled a little and said,

"No, it just chokes 'em a lot and seems to give some a lot of pleasure..." more laughter, "but, before they can die, they cut 'em down for the next bit – the 'drawing'... That's a bit of skill the executioner has to learn" said Tom. "The victims need to be close to death but still conscious, so they can really *feel* the second part"... this was said with a really nasty leer of relish on Tom's part!

"A couple of men will hold the victim up on his feet and the executioner will tear his chest and stomach open slowly with a dagger. He does it with care so that the dagger does not kill him either – if it was done too quick the victim might die too soon!"

"Then..." Tom let the word slowly out, "...he reaches in the victim's open stomach with his big hands and pulls – '*draws*' – the victim's guts out, slowly, slimy bit by slimy bit, until most of them are slopping around on the ground! If he's really good at his job, the executioner can get right to the end, with the victim still alive to see his heart slowly plucked out, beating in the executioner's hand!"

Young Jack's face was quite ghastly pale by now and Nicholas felt his own might be a shade or two lighter than usual!

"Then the executioner will squeeze the beating heart harder and harder until it stops beating" – Tom was almost drooling, telling this part of the story, and Nicholas began to think he probably wanted to become an executioner himself instead of butchering animals, the trade in which he was apprenticed.

Thankfully, the story was interrupted at this point before Tom finished his gory tale with details of the 'quartering'. At least Nicholas knew the outlines of this bit, so he could do without the details.

He knew enough from his previous visit to the capital city, that, on posts at various points of entry to the city, portions of body parts, in all sorts of states of decomposition, were always on display to warn visitors that the law prevailed in *this* town at least. And that punishment was always severe.

So, there might be someone's right leg on display, fresh from a quartering, someone else's left leg, hardly recognisable as a leg at all, more like a butcher's display might be if he had forgotten to clear it up several weeks previously, dripping stringy bits of muscle. Or, there may be odd bones missing, and removed by local street dogs as the bits fell to the floor.

There would often be a torso on an important city entrance, maybe fresh but more often in a state of sagging disrepair. And all the most important routes had posts with skulls still resting on poles, or if more recent, sightless heads. '*Why was it that the crows went for the eyes first?*' Many of the heads had straggly beards, and a look that suggested the head's original owner may still be writhing in purgatory.

Again, Nicholas looked for an opportunity to slide away unnoticed, but the crowd of youths got swept up in the now general movement towards the site of condign punishment. Tom was greatly disappointed to discover that they were not very near the front of the crowd and rather regretted their stop for a snack at the cockle stall. Nicholas, however, was thankful he had a somewhat obscured view of the proceedings to come.

Nevertheless, it *was* a new experience and part of his mind was still choosing to be observant. He had always been a curious person, by nature, and found he learnt a lot, even from events which otherwise disappointed, or upset, or even bored him, when he was able to analyse them later. Learning about human nature, he thought, even the worst aspects of it, was educational in the broadest sense. So he persevered.

In this case, he set to thinking about *why* Tom was obviously so enthused about something for which Nicholas felt a strong sense of overwhelming horror. Also why did he himself, Nicholas, feel so powerless, and seem unable to make the choice not to watch?

He seemed stuck to the spot and had a strong feeling that maybe, one day, he might feel uncomfortable, knowing so much detail about such an unpleasant event, but not quite knowing why. He found himself rather lost in a trance as events whirled on about him. Indeed, it was all happening much as Tom had described it.

There was a sudden flurry of activity and noise coming from the other side of the square from where the apprentices were bunched. Tom, in a voice that was slightly rasping with excitement, said – "I can see 'em!". He was a big lad and was a couple of inches taller than most of his friends and seemed to be watching over the top of other people's heads.

"There are two of 'em in the wagon – no, wrong, there are three. One is smaller than the other two and so I couldn't see him at first".

Nicholas could see virtually nothing of the wagon from where he stood, but, as the three men were prodded up the steps to the raised platform to which the gibbets were attached, a small fellow with black teeth and very bad breath elbowed past him. In doing so, he also pushed aside the tall man who had been standing directly in front of Nicholas, thus giving him an unwanted partial view of proceedings. Nicholas also had the 'benefit', if such a word could be used in these circumstances, of Tom's continuing commentary.

"They're taking off the smocks now."

The two taller men were shivering even though the day was not cold. They were trying to hide their embarrassment with their hands. The smallest man, however, seemed as though he was fixing his eyes somewhere else and seemed totally calm, and undaunted by his nakedness. His lips were moving as if in silent prayer, but he was showing no fear or discomfiture, as were the other two.

"The executioner is making them stand on small stools... and passing the nooses around their necks!" intoned Tom in a quieter voice, full of awe at his hero's work.

Nicholas noticed, with observant curiosity, that the stool provided for the smallest of the three victims happened to be three or four inches taller than the other two. So for the last moments of his life he achieved parity with them, which he may once have wished for in his youth. But still, his face showed little emotion, and he seemed to be at ease with his inner self in a way the others did not.

"He's got his two assistants to pull the nooses tighter and fastened the rope round two pegs at the base of the gibbet, so they have to stand on tiptoe!" Tom's eye for detail was disturbing, and slightly blood-curdling!

Carefully, slowly, the executioner pulled the stool from under the first of the taller men. The man appeared to gasp as the rope bit into his neck, perhaps wanting to scream? But he was unable to draw breath to make the noise. His face went very red and his eyes bulged. His hands were tied behind him, but he tried in vain to struggle free. As he did so, however, it merely tightened the grip of the rope.

Then Nicholas saw what the other apprentices must have been laughing at when Tom was relating this part of the story to the younger apprentice earlier. As Nicholas watched, the victim's manhood became as hard as iron and the women in the front row became raucous with their laughter, and comments, as it stuck out and bulged and throbbed before their eyes.

"oooh! what are YOU thinking of?"

"Nice one mister!"

"Can I swap him for my hubby?!"

The ribald comments continued and, if anything, got worse as the executioner slowly took the stool away from the second man, letting the rope stretch and tighten round his neck. Soon, the second fellow was as priapic as the first man, to the great delight of the ladies in the front row.

Indeed, one of the women had a small cane hoop, like the ones Nicholas had seen used for hoopla stalls on saints' days. She threw this hoop, perhaps hoping to win the first man by hoopla-ing his male member. Her aim was way off, however, and it hit the executioner on the ear, distracting him from his task. So much so, that he half turned towards her in a rage.

As he did so, his leg shot out and abruptly dislodged the stool of the third, and smallest, man on the scaffold. The stool flew off the scaffold into the crowd. The result was that the man dropped suddenly instead of sinking and stretching slowly, like the others had done. His head flew back as he dropped and there was a distinct crack as his neck broke.

The executioner shouted, loud and clear, at the offending woman, as pandemonium broke out, people shouting the odds, some women still enthralled at the wildly extended members of the first two victims. The gaudily dressed sergeant-at-arms quickly bustled the hoopla-thrower away from the scaffold as the executioner raised his arm to her as if to strike her heavily.

Strangely, however, the thing that caught Nicholas' eye was the wink the executioner had given the hoopla woman as she was bundled away.

As a child in Louth, he had always been fascinated by the Corpus Christi plays and he had grown accustomed to seeing acting at its best through his young life. It was as clear as day to him at this very moment, that this was as fine a piece of acting as he had ever seen.

'But, why? To what end? What had actually happened up there?'

ଔଔଔଔଔଔ

Tom was still commenting on the process as the first victim was lowered, barely alive, and soon to be ripped apart slowly by the executioner's sharp knife. The executioner began conducting this gruesome scene with apparent relish. He was using large gestures with the knife, playing to the crowd (*'more acting?...'* thought Nicholas.)

Meanwhile the two helpers had cut down the third victim, the short man with the broken neck. They had moved him, so the executioner would actually do this man's 'drawing' next, after he had finished with the first victim.

This he now did with despatch and sprayed quite a bit of blood around as he squashed the man's heart dramatically with his large butcher's hands. This man must have been well-and-truly dead already, however, his neck clearly broken in the fall as the stool was kicked from under his feet.

Then the executioner/butcher turned to the remaining victim, who was still alive. At this point his knife actions became bigger gestures again and he slowed his movements down to give the audience a good show.

He played up the agony the man went through as he was torn open and had his guts drawn out in a bloody mess. There was much baying from the people near the front, especially the hags on the front row. Nicholas, however, was thankfully lost in his analysis of the coup-de-teâtre which he was sure he had just witnessed.

Going over the scene again in his mind, the conclusion to which Nicholas came was that the executioner had clearly kicked the stool away *deliberately* when the hoopla hoop had hit his ear. The result was a swiftly broken neck and a sudden death for the diminutive victim, skilfully glossed over by a consummate actor. The whole artful scene was only given away by the tiny wink Nicholas had seen between the actors – the executioner and the hoopla woman. He wondered if anyone else had seen it.

Nicholas was convinced that the executioner had thus provided the third victim with a quick, and relatively painless, death. He could not know, however, whether it was as a result of bribery or from some other motive. Indeed, he was sure he would never know. But the conviction that this WAS the case, and that he had observed some consummate acting, would stay with him for the rest of his life.

Nicholas stated his view later that evening when the apprentices were drinking their meagre earnings away upon small beer, the very watery variety – which was all they could afford! Tom and the others, who had not seen the wink, or even the hoopla thrower, because they were concentrating on the first man, could not accept the argument Nicholas was proposing.

Somewhat tired and feeling in low spirits, after a day of sights he would rather not have witnessed, Nicholas chose not to make a big thing of it. But, he knew what he knew! He chose to let Tom think he had won the argument and then betook himself to a relatively early bed. He expected to be kept awake by his swirling thoughts but when he did wake in the morning he could not even remember laying his head down, sleep had come so quickly.

His thoughts swirled no longer when he woke, but he now knew for sure in his mind that he had been right about the acting. He was equally sure that the man with the broken neck had known in advance that his ending would be sudden and not a prolonged and painful experience. He decided that this must have been the reason why he had seemed so calm relative to the others, who were to be ripped asunder whilst still breathing.

ೞೞೞೞೞ

The Coat of Motley
An unexpected excursion

It was only a few days after this 'entertainment' that Cobbler Kirkkgarde had sprung a complete surprise on Nicholas. Indeed, he could hardly believe his ears when the shoemaker said they would be going, the following Wednesday, to Kirkkgarde's home town of Ghent. A niece of his, Marieke Molenaar, was getting married the week following on the Friday.

It was a surprise for Nicholas because it was nearly as much of a surprise for Kirkkgarde himself!

After her father died, when she was only fourteen, Johann Kirkkgarde had helped Marieke as much as possible with her upbringing – both financially and with her education. Now, she had just asked him to '*give her away*' at her wedding.

She had grown up into a very independent woman. She was now twenty five and she had a small millinery business. Her uncle had helped her by buying her first few yards of material, but the sewing and selling skills were her own. She had resisted family pressures to pick a husband for her, and had chosen her own husband, in her own time.

Kirkkgarde was, formally, her guardian. But his own rather negative experience of being found a bride contributed a certain sympathy to her search for true love. When he had moved to England a few years previously he had not required her to move with him as she seemed settled where she was.

Nonetheless, now it was about to take place, she wanted the wedding to be as traditional as possible.

Johann Kirkkgarde was thoroughly delighted to be asked, not having children of his own; he felt it was a special honour and was looking forward to it tremendously. Sadly his wife had chosen not to go because she got fearfully seasick and was afraid of travelling so soon after the English war with the French. So, although he had spent much effort trying to persuade her to change her mind, she had refused point blank to leave London. And, since Nicholas and he seemed to be getting along so well as apprentice and master, he had decided to take him along as a companion for the journey.

"'Tis a long enough journey and can be trying without good company. I have been here and back quite a few times over the years and I have always been miserable when travelling on my own. Besides, it will be an experience for you, young man! Broaden your horizons, eh? So much more edifying than taking yourself to executions, grisly and bloody as they are!"

He shuddered theatrically, having been given an expurgated version of Nicholas' day out with the apprentices!

Nicholas tried, half-heartedly at least, to be modest, and refuse the invitation, but Kirkkgarde would hear nothing of it; much to Nicholas' secret delight! He wrote a short letter to his parents telling them of his prospective adventure, but it was likely that he would be nearly at his destination before the letter reached them in far-off Lincolnshire.

As near as he could tell from the many questions he asked of his mentor, the journey was not many more miles on land from London to Ghent than from Louth to London. It was, however, made more difficult and time consuming by the sea journey from England to France. It crossed his mind that he would get to see Calais as well, of course. Whether he would be able to get to the bottom of 'Three-fingered Jack's' tall tale which he had recently heard in Newark's hostelry, he thought unlikely.

Kirkkgarde explained that a hundred years ago, "...*perhaps even only fifty...*" they would have been able to travel all the way from London to Ghent by ship but the canal from the sea to the port of Ghent itself had silted up these past forty years so "... 'tis said that nothing but a rowboat could make it all the way up the canal now! But my father told me he could remember seeing sea-going ships when he was young."

"So, my lad, we must needs ride to Dover, catch a barque to Calais and proceed overland to Ghent. I have been assured by the messenger who brought news of Marieke's wedding that travelling is straightforward for men of business such as myself – and you, of course! – so I sent word straight back via the same messenger that we should be there in time for the wedding. I have to say, the short notice does suggest to my mind that Marieke has, perhaps, been rather naughty and she wishes to be wed before a child is born! But these things happen and, anyway, I may be misjudging the girl – there may be a perfectly rational alternative explanation for her plight!"

They packed to travel light because Cobbler Kirkkgarde promised to buy them a new outfit of clothes when they arrived in Ghent "...'tis the capital of the cloth trade and I have a family interest in tailoring, so there will be no problem there!"

He made it all seem so matter-of-fact to Nicholas, who had assumed travelling between countries was so far out of his reach. They were on their way very quickly and there were no hitches on the way, either. Luck was with them, so much so, that they even managed to get passage on a Calais-bound ship the very morning after their arrival in Dover.

It helped that the cobbler seemed to know many of the sea-captains down on the harbour. He explained to Nicholas that he had always retained a number of customers in his hometown, and regularly came down to Dover to despatch several pairs of shoes each for well-off clients in the Netherlands. All his Ghent customers knew that their feet would be very comfortable with shoes made on the Kirkkgarde last, modelled directly from their feet, in the very finest leather he had managed to buy.

ରେ ରେ ରେ ରେ ରେ

Nicholas did not get chance to investigate Three-fingered Jack's story, for they left Calais almost as soon as they arrived. They went to stay at an inn known to Kirkkgarde just two miles outside the city gate. They were up betimes, and made good speed the next day too.

They were thus entering the west gate of Ghent less than five days after setting off from London. Marieke was surprised to see them with so many days to spare before the wedding. But then Kirkkgarde chided her for her surprise, and the short notice, saying he expected she must be "...with child", against his best advice when she was younger, and dependent upon him. She hugged him hard and laughed.

"I had forgotten just how resourceful you are Uncle Johann, to get here so quickly, but I am so very pleased you have done...you will be able to share in all the pre-nuptial preparations and celebrations...and NO – I am not 'with child'. Fie upon such a thought!"

All of this exchange had gone on in a foreign tongue, of course, so Nicholas was at a loss as to what was said and had to have it all explained to him afterwards. He was still rather bemused to be here and realised how strange it must all have been for Kirkkgarde when he first came to England.

Nicholas was made most welcome, too, by the family. And after they were shown their respective beds, they were provided with some light refreshments as a stop-gap until later. Then there was to be a festive supper for all the arriving relatives, who seemed to be numerous; a lot of cousins, and uncles and aunts from other towns and cities in the Netherlands. Nicholas was allocated a bed in a room with three male cousins from three different towns, only two of the cousins having yet arrived.

ଔଔଔଔଔ

It turned out that the explanation for the hasty wedding was at once complex, based upon the politics of nations and royal succession, and yet now rendered unnecessary by those same considerations!

Marieke's business as a milliner had attracted some customers from the court of the young King Charles (born in the same year as Nicholas, at the turn of the century) who succeeded to the throne in Ghent at the tender age of six, ten years previously. Marieke had attracted the interest of a handsome young sous-chef in the royal household who had, eventually, proposed marriage at a date to be determined in the future. He was a rather shy young man.

Charles was King of the Burgundian Netherlands, which title he inherited from his father, Philip the Handsome, who was married to Joanna the Mad, elder sister of Catherine of Aragon, Queen of England.

Charles was quite happy being king in his home town of Ghent. But his grandfather, Ferdinand, Catherine of Aragon's father, had just died. In their wisdom, the Spanish nobility decided Charles should not only be co-ruler of Spain, as regent, with his barking-mad mother, Joanna, as queen, but he should be *crowned* co-ruler as the first king of a unified Spain. The Spanish nobles said that this meant that he had to be *in* Spain to receive his crown!

That, in turn, meant that most of his court would have to move to Spain with him, not least his sous-chef, who was renowned for the wonderful creations of cakes and delicious sweet dishes in which he specialised.

And that, in turn, meant that Marieke had to marry her man straight away or lose him to Spain and the blandishments of Spanish senoritas. And *then*, having set the wedding date in short order, necessitating Johann's hasty journey from London, King Charles, the first of all Spain, suddenly decided he would only travel to Spain when it suited *him*.

And what suited him was to wait until next year – so the sous-chef and the milliner need not have rushed their wedding after all!

All of this, and several digressions, took Marieke quite some time to explain to Johann and much longer to explain it all in English to Nicholas, especially when some of Johann's relatives tried 'helping' with the explanation, in their very broken English; all of which tended to *hinder* Nicholas' understanding rather than help it.

The explanation was also interrupted when Johann's tailoring and cloth-making cousins arrived, and negotiations were put in hand to provide the cobbler and his apprentice with new clothes fit for the wedding. It was clear that Marieke had a significant influence upon the clothes her uncle would be wearing to give her away. For his part, Uncle Johann simply acquiesced to her decision making!

Nicholas discovered she was a strong-minded woman as well as good-looking in a blond Netherlandish way. So, when it came to his clothes, he was so pleased to be getting a new outfit that he anticipated simply saying "*Yes*" to her ideas, as his master-cobbler-mentor had done, to whatever was offered.

The discussion about his outfit was well under way when the tailor-cousin, Hans de Groot, said out of the blue...

"He could always have one of my new Motley Coats...?!"

Nicholas asked what had been said and, after Johann explained, he was no wiser.

"What is a Motley Coat?"

Johann explained that his cousin Hans had designed a coat which had caught the eye of fashionable people in Ghent and was boosting his business nicely. It was made from cloths of several different colours stitched together in panels. Marieke, who was good at sketching her millinery ideas for clients of hers, quickly showed Nicholas roughly what it would look like.

He nearly fell off his stool – it was so much like the multi-coloured shirts he had seen the fiddlers wearing in the Coronation procession in London, over which he had hung his nose.

"Oh YES...please, may I have a Coat of Motley!?" he enthused. Then he wondered if he had overstepped his host's kindness and tried to back away, but his enthusiasm had been noted and approved. He had no idea whether it was an expensive choice, or not, and felt very guilty that it might be really expensive. But the decision was made!

So, his new coat arrived the day before the wedding and he was thrilled with it. He was now one of the most fashionably dressed young men in Ghent, due to the kindness of his sponsor and his sponsor's tailoring cousin, Hans de Groot. So, when Johann suggested Nicholas might like to provide some entertainment at the party that night he had no hesitation in saying 'yes' – despite his consequent nerves.

His nerves nearly got the better of him, however, when he discovered that the 'party' was to be held at the palace! He thought he might have to perform in front of the king! But the party was not in the court, but in the large buttery next to the kitchens where Marieke's betrothed worked his cookery magic. And the participants were not the courtiers but the scullery maids, gardeners, cooks, footmen and grooms who were Pieter's daily colleagues. The only links with higher society were a few lowly pages who were regular visitors to the kitchens on behalf of their gentlemen and were, therefore, young sons of gentlemen themselves.

There was plenty of strong monastic-brewed ale flowing during the evening, so, by the time it came for Nicholas to perform his 'entertainments' he had lost his nervousness altogether! Thankfully he had not imbibed *so much* ale that would have spoiled his voice, but he did feel really *relaxed* as Johann was introducing him! He had explained the songs to Johann, in detail, in advance, so that he was able to give the gist of the story to the 'audience' before Nicholas sang for his supper *and*, of course, for his Coat of Motley!

With little encouragement needed, owing to the effects of the ale, he was soon standing on a bench so people could see him and he sang his first song "...a tune composed, and the words written by his most gracious Majesty, Henry VIII King of England... '*Pastime with good company'."* The song had quickly become a favourite at fairs, and church ales, all around England. He sang unaccompanied, apart from the beat of a kitchen hand upon a copper pot, his voice bouncing from the buttery walls!

I love and shall until I die
grudge who lust but none deny
so God be pleased thus live will I
for my pastance
hunt sing and dance
my heart is set
all goodly sport
for my comfort
who shall me let

Youth must have some dalliance
of good or ill some pastance
Company me thinks then best
all thoughts and fancies to digest.
for Idleness
is chief mistress
of vices all
then who can say.
but mirth and play
is best of all.

Company with honesty
is virtue vices to flee.
Company is good and ill
but every man has his free will.
the best ensue
the worst eschew
my mind shall be
virtue to use
vice to refuse
thus shall I use me.

His song was well received with some applause, making Nicholas smile. Then Johann explained that Nicholas would sing a song of his local county, Lincolnshire and people laughed as, between them, Nicholas and Johann explained the story of the song. Before he started to sing, Nicholas attempted to teach them the chorus...he sang the whole line first of all, then broke it down into three phrases which he repeated slowly...and got his audience to repeat as best they could, phonetically...

"..Oh...'tis my delight..."
"..on a shiny night..."
"..in the season of the year."

Then he began.....

When I was bound apprentice in famous Lincolnshire,
Full well I served my master for more than seven years,
Till I took up to poaching, as you shall quickly hear,
 "..Oh...'tis my delight...on a shiny night...in the season of the year.."

The chorus was jumbled to say the least...so he stopped singing and laughingly berated his audience..."NOOO – sing it again!" They did, with much better effect.

He sang the first verse again and the chorus was much better this time! So he continued:-

As me and my companions were setting of a snare,
'Twas then we spied the gamekeeper, for him we did not care,
For we can wrestle and fight, my boys, and jump out anywhere,
 "..Oh...'tis my delight...on a shiny night...in the season of the year.."

"Much better!!" ... then the third verse...

As me and my companions were setting four or five,
And taking on 'em up again, we caught a hare alive.

We took a hare alive my boys, and through the woods did steer
"..Oh...'tis my delight...on a shiny night...in the season of the year.."

I threw him on my shoulder and then we trudged home
We took him to a neighbour's house, and sold him for a crown;
We sold him for a crown, my boys, but I did not tell you where
"..Oh...'tis my delight...on a shiny night...in the season of the year.."

Success to ev'ry gentleman that lives in Lincolnshire
Success to every poacher that wants to sell a hare
Bad luck to ev'ry gamekeeper that will not sell his deer
"..Oh...'tis my delight...on a shiny night...in the season of the year.."

And then with a flourished repeat of the last line Nicholas took a deep bow to much applause and cheering from the buttery guests and jumped down from the bench, whereupon, several of the scullery maids came and took turns 'bussing' him on the cheeks. One dear lady of a certain age, and round as a barrel with rosy cheeks – he learnt later she was one of the cooks who worked under Pieter – came and gave him a smacker on the lips, holding his head so he couldn't escape – to general laughter!

In his fine new Coat of Motley he basked in the glory of his temporary fame, and at the wedding the next day many of the girls, *and* the rosy cheeked roly-poly cook, waved across the room to him and several blew him kisses! *"Definitely my lucky coat!"* he thought to himself.

The wedding itself went off wonderfully; Johann gave his niece away with aplomb and decorum and the wedding feast was a marvel. The meal was 'superintended' by Pieter of course, all his colleagues surpassing themselves in providing the food. And it was all washed down with more strong monastic-brewed ale!

Then home to London for Cobbler Kirkkgarde and his apprentice – in his fine new Coat of Motley.

ଔଔଔଔଔଔ

"A-huntin' we will go..."
A forest South of London

Meanwhile, on the same day that Nicholas saw a hanging, drawing and quartering for the first time a couple of weeks previously, the king, who had sanctioned this condign punishment at the behest of his counsellors, was taking very little interest in its outcome.

His Chancellor, lately Archbishop but soon-to-be Cardinal, Wolsey, was no doubt correct to say that the still-young king should assert his authority in a way that could be clearly seen by his people. But the king, more bent on pleasure than authority, chose not to spend too much time worrying about it.

He had been on the throne of England less than ten years and was mostly content to leave the matters of the realm in the capable hands of his council – and there was no doubting Wolsey's ability to run things for him. Indeed, the Pope was *also* pleased with Wolsey's ability, by all accounts, since he had just sent the necessary papers and his papal commission to appoint Wolsey a cardinal of the church.

Anyway, there were better things for King Henry to be doing (so Henry himself thought anyway!), such as jousting and hunting. This very day he and many of his courtiers, the ones that could keep up with him, at least, had been hunting down a fine stag in the royal forest south of the River Thames.

Henry was in his twenties and at the very height of his athleticism. The only man in the realm who could stay the pace with him was his great friend Charles Brandon, recently promoted to be Duke of Suffolk. They were the same height and build – "High and Mighty" some called them behind their backs. And they had the same huge appetite for life, and everything life could bring. Everything!

The size of the hunting group had shrunk, individuals dropping out as the going got too tough for them, so there were only a few left to see the actual kill. Suffolk leaned across towards the king and spoke a few words softly into his ear. Henry let out an exclamation of pleasure at whatever suggestion his friend had made.

"Ha!! An excellent notion!" He enthused.

Suffolk dismissed the rest of the hunt and quickly gave instructions to the bailiff and his men as to what should be done with the stag. Then he wheeled his horse and the two young giants trotted away, leaving everyone else to make their way back towards London and the court. No-one knew where they were headed and of course it was no-one's business but theirs, was it!? He was the king after all and could rather do as he pleased, could he not?

He had not realised where the great stag was taking them as it crashed through the forest in fear. Suffolk, however, had noticed a couple of local landmarks and it was their position that had triggered Henry's pleasure at his friend's whispered words. The track down which they trotted their sweating stallions led to a clearing. And beyond the clearing, they took the leftward rough track for about half a mile, when they came in sight of a small, but well-maintained, religious house, a priory whose prioress was some distant cousin of Brandon's.

It seemed that some watch was being maintained, for, as they came into the courtyard of the building, there were already two servants awaiting their arrival. They bowed low and took the horses to be rubbed down, and fed, and watered. There was no great ceremony, but nor were the servants surprised too much by the identity of their guests. It was evident that they had been before. Sister Agnes came into the courtyard to greet them.

"Your Majesty, Your Grace, you must be tired from your travels. Would you like a glass of wine to refresh you? We have some fine Rhenish wine chilled as you like it, or you could have a goblet of lemon posset if you prefer – to sustain you until we can prepare a table of meats for you?"

The Duke laughed.

"On past experience we'll have both, Sister!"

"Indeed you will, Your Grace!" laughing too!

"How are the young ladies, Sister?" The king's enquiry was about the ten or so girls whose education and upbringing was the responsibility of the priory. The house was funded from the royal purse and Suffolk acted as secretary for this particular house.

It served the needs of young ladies from families whose heads of household had suffered some setback, financially or otherwise, but whose connections were good at court. Sometimes it was simply that their parents were always busy on court business and, therefore, had little time or resources to care properly for their girls.

Sometimes it was the case that the young ladies had lost their mothers, or fathers, or both, and would otherwise be left to the mercies of sometimes unscrupulous guardians. So it could be said the royal purse had 'saved' them. And, therefore, it was likely that they would be pleased to be thankful to the royal purse and, indeed, the royal personage, for their wellbeing when they happened to pass by, as happened today.

The young ladies might enter the priory anytime between the ages of five to twelve, or so, and would be expected to leave at around seventeen or eighteen, having been found a good marriage with a well-regarded yeoman or minor gentleman, and having been educated in the household responsibilities of a well brought up lady. In the meantime it turned out that there was plenty of opportunity to thank the owner of the royal purse.

The two magnificent young men were taken through the priory, to a cosy withdrawing room, by the youngest girl in the house who had only been at the priory a mere three months since her mother died. Her father had a cousin at court who had recommended him and his daughter to the prioress as likely beneficiaries. She had the pretty eyes and features the prioress praised in a lady, and a quiet bearing that fitted in to the behaviour pattern expected at this genteel house of religious sisters.

The wine and the lemon posset were then brought into the room by two girls, carrying a small tray each. These girls had each been there more than a year now (they were both just fourteen) and they smiled sweetly to their benefactors as they handed the goblets to them.

"Your majesty"...."Your Grace"

They swopped places.

"Your majesty"...."Your Grace"

"Thank you my lovelies, how is your Latin grammar coming along? Your cheeks are looking very rosy Margaret! I think you must have been spending too much time outside picking fruit!"

Margaret giggled. "Thank you Your Grace; the grammar progresses, and one must pick the fruit when it is ripe, of course!"

Henry, not far off his twenty-fifth birthday, remained quiet as he accepted his posset from the other young lady, but his eyes were busy. For some reason the beauty of this young girl touched him in a way no other beauty had. She had a mass of wavy red hair, bushy and bouncy, and startlingly green eyes, features that had once appealed to him about his Spanish princess – now his queen, of course – when she had been younger. But this girl's hair and eyes were so much more stunning than Catherine's had ever been!

"How is your lute playing coming along Bessie? Have you mastered that tune I wrote for you to play when we called last?"

"I have indeed Your Majesty, thank you for asking. I shall be pleased to play it for you later after you have bathed and eaten."

"And had a relaxing massage!" added the Duke of Suffolk, laughing!

Rosy-cheeked Margaret, and the sumptuous green-eyed redhead Elizabeth Blount, each kissed a large whiskered cheek, the first kissing the duke, the second kissing the king and both coquettishly left the room, swinging their hips wildly as they went. Elizabeth Blount's father John was a courtier and her mother was a drunk – so Elizabeth had been sent to the priory to be looked after.

"What a grand day!" boomed the duke, who savoured the relaxation after the hunt as much as the hunt itself. "Three of our treacherous enemies hung, drawn and quartered in town, a fine stag brought down elegantly in the forest. And then some relaxation with some young fillies afterwards!"

His friend and liege Henry, the eighth of that name to rule this country, was less rumbustious than usual after such an invigorating hunt.

"Are you feeling unwell Sire, you are too quiet!?"

"Not unwell, Charles, no – just a little thoughtful! I think it is time we brought young Bessie here to court. It would suit me to see more of her, she fascinates me so."

"What would your dear wife think?" Suffolk had quite some latitude to question the king's motives and decisions, since Henry clearly trusted him with his most intimate life, as was witnessed this very day!

"'Tis no business of hers!" Henry snapped back. "She should be concentrating on bringing me a fine son, as you know!" Suffolk, recognising the tension in his friend the king, decided it might be wise to change the subject at this point and drained his wine glass.

"Let's go and get that hot bath now we have been refreshed! They have had time to get plenty of water to a good temperature by now!"

In what was once the dairy room of the priory, some of the royal purse had been spent on exquisite Italian marble tiles on the floor and two huge cast iron baths. Even though it was nearly midsummer there was a roaring log fire in the grate, for there was still a little chill in the air, especially for naked bodies. And the king and the duke *were* soon as naked as the day they were born, and immersed in hot water.

Each bath was attended by two scantily dressed young maidens (scantily dressed so they did not spoil good quality clothes in such a wet environment, of course – and for no other reason!) They were transferring hot water from an open boiler, heated by the fire, to the two cast iron baths which would otherwise lose heat and become too cold for the bottoms of their illustrious occupants.

After allowing their clients to soak for a little while, a third and fourth attendant arrived, one for each bath. Each new attendant was also a young maiden, perhaps fourteen, perhaps fifteen, and this time each wearing nothing more than a loose pair of pantaloons. And each girl carried a large sponge, transported all the way from the exotic southern seas, with which to rub down the bath's occupant. So, with the help of fine smelling soap, they could get rid of the sweat of a morning's excellent hunting.

It was strange how this process managed also to produce much giggling and splashing. Even stranger that the sponge carriers somehow ended up *in* the large cast iron baths without even their pantaloons on – one has to suppose they took them off to prevent them getting spoiled in the water.

Whilst the sponge carriers continued with their 'cleansing' tasks the other acolytes continued renewing the warm water, and eventually resorted to a mop each. It was their task to sweep excess water from the exquisite Italian marble tiles so that the baths' occupants would not slip when they needed to get out of the baths.

Once the bathing was finished and the royal personage and the duke had been towelled dry, they were escorted to the next room (which had once been a stable). Herein, were two sturdy leather-covered upholstered tables. Each massage table was covered in turn with a soft cloth and the two large men were made comfortable by their acolytes. Then, once they had been kept warm with another expensive soft cloth from the Low Countries, the men were left to relax a few moments nibbling at plates of tasty morsels of food, set beside them. There were cold meats, small rounds of bread with crab paste and little bowls of mussels in oil – and a goblet each of wine, of course.

After a little while, two full-bosomed girls of seventeen entered silently with aromatic candles which they placed near the heads of their clients, moving the food away to allow them room for their work. Just behind the girls who were charged with the pleasurable task of massaging these fine specimens of male form, Bessie Blount also came in with her lute. Another, older, girl came too, with a large recorder as well as the rosy-cheeked Margaret, carrying a small tambour, with which she kept the beat of their steps as they walked into the room.

The two older girls tasked with the massages, each of whom had spent time, of course, as wielders of sponges and loofahs when they were younger, were now quite the young ladies. They were deemed ready to leave the priory, soon, with serious faces and elegant posture. The prioress herself had trained them in the arts of massage, something she had been taught in her novitiate years.

And the two men of stature were soon feeling much relaxed in their riding muscles, chiefly their legs, their lower backs, their thighs and their glutinous maximus muscles, which some might call their buttocks.

The oils which these young ladies were using had been warmed and were applied by expert hands which slithered around the said muscles in quite a wholesome manner most of the time. Just occasionally the *wholesome* manner slipped a little and the young supple fingers strayed from the said muscles to nearby, more sensitive areas, eliciting soft pleasurable sounds from men more used to barking orders from the saddle.

All the time, getting on for perhaps an hour on the massage tables, Henry kept his eyes on the pretty fourteen-year-old Bessie Blount. He was checking, of course – as any good music teacher would – on his student's playing of the instrument. She, for her part, seemed able to play the instrument well enough without giving the body of the instrument or the strings very much of her attention.

Her vivacious green eyes spent most of the time staring straight back into the eyes of her king. She had very long eyelashes for a young girl and the king was struck by this as, indeed, he was struck by every other part of her young person. Her gracious hands held the lute just so, as they should, and her posture was excellent for a musician of skill.

She watched closely as the massage progressed and sensed when it was close to finishing and she saved the new song until the very end of the session. It was a delightful piece of music which the king told her he had written with her in mind, based upon the dress she wore the first time he had seen her at the priory.

He had called it 'Greensleeves' in her honour, for the pretty dress that had so caught his attention, the dress matching the colour of her eyes. It was a striking dress too, not least because she was very tall for her years, taller, indeed, than many boys her age.

The last notes of the song accompanied the last moments of the massage. By a coincidence of irony that may have amused the king if he had been aware of it, the massage ended with the same effect as the hanging had had on two of the three men hung, drawn and quartered earlier in the day. The same effect which had so pleased the hags nearest to the scaffold...

The king had not uttered a sound at this point, however. His focus was so clearly on the eyes of the lute-playing maiden, but a few moments later the duke was rather noisier in his appreciation of the skills of the buxom masseuse assigned to him. Noiser – and, it has to be said, somewhat coarser!

After several expletives which one must assume were expressing pleasure he called for another drink to slake his and his companion's thirst. He also despatched one of the girls to tell the stable boys to prepare their horses for their return to the court in London.

CRCRCRCRCR

Within days, despite looks of thunder on her face, Henry's Queen Catherine had a new Lady-in-Waiting.

Maria de Salinas managed, for the most part, to keep Bessie Blount occupied in such ways as to keep her out of the way of her mistress. Inevitably, however, there were times when everyone was in the same room – perhaps when they were busy sewing, for example. Then the tension would be palpable, especially if Elizabeth Blount were seated anywhere near the Queen.

Catherine knew, of course, that Henry had lovers. Indeed, all men of power were inclined to allow such power to turn their heads, but this was the first time he had chosen to flaunt his promiscuity in her face. He had normally been so discrete – and the girl was so young; pretty, she granted, but so young.

The girl was actually of marriageable age too, for arranged marriages, but, really! It was unconscionable that she should be placed in Catherine's own retinue, and with her father, Sir John Blount, often wandering nearby, what must he think!? '…And the blessed girl would keep playing "Greensleeves" on that confounded lute of hers. Did she not realise…?'

Catherine lost her concentration, and ended up sticking a sharp needle into the palm of her hand when her thimble slipped, which provided Maria with a heaven-sent opportunity to divert everyone's attention, and get young Bessie Blount out of the way on some minor errand that would take forever to carry out. She also patched the Queen's hand as best she could before dismissing everyone else, saying the Queen needed a little rest and silence for a time.

What she *actually* needed was the chance to shout and rave without everyone hearing her. Maria was such a good listener, however. Catherine realised she would miss her presence when she married that charming widower, Lord Willoughby, as she was destined to do very soon.

Willoughby was a bit of a country bumpkin, certainly, but so *nice*! Maria would, of course, still be at court *most* of the time but Catherine was so used to her being omnipresent. She now supposed she must allow her best friend *some time* with her husband-to-be.

Part of the trouble at this moment was that she expected the young strumpet, Blount, to be present at court for some considerable time. And Catherine would miss Maria's capable way of keeping the whelp out of her way.

And so it proved. Catherine had to put up with the king, her husband, mooning around over the girl in public, too.

She managed to steel her facial muscles when she was around the court, putting a brave face on the situation as far as the courtiers were concerned. In the relative privacy of her own quarters, however, she alternated between incandescent anger and sorrowful, heartbroken, sadness. She had thought she and her husband had once shared a true love. Maybe they had, as far as Henry *could* 'love'. His behaviour over this girl was demeaning and hurtful, however, and whatever love was left between them was but a shadow of its former self.

Then, when the Blount girl was about sixteen, the pretty young thing started getting heavier round the waist and it became clear she was expecting a baby. At this point Henry was *so* careful of young Bessie. He seemed as concerned as he had been with her, Catherine, when her first boy-child was born. However, when the boy had died, Henry changed and seemed much less caring during each of the subsequent failed pregnancies. It felt as though, increasingly, he blamed her, Catherine, for the deaths of their children. Things got a little better when little Mary was born and survived... but it was very soon after that that Bessie had first appeared at court.

Catherine bore all this as bravely as she could but, finally, in the middle of June 1519 Bessie dropped a fine healthy son and Catherine's heart felt so sore. It was as if someone had reached down her throat and was squeezing her heart from inside! She was still grieving, too, for the little girl who was born and had then died on the same day only last November!

Henry himself, however, was pleased as punch that he now had a fine bawling strong son, at least *he* was not to blame for his queen's inability to bear him a boy child!

Oh, of course, he was attentive to his Queen in public, and she to him, but Catherine felt empty inside, uncared for and, for the first time for a long time, she felt herself to be in a foreign country again. She was surrounded by cold-hearted foreigners, including, she now admitted to herself, her previously-beloved Henry.

The only discernible benefit in the "Birth of the Fitzroy", as she thought of the event, was that Henry stopped bedding Bessie (in fact he had stopped doing that about three months earlier!) Unfortunately, he was insistent she should stay as part of Catherine's retinue, but at least he stopped fawning over her in public.

Not that this made Catherine feel much better about herself, however. He had, by this time, allowed his roving eye (and probably his large hands, too) to alight on Mary Boleyn. She had been trained to seduce in the French fashion. At least he did not show his foolish side with her, though, as he had done with Bessie Blount. Mary was obviously just a sexual liaison for him, a fact with which Catherine felt more able to cope.

Indeed, Catherine was surprised he had not thrown himself at Mary's younger sister Ann, knowing his proclivity for *young* girls. It was that beast, Suffolk, who encouraged him in this unnatural lust for young flesh – she overheard them discussing it once, and Suffolk was so lewd. She found herself shocked, in fact, much to her surprise!

ଓଓଓଓଓ

Maria de Salinas had, yet again, found a way to minimise Catherine's discomfort with the Blount girl and her bastard child. Through her recent marriage to that nice Lord Willoughby in Lincolnshire they had met and recommended the young Lord Tailboys, another Lincolnshire man, as a fitting husband for Bessie Blount and step-father for her whelp. *His* father was as mad as a hatter apparently, but the boy was malleable and had tolerable lands to keep the ready-made family in distant comfort, with emphasis on the word 'distant'! Catherine was always intrigued by Willoughby's description of his home county; he always spoke of the place in glowing terms, describing the wide skies and rolling countryside and wonderful Cathedral with its huge spires. It made her want to visit, but Henry was adamant about not wanting to set foot in the foul place!

After Maria had suggested the idea to her, Catherine broached the subject with her husband, the king, one evening when they were in company and she could at least expect Henry to be civil with her. She was surprised to find, however, that he was not only civil, he was positively taken with the idea and without further ado made the necessary arrangements, snapped his fingers and it was done!

Lord be praised, it was one hurt taken out of her immediate vicinity. Thankfully, her mother, Queen Isabella, had had a long conversation with her many years before about what *men* were *really* like. She had stored the information away in her young brain and could feel her mother's comforting arm around her shoulder all these years later!

Just thinking about her mother now brought tears to her eyes. She suddenly realised that she had never properly grieved for her mother,

her death having occurred at a time when she had had to keep a 'court face' on nearly all the time, as had the deaths of each of her babies, too. Suddenly, she found herself with tears streaming down her face, gasping for breath as the sobs wracked her chest; very strange.

All the hurts in her world seemed to have hit her full on at the same time and knocked the wind out of her. She was alone in her chamber and for once it was unlikely that she would be interrupted – and, strangely, that felt comforting – she could actually be herself, a little girl of ten or eleven, as she sometimes felt herself to be in her secret heart, instead of *having to be* whatever everyone else thought she *should be*!

After a little while the wracking sobs abated, her eyes felt swollen but clearer somehow. She could get her breath again, and when a new tear fell she could feel it tracking down her cheek, hotly. Perhaps the recent death of her father, King Ferdinand of Castile, was grieving her overmuch?

When she shut her eyes, she could 'see' her mother, holding one of her babies and – oh, how she wished she could once have had her mother by her side, holding a grandchild! Catherine now thought it seemed 'right' somehow, that her mother was in heaven, welcoming her little angels for her.

It made her smile, in spite of herself, and she felt she could face company again, as and when she had to. Why, oh why, was she always expected to be '*on show*'? She sighed the same sigh as when she had been a child, pulled her shoulders back, took a deep breath and wiped the latest tear from the corner of her eye.

She rang a little bell which was on a small side table in her chamber and two Ladies-in-Waiting bustled into the room. Thankfully, neither was the confounded Bessie.

"One of you fetch me a cool moist cloth, I feel a little flushed just now. And the other run down to the kitchen and get me a warm orange posset – quickly now!"

The very thought of an 'orange' made her feel a little tearful again, as it reminded her of her childhood, her mother and father, now both dead... But she took *another* deep breath and, once again, was in charge of her feelings – *at least as far as the outside world was concerned*!

രുരുരുരുരുരു

Bubbling Broth:
The end of the first day
Monday evening 2nd October – 1536

Darkness had settled over the great Saint James' Church in Louth after events had taken such a decidedly violent turn earlier on the Monday. Nicholas had hoped all violence could be avoided and it was something they had talked about in Devotio Moderna gatherings over the long evenings of the summer. This hope was uppermost, as thoughts around the county, and further afield, had turned to the need to protest at the closure of the monasteries and abbeys in and around their communities.

But, as reports came to Nicholas and the guardians of Louth church from several villages and towns in the Lincolnshire Wolds, it was clear that anger was being stirred by the harsh words of some hotheads, and not everyone was being restrained!

The treatment of John Frankish, which had made Nicholas feel so uncomfortable in the morning, paled into insignificance against the violence committed in various places during the afternoon. And with feelings running high now, he thought it was probable it would get worse before it would get better!

ଓଓଓଓଓ

The large group of men who had walked to Legbourne earlier in the day had split into two when they arrived at the priory, because only one of the two commissioners was there, questioning the prioress, Mother Maria, about the dependencies of the priory. The other was apparently at his lunch nearby.

John Bellow, one of Cromwell's key men in dissolving the monasteries county-wide, was loathed and hated in Lincolnshire well before the closing of religious houses. Not a particularly well-educated man he nevertheless was gifted with more than his fair share of low cunning. He also knew he enjoyed the protection of a man, in Thomas

Cromwell, whose importance had taken several huge leaps forward over recent times. Firstly from being an entirely secular counsellor, to Chancellor, to becoming Vicar General of King Henry's English church, as was now his title.

Bellow was also a big man physically - it was mostly fat however, covering very little muscle - so he was not especially concerned at first when the mob pushed their way into what had been the receiving room of Mother Maria, in her role as prioress. Bellow now regarded it as his temporary office. Normally his presence, imposing as it was, in girth particularly, made men quiver with worry whenever he confronted them.

What he had not counted on – for how could he have known it – was the fact that the men composing the mob had been winding each other up for several miles about what they would LOVE to do to the miserable wretch if they had him to themselves for just a little while.

Several men in the party, farmers for the most part, had been on the wrong end of arguments with John Bellow over the years and had, between them, probably lost the best part of one hundred and thirty acres of land to his legal bullying. Some of them had even lost the sheep that went with the fields too, in questionable court cases brought by Bellow on behalf of high and mighty clients who paid court officers well for a favourable result. So their blood was running high. And they had strength in numbers, with men who were wiry and muscular from the hard work they did on the farms.

"Gentlemen, what can I do for you this afternoon?" Bellow started with unbecoming gentleness, standing up, his deep jowls flapping at the side of his jaw. Mother Maria had retreated to a corner of the room, looking pale.

For an answer, one of the wronged farmers whacked him on the shoulder – hard – with a long hazel walking stick he had brought with him. "You are to come with us to Louth, you unspeakable churl". The answer was clear.

"But I am work..." he started to say but was interrupted by a blow to the head this time by the same hazel stick. A trickle of blood rolled down his right jowl. And by this time, four strong men were holding his arms between them with another sizeable group now behind him, propelling him from the room.

He nearly fell just before he reached the door when a well-aimed kick struck his kneecap and he yelped in pain.

"Careful", shouted one of the men grasping his arm. "He has got to walk to Louth yet, and he needs his legs, because I am definitely not carrying the bugger!" Some of the violent tension eased at this comment with a laugh from several of the men nearby. But not for long.

They had just got him outside onto the gravel courtyard when he started to bluster again:-

"You will regret this you carrion, when my master hears of it..."

This was cut short by one comment from a voice he could not pinpoint...

"...by which time you may well be dead if you're not too careful!" said with some venom!

And he was dissuaded from starting to bluster again when another of the wronged farmers chose to actually put into practice the thoughts he had spoken of when walking from Louth.

First he spat in the man's face, then hit him full-square on the end of his bulbous nose. Some men nearby told later of hearing the crunch "...as the fat pig's nose broke!" and copious amounts of blood splattered those holding him.

At this juncture those with ropes which they had carried all the way from Louth proceeded to tie his arms tightly so they could drag him from a safe distance. One also tied a rope to his left leg just above the knee, handing the other end to two of the younger lads present with instructions to "...pull his leg from under him if he manages to run for it!"

By now Bellow looked a pretty sorry sight with blood all over the front of his shirt, his nose still pumping blood – they had not let him even hold a rag to his nose:–

"...let the bugger bleed to death!"

Bellow now tried a different tack and intimated to his captors that there might be much money to be earned in letting him go. This tactic, however, brought him just as much trouble as his earlier bluster.

"We don't want your blood money, you bastard!"

The response was accompanied by several further blows and this time he did fall to the floor. Judging by the grin on the face of the lads holding the rope attached to his leg, it was apparent that it was not just the force of the blows that had caused the fall.

When he managed to get up again his palms were bleeding too, after he tore the flesh on the gravel, protecting himself from the fall. His breeches were torn, too, and his shirt much dishevelled. He now made a wiser choice of silence for the remainder of the journey to Louth. Nevertheless, he still ended the journey with more blood, more bruises and more tears to his clothes as the miles passed by.

When they eventually did arrive in the market square in Louth, nearby the town Cross which had seen John Frankish's books turn to cinders in a bonfire earlier in the day, Bellow was unceremoniously stuck in the stocks. And the womenfolk who had not gone along to Legbourne had a little fun with eggs and mouldering cabbage leaves! Indeed, in one case a bowl of soup that had seen better days was used to great effect. In fact, the culinary collection just mentioned formed the best part of John Bellow's diet for the rest of the day, supplemented as it was getting dark by a little dry bread, with water to wash it down.

ରେ ରେ ରେ ରେ ରେ

Roger Millisent, Bellow's '*partner in crime*', as the good people of Louth saw it, was marginally luckier. He had taken four or five mouthfuls of his lunch by the time the breakaway group of Louth militia caught up with him. But for him, too, there was a lack of ceremony in the way his lunch was interrupted. No ceremony, but plenty of skyre and noise as the mob pushed past his host, to find the commissioner at his table.

Not so many people round-about had had former dealings with Millisent as with the loathsome John Bellow. His treatment was, thus, less personalised and marginally less violent. However, by the time he was sitting with his colleague in the second set of stocks in Louth, he had acquired a number of bruises no-one could – or would – specifically account for. There was also a little blood on his chin from a loose tooth which had not actually been loose earlier in the day.

When the bread and water arrived for the two men in the stocks, Millisent was less inclined to eat his, since one gentlewoman of the town had found a choice, fresh piece of dog-dirt. She placed it in Millisent's left hand had then got one of the stronger men, hovering

224

still in the vicinity, to force the commissioner's right hand to squeeze his own left hand. This left Millisent retching, with the foul odour clinging to him, just as the bread and water was placed nearby.

ଔଔଔଔଔଔ

When 'Captain Cobbler's Council of the Church' met late in the afternoon on that Monday in the Tower of Saint James's Church – Tom Foster had so named the preservers of the church silver, during Monday afternoon, and it had stuck – it was an expanded group from the men who had been there on Sunday evening and through the night.

In all honesty, the expansion of the group was not to everyone's liking – the group guarding the church treasures on Sunday night all knew one another intimately. They were friends and knew each other's opinions. They trusted each other to watch out for their backs against any interference from outsiders.

The day's events and the speed with which the events happened had, however, surprised many of them. Indeed, several men felt they may have bitten off far more than they could chew. Certainly, there was a feeling that help was needed from people who knew of different things than ploughs, or shoes, or handling wood. Or making beer, or selling home-made pies, or how to cut hedges, or sew coats.

Even the priest, Father Kendall, and Captain Cobbler, too, felt things were moving away from them into areas of activity and organisation beyond their normal scope. Nicholas had asked Jack Bawnus to use his mathematical skills to try and work out how many people were now sworn-in, and involved in the activities of the last couple of days.

Every new person bringing in information from other villages during the afternoon was first asked to give a general description of what each knew about his locality and what had happened during the day. Firstly, they were to tell Captain Cobbler and a group of five or six of his trusted companions.

Visiting priests and other religious men were then asked to give their reports to Father Kendall and three or four of his close colleagues from nearby villages who were now happy to submit to his religious leadership and stay here in Louth, ready to assist in whatever ways they could. Despite his earlier misgivings and the ill feelings that had been raised by his sometimes-unhelpful interventions during the day, Monk Morland now found himself part of this select religious band. This was, not least, for his clear and substantial knowledge of the legal standing of the monks and nuns of all the religious houses which had been shut down in the County.

Then each newcomer was asked to go and tell Jack Bawnus and two of his brightest mathematical students something of the numbers of people they knew, or thought to be involved. So, there may be "... *twenty men active here and seven gentlemen sworn in to the support of the commonwealth*" there. Or, perhaps, "... *at least forty active men in that village and a dozen gentlemen at least sworn in, three very reluctantly and only under threat of dire retribution if they did not so swear.*" And so on...

Or, perhaps "...*thirty active men with willing wives from this village and fifteen priests from this former monastery wanting to help and the former abbot sworn in to the commonwealth.*" And so on...

And so on and so on. The main complications facing Jack Bawnus and his helpers occurred when they had different people from the same village, but perhaps living a mile apart, who knew different people in the village and had differing views about the local gentry and their likely status of having been sworn in or not.

So when Nicholas asked Jack to come and give a report of what he knew the young man was very nervous about how good his intelligence was and what relationship his numbers bore to the truth?

When he arrived, it was supper time. Because there were quite a few more mouths to feed than on the previous evening, John and Pat Baker had decided to go for making a large stock-pot of bubbling broth as the mainstay of the supper. This would be served with a chunk of fresh-baked bread, doled out with each dish of soup.

Thus, there were several groups of men dotted around the church, each talking amongst themselves, dipping their bread and slurping their broth. And there was a buzz as the chattering increased, as they relaxed with food in their bellies.

And, separately, in the large space beneath the bell-tower of Saint James, *Captain Cobbler's Council of the Church* numbered about eighteen men. This now consisted of his immediate group, who had heard the 'lay' reports. Father Kendall, Monk Morland and the other religious who had taken the religious reports were there. And then, a few minor gentry who had been co-opted to the main core of planners. They had been called upon, either for possessing some expertise, or having some standing in the town, or simply because they were forthright in wanting to be there and had stuck their noses in.

A distant cousin of the Heneage family who lived locally was there, supposedly representing the Heneage interest. In fact, Nicholas rather doubted whether he had any real idea what the church administrator was thinking, nor what his cousin may do on their behalf, if anything!?

Also, there were a few minor gentlemen of Louth who were known to feel similarly to the original group of artisans and had been more than willing to be sworn in to the action. The word seemed to be spreading, too, that decisions were afoot which would inevitably lead to more activity over the next days. So, newcomers were coming into the church in odd ones and twos, and being allowed in, provided someone could vouch for them from the group which was already gathered in the church and which would continue their *'guardian'* role later that night

Pat Baker had organised a little coterie of her *'goodwives'* to help her, and husband John, with victualing the expanded group. However, the only woman present in her own right in the newly named – and so far informal – 'Council' was Nicholas' cousin Eleanor, Sister Beatrice. She was, formerly, the chief assistant to the Legbourne Prioress, Mother Maria.

Eleanor had been living with Nicholas and his family over recent days since the priory had been closed abruptly on the orders of Bellow and Millisent. Nicholas had always valued her thoughts on matters of a religious nature. She had a different perspective on the role of sisters and brethren of the church than did Thomas Kendall and Nicholas felt that would be helpful in current circumstances.

଼ ଼ ଼ ଼ ଼

Now sensing the need for a little theatrical magic, once things had moved beyond the original close-knit group, Nicholas organised the table to fill the centre of the space. He had placed himself at the

227

centre of the table, wearing his colourful Coat of Motley, which he always wore at meetings when planning the Corpus Christi plays each year. He knew, indeed he could feel, the sense of authority it conveyed and he was conscious that, on this night in particular, such a sense of authority would not come amiss!

Unfortunately that *'feeling of authority'* it conveyed, also scared the daylights out of Jack Bawnus for some reason. He was of a nervous temperament at the best of times, so much so that it had nearly deprived him of the power of speech this evening. He had been as fluent-as-you-like yesterday and, yet, today, he was attacked by the worst of stutters.

It was unpredictable, and very frustrating, for him *and* the people around him.

"W.w.wwwe ha...ha..have b.b..been t.t.t.t....terrr.." an explosive gasp and silence.

When he was like this, many people would try and complete his sentences for him, but Nicholas knew from experience that that would only make him worse, much worse. So he exerted his utmost patience, gave Jack an encouraging smile, and a nod to 'go on...'

"W.w..wwwe ha...ha..have been t...trying to get an acc...cc..ccurrrate p..picture..." he was getting hold of it now. His face sometimes screwed up as he concentrated hard.

"...picture of numbers of people involved in this commonwealth p p project. And although it is rather cloudy picture at best, I will try and give as good account of it as I c..c..can" ...Patience had been rewarded and he was almost fluent again now.

"Louth is of course the b..b..biggest town hereabouts, so we see the biggest numbers of men from here. And they amount to several hundred souls of the commonwealth involved and ready to follow the Captain's Council's lead." He smiled as he referred to the new name for the group sat before him and the shoulders of several present straightened back with pride in themselves and their leader, Captain Cobbler.

"As far as we can tell we have sworn in, in addition, at least forty five gentlemen of Louth during the day, including Mr Heneage, visiting, and the whole of the town council there present with him at his meeting this morning. As well as that there were at least forty religious persons in Louth today, for various reasons, all of whom have been sworn in to the commonwealth."

"As for nearby villages, we seem to have quite good information on most of them within ten miles of here. The common folk in these villages amount to many hundreds of people – perhaps about fifteen hundred, up to two thousand, who know what we are about. And who know what we are doing, to some degree. We also think between two hundred and sixty and two hundred and ninety landed gentlemen in the area have been properly sworn in, several tens of them apparently needing a little 'extra persuasion' than was provided for by a simple explanation of the events alone."

"Religious people and their lay colleagues and servants, currently in houses nearby that have **not** been dissolved, account for another two hundred and fifty or more persons sworn in that we are sure about. A similar, slightly higher number accounts for the religious from the **dissolved** houses." Monk Morland nodded sagely at this piece of reporting – it seemed to tally with his notion of the men out there with whom he had had dealings, one way and another.

"We also have information from further away – but that tends to be rather vague, partly because some of it is second or third hand and partly it is due to the fact that information about Sunday night happenings here in Louth took longer to spread to outlying villages. But we do know of some activity as far away as Boston, but without numbers. Also, people in Grimsby and Cleethorpes know what happened here on Sunday. We do not have information yet, as to whether alarms have been raised for further action in those places."

"Similarly, it is known that the Leach brothers, from Horncastle, were seen here earlier today. And, thus, the message of what went on will almost certainly be broadcast there by this evening."

Jack was just about to finish his report when Great James the tailor came over to Nicholas from the door of the church and whispered in his ear that "John Heneage is back with a number of gentlemen, hoping to talk to you all – shall I let them in? There are about six or seven of them, apparently."

Nicholas did not hesitate – "Yes, James, of course they must join us!" – said, perhaps, with a little more confidence than he actually felt!

Just as the gentlemen newcomers were being let into the church a flurry of black priestly cloaks arrived too and several of the priests who had been present that morning, and had just been sustained by the hospitality of Father Kendall and his housekeeper, were also admitted to the deliberations of the 'Council'. A black-cloaked Father Kendall swirled in just seconds later, having come through a different door and then via the vestry.

Nicholas drew a breath and, choosing to project his voice as if he were on the morality stage of Corpus Christi, bid them all a hearty welcome, thereby exerting his authority as the focus of the meeting. Rather than create a significant diversion by ensuring that pews were brought to the space from the nave to seat everyone, Nicholas turned to John Wilson and asked him if he would kindly make his stool available for John Heneage to sit on.

"Just to the side there, John, if you would be so kind, to accommodate Mr Heneage."

In this way he ensured he would not be directly facing the administrator as if in conflict with him! The move also ensured that Heneage could not easily take centre stage without appearing arrogant or churlish.

In fact it was so easily and charmingly done that Heneage probably did not even realise he was being stage-managed! The gentlemen with him felt rather disadvantaged, however, as they were not used to simple ploughmen, and websters, taking precedence over them insofar as seating went. Indeed, some of the ploughmen and working folk seemed uncomfortable at this fact too, but Nicholas chose to ignore such issues of civility, deliberately reinforcing his own authority in running the meeting for the time being. And, indeed, he also enhanced the standing of the group of *treasure protectors* who had spent the previous night guarding the church rood loft of treasures.

"Mr Heneage, Jack Bawnus here was just finishing telling us how many folk were party to what was happening here in Louth, so it might be helpful to ask him to summarise what he was telling us. Jack, go ahead."

Bawnus managed to keep his nerves under strong control now that he had delivered his main calculations. And the way Nicholas had invited him to summarise allowed him to continue speaking with fluency rather than reverting to the stuttering start he had made a little while earlier.

"Well, I think we know that there are upwards of fifteen hundred common folk in Louth and the villages around who all know and support what we are doing here and the word is spreading rapidly so far as we can tell. ...more, of course if you include all their women-folk and families."

"There are getting on for three hundred local gentry who have been brought in by swearing the oath. Similarly, there are getting on for six hundred religious and lay people from existing and former religious houses hereabouts who are known to be sworn in or committed to supporting us in what we do. All in all, well over two thousand people. And double that if you include all the family support they will get and that is increasing rapidly"

Jack Bawnus sat back and sighed slightly, pulling his shoulders back as he completed his analysis, pleased with his detailed report. Nicholas welcomed his report.

"Thank you again, Jack, it looks as though we have begun to get our message across that we mean to ensure our treasure is protected against the ravages of the chancellor but ..." and here he included all those present to consider his next words seriously... "What should we propose to do next?"

The way John Heneage moved in his chair suggested he wanted, indeed expected, to speak next and Nicholas, catching the movement, invited him to speak before he could presume to take over the meeting. "Mr Heneage..."

"Mr Melton, gentlemen and brethren, all. As well as conducting the main business of the Louth administration at our meeting today we were able to reflect on the points you and Mr Bawnus here were making this morning. We also considered the wider scuffling that took place later in the Square, as well as the violence that was meted out to Chancellor Cromwell's servants Masters Bellow and Millisent. Apparently they still rest in your local stocks in some considerable indignity."

Heneage's voice was strong and authoritative now...

"We feel sure that cooler heads ought to prevail than those who undertook or countenanced the violence against these men..."

Nicholas felt the tension rise markedly as Administrator Heneage became so critical, and he was minded to intervene but retained his patience and raised his palms a little to discourage those others who he felt might jump in....

Heneage continued... "and in summary, provided some conditions of peace are met, I am willing to travel to London to talk with the king.

231

I undertake to speak up for the more responsible amongst you, and will ask him to forgive the actions of the hotheads. Then we may scotch the many rumours that you have made me privy to today, all of which I feel considerable reluctance to give credence to, to be frank!"

There was much nodding of heads at this from the small coterie of landed gentlemen allowed into the church along with John Heneage – but it was clear, too, that his remarks had also ruffled a few feathers amongst others present and the level of background noise became considerably louder at this point, with some danger that disorder may follow – even though they were still within the confines of the church!

Nicholas raised his hands again in a peace-making gesture, and John Heneage continued,

"...and we feel one condition of peace is that there must be a resumption of dignity for the Commissioners Bellow and Millisent before we ..."

This was clearly too much for many present and several started to bestir themselves, the noise level increasing again to a point which prevented Heneage continuing! The discomfited gentlemen, with no seats to call their own, started to look severely ill at ease. Perhaps they wondered if their next seats would be the local stocks as well? This time Nicholas did not make any effort to hold the comments back. And, several voices started to speak at once.

"Dignity be buggered..."

"...and what about the dignity of the brethren from dissolved houses?"

"...never mind their dignity, they were lucky not to be strung up..."

This last comment was from John Sanderson who had earlier offered to donate wood to make the gallows, and clearly still felt aggrieved that his offer was not taken up!

"At least that bastard Bellows got the bloody nose he deserves"

Shouts of "...*aye!*" and some laughter greeted this comment and Nicholas wondered again if he should exert his authority and try and bring some order. Then the voice of Robert Brown, one of the lesser gentlemen of the town, who had been in the church for a while and was therefore seated on one of the benches, made a suggestion. This had the effect of defusing the tense atmosphere by accommodating the views of both sides...

"I think you probably all know I have just had a sturdy stable erected for my horses but they have not yet taken residence. It has a door which can be bolted and locked. If you were all in agreement, therefore, I am sure we could accommodate the errant commissioners in there and feed them slops for a time until this business is finished? Their "dignity" may still be impaired a little but not so much as it is now and yet they would not be able to continue their ill-begotten work whilst locked away, nor do other unimagined damage. May I commend this course of action to you all?"

"Thank you Mr Brown, I am sure this would appeal to most of those present!" Nicholas intervened quickly to move the discussion onwards. General support came in the form of grunts and the nodding of heads.

John Heneage simply *"Hmmph"*-ed and his face went very red for a while. But he chose to say no more on this particular. He clearly felt he might be shouted down, not a circumstance he was used to!

"Talking of commissioners..."

...another voice chimed in near to Robert Brown. Nicholas recognised it as Thomas Spencer, one of the churchwardens, but one who had chosen early on, just after the Sunday service in fact, to follow the path of the commoners. He was, therefore, a welcome ally in their deliberations. He was a member of Devotio Moderna, too, alongside Nicholas. And he had been party to many of the discussions over the summer amongst members of this thoughtful group, concerning the closure of so many religious houses.

"...Talking of commissioners... I know there will be a lot of them about in Caistor tomorrow. They are gathering there to assess the subsidy for next year and Lord Burgh is coming over from Gainsborough to preside over the meeting. There will be a lot of Lincolnshire's top gentlemen present, I know for a fact. Thomas Moigne, Lincoln's Recorder will definitely be there; and Sir William Ayscough, Sir Robert Tyrwhitt, Thomas Partington and several others will probably be there too."

"Our idea is that we go and meet them – all together, as the muster from Louth – and swear them all in to the action we are taking. If the villages hereabouts also muster and come along with us, we should present a formidable host, being all of the same mind. Then, once they are "in", we shall have the credibility of the senior men of affairs in Lincolnshire with us when our questions and demands reach the chancellor and king in London. Surely, then, they cannot then say us nay!"

Thomas Spencer's brother Jack and Robert Bailey, who owned large general businesses in the town and the Bishop of Lincoln's Louth-based farmer and the miller, William King, were all nodding in support of these last comments. They had clearly been talking about the commissioners' meeting amongst themselves during the course of the day and had decided greater personages needed to be brought in to the cause if they were not all to be swept away and swatted like flies. Or, worse, hung as traitors!

John Heneage was shaking his head vigorously during this discourse and, although it was clear that the general feeling in the room was supportive of Thomas Spencer's ideas he, Heneage, tried to pour cold water on the notion. His words were both scornful and scathing; and his voice was loud and strained...

"You speak as if these fine gentlemen will simply fall into your hands like ripe fruit in the autumn. As if they did not have minds of their own, nor the will to resist the urgings of a mob in full cry!" Heneage's blood was up and his face red with his urgings. His patience was clearly torn to shreds.

But as will sometimes happen to one whose urgings usually fell on *receptive* ears, he was much surprised to find himself on the wrong side of an argument for a change, and the ears around him not so receptive! Indeed, the mood was getting fractious now, and voices were becoming raised as the discussion flowed and ebbed according to the manner and form of the argument, from articulate to bluster, and back again.

Actually, it was probably mostly bluster, if truth be told! Nicholas, however, now began to be concerned when it appeared that the action, which had simply started out with the objective of preserving community wealth where it belonged, now seemed to be turning towards outright rebellion.

ଛଛଛଛଛଛ

Anger pervaded the air and each time one of the gentlemen present sought to calm the situation, louder voices would prevail.

Some of the loudest voices came from the substantial group of black-frocked priests, and former brethren, now present in considerable numbers in the church.

Twice more administrator Heneage had tried to intervene, but both times had been shouted down by the priests. Feelings were running high...

"*Go forward! Let us go forward and ye shall lack for no money!*"

This urgent call came from a brother from one of the houses yet to be dissolved and, the more the hesitant gentlemen of Louth council seemed to urge caution, the more vociferous were the black frocks...

Let us go forward and ye shall lack for no money

It became a refrain....

Let us go forward and ye shall lack for no money

"But the king and his chancellor will show no mercy for rebellion"

Let us go forward and ye shall lack for no money

Heneage and his coterie of members of the council of the town were finding their position more and more uncomfortable as the volume rose in favour of Thomas Spencer's idea. And the discomfort was not simply to do with the fact that they had had to stand whilst lesser mortals sat and shook their fists.

They had been sworn in in favour of the commonalty – under pressure, indeed – but their hearts were not fully engaged with the ideas they had sworn to uphold. Nor, if they were being honest, were they engaged with the people who espoused those ideas.

How was it all going to turn out if they backed down?

Those with businesses in the town were dependent upon the goodwill of Louth people for their ultimate wealth, it was true. But there was, of course, a higher order that everyone was bound by. They had, after all, been caused to swear their allegiance to the cause on the bible in the church earlier in the day. This was not a little matter to abandon quickly, when their immortal souls were now at risk.

John Heneage, however, was not uncomfortable. He was just cross.

He was doing his best for these people but they were choosing to ignore his advice. '*Well, they would be the ones to suffer in the end if they did not heed the advice of a man of position. What on earth were they thinking of, trying to upset the natural order of the world? Damned shoemakers, candle makers, priests and ploughmen? Whatever possessed them?'*

Suddenly, however, Heneage *was* really uncomfortable and it was that single thought that had done it. Perhaps they *were* all possessed, literally, by the very Devil!

He went pale as this disturbing thought took hold in his mind.

He started trembling and decided he really must get out of here and go back into the world he knew in Lincoln. He would write to the king, God bless him and preserve His Highness; he would write to the bishop and Chancellor Cromwell and in Lincolnshire he would write to Lord Hussey in Sleaford. Someone needed to take charge and turn this situation back from the brink of terrible, ungodly, works. And he must try and contact Lord Burgh and tell him what was afoot. He was sweating now, as all these thoughts whirled in his head, even though the church was cool on this October evening.

"Mr Melton, gentlemen, forgive me for, as you may see from my brow, I am feeling somewhat faint and unwell of a sudden. I must go. I ..."

Words failed him for a moment – he could not admit why he was feeling faint.

"I will write to the king, as I said earlier and, if he thinks fit, I shall go and see him to put to him the questions you have raised with me."

His voice was quavering now and his listeners really did believe he was feeling unwell, but almost certainly they did not appreciate quite *why* he felt so unwell!

"I am... I am sure you will find all this is but a molehill and not a mountain. Rumour rather than reality. I ...err... I... Goodnight gentlemen I must go..."

He stood quickly, knocking his stool over, the sound echoing round the stone walls of the church. He stumbled and one of the gentlemen of the council grabbed his elbow to steady him. The other gentlemen were taken by surprise and were not sure whether they should follow him out of the church or stay to represent him. Confusion was written on their faces.

"Yes, of course, Mr Heneage, you must go – of course – I hope you will feel better soon. Perhaps you will make sure to keep us in touch with your communications with the king."

Nicholas managed to respond quickly to the sudden change of direction with good grace, though it felt rather lame as he spoke the words. Several people exited with the bishop's administrator. And several others took the opportunity of the hiatus to relieve themselves outside, so there was a considerable amount of shuffling about before the meeting became ordered again.

A quiet voice from amongst the black frocks was heard clearly in a theatrical stage whisper to say *"Good riddance!"* as the administrator left the tower meeting area. At a more mundane level, John Baker took the opportunity to bring in another few platters of cold meats and other titbits for those who still had hunger to appease and Pat Baker and her team of goodwives cleared some of the earlier bowls and wooden platters and goblets out of the way.

John Baker also let everyone know there was a new barrel of ale which had just been breached, if anyone was gasping for a drink. More shuffling and the mood noticeably changed back to a more relaxed gathering of friends, now most of the stuffy nay-saying gentlemen had left, trailing after John Heneage.

His distant cousin had left the church with him. He had obviously had a brief exchange of words with Cousin John, and had returned, trying to look self-important but achieving only a sense of being out of place and out of his depth. Nicholas chose to ignore him.

"'Tis clear that Mr Heneage found himself outnumbered with respect to our intended action tomorrow and I think it is now also clear that we should make preparations to call the town out to muster first thing in the morning. We must get them ready to go to Caistor as a host and 'bring in', to our cause, the commissioners and other key gentlemen we may encounter there."

"We need to bolster our cause with respected men of affairs who are used to dealing with authority. Am I right in summarising our discussions so far?

A chorus of hearty *"Aye's"* greeted his words....

"...and, so, let us get on with planning the details so we can start betimes in the first of the light tomorrow, for I see it becoming a long day!"

CR CR CR CR CR

Meanwhile...

When John Heneage stepped into the fresh crisp air of the early October evening from the church he was still trembling, and it was lucky for him that others were at hand to offer assistance. For he was definitely flustered by his inner thoughts and disturbed by being rounded upon so publicly by his brothers of the cloth. The churchwarden, Mr Elwood, spoke quickly to one of his servants, who was seated on a horse and holding Elwood's own horse for him.

"Leave my horse here with me, and I will walk over the river yonder on the Lincoln road with Mr Heneage here. Ride like the fury to the stables behind the inn, brook no delay from the hostler to have Mr Heneage's mount saddled forthwith. Then bring the horse along to us as soon as you can. Go, man, quickly!"

Elwood took hold of the reins of his own mount as the servant swivelled his horse on the spot and headed east to the inn.

"I am sure he will not be long; my guess is that your horse should be a'most ready anyway, apart from having his girth tightened?

The administrator waved a hand carelessly to dismiss the other town councillors as he and Elwood walked down the slope to the bridge. The bridge was lit with sputtering brands against the autumn evening dark. There were four waxed brands along each side of the bridge, casting flickering shadows in a gentle breeze.

"I will wait with you by the mounting block there on the far side of the bridge, so we are still in the light." Speaking now for the sake of warding off an uncomfortable silence, Elwood tried to make light conversation but Heneage was far too distracted.

Thankfully for both of them, the servant returned in short order with the administrator's fine grey mount and Heneage was glad to be on his way.

"Shall I ride with you for a way along the Lincoln road?"

"No, please, Mr Elwood, make your way home, as I shall speed my own way onward to the City!" The relief to be leaving was evident in his voice.

"God speed, Elwood, many thanks for your help!

238

"May God be with you too Mr Heneage".

And with that benediction the two parted company. Heneage urged his horse into a fast trot and it felt good to be gone from the town. He had barely gone two hundred yards up the slope on the north bank of the Lud, however, soon to turn westerly onto the Lincoln road, when he was hailed by a rider coming in from the Grimsby road.

He recognised Guy Kyme, (though still young, Kyme was, nonetheless, one of the chief men of Louth, having recently inherited his father's substantial business) whom he, Heneage, and the council, had sent to Grimsby on business about which he would normally be anxious to hear at the earliest opportunity.

There had been reports of the unexpected discovery and arrest of a gang of pirates who had been troubling the east coast traders for months over the summer. Luck had been on the side of the Grimsby Constable for a change and someone with a grudge had provided intelligence which had proven correct – an unusual occurrence in the fish-smelling ale houses of the port, to be sure!

Guy Kyme was genuinely excited by this news but he found Heneage unwilling to stop to hear what he had to say – another unusual occurrence which surprised the Louth man. He had obviously missed some notable excitement of a different kind in his home town during his absence on official business and, trying to piece together as much sense as possible from the disjointed words offered by the still troubled administrator, he stood for a few moments watching Heneage disappear into the darkness of the Lincoln road. Then he went to the church where he hoped to find some answers to a new puzzle, different from piracy to be sure, but still novel in its own way.

He trotted over the bridge and round the west front of Saint James' Church, where he and his lovely betrothed were to have been married only a few short years previously.

There were still some men of the town standing talking outside the doors, huddled in coats against the chill now setting in for the evening as the breeze turned northerly. From them he heard the tale of John Frankish being chased out of town. This proved to be another surprise since he expected to find the man warming against the fire in his front room at home, a goblet of mulled wine in his hand. Frankish was an old university friend of his now-deceased father. Indeed, he had always thought of him as '*Uncle John*', though he was no blood relation!

He was not entirely surprised at the meeting going on in the church, however, since he had heard the rumours, before he left for Grimsby on the Saturday afternoon, of the commonalty perhaps seeking to take charge of the church treasures. But he had certainly not anticipated the escalation of events in the way they appeared to have unfolded so rapidly during the day!

Although his father had been rather aloof and arrogant about his success in the world of mercantilism, which had taken him quickly away from his roots in the town, Guy Kyme himself had always been much less of a snob than his father. His deep involvement with the Corpus Christi plays from a young age had also endeared him to those around him who were so much more involved in the social life of the ordinary townsfolk than had been his father.

He was, too, like many of those closely involved in the current protection of the church's treasures, a member of the Devotio Moderna grouping in the church. As such, he was always willing to lend a hand providing help and support for those within the church community who, for one reason or another, might be having a hard time. Just two weeks earlier, for example, he and a few others had spent most of the Saturday and some of Sunday morning sorting out the autumn clearing of the land of a widow woman on the Lincoln road. She had three very young children and her husband had been killed in April in an accident, whilst felling trees for his employer.

She had managed quite well during the summer, preserving fruit and so on, but had not had time to keep up with the necessary tidying up after the harvesting had been done. Guy Kyme's cousin was a friend of the widow woman so it was an act of friendship. But it was also more than that, and Guy and his friends in Devotio Moderna got much satisfaction from being able to help where they could in all sorts of ways and for all manner of local people.

Thus it was that, when his father died and he found himself naturally amongst the important people in town because of his wealth, his natural affinity was still with his previous social life. He found he was able to be himself without pretension amongst whichever group of people he encountered. There was, therefore, no suspicion of him when he bowled into the meeting in the church and boldly enquired...

"So, what transpires here, then? It seems I have been missing the fun whilst away in Grimsby sorting out pirates!"

He was treated to a quick summary of the current position and such was his popularity that no-one even thought to have him 'sworn in' as they would have done with any other member of the local gentry – he was automatically assumed to be *...one of us...*! Anyway, once brought up to date with the plans now afoot in Captain Cobbler's Council, he was enthusiastic about how they should go about planning for, and acting, the next day. As always, he wanted to take everything on personally, such was his enthusiasm, so Nicholas and the others had to hold him back to what was possible.

"So let me get this straight. The priests present are all going to go back to their various villages and will sound the common bell when they get home this evening to tell their people to be ready to move in the morning as if for a spring-time muster and target practice. They should be fully harnessed if they have the necessary armour. So everyone should get as early a start as possible, as we all will here in Louth?"

"Yes", Nicholas confirmed for Kyme as well as for all the others present. Kyme continued...

"We need the outlying villages to be moving first, since many of them will have further to travel than we will onto the Caistor Road. The gentlemen here present have suggested, wisely, that we should probably all muster together at Orford which is on the way for us. It is where we have often met for the larger spring musters, so everyone will have a good idea where they have to get to."

"And you want me to ride to Orford Priory this evening after our meeting has finished, to alert them in the priory to our arrival, and make sure there will be some refreshment for everyone. Make sure there are a lot of water barrels, and bread at least to make sure no-one faints away from all the walking."

"Indeed we do", Nicholas confirmed with a smile – there had been some chuckles at the idea of anyone fainting just for walking the few miles to Orford! Even though there were some small hills to negotiate on the way.

"And if you would be kind enough to include in your travels a personal action for me, Mr Kyme, I would much appreciate it" chimed in a voice they were all becoming familiar with today. It was the monk, Morland, speaking.

"My horse has gone lame today. I am not sure whether it is a muscular thing or whether he has picked up an infection in his hoof. But he is getting on in years, not unlike me! And he has had a busy few weeks with all the riding I have been doing of late. When I was out at the priory some weeks ago and talking with the prioress about horses, she said she had a young horse they had recently broken in and if ever I wanted to replace my old fellow, this horse was a calm sort and would make a good ride for me."

"I wonder, could you explain that I shall be walking to Orford with the Louth host tomorrow morning and it would be a most civil thing if I could take her up on her earlier kind offer. I should be much obliged to you." He seemed to have no embarrassment at asking for favours. His lifetime of service in the church had trained him to ask in a forthright way for things the church needed – and this seemed to cover things he needed personally as well.

Time was moving on, the soup was all finished and much of the latest barrel of ale had been drained and it was now apparent that some of those present who had farthest to travel were getting anxious to be off. No-one actually wanted to be the first to leave, however, in case they missed something that was important or interesting.

The person who picked up on the fidgeting had, perhaps, the quietest voice in the room but such clarity that no-one missed what she said when she picked her moment.

"Cousin Nicholas - 'tis perhaps getting to that time when some of our friends must leave. They have far to travel and then must rouse others and talk to them if our plans shall become actions on the morrow." Sister Beatrice had a bell-like timbre to her voice, both pleasing to the ear and insistent at the same time.

"You are right as always cousin Eleanor - and more observant than most of us who would continue talking until late..." He paused...

ଔଔଔଔଔଔ

242

Lady in waiting: Bridesmaid to Bride
Remembering... Cousin Eleanor free to gossip

As Nicholas and the other prisoners were wobbling along the cobbles from the Tower of London to their place of execution, in March 1537, in a pair of old straw waggons, it occurred to him that, *in extremis*, all men (and women, too!) can be humbled and brought low.

Amongst his companions on these two wagons were men who had mixed with some of the high and mighty of the County of Lincolnshire before the rebellion. There was the abbot of Barlings Abbey, Bishop Mackrell, who had been known to sup with Chancellor Cromwell and converse with the great Cardinal Wolsey, once Bishop of Lincoln. There was also Lord Hussey, perhaps the sorriest sight of all, who had been a favoured servant of the old Queen Catherine. He was reduced to tears on this, his last journey.

Now look at us all, in our common smocks! Nicholas thought...

...and the thought took him back – in that strange time-dilating way he had been feeling on and off from first light that morning – to a long conversation he had had with his dear cousin Eleanor one Christmas-time when she had been to stop at his house for nearly a month.

Legbourne Priory had suffered the loss of much of the roof of its dormitory in a great November storm, and many of the sisters had been sent to stay with nearby relatives whilst the repairs were being done. In view of the later role Legbourne Priory would take in sparking the rebellion, it was ironic that its steward and sponsor was the same Thomas Cromwell whose policy had eventually closed it down.

The prioress, Mother Maria, originally Jane Mussenden, had written hopefully to the chancellor when the closure became known, begging him to intervene for them. But the request fell on politically deaf ears!

Nicholas tried hard to remember which year it had been when the conversation with Eleanor had taken place, but could only reckon it must have been about ten years previously, perhaps in 1526 or '27.

It had certainly been quite a long time since he had seen his cousin before that. He remembered feeling a little embarrassed when he met her in town, to bring her to their home. He thought it may even have been the day he got married, when he saw her last – and that was in 1520.

"What do I call you at home when we get there – Cousin Eleanor or Sister Beatrice?"

She laughed a light wholesome laugh and flushed slightly and said she would answer to both or either!

"Perhaps for the sake of your two young boys and your lovely wife we might stick to the family name of Cousin! I don't want them to think me a strange being!"

She had settled in to family life quicker than Nicholas had expected and she told his two sons family stories that he had long forgotten. This seemed to amuse and delight them no end. His lovely wife, Eliza Jane, had found a sisterly bond with Eleanor from the outset. No doubt this was because she had grown up with older brothers and would so have loved to have a sister to keep her company against the antics of her brothers. In fact the deep bond started almost as Eleanor walked through the door. Since Nicholas had had no opportunity to report on his conversation as to how they should address her, Eliza Jane had started a sentence, hesitantly, with...

"Sister...erm..."

...and Eleanor replied quickly, to cover her hostess's hesitancy with...

"Yes sister...!"

Somehow she must have divined Eliza's need for a female sibling, and the two women, who had never before met, fell into each other's arms laughing their heads off, leaving Nicholas and his two sons somewhat bemused.

It was just before Christmas and they had, of course, all gone to church as a family several times over the next few days. They went to celebrate, and sing, and pray. So, it was probably a couple of days after Christmas Day that the conversation had taken place which Nicholas remembered all these years later.

It was the first time Nicholas had seriously contemplated the fact that the 'Great and the Good' were just people; that we human beings are all brothers and sisters under the skin, just as the bible teaches.

244

But how different the reality of the world was, he thought, with the 'Great' holding sway over the poor, and often treating their very lives so lightly. And the 'Good' moralised, whilst ordinary folk sometimes had to resort to a little cheating and stealing, just to survive.

Eleanor had been telling them about a Christmastime, perhaps ten years prior to this visit to Nicholas and family. Suddenly, as she was speaking, Nicholas realised that he was related to someone, who knew someone who was part of the royal entourage. How strange was that? Eleanor was saying...

"...it was all on account of the first Lady Willoughby's support of the Devotio Moderna and the fact that she had died tragically young. During Lady Willoughby's last illness, Lord Willoughby had brought her from his seat at Eresby House for the sisters to look after her and bring her peace. She showed great fortitude in such pain, poor woman. And we all got to love her very much in a short space of time, for her humour and for her grace."

"Lord Willoughby was really no great age himself – still in his forties I think – and was distraught and beside himself that he could not make his wife better or save her from the pain. She died just before Christmas that year, for I remember that Lord Willoughby was troubled that he ought really to be at court for the king's great festivities. But he was so loyal to his wife and her needs at the last."

"The king and his queen were still quite young, and hopeful then about their expectation of having male heirs to the throne. But I think the Princess Mary was just a toddler, and the queen was expecting again. So, they were celebrating Christmas with a will, but Lord Willoughby missed it all."

"Quite early in the new year, he came to see Mother Maria, who had only recently taken over as prioress. He gave the priory a significant gift of income from some of his lands, in perpetuity, in grateful thanks for our care of his wife. It was a nice gesture, and secured our position in being able to offer care for lady folk in distress for all time thereafter. It meant we could start looking after our herb garden better and extending it so we had more helpful, healing herbs on hand. We could also afford two servants to maintain the hospital beds, and the kitchens, and free our sisters up to provide time for caring rather than simply chasing about gardening and cleaning. It was wonderful!"

"I think most of us thought it would be the last we saw of Lord

Willoughby and he would be off at court all the time, not wanting to visit his Lincolnshire lands, his grief was so strong."

"But it was not much after that that we saw him again, when he brought his new bride-to-be to stay at the priory before their marriage. He was probably as surprised as anyone at how the world changes, even in grief. The queen had lost yet another of her children in childbirth and Lord Willoughby had been particularly sympathetic to her. He probably felt her grief alongside his own and that made him so much more supportive than many men can be when faced with great emotion."

Nicholas, whose wife had lost a little girl in childbirth only the year previously, was holding Eliza Jane's hand as the tale unfolded and Eleanor noticed his hold had tightened and that his eyes were glistening as she spoke. She thought it better not to mention this in case she provoked an unlooked for breakdown!

Anyway, Eleanor's tale had a happy ending, so she wanted to get on with the nice part of the story!

"At any rate," she sighed, "Lord Willoughby found that the queen requested his presence more often after this. And, as a result of his being in *her* presence he also found himself in the presence of her chief lady in waiting, Lady Maria de Salinas, from Spain. Now, my Lady de Salinas was still unmarried at the ripe age of thirty or thereabouts. As it happened, she and Lord Willoughby found they had much in common despite their widely different backgrounds, I think mainly because of their similar ways of thinking in a philosophical manner – they both supported Devotio Moderna, for example."

Nicholas smiled at this connection with his own life. He had taken an interest in the workings of the Devotio Moderna through the priest, Thomas Kendall, who had asked him to act as secretary of the Louth group. This group was raising funds to support charitable work through the Louth Park Abbey, Legbourne and other nearby religious houses.

Many of the group were ladies of some of the more important families hereabouts. They wished to support children of local families which had been broken by death, or disease, or poverty, and were active with both funds and prayers.

He found his thoughts were drifting off, but Eleanor's next words brought him back to the present discussion...

"Thinking back," she paused, "...it may be that the queen was doing a little matchmaking for her lifelong friend Maria – and Lord Willoughby was such a nice man! Maybe not the most handsome man in the world, but who am I to judge!?"

Her laughter at this point may have suggested she *was* in fact quite capable of judging handsomeness in a man, whilst also being able to ignore it as a distraction from her calling!

"Well, it was not long before he proposed marriage to the Spanish señorita and asked permission of the king and queen for her hand in matrimony."

"I understand the king burst out laughing when my Lord Willoughby broached the subject with him. King Henry went round the court for the rest of the day with a broad smile saying 'Well – and about time too!' He gave them a fine wedding gift as well – a huge oaken four poster bed, by all accounts, and I believe she was granted some of her own lands in Lincolnshire as well!"

Strangely for her, Eleanor was rather enjoying her chance to gossip, she was normally such a quiet spoken woman. But she felt a sense of being 'out of school' whilst she was staying with Nicholas this Christmas. Anyway, her story hardly classed as tittle-tattle did it!? Well, maybe a little – but it was harmless for all that!

"Since Lady de Salinas does not have any family in this country and Lord Willoughby wanted so much to have the wedding in his fine chapel at Eresby Place he asked Mother Maria if we would look after the Lady in the time before her wedding, to make sure she was properly chaperoned and cared for. Mother Maria said *'yes'* straight away, of course. So when Lady de Salinas arrived, I was deputed to be her welcoming party, and to look after her day to day needs. For the life of me, I do not know why!"

It was, of course, perfectly clear to Nicholas and Eliza Jane what the answer was to the question *'Why?'* It was because Eleanor was such a personable woman and a delight to be with, not at all stuffy like some religious sisters they had met over the years.

Almost as if their thoughts had contributed to the next words of his cousin Eleanor, she continued...

"Well, when my Lady de Salinas arrived, I found her so personable and a delight to be with! We just got on so well from the first moment we met."

Nicholas and Eliza Jane just looked at each other and smiled.

"She had a couple of servants with her, who looked after all her bodily needs. So, when Lord Willoughby's mother was well enough (for she was old and very feeble by then) my Lady de Salinas visited Eresby Place for an odd day or so whilst the Lord Willoughby was still at court. But, all in all, she stayed with us at Legbourne for about two weeks before her wedding, so I got to know her very well during that time."

"I showed her round, of course – you know, where we keep the bees – and our little fish pond, which is stocked so well with nice trout for Fridays. And I showed her the herb garden, for our pharmaceutical herbs and the vegetable patch, for our greens."

Nicholas laughed, saying "Quite a little farmstead you have there! I even recall the milking cows that were there the first day you arrived so many years ago!"

"Goodness gracious, yes! That turned out to be my first job! Milking the cows; I had forgotten all about that! Anyway, I was telling you about our famous visitor, Lady de Salinas... her English language was excellent, but she had a delightful accent when she spoke. And some words came out very oddly, which made me laugh more than it should! But she didn't seem to mind – and she told lovely tales of when she and the queen were just little girls back in Spain, of riding on the backs of lions and other beasts. But they were made of stone – I was pleased to hear that! She told of the colourful spices they sold in the streets, and about the marvellous palace which was her home for much of her childhood, and about the fearsome woman she referred to as 'the Duenna'."

"She told stories of their travels to England and the rough seas they encountered. It all sounded very dramatic and enchanting to a poor, un-travelled, girl from Lincolnshire!"

"She even told a tale of when the old king – King Henry VII – God rest his soul, first set eyes on them when the Spanish party was travelling to London. He thought maybe the princess was really an ugly little girl. He apparently barged into the princess's bed chamber in the middle of the night and pulled her veil to one side expecting goodness-knows-what features he might find! And all he discovered were the pretty eyes and face of a frightened girl a long way from home – how they laughed about it afterwards. But she said it seemed strange at the time."

"She also told me many things I cannot tell you because it would betray a trust she placed in me. So, I feel very privileged to have met her and become almost a close friend in a short space of time. But the thing that stays with me so much about her visit was the fact that although she is a lady-in-waiting, and so highly placed in court and all, she was also just such a lovely ordinary person, and so easy to talk to."

At this point she had turned to Nicholas' two little boys who were still very young and so wide-eyed in wonder at these tales of people in high places and said very seriously to them...

"Always remember – you should, of course, be respectful to people who hold mighty office, and people who are of socially high rank, but under the skin they are just the same as you and I. They are just folk, just boys and girls and men and women, our brothers and sisters under the skin, as the bible teaches us!"

Nicholas was not sure whether the boys would remember this tale, for they were very young at the time, but, all these many years later, he certainly remembered the moral of his cousin's tale.

He also knew that, for some people, being high on the social scale sometimes gave them chances to get even higher and join 'the Great and the Good' as equals, even though they were perhaps *neither* great, nor good!

ભ ભ ભ ભ ભ

Following that Christmas visit of his cousin, he had kept an ear out for what happened to the Willoughby family, who lived not so far away from this Lincolnshire market town.

And there was much gossip to be had over the years! Lord Willoughby and his Spanish wife had had a daughter, whom they named Catherine in honour of Maria's long friendship with their Queen Catherine of Aragon.

On the death of her father, Lord Willoughby, in 1527 the girl, who was about ten or so then, was made a ward of the great Duke of Suffolk, who had, straight away, betrothed her to his son so the Willoughby lands would come to his offspring – but the boy died before they could marry.

249

Not so long afterwards, the Duke himself became widowed again, and did not want to waste his investment in the Willoughby girl and her Lincolnshire lands, so he married her himself.

What she thought about being married at such a tender age to a great barrel of a man who was the king's greatest friend and brother in law (Suffolk's wife, who died, was King Henry's sister Mary, of course) the likes of Nicholas would never know. Nevertheless they could, of course, sympathise with the girl's plight!

The girl's uncle, Sir Christopher Willoughby, thought he had some rights to the land which had belonged to his brother. Such was Suffolk's sway at court, however, that Sir Christopher could not get his hands on what should by rights have been his. Or so the local stories went.

Rumour had it that he even had some of his men help him to break in to his brother's manor at Eresby to get papers showing his rights. But the Duke brushed him off like an annoying fly.

CRCRCRCRCR

It was during this same visit that Eleanor had tried to explain to Nicholas the 'King's Great Matter'. It was really supposed to be a state secret but so many theologians had been consulted that it had inevitably become something very widely known in the population as a whole. Or, perhaps one should say that highly coloured versions of it were known to pretty well everybody who had ears to listen to the rumours!

Everyone Nicholas knew was most concerned for good Queen Catherine, and felt sympathy for her for Henry's rejection of her as his consort. Nicholas himself had a closer interest in the theological argument, too, because, like King Henry, he himself had married his brother's widow. And yet he did not feel he had sinned. Nor had he been prevented from having two fine sons, so, when Eleanor was there with them, and everyone else had retired to their beds, he had asked her advice for himself and the well-being of his soul.

It was late in the evening and the two boys had been asleep for ages having had an exciting day playing in the first snow of winter that year. Nicholas had helped them build a snowman and their still tiny fingers had got *very* cold and wet but they were *so* excited.

Eliza Jane had had a busy few days feeding a host of visiting relatives who had been with them for a time over the Christmas period, wanting to see the boys, of course, but also wanting to say hello to Cousin Eleanor. All the visitors had now gone, and everything had been cleared up with a little family teamwork. Eliza Jane was so tired, however, and had taken herself to bed early with a headache, something she so rarely suffered from!

Nicholas had raised the 'King's Great Matter' with his cousin because of the rumours that the king believed it was a sin to marry his brother's widow. And that this was therefore the reason God had denied them a son. These rumours made Nicholas fearful for his *own* soul in case Henry's view was correct, since he had also married the wife of his deceased brother.

ೞೞೞೞೞೞ

Nicholas had been apprenticed in London, and had been there three years, when he heard that the 'girl next door', Eliza Jane, who had bussed him on the cheek when he was nine years old, had chosen to say *'yes'* to his brother Robert's proposal of marriage.

Nicholas and Eliza Jane had always been really good friends as children, more like brother and sister, in fact, but apparently, whilst he was away in the big city, learning his trade, she had grown into a young woman. And his brother Robert was around to see it, but Nicholas was not! He felt something he could not define, perhaps a feeling somewhere between jealousy and regret, maybe both?

Nicholas had, of course, gone home for the wedding and wished the couple all the very best, as a good brother should. It was a lovely, happy, event.

So, it was such a shock, less than a year later, to get a heart-breaking letter from his mother that the latest round of the deadly Sleeping Sickness had taken both his father *and* his brother and "*...could he come home and help them all in the aftermath of such a terrible loss?*"

He wasn't even twenty years old yet, but he suddenly felt himself a burdened adult rather than a carefree lad, and it hit him hard. He had, of course, experienced death before but it was always at a distance, an elderly aunt, an uncle he didn't know very well, the younger brother of

251

a friend... and so on... but nobody so very close as his own father and his brother. And he had not even been at home to help as he should.

By the time the news of their deaths had reached him in London they had already been buried, and he felt so helpless, feeling he should have been there for everybody. Honestly, though, his mother had actually been relieved that he was somewhere else, in case the sickness might have taken him as well... or so he discovered when he eventually got home.

His apprentice master, Johann Kirkkgarde, had been totally sympathetic when he heard about the family misfortunes and simply told him to go home and do his family duty. He was not to worry about the Kirkkgarde business,

"...'Twould be no great hardship to get another apprentice! GO boy, go to your family, they need you!"

And Old Willum van Planck had been really good to 'lend' him a horse for as long as he needed it. "...just go – ride like the wind!"

He hardly stopped on the way – just a couple of short breaks for the sake of his horse, rather than himself! And when he arrived home he wasn't sure whether the hugs he had received were for him, or whether he was hugging others for their sakes. It was probably a bit of both if the truth be known!

His mother was distraught. His sister-in-law and childhood friend, Eliza Jane, was distraught. She was still a teenage bride, and now was a teenage widow. How cruel was that? So, tears that had flowed once for the *event* of their deaths, now flowed again for the *explanation of the event*, and for the grieving of all concerned.

On a practical level he was immediately able to take on the business side of things, and that provided the financial support for everyone – he supposed he would never get his master's papers since he had a doubly broken apprenticeship, but it didn't seem to matter. Everyone concerned treated him as the master of his father's business and there were no surprises for him in how to run it. Johann Kirkkgarde had given him all the support he had ever needed, technically, and so he knew how to make and mend shoes as well as anybody else in Louth (actually – probably better than most!) so he quickly became established as his father's son and heir.

His mother was so proud of her son's easy mastery of the business and was happy to have him home.

Eliza Jane and Robert had still been living with Ma and Pa Melton anyway, so although they had talked of establishing their own home soon, the young couple had not yet moved out. So Eliza Jane had, of course, stayed on as company for Ma Melton in *her* hour of need.

But it was not very long before the lifetime friendship she had had with Nicholas had blossomed into love ...a love which at first made Eliza Jane feel guilty. It was as if she may have been betraying Robert's love and kindness, but it quickly grew into something new, and rich, of its own. Well, in one sense it was new, but she realised that her feelings for Nicholas had always been strong. Yet, even that realisation had added to her feelings of guilt and confusion, since she began to wonder whether she had truly loved Robert for himself!

Nicholas was a bit slow to recognise it as love, however, and needed a little prompting from his mother, who saw what was happening. She was also able to reassure Eliza Jane when she confessed her confusion. She loved her daughter-in-law and knew she had been a good and loyal wife to her elder son, even if it was only a brief match, and was delighted, of course, to have her continue to be a close family member.

In the end it seemed so natural, and everyone was delighted, when they named the wedding day. They had a spring wedding, many flowers, many friends and much happiness. Both Nicholas and his bride shed a few tears and had some difficulty swallowing, and speaking without the voice cracking, at odd moments when the recognition that people who *should* be there were not there!!

But it was a shared sadness and an uncle at the wedding had made them all laugh when he spoke so seriously and said in sonorous tones...

"My view, as you all probably know, is that a trouble shared..." and he paused...

"... is still a bloody trouble!" and he slapped Nicholas hard on the shoulder and added with a twinkle...

"...but she's such a delightful trouble I shouldn't worry about it!" Giving the bride a smacking kiss on the cheek, he went off and helped himself to another tankard of ale!

Within a few months of the wedding Nicholas found himself to be an expectant father and the process of becoming the senior man of the family kept moving on apace. Three years later he was the proud father of two young boys.

It did not seem much longer after that, that the first rumours started going the rounds that King Henry was trying to justify the annulment of his marriage to the queen, something to do with his 'sin' of marrying his older brother's widow.

At first Nicholas paid scant attention, primarily because he had no interest in listening to gossip, secondly the gossip was about the king and queen, and bound to be salacious, and, thirdly, he was so busy making his father's business into his own, keeping his young family fed and clothed.

He was also so very busy with the Corpus Christi play cycle, which he had missed very much when he had been in London, and which had welcomed him back so easily because he was GOOD at playing and organising and producing. He had quickly become the leading light of the Louth players.

Also Thomas Kendall, who had only been the parish priest for a short time at that point, found that Nicholas' production skills were much better than his own. Father Kendall could be guaranteed to offend at least one important member of the church every year without fail. So, he would always spend the next three months having to be so diplomatic in order to recover the situation.

Nicholas clearly had superb powers of persuasion without upsetting people – so the priest happily passed over the responsibility for the entire programme of plays to his friend.

But eventually the rumours about the King's Great Matter began to sink in, and Nicholas was left feeling as though perhaps he himself had, perhaps, done wrong as well, though the parallel was inexact to say the least. For one thing they had two fine young sons to show for their marriage. The one issue that made Nicholas really worry that he may have sinned was when their third child, a little girl they called Rebecca, lived but two hours after her birth.

Although he kept his worries largely to himself for the sake of supporting Eliza Jane in her obvious distress, in his quiet moments during the day he kept questioning himself. He would say special prayers for their souls when he went to church and sometimes even when he was riding around the town delivering new or mended shoes to his customers.

Thus, Cousin Eleanor's visit provided an opportunity for him to share his worries with someone who might be expected to have a sound religiously based view of the matter. So, in the quiet of that evening when his sons had gone to bed exhausted and his wife had gone to bed with a headache, he found a way to introduce the topic of the King's Great Matter to the discussion he was having with Eleanor.

Unsurprisingly, she quickly picked up on the fact that Nicholas was equally concerned for himself as for the king.

"So, tell me," he said, "why does the king think it may be a sin for a man to marry the widow of his brother?"

He tried to make the question sound light but Eleanor heard the worry in his voice and considered her words carefully. She watched his eyes carefully as she spoke...

"Well, from what I hear there are two theories about it and many different opinions on each theory. The first is that he has grown tired of being married to a woman several years older than himself, worn out by unsuccessful childbearing, and would like to change her for a younger lady!"

Nicholas smiled.

"Yes, I have heard that theory too, but I am sure that is just idle chatter, of course!"

His smile belied the words, his tongue firmly in his cheek, but he still seemed concerned in case that theory was *not* correct. Eleanor continued...

"The second and more substantial theory is that the bible specifically indicates that it is sinful to marry your brother's widow. I use the word 'indicates' deliberately because as far as I know from reading the bible every day for well over eighteen years, I have never read a verse which *states* such a thing categorically."

"I am sure there are theologians much more versed than I am in the scriptures, and I know from reports that King Henry himself was expecting to go into the church, as a priest, before his brother Arthur died and he became heir to the throne. So I understand he is enthusiastic in his biblical knowledge."

Nicholas pointed out that the rumours he had heard were that the king had consulted many universities in his quest to get the matter sorted out once and for all.

"Yes, indeed, I heard the same, but it seems to turn on just a few words here and there. And there are conflicting sets of words in the bible which give comfort to either view. The verse that can be interpreted to agree with the view King Henry believes, is short. It is from Leviticus, chapter twenty verse twenty-one... I know it now by heart!"

"If a man shall take his brother's wife, it is an unclean thing ...they shall be childless."

"My own thinking on this verse, however, is that it means when the brothers are still alive, so is referring to adultery. But more learned minds than mine decided otherwise!"

"On the contrary side there is a verse, which seems to me, anyway, almost a certain instruction. It says directly that it is the *duty* of a brother, in the unfortunate circumstances where his brother dies, or is killed, that he should do everything he can to provide, and care for, his sister-in-law."

"This does not seem to preclude taking his brother's wife as his own from that point on, as indeed you did after Robert died, with Eliza Jane. And I am sure you are both happy and have a beautiful family. Now, that verse comes from...ermm... *Deuteronomy*, I think, chapter twenty-five and says something like...

When brethren dwell together, and one of them dieth without children, the wife of the deceased shall not marry to another: but his brother shall take her, and raise up seed for his brother...

"So, personally, I think you have biblical testimony on your side, cousin!"

Eleanor reached out her hand and rested it with loving concern on her cousin's hand.

"And I know you have no reason to want to put your lovely wife aside – as our master the king perhaps desired, when he was debating the issue!"

"No, no, no, indeed I do not!" the words exploded from his lips, rather shocked at the thought his cousin voiced!

"And, so, I think the latter verse is the one you should read when you can, and include in your prayers. It seems to me that you have done all any responsible man can. We have one of the new Tyndale English bibles at the priory – I will copy the verses out for you when I get back after this little enforced break."

"You love Eliza Jane, and your children, I know. And the sad death of your daughter Rebecca so soon after entering this world is a blessing on the child, that she has been taken into God's arms as an Angel."

Cousin Eleanor was quietly speaking in her 'official' capacity as Sister Beatrice now, her hand still covering Nicholas' left hand. Nicholas looked quite far away and his eyes were glistening. They both stayed unmoving for a little while as the flickering flames from the burning logs on the fire cast shadows around them.

Suddenly Nicholas took a deeper breath and his eyes became focussed within the room again and within the present time. He shook his head a little, almost as if shaking sleep from his eyes. Eleanor's hand was still covering his and he moved his right hand on top of hers, looked her in the eye and squeezed her fingers to say "thank you". Then his lips moved as well, and he actually said...

"Thank you, cousin. You have set my mind at rest and I shall do as you say and read the verses you talked of. I somehow thought I should not really worry myself... but these things seem bigger and more important when you think about them in the dark hours of the early morning than they do in the daylight. I shall simply get on with life to my best ability and be thankful for the health of my sons."

ରେ ରେ ରେ ରେ ରେ

As the waggon bumped along the London cobbles, these many years later, taking him to meet his maker, Nicholas reflected that he had tried very hard to do as he had indicated to Eleanor all those years ago. And for the most part he believed that he had succeeded.

The 'prompt' that had taken his thoughts along this road for these moments had been his consideration of the way 'good Queen Catherine' had been brought low by the choices, and actions, of her husband the king. For all her social position, those last few years of her life must have been a miserable existence for her.

And, of course, it was only just over a year since Catherine had died, and, shortly afterwards, Henry's second wife, 'the Bullen girl', Anne, had had her head chopped off! How fortunes changed, sometimes up, and sometimes down.

And so, Nicholas reflected on *his* downward change of fortune, which had deposited him in this old straw waggon.

ଔଔଔଔଔ

Monday night Tuesday morning
2ⁿᵈ & 3ʳᵈ October 1536

☞ The person who picked up on the fidgeting in the meeting that Monday evening had, perhaps, the quietest voice in the room but such clarity that no-one missed what she said when she picked her moment.

"Cousin Nicholas – 'tis perhaps getting to that time when some of our friends must leave. They have far to travel and then must rouse others and talk to them if our plans shall become actions on the morrow." Sister Beatrice had a bell-like timbre to her voice, both pleasing to the ear and, yet, insistent at the same time.

"You are right as always, cousin Eleanor, and more observant than most of us who would continue talking until late." He paused...

"Gentlemen all..." his voice took on an authoritative quality which he used sparingly, but always effectively, in meetings...

"Go to your tasks with a will, and we shall meet at Orford tomorrow in great numbers and with determination of spirit in our breast for our communities' sake. Let us all be heroes of the common wealth, and turn our attention to saving our heritage for future generations to marvel at."

The black robed priests were first to stir themselves. The resulting flurry of black forms, rustled like a storm of corvidae bestirring themselves in a fierce wind, swirling and dispersing to various points of the compass. Some, generally those with furthest to travel, were horsed and their mounts awaited them nearby.

Some, indeed, had arrived that morning in a variety of harness, mostly consisting of armoured breast plates, and a few with upper arm protection. Perhaps they had a sword slung round their waists, as if for a muster. Honestly, Nicholas found this slightly disconcerting, for priests to be so forward in preparation for conflict.

The others, those without horses, took to their tracks in twos and threes, destined to split later into single 'messenger-crows', at junctions marked perhaps by a single stile or a rutted road fork known to locals only.

The monk, Morland, walked with a pair of priests, who were headed further than him, but in his direction. One of his companions took the opportunity to sound him out on an idea he had formed – but had not yet spoken about – in the meeting as a whole.

"William, I was too hesitant to speak about this earlier, because it seems the main emphasis for the common people of Louth was, justifiably I suppose, elsewhere. They want to protect their treasure from the ravages of a corrupt chancellor, who seems bent on self-enrichment at the expense of the body of the church."

Fortunately, they were well away from the town, and there was no-one to overhear him other than his two walking companions; otherwise his words would be self-evidently dangerous, talking openly of a *"corrupt chancellor"*! He continued...

"But my main concern is the ultimate truth of the church's teachings. They seem more at risk from heretic reformers than does even the treasure of the church loft. I know we are at one on this issue, and I want to make sure this is not overlooked as we go forward tomorrow."

"I am clear in what I think, of course, but my brain does not always instruct my lips to mouth the correct words. And I get twisted up when trying to explain my thoughts to other people in public. But you... I have always admired how you find the right words when you are dealing with complicated theological truths."

Morland merely allowed his lips to twitch into a modest smile of acceptance of this 'truth'. He always warned others about accepting out-and-out flattery, but clearly failed to recognise it when directed at him! His colleague kept talking...

"What I am trying to ask, is whether you would accept our nomination as one of the main spokesmen of religion when we gather tomorrow. I know we did not make any decisions about this tonight when it came up for discussion in the meeting. I understand this was because some of the probable spokesmen were not present, and the decision was put off until morning, so all was clear and everyone was present to be asked to their faces."

"But I noticed your name was not mentioned when the idea of

religious spokesmen was raised, and I would like to make sure you would be willing to have your name added to the list of religious spokesmen of the pilgrimage we are about to undertake?"

Morland was clearly pleased.

"Thank you for such confidence," he said, "I am indeed touched by it."

"I think I blotted my copy book with the Louth men this morning when I took the side of Brother Frankish when he felt so imperiled. So I am not surprised my name did not arise earlier in this context; but if you want to put my name forward, of course..."

He left the sentence modestly unfinished, accompanied by a vague hand gesture, knowing it would be acted upon.

"In that case William, we will pause briefly when we reach your cottage, and I will write a note to this effect to young Father Richardson who has recently joined Vicar Kendall as an assistant at Saint James in Louth."

"He only qualified recently, but he's a cousin of mine! And if the subject is raised in Louth tomorrow before we assemble in Orford, there will be someone to put your name forward. Otherwise, if it is not settled before we all meet in Orford, I will ensure the job is done there, so it need not embarrass you to have to put forward your own name!"

Their other companion nodded his enthusiastic assent to this idea, and the deal was sealed as they arrived at Morland's cottage. The note was duly written. And Morland took himself to bed, with a view to getting up early and hand-delivering the note to young Richardson, who had lodgings near the church.

His brother-in-the-cloth had solved an issue which might otherwise have been mildly embarrassing to him. It had been puzzling him how to achieve this end. His skin was quite thick, however, and no doubt he would have been embarrassed for a *very short time only* if he had had to put his own name in the hat. He smiled inwardly at this thought as he drifted off to sleep.

છ છ છ છ છ છ

Tuesday morning...

Monk Morland was not first to waken next morning. By the time he was stirring in his cottage just outside Louth, all the men who had spent the night again in the church in Louth were awake. Albeit that not all of them *felt* awake yet. It was still dark as they went about their ablutions in a water butt that had been brought into the vestry for the purpose, the room now lit by a few of the church candles.

Richard Nethercotts and John Wilson were the two leading bell ringers for Saint James' Church, and they were the most wide awake of those present. It had been decided last night that the common bell would be sounded at daybreak to fetch out everyone in the town. And these two had been darned sure no-one else would get their hands on *their* bell-ropes, *thank you very much*!

It was always the same if someone other than these two were allowed to ring the bells. There was always something wrong in the bell-tower afterwards. The ropes were "...not stowed and hung properly..." or "...things were left untidily on the floor..." Needless to say, they were very territorial about their space in the bell tower.

Neither would ever admit such a thing however, although each might hint, if pressed, that the *other* one of the two may, sometimes, seem to be a *little precious* about things in the tower. Mostly they would defend each other's rights, with respect to the church bells, to the death, and woe-betide anyone interfering.

All they were waiting for now was a word from their captain, Captain Cobbler, to set the bells ringing and fetch all their neighbours from their beds.

CRCRCRCRCRCR

Meanwhile...

Even the men in Louth Church were not first awake and stirring in the County of Lincolnshire, on today's business. Many miles away, Lord Burgh had left word with his servants that he was to be awoken in good time this Tuesday morning...

"...and, indeed, all the other gentlemen here present should be awakened in timely fashion too, for we have much to get on with in the morning"

Bugh's manner was somewhat imperious, it should be said, for he was a man of substance in the county. Indeed, he was one of the *chief* men in the county, and so was used to being obeyed! Along with the 'other gentlemen' he referred to, he was staying with Sir Robert Tyrwhitt in that gentleman's fine new house in Kettleby near Brigg. Thomas Portington and Thomas Dalyson were there, too, and a couple of other lesser gentlemen, who were involved in setting and collecting the subsidy in the north of the county. All had at least one servant along with them; Dalyson two; Portington three; and Lord Burgh himself had four. The four included his bailiff, who was very good with numbers – and even better at explaining them to Lord Burgh – who was, frankly, hopeless if left to himself with a sheet of numbers.

All in all, the household was very busy at daybreak, with servants dashing in every direction, carrying water, both cold and hot, carrying slops and worse, and carrying platters of cold meats and fresh bread and jugs of ale. It was no small feat that all the right things ended in all the right places, for all the servants were well trained and practised.

Actually, some of the smells from the slops and worse did end up attaching themselves to the servants with the platters of meat and ale but no-one was ignoble enough to point this out – or maybe they just didn't notice – it was very early after all!

૭૩૭૩૭૩૭૩૭૩

Meanwhile...

By the time the bells were rousing the folk in Louth, Lord Hussey in Sleaford had been awake for hours, and was pacing about in the large dining room in his house on the edge of town. He was muttering to himself, a habit that had got worse over the years and now, well into the seventh decade of his life, it was a habit he was never going to break.

The former queen, Catherine of Aragon, had tolerated his habit of muttering and mumbling. To her, of course, he had been a sympathetic and well organised advisor, as master of her household when she was isolated in the damp and unhealthy house at Buckden in her latter years – '*Oh, my Lord, was that only two years ago?*'. Thus, his muttering would sometimes help her to sort her own thoughts out, having been so cruelly and wantonly abandoned by her husband the king. Also, Hussey used to make a mental effort to try hard not to do it *too much* when he was in her presence. So, perhaps it was not *too difficult* for her to tolerate.

It was a habit, however, that irritated his wife enormously, which is why he was in the dining room doing it at this early hour, rather than in the bedroom. Sometimes the muttering was about current issues, such as the two letters he had received late the evening before. One was from the young Lord Clinton, of the village of South Kyme – most recent husband of the king's cast-off lover, Bessie Blount. And one was from the bishop's administrator, John Heneage, who had given him quite a long account of his unusual day in Louth.

"...silly young man..." – referring to Clinton.

"...hmmm, extraordinary..." – referring to Heneage.

Sometimes the muttering was about the indignity the queen had suffered at the king's hands. And sometimes the muttering was about the contacts he had had with the Imperial Ambassador Chapuys. He was always full of intrigue, and full of little hints that he had connections abroad which could provide an army who would come and help overthrow the heretic King of England if the people were willing to rise against him.

"...hmm...so unfair to the poor dear lady...."

"...never could believe a word he said...."

These hints which Chapuys made were never enough to get him into trouble if they were reported directly to the king or his ministers. So ambiguous, they could easily be denied. To a sympathetic ear like Hussey's, however, who had been so bitter at the appalling treatment of his queen, 'God rest her soul', the hints were magnified. They took on the possibility of credibility, despite the fact that they came from such a schemer as Ambassador Chapuys.

"...on the other hand...if they were only true...this might be the ideal time for a wider action..."

"...mm, Ann Boleyn recently dead... Princess Mary... (no, mustn't call her princess – Ha! ...wife was put in tower for saying that! ...silly woman)..."

"...silly fellow yourself!... only get into trouble... keep out of it... hmmmph... too dangerous..."

"...got to be seen to take the king's side here..."

And so Lord Hussey's muttering went on, mostly unintelligible, unless one could read the rest of each sentence in his mind! The trouble was, he was never anything other than a ditherer, and the dithering, like the muttering, was getting worse with age.

Lord Clinton's message, although it was (or, perhaps, **because** it was?) much shorter than Heneage's, was the more worrying of the two.

Scrawled very quickly, sealed and given hastily to a trusted servant to deliver to Lord Hussey, Lincolnshire's third most senior aristocrat (after the Duke of Suffolk and Lord Burgh), Clinton had intimated that Louth was really "...up in arms, so dangerous, and I cannot get my village to raise against the rebellion. I think they would rather take the Rebels' part!... what should I do?"

As the daylight started to brighten through the excellent glass windows of his new, magnificent, house in Sleaford, the dithering, muttering Lord Hussey carried on muttering and dithering.

ଔଔଔଔଔଔ

Meanwhile...

Similar rumours of armed rebellion had reached Horncastle by mid-evening on the Monday and were being spread by less dithering mouths. In fact, several related mouths. The Leach brothers, and their cousins, had been party to several discussions during the summer months as members of Devotio Moderna, about possible action in the autumn, to protest against the closures of the county's many religious houses. They had always said any action taken should be more forceful than other voices were calling for. So, when William was telling the story of what had happened in Louth during the day, he was quite happy to embellish the details for greater effect amongst his listeners.

William was a very successful sheep farmer amid the rolling hills of his beloved Lincolnshire Wolds and was built rather like the Wolds himself. He was a stocky, rounded man with big farmer's hands, not unaccustomed to carrying a full grown sheep on his shoulders when need arose. And he expected those around him to match his own enthusiasms and capacities (which few could!)

He was ruddy-faced, from the biting winds that sometimes cut across the hilltops and had a voice like a stag at bay. The problem with that was that he only had one volume, indoors or out, which could be intimidating, or simply annoying, to those around him. But when the man was paying you regular wages it was probably best not to show your impatience. Certainly, that had been the case for old Tom Dixon and a good few other local labourers, whom he had instructed to come and listen to what he had to tell about his day in Louth.

It was a mixture of truth and exaggeration but it had had the effect intended. They were still talking about it this Tuesday morning, as they made their way towards the church, billhooks in their hands. The long curved blades had been well sharpened to tackle the thorn hedges around William Leach's sheep enclosures and one or two of them wondered if the blades might draw blood before the hedges got trimmed?

"Mester Leach was in a lather about the silver chalices being took from Louth Church yes'day, warn't he Tom. I nivver seed him like that afore!"....said one of them to Tom Dixon, then he thought again... "except that time we chopped the wrong hedgerow down in Deep Meadow for 'un!"

"...and the time he caught us pissin' in his fish lake after that church ale t'other year!" chimed in a different voice, to laughter all round.

For all the turmoil and talk of armed rebellion, however, most of the men present regarded this outing as a day out from the daily toil of laboring. It was a day to be enjoyed rather than troubled over. Perhaps about half the group nearing the church had been present with Tom Dixon the previous evening, so it was for the benefit of those others that Tom now said,

"'Twas as much Mester William's cousin, Parson Robert Leach, as was in a lather! He don't quite match William's booming voice but he were just as angry last night as his cousin!"

"They were both of a mind that the commissioners would be here in Horncastle today to take our church treasures, like they did in Louth yes'day. He also told us that they Louth rebels, led by a fearsome warrior they call Captain Cobbler, (who's nearly seven foot tall, so they say!) had beat up them two scoundrels Bellow and Willisent real good and proper. And then had put 'em in the town stocks and oiled and tarred them!"

Not only did he mangle the name of one of the Legbourne commissioners but clearly confused the medium, wiry frame of Nicholas, with the sturdy frame of Great James! But it all added to the steam of the story, which got wilder at each telling.

"Parson Robert also telled of a bunch of priests in full battle array, you know, full armour, broad swords and battle axes a'spoiling for a fight, so whether we'll see 'im in 'is battle regalia I daresent say."

Clearly they had all got a good mental picture of the part-time priest of Belchford in full harness alongside his cousins William Leach, Nicholas Leach (also a religious man, as sub-deacon of Oxford) and Parson Robert's namesake-cousin Robert Leach. They were all hefty men – none quite as rotund as William, but a sight to be seen on the muster field as they rode along together. They always got a cheer in the field when it was muster time. If the sun was shining their armour glinted in the sunlight, bright as a beacon.

The group surrounding Tom Dixon turned a corner to bring the church in sight and there were the three Leach brothers, and cousin, Parson Robert, astride their horses. The early October sunshine was breaking through the clouds, reflected boldly from well-polished armour, bringing a goodly cheer from the men they often employed.

ଓଓଓଓଓଓ

By the time the October sunshine was glinting on the Leaches' armour in Horncastle, Captain Cobbler's bright Coat of Motley was attracting similar cheers from the gathering crowd in Louth, as he stepped out from the shadow of the church's great West doorway and clambered onto a low stone pillar to address the milling crowd.

One of the group of minor Louth gentry who had been present in the meeting the previous evening, John Taylor, (his name told of his trade but he always liked to tell his customers that he was a 'man of the cloth', always accompanying his time-worn humour with a self-deprecating chuckle), had vacated that same pillar just moments before. He had told the assembled townsfolk the outlines of what had happened in the meeting, to bring everyone up to date.

Nicholas held up his right hand to quieten the crowd and started speaking.

"As you all now know, we must move forward or lose all the momentum of our actions." His voice was heavy with gravitas and responsibility, but fresh and buoyant at the same time and he was using his full powers of thespian projection.

"Now is not the time to fall back by the wayside. We have brought many leading men into the fold in our support – most of them quite willingly!" Half-smiling at the understatement on delivering this last comment he knew that his audience would know of the pressure brought to bear on those who had wavered.

In fact, the rumours surpassed the truth as to how they had all been dealt with for the most part. But persuasion had been used and, perhaps unfortunately at times, the threat of violence lay not far under the surface!

"Now, we must go and persuade several more of the leading men of the county to come in with us and I believe we can then look forward to a successful outcome to this action."

"It is clear that most of these leading men are coming into our neighbourhood quite voluntarily today so we have decided to go and meet them and talk them into supporting us. Only, this time, we are going, together, as a host to Caistor. Our 'persuasion' will be much stronger if we are all together in this task and accoutered as if we may have to act by force."

"The paradox is that this show will make the *actual* use of force unnecessary! Such is our power of persuasion when acting in concert!!" He was speaking partly to convince himself as much as anything!

"What we need, therefore, is for you to go back to your homes and make sure you are set up as for a full muster. Bring weapons if you have them. Bring billhooks and sickles if you don't. Bring armour if you have it, with stout leather jerkins or similar if you don't. But – above all – act with a will – AND I KNOW YOU HAVE THAT APLENTY!!!"

A rousing cheer rang out in the hazy morning sun. Nicholas raised his hands to quieten the crowd.

"So, go now and prepare, bring food and water as well as arms. I know we have spoken before everyone is yet here from the outermost reaches of Louth but I rely on you to tell your neighbours what is afoot so we can get on our way sooner rather than later!! Hurry, we shall ring the bells again in half an hour at most and we need to be on our way as soon after that as we can."

Some people started to speak to each other, and one or two looked as though they might ask questions so Nicholas pre-empted further delay by his final words.

"Now is a time of action gentlemen one and all. Speak to each other as you move. Go! Be ready by the ringing of the next bell, and let us succeed in our task of protecting the common treasures of our town. Go now, brook no delay!" With this appeal ringing in their ears the good men of Louth hurried homewards to prepare for action and movement! With a will!

ଓଓଓଓଓଓ

Because it was a fine autumn morning men started reappearing around the church even before the bell was rung again. Rumours had circulated about what was to happen so most folk were ready anyway

269

– and excited, mostly, by the new sense of action. Better than waiting for their treasure to be confiscated.

Groups started to appear in Louth from nearby villages, too, whose path to Orford would take them through the town anyway. John and Pat Baker appeared on a horse-drawn dray, piled with baskets and wooden boxes, all laden with foodstuffs. John hailed Nicholas from the road and spoke over the heads of all the folk milling about between them. Nicholas was about ready to have the bell rung again, but paused to hear John's shouted comment...

"We are going to go off now, and will probably be at the Furrehill field at Orford before most of you are halfway there. I want to make sure we get set up on that flat patch near the entrance before it gets full of people with nothing better to do than sit around. My cousin Bill and brother Jeb will be coming through in a couple of minutes with a cart full of ale barrels. Make sure this lot let them through won't you! See you later."

He didn't wait for a reply, so Nicholas just smiled and waved them off and the dray took the little hill down to the bridge over the River Lud somewhat precariously. It was not long, however, before he was up and away on the other side of the river and round the bend, and out of sight amongst the trees.

John Taylor was the next person to want Nicholas' attention, and had a suggestion to make...

"It is getting crowded around the church now. It might be an idea to get the first groups off and away. Then I can get them in some sort of order when we get to Orford, and you can bring the rest as soon as they get here after the bell."

Nicholas was just in the process of nodding to Richard Nethercotts and John Wilson to ring the bells again so he turned back to John Taylor and carried on nodding, raising his voice as the bells started pealing...

"I think you are right, we need to clear this area so it can be filled again with the later arrivals. We should be ready to follow you in about ten minutes, all being well, and I will leave someone to bring along any stragglers later! See you there! I shall get mounted up and follow on soon."

John Taylor wheeled his own mount and spoke to the many people already assembled, projecting his voice as his actor mentor Nicholas had shown him for the plays...

"We are set on a task of great significance, this day, my friends. There are many of us here already as is plain to all present", he smiled a little as he realized that his rhetoric was a little obvious!

"All of you here gathered should follow me to the muster at Orford now and Captain Cobbler will come behind us with the main body of Louth people shortly hereafter. Do not straggle and try to keep in lines of four along the road, as we have been instructed in our marching drills. The gentlemen here and mounted will come with me in the vanguard and the walking host will follow us with the priests who are mounted bringing up the rear; ...*onward my friends!*"

At which moving behest, he wheeled his mount again with as much drama as he could within a tight space and headed off down the slope towards the bridge.

Hardly had the last mounted priests left the vicinity of the church, when the space began to fill again rapidly with people responding to the call of the bells. Some of the first arrivals thought they had missed the main event and started to chase after the rearguard of priests until called back by Great James, who again today was acting as Captain Cobbler's adjutant and bodyguard. When they realised that they had to await the next call to duty they crowded nearer the church doors to anticipate instructions.

Nicholas saw that his servant, Joshua, had brought along his horse, and so he decided to speak next from the saddle. Well enough off to have two servants (but not moneyed enough to be invited to be a churchwarden!) he was an excellent horseman. Though his horse would not have won him any prizes in one of the chivalric jousting tournaments so beloved by King Henry himself (for one thing she was not a stallion!) she had a delightful temperament. She was also very responsive to his instructions, often understanding by intuition what he was about to ask of her, too!

She was a fine mare, and tall – taller than Nicholas himself at her withers – and strong, too. Black as a winter's night, she had a white star on her forehead and seemed proud this morning to be at the centre of attention, when Nicholas started to address the gathering throng. She held her head high and snickered a little as if to warn folk that her rider, their Captain, was about to say something important!

With his bright Coat of Motley glistening a little in the morning sunshine (*he had deliberately moved out of the church shadow to ensure this very effect, his theatrical mind always working to create the most positive visual image!*) Nicholas raised himself a little in his stirrups to gain posture and ensure a good supply of air to his lungs.

"Good morrow, fellow citizens of Louth. You all know what we are about this fine morning! We are here to prevent a wrong being committed against the interests of the wealth of our commons here in our excellent town. We are protecting the treasures of this great Church of Saint James. We shall do this by 'bringing-in' the main gentlemen of the county to speak on our behalf to the king and his counsellors. We are to muster at Orford which all of you know from regular area musters and we shall march from there to Caistor, where the commission is to meet today, so I hope you are all well-shod!"

Shouts of "*Aye Captain Cobbler!*" rang out around the church and laughter filled the air.

"Once we are gone from here the church doors will be securely locked and the church guarded from within, as before. Let us go forward with a will, therefore, and be proud of our town and its wealth of fellowship and goodwill as we pursue our goals today."

He applied the lightest pressure with his heels and with his calves and hands and the great horse beneath him snickered again, tossed her head with pride, wheeled elegantly and led the column down to the bridge, over and away. Nicholas rode alongside Thomas Kendall, the vicar of Saint James who had held aloft one of the silver headed wooden crooks used for minor celebrations as a talisman of the march they were making this morning.

It was a symbol of the church and had raised a cheer as he wielded it above his head – almost as if it were a broadsword he would use in battle. It seemed everyone was in good spirits as the sun shone on their outing.

CRCRCRCRCR

Some of the gentlemen were in almost full harness with shining breast plates catching the sun's rays and an array of weapons in their hands, although none wore helmets. It was as if they wanted to be seen to be playing their role but at the same time not wanting to provoke anger when they met their peers later. So by not wearing helmets, they indicated they did not really expect violence.

Most of the ordinary menfolk of Louth were wearing their thick leather jerkins which stood in for the breastplates of the gentry. They might protect their wearers against all but a well-flighted arrow, or a direct strike from the point of a sword. And they were carrying a variety of sharp, or blunt, tools which would inflict damage to a head or an arm which was unlucky enough to be in the way of a strike from such a weapon. Billhooks or sickles were the main weapons of choice, though some of the bigger men relied on weight, rather than sharpness, to inflict harm, and were carrying very stout sticks or wooden clubs.

In the midst of the column, there was also a group of archers with sturdy long bows, which they had carved for themselves or which had been handed down in families of strong armed menfolk. It was not everyone who could successfully fire an arrow from one of these weapons and part of the reason for Nicholas' efforts with his horsemanship over the years was to make up for the fact that he had never become an expert using a longbow.

Loosely attached to the group of archers with their long bows were even a few men who wielded ancient foreign crossbows. These were probably confiscated by them, or their forebears, from mercenaries whom they had encountered as soldiers in days past with Henry's French campaigns, more than fifteen years previously. They were generally quite expert at using these weapons and liked to show off at musters by displaying their prowess using these strange and, to the English eye, quite alien bows.

One of the local blacksmiths, George Smith – with a name to match his profession – was the proud owner of a crossbow and had helped his little group of colleagues by fashioning replacement tips for their supply of bolts. They liked to find and reuse the small but deadly bolts as often as possible but inevitably they would lose a few every year in the long grass when one missed its target and disappeared beyond the straw filled dummies which served as 'the enemy' in their practices.

Even when they knew the direction a missed bolt took, the little projectiles could disappear in even the shortest of grass, slithering into the tangle of undergrowth. So George had to make a few new bolts each year. And George's ducks, which he kept because he so much liked a duck egg for breakfast, lost a few feathers each year as raw material for new flights for the crossbow bolts!

Just behind the archers and crossbow experts, a small group of former brethren of Louth Park Abbey who still lived locally, kept company with Monk Morland, who was trying to avoid showing his discomfort at walking with the host. It was a real discomfort, too, caused by an old injury to his knees, the foolishness of youth really. It happened when he was still a novice at the abbey, and he had been visiting the family of his older brother who farmed nearby, for a weekend off from his studies.

He had been playing the fool to entertain his young nieces whilst their mother was preparing Saturday lunch in the huge farm kitchen. He had jumped off a low stone wall, to hide from them behind a dense yew bush, intending to jump out and startle his nieces. But he misjudged the jump, heard a crunch, and felt something tearing in his knees, as they collapsed beneath him. The girls discovered him rolling around on the grass and went to jump on him thinking he was still playing, but quickly ran for help when he yelped in further pain and asked them, sharply, to fetch their father!

He had had to sleep on a wooden settle, downstairs, for two nights and was hobbling around for a couple of weeks, gradually able to resume his novice activities at the abbey. Subsequently, praying on his knees for any length of time had always been a trial which he bore, staunchly, as part of his service to his church.

For the most part, however, he had not been too troubled by his knees until he began to get grey hairs too. Alongside the other signs of ageing, he sometimes found his knees were aching rather more these days. He was hoping, sincerely, that his request to the prioress at Orford had reached her last evening, and that there would be a mount awaiting him after the walk. At the same time he was trying not to show his discomfort to his brethren, since even the walk from his cottage into town had started his knees aching on this bright but cool autumn day. Frankly, it did not help that he was carrying the additional weight of a breastplate, and arm protectors, as well as a sword. They would look fine, and be no bother when he was on horseback but, just at the moment...

"You know, brothers, that we have been talking about just this sort of action all summer long, since the first religious houses were dissolved from under our feet, so we must take advantage of the moment now it has arrived. The fact that it came about as a result of an event only indirectly connected with the dissolution process makes our hand stronger with the authorities. It cannot be seen simply as a matter of self-interest by "corrupted" brethren as it might have been portrayed if we had made the first moves."

He did not feel quite as argumentative as he sounded but the discussion was, at least, taking his mind away from his aching knees!

"But, Brother Morland," the voice was that of young Father Richardson, cousin of Morland's walking companion the night before, "how is it going to make a difference?" He sounded as though he needed convincing that he was doing the right thing, for himself and for his mother church.

"Well, Father..." the honorific would boost the young man's self-confidence, at least, Morland thought, as he considered his next words.

"...it seems to me that in a protest such as this, there will be room for quite a lot of demands to be put forward as pleas by the host, of which we naturally form a significant part. I do not think all of them will be granted, of course, but if we carefully lay out the main arguments and put the strongest arguments at the top of the list, I feel sure there will be concessions by the Privy Council and the Vicar-General."

"They will let us have some points, and we will let drop some of our weaker points, and so it goes, in order to keep face on both sides."

He was not entirely sure he believed his own words, so he was equally unsure as to the effect upon his listeners. Autocratic rulers, such as their bold King Henry VIII, never seemed to worry too much about losing face, as long as they lost no power!

But if he was going to be one of the religious voices at the head of this popular march for justice, he needed to practise the arguments he would make later but on sympathetic ears in the first place. The decision about who the spokesmen would be was to be taken at Orford after all, when all possible spokesmen would be present to say "Yea" to the task proffered to them. So he followed through on his words.

"The problem is that the advice the king has been given by his religious counsellors has been false and that way for a long time. We cannot revisit the advice he got about his 'Great Matter' – after all his wife the Queen Catherine died this year and his replacement queen, Ann Boleyn, had her head chopped off recently too. But we can suggest that the people who gave him this advice were working for the Devil, and were therefore heretics who should be burned at the stake!"

'*Hmm*', he thought to himself, '*that sounded more convincing!*'

It had, in fact, caused an intake of breath by some of his colleagues on the march for its audaciousness. They were not used to hearing such things said loudly in public!

"As you all know there are several heretic bishops in this regard, probably five we could name, including the Bishop of Lincoln, Bishop Longland. He was certainly one of those closest to the king, whose advice about the divorce brought us to this sorry state, along with the Bishops of Rochester, Ely, Worcester and Dublin."

Morland was now getting into his stride...

"I am sure we should also make it clear that we believe the current Vicar-General, Thomas Cromwell, as a man *not* trained in theology, is an unfit person to be in the post he occupies, advising the king about whether to close religious houses and ruling the roost on other contentious matters of holy law. In this respect we will have the common people supporting this view because they do not want any more monasteries closed. Indeed, there are many religious houses which could re-open quite easily."

"Sadly too, however, there are several houses which have been so pillaged by the greedy men of power in this county and in Yorkshire, in particular, that the only way they could support a religious fraternity again would be if they were rebuilt and refinanced. Given the feelings running hot amongst many of the gentry at the moment I cannot see this happening. So – we have to settle for what is possible. But that doesn't mean we have to *ask* only for what is possible!!"

With that thought rattling around several overheated brains, causing some to smile a little, this group of plotting priests walked on towards their appointed muster meeting place in a raised state of excitement, as others around them had other conversations on the go.

Just fifty yards in front of them was a group of ploughmen discussing the state of the soil in the fields they were passing after the heavy rain there had been at the end of the week before.

"Aye, 'tain't too bad up 'ere – that's 'cos we're atop this hill – but look down the bottom of the field there, watter is a'laying heavy in the dips. I can warrant our field is going to be too wet to plough for another week at least – and that's if it stays dry..." he looked up into an almost cloud-free sky at this moment but with the eye of a countryman for changes in the weather portending.

Just at that moment John and Ma Baker were already turning their waggon into the bottom of Furrehill field just beyond Orford brook. The ground was a little soft from the recent rains, but there wasn't "... *watter a'laying heavy in the dips...*" So they managed to manoeuvre the waggon into place not far from the entrance way into the field. There, they found several covered stalls already set up with refreshments of various kinds. The Sisters of Orford Priory had been busy, having been forewarned of the gathering by Guy Kyme's visit the evening before.

Many of the sisters must have been up virtually all night in the priory kitchens baking bread and preparing soup – mostly thin and watery vegetable soup in view of the large numbers they must have been warned to prepare for! As well as the soup, though, there was potted meat paste and several large wooden tubs of dripping, delicious spread on fresh bread with a cup of hot soup in your hand to wash it down. Just what foot-weary men-of-war needed to set them up for the next few miles of their journey!

The sisters had agreed to provide the soup, and bread, and dripping, and meat paste as their contribution to the community effort to stop the closure of religious houses, as requested. There were, however, also two stalls catering for those who would have a few pennies to spend for something a little more substantial. Indeed it looked as though the sisters had killed and butchered a sheep since last night – at least one and maybe two – judging by the stacks of mutton pies on the stall nearest the entrance.

Mother Baker was impressed, despite herself, by the labour that she knew must have been put in, in the last few hours. As a caterer of talent herself, she knew this display could not have been thrown together without much skill and planning. And it was obvious to her who had been in charge.

Indeed, it would have been pretty obvious to *anybody* nearby, from the high colour in the very plump and rosy cheeks of Sister Magdelene, but Pat Baker knew her from many years of cooking-comradeship. They were, indeed, mutually respectful of each other's skills.

The Orford sister was the archetype of everyone's favourite aunty. She always had a ready smile for visitors to the priory, and was prodigious with her provision of foodstuffs. No-one ever went hungry when she was around, and she was very sensitive to the emotions of people around her. She was singularly generous with her hugs, and it was very rare for anyone to leave her presence without smiling.

Whilst John started to unload their waggon, Pat Baker went over and greeted her friend with a huge hug which was readily reciprocated. And within seconds they were chattering away about the batches of cooking and preparation which each had been responsible for.

Sister Magdelene also acted as midwife for several villages around Orford and over the years had acquired a slightly quirky mannerism whilst standing chatting. Years of acting as a comforter of little babies and young children in her charge, meant she had spent many hours, altogether, rocking tiny children in her arms as a way to get them settled and off to sleep. This action had become so natural to her that she still did it when standing and talking to someone for a little while, even without a child to hold!

Her arms were slightly crook'd, as if holding a baby and she moved just a little from left to right and back again. At first it could be slightly disturbing to anyone who had not met her before, but most people found it quite mesmerising and comforting after a while.

"Looks as though I had better go and help John," Ma Baker said after a little while, "or he`ll be a`telling me off!!"

This was said with a twinkle in her eye, and Sister Magdelene knew it not to be true, anyway. If anybody did the telling off in their house she would have guessed that it was Pat Baker, and not her man John. Their partnership was always strong, but Pat was probably the tougher of the two! Mostly, however, she was sweetness and light.

It was a good job that she had moved when she did, because no sooner had they got their stall set up from the back of the waggon, than the first of the muster began to arrive at the field. These first arrivals tended by and large to be the younger element who had stepped out from Louth with their youthful vigour and energy and had kept up a speedy pace along the way. Some were a little weary by now but there was plenty of noise as they arrived – they were enjoying their day out.

Most stopped by one of the stalls and waited in good humour for one of the bustling sisters to ladle some soup into the tankard they had had attached to their belts. Some even had a wooden bowl and a spoon to sup from. A generous slice of fresh bread and dripping and then they might wander a little way off to enjoy their breakfasts, in small groups, as more arrivals lengthened the queues at each stall.

Only those walking had come straight into the muster field. The first phalanx of the host, the men on horseback, had peeled off to the left from the road and had taken the cobbled pathway that ran alongside Orford brook to the priory, set back a couple of hundred yards from the highway.

The priory itself was a handsome Lincolnshire stone building and was surrounded by mature trees, looking a delightful picture this morning in the autumn sunshine. Once through the stout wooden gateway, the mounted men were met by the priory 'grooms' – *young lads from the village* – who normally looked after the few horses stabled there which the sisters and the prioress used when they went about their business.

The lads had made sure the troughs were absolutely full of water for the horses, and ponies of the horse-born host. Four of the priory's sisters had been delegated to ensure this group of gentlemen and priests were welcomed with a beaker of small beer before they were offered a ladle of soup and a round of bread. The bread was spread with beef paste, rather than the beef-dripping presented in the main field. The soup was a little less watery too.

It was all efficiently done and, within a quarter of an hour, most of the gentlemen and priests on horseback were being encouraged by John Taylor, who had led this group off from Louth, to join the walking warriors in the muster field across the road. As they were leaving the cobbled path from the priory, the second half of the Louth host – *led by the colourful Captain Cobbler* – was just coming down the hill towards the brook. They had started perhaps half an hour later than the first group but had obviously been stepping out quickly and had made up ten minutes on the first half of the host.

Following fairly closely on the horsemen, the foot-soldiers of this group were actually marching in orderly fashion and singing away at the tops of their voices, led by the wonderful tones of Tom Foster in the centre of the first rank. John Taylor wondered whether they had been singing all the way from Louth but he thought it rather unlikely, given the speed they must have been walking. He put it down to the showmanship of Nicholas who had probably set them up to start singing just before they got to the brow of the hill yonder. They looked and sounded the part – a valorous group of men.

It had brought a smile to his face anyway, and now that the marching column was getting closer to the muster point and could be heard in the field over the way, a ragged cheer went up from the *first* arrivals, who were already full of dripping-smothered-bread and wholesome soup.

Indeed some of them had recognised the song (one of those songs menfolk will sing on a rowdy night carousing at the bar!) and had started to sing along. Some of the younger sisters from the priory could be seen blushing a little at the words of the chorus – it was a little bawdy!

A few minutes later the group of horsemen with Captain Cobbler were all moving across to the muster field from the water troughs at the priory having, in their turn, refreshed themselves. At the same time a final, slower, walking contingent reached the brook. These were mainly older members of the commonwealth who had lost some of the spring in their legs from when they were merely youths and striplings.

This final group included the group of priests which had gathered around Monk Morland, who was now noticeably favouring one leg and occasionally grimacing, as his knees played him up. All but Morland went straight into the muster field, to the right off the main lane.

Morland, however, took the cobbles towards the priory and was relieved to see that the prioress was awaiting him near the water troughs. She had a stable boy with her who was holding the reins of a strawberry-roan pony. Now, that looked a promising sight after his uncomfortable walk!

They greeted each other warmly; they had clearly shared many meetings during their years on this earth, and knew each other well. The monk had served as father-confessor to most of the sisters at one time or another, too, so he had an over-full store of transgressions (well, actually, mostly *imagined transgressions*, since the sisters were, for the most part, lacking in *real* sins of any kind!) which he had sometimes found it difficult to cope with in his own mind.

Indeed, he was thankful to the Prioress of Orford for helping him to manage the thoughts which sometimes plagued his mind after visits to the priory.

He was particularly thankful to the Mother Prioress, this day, for looking after the more physical needs of his damaged knees. He was, indeed, most effusive in his thanks but realised he must cut them short as he could hear that proceedings in the muster field were in danger of starting without him. He quickly hobbled to the nearby mounting block and was soon sat astride the small but sturdy pony. It was a pony the prioress of Orford used for her travels around the villages, hard by the priory. As the monk trotted the pony along the cobbled path back to the brook, the prioress, a truly handsome woman and his dearest friend, raised her hand, in farewell and benediction behind him.

The clacking of the pony's hooves on the cobbles meant that Morland could not hear clearly what was being said across the road, but he could tell that Captain Cobbler had started to rouse the gathered men of Louth, and its hinterland, to the task at hand.

ꏹꏹꏹꏹꏹꏹ

Nicholas, with his eye for theatricality, had positioned himself and his mount on a knoll about a third of the way up the sloping muster field, where he could see everybody and, more importantly, where he could be seen, and heard, by everybody. He projected his voice through the still-sharp autumnal air. Indeed, as he exhaled, or emphasised a point, a little of his soup-warmed breath condensed, catching the early rays of sunshine.

It was still not late in the day, and yet this large crowd had already covered nearly ten miles to get here from Louth. To be sure, some of the outlying groups of villagers had started well before light to get here from their homes beyond Louth itself.

Nicholas knew that it was now important to raise their level of anticipation for the further tasks ahead since they had another six miles or so to walk, or ride, to get to Caistor, where the commissioners were gathering to transact their business later on.

The muster ground at Orford sloped upwards from the entrance where all the refreshment stalls and waggons were located. As the crowds had arrived, the older villagers and townsfolk tended to stay on the lower levels and the younger, more energetic types had gradually worked their way uphill as the entranceway became more crowded.

Mostly they milled about in the groups they naturally formed at muster times, of neighbours and friends from the same localities. There was always a lot of noise and banter at the outset of a muster as folk greeted cousins and brothers, friends and acquaintances, fellow tradesmen, and suppliers, and customers, from different villages, whom they hadn't seen in a while.

It was not quite what you might call a natural amphitheatre, because it was too uneven a space, but about thirty or so yards in, at the lower end of the field there was a small raised knoll which had stayed unoccupied up to now. The milling crowds had left this space clear out of habit, for it was where the muster captains stood, often on horseback, to address the gathered hordes, and shout instructions during a muster.

It was known to all and sundry as 'the Captain's Table', and some of the local gentry were naturally drawn up in small groups nearby, as *they* were usually the ones giving out the orders, and they felt it was their territory. But no-one had yet ventured onto the knoll itself.

Today, as if to the manor born, Nicholas steered his mount to take up a central position on 'the Captain's Table' and a ragged cheer went up as people realised who it was who was getting prepared to address the throng. The banter peaked as Nicholas settled himself facing into the field and then subsided little by little as he deliberately waited for the attention to focus on him.

He let the silence take over the field and he could feel the tension rising, along with the expectation levels. His timing was impeccable of course, as a thespian of many years practice, and his voice projected clearly to the top of the field as he intended. He could feel that every eye was on him, every ear focussed on hearing what he had to say at this minute.

He pulled his shoulders back, took a breath, and started.

"My friends..."

"No doubt most of you already know, or will almost certainly have guessed at, the reasons we have called this muster. Many of us have been talking about this possibility during much of the summer – and the time has now arrived for us to step forward and act."

"We all just needed prompting. For us, in Louth, that happened on Sunday."

"So, I feel sure that most of you will have heard, too, that in the great church of Saint James in our fine town, we locked away the church treasures on Sunday night after the service. Indeed, some of us spent the night in the cold vestry, listening to Tom Foster's musical snoring..."

There was laughter at this, as Nicholas intended. Tom Foster was well-known in the town and round-about for his inordinate snores as well as his fine tenor singing voice. But the humour was just a brief cushion for the hard words that followed...

"We do not yet know the full extent of the chancellor's intentions in relation to our treasures. But, we are sure from his actions so far this year, in ravening the fine religious houses of the county of Lincolnshire and beyond in the name of the king, that he wishes to take more than the common wealth can stand."

"We believe he intends to take more than the king is yet aware of ...and we must petition the king to restrain him and his greed!"

A great cheer went up signalling wide approval of this sentiment

"Nor do we yet know the extent of the commissioners' inquisition of the vicars and brothers of the church which was to start this week. We are sure, however, that they are set on a course which will weaken our mother church! Brother Morland here will speak more of this later."

The Monk's timing was, accidentally, perfect, as he threaded his way on the prioress's pony close to the knoll where Nicholas was speaking from. But Nicholas had seen him out of the corner of his eye.

"We do not yet know what extra taxes might be imposed to overburden the entire commonwealth here present. But, we are sure it will be more than we can pay without pain."

"What we *do* know with certainty is that our Holy Days have been cut back and rolled into one 'All Saints day' and we don't think that is *right*!"

Great shouts of "*SHAME!*" from the assembled mass.

"We also know that we must go and tell the king and his councillors what we think..."

"Are you with me?"

A great shout of "*YES!*" rang round the mustering ground and Nicholas stood tall in his stirrups... and repeated the question.

"Are you with me?"

"*YES!*"... much louder.

"We do not WANT extra Taxes..."

Assembled muster – "*NO!*"

"We do not WANT an inquisition..."

Assembled muster – "*NO!*"

"We do not WANT to lose our treasure..."

Assembled muster – "*NO!*"

"We do not WANT the king to be advised by heretic bishops..."

Assembled muster – "*NO!*"

ജ ജ ജ ജ ജ

At this point, with the crowd in his pocket, Nicholas resumed his seat in the saddle and, in a calmer voice, briefly explained the next moves. He explained the urgency of getting on the road again quickly, in order to catch up with the county's important gentlemen. They were, at this very hour, expected to be assembling to assess the taxes, for the northern areas of Lincolnshire, in Caistor just a few miles up the road.

He then moved his horse a little to one side and handed over the key spot of 'the Captain's Table' to Monk Morland.

Morland, himself, now felt under some pressure to say his piece quickly. Although he had preached occasionally in churches nearby to Louth Park Abbey, he had never mastered the art of voice projection. So, although his words were well chosen, only the lower part of the field-full of people could hear him clearly.

These included most of the religious men from the closed abbeys and monasteries as well as the priests from most of the Louth and Louthesk churches, so he got a good reception for the points he made about purgatory, his views on the ten articles and so on. The younger villagers and townsfolk at the top of the muster field, however, were getting restless and a few voices started to barrack him, which made him rather flustered.

He was more than a little relieved, then, when, at Nicholas' prompting, Guy Kyme edged him off 'the Captain's Table', thanked him loudly and profusely, and started to bellow orders as to how the host should proceed from now on.

Kyme was well liked by his fellows amongst the gentry, but was also something of a hero amongst the mass of men present. He was a natural athlete, so, as well as being a star marksman with a longbow, he would mostly hold his own in wrestling and throwing skills, which tended to be the areas where ordinary folk might excel. These talents were somewhat unusual in a gentleman. They tended to stick to showing off their fencing expertise during the musters, and their horsemanship skills!

Great James, the Louth man who had taken on the role of personal bodyguard to Nicholas in the last few days, was the only man Kyme had never been able to beat in a wrestling contest. All the other larger wrestling 'stars' in this part of Lincolnshire had been embarrassed at one time, or another, by the modest frame of Guy Kyme as he upended them in the straw – or sometimes in the mud – of the muster field.

His speed and agility gave him the edge over their undeniably greater strength and it won him applause and great popularity in the musters. He also spoke well...

"Fellows and friends, one and all... We must hurry on to Caistor, so we need to leave the field now, in good order, and get ourselves on the road yonder."

"You will pick out and follow your normal Captains as for a muster (here, he gestured with his right hand to the gentry gathered nearabouts around 'the Captain's Table') – and we shall leave the field as we normally do after a muster. Louth men, being the most numerous will leave the field first, with their captains and petty-captains. Then those villages furthest from the muster ground will follow *their* Captains as usual, followed in their turn by menfolk from the villages nearer to the muster ground.

"Anyone who is unsure when or where to go, just latch on to someone you know well and follow him..." he paused...

"...Oh...and when you get to the gate, remember to turn RIGHT to CAISTOR, and do not turn left to home!!"

This last comment brought a huge round of laughter and a ragged cheer.

"The religious men here, from those religious houses which have been closed, should all follow behind the men of Louth, rather than attach themselves to their nearest villages."

All these directions for a massed group of several thousand men, from many villages, could have led to chaos as the field emptied. The pattern of leaving the field in that order, however, was well-established at muster practices, to ensure that folk all got home at a reasonable hour. The host's familiarity with this notion led to a remarkably efficient exeunt of those thousands in a very short span of time.

Each of the main captains made sure his followers knew where he was. It was quite a matter of honour that everyone moved into their familiar groupings easily and quickly in rows four or five wide across the main track leading up the hill and away towards Caistor.

Nicholas led the way with a small group of tradesmen on their mounts, along with the town's main gentlemen, Guy Kyme, Robert Bailey and the rest.

On the way past the stalls and waggons, Nicholas made sure to thank the Bakers for organising their refreshments stall. He also thanked the sisters of Orford Priory, too, for their wonderful work in ensuring that plenty of food and drink was available for the large numbers foregathered at the muster ground on this unusual day.

Great James positioned himself on the right shoulder of his captain; Captain Cobbler, his long-time friend, of whom he was inordinately proud on this day – and very protective, too.

ෂ ෂ ෂ ෂ ෂ ෂ

For their part, John and Pat Baker and their helpers would now tidy up and wend their way back into Louth. The Orford sisters, too, would dismantle their stalls and tidy things back over the track and along the short lane into the priory.

As the host spread out it made a long snake of humanity wending through the watery autumn sunshine between ragged hedgerows of thorn and bramble and overhanging trees. It was still damp underfoot after the rain over the weekend but the air was crisp and fresh and by far the majority of those present were in good spirits. Indeed some of the younger members were even in *high* spirits and there was a fair amount of larking about until some of the captains had a sharp word or two with the livelier youths to get them to show a bit of decorum – on the basis that they were "...*out and about on a serious business...*"

When the vanguard reached the top of the long Orford Hill and the going flattened out somewhat the snake began to stretch out so that after half an hour or so it was almost a mile between the head and the slower moving tail. The top road was quite undulating and at occasional high spots, which were also in open countryside, the marching men would sometimes be treated to a really long view over the county.

Relatively few of the members of the host were used to travelling along this road as far as they had this morning. Orford muster ground was the usual extent of their travels out of Louth or its surrounding villages. So there was an occasional buzz of excitement as one of these long views provided a distant sight of the wonderful Lincoln Cathedral with its tall spires glinting in the sun.

As the sun rose higher in the sky and warmed the leaded spires, the overnight condensation gradually dried and the glistening jewels of water droplets were replaced by the leaden grey needles against the pale blue sky – still an awe-inspiring sight at this distance. Indeed many of the host who had not seen this view of their mother church crossed themselves, as if blessed by the view itself.

Indeed, the magnificent view stimulated a number of conversations along the snake about the wonder of the building and those who had been fortunate enough to visit the county seat and enter the cathedral itself passed on stories of it to their neighbours and friends as they walked along, stories that they mostly knew anyway but were always pleased to hear again...

"...when it was being built all those many years ago, the Devil sent many imps along to interfere with the stonemasons' work, breaking scaffolding, throwing stones from the roof and so on, some of which broke heads below! In the end, of course, God got REALLY cross with the Devil, and his imps, and in a flash turned at least two imps into stone gargoyles and set them perfectly in the building itself as a warning to any other imps who wanted to take such liberties!..."

"You can see them even today, there's one outside the building on the south wall and one high up, just above a pillar inside the cathedral. He has one leg resting on the other knee, and his arms are folded across his chest – he was obviously feeling pleased with himself just before God turned him to stone – you can still see his little horns on his ugly head, above his piggy little face!"

With such stories and other more mundane day-to-day conversations the miles gradually unfolded and the snake became a little more raggedy and rather longer. The slower walkers at the back were now nearly two miles adrift of the mounted group with Captain Cobbler and the town's gentry at the front as the vanguard passed through Rothwell. They were now close to the top of Caistor Moor, which overlooked the town which was their goal.

Just outside the village, Guy Kyme pulled away from the other gentlemen and came to talk to Nicholas about how they were to go forward from here.

"Listen – this is not really my idea..." he said cautiously, knowing it may not go down too well, "...William King and his attorney friend, Richard Curson, were obviously talking about it before we got to Rothwell, and sprung it on us a couple of minutes ago..."

Nicholas sighed – although he did not yet know what was coming he expected it would result, somehow, in a backing away from their original goals. The town's bailiff and its chief lawyer were known to be very cautious souls at the best of times, so Nicholas had been rather miffed when their names had earlier been put forward as two of the 'temporal leaders' of the host along with Guy Kyme and Robert Spencer.

Some had said he should have insisted on putting himself forward for the swiftly held election, but he had gone along with the move to elect King and Curson, because he thought it would be best if he himself did not stand on ceremony. He was happy enough to take a less conspicuous role in the background as the popular 'man of action' now that the town's normal leaders were getting more involved.

Guy Kyme continued a little uncomfortably...

"Their view... encouraged, it has to be said, by that wretch of a servant to Lord Burgh, Nicholas...er... whatever-his-name-is...

"Weeks " chipped in another voice...

"...Nicholas Weeks. He will keep sticking his oar in about things! Anyway, their view is this. Rather than everybody piling in to Caistor, which they feel would be counter-productive, they suggest we should find some way to choose a smaller group to enter the town – about one hundred people as a maximum – and explain to Lord Burgh and his colleagues what is going on?"

His voice ended the sentence on an upward querying note, signifying a question, rather than presenting it to Nicholas and the others as a *fait accompli*.

"*NO!*"

The negative response was quick, and firm, and accompanied by a tight smile with little humour behind it.

"We have not brought the townsfolk here to stand at the top of a hill to watch the occasional cloud passing by and gossip with the sheep." Several grunts and other sounds of accord were heard as Nicholas stood his ground on behalf of the common folk of Louth.

The moorland they were approaching was covered in scrubby gorse and ferns, dying back at the end of the season. There was also quite an area of cropped grassland where sheep were often to be found. There were none there today, as it happened. Presumably, each of the local farmers who used this area as free grazing had taken their flocks onto their own pasture land, unaware that their actions would leave room for the leaders of a larger 'flock' of humans making a spontaneous decision to use the open area as a gathering ground of their own!

Kyme took the firmness of the Nicholas' "*NO*" back to the other three temporal leaders who were closely attended by fellow councillors and officialdom of Louth. His firmness was now being vociferously supported by an increasing number of foot-bound Louth men who were now catching up with the stationary riders and being brought up to date by their fellows.

Quite a few comments were of a ribald nature since the Bailiff, William King, was not particularly well-liked by some of the rougher element in town who happened to be in the first foot contingent to arrive in numbers. They took it ill that he may, perhaps, be betraying them.

Most vocal was a ruffian known throughout the town for the many times he had been put in the stocks on William King's orders for laying about him, and flattening anybody who might have upset him when he was well and truly drunk. Bill Corbett was someone you would not want to meet in a dark alleyway when he had had a few too many cups of ale. Actually you probably would not want to meet him *anywhere* if he had been drinking. Unfortunately he had a few pals who always encouraged him in his excesses – they seemed to enjoy the havoc he caused!

"...yer fat bugger..." he was shouting, "...yon horse is sagging under yer fat arse..."

"...wouldn't trust yer as far as I could spit..." his pals were laughing.

Rather than let this rant continue, Nicholas leant over to Great James, nearby, and quietly asked him to...

"Just shut Corbett up for us James, he's not helping matters just at the moment!"

It was no sooner said than done. Great James trotted his horse over to where Corbett was standing with his few mates, lent down from his saddle and hissed "...*shut it, Bill..!*"

Great James was about the only person in Louth who could (or would) say such a thing to this loudmouth without getting more than he bargained for. He had never liked bullies and Corbett was certainly one of those.

Corbett didn't *actually* shut up. But he had enough fear and respect for Great James's prodigious strength that he stopped shouting the odds at Bailiff King as loudly as he had been doing. He continued, however, to growl and mutter indistinctly, but Nicholas thought that a considerable improvement. At least the vociferous support was now no longer personally disparaging since others nearby *had* taken on board the message that Great James clearly imparted to Corbett to get him to quieten down.

After a few minutes of what seemed like heated discussion within the leading group of gentry, Guy Kyme came back to report that they had decided, since Bailiff King's original suggestion had been scorned, that they should, at least, send a small posse to go and reconnoitre the lay of the land inside Caistor. They would quickly report back to the main group before everyone moved off into the town. The suggestion was for sending...

"...two of the four temporal leaders, William King and Robert Spencer, and two of the religious leaders, Monk Morland and the guild priest, Sir William More, and four or five more, including Lord Burgh's servant, Nicholas Weeks. He would at least be able to vouchsafe to his master what has happened in Louth over the last few days..."

Nicholas pondered the point slowly...

"All right," said Nicholas, eventually, "but I want John Taylor and Richard Nethercotts to go along with them so we get an accurate tale when they get back from our outlook too. The commonality deserves nothing less."

Taylor and Nethercotts nodded as Nicholas insisted on their inclusion in the posse, and they quickly made their way over to the group of gentry, as Guy Kyme went back to them to report his discussion with Nicholas. And, with that, they were off. They all set off at a slow canter, and were soon out of sight, along the track which curved around the hill on its way down to the town.

CRCRCRCRCR

Meanwhile in Caistor – Tuesday Morning
3rd October 1536

Tuesday morning in Caistor seemed, to most people in town, to start as a normal day in October – sunny and pleasant after the weekend rain squalls, but normal for all that. There were, however, quite a few visitors from outlying villages here, who had come to listen to the discussions taking place about the next year's subsidy expected from each of the wapentakes – the local councils they represented. This was, after all, the stated reason for Lord Burgh's presence in town, along with the other leading county gentlemen.

It was at this apparently-relaxed moment that Lord Burgh's bailiff had quickly scouted the centre of town, having been sent in to see what was happening. Following earlier rumours, Lord Burgh's party was more than a little anxious about the reception awaiting them, so when bailiff Robert Applewhite returned to the apprehensive knot of commissioners, smiling and saying...

'...it's like a spring Sunday in town, everyone is in their Sunday best and wandering round in the sunshine until we all arrive..." they all relaxed a little and set off towards town, aiming for the corn exchange in the centre. Little did they know that things were to change significantly before they got very far!

Indeed, barely had bailiff Applewhite turned his horse around to leave town and return to the main party, than the situation changed. Several groups who were, *indeed*, dressed as if for a day out came across, much to their surprise, some rather more warlike visitors from nearby villages. These men, dressed for a muster, had clearly got wind of what had happened in Louth at the weekend, and thought they should come to Caistor prepared.

So, there were many animated conversations in the street as explanations were sought and given for the wearing of stout leather jerkins, and in some cases body armour. Some were carrying weapons too. There was an increasing tension, as it was rumoured that the

real reason for Lord Burgh's presence with so many gentlemen, was to confiscate everybody's body armour. Then, they would be unable to defend their churches' silverware!

The tension was dramatically increased when a party of about twenty priests from villages roundabout, who had been required (*was this a coincidence?*) to come to Caistor to be examined on the Ten Articles, now became involved in one of these street discussions. The Caistor locals suddenly saw threats where none had been clear to them before. It all seemed rather *too coincidental* for their liking!

No-one was able to say afterwards whose suggestion it was but this particular discussion migrated to the nearby Caistor Church. At the same time all sorts of rumours started flying about the town, each overtaking the last and being inflated on each telling and retelling. The one consistent thing about the rumours was that "*...everyone is gathering at the church, we must get there soon...!*" so numbers kept swelling in the church and the noise level kept rising. No-one was really sure what was happening and there was a real sense of fear and apprehension.

ରେ ରେ ରେ ରେ ରେ

Thus it was, that when word came from the commissioners that they were nearby and wanted the people of Caistor to come and meet them just outside the town, most people were too afraid to venture far. Nevertheless about one hundred men – nearly all of them wearing some form of protective jackets or armour – did decide to go and see what the commissioners had to say.

It was around this time that William King's '*posse*' came into town. Being quickly apprised of the rumours, they were making their way to church. But, as it happened, they did not cross the path of the men going out to listen to the commissioners, even though at one point they could only have been the length of a short street apart!

On the way in, however, Lord Burgh's servant, Nicholas Weeks, saw an acquaintance of his in the town who was making his way to the church. Weeks asked if the man had seen Weeks' master, Lord Burgh...

"....aint seen 'im in town, Nicholas, but I saw 'is bailiff Bob

Applewhite ride in earlier and ride out again on the Market Rasen road, so p'raps they'm still comin' in....?"

Weeks glanced at the disappearing backs of the Louth posse. Then with a quick and, it has to be said, rather quiet "I'll just go and see how far he is from town..." addressed to no-one in particular, Weeks wheeled his horse and set off quickly down a short side street that led to the Market Rasen road.

A couple of men in the posse half heard him but considered they should stay with the main group headed for the church. John Taylor saw him leave, too, and had a quick conversation with Richard Nethercotts, as to whether they should follow him. They took the view, however, that they were best employed keeping an eye on William King and *his* activities. Nicholas had seemed most suspicious of Bailiff King's motives!

ಢಢಢಢಢ

Several Caistor people near the church saw the small party coming along the street and recognised at least some of them as Louth men. So, by the time they had covered the last hundred yards or so, dismounted, and entered the church, their entrance was fully anticipated. John Taylor even got a smattering of applause as he walked in – he was well-known in Caistor anyway, and his recent role alongside Nicholas Melton was also known by at least the armed and armoured contingents in and around the church. In other words, those who had heard of Sunday's goings-on in Louth knew who John Taylor was – one of Captain Cobbler's lieutenants!

This unexpected reception rather disconcerted William King but John Taylor acknowledged the brief greetings of several folk as he walked down the aisle of the church. He decided to take the initiative, and spoke out about why they were here and quickly related Sunday's lock-in at Louth church. This drew many approving comments from those present but, as he paused to draw breath, William King chose to take back the initiative. And, in a remarkably deep voice, he said...

"It is clear that Lord Burgh and his fellow commissioners are yet to reach Caistor. Does anyone here know when they were due to arrive and where they may be now?"

As it happened the same man who had spoken to Lord Burgh's servant Nicholas, had now arrived in church, too, and was first to try and answer the question. Thus, in a slightly surprised voice he said...

"...well I just told that to one o' your party only a few minutes ago. Nicholas Weeks was riding with you and when I said the commissioners were on the Market Rasen road, he turned round and chased off that way, quick as yer like...."

Again, William King looked unsettled and gave the appearance of simply not having realised that Weeks was no longer with them. He had, indeed, been at the front of the posse, so this brief transaction *had* taken place behind him. Observing King's reaction, though, John Taylor wondered whether he should perhaps have followed Weeks after all. Something seemed to be going on but he was not sure what. He wondered if Bailiff King had known Weeks had left the posse after all and was just keeping quiet?

Half a beat later his mind went off in a completely different direction, as several people all started to talk at once, and it became clear to Taylor and the others that they had, in fact, just missed seeing the group of Caistor men going off to converse with – perhaps even confront – the commissioners. No-one had said anything about it initially, perhaps assuming the visitors *must* have seen the party leaving town!

It was at this point that some locals, who lived nearby, but were not wearing leather jerkins, or any kind of body armour, quickly betook themselves home to get 'dressed' for conflict. And, as a result, the rumours started getting inflated again!

By now some Caistor men were convinced that Lord Burgh was at the head of a large body of men come to snatch their arms and armour to take it to Bolingbroke Castle. They would arrive at any time, "...*we need to hurry!*" Yet at least they also now knew the hard fact that the Louth host was not far from town and intending to come in soon. So it seemed to many that there was a strong probability that there would be fighting before very long.

ଔଔଔଔଔଔ

In point of fact, however, a little way outside town, there was no 'large force', merely a modest-sized group of now-worried gentlemen.

Lord Burgh had been in a huddle with his bailiff, Robert Applewhite, and Nicholas Weeks for quite a while, just out of hearing from the other gentlemen present. Sir Robert Tyrwhitt, the lawyer Richard Moigne, Sir William Ayscough, Thomas Dalyson, John Mussenden and the others were now having their own huddle, following Weeks's urgent news that the Louth host was already gathering at the top of Caistor Moor. Several took the view that they should simply turn and take themselves out of the danger area. But Dalyson was arguing strongly that this would just make matters worse, and that they should address the large group of Caistor men who were now in sight along the lane.

As the only lawyer used to addressing judges in court, Moigne, though still only in his twenties, drew the short straw to speak. With the other gentlemen arrayed either side of him, and behind him, he faced the newly arrived Caistor group and tried to argue his case persuasively. He was just getting into his stride...

"...and place not your trust in such base rumours that His Grace the King would take church jewels to himself. Why would he soil his honour in such a way? Fie!! Is he not now the supreme head of this very church anyway?"

There was some murmuring as he made this point but he could not tell whether the murmuring was *in accord with* his point or *antagonistic to* his point. He ploughed on.

"As for the subsidy, which we are coming to Caistor to consider this morning, 'tis no great burden. And anyway, it was freely granted by the assent of the realm in Parliament. Fie again!!"

"...you are knaves to give such light credence to such false rumours. Take yourselves home. Attend to your daily business. Pay no heed to calls for unlawful assembly as you appear to have done this morning..."

He was just winding himself up into what would, of course, be a fine peroration when he was shocked to hear the Caistor church bells begin to ring, calling all the townsfolk out for an emergency. It stopped him in his tracks. Even the Caistor men listening to him were caught by surprise at this turn of events but, of course, **they** did not know yet about the Louth host having arrived, after missing the posse on the streets of Caistor by less than a hundred yards.

Thirty or more separate conversations started up noisily both in the Caistor party on foot, and amongst the gentlemen present, mounted, as they were, on restless horses which were reacting to the general sense of confusion, bordering on panic.

The Caistor men turned, almost in unison, and started back to the church in haste, responding to the call of the bells. The mounted gentry urgently agreed the need for them to depart, and meet the next morning *"...away from this treachery..."* as one of them succinctly put it, in what they hoped would be the safer haven of Spital, north of Lincoln. They also agreed that Thomas Moigne should write to Lord Hussey and update him on what was happening today, knowing that Moigne, with his legal brain, would marshal the facts more clearly than any of them!

Everything was in turmoil back in Caistor too. Just before the common bell was rung on the orders of John Pormon who had hastily been elected Caistor captain by those present, two of the leading clerics, the Deans of Grimsby and Rasen, had urged locals to *"...fetch out and burn any hateful books they had..."* As a result, many such books were duly fetched, and soon created a smoking bonfire in the town square: Lutheran words fluttering up into the sky, English New Testament sentences shrivelling in the flames, and heretical paragraphs melting away in the heat.

As soon as the posse from Louth realised that their quarry was actually nearby they remounted swiftly and rode away along the Market Rasen road, soon passing the one hundred or so Caistor men they had so narrowly missed earlier, getting a rousing cheer as they rode by. Indeed some of the Caistor men decided to run after them on foot and turned once again in the road. Those who felt less energetic, however, wended their way back to the church to bring themselves and their neighbours up to date.

ପ୍ର ପ୍ର ପ୍ର ପ୍ର ପ୍ର

Meanwhile, atop Caistor Moor, the usually-quiet Great James was offering a rare comment to Nicholas as they waited on events, suggesting they should wait for the whole host to arrive before thinking of moving off again...

"...and I think the best reason for waiting for the laggards is that we make an impressive sight as a large host and we need to make an entrance..."

He never made it to the end of the sentence – there was a huge shout from Robert Norman. Along with a couple of others, they had taken their horses to a higher spot about twenty yards away from the main group just to get a better view of the lay of the land down into Caistor, ready for when they would move off again.

"Gentry in view below!!"

The shout was, in fact, so loud that it was likely that the group of gentlemen to whom he referred had also probably heard it. Perhaps not all of them, but those with the keenest hearing might well have heard!

The party of about twenty riders which Norman had espied had just emerged from scrubby woodland cover to arrive at this crossroads at the lowest spot of Caistor Moor. They were barely half a mile below where the Louth horsemen were now milling about in excitement.

In fact three of the party below *had* heard a shout, but none of them heard it clearly enough to know exactly where it had come from. Nevertheless, they guessed it must have been from somewhere towards the top of the moor. None of them could see the lookout Norman had left posted to watch them, since he had moved slightly. He was now behind a scrubby patch of gorse, where he could still see those below quite clearly without, himself, being in full view.

Fatefully for them, their reaction was to stop and discuss their options, instead of simply spurring their mounts to even greater speed.

Robert Norman, cross with himself for having let out such a full-blooded roar, was now being more circumspect as he told the others what he had seen. *"...at least ten gentlemen in fine robes..."* and, adding their servants and entourage and, perhaps, two pack horses with no riders, *"...perhaps thirty to thirty-five altogether..."* It was not really a conscious exaggeration of numbers, merely excitement getting the better of him!

The assembled group of horsemen here, atop the Moor, numbered about one hundred altogether and the first of the walking groups had now arrived too, perhaps another hundred well-armed men in total, including ten of the most accurate archers in the locality.

Nicholas, Guy Kyme, and three or four others amongst the leading group had, in fact, discussed the possibility that they might see the Lord Burgh party before the posse got back from Caistor. They had talked about what they might do if they *did* see them. So they had already considered several possibilities and weighed them up in advance. They were now very pleased with themselves, for it meant they were able to be swift in their decision as to what to do next.

It was Kyme who spoke up clearly.

"Robert..." he addressed himself to Robert Norman first "...take these archers and the first fifty men of the host to where you were when you saw the party below. Give us two minutes start and then stand tall on that rise over there – so they can see you. Particularly, so they can see the archers. No need to load the bows of course – just make sure they can be clearly seen at the front of the host with their bows in hand. As more men arrive get them to join you in full sight from below."

"We shall chase down the track to surprise them, if we can, before they disperse. The rest of the men on foot should jog down after us looking menacing! But no blood-curdling shout needed just yet!"

He smiled broadly as he said this loud enough so the men on foot could hear him, then turned his attention back to the mounted group.

"The rest of you horsemen follow me down the track – as fast as you can. If they have managed to get started on their way before we get to them, Robert Bailey and I will turn left on the Market Rasen and Lincoln road. Nicholas and William Hert will go straight on along the Kettleby road. And William Ashby and a small party will go along the Caistor road if it looks necessary. The rest of you know who you are following?"

It was largely a rhetorical question because, before he had finished speaking, he was wheeling his horse and taking off at a canter. About four hundred hooves thundered after him, and the horsemen were halfway down the hill before the archers came into sight of the party down below.

As for the quarry of this large hunting party, they were somewhat in disarray and were milling about questioning each other as to what they should do. The most decisive by far was the leader of the party, Lord Burgh himself, who, without further ado, and with little inclination to discuss further options, now took off at the gallop along the Market Rasen road. This was his nearest way home to Gainsborough, and he was closely followed by his bailiff and Thomas Moigne.

These three were away and under cover of the trees before the Louth horsemen appeared in plain view.

Rather slower to react but taking the Kettleby Road was Sir Robert Tyrwhitt and several others who had decided, after some debate, to head for home as quickly as possible. But 'home' seemed a long way off just at this moment! They could now hear the thundering of hooves of the mounted party chasing down the hill and the shouts of the host, on foot, following on behind.

Sir William Ayscough and John Mussenden, (cousin of Jane Mussenden who was Mother Maria, prioress of Legbourne Priory) were the two who knew the area most intimately. So they had taken a small track just off the Kettleby road with their servants, thinking to get away quickly. However, although they were out of sight of the main Louth group, they *had* been seen by Monk Morland and Sir William More who were the first of the posse from Caistor to arrive at the crossroads. They both belied their priestly backgrounds, and were very well-armoured.

William Ashby, Louth's Constable, saw the two clerics in pursuit of someone and realised that he need not go along the Caistor Road after all. The posse was coming rapidly towards them and would clearly be blocking that route if anyone had fled that way. He decided, therefore, to follow the monk and the cleric chasing Ayscough and his party. He signalled his intentions quickly to the dozen riders assigned to him, and they duly followed along too, most of them enjoying the excitement of the hunt!

Thomas Dalyson, who had been arguing that they should stay, and Nicholas Weeks who was under secret instruction from Lord Burgh to delay pursuit if he could, followed in Lord Burgh's tracks. Guy Kyme, Robert Bailey and their following group had them in sight, however, as they took the Market Rasen road. They had about half a mile start on their followers and were occasionally hidden by trees – but, for the first couple of miles, it was quite an open track and it was clear that the pursuit group was riding harder than the quarry.

Dalyson could see this and, recognising his acquaintance Kyme at its head, he decided to pull up and wait for them to catch up. Kyme paused long enough to say to Robert Bailey... "Swear him in and take him back to Caistor" ...before taking off after Weeks, and whoever may be ahead of them.

Bailey was happy enough to comply. He never had enjoyed the hard riding of a hunt (which this exercise was now beginning to resemble), and he and a small party of helpers trotted the 'captives' back towards Caistor.

Kyme and the larger part of the group carried on after Weeks, eventually catching up with him after another two miles just as the track split into three. He was taking the central track, but when Kyme asked him if this was also the route Lord Burgh would have taken no-one actually believed him when he said "*Yes*".

By now, Kyme thought it would be prudent to get back to the crossroads and see how many of the original group had been collared. Lord Burgh was an important quarry. But it seemed more important that the host did not become too dispersed chasing after individuals, and, perhaps, losing the vital core objectives of the day's activity.

He thought that everybody should be brought up to date with what was happening and he was, himself, anxious to discover what had gone on in Caistor earlier. He gave instructions to four of his colleagues to ride in close formation around Weeks to stop him making a break for it again and, as a group, they made their way back towards Caistor at a steady canter.

ଔଔଔଔଔ

As it was, they found they were the last party to make it back to the crossroads. Everyone else had returned with their 'captive gentlemen', all of whom had already been sworn in to the commonwealth on a bible Monk Morland carried with him. Then they had all made their way into the centre of Caistor, back to the church. A rear-guard had been left to let the Kyme group know where everybody had got to. So, by the time Kyme arrived at the church, he found it was crowded to overflowing with local men, many of whom now sported leather jerkins or, for those who possessed it, armour, ranging from chest plates, through to full body armour.

Outside the church, were all the Louth mounted gentlemen, and others, surrounded by the first two large groups of the walking host, the rest having been persuaded to stay for the moment at the edge of town. Nevertheless, there was more than enough noise, and a fair amount of pushing and shoving as anger filled the air. Kyme found he had to raise his voice considerably to report his capture of Nicholas Weeks and the apparent escape of the main target, Lord Burgh.

The mood of the host was pretty hostile anyway, and now they had a focus for their anger. Many felt that Weeks had deliberately betrayed his oath to the commonwealth in favour of his master Lord Burgh. As the story unfolded of his disappearance from the Louth posse, when he rushed to Lord Burgh's presence, the crowd's anger became a physical thing. Neither Kyme, nor Captain Cobbler was able to cool the mood as quickly as it had become heated. Also, the other authority figures were somewhat under suspicion, anyway, and none of them near enough to Weeks to have been able to change the course of what happened next.

The general skirl of the crowds and the manifestation of anger had unsettled many of the horses and there was much tossing of heads, and laid back ears, as the horses were pushed hither and thither. Several hands grabbed for the reins of Weeks' horse and just at that moment, someone threw a coin in the direction of the hapless servant. The coin hit the horse sharply on the muzzle, just as three sets of hands pulled his reins downwards and, not to put too fine a point on it, the horse decided he had '...had enough, thank you'.

The horse reared up. Normally, Weeks, who was a good horseman, would have been able to grip on with his knees and stay seated, but the crowds had knocked his right foot from the stirrup and he ended up slithering off the back of his horse, landing on his back with a 'whumpf!' as the air was knocked from his lungs. Unfortunately for him, he landed right at the feet of the loud-mouthed bully who had been shouting insults at the Louth bailiff earlier in the day, Bill Corbett!

Corbett needed no further provocation to take this personally, and immediately took it upon himself to kick Weeks in the balls. Corbett's mates were all nearby and decided to join in and support their hero. No amount of authoritative shouting could make this attack cease in the next few moments. Indeed, it seemed as though the additional shouting was making matters worse rather than better, whilst everyone's blood was up anyway!

Weeks did manage to scrabble to his feet, and initially tried to take cover amongst the horsemen, but the angry crowd chased him and rained blows on him ranging from fists to feet, and from billhooks to fence-posts. He did manage to run a hundred yards or so, but he was constantly harried and hounded, and knocked to his feet more than once.

The attack did eventually cease but, by then, Weeks was a bloody mess. The appeals for calm from some of the more responsible citizens had ultimately worked – either that, or the bullies were simply tired of kicking. One of those kicks had broken a rib which had penetrated his left lung, another had broken his jaw and Weeks lay there winded and coughing up blood. Both eyes were swollen and the right eye was bloody and closed altogether.

Someone called for a priest to comfort the man but by the time Monk Morland had worked his way through the mob he discovered that all he was able to do for him was to administer the last rites and shrive him for his journey into purgatory.

His death sharply changed the mood of the gathering and several people remembered the prophetic words of the Louth butcher, William Hert, from the day before, who had said "woe betide us all if mayhem is let loose".

The Bailiff, William King, who had witnessed the action directly himself, acted surprisingly quickly and arrested Corbett and Jack Bligh, the most obviously violent of his henchmen who had been seen to kick Weeks several times when he was down. These were the two men most clearly responsible for Weeks' death. He ordered them to be placed in Caistor stocks until the host was ready to return to Louth, when they were to be tied hand and foot, draped over two stock horses and sent post-haste to Louth, with a small contingent of gentlemen to guard them, ready for a summary trial later on.

The Bailiff's speedy action had a sobering effect on the others who had partaken in the common violence. Although there was a general feeling that Weeks had probably deserved his punishment at the hands of the mob, no-one really liked Corbett enough to object to his arrest. In fact several of those who had also treated Weeks to a few blows in the heat of the moment seemed to think themselves lucky that only two men had been arrested. Then they tried quietly to move away from the area of the assault in case the Bailiff reassessed his actions.

Everyone by now seemed to have had enough excitement for the day and "...*back to Louth*", became the general message – without any single order being given by any single individual. The newly-sworn-in gentry, who had been attending Caistor for their meeting, were not to be allowed home, but were escorted to Louth in the midst of a large contingent of horsed men. They were surrounded, in their turn, by about a third of the foot-weary host, the rest making their way back home in straggly groups, stretched out along the way. Some of the younger men were first to get back to Louth and their much exaggerated tales were worrying some of the women, who then became concerned for the welfare of their slower-to-return husbands and sons.

෬෬෬෬෬෬

Guy Kyme invited the 'captive' gentry to dine with him on their arrival in Louth where, with a degree of peace afforded to them in such elegant surroundings, they felt able to think through what their next steps should be. It was clear that they should write directly to the king and inform the court what was happening as soon as possible. Knowing that Guy Kyme was heavily involved on the side of the rabble (or, at the very least, was very sympathetic to their views), they chose to be circumspect in what they wrote. They chose to simply state what they knew had happened, as far as possible, and clarify, for the record, as clearly as possible, the main grievances of the commonwealth.

Sir William Ayscough did manage to find a quiet place where he could write more directly (and privately) to Lord Hussey, and call upon him to raise a force to 'put down the rebellion'. He sent this missive off quietly, in the hands of a servant, to Hussey's Sleaford home, about twenty miles distant.

The main text to the king took much longer to write, and by the time the key points were drafted and agreed upon, and then were copied in a fair hand, it was well into the early hours of Wednesday morning. They chose the youngest and fittest gentleman present to ride them down to the court and young Edward Maddison was pleased to be acting, at last, instead of reacting.

Now in his early twenties, he had spent a few years travelling to and from the royal court, so knew where he was headed, and he had a fine horse to get him there. Even so he thought he would have to change horses at least once on the journey, and decided to race through to Baldock on his own horse, thinking that by the time he was there, there should be enough people up and about to be able to change horses for him, without undue delay.

He was getting restless to be off, as the fair copy was being prepared, so even though he had sent his servant to get his horse ready, he chose to go out to the stables and supervise the preparation himself! Since he knew he would be travelling fast all the way he chose to shorten his stirrups by a couple of inches to save his backside the pounding it might otherwise suffer. He knew it would probably be less comfortable when he was trotting, if his stirrups were too short, but he did not expect to be trotting that much anyway!

He decided to mount up as soon as the horse was ready and went round to Kyme's front door. He asked his servant to let them know inside that he was ready to go as soon as they had the document sealed for him. His horse clearly felt his rider's impatience and responded in kind, snuffling and whinnying, throwing his head and fidgeting on the gravel of Kyme's long driveway.

Kyme himself and four or five of the other gentlemen accompanied Sir William Ayscough who was carrying the finished document. It had been signed by all present except Maddison who had been in the stables! Ayscough insisted on giving Maddison a last minute sombre message of Godspeed, which he found very difficult to stay still for!

"Farewell gentlemen – I had better make a start!"… so saying Maddison turned his horse and trotted slowly and uncomfortably down the drive, in order not to spray the farewell party with gravel.

Once he reached the gate, however, he spurred his horse into a steady canter, turning right out of the gateway and onwards to London. In the quiet of the night, the group standing on the driveway could hear him and the beat of the hooves for a good half a mile until a large stand of trees blocked the sound. At that point they drifted back indoors and off to bed, believing their duty to be done.

The fact they had written to the king should quiet the commonwealth and perhaps the deuced rebellion would subside peacefully. The commons would have to stay quiet until a response from the king was available at the very least… or so they all thought!

The night was clear, and there was enough of a moon to give good light on the road, except through the thickest of tree cover. So Maddison was happy to keep up a good paced canter most of the time. There were a few small hills where he gave the horse and his own legs a rest by walking a little way but most of his journey was undertaken at speed.

He was right about making it to Baldock as the place began to come alive. At the edge of town he passed a coach which had been travelling down from Stamford and one was just setting off north from Baldock on the same road, so there was plenty of activity at the first coaching inn he pulled into.

His horse was lathered with sweat and his legs were weary to say the least. The inn-keeper was in the yard so Maddison shouted to him even before he had stopped his mount in a slithering braking movement.

"I am on the king's business. Get me the fastest horse you have available so I can be on my way in a few minutes! And be quick about it!"

The innkeeper snapped his fingers at the stable lad who went off into the stables as another lad took charge of Maddison's tired mount and started undoing buckles and straps.

"Fetch me a small beer, a hunk of fresh bread and a slice of pork whilst I relieve myself. And make sure my horse gets the best care whilst I am in London."

He threw some coins into the innkeeper's hand. The innkeeper raised an eyebrow and nodded as he counted the coins – it would definitely be in his interests to keep this gentleman's horse in good condition for his trip back, so he passed on the order for speedy service from the kitchens, as Maddison flew into the inn for relief and to splash some fresh water on his face.

A few minutes later he came out stretching and rubbing his lower back. The innkeeper's wife – who had seen and heard his arrival – handed him a plate and a tankard, and even dropped him a little curtsy as she did it. It wasn't the most elegant curtsy he had ever seen, since the woman was a little on the tall side and all elbows and angles, but it was well meant and delivered with a smile. So he smiled back and took his vitt'als, perching on the mounting block in the yard whilst the stable lads finished swapping horses over for him.

His own horse now had a blanket over him, and his head in a bucket of water, slurping greedily, as Maddison's saddle was being tightened on the new mount. A fine looking horse it was too, black as night with a thin white stripe down his nose. He guessed the horses themselves had had a brief conversation whilst he was in the inn, since the black stallion was now showing his impatience to be off on this important mission. He was scratching the cobbles in the courtyard with his right forefoot as the stable lads worked on him.

Maddison finished his beer and checked the tightness of the girth, and length of stirrups before getting up on the back of the strange horse. Once mounted, he threw a small coin to each of the two stable hands, bid everyone farewell with his hat, slewed his mount round, and headed out of the courtyard in a hurry. The innkeeper cuffed one of the stable lads, and his wife took charge of the coins each of them had received. *'It's only right,'* she thought, *'since we board and lodge 'em for free...'*

The looks on the faces of the stable lads suggested that their thoughts were of a very different order than those of the innkeeper's wife!

It was late morning as Maddison cantered steadily along the Strand, the sounds of his mount's flying hooves generally alerting foot traffic to his fast passage, and causing them to get out of his way as quickly as possible. He got a few pestilential looks as he passed by, but the sweating animal bespoke a long ride at such speeds, so there was probably a general presumption of *'important business afoot'*. Thus, nobody did more than swear quietly under their breath at this gross breaking of etiquette in the main city thoroughfare.

As he reached the outer yards of Whitehall, he slithered his mount to a gravelly stop, handed the reins to a stable boy and ran into the palace. Just inside the door, the Lancaster Herald, Thomas Milner, was holding a quiet conversation with two legal looking gentlemen, apparently from Lincoln's Inn. The Herald recognized Maddison, who suddenly looked a little lost and vulnerable, not quite knowing where the king might be at this hour, but pleased to recognize the Herald standing there.

"Ah, Lancaster, would you be kind enough to tell me where His Majesty is at the moment – I have a communication of significance which he should see immediately."

308

He managed to sound more composed than he felt.

The Lancaster Herald quietly apologized to the two men, smiled to Maddison and beckoned him to follow him. Maddison tried to keep up with the Herald's brisk pace along the corridors without showing pain, but his thighs were screaming at the simple task of walking, after so many hours in the saddle.

They eventually reached the king's day chamber, and it was apparent that he had with him several members of the Privy Council. The Lancaster Herald left him in the corridor and went in to announce his presence. Another thing that was apparent was that Henry was not in the best of moods. His leg ulcer had burst again after his ride out that morning and, although the Royal doctors had applied leeches and then re-dressed the suppurating wound, the discomfort was clearly making him irritable, to say the least.

In truth, he was also still grieving for his son by Bessie Blount, young Henry Fitzroy, who had died only weeks before, up in Lincolnshire, after a short illness. The doctors could tell him nothing much about what had afflicted his son so suddenly at only seventeen years old. Of course, rumours abounded that the boy had been poisoned; but, if so, by whom?

The people closest to the king were very wary about his suddenly changeable moods these days...and this particular day was NOT a 'good-mood' day!

His voice was loud and sharp as the Herald entered the chamber. "What now, man!"

Lancaster blinked but was, by his nature, inured to the king's moods, both bad and good, having borne them for years.

"Sir Edward Maddison, Your Highness. He has ridden in great haste from Lincolnshire with an important message..." He let his voice tail off when he was finishing his sentence as he had found this tended to relax the king's mood just a little...sometimes, anyway!

The sweating horse-rider, still in the corridor, heard the king mutter an aside... "Maddison? Which one is he? Does he know something about Fitzroy?" before shouting at Lancaster... "Bring him in then, man!" No-one responded to Henry's question, as it was clear he would soon see for himself.

The Duke of Suffolk, with his back to a roaring fire, was the first person Maddison saw as he entered the room and he looked so similar to Henry in height and bulk that Maddison, in his highly nervous state, nearly handed the letter he carried to Suffolk instead of the king. It was only as he had fully entered the room that he saw the king sitting on the window seat. He had been obscured by the open door, with his offending leg stretched across the seat.

Maddison gulped as he realised the potential for embarrassment which he had, thankfully, avoided! Indeed, it was only in the act of beginning to bow his head to Suffolk that he had chanced to see the king out of the corner of his eye. He was able to turn the bow to a mere nod of the head and re-orientate himself to focus on Henry's now-bulky majesty and perform a deeper bow before handing the letter over to the king, thus saving face. In his discomfort, however, he knew that Suffolk had probably realised his mistake and was clearly amused by it. It was also likely that he would tell Henry later – but, by then, Maddison would no longer be nearby to suffer too much embarrassment, all being well!

"So, sir, what is this all about?"

Henry's question was brusque, pain and irritation plain in his tone. He still thought it might be some belated news of his son's final illness...but nothing would change the fact that Fitzroy was dead. After Anne Boleyn's execution for adultery and treason Henry had insisted on a new 'Act of Succession' which placed Henry Fitzroy, Duke of Richmond as the first in line to the throne after he – King Henry VIII – died. He now considered that *all three* of his children were, officially, bastards. Fitzroy's death had, therefore, been a double blow to him, as a king and as a father.

Maddison had, of course been briefed to expand on the letter as necessary but, unaware that the king might have thought he was going to talk about Fitzroy's death, he chose to suggest that...

"The letter, your Highness, should speak for itself." ...he paused... "...but in short, there has been some, er, ...'ruffling' in the county of late, that we felt Your Majesty should be apprised of as soon as possible..."

He chose the word with care so as to make it seem less dire than, perhaps, the word 'rebellion' might have indicated.

Both disappointed and relieved that the information was NOT actually about his dead son, Henry broke the seal with a studied lack of care. He quickly took in the signatures of many of the leading men of the County of Lincolnshire and started reading the finely scripted hand of Richard Curson, who had been delegated to act as scribe. The contents had been carefully crafted, too, so that it gave a straightforward account of the events of the previous days. It then provided a summary of the grievances of the commons and ended with a hope that the king would extend his merciful pardon to them after considering those grievances and...

" *'Od's teeth!...*"

The letter may have been able to speak for itself, but it was rich meat for the mood Henry was in today, with his leg throbbing painfully to the rapidly accelerating beat of his heart.

His exclamations were loud and raucous, his breathing became rapid and ragged and his face became a dark shade of red behind his beard. Maddison tried to shrink into the floor, as Henry glared in his direction. The privy councillors present grew restless at the rising anger apparent in the king's demeanour, though they knew not why.

The senior privy councillor present, the Duke of Suffolk was the only one who dared to move. He went to stand behind his prince to read the offending material over Henry's shoulder. The rest of the councillors could only attempt to reconstruct the contents of the letter from the odd words Henry spat out with disgust...

"*...ruffling...pah!...*"

"*...taking an oath! ... commonwealth!?...*"

"*...monks and clerics?...shoemakers and ploughmen!!?? ...pah!...*"

"*...books burnt ...commissioners in stocks ...unbelievable!!*"

Finally he banged his fist down hard on the table next to him and shouted for the Lancaster Herald, who he knew would be hovering just outside. He would be trying to listen to whatever was going on, as he always did whenever the opportunity presented itself. Then Henry flinched, and then muttered loudly as his leg responded to the sudden movement with a stab of pain.

"*Lancaster, LANCASTER... Arrgh, by God's blood, this leg will be the death of me*"

The Herald glided smoothly into the room, as if he had been just passing by... bowed and said quietly...

"Yes, Your Highness?"

"Arrest this wretch, take him to the tower and arrange to have him executed at sunrise."

Lancaster showed no surprise or anxiety at the peremptory order, rather contrary to the wealth of anxiety and surprise which Maddison felt. His face was now drained of any colour at all, as he shrank back at the Herald's approach.

The privy councillors present were all showing surprise, too, at the king's sudden fury and plenty of puzzled looks were being exchanged. Besides Lancaster, the only other person in the room who showed no overt emotion was the Duke of Suffolk, who had picked up the letter and quickly finished reading it, after Henry flung it to one side.

He cleared his throat....

"Before Your Majesty allows the Herald to take Maddison, here, away to the tower..." he spoke as if it were Lancaster Herald's idea, plucked from the air... "it may be that we can gain a clearer knowledge of what happened by asking him a few searching questions."

Still most of the occupants of the room had little idea of what was going on. So there was a general murmuring of agreement for the duke's suggestion and no immediate dissent from Henry who was rubbing his thigh hard as if that would remove the pain from his calf and the worse pain in his mind.

Taking the silence as permission, Suffolk launched his inquiry straight away with a tactic that would at least bring the rest of the privy councillors to an approximate understanding of how things stood.

"Sir Edward," the duke's tone was conciliatory, calming, "perhaps you would very quickly summarise the contents of the letter for those of us who have yet to digest the details." His casual hand gesture indicated the privy councillors who, for the most part were trying to look knowledgeable, though few were succeeding.

The immediate threat of incarceration and summary execution had abated, but Maddison still felt shocked by the king's venomous response. It was not at all what he had expected – and he had trouble forming words in his mind. Also, because his mouth was dry he had trouble uttering those words that he *had* formed, so he stumbled through a few incoherent sounds that helped no-one. But then he gradually got a grip on himself. The story tumbled out, at first rather disjointedly, but then Maddison got into a rhythm, much as he had with his mad ride down to London overnight. Gradually the privy councillors got a grip on the tale as well, and began asking questions.

Whilst this was going on, Henry had sent a hovering servant away to bring back some of his favourite Rhenish wine. He found it soothed his pains more than any concoction the quacks dreamt up. He had, by now, formed a pretty low view of the entourage of doctors who were generally never far away from the king's person.

By the time Maddison had finished his story and dealt with most of the questions the privy councillors raised, Henry's leg was throbbing rather less. Maddison sensed that the king seemed to have forgotten he had ordered him to the tower. Thankfully, none of the privy councillors seemed as if they would risk reminding him, though Maddison himself continued to be on edge in case the threat re-emerged. In fact, he supposed that the order may still be in place, and he might yet be executed at sunrise?

Although Henry had busied himself with his wine he had, of course, been listening to all the questions from his councillors and the answers they had elicited from Sir Edward. In fact, very little *had* emerged as a result of all this questioning that had not been included in the original written report. So, either the report had been well written, or Maddison knew little more than the report contained. Or – what Henry thought most likely – the questions so far had not been very incisive. Just as he was thinking this, Suffolk chimed in with a question of his own, after being strangely quiet thus far...

"...and where does Lord Hussey stand in all this...?" Henry had acquired a genuine dislike of Hussey for his support of Catherine in her declining years, so was delighted with the question. Suffolk continued, "...and what of my Lord Gainsborough? I mean, of course, my Lord Burgh of Gainsb'ugh".

Suffolk played with the place name making it sound like Lord Burgh's name and he and Henry exchanged an amused glance – they both thought Lord Burgh was a stuffed-shirt, and self-serving, speaking of things "for his own Gains..." as they suggested in their private conversations!

Maddison missed these nuances (he still felt somewhat on edge!) and answered straightforwardly...

"We had not heard from my Lord Hussey before I left last night, although I believe Sir Thomas Moigne would have written to him, in brief, early in the day. He said, before he escaped the Louth host, that he would if he could."

"Also, I believe a letter was being prepared for him from the gentlemen in Louth, in similar terms to the letter I have just delivered to you, which someone else would have taken to Lord Hussey's house in Sleaford last night.

As for my Lord Burgh, he managed – almost alone amongst us, along with only Sir Thomas Moigne, as I said – to make his getaway clean from Caistor. I understand, from something Sir William Ayscough said, that Lord Burgh's intention had been to ride swiftly on to Nottingham. Once there, he would talk with Lord Derby about raising a force to send into Lincolnshire..." his voice trailed off.

"At last!! Someone with a bit of steel in his backbone!" exclaimed the Duke of Suffolk, though this was said for its effect on the privy councillors, rather than because he genuinely believed Burgh really capable of a steely response. In fact both he and the king had rather a dim view of the noble lord.

At this, Maddison bridled somewhat, feeling that the duke was being harsh on the gentlemen, including himself, who had been taken by the Louth host. The duke had not been there, faced with thundering hooves and the clear threat of violence from the archers on Caistor hilltop.

He judged that he should, perhaps, not say anything at this point, however, since his position was still at risk, *vis-à-vis* the tower!

Lancaster Herald was not, of course, a member of the Privy Council. But everyone in the room was so familiar with his presence around the court, that no-one had raised any objection to him being there. He caught the duke's eye and mouthed a quick "May I?" – indicating he would like to ask Maddison a question. Suffolk liked him, and knew Henry did too, so with a quick hand gesture back, indicated that he had the floor.

"I am not sure I understand all the ins and outs of the objections the commonwealth seem to have, for I am but a simple man. But you rather skated over the fact of the murder of Lord Burgh's servant, Nicholas Weeks, and other dire deeds of violence that seem to have been perpetrated on officials going about their proper business."

"It strikes me", Lancaster continued, "that *everyone* involved, down there in the wilds of Lincolnshire, must somehow share a little in the responsibility of that poor man's demise. Tell me, as a simple official, what is being done to protect my fellow officers from the wanton acts of a murderous populace!?"

Maddison blanched at the question and the quiet tone in which it was wrapped up, but it seemed clear that Lancaster still wanted to escort him to the tower. It was clear, too, that the king liked the question being put in these terms. He thumped the table next to him hard a couple of times and shouted...

"Hah!! Good question Lancaster - to the nub of the problem as always!"

With a small inclination of his head, the Lancaster Herald acknowledged the compliment. Maddison gulped before launching into an answer that he hoped would save his head from an axe he could almost feel already.

"Your Majesty..." he addressed his answer to the king, of course "... Your Majesty, it was not my purpose to skate over any such incident. But so many events have piled one upon the other in recent days, I thought it was most important to bring you up to date with a *summary* of the chief events as they unfurled."

"The death of Lord Burgh's servant Nicholas was, indeed, a dastardly deed, but as I hope I managed to convey, it was dealt with swiftly. William King, the Bailiff of Louth, was nearby – not near enough to prevent it I am sorry to say – but near enough to quickly identify the main instigators of the violence. The men were one William Corbett, and an unruly kinsman of his, Jack Bligh, who were at the heart of this violence."

"They were immediately arrested and placed in Caistor stocks until everyone was ready to return to Louth. They were taken thence, draped uncomfortably over the backs of pack horses, and placed under lock and key. They will, of course, be tried when all this ruffling has ceased."

This was a perfectly competent and truthful answer, but it pleased the king not one little bit. He thumped the table again and leapt to his feet, forgetting for just an instant his ulcer, screeched in pain in an un-kingly way, and sat down hard again.

"Damn this leg of mine! *'In the stocks'*, you say... *'draped uncomfortably over pack horses'*, you say! Why were they not taken and immediately hanged from the highest tree nearby? Why were their balls not cut off and stuffed in their mouths? Why were they not accompanied in this path of rectitude by the other ruffians who must have helped them kick this man to his death?" Henry's face had

315

turned deep red again, and he swept the carafe of wine, and his goblet, crashing to the stone floor.

"Take this man and place him under lock and key until we need to question him again and let us get this matter sorted out! You…" Then, he pointed to the servant standing by the door. "Fetch some more wine and clear this mess up. Bring some more food too …and hurry yourself about it."

The young man, whose name was William, was the son of a fine gentleman from Sussex and had yet to be broken-in to respond immediately, and without question, to peremptory orders. He stood gaping with an open mouth for too long! Lancaster Herald decided he would have to have a sharp word with the boy later.

Maddison was now fully expecting to be carted off to the Tower. But he was simply found a room nearby, with a lock, and shoved inside until further notice.

William, the Sussex gentleman's son, having cleared up the king's mess, and brought more wine and food, was then sent in to Maddison a while later with a tray of food and some wine. So, they hadn't forgotten about him! But his accommodation was sparse – one hard wooden chair, no table, no other furniture. Nevertheless, he was so tired from his ride the previous night that, with food and wine inside him, he was soon to be found asleep on the floor. In the meantime Henry and his councillors started work on their response to this crisis.

ଔଔଔଔଔଔ

Captain Cobbler – a sleepless night
Taking Responsibility, Wednesday 4th October 1536

The dawn of Wednesday morning in Louth, just a little while before Maddison had even reached the inn at Baldock to change horses, was one of hazy autumn sunshine. But Nicholas Melton – Captain Cobbler – hardly noticed the lightening sky. After a wakeful night, his head was full of gloom, which he thought would take more than a few rays of sunshine to disperse. The truth was, he was feeling guilty at the turn of events the previous day. He was a very open person and no doubt his feelings showed on his face, for every one of his friends had spoken of it to him on the way back from Caistor the previous afternoon.

"Tis not your fault that bully Corbett took it into his head to commit murder...' was the consensus view they took. And, of course, it was true that Corbett, Bligh and the others would have to answer to their Maker for their foolish and brutal actions. And that was after they had answered the local, mortal, powers-that-be.

But... Nicholas could not shake the strong feeling that it was all his fault. He had been at the centre of this since it all started off on Sunday. He was, indeed, a key partner in all the many discussions that had been brewing for months before. These discussions had even foreseen some actions on the part of the ordinary people of Lincolnshire, Yorkshire and beyond during the autumn, after all the harvests were in. It was intolerable that the king's advisers were dismantling the very structure of ordinary life in the countryside by attacking the religious houses; and threatening to do the same with the church; and *somebody* had to make a stand...

'...*but why me, Lord...?*' had been the over-riding question that had kept him awake all the previous night. He had been to a late mass in the church yesterday evening. The guardians of the church, including Nicholas of course, had now arranged to unlock the doors for regular services and lock them straight away afterwards. Not that many people were actually choosing to go to church since Sunday's large turnout, however.

Nicholas went into the confessional afterwards, having caught Thomas Kendall's eye during the service and nodded his intention of needing his priestly support. Once inside the secrecy of the confessional, he had carefully owned up to his sins during the week, identifying the sin of 'Pride' as the most likely cause for his feelings of gloom now.

He had been proud of the way people had listened to him on Sunday... and on Monday morning, too. And the fact that everyone had come out and taken part in action he said was needed made him proud. He had felt a huge surge of pride at the wonderful reaction to his rousing speech from many thousands of men at the muster ground on the way to Caistor... and the way the men were following *him* along the winding roads of his beloved countryside. It was as if they were following him to battle...!

And *that* was it – to battle! Battles had casualties, and Nicholas Weeks was a casualty of that battle yesterday. But the 'battle' shouldn't have caused anyone's death, it was a battle of truth, and belief, and community, not violence. And yet it was *his* battle, so, therefore, it was *his* fault that Weeks had died, and he felt dreadful about it.

Father Kendall, as his confessor, had sympathized with his troubled mind, and had sought to lessen the guilty feelings Nicholas was displaying, by going over all the arguments for their action, arguments that Nicholas knew by heart anyway. It had made him feel a little better in the darkness of the confessional, but his doubts kept rebounding in his brain as soon as he was out of reach of Kendall's soothing words.

He remembered thinking that the feelings he had had after his speech at the muster ground had been much more intense than even the wonderful feelings that surged through his veins when he had put in a good performance during the Corpus Christi play cycle each year... *much more intense...*

He had held the attention of thousands in the palm of his hand!

After the mass he and his colleagues, who had taken over the guardianship of the church treasures on Sunday, all met up to discuss the day and what should be done next. Everyone there tried to boost his morale – he was obviously showing his dejection! This morale boost had worked to an extent, since he managed to put a smile back on his face. But he wondered afterwards, in the stillness of his sleepless night, whether he might simply have been 'acting' his smile for their benefit? Great James had probably provided the most comforting words for him when he said...

"You **know** we tried to keep Corbett in line earlier in the day. But clearly the Devil had worked his way with the foul-mouthed wretch... and none of us are a match for the Devil, when he plays with a man's mind!"

Sadly, that comfort did not last very long when one of the men there (Nicholas did not recognize the voice – so it was not one of his close friends) said, in defence of the brutal action...

"Weeks probably had it coming to him anyway, the devious bugger. Sneaking off like that allowed Lord Burgh to get away, I am sure. And the noble Lord may, at this very minute, be raising a force to put this rebellion down."

That made Nicholas feel worse, the fact that someone could seem to justify such a brutal death, whosoever it was. It made it no better, that Lord Burgh might be *'raising a force'* ...*and* that someone in this circle – wider than it was on Sunday, of course, when it had been just his close friends – could see this as a *'rebellion'* anyway!

'Surely,' he thought, 'it was just a coming together of the community, the commonwealth, against faulty advice from the king's counsellors and heretic bishops...?'

"Perhaps we are in a battle," he muttered, but thankfully no-one seemed to hear what he said. At this point he took a deep breath and the meeting got on with planning who should do what in terms of guarding the church treasures over this night. They considered what they might have to do next morning – mostly they were expecting a quiet morning after the gentlemen with Guy Kyme had indicated they would be writing immediately to the king, so they would have to await a reply.

They also thought about what they had heard concerning activity in neighbouring areas. Several people, with relatives and friends in surrounding villages, and nearby towns, even far-away towns like Grimsby and Boston, had been dispatched with messages and/or instructions to do some fact-finding and report back early in the morning.

Anyway, the result of this meeting and its business, and, indeed, its busy-ness, gave Nicholas a headache. Additionally, the anxiety over his guilty feelings, and the swirling thoughts about where all this action was headed, kept him tossing and turning in his bed after he had eventually retired for the night.

He had arrived home much too late to see his two sons awake, they had gone to bed much earlier, but his lovely wife, Eliza Jane, welcomed him home with one of her tasty meals, kept warm in the stockpot. She was troubled when he ate but a few mouthfuls, and when he declared how bad his head was, she bade him sit on the floor between her knees and try to relax.

With her knees, she squeezed the muscles outside his shoulder blades whilst her delicate but strong fingers tried to unravel the knots in the muscles of his neck and upper arms. He started to talk about the day but she firmly 'shushed' him, and kept easing the physical knots until his back began to feel less tense and his shoulders dropped. He felt drowsy at this point, but the physical activity involved in going up to bed woke his mind again, and despite having Eliza Jane's comforting arm slung across his chest, he could not settle again.

Eventually, knowing sleep would not come, he quietly slipped out of bed – by this time Eliza Jane was breathing deeply and steadily – and settled himself in a high-backed rocking chair that had been his mother's favourite place when she was alive. As he rocked back and forth, he allowed his mind to wander slowly over all the events of the week and weigh their implications.

ଓଓଓଓଓ

So that was how dawn found him, still in the rocking chair, and still somewhat gloomy, but perhaps beginning to feel that, despite the unfortunate consequences for Lord Burgh's servant, they had to carry on and not give way now. His slightest movement, getting out of the rocking chair, woke Eliza Jane, and she insisted that he had something to eat this morning to face the day, whatever it would bring.

She scrambled some eggs for them both, and although it was too early to get any fresh bread from John Baker, they had enough bread left from the day previously to be able to cut a few thick slices, and toast them in front of the log fire that Nicholas had poked into red heat a few minutes earlier. They had a long brass fork just for this purpose resting with the other fireplace implements ready for use. The handle was shaped in the form of one of the imps from the Lincoln Cathedral, one short leg crossing the other at the knee. It was ugly, but for some reason made him smile every time they used it, a smile that came naturally and made him feel better as soon as it took charge of his face.

Butter soaked deeply into the hot toast just as the eggs were ready. Eliza Jane was right as usual – he immediately felt better with some good food inside him. Tired, but better. Washed down with a ladleful of clear, very cold, water from the drinking barrel outside, his breakfast brought a positive slant to the day. A day which, in the dark hours, had looked to be a very dour day in prospect.

ଔ ଔ ଔ ଔ ଔ

Nicholas was not the only person who had had a sleepless night. The young lawyer, Sir Thomas Moigne, who had managed to get away from the thundering hooves of the mounted men of the Louth host on Tuesday morning (almost as quickly as Lord Burgh, in fact) had made his way home to North Willingham. He had paused briefly at a friend's house, in Usselby, a scant few miles from Caistor, where he had written a summary of what had happened that morning, which he then sent to Lord Hussey in Sleaford by the hand of one of the household servants.

It was a hasty note, to be sure, since he had been afraid that the chasing horsemen would somehow know where he had stopped, and catch up with him! He sealed the note quickly, too, and sent his friend's servant chasing off to Sleaford as *'quickly as he could ride'*... before resuming his own speedy way homewards.

Once home, he intended to raise the village to defend the county against the rebels, but discovered it was empty of active souls, all of whom had gone off early in the morning to join the muster at Orford! Frankly he was not sure what to do because he did not want to leave the house to the mercy of the rabble if they came back to get him, but on the other hand he could not go far without leaving his wife ill in bed. She had woken one day the previous week with a fever and servants had been scurrying up and downstairs since then, with cold water to cool her, and chicken broth to make her feel better, neither prophylactic achieving any real success. Her husband was worried she might die if he left her now.

Because *inaction* did not seem to be appropriate, he spent some time looking out his household's arms, long bows and arrows, spears and billstaffs, as well as his own armour. He had managed to gather quite a display of weaponry together, when he had a visit from a messenger, from a cousin of his wife's, who lived in Croxby nearer the coast, enquiring about her health.

The man had been directed by a scullery maid to find Moigne in the stables, where he was now sorting through these arms, scratching at a bit of rust here and rearranging a scuffed flight on an arrow there. Indeed, he was fidgeting about in general, but to little real purpose.

The impression this left on the messenger's mind, however, was that Moigne was seriously preparing to defend his house. Thus, when the messenger, a man called Doughty, was on his way back to Lady Moigne's cousin in Croxby, he had to pass through the Louth host which was returning from Caistor. They enquired who he was, where he had been, and where he was going. When he told them that information, he was then pressed about Moigne himself. In reply he could do nothing but say, "Sir Thomas appeared to be getting set to defend his house, with weapons and armour spread throughout the stables!"

This information quickly found its way to the group around Captain Cobbler, and *their* immediate reaction was to say, in return, "*...well, we'll have to deal with that traitor in the morning...*" It was a fairly open-ended threat, one which was later conveyed to Moigne, himself, via men returning to their village of North Willingham, after their excursion to Orford and Caistor.

Since some of those North Willingham men did not like their local gentleman very much – he did have a tendency to be overly arrogant, it has to be said! – this threat may well have become exaggerated by the time it reached the village. Moigne tried to send his bailiff to Ayscough, to ask for his protection, but he was really not sure of Ayscough's whereabouts. He was increasingly coming to believe the truth, that Ayscough had been captured by the Louth host.

To make matters much worse, Moigne then received a message

from his sister-in-law, who only lived a little way along the road, that the whole area was being watched so closely that they '...*would not be able to join Sir Thomas*...', as they had been planning to do, in his hastily devised notion of escaping on horseback to Lincoln.

So, by midnight, Moigne was in a high state of anxiety and worry, pacing the ground floor of his house. He was concerned over his wife's health, and his servants' loyalty. And he was expecting to be attacked at dawn.

As it was there was no dawn attack. Indeed, just a little time after dawn, Sir Thomas received a very reassuring note from Sir William Ayscough in Louth. It had been written after Maddison had set off for London. In the note, Sir William expressed the view, which he shared with the other gentlemen now present in Louth, that this action would '...*keep the commonwealth quiet for a time*', waiting for the king's response. Ayscough advised Moigne that he should, therefore, carry on as normal, and take himself off to the Isle of Axholme in North Lincolnshire, where they had been due to hold Great court there later in the day.

"I believe the duty should not be too onerous," Ayscough had written, "so I trust you will easily manage to cope on your own there. It seems we must, perforce, stay in Louth yet another day, at least..."

Moigne was, as a result of receiving the letter, feeling decidedly better about things now, not least because his wife had started to recover from her fever, which had peaked just after midnight. This left her able to get a few hours' sleep, which seemed to have done her good.

So it was that Sir Thomas had just decided to break his fast, and had sent for something to eat from the kitchens, when there was a quickly approaching 'barrelling' of noise, like a rolling thunder cloud, and a great many horsemen came untidily into his yard, followed, soon thereafter, by a large assembly of angry men on foot. They were making a hue and cry, and waving various pieces of sharp weaponry around, none too carefully!

Moigne's heart sank again, but rallied quickly when he recognised Sir William Ayscough's two sturdy sons in the midst of the horsemen.

It was at this point, however, that he suddenly realised that Francis and Thomas Ayscough were not *leading* the horsemen, so much as being treated as *hostages* by the noisy group. It was particularly noisy, too, because there was no leader as such; it was really just a 'mob'. So, everyone was shouting at once, and Moigne really had no clear idea of what was happening.

Eventually a little order was established, enough for Francis Ayscough to be able to identify, for his father's friend's benefit, that the *third* hostage being held was a man called George Eatton.

Ayscough explained, with much baying from the mob after almost every sentence – and often in the middle of sentences, too – that George Eatton was, in fact, a messenger from Lord Hussey. Hussey had received Moigne's letter from Usselby, and had written back to the gentry, not then knowing they had been taken en masse.

Not only that, but Hussey had also written to Robert Sutton, Lincoln's Mayor, in similar terms. And Robert Sutton had written his *own* letter to the gentry group agreeing heartily with Lord Hussey's view and offering his support.

The trouble was that Lord Hussey's '*view*' as expressed in the letter was that the gentry should use their good offices to raise a force and put down the rebellion as quickly as possible, '*not sparing the rod*'. Of course, the much-dithering Hussey had in the end dithered in the 'wrong' direction, when seen from the viewpoint of ordinary Lincolnshire folk, and had not anticipated that his letters and those of Mayor Sutton might fall into the hands of the '*rebels*'.

It was unfortunate for Sir Thomas Moigne, George Eatton and the two Ayscough boys that those 'rebels', now making such a fuss, did not know how much Hussey had dithered in *their* direction before plumping for orthodox security. Otherwise, they might simply have had a good laugh, and slapped their captives on the back, saying '*we are all in the same boat now, my boys!*' They just saw, and heard, the words as they had been quickly scrawled in Hussey's own hand... threatening the rebellion with force!

The mob therefore hustled Sir Thomas onto his horse, and was all set to force-march them all to Louth as soon as possible. But then John Chapman, a butcher from nearby Langworth, took himself into Moigne's chapel, nearby the house, and brought out a holy book. On this, they forced Moigne, the Ayscough brothers, and George Eatton, to swear an oath to '*the commonwealth, the king and the mother church*', before they were happy to proceed onwards to Louth.

"Let us see if they are so ready to raise a force to suppress us now they have sworn to God that they will support the commonwealth and the church!" Chapman exclaimed with vigour after the oaths were taken.

Chapman, and the other men on foot, insisted that the group as a whole should move at their pace, so they could keep a very watchful eye on the newly sworn in gentlemen all the way to Louth. Louth was some two hours walk away. They did suggest, however, that two of the *tradesmen* with them on horseback should ride on quickly ahead, and let them know in Louth about the letters and the capture of Moigne and the Ayscoughs.

One tradesman was a tailor, William Blake; and the other, John a' Bardney, was a shoemaker who knew Captain Cobbler personally. Neither Blake nor John a' Bardney were very young men, so they did not gallop along the lanes. But they were, nevertheless, quick enough to be riding over the Lud river bridge, just below the impressive Louth Church, before an hour had passed.

ର ର ର ର ର ର

Sir William Ayscough, Dalyson, Portington and the other gentlemen of the Caistor Commission, who had been captured and 'brought-in' the previous day were, just then, leaving the church with Robert Bailey, William King and Guy Kyme, having all been to early mass. However, they were leaving through the South door, on the opposite side of the church to the river, so they were out of sight of Blake and John a' Bardney, as they were crossing the bridge. These gentlemen were on their way back to Guy Kyme's substantial house to break their fast, and were, therefore, unaware of the new arrivals.

These same gentlemen all felt at ease, too, as Louth was peaceful now, and looked as though it may stay that way until they heard back from the king. They were pleased at their evening's work the previous evening, and were looking forward to breakfast. They knew, now, that Kyme kept a good table, having all of them been fed very well the day before.

The monk, Morland, who had been speaking with several of the gentlemen for a little while before they left the church, was still hovering in the south doorway. He was now talking to a group of his black-gowned religious brethren, including the young priest, Richardson, who had nominated him as one of the religious leaders of the host the morning before.

Morland was currently feeling pleased with himself, that many of the points he had been making the day before had, now, apparently, found their way into the correspondence which the gentlemen had sent to the king. He was optimistic that some good would come from his actions. Without boasting too much (he thought), this was the message he was passing on to his religious colleagues.

"Sir William Ayscough himself, just acknowledged to me that the points I was making yesterday were '*very logical and well-thought-out*'..." Morland was saying...

He paused as two riders trotted round the west end of the church and came into view calling for someone to direct them to where they could find 'Captain Cobbler'. Great James happened to walk through the Church door just at this point, and recognized William Blake as a fellow Lincolnshire tailor. He also felt he had seen the other man before in Nicholas Melton's company, and thought he was probably a cobbler too. He could not recall his name, however, until Blake introduced him as John a' Bardney.

Great James towered over the monk and his brethren, of course, as he did over virtually everyone. He quickly instructed one of the boys, hanging round the church precincts, to take charge of the two slightly-sweating horses, whilst he took the visitors inside.

"Nicholas is 'holding council' with Thomas Kendall and our central group in the vestry," he explained. "I was just going to find John Baker and his wife to organize some food for the meeting, because it looks as though they might be talking for quite a while! But it looks as though you have been riding hard and must have some news for us?"

His voice tailed off with the question, and Blake was quick to respond.

"We do, indeed, have some important news to give you all, so the sooner we get to see everybody, the better!"

Great James had never known his colleague, Blake, to be so peremptory in tone, so thought it must be important news indeed. William Blake was normally a very warm and thoughtful man, and very gentle in his manner, so his brusqueness was highly unusual.

Great James took them through to the vestry, and introduced them around, before taking himself off to carry on with his task of searching for John Baker to organise the food for later. He knew someone would tell him what the newcomers had said when he got back!

By the time they were in a position to tell their tale, a curious Monk Morland, and an equally curious Father Richardson, had also managed to squeeze themselves into the vestry, which was quite full, especially for a weekday morning! As the news from Willingham unfolded, Nicholas felt some brief pleasure at the fact that Sir Thomas Moigne had been detained after all, and brought into their action, albeit unwillingly.

But then all of them felt shock and anger, at the real threat of a force being raised against them, which was apparent from the Hussey and Sutton letters! Several voices were raised immediately, to say they should ring the common bell straight away and get themselves in readiness to fight for their lives. Nicholas, however, was still feeling the guilt he had been experiencing during the night, and felt very hesitant to give the noisy ones their heads in this matter. He was not, however, immediately able to counter this view, which was clearly taking hold, as the arguments developed.

Monk Morland, so pleased with the way the gentry had appeared to respond to his ideas yesterday afternoon, did not want disturb this peace, and spoke up very firmly for a quiet period of grace. This, he said, would allow the king to digest the excellent points they had all made (he meant his own, of course!)

This discussion was getting noisier all the time, but was not yet resolved, when *more* visitors arrived, this time from Horncastle. There were six of them, led by Thomas Dixon, and when they came into the church they were followed by another half dozen, or so, Louth men, who had been expecting them. This sudden influx of people meant the vestry would not cope with the crowd, so Nicholas bid them all move to the larger space under the church tower, where they had had their first meetings only three days previously. It seemed to Nicholas such a long time ago, already!

ଔଔଔଔଔ

The physical transfer of the meeting to the bigger space took much longer than it should have done; to move a few people a matter of thirty paces at most. It was also much noisier than it should really have been, too, in church. There was so much news to exchange, however, between people who saw each other so infrequently, so that about twenty different conversations were now going off all at once.

Suddenly, frustration with all this noise, and skyre, got the better of Nicholas. His sense of inadequacy, and feelings of guilt, vanished, and he became 'Captain Cobbler' again, projecting his voice, loudly, throughout the church.

"Gentlemen, enough!"

In the silence that followed, you could have heard a pin drop.

"Let us please be orderly about this..." and he proceeded to summarise, for the benefit of the newcomers, the information Blake and John a' Bardney had brought, about the 'capture' of Sir Thomas Moigne. Also, that Moigne, Ayscough's sons and Eatton would be arriving in Louth very shortly; and, also, about the letters that had been discovered, written by Hussey and the Lincoln mayor, Sutton, about raising a force. He paused.

"Now, let us hear what has been happening in Horncastle. Briefly please Mr Dixon."

Nicholas knew the Leach brothers and cousins, through his links with Devotio Moderna, though he could not honestly say he liked the family that well – all of them were rather too bombastic for his taste. But he knew Thomas Dixon to be an honest, if poor, foreman, in the employment of William Leach. He had gathered, in the several minutes when they were all moving round the church, that Dixon had been deputed by the Leaches to carry the message, to the Louth host, of what had happened the previous day in Horncastle.

Nicholas thought that maybe the Leaches had also written letters to the gentlemen of Louth, but had favoured Captain Cobbler and his friends with someone who he had decided would communicate with them on the same level, labourer to labourer and tradesman to tradesman. Strangely, it was a thought that made him feel really cross all of a sudden, but without quite realising why?!

Dixon – a taciturn man at the best of times – was, indeed, quite brief in his story. But it was a story with embellishments from the others with him. In particular, Davy Bennett, who was a weaver by trade, also liked weaving stories too, seemingly.

Referring, apparently, to the Leaches themselves Dixon said...

"They was all finely arrayed in their armour, glinting in the bright sunshine, and an imposing sight they were, as we set off to 'bring in' all the surrounding gentlemen. We first went to Scrivelsby Hall, as you know being the seat of the King's Champion. Old Sir Robert Dymocke was there – retired and quite frail. His sons Edward...and ..."

"He's the County Sheriff, of course, as we all know..." embellished Bennett unnecessarily. Then he paused "...and William Leach goes a'huntin' with Sir Edward Dymocke, often-times..." he concluded. Dixon gave Bennett a hard stare and resumed.

"Dymocke's sons, Edward and Arthur, were there as well as a couple of commissioners for the subsidy, who were staying there. Dighton and Sanderson, I think they was called." Dixon managed to finish his sentence.

"Sanderson's father in law, Sir William Sandon was there too..." Bennett butted in, undeterred, "...but he didn't come out to meet us. And Sir Robert's cousin, Thomas Dymocke, was there as well." Dixon gave his friend a withering look again, to try and quieten him, and carried on.

"Rather than go to the front door of the hall in such a crowd, 'twas decided to send a little group ahead, to get them out to see us. As it was, they had time to come all the way out to the main gate of the hall to meet with us. All except Sandon, that is."

Bennett could not resist another embellishment and informed the group under the tower of Louth church that...

"...Sir William Sandon had apparently said that we'd 'started such a business as would get us all hanged for our troubles', which managed to get William Leach in a lather! Well, William Leach is a burly man as you know, and he grabbed the Sheriff by his bosom and stuck his nose in his face and snarled, 'if you dosent do what is the Commons will, then you'll all die on the end of a rope from yonder tree.' They had more words which we couldn't hear, and then it appears that they agreed to swear the oath, at which we all cheered."

Bennett paused, but this time Dixon waved for him to carry on, since the Louth men seemed to be hanging on his every word!

"But then, it was clear that Sandon had refused, anyway, so a group of us fetched him bodily out of the house, and put him on a horse, for we were all bound into Horncastle; so we took all the gentlemen with us. Once we got 'em there, they were all sworn in, official-like, in the Moot Hall. Then William Leach took Sandon and Arthur Dymocke with him, when he and other mounted men went out in the afternoon to round up more of the gentry near-about."

Dixon then resumed the tale, looking round at his audience...

"I wasn't with them, but another group of Leach's workmen went off to Old Bolingbroke – for there were some gentlemen there to bring in. And the Lincoln bishop's chancellor, Dr Raynes, was there, too, in his sick bed."

Nicholas and several other of the Louth men present recalled Thomas Kendall's description of the inquiry Dr Raynes had chaired – *'was it only last Saturday?!'* They remembered that Kendall had spoken of Dr Raynes as looking *"...very unwell"* by the end of the afternoon. The damp atmosphere, in the castle, in Old Bolingbroke, probably did not make him feel any better for it was run down and very damp, but he was obviously too ill to move to a better place. Dixon continued his tale...

"The main man in that group was Phillip Trotter, who is a merchant in Horncastle. So, when some of the men with him were about to drag him off his sick bed, old Dr Raynes turns to Trotter and begs him save him. He offered him twenty shillings to save his soul! Trotter told me this morning, before we left Horncastle, that he thought the twenty shillings would come in, to pay for our struggle to go ahead for longer. So, he decided to get his people to leave Raynes alone at that time, pocketed the twenty shillin's and they went off after other 'prey'!"

"All in all", Dixon concluded, as if he had covered the whole day in close detail, "we bagged about thirty gentlemen of high importance, many other gentlemen of lesser importance. And, of course, we livened up many folk of our own ilk in the process! I was told to tell 'e all that it was many hundreds, but I nivver knowed, myself, however many 'twas, seein' as I cannot count above ten!"

He finished with this uncharacteristic flourish, which made his fellows laugh because they knew he *could* count much higher than that if it concerned his backdated wages! He was unused to making such long speeches, though, and his cheeks were quite flushed when he had finished.

It was clear to Nicholas, and the other Louth men at the meeting, from the several embellishments that had accompanied his tale, that much of what had happened in Horncastle was a direct result of what they had heard there, about the actions in Louth itself on Sunday night. It seemed that the Leaches had perhaps over-emphasised the rebellious nature of the kindly folk of Louth when stirring people up on the Monday. For example one of the men from Horncastle, said, "... and we heard that Captain Cobbler, here, was nigh on seven feet tall! He don't look it now"

That made Nicholas laugh aloud, and he said,

"That is just a mistaken identity – you wait 'til you see Great James when he comes back from his errand!"

Almost as if on cue, the man himself walked back into the church, through the south door, blocking a goodly portion of the weak autumn sunshine as he did so. He was followed in by another messenger from the North Willingham group coming to Louth with 'prisoners'. The messenger had been sent on ahead, over the bridge, to warn them they'd "...*be here in about ten minutes!*"

This news caused a bustle, and a noisy debate broke out again about sounding the church bells. This time 'Captain Cobbler' was back in charge. So, under 'Captain Cobbler's' watchful eye, Nicholas felt his doubts no more. Thus, he now declared that everyone in Louth should know there were many developments afoot, and he set Richard Nethercotts and John Wilson to their favourite task of bell-ringing.

"Go! Ring the common bell, loud and clear!"

They were moving around to where the ropes were neatly coiled and hung, but Monk Morland suddenly insisted they should not be used...

"... for the love of peace!"

...and threw both rope coils up and away, into the high window sill of the narrow tower window. One rope stayed up there, but the other fell back down, so he quickly picked the tangle off the floor, and threw the rope as high as he could again.

He was busy shouting that they should all hold on to the peace that reigned in Louth while the king was busy replying to them. Frankly, however, he did not really have much support. Some, vociferously, came from the young priest, Richardson, who was with him, but that was all.

His second throw made *that* rope get taffled with the first rope that had stayed in the window. And the weight brought both ropes back down again. Before Nethercotts and Wilson could recover their precious ropes, however, Morland managed to scoop them up again and once more throw them onto the ledge of the window. They very nearly stayed there in a jumble but by this time several hands had grabbed Morland himself. There was a very unseemly period of scuffling between Louth tradesmen and a dark-robed monk who found himself in the centre of many grasping hands.

The scuffling stopped quite suddenly as Great James grabbed the monk's black gown in two hands and literally lifted the man off his feet, pushing him back against the wall. Morland sputtered as if to start speaking again but James' face was only a couple of inches from his. No-one had ever heard a serious threat ever come from the gentle giant's lips before. But now he growled at Morland, that...

"...if you try and do that again, I shall take one of these ropes and hang you from its end, in the tower here!"

It was quite clear, even to the now-quiet Monk, that this was no empty threat, and that his life was in real danger if he persisted. In this short hiatus whilst the monk was still airborne, the two bell-ringers had reacquired their possessions, the precious ropes, and were about to start the bells a' ringing, calling the men of Louth back to the church precincts to hear the latest news. They were both flushed with the scuffle but their bell-ringing honour had been restored.

Nicholas placed a hand on James' shoulder and said quietly but firmly.

"Escort Morland and Richardson outside and let them cool off in the autumn air! As for you two..." his eyes encompassed the still floating monk and the young priest, whose arms were being held tightly by as many as five pairs of hands, "... it would probably be best for your continued health if you were not to come back into this church at any time in the near future. Thank you for your help so far, but you are no longer welcome."

He spoke gently, but with tough steel underneath the gentle tones.

ଔ ଔ ଔ ଔ ଔ

...breakfast at the Kyme household

Meanwhile, breakfast at the Kyme household was proving a very relaxed affair, the sideboard in the dining room almost groaning with the weight of comestibles perched thereon.

Guy Kyme was not yet married. He had been betrothed, when he was still only sixteen, but, just a month before his twentieth birthday, which was also to be his wedding day, an outbreak of sweating sickness (the same disease which had taken Nicholas Melton's father, and brother, Robert) deprived Guy Kyme of his bride-to-be, and of *his* father too. This was less than eight years before.

He had, of course, inherited the extensive estates and the business interests his father had built up, both of which needed care and attention. The loss of his young bride-to-be had affected him deeply, however. When first betrothed, it had not been a love match, simply the proposed joining together of two successful mercantile families, each with only one surviving child. In the long period of their betrothal however, they had grown to love one another, and shared a great enthusiasm for life.

Her name was Rebecca, and Guy missed his Rebecca every day of his life. She had grown into a vivacious young woman with long black wavy hair and she was a very tough act to follow. Prospective mothers-in-law, therefore, found it very difficult to present *their* daughters in a sufficiently favourable light for the prospective bridegroom to notice! Nor did he even *want* to notice, if he was honest with himself.

No doubt, in such circumstances he could have been easy prey for the Devil and might have become a wastrel, but he had turned into a serious young man of business. He was an avid supporter of the charitable Devotio Moderna and its good works. And he was something of a thespian too, playing increasingly important parts in the Corpus Christi plays in Louth. So these involvements brought him into close contact with Nicholas Melton and Father Thomas Kendall. Over time they became firm friends.

Rebecca's father, George Tuxworth, died less than a year after his daughter, most people attributing his death to a broken heart. With no close family to leave his business to, therefore, it was his will to leave the management of his growing mercantile enterprise to Guy Kyme. Kyme was rather shocked by this eventuality, but he had, anyway, been helping to run the business during the last months of Tuxworth's final illness, so he accepted the formal responsibility without demur.

As executor of the will, too, he oversaw the sale of Tuxworth's house and the disbursement of those funds to various distant relatives (Mrs Tuxworth had died in childbirth ten years since, together with Rebecca's expected sibling). Once the funds were dealt with and the house closed, he had incorporated the key members of the modest household staff into his own household.

One of these acquisitions had been Mrs Hempsall, the cook, and she it was who still presided over Kyme's kitchen. As such, she was responsible for the groaning weight of food on display for Kyme's guests on this delightful October morning.

Centrally placed on the oak sideboard, was one of Mrs Hempsall's locally-famed pork pies, and Sir William Ayscough was helping himself to a generous slice as Richard Dalyson, at his side, was reaching to the very back of the oaken board, for a helping of the mustard-pickled-cauliflower to compliment his own slice of pie.

Dalyson was speaking, as well as reaching, too.

"It was good to see Louth so quiet this morning as we came from the church. I was fearful that things might deteriorate further still from the depths of yesterday's dreadful events."

Another of the Caistor commissioners, Thomas Portington, already seated at the table, and with his mouth full of deliciously cured ham, wondered aloud...

"...I wonder how Maddison is doing on his ride to see the king and present him with our letter. I must say I did not envy him the journey up to London!"

Guy Kyme came into the room halfway through the sentence, having been giving Mr Hempsall, who was now his head gardener, instructions about tending the estate. Mr Hempsall was a prodigiously large man, a fact which spoke volumes about his wife's culinary abilities! Kyme picked up from a curious point in Portington's comment.

"I suppose it is true that because London is our capital city, we should always speak of 'going *up*' to London, but it has always been my view, from Lincolnshire, that because we appear above London on any map you see, we should really speak of 'going *down*' to the city, if and when we pay the city a visit!"

No doubt on any other day, such a throwaway comment might have started a noisy debate in the crowded room about the merits and demerits of going *up* or *down* to the capital city! Just at this point, however, there was an interruption to the seeming normality of such discussion. It was Kyme's bailiff, who had been on his way out of the house when a visitor had turned up in the yard. The visitor's sudden arrival in a small spray of gravel, as he stopped the horse quickly, suggested some urgency about his business.

Realising straight away that the visitor, who said he was from Horncastle, probably wanted to speak with all the gentlemen present, the bailiff did not sidle up to his master and quietly tell him of the arrival, which he thought most of the in-house staff would have done. He took it upon himself to bring the man into the house, and announce the visitor openly to all.

"Mr Phillip Trotter, of Horncastle, bringing a message from the Sheriff of Lincolnshire, Sir Edward Dymocke."

Mr Phillip Trotter, thereupon, entered the dining room, his eyes revealing some mild surprise at finding quite so many gentlemen crowded at breakfast in the room! At first he was not quite sure where, or to whom, he should address his remarks, but then his eye lighted upon Guy Kyme. He was well-acquainted with him from his business dealings, so he faced his host, but encompassed all the gentlemen present, as he spoke.

Trotter was a small swarthy man, neatly attired but with a rather fidgety demeanour, his hands constantly fiddling with the brim of his hat which he still carried. The bailiff was not a man used to the correct behaviour of indoor servants, so he had not relieved Trotter of his headgear before announcing his presence.

"The sheriff, Sir Edward Dymocke, and Mr William Leach, bade me come to inform you all as to the activity in and around Horncastle yesterday, following the raising of Louth on Sunday night, and Monday. Firstly, Sir Edward asked me to discover whether Lord Burgh was amongst you? Or, if not – and I can, of course, see for myself that he is *not* here – I was required to ask whether you know aught of his whereabouts and actions?"

There were various 'meaningful' looks in the room at these

questions, but Trotter was at a loss as to discerning the meaning of any of them! No-one seemed about to enlighten him at this point either. Some of the gentlemen, perhaps, felt that because Guy Kyme was in the room, and, despite his kindness of hosting them at his house, thought that he may be a bit too close to Captain Cobbler. They chose to guard their tongues.

Others, perhaps, chose not to speak, as they realised that they should hear what Trotter might have to reveal first about the happenings in Horncastle the previous day. Some of them knew, too, that William Leach and Sir Edward Dymocke were occasional hunting partners, but that Sir Edward's view of Leach was jaundiced, to say the least, by legal moves on Leach's part which could have been detrimental to the interests of the Dymocke family. There seemed to be little love lost between them, in fact.

Trotter paused, until the silence was long enough for him to guess it would not be broken. So then he continued his designated task of bringing knowledge of the Horncastle events to Louth. Despite his fidgeting hands, his summary of events was fairly crisply delivered. He skimmed quickly over the first raising of Horncastle, attributing it to the enthusiasm of the Leach brothers, and cousin, in passing on information about the raising of Louth at the beginning of the week. He also referred to the upset, caused amongst the priesthood, by the bishop's chancellor, Dr Raynes.

"I myself was leading a party which visited Dr Raynes in his sickbed in the run-down castle at Old Bolingbroke yesterday. He is definitely not a well man, but I had a job restraining the host with me. There were a lot of poor men, who were all for rousting him out of bed and taking him over to the church, just outside the castle grounds, to swear him in to the cause. They were too rude for my liking, as I had told William Leach earlier in the day, when we went to the Dymocke's estate. But he merely smiled, and said to me not to get fussed about them – *'a little rough behaviour might persuade the sheriff of our capability and seriousness more quickly'*. Dr Raynes reaction to our visit may have proved Mr Leach correct!"

"The chancellor pulled me over to his bedside, and hoarsely whispered in my ear, that he would willingly pay well to be saved. In case the ruffians with me had heard him and thought he was offering me a personal inducement, I said out loud that I was sure a generous

336

payment for the well-being of the men with me would allow him to stay abed. He thereupon instructed his body servant to find twenty shillings from his saddlebag to give to us."

"But, as I have already said, the most significant happening yesterday was the 'bringing-in' of the Lincolnshire Sheriff and his family. The poor men who were in the host when we went to Scrivelsby Hall were very pleased to hear the Sheriff's words when he came out to meet the host – 'Masters, ye be welcome…' and when he was asked to take the oath he said – 'Ay masters, with a will' – though, in between, there were some sharp words said between Master Leach and the Sheriff which I did not hear. It was all smoothed over in a trice, however!"

"Mr Leach asked me to tell you clearly what had happened, and Sir Edward Dymocke asked me to wait for your response, once you have had opportunity to discuss the ramifications of all the happenings of the last few days in our two towns and the surrounding villages."

"I have to add, on my own behalf, that the people I know best in and around Horncastle now have high expectations that this matter will go forward with bravery and determination, not least now that the very Sheriff of our county is 'brought in' to take charge of the matter."

Trotter's shoulders twitched back and his chest expanded forward as he added his personal views of the matter in hand. He was clearly proud of his own role in events thus far.

"I will leave you gentlemen to cogitate upon what news I have brought you and will take my temporary leave of you…" and in a quiet aside to Guy Kyme he added…. "Perhaps you would be good enough to point me in the direction of your kitchens, sir, since I left Horncastle very early this morning and have not yet had chance to break my fast, begging your pardon, sir!"

Kyme smiled at their visitor, placed a guiding hand on his shoulder and eased him towards the door.

"Indeed Mr Trotter, I think you are wise to believe the gentlemen present will wish to talk freely, otherwise I would simply invite you to take a plate and join us. I will walk you along to the kitchen. It is but a few steps away, but there are several doors off the route we shall take, one of which leads you to the middens, not a place you might wish to visit at this hour."

Not only was this a fair representation of Kyme's hospitality in general, but he recognised the gentlemen present might also want a few moments to talk without his presence, too. He was not immune to the occasional awkward moments of either silence, or a redirection of the discussion, sometimes engendered by his sudden arrival in a room where the said gentlemen were talking.

It amused him, somewhat, and concerned him, somewhat, but, overall, his confidence in his own abilities was such that it irritated him, rather than worried him. He was content enough simply to let the issues slide away, as water off a duck's back. After all, it was he who was the host to this gathering, and he had several close friends present who would defend his honour if need be!

His instincts were accurate, however, and no sooner was he out of earshot, but Sir Robert Tyrwhitt coughed gently and spoke. Tyrwhitt, though sharing Kyme's breakfast table, had not stayed at Kyme's house overnight but, along with two of the other gentlemen, he had stayed at the house of a cousin of his wife's, a little further along the same road. The cousin had been gracious about putting them up, of course, but had then seemed more than a little put out by the fact that his guests had not arrived at his house until the early hours, well after midnight. In other words, until after the letter-writing marathon had concluded, and Maddison had galloped off to London. The cousin's irritation seemed to have rubbed off on Tyrwhitt himself, this morning, and his voice was tight as he spoke...

"Reading between the lines of what this man Trotter had to say, it seems that the Sheriff was coerced, as many of us were, and he is looking for a way to call a halt to this rebellion. It may be difficult, but we need to keep the rabble occupied, but quiet, until we get an answer from the king. And we need to do that without alerting Kyme, here; otherwise we will all find ourselves in trouble with the mob! He is too close to them for my comfort at least."

Tyrwhitt was not known for diplomacy in his dealings with people, nor for his abilities in reading other people's faces, or he would have known that several of those present would cheerfully have cut his tongue out at that moment for his unthinking insult to their host.

Sir William Ayscough was cut from a different cloth, however, and was not only a smoother operator – some would say 'slippery', perhaps? – but he recognised that in order to succeed in diverting

338

the action of the rebels, a little underhand manipulation would be necessary. So, feigning agreement with the commonwealth causes may be needed in the short run, in order to overcome the reactions of a potentially unruly mob.

He also realised he must carry his own colleagues with him on this sensitive issue, otherwise they may be putting themselves in mortal danger from the local citizenry. Alternatively, if they showed too much enthusiasm for those causes they may be putting themselves in mortal danger from their king and his moral outrage!

So, conscious of the tightrope he was stepping onto, he adopted a light, almost humourous tone for his next remarks, directed as they were, ostensibly at Tyrwhitt, but with Kyme's friends, present here in the room, at the forefront of his mind.

"I feel sure the sheriff would feel differently if he were to have breakfasted with us and tasted Mrs Hempsall's fine pork pie..."

"...and her mustard pickled cauliflower!" interposed Dalyson, in the same tone. Ayscough smiled a tight smile and continued...

"...but we do have to deal with the problems we actually have in front of us, rather than wish they might not have arisen. Now that the sheriff is 'brought in', as we have been ourselves, I am sure he would want to use his powers of leadership to make sure this – what shall we call it? – 'ruffling', were carried forward in the safest, least threatening way for all concerned."

"Perhaps that means taking the road to Lincoln with the combined host, and discussing these weighty issues, en masse, in the capital of our fine county of Lincolnshire. After all, the trip to Lincoln would help walk off some of the extra weight Mrs Hempsall has unwittingly imposed upon us all."

He was awarded a few gentle chuckles from around the room for his success with the right tone. Tyrwhitt, however, threw him a rather haughty toss of the head, and an indiscernible mumble. The quietness of the mumble, however, probably indicated that Tyrwhitt at least saw the rectitude of the Ayscough approach, in the face of overwhelming odds of the local ruffians and those now apparently loose in Horncastle too. But he privately thought it would get much worse before it got better!

CRCRCRCRCR

Kyme returned to the room soon after Ayscough's intervention, so the gathering then set-to, in order to decide how best to take the 'ruffling' forward to Lincoln, in a controlled manner. As they were doing this, they were startled when the Louth Church bells started ringing out, calling local folk to action – again. Ayscough immediately stood and made the decisive move to take charge of the situation, rather than let the situation take charge of them!

"Whatever the cause for the bells, we must be amongst the first to get down to the church, so we can take the lead, instead of being led by the commonwealth."

Almost under his breath... (almost!)... Tyrwhitt said...

"You mean, 'by the rabble!'"

And Dalyson stood, side by side, with Ayscough, saying nothing but picking up another small portion of pork pie to take with him. He was tempted to take some pickle too, but decided against. They then led the way out of Guy Kyme's spacious house and walked briskly towards the church with a trail of well-dressed gentlemen following on behind, Portington, Skipwith, Mussenden and the others. Guy Kyme brought up the rear alongside Phillip Trotter, who was also still munching a piece of pork pie.

In the few minutes it took them to reach the church precincts, the area outside the south door was already full of noisy residents who had had less far to walk, with more arriving all the time. Quite a few were already dressed for possible 'action' in their leather jerkins, with hedge-cutting blades or heavy clubs in hand, milling around trying to find out what was happening.

Alongside the Louth men were faces none of the locals recognised. In fact, the North Willingham contingent had arrived!

The newcomers on horseback had already dismounted. A very nervous Sir Thomas Moigne, the two Ayscough sons, and the unfortunate messenger from Lord Hussey, George Eatton, had all been hustled inside the church; rather roughly it has to be said. Their horses had been quickly taken out of the way onto a patch of rough land across the road from the west door of the church (its main entrance on high days and Holy Days)

A very small number of the foot contingent from North Willingham had been allowed into the church, too. But most had been left outside and were now sharing their information with the locals. As each new conversation started the previous ones had to get a little louder to compete, so the noise level was rising quickly as more and more people arrived and the information – *or quite often mis-information!* – was being shared around.

The monk, Morland, and his collaborator, the young priest Richardson, had not gone far away earlier, when ousted from the church. Now, they were back, on the edge of these crowds, with a number of black gowned religious colleagues.

They were not having an easy time in their discussions either. Quite a few of the brethren were as horrified at Morland's actions in trying to stop the ringing of the common bell, as had been the protectors of Louth Church inside earlier. Clearly Morland had misjudged the mood of his *religious brothers* as well as the mood of the Louth host. He and Richardson were not getting a very sympathetic reception. It was at this point that Sir William Ayscough and his colleagues were arriving on the scene.

Morland saw, from the corner of his eye, the trail of gentlemen following Sir William Ayscough, and he realised that *this group* might well be more appreciative of his actions than were his fellow monks and priests. So, he broke away from the black gowns, and placed himself in the path of Ayscough, Dalyson and the others. To give them their due, they did pause in their stride to listen to the monk. But, as soon as Ayscough heard that his two sons were now inside the church, along with Sir Thomas Moigne, and possibly being harshly treated, he pushed roughly past the self-serving monk, and tried to make his way to the south door which was the nearest point of entry from the direction whence he came.

In normal times, the local residents would have melted to either side to allow such a well-dressed gentleman easy passage. It was clear, however, that these were not considered 'normal times' and quite a few burly men took a half step *towards* Ayscough's proposed route, rather than a half step away, so that he found he was 'hampered' to say the least. Not only that, but the 'hampering' sometimes took the form of a hard shoulder or elbow in the ribs.

But Ayscough was in a fury by now. What man wouldn't be who would protect his sons? And he quite literally gave as good as he got, using his own elbows and shoulders with little mercy to clear his path.

CICICICICICI

...inside the church, Louth

Inside the church, it was at least as noisy as it was outside, and not much less confused. George Eatton, in particular, was getting some rough treatment from some of the North Willingham group, as he was induced to explain to Captain Cobbler the contents of the letters from Lord Hussey. These were the letters which called upon Moigne, Ayscough and the others, to find a way of stopping the rising in its tracks, a view that was affirmed by the letter to the mayor of Lincoln, Robert Sutton. Then there was Sutton's own letter to the gentlemen concerned, reinforcing Hussey's view.

Some people were surprised that Lord Hussey had written what he had, in the way that he had, because they knew him to be sympathetic with the views of Devotio Moderna, which had effectively spawned this action during the summer. Most knew, too, that he had faithfully served Queen Catherine of Aragon in her time of distress, when the king had been so unkind to her. But he *had* written those letters, and that was that.

CICICICICICI

Adding to the noise was a new rumour that had only been brought into the church a few minutes before, by Guy Kyme's bailiff. He said he had...

"...clearly heard Phillip Trotter, from Horncastle, say that Lord Burgh was raising a strong force in West Lincolnshire and Nottinghamshire to put the rising down..."

No-one inside the church yet knew that that was not quite what Phillip Trotter *had* said, so the rumour was being treated very seriously...and noisily, of course!

342

As if all of that was not enough to cause confusion, another large group of men had just arrived from Alford, a town between Louth and the Lincolnshire coast. They said that the whole area around Alford was now 'up', and looking to Louth for a lead as to what should happen next. The leaders of the Alford group had been allowed into the church – they had been on the go since five of the clock that morning, and many were sat in the pews at the back of the church looking very weary.

Another thirty or so men from Alford, and the nearby village of Bilsby, were amongst the crowd milling about outside the church. The remainder of the Alford contingent, about one hundred men altogether, were expected to arrive within the next half hour. Altogether, the church was now very full inside, with quite a few men spreading into the pews, large knots of men gathered into various spaces around the sitting area of the church, the whole thing very noisy and confused.

Nicholas Melton, himself, suddenly felt rather overwhelmed by the reactions to their action in Louth on the previous Sunday, but the personage of 'Captain Cobbler' came to the rescue, as Nicholas wavered. Captain Cobbler was dressed, of course, in his very fine multi-coloured Coat of Motley and Nicholas asked himself what such a leader of men would do in these circumstances. The thespian in him answered... *"Take charge!"*... a simple enough response!

So, Captain Cobbler it was, who broke out from the centre of the huddle in the space under the tower at the west end of the church. He walked purposefully down the central aisle and up the spiral steps to the pulpit where his friend, and priest, Thomas Kendall, was normally installed each and every Sunday. Great James, nearby as always, saw he was about to move, and took station on his right shoulder. And, whereas Sir William Ayscough was still struggling to get into the church, Captain Cobbler and his bodyguard, Great James, made smooth and swift progress through the knots of men inside the church.

Nicholas was not quite sure what Captain Cobbler would say when he got into the pulpit but clearly the great Captain Cobbler, himself, was very confident in what should be said. And he said it with verve and charisma... and great volume...

"Friends, gentlemen, SILENCE! ...please... ...thank you!

The noise level had fallen a little, as men round about saw Captain Cobbler's intention of taking charge of the chaos, as he began to stride towards the front of the church, authority strengthening with every step. It had fallen further as more men from outside Louth, saw that someone they had yet to meet was being purposeful, and they paused in their passing on of information. And so, the noise had actually stopped within a couple of seconds after the word 'SILENCE!' had reached their ears.

The noise outside the church continued, however, but was diminished a little as the men nearest the open doors of the church, also responded to the barked order for quiet coming from the pulpit.

Nicholas felt a new, and strange, sense of calm come over him as he stood firm and tall in the pulpit. He felt as though, just at this moment, he held the destiny of the fine church in his hands. It was as if he controlled ALL the strings of a fairground puppet theatre, and everyone and everything would simply dance to *his* tune. The church was silent, and there was a sense of expectation, all eyes drawn to his brightly-coloured coat, all ears attuned to what he might say next. He felt, too, that time had slowed down for him so that he could measure, finely, exactly what he said, and was about to say.

He had rarely been in the pulpit, apart from the times they had used the inside of the church to rehearse the Corpus Christi play cycle, and he had always had a sense of being out of place – it was '*owned*' by Thomas Kendall, who used it every week.

But, today felt different – he felt entirely in his element, in control. His voice resonated against the church walls.

"We have a lot of new information this morning, some of it accurate, some of it in the form of rumour – but we should ignore the rumour only at our peril."

"I will try and summarise briefly what we actually *know*. Then we should try and get to the bottom of the rumours. And *then* we need to make some decisions about what we should do next – and, as you might expect, I have some thoughts you should hear about that."

"We must be brief in our discussions in here, too, because we must then share *all* this information with our brothers and friends who are now gathering outside the church. We must move forward as a commonwealth, working together for the common good, for the church, and for the king."

"Firstly, let us remember why we are here in the first place. We believe events are conspiring towards the possibility that Chancellor

344

Cromwell, and the king's advisers have persuaded, or are in the process of persuading, the king to start taking the church treasures to the king's national treasury. They have already stripped many religious houses of their treasure."

"We are unhappy, too, about the huge changes being made to the practices of the church, and its usages."

"Beyond that, there are those that are unhappy about possible extra taxes to be imposed. And, many other threats to the common good have been cited, and denied. Above all, however, we are concerned for the continuing 'health' of the Common Wealth, literally all that treasure that we, together over the years, and our fathers before us, have vested in this, the community of our church. Not simply this church in Louth, but in the mother church to which we all belong, and in Horncastle, in North Willingham, in Alford, Bilsby, Grimsby... to name just a few of those churches represented here today."

"We started this action in Louth, because this is where these threats seemed first to be manifested. But, we hear today, that Horncastle was 'up' yesterday, that Alford and Bilsby and surrounding villages were 'up' this morning, that Grimsby is expected to be 'up' tomorrow. North Willingham and Rasen have also been 'up' since early this morning – and for a very particular reason."

"Many of the senior gentry in this wonderful County of Lincolnshire have, apparently quite willingly, joined us in our endeavours to right these wrongs. Many more of them have been persuaded it would be in their best interests to join us in our actions. It is certainly true that the more we can all show a united front, the more likely it is that we will be heard, with sympathy, in the high courts and circles of this land."

"And yet..." he paused eloquently, letting the word hang in silence. Then he lowered his voice and continued. "...and yet, there are those who would bring us all down and whose 'trumpets' would bring the walls down upon our heads if they could. As most of you know we went to Caistor yesterday to 'bring in' to the cause certain gentlemen meeting there, who *said* they were there to discuss the subsidy."

"When we were close, and they could have talked to us with quiet calm, they took flight, and some of them got away before we could have our discussions. The two most notable gentlemen to escape our clutches were Sir Thomas Moigne, and, of course, Lord Burgh from Gainsborough."

Nicholas looked directly at Moigne and said...

"It was good of you to grace us with your presence today sir, but I do not believe it was an entirely voluntary action, was it Sir Thomas?"

Sir Thomas did his best to look suitably humble, though without conspicuous success... Nicholas smiled benignly at him and continued...

"Lord Burgh is not with us today." Nicholas looked around the church as if to check... "As you know, the noble Lord is the subject of a wild range of rumours; having apparently *BEEN* successful in raising a force in Gainsborough to come and 'quieten' us. Or having fled to the relative safety of Nottinghamshire, where he *IS* raising an army to 'crush' our 'rebellion' Or... but let me come back to those rumours later. Let me get back to the man in our midst, Sir Thomas Moigne."

"Now, Sir Thomas, here, decided, not unnaturally I suppose, that other senior members of the County gentry should be made privy to the happenings of yesterday. Although we have not seen his original letter, we have seen and heard the response it occasioned from Baron Hussey. Some of you have expressed surprise at the things Lord Hussey said in his letters to other gentry in Lincolnshire, because it was thought from previous contact with him that he might be sympathetic to the views we espoused."

"It is quite clear, however, that such thoughts were misplaced. Or, perhaps, Sir Thomas's letter to Lord Hussey was misleading as to what we were trying to achieve?"

He was about to go on, to explain why such thoughts were misplaced, but he was interrupted by a noisy scuffling coming from the area near the south door... and a loud voice broke the silence of his pause in speech. Sir William Ayscough would brook no further denial of his entry to the church.

"Let me through, I say, my sons are here as hostages!"

Ayscough had eventually managed to elbow his way through to the door and was clearly not taking "no" for an answer. From anyone!

Captain Cobbler got no further in his speech as pandemonium broke out.

Ayscough was allowed through to his sons, who both hugged him, and clearly let him know they were still OK. But the men around Moigne would not let him talk to Ayscough, and hustled Moigne quickly away into a side chapel nearby.

It was clear there was some disruption outside the church too. Although Ayscough had been eventually allowed through, none of the other gentlemen captured the previous day were being allowed into the church itself, and there was quite a bit of scuffling as they tried to force their way in. The only other person who was allowed passage was Guy Kyme, known to be a sympathetic local gentleman.

So Dalyson, Portington, Skipwith and the others were being restrained outside with quite a bit of strong language. It was *loud* strong language, too. It was clear that the reaction from Lord Hussey and the rumours about Lord Burgh had brought suspicion back onto the gentry. And that their current behaviour had somehow encouraged such a response, instead of doing what they had promised to do on behalf of the commonwealth.

Everyone was aware, too, that the gentry had sent one of their own down to the king with a letter about yesterday's happenings. And now, following the Hussey and Sutton letters, questions were being asked what that letter might have contained. The noise level was escalating again.

☙☙☙☙☙☙

Sir William Ayscough was trying to speak above the noise, but was shouted down by those around him – not something he was at all used to, he normally received a respectful silence when talking to common people. He looked flushed and flustered and his sons were anxious for him – this was outside the realms of their experience too.

It was clear that Sir Thomas Moigne would have liked to speak as well but the men of North Willingham and Rasen, who had him surrounded, would have nothing of it.

"Friends, gentlemen, brothers... let us have some peace... ... SILENCE!!" Again, Captain Cobbler was exerting his authority.

"Open the west doors wide, please, and let us move out into the sunshine. The fresh air will do us *all* good! Quickly please, if Lord Burgh *is* on the move, time is now of the essence!"

Although the noise of voices quietened down quite a lot, the general noise level stayed high, since over two hundred men were now trying to make their way out of the church. Normally this might have been achieved fairly quickly, but the problem today was that there were already many hundreds of men gathered outside the church, all trying to get closer, so they could hear what was going on.

The cobbled road outside the south door, constrained as it was by the vicarage wall on the other side of the road, was absolutely solid with people, including the gentry who had been at Guy Kyme's for breakfast, so virtually no-one was making progress through the south door. The west door was a bit easier, since the land fell away to the west, and it was not bounded by a stone wall, so the men there could be eased away from the church as those inside moved out.

As Nicholas reached the open door, he could see over the tops of the heads of the people standing a step or two below the entrance. There were many more people than he had ever seen at the church, even including the crowds for the big theatrical events of Corpus Christi. There were crowds of folk, stretching away along all the approach roads as far as the eye could see.

There were men in the fields across the way, with the horses from the North Willingham contingent, and there were groups sprawling round to his right, down the curving road that led across the bridge over the River Lud. All the green space nearby was covered with people, including many who were trying to be reverent as they were trampling over the graves in the churchyard in the rather cold shade to the north of the church, before the land dropped away to the river.

The men outside were shouting questions and comments, wanting to know what was happening, and Nicholas managed to achieve a reasonable degree of quiet simply by raising both arms aloft and waving gently downwards with both hands. When it seemed quiet enough, he spoke with full projection of his voice and said much the same as he had inside the church, bringing people up to date.

He had to pause several times, as men reacted to the different items of news, or rumour, that he regaled them with. He could feel the palpable anger as he told them about Lord Hussey's letter and the supporting letter from Lincoln's mayor Robert Sutton to the gentry, whom both of them had thought were still free agents.

He allowed the anger to build a while, as he kept telling his story. It seemed to be unifying the multitude surrounding him, and was resonant with his own anger, too. He thought the gentry were playing a dangerous game, pretending on the one hand to appear sympathetic, yet clearly some of them despising the whole enterprise.

He knew, for example, that quite a few of the richer families in the County had already benefitted by buying stone cheaply, or simply *taking* stone, or carved wood, or metalwork, from some of the suppressed religious houses. And goodness knows what other riches had been stripped away. The anger was real, but it needed focussing to achieve change. So, he presented them with his idea...

"...and so it seems to me, that we must take the action further, and make our feeling clear, by going on to Lincoln. As far as I can gather from all the news this morning, we now have the weight of the sheriff of the county, Sir Edward Dymocke, working with us rather than against us!

The massed ranks of men in front of him let out a ragged cheer at this news.

"This will all require a considerable degree of organisation, and it is clear that we will have to entrust quite a bit of that organisation to many of the gentlemen with us here today..."

Shouts of dismay replaced the cheers. Indeed, when some of the gentlemen in the crowd, tried to start speaking about such organisation, they were ALL, without exception, shouted down, some of them with none-too-gentle prods from elbows or knees to keep them quiet. Indeed, several began to look rather afraid of the mood here today. Nicholas, too, felt he had to take care not to let things get out of hand!

"I am going to ask Guy Kyme, here, to explain what should happen next."

Another ragged cheer greeted this piece of news, he was really the only gentleman around who was widely liked and trusted by the general populace. Before Kyme actually spoke, Nicholas had more information to impart...

"While he is speaking, I am going to start talking with John and Pat Baker about what needs to be done about food for the next few days." – This comment generated another cheer! – "I know quite a lot of you are already rather a long way from home, and we need to keep you fed, if we are all going to be able to work together getting many thousands of people to Lincoln without starving or dying of thirst!"

The cheer which had started in the midst of this sentence became louder and more protracted as he finished speaking. The crowd was clearly pleased with him for dealing with such a practical problem close to their hearts (their stomachs!) And so, a beaming Captain Cobbler stepped down from the stone plinth he had been using to raise himself above the milling crowds. Guy Kyme took his place.

"We are going to Lincoln!" He shouted as soon as he stood upright... Guy Kyme knew how to carry a crowd with him, too! Cheers filled the air...

"...and the County Sheriff is coming with us, to ensure a welcome when we get there!" Another loud cheer.

"But we need to be organised."

There were a few groans, but Kyme carried on speaking as if nothing happened.

"So, we are going to leave here and reassemble at Julian's Bower. For those of you who are strangers to Louth, Julian's Bower is our turf maze, with plenty of space around it and it is just over a quarter of a mile in that direction."

He pointed almost due south to the edge of Louth township. It was a favourite place for local gatherings of any size. Many of the best church ales were held there, as all the locals well knew!

"Make your way there now, and we will organise everyone into reasonably sized troops with captains and petty captains to keep order – and to make sure you all get fed, if you are visitors to Louth."

"We expect Louth men to make sure they have their own food and water for at least today and tomorrow, when we shall be setting off to Lincoln. If you have room for a few guests tonight, let your captains know and we shall try and put up as many visitors as we can under a roof tonight. If we cannot manage home billets for all, there are some comfortable barns ranged round the south of the town, and you will be directed to one of these."

"Those of you who are local make sure you organise some clothing to keep the water off. Also, in groups at least, make sure you have a good canvas cover, because we may be sleeping under the stars tomorrow night, and Friday night at least – and it *is* October, remember. The sun is shining now, but we all know that is not guaranteed to last – my farming friends say we should expect some rain over the next few days!"

"Right my friends – let us move!" And on that note, men started moving off in the direction Kyme had pointed and the noise level rose again, but it was a much better-humoured sound than previously. It was interspersed with laughter, as locals pulled the legs of strangers who had never visited Julian's Bower, nor even knew of its existence.

ଔଔଔଔଔ

Kyme and Captain Cobbler, John Baker, and several other key Louth men, all went back into the church, to get started on the necessary organisational details. All the gentlemen who had been 'pressed' into support the previous day also entered the church. Sir Thomas Moigne, the two younger Ayscoughs, and George Eatton had never been let OUT of the church.

Sir William Ayscough now started to say how important it was that the key gentlemen should be properly arrayed in their armour and that ...

"...we should all get home to collect our harness..."

...but Captain Cobbler nipped that suggestion in the bud, and turned to face Ayscough, who had remained standing in the doorway of the church, just behind him, as Nicholas spoke to the crowds. His movement brought the two men face to face and in very close proximity.

Normally Nicholas would have stepped back a little to give the gentleman more room but now he chose to keep his face just two or three inches from that of Ayscough. Since he was so close, he had no need to shout, but the men roundabout could hear every word, clear as a bell. It was Captain Cobbler at his most commanding.

"Let me make it quite clear that I do not trust you as far as I could throw you! Nor should you, or any of your colleagues, have much expectation of gaining the real trust of the men of the commonwealth of Louth, and beyond, given all that has happened in the last couple of days."

"So, you may, of course, send servants, or local men, to fetch your harness, ready for the early-morning start tomorrow, but you will all stay within the confines of the town of Louth this afternoon and evening. We need you to help us organise and plan for the needs of this large host of men, for the next few days. We also need to keep you clearly in our sight, and make sure you get up to no more letter-writing."

At first Sir William started to splutter, since he was not used to being talked to in such a manner by a cobbler, for goodness' sake. He quietened down, however, when he saw the look he was getting from Great James, glowering over Nicholas' right shoulder. Great James said nothing, of course, as he was noted for being a taciturn man; but it was pretty clear from his scowling face, what he was actually thinking.

After a brief discussion in the church Captain Cobbler encouraged the key gentlemen of the county to go back to Guy Kyme's house, where they were told they should discuss firm plans for getting a large host of men, efficiently into Lincoln the next day. But first they all went along to Julian's Bower, to make sure the host was being organised properly in the field.

No-one knew for sure who really owned the fields there, or why the owner chose to remain anonymous, but the farmer who kept sheep on the land was always careful not to divulge anything, and the whole area was more or less treated as common land. The turf maze at its centre was an important 'play area' for the town's children, and had been for decades at least.

There was barely an adult of Louth who had not at one time stepped carefully onto the entrance stone, and pretended to be lost in a real maze with high hedges, as princes and princesses faced in the famous Hampton Court maze. Indeed, there were some lucky adults who could still pretend they were lost and were for that reason seemed able to retain some of the innocence of childhood! But childhood innocence was a long way from the thoughts of most of the town's menfolk in the Bower today.

Jack Bawnus and his helpers were there, again trying to keep a reasonable head-count of how many men there were at the muster, so that plans could be made for feeding everyone. Nicholas had asked Jack Bawnus to report his numbers to both John and Ma Baker and then to Great James who would pass the numbers on to Captain Cobbler, himself, of course. Nicholas would, in turn, ensure the gentlemen were given accurate numbers for their planning purposes.

It was clear that numbers were significantly higher than even on Monday, and were expected to get much higher too, since Horncastle was 'up', as was Alford and surrounding villages and it was expected, on strong rumour, that Grimsby would be 'up' in the morning too. Guy Kyme had been on business to Grimsby only last week and had good contacts there who were now sending him up-to-date information.

Even before all the organising into 'troops' that was happening at the field had finished, Jack Bawnus had a pretty good idea of the likely numbers – he had tallied the 'extra' numbers from the incoming villages, and added them to the totals they had worked out for Monday's outing to Caistor. He left his helpers at the field, attempting to get better figures, but he was confident enough of his own estimate to go and talk to John Baker. Baker had stayed home, and was busy baking bread for today. Ma Baker was equally busy baking pies. They were covered in flour, and Jack smiled as he decided Ma Baker must have won the flour fight they appeared to have had.

"Y-y-y-ou're b-b-b-oth a d-d-d-ifferent colour to the last t-t-time I s-s-saw you!"

He didn't normally attempt humourous banter with anyone because he sometimes stuttered so badly. But he always felt comfortable with the Bakers, they were such friendly people. John and Ma Baker looked at each other and burst out laughing.

"I see what you mean Jack," John Baker chuckled. "I think we both have a couple of minutes before the next things need doing – so speak up and let's hear the numbers so far!

Jack gave them his estimates and John sat down with a 'thump' on the wooden seat in their kitchen. "'*That IS a lot of mouths to feed!*" He paused, thinking.

"We can get through today with no trouble, I am sure, because most local people will be living at, and eating from, home in Louth of course. So, we will only have the non-locals to feed. And that, as you see from our flour-covered faces, is a process which is 'in-hand' – we are busy because we know there are a lot of them! I don't think we realised quite how many!"

"When you tell the group of gentlemen doing their planning at Guy Kyme's those numbers, you probably also need to tell them – from me – that they will have to arrange to pick up quite a bit of meat 'on the hoof' on our journey through to Lincoln. We will be able to carry enough for tomorrow and breakfast on Friday but we will need fresh meat and general provender after that."

"In the meantime, I will talk to all of our butcher colleagues, and ask them to make sure they bring along their tools and trestle tables for killing and cutting up the sheep – or beef cattle, if we are that lucky?"

Baker was speaking quickly because that was the way his brain worked, he seemed to be doing a lot of calculating as he was speaking...

"They will also need to make arrangements, ahead of the march, to get sacks of flour ready to use wherever we stop." He ceased speaking suddenly, as if pondering a big question... "I believe Mr Dalyson is there with Guy Kyme? So, your numbers will mean most to him, and he will be able to work out how much flour and stuff we need. I know that he does that kind of thing for the major musters in the north of the County, because we have spoken about these matters before. Tell him, if he needs to talk to me, he will have to come here, because we are busy cooking at the moment, and cannot leave things unattended!"

Ma Baker chose to add at this point that...

"The Alford group was raised early this morning by William Wilson, Alford's miller, so they knew well enough to bring along their own flour and meat for today! That is why I am so busy with pies already; he set me to work using their stocks! All being well we should be able to get enough cooked today, in order to have some in hand for tomorrow as well. I have got quite a few of the Louth ladies cooking pies this afternoon! So we are all working for the common good!"

John and Ma Baker smiled knowingly at each other as she was speaking. They both knew they were always working for the common good, they felt strongly it was their special duty. It was more of a calling really and was always done with a good will. They knew (*perhaps they hoped, anyway*) that they would get their reward in due course in Heaven. They always felt the goodwill of the community was with them here on earth too!

"And goodwill is all the reward we ever need, isn't it Ma?" said John with a smile. "So we'd better get on and earn it Bawnus, my dear fellow! Back to the ovens, Ma, for both of us!"

CRCRCRCRCR

Jack Bawnus took his leave of them, and walked the short distance to the church, which he found a lot quieter than it had been only a little while ago. Because there was a light breeze from the south, he could still hear the sounds of the muster coming from Julian's Bower nearly half a mile away, with captains and petty captains being appointed, and formally recognised by their troops.

Mostly, of course, it was a question of reaffirmation of known relationships within villages and locales within towns – but there were always a few changes as people died or retired from their roles, as generations moved ever onwards. So, the men were expected to pay full attention, as if going to war – duty and loyalty demanded it! Certainly it sounded as though each appointment was presaged by a short roll of drums, muffled though they sounded from this distance.

It seemed as though some of the gentlemen 'brought in' (*reluctantly*) from Caistor the previous day, were actually beginning to get involved voluntarily, now that the news had been brought that the Sheriff was 'in' too! The volunteering was most apparent amongst those gentlemen who had been party to the discussions that had taken place quietly in Devotio Moderna meetings during the summer.

For the most part, such was the commitment to charitable work of these men that they were in full sympathy with the needs of the ordinary working families that had been pressing for *some* kind of action to stem the tide of monastic closures. And when their *churches* seemed to come under threat, there had been a marked change of mood in their normal acceptance of the way of things, as it were being stripped from under them and their extended families by newly raised-up 'counsellors' to the monarch.

In particular, on this day, Thomas Mussenden and John Booth, who had both been with Sir William Ayscough's party of commissioners to Caistor, were scuttling between the meetings in the church and in Guy Kyme's house – for, by now, most of the senior gentry had left the fields at Julian's Bower. It was, after all, getting cooler now it was late afternoon and the sun had gone in!

The main group in Louth Church comprised Captain Cobbler and his supporting group of Louth artisans, labourers and lesser gentlemen; plus Phillip Trotter from Horncastle. There were also two men from North Willingham area (most of the rest were still at Julian's Bower, being mustered and captained). Also there, in the church, was the miller William Wilson representing the Alford, Bilsby and Markby group.

Again, the rest of the men from the Alford area, were at the muster. There, with yet another roll of the drums, their two main local gentlemen, Sir Andrew Billesby and Edward Forsett had just been declared captain and petty captain of upwards of two hundred men. Coincidentally as the drums rolled for them and two hundred men were cheering them to the sky, William Wilson had just been telling Captain Cobbler and the others in church, that they should be rather wary of Sir Andrew, in particular, because he had tried to stop them raising the village that morning. And he had only been over-ridden by sheer weight of numbers and "...*not a few muttered threats!*" Wilson was continuing...

"Most of the threats could not be heard very clear, but the atmosphere you could slice with a scythe and then there was one shout (I reckon as I know'd who shouted, too, but I ain't saying nothing!) This shout made Sir Andrew go white as a sheet, and very quiet like! – '*String 'im to yonder oak*' was the words! At that point he changed tack and said – 'Gentlemen – as you will' and let us get on wi' it!"

A bitter chuckle escaped his lips, but he was smiling because they had got their way after all!

John Booth had heard the whole of this story, because he was spending most of his time with the group in the church. But the cousin of Legbourne Priory's Mother Maria, Thomas Mussenden, only heard the last half sentence as he had only just walked in, having come from the Kyme household.

It was the young Sister Maria who had greeted Nicholas Melton's cousin Eleanor those many years ago. Nicholas could still picture the rosy-cheeked girl who had met them all at the priory gates with fresh milk to drink with their picnic lunch of bread and bacon! She had got on so well with his old "uncle" Tom who had passed away these many years. Nicholas had not met her since then, but had had a conversation with Thomas Mussenden about the memory, only a couple of hours previously, as they were getting to know one another.

Mussenden had smiled, and said, "...that was typical of our Jane..." and from that point forward Nicholas felt a strong affinity with Mussenden, a feeling that seemed to be mutual, because of their shared cousinly relations in Legbourne. Indeed they were already on first-name terms! Nicholas noted his entry to the meeting...

"Welcome Thomas, what news do you bring of the discussions amongst our senior gentry at Guy Kyme's? Jack Bawnus, here, has just given us his preliminary numbers and he and John Booth were just about to go with those numbers to the gentlemen you have just left!"

As the newcomer started to speak, the priest, Thomas Kendall, was walking round with a taper, lighting the candles, as the afternoon light was now quickly fading. It was likely that the muster would be breaking up soon, if that process had not already started, so that the strangers to the town could be found shelter to spend the night, before full darkness settled in.

Mussenden had given a brief account of the main organisational discussions by the time all the candles were lit. Much of it was straightforward information, mostly anticipated, or spoken about, by the group in the church during their own discussions. He finished up, however, with two genuinely new pieces of information which grabbed the attention of everyone present...

"...two pieces of important news to finish with. Firstly, the gentlemen are suggesting that we aim for the main muster tomorrow at Grange de Lings. It is about three miles north of the city's north wall, and the Newport Arch entry into Lincoln. It will take the numbers anticipated, and many more besides if necessary! It is on the Lincoln Edge high ground and is apparently well drained for the most part, which may be important if it rains, as the local farmers are suggesting it may."

"It is also the largest natural muster point as you come from this direction, so it should be the lowest journey time for the majority of us. It is also easily accessible from Lincoln – as far as delivery of food, and supplies, is concerned."

"The second piece of news, about which I shall enlighten you in a second, turned out to be the deciding factor between Grange de Lings and the other possibility – which was the West Common Land. The West Common would also have been large enough for our numbers and, indeed, just as accessible for many of us."

"However, we have now heard that Grimsby will definitely be UP tomorrow – *and they will be bringing their cannons*! They might have some difficulty crossing the River Witham to get to the West Common, without going through the outskirts of town and the gentlemen thought that would be too provocative, given the Mayor's views. So, Grange de Lings was chosen."

Mussenden was smiling broadly as he finished speaking, mainly because of the effect this last piece of news had had on the group listening. Several jaws had dropped, since there had been no inkling of "cannon" in any of the rumours coming out of Grimsby. Mussenden continued...

"We don't know exactly how many cannon there will be, but the information coming to Guy Kyme from his Grimsby friends was very definite about it. It was definitely in the plural, rather than a single cannon. Indeed, we think they may already have set off with the weapons today, since it is normally a slow job hauling those things, even the smaller ones. So, they may have tried to get a couple of hours start in the daylight today, so they can be close to Lincoln before eventide tomorrow."

Suddenly, Nicholas' mind flew back to the time he was sixteen or so and travelling down to London for the second time. He remembered, in vivid detail, the tale of Big Saint John the Evangelist falling into a ditch in France, and the blushes he was spared, by not saying out loud that "...such a thing never happened..." And that reminded him of his shared journey with Bill Cole, which had proved to be so dangerously eventful the next day.

He had not seen Bill, in these twenty or more intervening years, but he had heard by a circuitous route that Bill had taken the cloth of a friar after being treated so carefully and well in the monastery when he had broken his leg. He also gathered that Bill was based in a religious house somewhere in Yorkshire but Nicholas knew not where. *'Was he even still alive?'*

'Well, well, it has been a long time since I thought about those long-ago events'. He was so lost in his own thoughts for a moment, that he completely missed the question he had just been asked, only realising at the last second that he had even been asked a question!

"I am sorry, my mind was distracted for a second or two there, Thomas, thinking of times past! What did you ask me?"

"I said, Sir William Ayscough was of the view that we should send an urgent message to Grimsby to say the cannon should immediately be secured in Grimsby, but be made available to be called on if we should need them. There were those who argued against him, and I wondered if you have a view to share with us about that?"

Nicholas was smiling as he answered.

"I am glad I asked you to repeat the question, then, Mr Mussenden. It seems to be an issue of some importance! And, judging from the wry smile on your face, I suspect you have an idea how we may choose to answer that question!?"

"I am sure my colleagues here will have views to share with you as well, but I think it safe to say they will agree with me when I suggest Sir William is spitting into the wind here! I hope, of course, that the occasion will not arise where we should need to fire the cannon. But my view is that we should have every strength at our disposal if worse came to worst. So the cannon *will* be taken to Lincoln as the Grimsby host has planned. They should be made clearly visible for all to see, when they are there, too, with firing-training taking place for those who may be called upon to use them."

Sounds, and nods, of affirmation came quickly from all those present. Nicholas looked around the meeting, and then smiled as he spoke.

"Yes, Thomas, it is clear what answer you should take back to Sir William; the Grimsby cannon will come to Lincoln! Tell him Captain Cobbler has spoken!"

ରେ ରେ ରେ ରେ ରେ

At this point Thomas Mussenden changed the subject...

"The only other thing I was asked to mention, is the issue raised by Phillip Trotter's ambiguous comments this morning about the whereabouts of Lord Burgh..."

Trotter was still in the church, having chosen to stay with the group wherein he felt most comfortable, and welcome. He immediately intervened here, before Thomas Mussenden had even finished speaking.

"My comments were not in the least ambiguous! I was merely asking if anyone knew of Lord Burgh's whereabouts! 'Twas a straightforward question!"

Mussenden raised his eyebrows at the interruption, and continued...

"Well, whatever the comment – or question – it was decided that we should send some small scouting parties out to try and establish the truth of the matter. So, the monk, William Morland, went out and about with William Hert, the butcher, in one looping ride. And the Bailiff William King and another man, whose name I do not know, went off in a different loop to see what intelligence they could discover. Both pairs have been out several hours, but all have recently arrived back. They brought no comprehensive news, however, only echoes of the rumours that were bandied about this morning."

Several secondary conversations started at this information, and Nicholas had to raise a hand to bring the meeting back to order.

"Mr Trotter, you have the floor..."

Phillip Trotter clearly wanted to clarify his earlier position, worried that more people might still think his words had been ambiguous, though he felt they had not been so.

"It was what the Sheriff, Sir Edward Dymocke, said, and the concern in his tone that may have coloured my words." Trotter said, a little defensively.

"Obviously, the Sheriff was rightly concerned that Lord Burgh may have thought the 'ruffling' here was a small matter, and the noble Lord might have thought he could raise a force from his local area of Lincolnshire to put down any discontent quickly and easily. WE know, of course, that he would be mistaken, but he might try anyway. So we clearly need to be aware of the danger, and curtail it if possible."

Nicholas took up the thought, and followed through with a question.

"So, does anyone here know anyone, or have family, or friends, in the Gainsborough area? Or, failing that, is there anyone who has contacts or family in **Lincoln,** who may have contacts in Gainsborough?" He paused.

"No, I rather thought it was a long shot, leading us nowhere. So, apart from suddenly finding Lord Burgh at the head of a marauding army in our backyard, intent on destroying us, does anyone have any sensible thoughts as to what we should do?"

As he was beginning this last set of thoughts, he was rather surprised to see John Booth come back into the church. Booth had gone off with Jack Bawnus, not very long previously, to provide the gentry at Kyme's house with the tally of men committed to this venture tomorrow. Nicholas anticipated he would be there for quite a while.

Booth straight away explained his reappearance...

"I can see that you are all surprised I am back so soon, but, as it happens, I have been sent back to pass on a message relating to the very point Captain Cobbler was just raising. The gentlemen had been discussing this same point just before we got there. And Monk Morland and the Bailiff William King had not long been back, having achieved little reward for their efforts at fact finding – all of which I believe you now know from Thomas Mussenden."

A nod of heads between Booth and Mussenden confirmed this. Booth went on...

"The suggestion Guy Kyme made, was that a moderately small but highly mobile group of knowledgeable, and committed, men should set off from Louth, on horseback, before first light. They should go at least as far as Gainsborough, into Lord Burgh's back yard – to use Captain Cobbler's allusion just now – to discover what the situation is. And then head back to Lincoln, to meet up with the host at the Grange de Lings muster later in the day."

"Clearly, this group would not be able to fight if there was a force being raised but it *would be able* to report back quickly if something was afoot. He strongly made the point about it consisting of committed men, so that villages and towns on the journey could be persuaded to join us at muster – or be dissuaded from attacking us – depending on what course of action was expected in any location."

"Mr Kyme suggested, Captain Cobbler, that you and he should lead this party. And that it should include a number of the horseback contingent from Alford, and some from North Willingham, as well as yourself, of course, and a small number of your horsed colleagues from the Louth area."

Booth was clearly not one used to making long speeches – and for him this *was* a long speech! – but he seemed pleased that he had carried it off so well. Indeed, he was even more pleased when there was a little ripple of applause which greeted the idea, and smiles all round!

"Thank you John; that was a timely entrance and report! I think I speak for all of us when I say the efforts you and Thomas here are making, to liaise between mutually suspicious groups, is helping very much."

Nicholas then spread his hands wide and asked...

"Friends, what say you to this latest idea?"...as if he didn't know from the applause!

Affirmation was swift, and changed the mood of the meeting in a way Nicholas could not quite define? Certainly the atmosphere felt more charged, like the air felt just before a lightning strike close by. More purposeful, too, maybe... not that the meeting felt without purpose before, of course, but it seemed less 'hypothetical' now and more 'real'.

Captain Cobbler took a breath and resumed.

"Aye, well then Mr Booth, perhaps you would be good enough to return directly to Mr Kyme's house and confirm that we concur with his idea, and the party from this end will be..." he paused, looking round the meeting, catching an eye here and an eye there...

"...let us say about sixteen men altogether, plus Mr Kyme and two or three of his party of gentlemen? Say twenty at most. And we should be ready when the church bell tolls for four of the morning clock."

John Booth smiled a satisfied smile for his part in this initiative, nodded once to Nicholas, and a couple of times around the assembly, and took himself back to the Kyme household.

"Well, that was all swiftly concluded" ...chimed in the deep voice of Great James...

"...and in view of the hour, may I suggest we begin to draw the previous discussions to a close, so that those of us needing an early start in the morning can organise our provisions for the day. We need to get ourselves fully ready, to ensure we do not have to delay the start of this enterprise come the hour!"

"Sound thinking, James..." Captain Cobbler concurred, "...let us quickly review where we were in our planning, and make sure that those, who have had specific tasks allotted to them, know what they are, and how everything fits together tomorrow."

"Rather than indulge in more talking for the sake of it, may I make the assumption that we were already reasonably clear..." nods all round "...and let me just ask three or four key questions. If the answer to each is 'yes', then perhaps the meeting can break up into smaller groups to put our plans into effect...?"

So, Captain Cobbler asked his questions and the answers came back as "*YES*", "*AYE*", "*YES*" and "*YEA*" from varying sources in the meeting. The meeting then broke up, noisily, into several smaller groups, seemingly everyone talking at once. Nicholas decided he '*had better...*' – but even before he had finished the thought of what he ought to be doing, he was interrupted. Great James laid a big hand on his shoulder and said quietly...

"We are going to have to be up very early in the morning, and there is nothing more *you* need to be doing here. Go home to that lovely wife of yours, and see your boys before they go to bed. You have been so preoccupied with everything, and everybody else this week, your family has hardly seen you."

"We are going to be away for a few days at least, so go and get your things ready for morning, and get an early night's sleep. We need you bright, and refreshed, in the morning to take charge – Captain Cobbler!"

This last reference to his new-found status was so much over-emphasised with deliberate melodrama, that it made Nicholas laugh. Great James smiled in response and then concluded...

"I will make sure all the Alford and North Willingham people concerned, are safely sequestered for the night, and everyone knows where to meet in the morning. And you know that if there *are* any problems, I can easily walk down your road and check with you anything that needs checking. So just relax!"

Great James lived by himself, having been widowed eight years previously when his wife died in childbirth. They had had no surviving children, so he just had himself to look after. And Nicholas did feel relieved that someone was "allowing" him to go off duty for a while.

He had hardly seen his wife, Eliza Jane, and their two boys, Robert and Arthur, at home, for over a week. At fifteen years old, however, Robert had been old enough to go with the host to Caistor. Even then, Nicholas had seen little enough of Robert, as he himself had been on horseback, of course, and Robert had been walking with his uncle, Tom Foster, (Eliza Jane's brother), and an older, second cousin of Nicholas', Joe Waterland. 'Uncle Joe', as Robert called him, had kept them all amused, with tales of pranks from musters over the years, mostly involving himself and Nicholas.

Robert really liked his Uncle Joe; he had a very expressive face and an infectious laugh. Sometimes, for no sensible or rational reason, he would crease up with a giggling fit, tears streaming from his eyes, hopelessly unable to stop laughing. As he was beginning to recover, someone would ask what he was actually laughing at, and he might start to try and explain, but after about three words, the quest would get the better of him, and he would collapse into another helpless fit of giggles.

By the time he had tried, three or four times, to say what it was he was laughing at, he would be gasping for breath, and everyone else would be laughing, too, even though they had no idea what at! Smiling at such recollections, Nicholas started to make his way out of the church.

Although several people tried to engage Nicholas in some conversation, which seemed important to them, Great James would ward them off, as he was guiding Nicholas out of the church doors. Nicholas was quite happy for his huge friend to do this, for he suddenly felt himself to be very weary indeed. As they got to the heavy south door Great James grabbed Richard Nethercotts by the shoulder, physically turned him round to face them, and said...

"Richard, just take a few minutes to escort our Captain Cobbler to his house, making sure no-one tries to engage his attention. I have to go back inside to attend to some final arrangements for the morning. Once he's inside his house, come back here, there are things we need to discuss for tomorrow."

Nicholas reflected that this responsibility for making things happen seemed to be making James a more sociable person than he had been for a while! It was doing him good. He had sheltered for too long in a silent world of grief when his wife died. Not that he had ever been a really outgoing type, anyway!

୨୧ ୨୧ ୨୧ ୨୧ ୨୧

Nicholas' son, Robert, had been home for quite a while, excitedly telling his mother and his 13-year-old brother, Arthur, all about the muster at Julian's Bower; Cousin Eleanor was there too. Robert was also regaling them with what he had heard about plans to "...*attack the king's troops in Lincoln*". This was a *much* exaggerated tale, which had, nonetheless, had the effect of seriously worrying his mother, whilst filling young Arthur's mind with excitement and disappointment – that he would have to miss it. Cousin Eleanor had done what she could to downplay Robert's overly-exuberant joy at the thought of 'serious action', but his mother had definitely been disturbed by it.

When Nicholas walked through the door, much earlier than anyone anticipated, he was immediately faced with the task of trying to comfort his wife, without undermining his son's enthusiasm too much. He had heard Robert's mistaken view that they would be attacking the king, so at least he was able to scotch that rumour, straight away.

"There'll be no attacking done my lad – it is much more about negotiating than attacking! And, as far as anyone knows, King Harry is still in London."

He looked directly into Eliza Jane's eyes as he said this, to ensure she got that message clearly! She looked a little relieved, but still seemed rather tense. It was bad enough having her husband "...*going off to war*". But her firstborn son was going to be there, too, facing goodness-knew-what dangers!

"You're home early!" she said feeling relieved, and worried, at the same time.

"Yes," he said with care, not wanting to set her worries off again, "I will have a really early start in the morning – before even Robert here will be awake, and *he* has to be up for dawn!"

"So – let's eat now and then we can all get a nice early night," he said, rubbing his hands together with enthusiasm to ward off too many searching questions – although he knew he would have to face them later. Eleanor saw the need for some diversion, and suggested the boys should "...go and sluice some of the day's dirt off your faces!"

Because she had not known what time he would be coming home, Eliza Jane had put something in the stock-pot so that it would be ready for the boys, and her, and Eleanor, to eat. It could then be left, keeping warm, for whenever Nicholas got home. It had been late, on the previous evenings when he *had* come home. And there were at least two nights during the week when he had stayed all night at the church, so she was feeling rather frazzled, and was missing him madly.

Eleanor had tried to keep her company as much as possible, but it was obviously Nicholas whom she needed!

She hugged her husband tighter than usual, and held the hug for longer than usual, but he wasn't about to complain, and hugged back accordingly. When the hug finished, Nicholas noted that her eyes were glistening a little in the candle light, but she busied herself round the kitchen, saying nothing more. Eleanor helped her organise, setting the table with the big wooden bowls they usually kept for 'best', when they had guests to dinner.

They had had these bowls 'forever', and they were very smooth with use and cleaning. They had been made by Nicholas' brother Robert, for Eliza Jane, when Robert and she were first married. Eliza Jane was not very sure that she should ever use them again after Robert died, but Nicholas soon persuaded her that they would be an ever-present reminder of Robert's life on earth. He had always been very good working with wood, and had spent many hours working the treadle to spin the wood, and get such a fine even curve to them all – *so it would be ungracious NOT to use them*!

The stock pot was full of all sorts of delicious things. The meat was a late season lamb, rather than the tougher mutton that sometimes served to fill the pot, and there were whole shallots, that had been freshly hung to dry a couple of weeks previously, from the kitchen garden, which the boys were now old enough to look after with a will. There were green beans, too, and carrots from the garden. There was also a huge turnip that Uncle Tom Foster had brought them at the weekend from his garden. And the stock pot had been bubbling quietly for ages, so the juices had blended and thickened, as they all liked it.

The bones had been left in, of course, so all the marrow jelly had added its taste to the pot... MMmmmm – delicious! The bread was freshly made that afternoon, too, so just the smells in the house were absolutely mouth-watering.

Eliza Jane had acquired many of her culinary skills from Ma Melton, when she had first moved in with the family. Her own grandmother had been quite good in the kitchen but Nicholas' mum was the real expert cook, and had willingly passed her skills on to her daughter-in-law, delighting in the opportunity, since she had not had a daughter of her own.

Nicholas *had* learnt a few lessons at his mother's side when he was a little 'un, enough to be able to look after himself in a basic way, anyway. But he was *so* glad his mother had been so generous with her schooling for Eliza Jane! He had always been quite a slight man, and wiry, but he did enjoy his food, and he managed to pack away more food than it looked as though he could!

By the time they had all finished eating, and doing their share of chores, Nicholas declared it was time they were getting into bed. Young Robert would have to be up by dawn, and he knew he himself would have to be on his way long before then. The boys went up to bed first, followed soon thereafter by Eleanor, pleading a "...*long day*", and Nicholas was just about to go up, too, when Eliza Jane laid a hand on his forearm...

"I know you have to get to bed, but can we just talk for a few minutes. You know that I am worrying about young Robert..."

Nicholas interrupted and was about to say..."You have no need to fret yourself about him..." but Eliza Jane put her right hand on his lips, so he got no further than the first two words. And so, she continued...

"...BUT, I am much more worried about you." Nicholas wanted to speak again, but his wife's hand was still keeping his lips closed.

"I know all about your principles, and your heartfelt feelings about the church, and our community, my love. And I know your heart is in the right place, and the community is much luckier than it realises to have you as their champion! And you know I do not disapprove, and that I support you to the very ends of the earth for the good you are doing."

"But I heard all about the violence, this week already, and I feel sure this will not be the end of it. There are some foolhardy people out there, and my worry is that it will all fall on your head at the end of the day. And it is *your* head that is precious to *me*. I don't want it to be chopped off, or get stuck in a noose for anyone."

"Now you come home and tell me you are to go off, chasing after this Lord Burgh – who might be '*raising an army to put the rebellion down*', is how young Robert phrased it for me earlier today! And I worry that I might never see you again! I love you and, there, I have said my piece! I love you dearly, Nicholas Melton, father of my children. I don't want you to disappear!"

Nicholas knew that this was not a faint-hearted whimper that could be gently put off with a few well-chosen words, so he paused and took a deep breath before attempting to reply in kind. He sat them down on the two chairs they had been sat on for their supper. They were close enough that their knees were touching, and he took both of her hands in his before speaking.

"First things first," he said. "You know that I love you more than life itself, and you fill my heart from waking to sleeping. You know, too, and you have just said it again... you *know* how I feel about this community of ours, and the punishment it has had to endure this year. Something had to be done and somebody had to do it and, it may be the sin of pride on my part, but I felt I was being 'called' to do, and say, what I have said and done, all of which started this whole thing off in the first place. But I did feel 'called' and there it is!"'

He sighed, feeling the responsibility of it all, and paused, looking down at his feet. Still holding Eliza Jane's hands in his, he took a breath and went on...

"...And I know, too, that you have supported me in all of this, without murmur or restraint, and I love you for all of that too. But I won't try and 'soft-soap' you, and say, with unjustified calmness, that 'everything will be all right, and I will be all right'... because I know there is a possibility that it will not!"

"But, having said that, I do believe strongly that everything *will* be all right. If I am wrong though, for whatever reason I cannot discern, I believe it must be God's will that I *be* wrong on this issue at this time and I will have to suffer the consequences of that."

"What I cannot bear, is the thought that you and our family would **also** have to suffer those consequences too, and that has given me much pause, this week particularly. And after yesterday, and today, even more so ..." he stopped, leaving his last thought unspoken.

"But my heart is full of conviction that I am doing the right thing, and I MUST continue to do the right thing. It IS as if I have been 'called', and I know that we have family and many friends who will ensure you and the boys come to no harm, should bad go to worse."

"We have talked all of this through before, and it always seemed so far away as to be not 'real'... but if anything should happen to me, God forbid, you know you must take the boys and yourself to the safety of your cousin, on the coastal marshes, up near Barton on Humber?"

"Yes, but..." she hesitated, not quite knowing how to say what burdened her heart.

"There can be no 'buts' my love. I **must** know that you will be safe, and the boys out of danger, if everything does not work out well with our quest. Otherwise it *will* surely fail, for lack of sanity in Captain Cobbler!"

His attempt to lighten the atmosphere was heavy-handed at best, but to his great surprise, it not only lightened the atmosphere – it changed it altogether. Eliza Jane smiled, took his face in both hands and kissed him firmly on the lips. Still smiling she looked him deeply in his blue eyes and said...

"The trouble with that statement, my husband, is that it assumes Captain Cobbler to be sane in the first place... a fact I seriously doubt!"

He didn't know whether to laugh, or cry. To laugh at her cheeky comment; or to cry at her bravery in making it, for it must have cost her such a burden in anxiety, and love, to attempt to set *his* mind at rest. She did that, however, knowing that he had a tough task ahead, and not wanting him to be burdened by worry for his family.

He ended up neither crying, nor laughing... but simply smiled, and then kissed her back, long and hard. She responded in kind, then suddenly turned away saying nothing, took hold of his hand, and led him up the stairs. Sleep would just have to wait a little while!

Cousin Eleanor, quietly in bed already, was very much aware of the earlier tension in the house, and had heard very little of the detail of the conversation. But she did hear Eliza Jane's last statement, which was followed by a period of deep silence, and then the tread of two people coming upstairs, one close on the heels of another. She smiled to herself, and whispered silently, "God bless you girl! You always were able to do the right thing at the right time!"

০৪০৪০৪০৪০৪০৪

An Unhappy Christmas:
Christmas 1535
Missing her grandson, missing her friend...

Maria de Salinas, widow of the 11th Baron Willoughby of Eresby, awoke to the sound of her grandson, little Henry, crying to be fed, when it was barely light.

It was a Saturday morning, and Christmas Day, in the Year of Our Lord, 1535, was only a week away, yet she had to go up to London on the morrow. She had been ordered to court by the king for the Christmas festivities. Not that she felt at all festive this year. She could do without all the 'splendour' of court, and would give anything to stay with her daughter and new grandson, Henry, this year. But, if the king says you have to be at court, you have to be at court!

Indeed, she was surprised that her daughter, Catherine, had not also been ordered to court as well, to show off her firstborn to all and sundry, but it seemed that her doctor's view had prevailed – that she was still too weak to travel. It had been a difficult birth at the end of September. She had lost a lot of blood, and was only just now beginning to recover her strength. They had a wet-nurse for the child, the doctor was not very far away, and the household was well-managed. So Maria knew she should not worry – but that did not stop her worrying! Catherine was still only fifteen years old after all, barely out of childhood herself.

And, of course, that was not all Maria was worrying about. She knew that her great friend, Catalina, had been very ill, but all of Maria's requests to visit her had been rebuffed by the king. He seemed to be afraid that Catherine would conspire with her to bring about a rebellion in favour of their daughter, Mary, and wanted to keep her isolated from the world as much as possible. Maria knew that this was a complete nonsense, of course, but Henry seemed afraid of his own shadow these days, yet covered his fears with bluster of the worst kind, egged on by his greatest friend, Charles Brandon, Duke of Suffolk.

The fact that Suffolk was now Maria's son-in-law, and father to her grandson, made very little difference. He was a horrible man, and she liked him less and less, the more she got to know him. He had helped a lot, when Maria's little Catherine was made his ward, after Baron Willoughby died. The baron's brother, Sir Christopher Willoughby, had tried to wrest the title, and property of Grimsthorpe castle, from its rightful owner, Maria's daughter, the twelfth Baroness.

Being the Duke of Suffolk had helped the law take its proper course, then; greasing a few palms had probably helped too! But that didn't really help Maria to like him at all.

Then the duke had realised that if he *married* his young ward himself, instead of letting the planned wedding to his son, the Earl of Lincoln, go ahead, he would *always* have the income from the Eresby property, as well as having a comely young girl to bed for himself!

Maria had always known, well enough, about the debauchery that Suffolk had led Henry into, from the reports that came to her from Eustace Chapuys, the Imperial Ambassador, to pass on to Queen Catherine – meddlesome man! Quite how he got the information he was able to get, she did not know. He must have spies everywhere. Nevertheless, Maria also held a very dim view of Suffolk's penchant for young girls.

So, she did not really want the duke as a son-in-law, but was in no position to do anything about it, if Henry gave his permission. And that had always been a foregone conclusion as far as Suffolk was concerned. So Maria gave her daughter what advice she could, but she felt sure it would never be enough to protect her against such a foul beast as Brandon appeared to be.

The only woman he had appeared to treat with reasonable respect had been his third wife, King Henry's younger sister, Mary, whom he seems to have seduced rather than debauched. Certainly Maria thought Mary Tudor had been in love with the 'idea' of the handsome Charles Brandon since she was a little girl, watching her older brother and his even older friend together. Whether Mary found that he lived up to her ideal, Maria de Salinas did not know.

After Mary Tudor's brief political marriage, engineered by her politically astute brother, King Henry VIII of England, to the wizened old French King (with gout and a pock marked face) Brandon had 'rescued' her from *another* political marriage after King Louis died, by secretly marrying her in France at some risk to himself. He was relying on his friendship with Henry being strong enough to withstand Henry's short term annoyance. The bravado worked, and Mary Tudor had loved him for it, but Maria de Salinas, the eleventh Baroness d'Eresby, had always thought it more self-serving than self-sacrificing.

One little thing Maria had always remembered, was once coming across Mary in the gardens at Richmond, quietly sobbing. And, in a moment of unusual vulnerability, Mary admitted, to her sister-in-law's best friend, that "Charles could be very cruel in bed..." Then she covered her mouth with her hand, as if realising she had already said too much. But those words kept coming back to haunt Maria, when she thought of her fourteen year old daughter, swept legally into the same bed of the soon-to-be-fifty duke.

The fact that the marriage bed had quickly produced a pregnancy, and that the duke was most often at court, rather than at Grimsthorpe Castle in southern Lincolnshire, was a comfort to Maria, who chose to spend as much time as she could looking after her duchess-daughter's welfare!

Little Henry's cries had now quietened, after the wet-nurse picked him up to suckle him. She was a nice friendly country girl, though not too bright. And she was very loving to the little boy. His cries had set the household moving, too, and now servants were bringing wood, and coals, for the fire. Maria's ladies were laying out her day clothes, and Catherine's ladies were washing the duchess, who was preparing for another day reposing in bed.

Once little Henry (named after the king, of course!) had had his fill of milk, Maria took great delight in walking back and forth across the chamber, with him over her shoulder and patting his back. She had, perhaps, a closer relationship with her grandson than ever she had been allowed with her daughter, since she had had to bring her daughter into the world in the intensely closeted environment of the court. She would miss him terribly when she left for London tomorrow.

As she walked round the chamber she was thinking of her friend Catalina, too, stuck in cold, damp, Kimbolton Castle with a bare minimum of servants to look after her day to day needs, but with no friendly faces to support her. Maria had been writing regularly, and she was getting some replies, but she was not at all sure Catherine was getting *all* her mail. There were always some gaps in her replies that suggested she had not got *this* piece of news, or *that* bit of gossip. She was fairly sure, too, that the letters in both directions were carefully vetted, for the least suggestion of conspiracy, so was always circumspect in what she wrote.

It was now over two years since she had last seen her best friend in the world, and she was now very worried about Queen Catherine's health. *She still thought of Catherine as queen even though Henry had forbidden anyone to refer to her as such.* She was formally to be known as the Dowager Princess of Wales, referring to her brief marriage to Arthur, Prince of Wales all those years ago!

The queen had written to Maria at the beginning of this December, 1535, that she had had serious pains in her chest, so Maria thought she had perhaps had a heart attack, though the doctors apparently said not? Then her last letter, which arrived only a couple of days previously, indicated she had felt much improved on the 17th of December, well enough to 'celebrate' her fiftieth birthday, with a short walk to the "*lovely little chapel in the walled garden...*" where she had "*...given thanks to the Lord for a long life.*"

Maria had allowed herself a small ironic smile at this last sentence since, when they were small children, they had always talked about wanting to have a '*Happy Life*' in preference to a '*Long Life*'. Catherine would have known that Maria was the only person in the world able to read between the lines of *that* sentence!

The smile was quickly followed by just two hot tears, one from each eye, which trickled slowly down her cheeks at the sadness embraced in those words. And yet Catalina was always so loyal to her husband, the king, much to Maria's disapproval. Catherine still really loved her Henry, despite his many faults.

Maria had been so relieved by that last letter, but she still wished she could go and talk to Catherine and tell her of all that was happening in her own life here at Grimsthorpe.

"*Oh, my Lord, I DO miss her very much...*" she breathed quietly into Little Henry's ear, "*...and I shall miss YOU very much, too, whilst I am away! I hope you will be a good little boy for your mama!*" She nuzzled his neck and took a deep breath of his lovely sicky, milky, baby smell!

The next day she gave her daughter a huge hug and her grandson a huge cuddle, before setting off with two of her ladies, and a quartet of guards for the long ride to court in Richmond. After nearly three hours of travelling they reached the fork in the track, where they had to take the London Road instead of the road which would quickly have taken them to Kimbolton. It took all of Maria's willpower not to turn her horse along the Kimbolton track! She could have been there in less than another hour, perhaps even in half an hour from that point, if she cantered her horse rather than trotting! It set her mind working as to how she might have gained access, for she knew Kimbolton would be well guarded. These thoughts carried her onwards, barely conscious of her progress towards court.

She was tired when her party eventually reached court in the gathering darkness. The guards with her found some servants ready to take their horses and belongings in charge. Maria set off with long strides after a servant carrying her bags, to her allotted chambers. She was followed closely by her two ladies, who knew they would have little time to get her ready for the banquet she was expected to attend this evening. Most of her best gowns had been left at court, so they knew there would be something ready she could wear, which would look well on her still-slender frame.

Maria tried, as hard as she might, to give herself over to the various festivities leading up to Christmas Day, but her heart was not there at all. Many were the times when some acquaintance, or friend, came up to her and spoke, but she had to ask them to speak again, for she had not registered what they were saying. By and large, she also tried to keep out of the way of the 'royal couple', in case she should offend them by appearing disrespectful. It wasn't as if she actually hid herself, but she did try to stay on the fringes of any activity, and kept out of the most brightly lit areas.

In the end, it was this strategy which caught her out, when, in the shadows, she literally bumped into the Duke of Suffolk.

Well, he probably bumped into *her* since he was a little the worse for drink, it being quite late in the evening – the carousing having been going on continuously for several hours! He rocked a little on his heels, then broke into an ungracious laugh.

"Well, if it isn't my mother-in-law!" He put his free hand round her shoulder, the other hand unsteadily holding a tankard of strong ale.

"How are you enjoying this feast, Mother?! And how does my

wife, and our child, in Grimsthorpe?" ...all of which was said in an unnecessarily LOUD voice.

"Little Henry and Catherine are well now, Your Grace, thank you. Catherine is still weak, but now able to get up for short periods during the day." Maria hoped that giving him positive news in a civil manner might get rid of the man sooner than trying to ignore him. Sadly, she was mistaken.

"So delighted to hear it, my dear mother-in-law! Come and make your report to the king, too! Come...come!" He had hold of her arm, and was more or less dragging her into the chamber, wherein sat Henry and his pregnant wife, Anne.

The king seemed pleased to see her, whereas Anne's face turned into a worse scowl than usual, on seeing her.

"Mary Willoughby, as I live and breathe! How are you?"

Henry always anglicised her name, and had once called a ship of the realm after her. It had once amused her, as it had amused Catherine, but the amusement soon wore thin. All of Maria's long years of practice and training came into play, however, and she smiled her sweetest court smile, and curtsied low.

"Your Highness. I am well, thanks be to God. His Grace, the Duke, asked me to let you know how my daughter and grandson are faring at Grimsthorpe. As I just told him, they are both quite well now, and Catherine is getting stronger day by day."

She hoped if she kept the report brief and factual she might just be allowed to go. She felt very uncomfortable in the presence of Anne Boleyn, who now styled herself Queen of England with, of course, the king's blessing, but in the most arrogant and obnoxious way. The king, however, mellow with drink and fine entertainment, wanted stimulating company, and he had always enjoyed Maria's sharply amusing tongue and her ability to hold her own, in any conversation, about anything. It was not a trait that was always evident at court!

"Sit, my Lady, sit! ...Bring some chairs over here now!" he bellowed at a passing servant, who jumped out of his skin, but responded with aplomb.

Chairs were duly brought, and Anne's nose was rather put out of joint, when she had to shuffle round to make room for the newcomers, the Duke of Suffolk and his 'mother-in-law'.

Maria had to relate all about Catherine's recovery, and how little

Henry was doing. And, in truth, she actually felt better now that she *could* share her pleasure at being a grandmother! She felt more relaxed with a couple of goblets of wine inside her too, and suddenly she felt *bolder* as well.

"Your Highness... as you can tell I am thrilled to tell you about my grandson..." she took a deep breath and tried to choose her words carefully, "...and as you can imagine, I would love to be able to tell my good friend, and countrywoman, the Dowager Princess of Wales..."

The words nearly choked her, but she knew if she did not bend a little, Henry would explode...

"May I have your permission to visit Catalina, in Kimbolton, after Christmas?"

She hoped her reference to Catherine as Catalina might disarm him... and so it nearly did. He smiled almost fondly, until a loud and unladylike snort reminded him of Anne's presence. His demeanour changed very quickly, and his mellowness disappeared.

"No, my Lady Willoughby, you may not. And you shall not speak of this again in my presence. Now, please leave us."

The look on Anne Boleyn's face would haven frozen a volcano in mid-eruption, and her gloating eyes would forever haunt Maria's dreams. Nevertheless Maria would not allow the witch the satisfaction of seeing her beaten. She rose gracefully from her chair and bid them all a calm "Good evening." She swept slowly from the chamber with as much grace as she could muster, and reached her chamber with her head held high, breaking down in wracking sobs only when the door was firmly closed behind her.

For the rest of the Christmas period she managed to show herself to be *at* court, so that a few people saw her around, but also managed to keep well out of the central areas, so she could keep out of the way of Henry and Anne; and, particularly, out of the way of the Duke of Suffolk.

On Christmas Day itself she did appear at the feasting – otherwise the king would have noticed her absence, and would probably have had her fetched, and paraded, to embarrass her. But she avoided, as much as possible, from being near the king. This, in itself, was unusual behaviour at court, since *most* people there *wanted* to be near, and to be seen to be near, the royal couple. She did have to talk to Suffolk once or twice, but, since a lot of people wanted to be seen to be near *him* too, there were several natural opportunities for her to slip away again.

ରେରେରେରେରେ

On the twenty-eighth of December, news came from Kimbolton that Catherine, the Dowager Princess of Wales, was taken seriously ill again. By now, Maria had given up hope of getting permission to go and see her friend, even though it was rumoured, a couple of days later, that Eustace Chapuys had managed to get permission, since it seemed likely that Catherine was now expected to die very soon. Chapuys left court on January the first, and was expected to be in Kimbolton the next day.

Maria kept as quiet as possible, and as much in the background as she could. But she had hatched a plan, which she shared with no-one.

She told two of the four guards who accompanied her up to London, to go directly back to Grimsthorpe, accompanying her two ladies-in-waiting, since she would be "...*staying alone at court a little while longer, and they should resume their posts on behalf of little Henry...*" She asked them to say nothing to their colleagues, and just go as soon as possible. The two remaining guards were men who had been in her service for several years, and she knew she could trust them to be discreet.

Then, on the fourth of January, she bustled around the court, saying loud goodbyes, to as many people as possible, telling them she was going back to Grimsthorpe to be with her daughter and grandson. She even had quite a long conversation with the Duke of Suffolk about going back, and she was ready, early on the fifth, to set off with her two remaining guards.

By early afternoon, the three of them had passed the fork in the road which she should have taken if she was going to Kimbolton, for she did not want to get the guards into trouble. It was a little frustrating for her, but she needed to be firm with herself!

Two or three miles further on, she pleaded a headache, and told the guards she would take shelter in...

"...yonder priory. I know the sisters in there. But it is a strictly women only place, so you must carry on to Grimsthorpe, and let them know I am safe, and that I will be there shortly."

The guards protested a little, and offered to stay in the village just along the way, and come back for her in the morning. But she was firm with them, and they knew her to be both strong minded and a capable woman; and it was only about twenty miles further to Grimsthorpe, so they did not argue. Because they would be in sight for a while, she actually had to go *to* the priory, and speak with the prioress. But she found some excuse for a conversation with her, which was more or less plausible, but she did leave the prioress a little confused, when she left quickly.

The sky was full of dark snow-clouds and the afternoon was progressing quickly, so Maria knew she had to make good time now. It was bitterly cold too, though she was well wrapped up against the cold wind.

She soon retraced her steps to the fork in the road, where she could now take the right turn that would take her to Kimbolton. From there it was about another fifteen miles to the castle, but no sooner had she turned than the snow started to fall. After a couple of minutes, the snow-flakes had gone from being tiny swirling specks, to large fluffy flakes, settling quickly on the already frozen ground. The wind had dropped, so it was not actually a blizzard, but it was not very long before the ground was white over, and getting thicker underfoot.

The sound quality changed as well, since the snow acted as a baffle. The trotting hooves of her mount now sounded much muted, and there was no echo either. Thankfully, the track was well defined through the trees and hedgerows, so she was not expecting to lose her way, but she was a little concerned her plan was rather foolhardy... '...*what if...?*'

"*Stop that at once!*" she spoke the words out loud to herself, and took tighter hold on the reins!

A little over an hour later, she suddenly saw the castle, on a small mound, as she rounded a corner in the track. The heavy snow had stopped falling, but the ground was quite deep with fluffy white snow. She pulled up, and with great effort of will, turned back around the corner, for a few moments, and dismounted from the horse.

She walked over to a nearby tree, and carefully banged her forehead against the trunk, scraping her skin a little. She also rubbed her outer coat against the tree, so it had a smear of green moss along it, and then, for good measure, she tore her cape's hood a little as well.

She thought a little while, and decided she should also make the boots look damaged too – '...*pity though, they are brand new boots*!' She scraped her right boot against the green of the trees, and then she let herself fall backwards into the snow, so her cape was well covered with white, though, to be honest, it probably already was snow-covered from the ride. She was beginning to enjoy this!

She remounted the horse, which had stood patiently, watching her rider behave oddly. Then she cantered the rest of the way to the castle gateway. She had to ring the bell-pull several times before anyone came to see who was making the noise on such a terrible winter afternoon.

Two guards showed themselves above the gate and the older one said...

"Who goes there?"

"Dowager Baroness of Eresby, mother-in-law of the Duke of Suffolk, let me enter now!"

The two guards conversed briefly and again it was the older man who spoke.

"I am so sorry, my lady, but we have very strict instructions not to let ANYBODY inside the castle!" He sounded very concerned that he was perhaps insulting someone of a very important nature, but his orders had been *very* explicit.

"Well, I know for certain that that is not correct because I know the Imperial Ambassador, Monsieur Chapuys, is visiting the Dowager Princess of Wales. And, also, a court officer was sent here, from Richmond Palace, in haste this very morning, bringing orders to let me in to see my cousin, and friend, on her deathbed."

Maria deliberately let her Spanish accent show, rather more than it usually did these days. Very few people noticed she had any accent at all, after all these years in England. Talking of Catherine as her 'cousin' was a little exaggerated, too, although she believed her father's mother had been somehow related to one of the Spanish royal families, if, perhaps, rather loosely!?

"I am sorry my Lady, but no-one has brought such new orders and my orders are very explic..."

Before he could finish the sentence, Maria shouted up tearfully and indistinctly...

"I am ...mbl..indistinct...jumble ...sob...and I fell off my horse a mile back ...and mbl...jumble indistinct...and ... sob; ...sob;...COME DOWN HERE AT ONCE, AND SPEAK WITH ME!"

The older guard was hopeless with women's tears and had no idea how to respond. And the younger guard was, frankly, just hopeless. The imperious nature of her last words made the older man move, however, and he came down from above the gate, and opened a doorway in the main larger gate – just a little.

Maria leaned down, so that he could see her 'head injury', and the torn cape hood, and started crying...

"I have come all the way down from court in London, it has taken nearly all day...sob;...sob;...my guards took a wrong turn, and I lost them in the blizzard ...sob;...sob;... My only friend in England is dying, and I must see her...sob;...sob; I fell off my horse after banging my head on a tree branch a mile back...sob;... I am hungry, and weak, and the king will be furious if I die out here in the snow whilst my cousin dies!!"

By now she was crying *real* tears, because the underlying truth was now really hurting. Catherine *was* dying and she *was* really all alone in a foreign country, with no friends around her.

The guard was hopelessly torn between his required task and his humanity. He had suspected, before, that Maria was putting it all on to befuddle him, but he recognised real pain when he saw it – he had lost his old mum just last year.

And suddenly the gate was open and Maria was riding through into the snow-covered cobbled courtyard. She dismounted, and handed the horse over to the care of the younger guard, who had remained silent throughout, allowing the older man to make the decision.

Maria then headed for the main doorway, and someone must have been watching through one of the windows, because the door had opened before she knocked. A girl came to take her cape, and showed her into a small room with a roaring fire.

"*My Lady d'Eresby!*" Eustace Chapuys came from near the fire to greet her.

"You have obviously had a hard journey! Let me call for a warm orange posset for you."

Chapuys spoke excellent Spanish, but he chose to speak to Maria in English, since it was more than likely that Cromwell would have his spies listening in. And, if they spoke in English about the weather, and orange possets, Cromwell could have no grounds for thinking they were conspiring against the English crown.

For her part, Maria had to keep to her story of permission being granted, but not having arrived, and the fact that she had fallen from her horse on the way, again, just in case others were listening in. So their conversation was somewhat stilted, to say the least.

Chapuys explained that he had been talking with Catherine earlier, and, although she had been in considerable pain in the morning, she had rallied a little and they had conversed about "...*this and that*..." for an hour or so before she tired, and sent him away so she could sleep a little. That had been only half an hour or so previously, so Chapuys suggested Maria had a little time to settle herself before Catherine was likely to surface again.

"I will probably do that, indeed, Ambassador...and I would be so pleased for you to order me a warm posset... But I have travelled long and far, and it would be ungracious of me if I were not to look in on my friend, and just peek to see if she is yet awake, even if 'tis only to let her know I have managed to get here at last."

Then, more to herself, than to Chapuys

"...it has been *such* a long time. I should have come before!"

She managed to seem calm, and ask the ambassador how to discover Catherine's chamber, as casually as she could. But, really, she was desperate to just run up the stairs, and fling all the doors open, until she found the right room! Having listened to, and understood, his directions she *just* managed to restrain herself from dashing away; and, in fact, her exit from Chapuys' presence was almost graceful. As she left the room, Chapuys was pulling a silken cord attached to a bell in the kitchens to order the confection for her. She heard a distant tinkling as she was going up the first half flight of steps. Then throwing caution to the wind, she ran the rest of the way.

Then she forced herself to slow down, just in case Catherine was asleep, and managed to open the door quietly, peeping her head round the door frame as quietly as she could.

CRCRCRCRCR

With her head and shoulders propped up about thirty degrees from the horizontal, Catherine looked very pale and shrunken in the big down pillows, with her hands resting down by her sides over the top of the covers. Despite the very cold weather outside, Maria was very pleased to find the chamber was toasty and warm, with a log fire providing heat – and a flickering light – in the gloom of late afternoon.

Seated next to the bed, was a young woman of around eighteen or so, slowly embroidering a silken handkerchief. Maria did not recognise her, so she presumed the girl was an older child of a local gentleman's family, rather than a member of the former queen's retinue from the court – most of whom had been sent away anyway. For her part, the girl probably did recognise Maria, and smiled sweetly as she welcomed Maria to the Dowager Princess's bedside. She showed no surprise at having another visitor.

Maria made as little noise as possible, but a rustle of a skirt, or a quiet scrape of a shoe on the floor was enough to make Catherine open her eyes. At first, rather unfocused, she looked at Maria and looked away, and then Maria became the centre of her focus and her eyes shone with the pleasure of recognition...

"Maria, is it really you...?"

Maria could not utter a word, not even a syllable. Her eyes filled with tears, her throat constricted with a lump the size of an orange, but she moved close to the bed holding her hands out, taking one of Catherine's hands, and holding it to her lips. She managed to nod her head, and make a "*mm*" sound of affirmation. She was SO pleased to see her friend, and yet SO hurt to see her in this predicament, no words seemed adequate.

"Did the king give you permission to be here with me, has he relented...?"

Maria laughed a slightly hysterical laugh, tears now streaming down her face...

"NO!! The king did NOT give his permission – I slipped away from court, sent my guards packing to Grimsthorpe, pretended to go to a priory, left the prioress in utter confusion as to why I was there and then had to rush off – I think she thought I was mad – I think perhaps I am a little mad! I rode like a madwoman through a blizzard, acted as foreign as possible for the guards, telling them that Henry would be furious if I was not allowed in, ripped my cape; deliberately banged my head against a tree and rolled in the snow, sobbed and cried, real tears as it turned out, left Eustace Chapuys in the chamber below ordering me an orange posset; and came running up the stairs thinking you might fade away before I got here; and now I am having hysterics and rambling like a madwoman again!..."

...at which point she had to take a breath. Catherine squeezed her friend's hand tightly – stronger than Maria expected! – and just smiled a little smile.

"Maria, my dear...can you start the story again. I am not used to having conversations with a madwoman at such a speed. Take a breath, and tell me all of that again, slowly. Young Frances here will go downstairs and ensure the orange posset is delivered here to my chamber; and that Monsieur Chapuys is left downstairs so we can chatter together undisturbed – won't you Frances?"

Catherine looked across at the girl, who had discreetly moved away from the bed. She smiled, curtsied and went off willingly to do Catherine's bidding.

"She's a lovely girl, very sweet natured, but not much of a conversationalist!"

Worried about her friend's strength, and concerned she might tire her, Maria asked how Catherine was feeling.

"Tired. Tired of dying, tired of living, but so happy to see my best friend fooling the monarch and battling the weather, *and* my guards, just to see me! Bless you girl!"

"GIRL?" Maria exclaimed..."I am a grandmother, for goodness sake!"

"Yes – so I heard. I am not completely cut off from important news, you know. I was so pleased for you ...and your grandson may be a Duke one day!"

"We have so much to talk about, I have so much to tell you, but I have no idea where to start..." Maria suddenly felt speechless again.

"Well, you can take a breath, and try and tell me again how you managed to get here – but take your time this time; I want to understand it all! Sit down as well – now you are here, we might as well get comfortable."

Maria was amazed at how calm Catherine was, and how 'at ease' she felt now she had achieved her goal of simply being here.

They talked... and talked... and talked. In fact Maria did most of the talking, telling her story again as requested, this time with all the little details and diversions that she did not realise she had noticed. She told Catherine about her daughter, and her grandson "...*he has such blue eyes!*..." and her dislike of her 'son-in-law', even though he is the father of her grandson.

It was as she was relating this that she realised Catherine was, literally, the only person in the world she could say these things to. She briefly broke into her narrative to say...

"Mi Dios... I have missed you *so* much!"

The orange posset was brought; and sipped; and ignored; and eventually drunk, without Maria even realising they had been disturbed. They just talked and talked. It was as if they had never been parted; let alone being apart for more than two years now!

For her part, Catherine asked after Henry – she still loved him it seemed, despite the real cruelty she had suffered at his hands. She talked a little about being housebound for so long, and being virtually imprisoned for the last two years with nobody but strange new servants who all seemed distant and disengaged. Apart from young Frances, apparently, who was, indeed, sweet-natured.

"She talks very little," confided Catherine, "because she has this most awful stutter and is always so embarrassed when she tries to speak. She is a little better now; I have tried to encourage her just to relax when she talks to me. And, just occasionally, when she forgets who I am, and why she is here, she can be quite forthcoming. Then she remembers who she is, and where she is, and her ability to talk disappears."

It was as Catherine finished this sentence that Maria noticed how strained her friend was looking now.

"You look so tired. Let me leave you to sleep, and we will talk again in the morning..."

She began to get up, but Catherine held onto her hand.

"Don't you dare leave me now. Yes, I am tired, but I am now certain I shall die very soon and I can sleep then! Peacefully, if God wills it!"

"If I was in real pain, as I have sometimes been of late, I might have a problem talking, or just listening. But, even though I am tired now, I *can* listen and we have so much to catch up with – even just to remember! When I saw you there my mind immediately went back to when we were children. It seems just like yesterday that we were scuttling about that big old palace at Alhambra, and pretending we were in the jungle on those old lions!"

"And the heat..." Maria took up the memory... "...why is England so *cold*? Even the summer here hardly matches the winter in Spain!"

"WHAT?! Have you forgotten the snow we had in the winter in Alhambra? It could be quite cold there in the mountains!"

"Mmmm... QUITE cold. But not as cold as it is here, by a long way!" Maria shivered theatrically, even though the room was hot with a roaring fire!

"I could have ended up in a block of ice today, if I had lost my way! There are stories each year about poor people getting frozen to death when they miss their way home. One of the Greenwich Palace servants was lost last year, and it was two weeks before they found her, huddled up under a tree, frozen solid. She had taken a wrong turn on the path home!"

"I remember some warm English summers..." Catherine started to say...

"Is that one day or two?!" They both laughed.

"Do you remember that year when Henry went off to have one of his wars with France? His 'French Campaign', when he was still little more than a boy? What was it, about fifteen years ago?"

Maria chuckled... "More like twenty, maybe twenty two? I think it was 1513 in fact!"

Catherine thought a little...

"Good gracious, you are right. Where has the time gone? Anyway, I certainly remember that as a VERY hot summer. There were many people who died on 'Hot Wednesday' that year...sometime in July I think. Then it got very wet."

"Henry left me here as his Regent. I don't think he was quite sure whether I was up to the task, and the Scots must have thought I would fail too, so they invaded the north. But I sent my army into battle at Flodden with the Scots, and we won handsomely in the wettest weather for years! The Duke of Norfolk sent me down that bloody jacket of James IV, killed in battle. I think Norfolk thought I would be too squeamish to know what to do with it!"

Maria finished the story, as friends do.

"...but you sent it on to Henry with a note, I remember it so well! You were pregnant that summer, too, you must have been so uncomfortable in the heat…"

A look of infinite sadness overcame Catherine at this point, and Maria was kicking herself for raising the subject.

"I seem always to have been pregnant over those years…and just one little girl to show for it all – all my poor little boys gone to Heaven. How *is* Mary? Does she fare well? I miss her so much!"

"Yes, she is well. She has been asking many times to come and see you but she has been getting the same answer as me. And her father can keep a much closer watch on her than he ever could on me, so I cannot see how she would be able to get away as I have done."

"She will be nineteen next month, and I fear I shall not see her again…" Tears filled Catherine's eyes but not one escaped onto her cheeks. She had cried into her pillows so much, yet her years of having to be strong in company staunched the flow for the moment – even though it was just Maria there, on her own, her closest friend and confidante.

"Henry and his counsellors are so worried about your general popularity, that they think you and your daughter, Mary, with a little help from the efforts of Monsieur Chapuys, downstairs, and his contacts in Europe, could raise, and win, some sort of popular rebellion!"

"Chapuys has even talked quietly to me about it a couple of times but I have told him in no uncertain terms that neither you nor I would ever consider such a thing…"

"…Oh my goodness …he hasn't said anything to you since you have been here has he?" Catherine was clearly panicked such talk would be overheard, downstairs at least.

"No," laughed Maria, "…all we had time to talk about, downstairs, was getting me an orange posset!"

Catherine started to be concerned about her visitor.

"Talking of which," she said, "you must be getting hungry now, if you have had nothing but the orange since you broke fast this morning! Pull the cord there and we will arrange for food to be brought up… and Chapuys too. He has been so kind since he has been here, nothing has been too much trouble for him. The least we can do is reward him with a little company."

"And… Maria… will you do me a little favour?" Catherine looked guilty for even enquiring.

"Of course, how could you doubt it? Just name it!" Maria was slightly surprised even to be asked such a question!

"There is a truckle bed in the room, here. Frances has sometimes used it when I have been most incapacitated. Will you stay during the night, so that if I awake I shall not feel alone... it can be SO lonely in the darkest hours!"

"Of course, my dearest Catalina, I was going to ask you if I might stay anyway."

ରେ ରେ ରେ ରେ ରେ

So, with that, all necessary arrangements were made. Some food was provided for them all, albeit that Catherine tasted very little of it. Eustace Chapuys entertained them with tall stories from his youth – daring escapades, every one slightly less believable than the one before! All of them were amusing, Chapuys himself being the butt of most of the amusing tales. He was *the* most charming of men, especially when he was not being 'political' – and he managed to steer clear of politics all evening.

The two Doctors of Physic who were charged with Catherine's health, came in, with many pardons, at around nine of the clock to check on their patient, and the 'party' had to break up. Chapuys excused himself, and went off to his chambers. Maria stayed in the room in the background, talking to Frances and two of the servants about her own arrangements for the night. And, as soon as the doctors had discharged their duties, Catherine was cleansed and readied for sleep. Maria sorted her own ablutions out, and settled down into the truckle bed.

Maria became much more aware at this point just how weak Catherine was, and how the process of moving her about to cleanse her was obviously very painful. She was very thin, having had little sustenance for many weeks, and Maria noticed a large lump on her chest, over her heart, which she had not seen whilst Catherine had been snuggled under the covers.

It was perhaps ten o'clock by the time everything had gone silent again, and both women were in their beds ready to sleep. Having said *"Goodnight"* to each other Catherine had dropped almost straight off,

388

helped, no doubt, by a sleeping draught the doctors had given her, leaving Maria to ponder alone on life and death and her mad ride to Kimbolton. Her pondering lasted only for very few minutes, however, and she herself was asleep in hardly any time at all, though she did manage a small prayer...

"Oh my Lord, thank you for getting me here!" ...and with that little prayer she fell asleep.

ପ୍ରପ୍ରପ୍ରପ୍ରପ୍ର

She was awakened about four hours later, however, by a loud and excruciating scream of pain nearby, and for a few seconds wondered where she was and what the matter was. And then she remembered – she was at Kimbolton Castle, and it was her best friend in the world screaming in pain. The door flew open, and Frances rushed in, closely followed by the young guard who had chosen to say nothing when Maria arrived at the castle just a few hours previously. They had clearly been sitting just outside the chamber to be available if needed.

Frances went to her mistress, and tried to calm her a little. At the same time she instructed the guard, apparently named Richard, to "Run and get the doctors! Quickly now!" with not the least sign of a stutter! In fact, however, he did not have to run very far, because the doctors had heard the scream, too, and were hurrying to find out what was the cause.

Catherine was writhing in an agony of pain. Maria felt so helpless, and just had to watch as one of the doctors instructed Frances to pour a tumbler of water. He took a small phial from his coat, stirred the contents into the tumbler, and held it to Catherine's lips.

"Here, drink this Your Grace. This will help with the pain..."

Within a minute or so, Catherine was calmer and the pain had diminished, but her eyes were unfocused and she was mumbling incoherently. Indeed, it was only a few minutes before she was sleeping again – in what seemed a very deep sleep, breathing heavily, almost snoring.

Maria, on the other hand, was very wide awake now, her mind whirring along, worrying about Catherine and disturbed by the obviously agonising pain she must have been in to scream so much.

As the others gradually left the room, now that Catherine was asleep again, Maria asked the older of the two doctors to tell her more of Catherine's illness.

"My lady, you are clearly a very close friend, so may I be frank with you...?" he asked tentatively, he seemed much less arrogant than most doctors Maria had met.

"I would expect nothing less!" returned Maria at her most assertive. The doctor smiled a tight smile and inclined his head, measuring Maria's capacity for the truth.

"I think you are aware that the Dowager Princess is dying, then?" His eyes asked the question as well as his words.

"Yes."

The doctor paused a moment, but obviously decided candour was the most appropriate option...

"She has a canker in her chest that has been growing quickly, and at times it is clearly restricting her heart, sometimes affecting her lungs and her capacity to breathe. The pain we just witnessed suggests it is in the final stages of killing her, and it will be a matter of days, at most, perhaps even hours, before she succumbs to its ravages. As you saw, I gave her some medicine – it is quite new and is called laudanum. Quite evidently, (he nodded over to the bed) it is very effective at combating pain, but it seems to have serious side effects, and sometimes makes patients very angry, or very depressed, but at the extremities of life it can be merciful."

"I think when the Dowager Princess wakes in the morning, she will have little memory of being awake in pain just now, but she will probably be very foggy in her mind generally. But my judgement is that, though this drug is very expensive, and can be dangerous, its effectiveness makes it valuable in cases such as this."

Maria acknowledged the doctor's candour with a brief nod.

"Yes, I have heard of the drug at court, now you mention its name. I have heard, too, that some of the richer young courtiers have tried to use it as a way of getting very intoxicated, causing much upset with their subsequent behaviour!"

The doctor nodded back.

"It is certainly very expensive to obtain – but the king gave us very specific instructions that no expense was to be spared in the care of the Dowager Princess!"

The revelation of this last piece of information rather surprised Maria, though, of course, she did not let her surprise show on her face. In the company of his new "queen", Anne, he was very dismissive of Catherine, but the doctor's comment revealed a continuing affection, perhaps even 'love' – '...Goodness, Henry is a puzzle!' Maria thought.

ଔ ଔ ଔ ଔ ଔ

Eventually Maria had gone back to bed and drifted off into a fitful sleep, dreaming unpleasant dreams and being startled awake when a servant came into the chamber to stoke up the fire for the morning.

'...at least I won't freeze!' she thought.

She must have slept longer than she imagined, because it was now well into the morning, and there were sun rays reflected off the snow shining onto the ceiling, through a little gap in the heavy damask curtains in the room. Catherine was still quite heavily asleep, despite the noises around the room, as things were being done. So, rather than open the curtains here, Maria decided to leave Catherine sleeping peacefully. And, since the sun seemed to be shining brightly, perhaps she might take a little stroll in the fresh air.

As she walked into the corridor outside Catherine's bed-chamber, Maria stepped into an almost blinding brightness, on leaving the heavily curtained room. All the curtains in the corridor were open, and when she looked outside it was clear that there had been a very heavy further fall of snow. It must have been snowing all night in fact.

She could tell from the sloping roof just outside one of the windows, that there must have been over a foot of snow altogether. The world outside the windows was totally white over, and silent indeed, but the sky was pale blue with just a few thin clouds here and there. The sun was shining brightly and reflecting into the building from the courtyard and one of the roofs opposite the windows. The cold English weather did have its compensations after all – it looked delightful from inside the building!

After breaking fast with a fresh bread roll covered in honey, and drinking a silver goblet of small ale, Maria put on her cape (the torn hood of which had been miraculously mended during the dark hours

391

of the night!) and her new but badly scraped boots and went for a walk in the sunshine. She might not have been the first occupant of the house to venture outside (someone had been out to fetch wood, at the very least!) But she was definitely the first to exit the house from this particular door, into this particular courtyard! The snow was pristine, and she delighted in sinking her boots into the deep snow.

They were fine leather boots, and although she had on two pairs of stockings against the cold, it quickly found its way to her toes. She would not stay outside for long in that case. But she took a turn about the courtyard, and found a doorway which probably took her into the garden where the chapel was located which Catherine had told her about the previous evening.

Thankfully, the gate into the garden had been protected against the prevailing snowfall by a wall so she managed to open it just far enough, before it got stuck in the deep snow, to be able to squeeze through. The walled garden was probably a delight to behold in the summer months, with roses blooming. And although she did not like rose plants in the winter, normally, because they looked so bare and spiky and dead, the snow had given them a completely different look today. They were like so many large white cannon balls lying in the garden, with melting flakes making them glisten in the morning sun.

There were a couple of blackbirds scratting around at the base of two of the 'cannon balls', to see if they could find leaves, under which there might be insects to nibble. One was successful, but one had chosen the wrong place to look, as Maria stood silently watching them.

The shape of the pathway across the rose garden was reasonably clear from the way the snow had fallen, and settled, so Maria set off towards the chapel, leaving a trail of deep footprints again. When she got to the chapel door there were other footprints arriving from a different direction, so someone else had been there this morning. The door was slightly ajar so she went inside and whoever had left the footprints was still there sitting, head bowed, near the front of the little space.

She genuflected, crossing herself, and quietly made her way down the aisle towards the small altar at the front. One small window had been glazed with coloured glass whilst the other windows were just plain. The sun was shining brightly, lighting the floor near the altar with beautifully coloured lights. The other person in the chapel was obviously Eustace Chapuys, but he appeared deep in prayer, or thoughtful reflection, so Maria simply bowed her own head, and silently spoke her own prayers to the Virgin Mary, and God Himself, rosary beads marking them off through her fingers.

After a little while Chapuys moved, and Maria had completed her rosary, so when he stood and spoke softly to her she was able to respond accordingly.

"Good morning, my Lady."

"Good morning, Ambassador."

"May I sit and converse with you a while?"

"Of course."

"How does the queen do this morning – I heard she was in pain during the night?"

"I believe she is probably still asleep, the doctors gave her laudanum last night, and she was sleeping soundly still this morning as I left her chamber less than an hour since. It grieves me to find her thus reduced to pain and suffering, but I am so glad I managed to get here!"

"As am I, my dear Lady, as am I! May I speak frankly with you whilst we are alone here in the Chapel? I took the liberty of checking it out when I arrived. All the outer doors, apart from the main entrance door, were locked, and there were no footprints approaching in the snow, and no-one has arrived nearby since you came in..."

Quite how he knew this for sure, Maria could not tell, but she took him at his word since she had heard no sounds during her brief time there either...

"...so I am as sure as possible we cannot be overheard. Especially as we are talking so quietly!" He certainly was, and Maria was saying very little anyway, so she inclined her head in acquiescence, though feeling somewhat uncomfortable doing so.

"These are trying times with the Bullen whore on the throne, bringing Lutheranism so brazenly into the country."

Maria would not, of course, have used such strong language, but found she could not disagree with the sentiment behind the words! Chapuys continued...

"The Bullen usurper must be pleased that the Queen appears to be dying... and I feel sure it will not be long now! There are rumours around that Bullen is slowly poisoning her somehow, but, even now I am here, I can find no evidence of the fact. And I have examined the kitchens closely, and watched the staff very carefully!"

"I know that neither you, nor the queen, are at all likely to wish to be involved in any plan to overthrow King Henry, and that is not the reason I am here. But, there are factions, including people in this country, who would welcome such a change if it were to be in favour of the queen's daughter, Mary, who is now of an age to be able to rule without a regent."

"The Queen's nephew, my master, Charles V, the Holy Roman Emperor, asked me to come and see his aunt, as she is dying, to convey his love for her and encourage her to make a deathbed confession, consistent with the position that she has always taken. In other words, to affirm that she never consummated the marriage to Prince Arthur. Thus, Henry's strategy of 'putting her away' from him and seeking to annul the marriage was, and remains, unlawful in God's sight, and according to canon law, and according to the law previously existing in England."

"My Lady, I believe the queen will probably do this because she has been so steadfast in her position. And such a strong indicator of truth as a deathbed confession, given that it would prove her soul is pure, would help bring this country back to the mother church. It would do this, either by placing Henry in such a bind that would have to reverse his position, or by providing a platform for continuing action by the church authorities to bring Henry to heel!"

Chapuys was still talking very quietly, and hardly taking a breath between sentences.

"The Emperor is stretched right now, in keeping the empire together, and cannot assist in a rebellion anyway, but would certainly be sympathetic to such change. He may be able to afford to pay for mercenaries if necessary and appropriate, as long as he does not have to provide men, or arms, of his own commands. Cash would not be a problem, and could be routed through sympathetic religious brothers and sisters, particularly associated with the Devotio Moderna that you, and Queen Catherine, so nobly support!"

"I think Henry may have got wind of this, and it may be a factor in his obsession with closing many of the religious houses around the country, the other being his desperate need of money of course! Queen Catherine knows all of this because I have managed to speak with her about it since I have been here but, if I am being frank, I am not quite sure whether she really trusts me. And she may welcome a sounding board who is attuned to her ways of thinking. In short – *you*!"

"I am sorry to have been so frank, and so blunt, but I needed to tell you all this quickly, whilst we had time to converse in 'secret'. I have an enormous respect for you and your wisdom, and I know I can trust your discretion, at least for the sake of our mutual friend the queen. Indeed you may not trust me either. I cannot tell, and you are very good at covering your emotions! But I will have to trust your own judgement of me, and the queen, and of the situation here in England, I can do no more. Forgive me."

"I shall leave the chapel now, and return to the house using the route by which I arrived here. None of the entrances of the chapel are visible from the house, so unless someone has recently come into the walled garden, and sees me leave, and then sees *you* leave, it will be almost certain that no-one will know we ever had chance to talk privately. May I suggest you stay here just a few minutes, and then return to the house via the same route whence you came. Then when we meet in the house, as I am sure we will, it will, of course, seem to be for the first time today!"

He smiled an enigmatic smile, and before Maria could respond, he had swept his cloak around himself and left the chapel silently and quickly. Maria herself was almost breathless with worry and concern over the meeting, and over what Chapuys had said; and, even more, what he had intimated without saying! His advice to stay put for a few minutes was not really necessary since she needed a few minutes silence to calm herself down before she could trust herself to remain discreet! The silence in the Chapel was now dramatic, and the sunny silence outside was perhaps even melodramatic – at least, it seemed so, as Maria was feeling now.

"*Dios en el cielo - Tengo que calmarme!*" The fact that she had appealed to God in heaven, and just told herself to be calm, all in her native Spanish, told her that she was definitely *not* feeling calm at this moment. So she sat for a few minutes as Chapuys had suggested – and tried breathing deeply.

By the time she left the Chapel, the sun had gone behind dark grey clouds, and long icicles were beginning to form on the guttering, as the melting snow on the roof started refreezing as it dripped. Maria shivered, and her mood had changed very much from what it had been earlier. Even the sound of the snow had changed underfoot! How strange?! It crunched more crisply than it had done in the sunshine earlier! The temperature must have dropped quite dramatically in the short time she had been out in the chapel. She was thankful to find roaring fires in the rooms inside the castle as she moved in and took off her cape and boots.

The girl, Frances, happened by (*though it might **not** have been happenstance!*) and said her mistress was now awake and had expressed her desire to see Maria as soon as possible.

Maria went up the stairs quickly but paused outside Catherine's door to try and take off the 'worried, unhappy face' she was wearing, and replace it with a 'stoic, unworried face', though she wasn't sure it had entirely worked? There were still servants scuttling about tidying pots away, though most looked untouched... '...*the pots, that is*...' Maria thought to herself, smiling slightly at her strange mode of thought!

"Good morning, Maria, did I disturb you last night? Listening to the servants chatter it sounds as though I probably woke the whole household...?" Catherine looked as weary as she sounded, worn out with coping. She was now propped up a little on pillows of swans' down, her eyes tired and drawn, with dark circles beneath them.

"You had some pain, which you shared with us a little..." Maria always told her the truth, though perhaps a softer version of reality than she might... perhaps a little understated. Her tight smile was enough to tell Catherine the truth in full.

"I recall very little, except as if it were part of a strange dream? I know the doctors have been dosing me with laudanum from time to time, and it always feels the same the next morning, so I am guessing they resorted to the poppy again last night...?"

"I'm not..." Maria began, intending to disclaim any medical knowledge... then Catherine interrupted...

"No, I know you are not ...qualified... a doctor; whatever... and I am not really asking anything, it was more a rhetorical question. I feel hazy in my head, and I feel background pain over my heart, so I also guess the laudanum is still working in my body somehow. But I am awake, and capable of speech, so let us talk a little more whilst we can. Each time I wake I feel weaker than the time before, so I think it will not be long before I meet my Maker, and have to atone for all my sins..."

"Shhh. Let us not talk of sins..." Maria began. But Catherine waved her hand weakly as if to dismiss Maria's caring thoughts.

"I know where I have sinned," Catherine continued... "...and, more than anything at this moment, I also know where I have *not* sinned. And that includes the '*Great Question*' of my husband, and Lord, Henry. I know in my heart that Henry is wrong, and has been wrong all along, for the last ten years or more. And, for the sake of my soul, I need to be clear about this whilst I can. The end is near..."

Maria's eyes started glistening at this point, but she took a few deep breaths so as not to upset Catherine too...

"...and I want to unburden myself whilst my mind is still capable of fashioning rational thought, and I still feel strong enough. Will you organise for my priest to come to me very soon, and let us get this done."

She added in a whisper, meant only for Maria's ears... "...*not for Chapuys, either, but simply for my soul!*" and squeezed Maria's fingers a little.

Maria, not knowing how long her queen would stay in this relatively calm, almost pain-free, state, set about discovering the whereabouts of the priest, and soon it was done. Frances and the commander of the guards (a man Maria had not yet seen) were there too, invited to be independent witnesses of at least part of her deathbed confession, and Eustace Chapuys came in for a while, too. After a little while, however, the priest asked everyone to leave for the more 'private' confessions he would hear, and forgive, on God's behalf.

Whilst they were all still present, Catherine asked for forgiveness for her anguish, and her "...sin of anger..." that she had been disbelieved about the status of her marriage to "Prince Arthur of Wales."

"The truth was that we were very young and inexperienced in life. He was busy with affairs of state, and we saw each other infrequently, and although we shared a bed a very few times, not once was the wedding consummated before he died suddenly of an illness we also shared. It was an illness which I survived. He did not, due to a weakness in his constitution, and in the light of God's will to take him to a better place, where, I doubt not, I will shortly see him again very soon!"

Whether it was the effect of taking a weight off her mind or simply the efficacious effects of her medicine – the doctor had given her another much smaller dose of laudanum this morning – she expressed herself to feel much better after the priest had left. So much so, in fact, that Chapuys had decided he should leave Kimbolton so that he might attend to other matters of state. The sun had come out once more, and he deemed it good travelling weather.

Maria was not sure if his sudden departure had anything to do with the deathbed confession. Perhaps he wanted to make sure the information was widely known before the queen *actually died*? But, for Maria, it meant she really had her friend to herself for a time, so she was rather relieved that he had gone.

Catherine sounded much stronger and in good spirits again. For one thing, she declared the curtains should be drawn "...right back, to make sure we can see as much sun as possible this fine day!" Suddenly, she asked Frances to bring her a mirror, and exclaimed loudly at the image she saw there...

"Oh my goodness, what have you all had to put up with looking at me, and after me, in this state. My hair feels dreadful, it needs washing and tending to. Frances – set to at once!"

Frances was, of course, delighted to be called upon for such a positive task, and organised her two fellow maids to make much hot water and to find some soft soap. All this time, Catherine was chattering to Maria in her native Spanish, something they had not done for SUCH a long time... *such a LONG time*! Frances knew hardly any words of Catherine's native tongue so was unable to follow their conversation but, yet, she did catch a few words she recognised. Try as she might, however, she could not make a sentence make any sense which contained the words for LIONS, ORANGES, and SPICES... so maybe she had misunderstood the words.

The exchange had also had a reference to a Donna Elvira (whom Catherine had mentioned to her one day when she had been sitting with her mistress) and a man, at least she *thought* it was a man, called Geraldini (whom she had *not* mentioned before). Whatever story they were sharing it made both of them laugh a lot, a sound she thought she might never hear in Catherine's presence, she had been so low-spirited for such a long time here.

Finally Catherine's hair was as she had wanted it, clean and tidy! Frances and the maids were now dismissed for the moment, and Catherine became serious again with her friend.

"If I were to dictate a note to you for my husband, will you be able and willing to write the note for me? I am not sure my hands are strong enough to write without making it appear as if a spider has crawled across the page?"

With a slightly exasperated "*Of course!*" for having been asked, Maria found quill, ink and paper to undertake this task. Catherine thought for a little while, and then in a strong voice which belied her physical state she started...

My most dear Lord, King, and husband.

The hour of my death now drawing on, the tender love I owe you forces me, my case being such, to commend myself to you, and to put you in remembrance with a few words of the health and safeguard of your soul, which you ought to prefer before all worldly matters and before the care and pampering of your body, for the which you have cast me into many calamities and yourself into many troubles.

For my part, I pardon you everything, and I wish and devoutly pray God that He will pardon you also. For the rest, I commend unto you our daughter Mary, beseeching you to be a good father unto her, as I have heretofore desired. I entreat you also, on behalf of my maids, to give them marriage portions, which is not much, they being but three. For all my other servants, I solicit the wages due them, and a year more, lest they be unprovided for.

Lastly, I make this vow, that mine eyes desire you above all things.

Maria made a fair copy and then Catherine signed it and passed it back to her for onward passage to her liege Lord and husband, King Henry VIII of England. Catherine then got Maria to write a letter to her nephew, Charles, as well. And then, despite the fact that it was strictly unlawful for a woman to write her will whilst her husband lived, she wanted to be sure her disposition of worldly goods was as *she* wanted it to be. When Maria reminded her of the law in England, she said...

"Well, what of it? What is the worst they can do to me, sentence me to death? I shall be long gone 'ere they can pass sentence!... Anyway, 'twill be a fine paradox for Henry to resolve... either I *am* his wife and therefore it *is* unlawful, but I shall be dead anyway... or I am *not* his wife, so how *could* it be against the law!?"

First of all Maria felt shocked by Catherine's acerbic wit, then laughed a little, which made Catherine laugh... and soon they were both laughing helplessly. Until Catherine started gasping with breathlessness and a sudden pain, which made them both sober up very quickly!

"Oh my Lord... Catalina... I am so sorry" whispered Maria, hand over her mouth.

Catherine placed her hand on Maria's free hand and squeezed. At that moment she could not speak, but when she had enough breath she said... and it was also barely above a whisper, for she only *just* had enough breath for the sentence...

"Maria, stop fretting... laughter with you does my soul good. And, since my soul is about to go on a journey though purgatory, I shall recall our laughter, and it will surely shorten my journey. Or, if not shorten it... make it more bearable."

"Let me rest awhile, and you must go and have something to eat, then we shall talk again whilst I feel strong. I must finish my will, too... You shall have that lovely gold collar that came with me from Spain and, because it is *so* cold here, you shall also have all my fur coats! Then I shall pray for a time, for my soul's sake, with you by my side, if you will be so kind?"

Maria was about to protest, about having something to eat, and about the collar and the furs, and at being *asked* again... but, looking at Catherine, sunk again into the pillows, she decided to leave her in whatever peace she needed to recover.

Maria did not really feel hungry, but a visit to the kitchens would probably be soothing, she thought. There *were* some appetising smells drifting through the house at the moment – life seemed to keep on going on, come what may. It was something she had noticed when her husband had died. She had felt the world come to an end, but the household staff needed to be doing something that felt normal. It had puzzled her at the time but she had seen it happen with other deaths, where she had not been one of the central characters, and it all made a kind of sense to her now. It was true that this house was being run on a bare skeleton of staff plus doctors and a priest, but she guessed the principle still applied – humans needed continuity in their lives – the continuity of living!

A light meal and another orange posset – the kitchen seemed well-stocked with Spanish oranges at least! – and Maria did feel more refreshed than she had expected! She went back upstairs and carefully opened the door to Catherine's chamber in case she was asleep. She was pleased to see her friend looking a little better again, there was a little colour in her cheeks now!

It did not take them long to sort out Catherine's will, and there was very little writing for Maria to do, mainly since there was no large estate to dispose of. It was mainly jewellery and clothes. The king had effectively disposed of most of what Catherine thought of as hers, anyway, after he had had her isolated over two years previously. Lord Mountjoy had been directed to act as her chamberlain, as he had done before, and had had strict instructions from Henry as to how to sort out her belongings! Intelligent and learned as Mountjoy was, he was not the most likeable of characters, and Catherine (*and* Maria too!) much preferred Lord Hussey and his slightly odd wife.

Once her 'business' details were sorted out, Catherine asked Maria simply to sit with her whilst she prayed to "...our Lord..."

Catherine held her rosary beads between her weakened fingers, and used them as a comforter, as she prayed to God to forgive her, for her sins, and to forgive Henry for *his sins* (unspecified!) She had her eyes loosely closed, and occasionally Maria saw her eyelids flutter as she whispered her prayers. Catherine's face was mostly in repose during this lengthy period of individual prayer, most of the requests being targeted at her own situation.

She prayed mightily for her loving daughter, Mary, and for the continuing peace of her adopted country, and good counsel for her husband, King Henry. She prayed for the wellbeing of her great friend, Maria de Salinas, Dowager Baroness of Willoughby, and her daughter, and grandson – a prayer that brought a tear to the eye, and a lump to the throat, of her aforesaid friend! She prayed for the future happiness and wellbeing of Frances, and her other maids, and her household servants and former servants. She prayed for her nephew and family members and so on... and so on.

Mostly, however, she prayed for her soul's passage through purgatory, acknowledging, of course, the need to spend time there to purge her sins, great and small. In fact, Maria thought several of the sins Catherine referred to as *great* were, in truth, matters of small moment, when compared with the behaviour of many people known personally to Maria herself!

For quite a long time after she had finished speaking out loud to God, both Catherine and Maria fell quiet and sat in thoughtful peace. Thinking she perhaps should leave Catherine alone with her thoughts for a while, Maria quietly said...

"I am sure you need a drink after all that prayer... let me go and get you a drink... I know for a certainty there is another large wooden cask of oranges in the kitchen which your nephew, Charles, arranged for you to have from Alhambra Palace gardens..."

"Yes – I would love a drink of freshly pressed juice from Spain... but – NO – *you* will not leave me! Call for Frances to go, and let us talk about worldly matters for a time – there must be a lot of things you have yet to tell me. Not that you were ever one to gossip wildly! Just think of it as providing a summary of affairs of state for your Queen!"... and she laughed!

Maria called Frances to get them both some freshly squeezed juice, and then went back to sit on the little chair by the bedside. It was strange that the relationship had almost reverted to the informality of their childhood. They had, of course, had their moments of informality over the years, but that was it... merely moments. Right now, it felt much more intimate, and several items of true 'gossip' were passed on, but nearly all of them related to the goings-on of former ladies-in-waiting, to Catherine as queen. Maria quite consciously steered clear of the Boleyn family, for obvious reasons, but she felt she had to bring Catherine up-to-date on Bessie Blount, and her son Henry Fitzroy, the Duke of Richmond, since his position affected Mary's future.

Catherine's original 'hatred' of Bessie Blount had calmed over the years, worn away by more recent hurts, and slights and, perhaps strangely, by the nature of Henry Fitzroy himself. He had inherited his father's natural charm, and at the age of ten or so, when he had been at court for Christmas, he reminded Catherine of how Henry had been when she first met him all those years before, when she had set foot in England for the very first time. He had not inherited Henry's robust health, however, and was thin like his grandfather and, indeed, like his uncle, Catherine's first husband, Prince Arthur, with a similar tendency to ill health.

So, Catherine, despite her natural prejudice against the boy, ended up liking him for the sake of her memories! And that eased Catherine's pain, from Bessie Blount's role in her life, too, and she had, of course, spoken of this with Maria many times before. Maria had also discovered, by happenstance and practice, that if she referred to him as 'Fitzroy', it took the sting out of any residual pain.

"Fitzroy was at court over Christmas, not that I spoke to him at all, since I was assiduously keeping out of everyone's way ...but I heard him often enough, and he was taking part in many of the 'disguisings', just like his father always did! His voice is surprisingly deep, too. When he sings, he always takes the low harmonies – must be the long neck he has – a bit like one of those deep organ pipes, the long ones!"

They both laughed at the mental picture Maria's words had conjured up!

"As far as the gossip goes, he has not yet, apparently, had opportunity or inclination to consummate his marriage with Norfolk's daughter Mary, but she is still very young and he's still only sixteen, so there's time yet!"

"And how IS the Duke of Norfolk!?" Catherine asked the question in a tone of asperity, because, of course, Anne Boleyn was Norfolk's niece. He was also, however, very often the cause of troubles at court by disagreeing with Henry in public, over trifling matters (usually) which irritated the king. But Henry often consulted him when he *really* needed help, especially with matters of martial concern.

Especially after his defeat of the Scots at Flodden, Catherine thought of Norfolk as England's leading warrior, but she knew he had had his nose put out of joint by the young Duke of Richmond's promotion as Lord Admiral, a post Norfolk had previously held.

"Physically he is well, but he is very disapproving of Fitzroy! Even though he is the boy's father-in-law (actually, it is probably *because* he is the boy's father-in-law, now I think about it!) He was bemoaning Richmond's behaviour when away from court."

"Why...? What has he been up to?" Catherine seemed genuinely intrigued by this piece of information; clearly it was not something that had filtered through to her in Kimbolton!

"Well…" Maria started hesitantly, since she did not want to do Fitzroy an injustice, then she remembered they were alone so she took a breath and continued…

"Well… all the following information stems from my Lincolnshire connections, by the way… I think it is partly to do with his relationship with his new step-father. He always seemed to get on quite well with Bessie's first husband, Gilbert Tailboys, and he was upset when Gilbert died, if you remember. But when Bessie married young Lord Clinton not long ago, Fitzroy seemed quite jealous of him, and persuaded his father to give him a bigger household of his own in Collyweston, near Stamford."

Maria, having got into her stride with this tittle-tattle, continued…

"He is always bragging at court about his 'private army' – he seems to have collected a lot of the better-off Lincolnshire 'younger sons' as his hangers-on; the ones who have limited expectations because their patrimony will go to an older brother, for example. They go around ripping through the local countryside in a big 'pack' when they are out hunting, often causing havoc with the tenant farmers, trampling crops everywhere. And, when they aren't hunting deer, they are hunting and harassing the local girls – and even married women! And, of course, the local people cannot do anything about it – he is the king's favoured son, even though he is a bastard son!"

"Talking of which…" Catherine interrupted, "…did I ever tell you of the letter Henry got back from one of the European dukes, when he was trying to marry Fitzroy off to one of the smaller Royal households? I cannot remember just who it was, but I do remember that after the first sentence, which started with the words '*I regret…*' the second sentence said something like… '*…we have enough bastards of our own!*' It amused me very much, but I dare not let Henry see I was smiling!"

In fact, Maria *had* heard the story before, several times, but she thought it best not to say so. Instead she changed the subject a little…

"Had you heard that Fitzroy, despite his sins of youth, has also joined the ranks of Devotio Moderna, which you and I so much enjoy for the 'Good Works' we can be involved with through that organisation…" She lowered her voice at this point…

" …but since my talk with Eustace Chapuys this morning I fear my thinking about that may need re-examination. He seemed to imply..."

She lowered her voice even more until it was barely above a whisper...

"...he seemed to imply that Devotio Moderna was somehow connected with a conspiracy to bring money into the country from your nephew Charles. I tried not to listen but he was determined to finish his comments before he left the chapel!!"

Catherine, too, kept her voice to a bare minimum so that only Maria could hear.

"I am never quite sure whether he is *really* such a schemer as he makes out, or whether he lives in a fantasy world of his own making, but he does sometimes surprise me with the things he knows. He does seem to have an extensive network of spies!"

Maria said quietly, "How on earth did we get onto this subject so quickly? We were talking about Fitzroy... perhaps we should change subjects again."

So they did – Maria waxed lyrical about her "...adorable grandson..." without once mentioning the boy's father, which might have set them off on politics again.

At almost the exact same time as Maria was speaking about little Henry, it so happened that Eustace Chapuys was seated at a tall writing desk, in the quiet seclusion of the copying room of a Carthaginian Monastery, on his way back to London. He was scratching a few words to his master, Catherine's nephew, Charles V, the Holy Roman Emperor. The letter contained these words in cipher...

Maria de Salinas, the Dowager Baroness Willoughby, is the most virtuous woman I have ever known and the highest hearted, but too quick to trust that others were like her, and too slow to do a little ill, that much good might come of it.

ॐॐॐॐॐॐ

Not many minutes later, the Doctors of Kimbolton Castle came on their rounds and pronounced Catherine to be "...*looking tired, but in*

405

a good way of spirits owing to her friendly converse today." It was time for ablutions to be performed and for the two friends to cease their 'friendly converse' for the night.

The doctors decided not to give Catherine any laudanum this evening, but to use a less potent sleeping draught, believing that their charge might find her own way to sleep, which proved to be the case. Maria, too, fell into a sound sleep without the benefits of any sleeping draught at all.

ର ର ର ର ର

Friday 7th January 1536 – a dark day!

Catherine awoke whilst it was still dark, feeling uncomfortable but with occasional stabbing pains too. She tried moving a little in bed, but also tried not to disturb the still-sleeping Maria. She was not successful with either endeavour and Maria awoke, feeling slightly groggy, and unfocussed. Then, upon hearing a small involuntary exclamation of pain from Catherine, Maria became all-too-aware of where she was, and why she was there.

She carefully clambered from under the bedding and slipped her heavy robe around her shoulders, trying not to lose too much warmth in the process. The fire had died down overnight, and it was much colder again this morning! She moved the few feet between her truckle bed and the slightly raised platform which held Catherine's bed, and perched carefully on the edge of the bed, resting her hand over Catherine's...

"You are in pain again this morning?" it was almost as much a statement as a question. "Can I get you a drink? Water, warm milk... a glass of ale?" she smiled, trying to make light of her caring question!

"Yes, in answer to the pain... my chest and stomach hurt this morning... and no, thank you, about the drink...", she tried to smile back, but her lips failed her.

"I had a sip of water from the goblet on the bedside table and I think nothing else would stay down! I am feeling very sickly this morning!"

"Shall I call the doctors to see you...?" Maria felt sorely troubled.

"No...dear Maria...they would probably just give me a large dose of laudanum, so I would end up sleeping my way into purgatory!... oh, hnnnh..."

Her body stiffened briefly in pain...!

"...I feel very weak this morning, I think my time on this earth is soon to end. Just stay with me so that I know you are there. I can die happy, now that I know I have not been deserted!"

"Let me get Frances or someone to see to the fire, so that at least we are warm!"

Maria tried, with reasonable success, to keep her voice strong and positive, though her feelings were far from being so! She tucked Catherine's hands under the quilt to try and warm them up, and quietly walked over to the door. As was the case the previous night, Frances was just outside the door. The guard was nearby too. Maria tried to recall if she was right in thinking his name was Richard? Speaking quietly she said...

"Frances, can you organize to have the fire built up for us, and then let the doctors know that the queen is not at all well this morning..."

Richard, the guard, shot a warning look to Frances when Maria used the word "queen" to describe his charge. His instructions did not cover what to do in such a case, however, since it was assumed that all who came into the castle would know only to refer to her as the Dowager Princess of Wales!

"Please do not let the doctors come straight into the chamber when they get here, however. Fetch me to speak with them out here, please. And can you organize a warmed drink of orange for me – but, again, do not bring it into the room since the queen is feeling nauseous this morning – I will come out here to drink it." Maria's voice was much stronger now... she was taking charge!

She had felt like a visitor to Kimbolton up to now, but her sense of natural authority was coming to the fore in this crisis – as it had all those years ago when the old King Henry VII was about to come charging into the chamber to check whether the child Catherine was a pox-ridden dwarf, or worse, when they first arrived in England!

Indeed, she now decided to make a pre-emptive strike on the guard...

"Richard!" her voice was now almost imperious... "You looked askance a moment ago when I called the queen, 'the queen'. It may well be her last day on earth and I shall call her what I may today! If you have a problem with that, feel free to do as you might afterwards. But, for today, keep quiet, and find some way to make yourself useful!"

With that, Maria, turned on her heel and went back in to the bed-chamber, shutting the door on Richard, who was left with his mouth hanging open. *'My word; that felt good!'* she thought.

A very little while later, one of the maids came in with a young man carrying a basket of logs, and between them, they stoked the fire into flame. Then Maria's orange drink came up from the kitchen, and she quickly gulped the drink down so as not to leave Catherine for long on her own. Finally, Frances came to tell her that the doctors had arrived.

They dutifully stayed in the corridor until Maria came out to see them. And she spoke to them quite firmly.

"Whilst I am not trying to do your job for you, I want you to know that the queen has requested that she should not be 'put to sleep' with laudanum today. By all means, give her a little, enough to dull the pain, but not enough to knock her out. She expressly wishes to remain conscious for as long as possible, even with any associated pain. I wanted you to know that before you go in and end up making her feel worse because she has to argue with you!... Thank you."

The older doctor responded, the younger one nodding along with the words of his colleague.

"Of course, my lady..." He nodded his understanding, graciously.

Then they both went in, followed by Maria, who stayed close by, as they undertook their tasks. It was clear that the attention of the doctors was troublesome for Catherine; just moving for them caused her some distress and pain. The older man, as before, brought out a phial of laudanum and put just a few drops into a goblet of fresh water, which he caused her to drink. After only a short while she seemed somewhat eased of the pain, at least.

When the doctors left, Maria went again to the bedside and took Catherine's hand, just this action bringing a ghost of a smile to her lips. When Catherine spoke, she spoke quietly, her voice tired beyond belief, but her spirit strong.

"Maria, my dear, dear friend; we have been through many years together, from childhood to this older age – I won't call it 'old age' – and sometimes it seems such a brief and fleeting dream. Sometimes happy, and sometimes sad, sometimes frustrating, and sometimes bad. But I am *so* pleased you are here with me at the end – and I fear this day will be the end of my life here on earth. I believe it is time, and I think you should call the priest to come and perform 'unction in extremis', so that I may die with my soul at peace. Go, but come back then and stay with me. And no more doctors, please."

Her last few words were heartfelt, and Maria squeezed her hand in affirmation, and went to do her bidding. It all took very little time, because it seemed that everyone was expecting the end to come soon, and was just marking time awaiting their specific tasks to be allocated.

The priest came and, since there was time to perform the longer ritual, he was careful to do everything smoothly and calmly. He took the sweet anointing oil and Catherine visibly relaxed as he applied it, with his prayers, to her senses, of sight and hearing, and so on. It was as if all her remaining cares were being taken from her. She was clearly comforted by the taking away of her sins, slight as Maria thought them to be! Having performed this sacrament, he heard Catherine's final confession and then withdrew to a chair in the shadows, to be on hand if needed again.

Maria took her seat at the bedside, Frances stood nearby, and Richard, the guard, stood to attention by the door. It was largely silent for a long time, just occasional murmured conversation between Catherine and Maria, as stray thoughts moved through Catherine's mind – "...*say this to so and so – or that to such and such...*" For the rest, there was just a faint susurration, as Catherine murmured her final prayers, for her soul. Occasionally Catherine would move restlessly, and suppress sounds of being in pain.

Once or twice Frances urgently whispered to Maria that perhaps she should "...*fetch the doctors...?*" but each time Maria would quietly tell her "*No!*" on her mistress's behalf. As time passed by, throughout the morning, one or other of the persons in the chamber might quietly leave to stretch taut muscles, attend to calls of nature, or betake themselves of a little refreshment.

Catherine continued to show some distress at the pains she was getting, and she had problems from time to time with her breathing, but her decline was relatively slow and undramatic. Maria was ever-present, disciplining her calls of nature just to wait, holding Catherine's hand all the time. Then, in the early afternoon, Catherine suddenly started gasping for breath, as if being suffocated from inside, and tried to sit up, the better to take her breath. Maria moved from her seat to help her queen to sit, putting her arm round Catherine's shoulders.

Catherine shuddered and managed a relatively deep inhalation, her face a little panicked at her sudden shortness of breath. Then she just fainted away in Maria's arms, her soul slipping silently away on its journey. Maria simply sat there, holding her best friend closely to her bosom, two tears sliding warmly down her cheeks, depositing a little salt on Catherine's recently-washed hair. One sentence, only, left her whispering lips...

"Oh... Catherine my dear friend... Godspeed on your journey..."

୯୬୯୬୯୬୯୬

Frances, seeing her mistress take her leave of this world, stifled a sob of her own, and then waited a few moments to allow Maria her final silent hug. Then she quietly walked over to the bed and helped Maria lower the former queen's body onto the bed with dignity. Between them, they shepherded the men from the chamber intending to cleanse the body ready for its final journey.

Within moments, however, the chamber door opened again and Richard, the guard, came back into the room with the two doctors. This time it appeared that the younger doctor was the more authoritative, for he spoke first, and his voice was firm, and commanding.

"Ladies, please forgive us, but we must insist that you leave the Dowager Princess's body untouched, and leave immediately!"

Frances looked totally shocked by the intrusion, and Maria was about to deal blows, left and right, to physically eject these black-frocked men who would not call her queen by her rightful title. But the younger doctor, anticipating just such a reaction, held his hands up palms forward and said, in his stern professional voice...

"Stop, my lady, before you start!"

"We were under the king's direct command to look after the Dowager Princess during her life. But we have equally compelling instructions from his Majesty to perform an autopsy immediately, should our patient die. You will all leave us to perform this task in private, apart from the young guard here, who is instructed to monitor our work. Once you have gone, the other guards, now outside, will come to transfer the body to a chamber we have prepared for this task. It will all be done with decorum and dignity, as our profession demands."

At this point, the older doctor smiled his ingratiating smile at Maria and sought to reassure her.

"My colleague may look young in years, my Lady, but he has studied the science of autopsy at Cambridge, and before that in three universities in Italy and the Netherlands. He is, I am convinced, the leading expert in this science in all of England and I do not say this lightly, for I am no slouch myself!"

His charming manner was just enough to quell Maria's most murderous thoughts. *Just!*

All the time the doctors were speaking, Maria was watching the guard, Richard, from the corner of her eye, and he had been clearly prepared to eject Maria forcefully from the room if necessary, and was obviously still fully alert to that possibility right now. She judged it best for herself, and for the dignity of her queen, that she should comply with the wishes of the doctors, however odious they seemed. So, without a further word, she turned on her heels and took Frances along with her.

Maria now felt that there was nothing more she could do at Kimbolton Castle for her friend, and she decided it was important that she should be back at court when the results of the autopsy came through. Her grandson, little Henry, would have to wait a little while longer for the attentions of his grandmamma!

Indeed, since there was just a couple of hours of daylight left, Maria made a quick decision to leave Kimbolton straight away, and get back to court this day, if at all possible.

Her decision was helped along as she heard the gates being opened and the sounds of a messenger leaving for court at that very moment. Someone must have had a messenger standing at the ready all morning, and into the afternoon, to have reacted this quickly to the queen's death. Indeed, once having reached her decision, it was not much longer before she was on her way back to London herself, although it was dark well before she arrived.

When she arrived back in court, almost the first thing she heard was that the Solicitor General, Sir Richard Rich, had been sent to Kimbolton Castle that very afternoon to advise the king on the disposal of Catherine's worldly possessions. This information made Maria sigh, for she knew Rich to be a low, scheming villain, who had lied under oath at the trial of the worthy Sir Thomas More not so very long ago!

ରେ ରେ ରେ ରେ ରେ

On the very day that Catalina was to be buried at Peterborough Abbey, her successor as Queen of England, Anne Boleyn, was stricken from her pregnancy and miscarried a male child. There were those of a superstitious nature who could not but conclude that the spirit of Henry's first wife must have cast a spell on her deathbed. But most people thought Catherine was too pure of heart to be capable of such a hateful act. And Maria was always very cross if anyone said such a thing in her presence

And then there were others, of a more worldly disposition, who said it probably had more to do with the apoplectic fit Anne had had when she flew into a rage, having caught the young, and rather pretty, Jane Seymour sitting on her husband's lap.

Eustace Chapuys was overheard to remark, drily, to Lord Cromwell that it appeared that Anne had "...*miscarried of her saviour!*" Cromwell made no response but was seen to smile briefly. Very soon afterwards King Henry spoke openly and rather loudly about being seduced into the marriage by the French practice of 'sortilege', a form of deception involving 'spells' which Anne Boleyn must have learnt when she was part of the French court, with her older sister Mary, years earlier.

Whatever the truth of all this it was certainly the case that Jane Seymour was very soon moved to a suite of rooms quite close to the rooms of King Henry VIII himself.

ଦ୍ୱ ଦ୍ୱ ଦ୍ୱ ଦ୍ୱ ଦ୍ୱ ଦ୍ୱ

To Lincoln: A show of Strength
Thursday 5th October 1536; very early morning...

Nicholas tried to get up without waking anybody else, but inevitably Eliza Jane woke as soon as he moved from the bed and their son, Robert, was so excited by his own expectations of the day, that he was roused by the slightest of sounds. Arthur, just 13, remained asleep, and Cousin Eleanor stayed out of the way in her room until Nicholas was almost ready to leave. Then she popped down, despite the early hour, to wish him a quiet "Godspeed!" and give her cousin a hug, before retiring again, and leaving Nicholas to his wife's farewell.

"Take care, husband of mine! Don't gallop too fast on that mare of yours – I want you back in one piece, living and breathing!"

"I will. I am not sure how long we will be away. Robert will probably object to my idea, but, if necessary, I shall ask him to run messages to and from Louth, so I am sure you will know before anyone else here!"

Nicholas paused and a smile suffused his face. He spoke quietly whilst they were out of Robert's hearing...

"Don't tell him this before Cousin Joe gets here, because it might not happen. But Joe said, yesterday, that as well as riding his old mare to Lincoln, he was going to try and bring that new young pony he was breaking in recently for Robert to ride, assuming the pony accepted the saddle! He is still very green, but Robert might well enjoy the excitement of riding a new pony... I know I did at his age."

Eliza Jane gently squeezed his arms in affirmation.

"Godspeed, Nicholas. I am so proud of you..."

Her eyes were moist, but she was determined to be brave. The truth be told, Nicholas also had some moisture in his eyes, too, and his last hug for Eliza Jane was tighter than he intended, making her gasp, and then smile!

It took a few minutes for him, finally, to get his horse ready for the trip ahead, and he made sure to cinch the girth a little tighter than usual, since they might be travelling at speed for quite a distance. There was still a half-moon, so it was light enough for Eliza Jane to see him for a little way to the corner, before she lost sight of him in the trees, so she and Robert waved him away into town.

If he had been travelling alone to Gainsborough, he would have left home in the opposite direction, and crossed the river upstream a few hundred yards, but he had to meet everyone else by the church, as designated the previous evening. So, they would cross the River Lud, by the stone bridge just north of the church and take the Market Rasen road.

As he neared the church, he moved from the packed earth road onto the cobbles that surrounded the church and he could hear, even over the clopping of his own mount, the clattering of several sets of hooves, as others approached the meeting place. Some of the party were already there, and the steaming breath of men and horses drifted up in the cold, still, October air, reflecting the moonlight in a misty swirl.

A few lighted candles shone through the church windows, since there was still a strong group of citizenry guarding the silverware of the commonwealth. John Taylor was taking charge of the watch this night, and he and two others were standing outside the west door, talking to the early arrivals as they waited.

"It is a good job we are not from Cromwell's commissioners," Nicholas teased John Taylor, "or we could sweep in, and make off with the silverware, now you have the door wide open!"

"That is where you are wrong, good Captain Cobbler," came the reply, "it takes us but a few seconds to nip in the door and slam down the wooden spar which would keep you out until we had the door securely locked against you. We have practised this manoeuvre several times tonight, before you arrived. And in a dire emergency, the men inside are instructed to close the door with us outside if the threat seemed serious!"

Nicholas smiled at the response, but felt a glow of pride in his men that they were all taking the task so seriously, to have considered all possible actions against the common good, including risks of even an unlikely nature!

About half the expected group was already there, and it was only a matter of minutes before the rest arrived. The last four to arrive were Guy Kyme, and his three colleagues, as had been agreed the previous day. Kyme was wearing a chainmail suit of his father's that

416

had recently had a polish by the look of it, shining in the moonlight. Also, one of the gentlemen with him had a breast plate, armguards and a helmet; and, of course, all four gentlemen wore swords.

Nicholas himself had his sword on a belt beneath his Coat of Motley, and the armaments of the rest of the group consisted of a few purpose-made daggers, and quite a few large knives, as well as some very sharp hedging knives – with recently-sharpened blades catching moonbeams, now and then.

"So...we are all present and correct. Let's move off without more ado!" Nicholas took charge of the action in an understated way, turning his horse down the lane to the bridge. Guy Kyme joined him at the front and the others all paired off behind them. Once over the bridge and up the slope on the other side, they moved into a steady canter for the first section of the journey, mostly without trying to talk.

The track was good and clear in the moonlight, so they made good time and in just over half an hour they were just entering the little village of Ludford where they stopped briefly to give the horses a breather and a drink of water from the stream. They then trotted the horses, for the next hour or so, and were arriving into Market Rasen as it was getting light.

Guy Kyme, who probably travelled further, and more frequently, than the rest of the group put together, guided them through the town to stop at an inn on the western outskirts of Market Rasen, on the Gainsborough road. By this time, a few of the human legs were weary, never mind the legs of their mounts! The inn keeper was already up, and busy, but he was a little surprised to have such a warlike bunch of guests this early in the day. As soon as he heard it was Captain Cobbler, however, he jumped-to, and made sure all his staff jumped-to as well, cuffing one of the stable lads who was somewhat slow on the uptake!

The stable lads made sure there were buckets of water, as well as a well-filled water trough, for the horses. And buckets of grain were brought out to give them a boost of energy. For their riders, several platters of cold pork and freshly baked bread were made available, and it was all 'on the house'. The inn-keeper shook Nicholas by the hand several times and said he would "...*be able to tell my grandchildren I have shaken the hand of the famous Captain Cobbler!*" This left Nicholas a little bemused, to say the least.

Refreshed and enthused, they were ready to be off again in a little over half an hour, and they walked a little way to take care of the horses' digestion, as well as their own. After a couple of miles, Nicholas looked around and asked if all were ready to speed up again and with no dissenters, they broke into a trot, and then cantered again for about half an hour, bringing them to Normanby-by-Spital.

The priest there was just walking across to the church to say a morning mass so they stopped briefly to speak with him, and he was able to confirm that Lord Burgh had, indeed, passed through the village at high speed the other day, in the direction of his home in Gainsborough.

Barely a couple of miles further on, and they came to the famed Ermine Street, reputed to have been built by the Romans from London to Lincoln, and then on to York. Straight as an arrow, it cut along the top of the Lincoln Edge, and, as they moved through a copse of trees to the clear roadway, they had a brief glimpse of the spires of Lincoln Cathedral about ten miles to the south. Then they suddenly had the benefit of a wonderful long view, straight ahead over the Trent Valley.

After the rain on Saturday, and some brief squalls on Sunday, they had had a very sunny week. And today continued with the autumn sunshine, giving them a clear crisp view of their way ahead to Gainsborough. The church tower was visible, even from here, nearly ten miles as the crow flies – just a little further by road. A quick canter north along Ermine Street and then down Hemswell cliff, then a steady trot along an occasionally meandering road to Gainsborough (clearly part Roman, part English!) would take them, in just over an hour and a half, to the edge of the town.

As they walked their mounts, jarringly down the track from Hemswell into the Trent Valley, Guy Kyme asked his friend Captain Cobbler...

"What do you think are the chances of finding Baron Burgh in residence in the Hall with his feet resting on a stool in front of the fire, sipping Malmsey in peace?"

"About the same as seeing you fly over that tall tree in your chain mail, I should think. My opinion is that he has fled into Nottinghamshire, discovering the good people hereabouts have no wish to '*put the rebellion down*'. But we do need to find out for sure. By all accounts he is an unpleasant man at the best of times and may be nearly as mad as his father was."

Nicholas related the stories he had heard about Lord Burgh...

"He threw his daughter-in-law out of the house, according to gossip, and had his grandchildren, by her, declared bastards. He was Anne Boleyn's chamberlain, and then he also sat on the council that decided she was guilty of the terrible crimes of which she was accused, and should have her head chopped off! I would much sooner have him as an enemy than as a friend to be honest, so I hope he is NOT home. Even if he took an oath to our cause, I wouldn't trust him as far as I could spit."

"That is unusually harsh of you Nicholas! You more often than not believe the best of people, even when it is not always warranted!"

Nicholas was not quite sure whether Guy had meant that as a compliment or not...

"I met..." he paused. "No, let me start that sentence again – I was about to say I met him once, but that is not strictly true. I was in the same room as him once, years ago, in Lincoln. I had made three pairs of shoes for a gentleman who lived in Wragby but, for some reason, he had to be in Lincoln and wanted me to deliver the shoes to him there. He was stopping at the Cardinal's Hat – you know the rather superior hostelry at the lower end of Steep Hill. Indeed, I think it may have been the year it opened its doors as an inn?"

Kyme nodded – he knew it well.

"Anyway, there I was, talking to my customer about his shoes, and the world in general, when Baron Burgh barged in to the room and elbowed me out of the way, as though I was a common street dog, and said something unbelievably vulgar to my customer about his sister. She was a thoroughly charming lady by the way. And then he disappeared out of another door on his way to meet *'someone of importance'* ... was the way he expressed himself."

Nicholas shuddered.

"You know that expression we sometimes use when speaking... *'he made my hackles rise'*... which we say about someone who is unpleasant or rude? Well it is the only time, ever, in my life, that I actually FELT my hackles rise for real! The hairs on the back of my neck were stiff and my shoulders were tense. I felt a really visceral dislike of him at a very basic level, like an animal does with a cruel master! Horrible man!"

"Well, well... I hope you feel better for that!" Guy Kyme chuckled at his friend's discomposure. "Let us hope he is not at home or we might have a duel on our hands!!"

Nicholas laughed along with Kyme too, "Until a couple of minutes ago when I started telling you the story, I would probably have been able to say in all honesty, that I have no strong feelings of dislike or hatred for anyone. But it appears most likely I would have been telling a fib! I didn't realise my dislike of him was so intense. Something for me to admit, next time I go to confession!"

Nicholas decided it would be a good thing if he shared his next thoughts with everyone before they went further, so he and Guy Kyme stopped at the bottom of the steep track and let the others catch up and gather round.

"In the unlikely event that Lord Burgh is at home and we are sufficiently numerous to arrest him that is what we should do. There remains the strong possibility, however, that he has men and arms to outnumber us and put up a fight. If we can contain him in the hall without danger to ourselves we should and will send a messenger to Lincoln to bring reinforcements sufficient to finish the job."

Guy Kyme agreed, and added...

"...If he has forces that are a threat to us, they may also prove to be a threat to the host meeting in Lincoln, so we would then have to take that knowledge safely back to them sooner rather than later, so it can be dealt with appropriately."

Nicholas then went on to say what they should do if he was NOT at home – the most likely scenario.

"Probably the most significant part of our task, then, is to let people in this area know what we are doing at Lincoln so they can join us if they wish to, so at that point we will split up into four groups as we have spoken about before..."

He looked round to check if everyone was still with him, and knew which group they would be part of, getting nods all round...

"...and make our way back to Lincoln and the muster at Grange de Lings, calling at as many villages as we can. We have ridden hard and fast to get here as quickly as possible so I think the return journey can be taken more slowly for the horses' sakes as much as our own! Each group will make its own arrangements accordingly, but I expect we will all find somewhere to stop before it gets dark or soon thereafter, even if it is a draughty church!'"

"I will take the most direct route back, coming back along here to

Hemswell and then along the cliff-bottom villages towards Lincoln." He nodded in a southerly direction to emphasise his point.

"John Booth and his group will come with us as far as Corringham and then branch south through Upton and Stow and the villages along that road. Tom Mussenden will take his group along the Trent bank villages as far as the Fosse Way, then north east to Lincoln. That is by far the longest journey, so it will be late tomorrow before we see them again!"

Thomas Mussenden chimed in... "Tomorrow? It will probably be Saturday before we all meet again!" before Nicholas could continue...

"...and Guy, here, will take his group in a northward loop from Gainsborough before picking up the Ermine Street and heading south again towards Lincoln."

Nicholas looked around at his group of 'warriors' and asked...

"...is everyone clear what we are about, gentlemen? If any of us picks up worrying news about large forces on the move, then it becomes most important to get that news back to the host, near Lincoln, as soon as possible!"

There was a general chorus of agreement with this last remark from Nicholas – all of them were worried that it was still possible that a crushing force from Nottinghamshire and Derbyshire could already be gathering on the other side of the great Trent river, to sweep them all away. Whereas the information being fed back to them, through Devotio Moderna contacts over the summer, from Yorkshire, and the counties north of Yorkshire, was always positive, and in accord with their thoughts, they had got much less information from across the Trent, and not all of the news they received was good news, either.

Maybe it was because Yorkshire, and the North, had a large community of great religious houses similar to those in Lincolnshire, that they felt the same way. It could have been something indefinably different, of course, but it was enough to give them pause, that Nottinghamshire and Derbyshire were apparently much less sympathetic to their views.

"Right my friends. Let us get on with our task!" So saying, Nicholas turned his horse and led them onwards, every inch a warrior-leader in his colourful Coat of Motley.

As they entered the outskirts of Gainsborough, even though Guy Kyme knew exactly where he was headed, Nicholas thought it prudent to ask the way from one of the townspeople they came across on the road, in the hope they may get 'free' information. And so it was...

"...down yonder hill, and when yer reaches the river, turn right 'afore yer 'at floats! But if yer after me Lord Burgh – an' yer looks mighty fierce as if yer might be – 'e ain't there! By all accounts 'e went a'chasing off to Nottinghamshire earlier in the week, as if 'is life depended upon it. An' by the looks of yer lot, p'raps it did?"

The man they had stopped, who had quite an age to him judging by his lack of teeth, turned away after imparting this information, but then turned back to them with an afterthought...

"But, if yer bent on plundering his hall, 'ave a care! 'E left a guard there, and they are precious well-trained, an' might give ye an 'ard time of it, even with yer swords an' sharp knives!"

His observant concern for their welfare was duly noted, and Nicholas thanked him before they moved off again.

As they rounded a bend at the bottom of the hill the westering sun glinted off the great river Trent. It was their first view of the water, hidden as it had been by the trees and the lie of the land. The river was still running fairly full from the rains of last week, which fell on the hills of Derbyshire, and were only now finding their way towards the Humber estuary and the North Sea. There were barges, and boats, tied to the wharves, and, in general, it looked a busy scene, after their ride through the quiet countryside. Grain was being loaded, and timber being unloaded, as they passed by. Where it was going to, or where it had come from, they did not know, but for most of them it was an unfamiliar sight.

For Guy Kyme, however, it reminded him of the pirates he had been sent to investigate in Grimsby, only the week previously, and he realised he had not yet told anyone of his story – he had been pulled, dramatically, into a very different story the minute he arrived back from Grimsby. Perhaps it was a tale he could tell around the camp-fires of the muster near Lincoln, as they all waited for the king's response to their letter, which had been sent to him on Tuesday, still less than two days previously!

As soon as they turned right onto the road which ran alongside the river bank, they espied Lord Burgh's fine hall. Apart from Lincoln Cathedral, it was the finest building Nicholas had seen outside of London. One thing that struck him straight away was that *all* the windows had glass in them, and there were a lot of windows, so the glass alone must have cost an absolute fortune. The walls round the property would not have withstood any bombardment from cannon, but nor would they be easily breached *without* cannon. Not that they were planning to try and breach them at this time anyway!

They made their way along the wall to the gates, which were oak and very substantial. In the 'battlements' of two small towers, either side of the gate, there were about six, apparently well-armed, guards, two of whom had crossbows, disconcertingly pointed at Nicholas and Guy Kyme. Even Kyme's chain mail would probably not stop a crossbow bolt; though it might slow it down enough not to be fatal... but the Coat of Motley Nicholas was wearing would not deflect an arrow fired by a child, never mind the penetrating power of a cross-bolt! So Nicholas decided to pre-empt any warlike approaches with good humour.

"Hail gentle knights... We come in peace for converse with Lord Burgh, is he at home today?"

The reply he received lacked the same warmth of tone, however.

"...'Tis none of your business where my Lord Burgh may be, so take yourselves on your way and begone. I am sure he would wish for no converse with you!"

Guy Kyme followed up in the same warm tone that Nicholas had used...:

"Perhaps we can leave a written message for when he returns... perhaps I might come in and draft a note to him?" Kyme asked disingenuously. "Or would we be better trying to speak with him when we get to Nottingham. Is he likely to be with Lord Derby?"

"You may do as you see fit... but he left specific instructions not to let anyone in to the hall grounds..." The guard's voice trailed away as he realised he had given too much information out to these strangers! Nicholas and Kyme exchanged a brief glance, trying not to smile and embarrass the guard unduly, since his colleagues were still aiming their weapons at the pair of them.

Although they may have bested the guard verbally, Nicholas

realised the crossbow bolts were all too real! So, fearing the crossbow-men may have light trigger reactions Nicholas raised his hand in farewell, and bid the guards a good afternoon, moving slowly so as not to provoke such a reaction.

"Thank you, we will make haste to Nottingham in case we can find him there – we'll bid you farewell!"

They turned and took the road back the way they came as they would have had to if they really were going to Nottingham. On the way back, they detoured down onto the quays and spoke to several of the local men who were loading, or unloading, boats. Most seemed to have realised who they were before they came to speak. Several gave nods of complicity, but spoke no favourable words, in case Lord Burgh's spies should report back about them later. They were quite happy to confirm Captain Cobbler's suspicions that Lord Burgh had not stopped in Gainsborough more than an hour or two on Tuesday. The noble lord must have realised quickly that he would not be able to raise any kind of force here to go against the Louth uprising.

Nicholas and Guy Kyme left information 'hanging in the air', that there was to be a muster near Lincoln on Saturday. But they both knew it was unlikely that any contingent from Gainsborough would be there, since Lord Burgh was a local tyrant, and woe-betide anyone who went against his wishes. He had a troop of full-time soldiers, who kept strict order for several miles around and they were not averse to a bit of house-burning, if they thought some punishment was deserved in the eyes of their master.

On reaching the bottom of Corringham hill, Tom Mussenden and his party bid the others farewell and took the road that wound close along the river bank towards the Fosse Way and Newark. They took off at a gentle trot knowing their horses had worked hard for them all of that day and that speed was no longer a primary factor.

Captain Cobbler and the others walked a steady walk up the hill, for the same reason, breaking into a trot only as they crested the hill. Then they separated into three groups at Corringham, taking three different directions; Nicholas leading the only group to retrace its earlier steps from Hemswell. The only difference from the outward journey was that they now stopped in each village to tell people what was happening, hoping to get folk out of their houses, to swell the numbers converging on the county town of Lincoln. Progress was therefore quite slow, even though each conversation was relatively limited; so it was getting dark by the time they got to Hemswell.

Nevertheless, they decided to carry on back to Normanby-by-Spital. It meant crossing Ermine Street again and would take them a couple of miles out of their way. But Robert Sleight, one of the men in the small group with Nicholas, had a cousin at Normanby who would probably be able to put them up in reasonable comfort for the night. Otherwise they would, more than likely, end up in a draughty church, as Nicholas had joked earlier.

Once they were up on the Lincolnshire Edge, it was a flat ride to Normanby, so they were able to trot on, and were in the village in little more than a quarter of an hour. The problem was that Sleight had never been to his cousin's house, so they first had to find someone to ask where it was. In the end they chose to call on the priest and ask him. They were lucky enough to discover that Jack Sleight lived just round the corner from the church. Needless to say, he was mightily surprised to see them, but was surprised in a pleasant way and was delighted to meet Captain Cobbler in the flesh.

Jack Sleight was a farmer in a small way, with about ten acres to his name, so he had some stabling for the horses, and there was a straw loft above the stables. So Nicholas and his colleagues would be able to keep warm and cosy for the night, above the body heat of the horses. Jack, and his wife Jane, had a truckle bed which they offered to Nicholas but he thanked them warmly, and insisted that their cousin Robert should take the truckle bed – and he would be "...*more than happy to curl up in the straw...*" above his horse, who had been a faithful servant that day!

The Sleights had plenty of vegetables put by from their annual crops, so it was but a matter of minutes before Jane had a pan of soup started over the fire. She had cooked a chicken a couple of days earlier, so the carrots, turnips and onions went into a fine smelling stock conjured up from the chicken carcass. And whilst they were waiting for the soup to cook, they all spent some time caring for their horses – all of which were looking very weary after such a long day.

Nicholas had brought his best wire brush with him, so he spent quite some time brushing his mare, and talking softly to her as he brushed. She slurped her way through the best part of a whole pail of water, and had appreciated the large carrot she had been given as a reward for her hard work. She was happily munching at a hay bag as Nicholas groomed her, enjoying the personal attention of her master – this was usually a job he left to his younger son these days, now the lad was tall enough to reach up to do the job properly!

Once the horses were all groomed and watered and fed, Nicholas and his men were able to sit down to the soup. Jane Sleight apologized there was no fresh bread, only two day old bread that would "...*soften in the soup!*"

"No apology is necessary Mistress Sleight! We descended on you without any notice – indeed it is good of you and your husband to put us up for the night. This soup is delicious, too, as tasty as you could wish for! We'll sleep warm and contented this night, I am sure."

Once they had relaxed a little and done with pleasantries, the talk turned to what had been happening over the last few days and Jack and his seventeen-year-old twin sons promised to raise a group of menfolk from the village, to join the muster the following day. This did not entirely meet with the wishes of the boys' mother, but she held her tongue, knowing it would do no good to argue the contrary; not with Captain Cobbler in the household, at least!

It was all Jack Sleight could do to stop the boys going out in the dark and telling everyone what they needed to be doing in the morning. "We'll all be up at first light, my lads, so 'twill wait until then." Nicholas concurred, and said he thought it would be good for everyone if they all got an early night.

"I am sure I need an early night, if no-one else does! We covered an awful lot of miles today. And I know we were sitting down much of the time..." his men laughed at the understatement, "...but it was the most tiring sitting down I have ever done!"

At this they all got up, and bid their hosts a good evening, making their way to the stabling area, just across the yard.

Robert Sleight and his cousin Jack came out with them to light their way. Jack Sleight took his candle over to a stone bowl in the corner of the stable and said...

"I will leave this light here gentlemen, but would appreciate it very much if you would ensure it is safely put out before you all bed down... there's as much straw and hay in here at this time of year as we have in here at any time during the year. So it would be a real shame if we were to lose it (and *you*) by accident!"

So saying, the cousins left them to get comfortable and betook themselves back into the house. As the men were shuffling about to find the best position to be assured of a good night's sleep, an incongruous thought made Nicholas chuckle out loud, so of course he had to explain what had caused him amusement.

"I was just thinking about Guy, and his chain mail, and wondering what their sleeping arrangements were tonight. I know chain mail affords good protection ...but if you are sleeping in a hay-loft, as we are, it must be a bugger to get out of in the dark, goodness knows how long it takes him to take it off and put it on every day. It certainly cannot be comfortable to sleep in! And here I am; all I have to do is take my coat off and lay it back over me when I lay down. Easy!"

"Sleep well my friends – we had a long day today – at least we can sleep easy, knowing Lord Burgh is not going to run us over with a marauding army as we sleep."

છ છ છ છ છ

A force to be reckoned with
Friday 6th October 1536

Nicholas awoke with a start the next morning and realised he had been dreaming, but some noise had startled him awake. As he lay there listening for whatever noise it might have been, he tried to recall what the dream had been about – but, in the way of dreams, the more he thought about it, the more it disappeared in a haze ...something to do with castles and knights in armour...? Had he been wearing armour in his dream?... he seemed to recollect feeling heavy – it must have been thinking about Guy's chain mail the previous evening that had set his dream-mind working!

There was the noise again! His dream-state disappeared and he worked out what the noise was. It must have been one of Jack Sleight's milking cows kicking out at a wooden bucket. Nicholas was not used to sleeping in the hay loft of a stable, with a barn next door containing half a dozen milking cattle. Now that he was concentrating on his hearing, he could just make out a murmured conversation coming through the wooden walls of the stable.

He was the first awake in the hay-loft, and it was already light outside; they must all have been really tired last night and they had certainly all been very comfortable. Three of them still were! Mind you, they might as well sleep on a while; there was no particular rush this morning, it was only a few miles down the road to the muster, and it would be quite a while before everybody *there* was awake and organised!

Nicholas hoped everyone had reached Grange de Lings safely and got settled in well, but he doubted they had had such a good night's sleep as he had in the hay loft! As quietly as he could, he clambered down the loft ladder and went to relieve himself in the yard. Jack had left a jug of water and a bowl near the kitchen door so, again, as quietly as he could manage, he splashed water on his hands and face, and dried them on the cloth Jane had provided – all very civilized for a surprise visit!

"Brrr!" ...the water was cold! Still the others slept on in the loft. He could hear steady deep breathing from all three of his colleagues, so he left them to their slumbers and walked round to the barn door, to say good morning to his hosts.

Robert Sleight was leaning on a post in the barn, watching his cousin Jack milking one of the cows. They had clearly both been up and about for a little while already, and Jack was talking away quietly without seeming to pay much attention to the milking process, which must have been almost automatic after many years farming. He nodded to Nicholas as he entered, and immediately apologized.

"Sorry if we woke you...Lucy here was being temperamental! Jane and I take it in turns to milk the cows and this week it has been Jane's turn through 'til Sunday. But, since me and the lads will be away for a few days, I thought I should take my turn today at the milking. What I didn't reckon on was that Lucy, here, must have a sense of time passing and knew it should not be me doing the milking today... and got grumpy when I started. She doesn't usually kick the bucket when we start, but she was just letting me know that Jane has kinder hands!"

Nicholas smiled at the explanation for the noise! And took his turn to apologise...

"Well, Jack, please pass on my own apologies to Lucy, then. Clearly we have disrupted the animals' routines as well as yours this week! I think there will be quite a few beasts around Lincolnshire that will be demanding an apology from their masters when they get back home!"

"...And some who will live a little less time, in order to feed the muster, too!" added Robert with a black-humoured chuckle.

"Aye, indeed... I suppose your farm is one that is close enough for the quartermasters to come round calling to see if you have beasts for sale, too, Jack. So, I reckon you probably need to leave word with Jane what you can sell, if they come to you."

"We've no cattle ready at the moment. Lucy's calf and the other calves are still too young to have much meat on 'em. But we have a few porkers which are about ready for the market, so they could have those. How much do you think we should be asking for them?" He was clearly worried he might be making a loss on them.

Nicholas tried to be reassuring...

"I am not an expert on pig prices, Jack, but I know you will be offered a fair price. We have talked about this in some detail, and I know there is money set aside to buy meat and provisions, from the funds provided by some of the gentlemen, and many of the religious houses. Such provision of cash has not always been entirely voluntary, I have to say!"

"We agreed that anybody farming in a modest way, like you, should be paid the market rate. Some of the bigger (and, therefore, richer!) farmers will be expected to 'kindly donate' their beasts to the cause! I don't doubt there may be a few arguments at the margin between small and larger, but I made it clear that no-one should be paupered for the sake of the commonwealth, so I expect allowances will be made if the need arises!"

"Well, I am relieved to hear that, Captain Cobbler, sir!" Nicholas smiled at the slightly tongue-in-cheek obsequiousness – clearly Jack Sleight had an unusual sense of humour.

"The past three years have not been easy ones for smaller farmers like me – with all the wet summers and cold winters we have had, the crops have been lower than we'd like! This year we have not done too badly round here, though, and the harvest has crept up a little from last year, so we hope for better things. I would hate it if the commonwealth actions resulted in making the benefits of a slightly better harvest disappear!"

Nicholas agreed… "So would I, Jack, so would I."

At this point they all heard significant sounds of movement from next door – clearly the sleepy-heads had all woken now, and were on their way to being up-and-about. By the time they were all spruced-up, Jack had finished his milking, and it was time to break their fasts. They all walked over to the house, and the smells that assaulted their senses were overwhelmingly delicious. Nicholas had noticed a haunch of smoked bacon hanging in the kitchen the previous evening. It was no longer hanging there this morning, but the scent of *cooked* bacon, and the sizzling, gave the game away as to where it had ended up!

Much of it had been sliced off expertly with a large kitchen knife and had clearly been in the pan for a while, because it was getting nice and crispy the way Nicholas liked it. Added to this scent, was the similarly-delicious waft of freshly-baked bread. Jane, probably a little embarrassed at having her guests eating two-day old bread the previous evening, softened in the soup, had prepared a batch of bread after everyone else had retired to bed, and it had gone into the oven first thing this morning before anyone else had stirred. It had been out of the oven, just long enough so that it could be cut with a knife without falling apart.

The heavy kitchen table was set with wooden platters enough for family and guests, with just enough space for a large dish of golden yellow, home-made butter. The sight and the scents had all of them salivating, and rubbing their hands together in anticipation. As they were preparing to sit themselves down, the twins, Richard and Henry, came in through the front door and told them all that the church bells would be ringing in about a quarter of an hour, calling the village out. They both started to speak at the same time – then looked at each other and smiled, Henry deferring to Richard, the older of the two by an hour, who informed everyone that...

"We have spoken with several of the nearest families, and asked them to pass the information onwards, and outwards round the village. Then we went to see the priest, Father Blackwell, and he was all for ringing the common-bell straight away, but we told him Captain Cobbler had not yet had his breakfast, and would be very disappointed if he had to miss it! To be perfectly honest with you, sir, we were also worried *we* might have to miss our breakfasts, too!" and both boys gave identical embarrassed chuckles; chuckles that were immediately echoed by the others in the room; the expectation of a hearty breakfast putting everyone in good humour!

"You are perfectly right, young man," Nicholas did not try either of the names since he could not tell the boys apart! "Captain Cobbler would, indeed, have been mightily disappointed!"

At that, everyone set-to, and between them they ate every last scrap of bacon, all of the fresh bread, and more than three quarters of the home-made butter, all washed down with copious quantities of warm fresh milk. Sitting back, full of the contentment of well-fed animals everywhere, they relaxed for a few minutes more, before the church bells were rung. It must have been the best part of half an hour, rather than the quarter hour the boys had specified! For which they were very thankful.

Nicholas was first to break the silence.

"Well, my lads, it is time we moved on! Jack, we will come with you all to the church and tell our story, and then we will leave you to gather everyone together and make your way to the muster ground at Grange de Lings. I take it that is where you would meet for a muster, anyway, so you know the way?"

His enquiry was met with a nod from Jack Sleight...

"No doubt we will see you there at some point, but just in case we don't, let me say a very hearty 'thank you' for your hospitality at such short notice – and to you, Jane, for your excellent provision of foodstuffs! We really are very grateful – it made a very long day much more tolerable to be so comfortable at its ending. And for the beginning of today... well, what can I say! *Wonderful breakfast.* I dare say we will not be eating quite so heartily for a good number of days at least. We will certainly not be breaking our fast so thoroughly each day, for sure." Various enthusiastic sounds of agreement for this sentiment were expressed round the table as everyone was getting up ready to go.

Jane Sleight blushed at the overwhelming enthusiasm for her hospitality. Clearly her embarrassment about the bread had been eliminated by the reception for this hearty breakfast.

Nevertheless, it did not stop her worrying about her husband and sons going off to goodness-knows-what today. 'Captain Cobbler' had made it all sound very innocent, and inevitable, the previous night, but Jane had her doubts about the outcome for her family if things worsened, as they might.

Her Jack's cousin, Robert, had even suggested that, if there was no positive response from the king, it might even be necessary for the host to march down to London, and insist he should pay them real attention, because their demands were just and fair.

He felt that the king *had* to get rid of Cromwell, at least, since he was at the centre of the closures of the religious houses. And it was that, more than anything, that was damaging the commonwealth... "... everyone knew that!..."

Captain Cobbler had not disagreed with Robert's analysis, but had been more optimistic about how their march on Lincoln would be "...persuasive..." to the king and his privy council. But he had then sounded a note of warning...

"If you are correct, Robert, that further persuasion is needed, and a march down to London is the only way to force the king's hand, then I fear that the gentry may well find a way to back out of their commitment. For most of them, it seems a half-hearted commitment at best, so I do not think they would be as ready to move south, as we might think they should..."

None of the others commented, but Robert Sleight thought it was the first time he had heard anything but optimism from their Grand Captain. Perhaps it had been just the weariness of a long day showing through? He certainly seemed in better spirits this morning, after a good night's rest!

ଓଓଓଓଓଓ

It took about half an hour, after leaving their breakfast, before all the horses were saddled, and all the riders mounted. So, by the time they had walked them out of the stables and round the corner to the church, most of the village menfolk were ready and waiting. Quite a few of the women-folk of the village were there, too, to hear what was said. The rumours had, of course, been flying, and grew as they flew; rumours of what was ahead, but also inflated rumours of what *had been* happening earlier in the week. It was a small village, however, so there were probably less than a hundred people there altogether.

Nevertheless, they managed a rousing cheer when they saw the charismatic Captain Cobbler appear round the corner in his Coat of Motley. He acknowledged the cheer with a wave of the hand, and a beaming smile. As he passed the priest he leaned down from his horse, and spoke a few quiet words of thanks for getting the village roused this morning, and then spoke to the assembled villagers.

He told them briefly of the first actions last weekend at their own church in Louth, and made them laugh with him about the mixed reactions of some of the bigger farmers who had been affronted when not allowed to leave the church in their normal order of exit... and the huffing and puffing it had caused. He told them of the host visiting Caistor and their 'capture' of the gentry, who were meeting there. He spoke of the letter sent down to the king, and the worrying developments of Lord Hussey's letters about 'quelling the rebellion', and of their fruitless journey to Gainsborough the previous day to check on the whereabouts of the escaped Lord Burgh.

434

He then told them about the next actions, which were expected, and the muster planned to happen just along the road, towards Lincoln today. He spoke, too, of his hopes that they would come and join the assembled people of Lincolnshire to boost their numbers and their morale. He raised both arms in an inclusive gesture, as if giving all of them a hug... it was an unconscious gesture which marked nearly all of his speeches! It made most people smile without quite realising why!

"We know we have right on our side, but we do not have the 'might' of the king and his army. But we need to show the councillors in our capital that we, the people of this, our great commonwealth, are of one mind about the abominable treatment of our wonderful cultural heritage at the centre of our communities. We need to reject all the threats made to strip our churches of community property, silverware and church jewels to pay for the excesses of some of the Privy Councillors; Cromwell, and his ilk. And we are distressed at the heretical views of some of our bishops, taking the church away from the mother church in Rome and supporting the advice of Chancellor Cromwell, as he misleads the majesty of our King Henry."

He finished on a lighter note...

"Not least, we are upset at the reduction of our Holy Days during the year – we all work hard, so we need to rest, sometimes! So, go and get ready to follow us to Lincoln, and support this cause. It is central to the commonwealth of Lincolnshire people. My colleagues and I will leave you now to get organised, and get your things together, but we will see you all at the muster in Grange de Lings in due course. Let us all go forward together!"

He stood in the stirrups to deliver his last sentence with the gusto of a fine performance, and earned himself another rousing cheer from the assembly, who then started to disperse back to their homes to get leather jerkins, and any sharp weapons that might come to hand! Finally he leaned down from the saddle again to thank Jack Sleight once more, shaking his hand firmly, before taking his leave and setting off along the road to the muster.

Jack had explained fairly carefully (and more than once!) the way he and the Normanby villagers would be going, which was shorter and quicker than going back to Ermine Street, which they had crossed the previous evening, although it involved a few turns along the way which were not all well-marked or signed. On foot it would save the villagers nearly an hour against the longer route but, for a trotting horse, it might save perhaps twenty minutes, or half an hour.

So, instead of going back along the road upon which they came into the village the previous evening, they took the road south out of Normanby and were soon in Saxby, then, soon after that, Spridlington. They had left instructions for Jack and the rest to raise these tiny villages along the way, so there was no need for them to stop, nor was there anyone about much to stop and talk to anyway.

Unfortunately, they must have missed one of the turns Jack had talked about, since they were expecting to ride into Hackthorn, but no village appeared. Then there was a lane going off sharply to the right with a sign telling them that Hackthorn was a mile away, but if they carried on the lane they were on, they would soon be in Welton. Jack Sleight had said they *could* also go through Welton, but it would perhaps be half a mile further. However, the road improved after that, so there wouldn't be much in it as far as time was concerned.

So they chose that slightly longer ride to Welton, and just beyond there they joined one of the main routes into Lincoln. As they were about to turn right towards Lincoln and the muster ground, they caught sight of a group of men with what looked like some kind of machinery on wheels cresting the hill a couple of hundred yards to their left. Suddenly Nicholas realised what the 'machinery' was – it was one of the Grimsby cannon!! Or, since there was only one, perhaps it was the *only* Grimsby cannon!?

"Let us go and have a word with them – they look as though they are struggling with that thing!" So Nicholas wheeled his horse and the group cantered up the slight incline to meet the Grimsby men. They must have recognised the reported outfit of Captain Cobbler, because they managed a ragged cheer despite their apparent difficulties. They managed to turn the wheels of the cannon so they were not pointing downhill and got the thing stabilised before the horsemen reached them (just!)

"Hail, Captain Cobbler, can we presume?"

"Aye, you can..." Replied Nicholas "what goes on here – I thought there were several cannon headed for Lincoln; are you on your own? And do you need help?"

"There are; we are; and no thank 'ee sir, - in answer to your three questions! We are managing - 'tis a matter of pride now! Indeed there are eight cannon we are bringing from Grimsby, and we think seven of them will already be at the muster-ground. Each one had a horse pulling most of the weight, with a team of men, guiding, and helping pull and push, up and down, the hills."

"Unfortunately, we hit a rock when we was going down an incline, which tipped the cannon on its side. That, in turn, pulled the horse over, and he broke his leg, poor thing, so we had to put him down and struggle on, on our own."

The story reminded Nicholas of his own epic journey down to London those many years ago, when he had to rescue his companion from the river, and put the horse down because of a broken leg.

"Bravely done then, men! I think you only have a couple of miles to go now – do you want us to tell them we saw you coming..?"

"Again, no thank 'ee, sir. We'd like to make an entrance if we may. We might get a bit of ribbing for being late, but we'd like to be able to say we made it on our own!"

After a bit of good-humoured banter all round, Nicholas and his group of horsemen took their leave of the Grimsby men, and trotted off to the appointed muster meeting place. Less than a quarter of an hour later, they came across a large wooden board with an arrow painted on it in whitewash, together with the words "GRANGE DE LINGS MUSTER GROUND" also whitewashed on.

From there, onwards, they came across little groups of men going one way, or the other, on some particular errand. And each group they passed gave a cheery wave and made a few welcoming remarks or shouted encouragement as they recognised the newcomers. One incongruous group consisted of three monks, all befrocked, droving a small 'flock' of sheep towards the muster ground. It turned out that they were from Barlings Abbey and the sheep were the abbey's contribution to the feeding of the host!

A little further on, they found a gate with another whitewashed signpost, and when they entered, through a little copse of trees, they found the first muster field with scores of men building and tending bonfires of varying sizes. Most fires already had metal tripods at either side, and some of them had an exceedingly large metal spike across the tripods skewering through an animal carcass; some were bovine and some porcine. Mostly, they were still red, or pink, although some were beginning to sizzle, and brown, as they turned on the spit.

Captain Cobbler's group was apparently entering through the 'kitchen' area!

Gradually, the men tending the fires recognised the leader of the horsemen, and started shouting and cheering. This noise brought other men from the adjoining field to see what the fuss was about, and the five fellows on horseback soon found themselves surrounded. They were almost being herded into the next field, where the greeting shouts just got louder.

To start with, Nicholas and the others, leant down to shake a few hands, but as the crowding and shouting grew in intensity, Nicholas kicked his horse into a trot, in order to make it clear he was *leading* the group rather than being bundled forward out of control!

After the first two fairly small fields, the site opened up into wide-ranging pasture land, fairly flat but with a few small undulations, and Nicholas could scarcely believe his eyes. There were men, and horses – and indeed quite a few women too – as far as the eye could see. There were more people in this space than he had ever seen before in his life.

About a quarter of a mile across the pasture, there were three very large tents set in what seemed to be a fairly formal pattern, with a number of large wooden boards laid on the earth around them, to stop the earth getting churned up if were to rain. It struck him as a likely site for the "headquarters", so he set his horse's head to go in that direction. The men all around crowded closer, but left a pathway towards the tents, so it felt as if Nicholas and his colleagues were walking through an honour-guard. Gradually the general cheering and shouting resolved itself into a chant...

"Captain Cobbler... Captain Cobbler... Captain Cobbler!"

Nicholas began to worry he may be falling into the sin of 'pride' again, but that brought the recollection of Father Kendall's words in the confessional, when he told Nicholas that his actions were necessary, and "...protected the church and the community. A certain amount of justified pride is actually a good thing sometimes. And we can say your pride is certainly justified!"

So, as he rode along towards the 'headquarters' the chant continued...

"Captain Cobbler... Captain Cobbler... Captain Cobbler!"

...he felt his heart swelling with 'justified pride'. He smiled as he waved back to his honour-guard. Just before he reached the tented 'headquarters', he started seeing a lot of faces he recognised, and realised he must be somewhere in the midst of the Louth contingent. Many of the faces reflected the pride he was feeling – their pride taking the form of pride in 'their' man... their very own Captain Cobbler. Then he saw two faces which seemed to be positively *glowing* with pride. They were the faces of his older son Robert, and his good friend and protector, Great James.

He looked round a last time from horseback and gave a large general wave, to all and sundry, and then quickly dismounted, handing over charge of his horse to Robert, giving him a hug and speaking quietly and quickly in his ear...

"I hope you had a good walk from Louth? Tell me about it later – I think I should go and report to the sheriff on my expedition to Gainsborough. Can you look after my horse well, she worked hard yesterday and needs a bit of a rest?! Mind you, I think she enjoyed the welcome we got nearly as much as I did! Look at her ears pricked up with pride...!"

"I didn't walk from Louth!" Robert replied, "...and I think you already knew that!? Thanks for arranging with Uncle Joe to give me that pony – he's superb!"

"Your Uncle Joe?" Nicholas queried, teasingly...

"Nooo! The pony! No...YES! ...*and* Uncle Joe as well!"

Nicholas smiled indulgently, proud of his son in his new role as 'Master of Horse' for the Melton family! He then turned to his good friend James Long – Great James himself.

"James, perhaps you would come with me and the others as we report in, and then bring me up to date with events as you have seen them over the last day and a half."

Great James, smiling broadly as he resumed his job as Captain Cobbler's bodyguard, soon cleared a space for them all to move over to the headquarter tents. Robert Sleight, and the other horsemen with Nicholas, found 'grooms' to leave their horses with, from amongst the surrounding crowd.

As they all dismounted, and were thus lost to sight of people further away, the cheering gradually diminished, and everyone started moving back to get on with whatever they had been doing before their Grand Captain, Captain Cobbler, arrived amongst them. Even so, there were still many men nearby who wanted to slap Nicholas on the back, or shake his hand. At least, there *were*, until Great James turned and scowled at them all, when they suddenly discovered they all had something better to be doing.

"I am overwhelmed at the numbers here today, there must be 20,000 or more…"

Great James told him that Jack Bawnus reckoned it was somewhere between twelve and fifteen thousand, but that was "…*guessing rather than knowing*". They were basing their catering needs on fourteen thousand and hoping that was nearly right.

They may get a better, more accurate, number, after the next day or so. They needed to, because the sheriff, and his fellow gentlemen, and the purse-holders of Devotio Moderna, had taken a decision to pay all the men from Monday onwards, at twelve pence per day, so they needed accurate figures by then.

"Well, whatever the number, I think we can say it is *a lot!*" Nicholas allowed himself to be over-ruled, and laughed. And, with that, he directed his footsteps towards the tents, together with his small coterie of colleagues, Great James at his right shoulder, as usual.

As he was entering the tented area the first face he espied which he recognised was that of Guy Kyme. He was really quite surprised that Kyme had arrived before their party, since the Kyme-led group had branched off northwards, looping up as far as Messingham, before coming back south again. Guy came over and greeted them warmly, but was quick to reassure him that everything was all right, and he had only been there about five minutes, before Nicholas himself arrived.

"We hadn't even had time to report in before we heard the cheers, and it was easy to deduce that YOU had arrived. We looped up as far as Kirton in Lindsey yesterday afternoon, and had quite a chat with the priest there. We gathered from him that all the villages along the low road beneath the Lincolnshire Edge were already primed to be "UP" this morning so, instead of going as far as Messingham, we took a quick turn right and picked up Ermine Street again. We stopped at the Hospital at 'Spital crossroads so we did not have far to come this morning and, as I said, we only got here a few moments before you arrived."

This was all said very quickly, and very quietly, chiefly to reassure Nicholas that everything was well and that they were not there to report on finding Lord Burgh, with a large army of Nottinghamshire men, or anything as untoward as that! As he was speaking, they were making their way to the biggest of the tents. As they arrived, the men inside came out to greet them.

The chief of these was the Sheriff of Lincolnshire, Sir Edward Dymocke, who gave every indication that he had taken charge of the proceedings. He was wearing chain mail, and from the corner of his eye Nicholas could see a full set of armour resting on a trestle table towards the back of the tent, clearly ready for any action. Dymocke was first to speak...

"Captain Cobbler, I imagine, from all the reports I have had? I am pleased to meet you at last, having heard so much lately!"

Nicholas was not entirely sure whether his voice showed genuine warmth, but, under the circumstances, he was prepared to accept the greeting at face value, and responded with a warm handshake of his own. Dymocke went on to introduce his retinue...

"This is my father, Sir Robert Dymocke, the King's Champion. Sir William Leach, you probably know... and various of his cousins and brothers. Sir Robert Tyrwhitt and Sir William Ayscough I think you have met already... and various others with whom you will, no doubt, become acquainted in due course..."

He waved a hand vaguely around him, as if it would do as an introduction. It was not often a cobbler was afforded such a welcoming introduction, and Nicholas was smiling inwardly at the backhanded compliment it represented, even if it did not feel entirely genuine.

Nicholas responded in kind by introducing some of the men around him...

"Guy Kyme, I think you will all know anyway, Robert Sleight and these other gentlemen accompanied us to Gainsborough yesterday. This is James Long but everyone knows him as Great James. And Father Thomas Kendall, here, is the priest in Louth."

"Just to report quickly on our scouting trip yesterday: we discovered that Lord Burgh had left Gainsborough as speedily on Tuesday afternoon as he left Caistor in the morning, and he is reported to have gone directly to Nottingham where, presumably, he is trying to raise a force to put down or contain the uprising here."

It still felt strange to him, even to think of what they were doing as an 'uprising', but it seemed to have slipped into common parlance now, so he used it as a convenience of speech. Nicholas continued... or, rather, 'Captain Cobbler' continued, and Nicholas felt as though he was 'looking on'.

"We spent some time, as we returned, alerting the villages north and west of Lincoln about the muster here, so I should think we will be joined by a few hundred more men later today or early tomorrow."

"For what it is worth, we also spoke to a number of farmers, who were out and about, and the consensus is that the spell of fine weather we have been benefitting from for the last week is soon going to break. We will be getting showers soon, perhaps turning to heavier rain in the next few days. But my own experience of farmers is that their forecasts are only ever half right and it is never clear which half is right! So – goodness knows what the weather will *really* do!?"

William Leach decided it was time for him to step into the conversation now and establish his presence... He had a loud rather raucous voice, which always set Nicholas' teeth on edge.

"Aye. We reckon there'll be rain soon, as well, and only about half the men here will have some form of shelter from the worst of the weather when it turns – which means that half of them won't! Quite a high proportion of the gentlemen here have been able to arrange lodgings in Lincoln itself, and it seems some of the ordinary menfolk have relations there, too, who will put them up under a dry roof!"

"Lincoln's mayor paid us a visit yesterday afternoon when we arrived and asked us to make sure the behaviour of the men was civilised whilst in the city. I told him we couldn't guarantee any such thing!"

Leach and his brother, and cousins, laughed; and one or two others with them laughed along as well but, mostly, his last comment was treated warily by the others present. Nicholas made a mental note to ask someone what the laughter was about once they were clear of the Leaches. Something did not feel right, but he could not put his finger on what it was?

Sir Edward Dymocke, the sheriff, laughed along with Leach, and that did not 'feel' right to Nicholas either. But it would have to wait. Dymocke took over the conversation again when Leach had finished, speaking directly to Captain Cobbler.

"You and your colleagues will, of course, join us in a Great Council meeting planned for later, to discuss what our status is: where we should go from here: and how we might get there. This Great Council, for your information, will consist of just the grand captains from each of the areas plus their key advisers, sometimes captains themselves, or sometimes people with specialist knowledge of catering, weaponry, or specific local knowledge of Lincoln itself."

"We have been assured by the mayor, Sir Robert Sutton, that the castle will remain open to us at all times, and we may establish a small force inside the castle to guarantee it is not used against the host. Once this Great Council has met and discussed these things, the grand captains will be responsible for passing information on to their captains and petty captains and their own wapentakes, so that everyone is properly informed."

"The bulk of the host, including a few from Horncastle and beyond, is here and will be moved later to the proximity of Newport Arch in the city's north wall. The majority of the Horncastle host, and those who have ventured from southern Lincolnshire, have already mustered at Myle Cross between Nettleham and Lincoln and will remain there for the time being."

This information was presented to Nicholas and his colleagues as a decision already made, but a moment's reflection prompted Nicholas to call at least some of it into question before it took the form of a commandment written on a tablet of stone.

"Forgive me Your Worship..." he was not at all sure this was the correct way to address the authority of the Sheriff, but he decided it would have to do...

"I think you may be forgetting how this all started. And I need to make it plain, from the outset that we, the commonwealth of Lincolnshire, will not accept any plans made without our full knowledge and involvement. So, for a start, this 'Great Council' you propose will have to include more than just a few so-called-experts."

"Let me make it clear, that there will be representatives of *all* the wapentakes, sitting with you as these decisions are discussed, and made, not just the token presence of 'Captain Cobbler' and a few of my friends. There will be representatives of all the religious houses there too, both those that are still working houses, and those that have been closed."

"And, let me also make it clear, that we will be there, not just for show, but to make a real contribution to the decisions, as time goes on."

Sir William Ayscough looked to be ready to intervene, with an objection to both the content, and the manner of Captain Cobbler's words so far. But a severe look, and what seemed to be a growl from Great James, stopped him in his tracks!

Not that he was afraid of the huge Louth tailor, oh no! But he considered his comments might have been taken the wrong way by the big man, and he wouldn't want the day to get off to a wrong start. Of course!

So Nicholas continued speaking...

"If the weather stays fair, I suggest we have such meetings in the castle grounds, if only to test the goodwill of Mayor Sutton! He has some ground to make up before the men will trust him entirely. You will remember he wrote a letter supporting the idea that this 'rebellion' should be put down!"

"I remember being taken inside the castle when I was a child, and I remember there is a natural embankment, a sort of amphitheatre which would work well as a meeting place. Alternatively, if it is raining, we should meet in the chapter house of the cathedral. This commonwealth action, at its heart, is, after all, about the mother church, and I know the chapter house would take a large meeting, without being too much of a squash."

"I suspect Bishop Longland might object, but, by all accounts, he is not currently present in the city. And, again, after the events of earlier this week, we need to test the goodwill of the deans and other church authorities towards the commonwealth."

Almost everyone present was quite taken aback, by both the confident manner with which Nicholas dealt with what could have become a source of confrontation, and the detailed knowledge he was showing, of potential meeting places. After all, he was just a cobbler from Louth! The only three to show no surprise at this confident display of tactical thinking, and presentation, were Great James, Guy Kyme and Father Kendall.

All of them, of course, knew him well, but they also knew he had recently been to two or three meetings of Devotio Moderna, as the secretary/administrator of the Louth branch of the charity, and at least one of those meetings had been held in the cathedral chapter house! They knew this because he had waxed lyrical about the wonderful design of the place, and the clarity of hearing, for everyone at the meeting.

The chapter house was where the deans and sub-deans met to talk church business, and was twelve sided, but seemed circular, and had excellent natural acoustics. You could talk very quietly, and still be heard across the other side of the space.

And just outside the chapter house were the cloisters, a charming quadrangle built for quiet contemplation, but, although entirely enclosed within the huge cathedral, it was also a beautifully sunny spot, once the sun was high enough in the sky to reach over the cathedral roof! Then again, of course, if it was raining when they met in the cathedral, there would be no sun in the cloisters!

ଓଓଓଓଓଓ

Father Kendall was listening to his friend being authoritative about the meetings and was just thinking that perhaps the cloisters would now be a place '...where men of modest birth and background might influence matters of state for the better?' Then the priest had to bring his mind back from contemplating philosophy, to the present, when he realised Nicholas had actually asked him a question...

"Sorry Nicholas, I was contemplating; my mind had drifted off... and I missed your question...?"

"We were just talking about the list of entreaties to the king, and the privy councillors, being drawn up by the gentlemen, and our religious brethren, on behalf of the commonwealth. I gather a lot of progress was made yesterday on the way to the muster, whilst we were off chasing Lord Burgh, and rather than try and go through the details here and now, I was asking you if you think we have just about got the balance right, since you have been our eyes and ears on the 'drafting council'!"

"W-e-l-l..." Nicholas could already feel the doubt, with such a long-drawn out 'well' from his friend..."there are many points which have somehow made their way onto the list of articles so, at the moment it rather looks as though we want everything that's nice under the sun. And everything takes priority over everything else!"

"The list needs some judicious pruning, to become a little more realistic, and believable. There are a lot of items included on taxation issues, as well, that only affect a few of the richer people here, so we might be able to cut back on the number of issues addressed. More importantly, some of the matters concerning the practices of the church have been gradually slipping down the list, and need raising back up again..."

It was a longer answer than Nicholas had been expecting, but telling for all that. It sounded as though he needed to gather more opinions from the ordinary people of Louth, before the final definitive list was drawn up. The trouble was, they needed the gentry on board with them, to give credence to their movement, but by giving them such a free hand it meant that the real problems of the commonwealth were getting put into second, and sometimes even third, or fourth, place.

His mind now turned to the timing of the meetings.

"Sir Edward, you said a few moments ago the new Great Council would probably meet in Lincoln itself at two o'clock this afternoon. Can I make two specific suggestions now?"

"The first suggestion I need to make, arises because we need to have members of the commonwealth there in significant numbers and it is about an hour's walk to Lincoln (and, of course, *from* Lincoln as well!) I think we should move the time forward an hour – for the meeting to start at one of the clock – and plan to get most of the business conducted by three o'clock, so that the men walking to and from the meeting can set off home again whilst it is still light. The gentlemen living in Lincoln, and those of us on horseback, can stay longer to finish any unfinished business, of course."

"The second point I want to make, is one I have already touched on, and that is that we should hold the meeting either in the castle grounds or, if it is raining by then, in the chapter house at the cathedral. We need to start as we intend to go along."

This time Sir William Ayscough could not hold himself back from commenting...

"You arrogate a lot to yourself Cobbler! The leading minds of Lincolnshire have spent much time on considering articles to be put forward to the king, and the king's Privy Council. We have asked the men along the way whether this or that article found favour with them. You speak of testing the goodwill of the Mayor of Lincoln, and of the church authorities, and to what end, may I ask...?"

446

At this point, Great James showed signs of being willing to throttle the said Sir William, but Nicholas quietly laid a hand across his chest to restrain him. His words, too, were quiet, but his tone was sharp; very sharp!

"And *you*, Sir William, seem to forget what the Mayor wrote to you and the other gentlemen, at Lord Hussey's behest... something along the lines that the rebellion should be 'put down' wasn't it? Oh... and what would the 'leading minds' have been doing if we, the common people of Lincolnshire had *not* started to object to the actions of Chancellor Cromwell? Perhaps they would be thinking of ways they could use the fine stone and other materials in the closed religious houses ...I dare say you might know about this already, having used such stone to 'make pretty' your house and those of your sons!"

Ayscough blinked a couple of times as the outburst from Nicholas caught him off-guard – he was not used to being talked down to by a common cobbler! But Nicholas himself had not yet finished...

"And the goodwill of the church authorities? Hmmm, were those very authorities not visiting churches around Lincolnshire checking into their worth, and the worth of their silverware? And who was it who stopped them from their devious actions?"

The question was largely rhetorical.

"Yes, it was *us*, the common people of the county; cobblers, and craftsmen, all – and you think I am 'arrogating' much to myself. You and your kind are too used to 'arrogating' things to yourselves for us to be able to trust you entirely, so please forgive my strange lack of trust for the mayor and the church authorities, at this moment!"

It was so unlike Nicholas to let rip, but the arrogance of Ayscough really irritated him and, he had to admit to himself, he had quite enjoyed the look on the man's face as he was speaking. It was clear that others enjoyed it too...

"You tell 'im.."

"Good 'un Captain Cobbler..."

"Time someone told him what for..."

"Snobby bastard......"

As Nicholas finished speaking, the Lord Sheriff of Lincolnshire obviously felt he should intervene to keep the peace, since Ayscough was now looking quite apoplectic, and set to explode...

"It is clear," Dymocke was saying, "... that we might have to agree to disagree about motivations for our actions, but the fact is we *do* now have to act together, so I am prepared to take on board the points you make Captain Cobbler, and grant that the meeting should be moved an hour, and shall take place in the castle grounds – or, indeed, the cathedral – no harm will come of this decision."

"Let me also suggest that apart from the Grand Captains, and our advisors, there should be no more than, say, one hundred men of the commonwealth present, otherwise no sensible business will be done in the time span you mention. How you organise the representative nature of these one hundred persons is up to you, of course."

And, with that, he waved his hand vaguely again and turned away. So, it seemed clear the meeting was over. Nicholas was conscious that one of Sir William's sons was physically holding his father back from further intervention, probably not least because of the real threat of retaliatory violence from Great James if he persisted! The look on James's face told its own story!

As he was about to leave, Dymocke turned and said, as if it was an afterthought...

"We have also decided to send a group to Sleaford to 'bring in' Lord Hussey. The group will be led by Sir William's cousin, Sir Christopher Ayscough, who is a Grand Captain of Louth, as, of course, you well know. Monk Morland, here, will accompany the group as Hussey knows him well."

Nicholas immediately felt wary, partly because an Ayscough would be leading the group, but partly because the monk was also involved. He exchanged a brief unspoken conversation with Guy Kyme with his eyes, an inclination of the head towards Sleaford, and a questioning uplift of his eyebrows – receiving a barely discernible nod from Kyme in return. Then he spoke up...

"It seems to us that this task, of 'bringing in Lord Hussey', would be more likely to happen, the more people there are in the party, committed to our cause, so Guy Kyme, here, will join the party with as many Louth men on horseback as we can muster for you in the next half hour, probably about a hundred. How many were you thinking of sending, anyway?"

Caught off-guard by Captain Cobbler's swift tactical intervention, Dymocke almost stumbled over his answer.

"Well…" he glanced at Ayscough, "…there will be about one hundred and fifty…"

"If Hussey is as sympathetic to our cause as he has sounded all summer, that would be more than enough, but if he feels as dogmatically opposed as he sounded from his recent letters to Sir William here, and Mayor Sutton – and, *indeed*, if he has raised any kind of force from South Lincolnshire – we may need to meet strength, with our own strength."

What Nicholas was really worried about, however, was the chance that, if Hussey had raised a force, and it was joined by a one-hundred-and-fifty-strong force led by Sir Christopher Ayscough, they might somehow turn the tables on the Boston-based host known to be meeting at Ancaster to the south of Lincoln, and weaken the commonwealth before it got started on achieving its goals with the king's councillors.

Dymocke recovered his composure and smiled…

"So, Captain Cobbler has spoken! I hadn't realised the extent of your 'generalship' in military matters. I am not sure that Lord Hussey poses the threat you are suggesting, but I have no objection in principle to minimising the risk he may represent."

Nicholas smiled rather sourly at the '*damning with faint praise*' contained in Dymocke's tone. He would rather be safe than sorry, and the fact that Guy Kyme easily went along with his unspoken question, reassured him that he had done the right thing.

He turned and spoke to Kyme and Thomas Kendall who were nearest to him but his words were intended for the wider audience around them too.

"There is, no doubt, much to do, and discuss, before we go to meet in the Great Council. Let us start the muster for going to Hussey in Sleaford, and then compare notes as to what we have all learned in the last forty eight hours…"

As he turned, the men who had been crowding around to listen to the meeting, between 'their' Captain Cobbler and the sheriff, parted like the Red Sea had parted as Moses raised his staff. So, Nicholas, Great James and the priest, Father Kendall, took the pathway thus formed, to the centre of the gathering of Louth men, thirty or forty yards away, where a large canvas sail-cloth had been strung on four stout poles. The poles and the centres of each side of the sail cloth had been securely pegged taut, to provide an extensive, sheltered, area, acting as a local headquarters for the grand captain of the Lincolnshire uprising, Captain Cobbler, and his captains and petty captains.

Nicholas also learned as they walked over to it, that it would provide a sort of shelter for about twenty men sleeping in the open and it had been assumed that he and his son Robert would be two of those twenty souls; '...*unless they had made other arrangements of course?*' Nobody wanted to presume on Nicholas' goodwill!

Guy Kyme had come over with the Louth group, too, and spoke quietly to Nicholas.

"I think you were exactly right to bolster the group going after Lord Hussey, and I am more than happy to lead the Louth contingent keeping an eye on Ayscough! I am guessing we shall all be back in Lincoln again by midday, tomorrow."

"I also thought you should know that I have made arrangements whilst we are here, to stay in Lincoln, with a cousin of mine, who lives up the hill. It is not far from the Cathedral, as a matter of fact, so if you need accommodating in town after any meetings there, there will be a place for you, whenever you wish."

Equally quietly, Nicholas responded.

"Thank you, Guy, the offer is appreciated, and I may take you up on the invitation, if the need really arises, but I think, for the most part, I should stay with my colleagues – and my son, Robert, of course! – here amongst the people of the commonality!"

"Understood... just know that you are welcome, anytime you need."

Nicholas patted his friend on the shoulder in thanks, but then spoke louder for everyone to hear.

"So what happened yesterday whilst we were all off chasing the ghost of Lord Burgh...?"

ରେ ରେ ରେ ରେ ରେ ରେ

Several people started talking at once, and it all sounded very confused at the start, but the story gradually unfolded.

To a large extent, the host's journey to Grange de Lings was just a long walk by a lot of people and, since the weather was still treating them kindly for October, it was probably an enjoyable walk for the most part. At various points they joined up with other groups who had started off from other places before them, and were tiring; or others, who started after them, and moved faster. Some of the younger ones – against the advice of the more mature – made it a bit of a foot race to see who could get there first! Some of them were now paying for that competition with large blisters!

The outcome of this blending of groups was that the Louth men heard something of what had happened in the Horncastle area on the Wednesday, and, for Nicholas, it made for dismal hearing. He had been concerned at the level of violence on Monday in Louth, but it turned out that that had been tame, compared with the death of Nicholas Weeks near Caistor on Tuesday. And now, even that seemed modest, in the light of what apparently happened in Horncastle on Wednesday.

What had happened to Weeks at Caistor could, at least to some extent, be almost justified by the deviousness of the man in helping Lord Burgh get away, to the possible endangerment of the lives of the Louth host in the long run. But what had happened in or around Horncastle seemed to amount to cold-blooded murder. Nicholas could only presume that this was the mysterious cause of the Leaches' black-humoured laughter earlier which had made him pause in puzzlement?

Chancellor Raynes, who had escaped a beating on Tuesday, according to Phillip Trotter's previous report, was dragged from his sick-bed in Old Bolingbroke by another group on the Wednesday, a group including one of the richest men in Horncastle, John of Hawmby. Raynes was then forcibly, and roughly, sent into Horncastle, surrounded by shouted hostility from the men accompanying him. When he arrived there he was dragged off his horse, and beaten to death, with priests and former monks looking on, and encouraging the violence to his person.

"They were chanting 'Kill him; kill him; kill him'" Great James reported, "very unreligious by my reckoning!'

All this had apparently happened in plain sight of the county sheriff, Sir Edward Dymocke, and Sir John Copledike, a leading Horncastle gentleman, neither of whom had lifted a finger to stop the beatings and, from all accounts, both men had been giving their undisguised blessing, or support, to the action. Indeed Dymocke had supervised the sharing out of Raynes' clothes, and money, amongst the group who perpetrated the murder. This was not really what Nicholas thought should be the 'responsible' action one might expect of the County's chief law-keeper.

Also, there had been another death which Nicholas could not distinguish from murder. Again, it was apparently encouraged by priests affected by some kind of blood-lust. The victim was a servant of Cromwell's who, for reasons unknown, happened to be in the area, and who had, somehow, been identified by, or to, the mob. His name, Thomas Wolsey, unfortunately reminded locals of another previous chancellor – Cardinal Wolsey, of course, whose policies had often been unpopular in the county! And, the fact of him being a servant of Cromwell's sadly sealed his fate.

Apparently, this beating had also been witnessed by the monk, Morland, who had been sent by the Louth gentry, to Horncastle, to find out what was happening there. By the time Morland had got back to Louth, though, Nicholas had already gone to bed early, for his early-morning departure to Gainsborough. So he had missed out on this news.

Similarly Kyme had already left his house the following morning, before Morland called there, to report in to the gentry collected there, so neither Nicholas nor Guy Kyme were aware of this until today. Nicholas felt sick to the stomach, hearing now about all this unnecessary violence!

"So, this is what that strange exchange was all about when we were with Leach and the sheriff earlier," Nicholas muttered more or less to himself, sighing. Father Kendall, sitting close-by, laid a hand on Nicholas' arm and said quietly...

"Do not feel responsible for the actions of others, under their own free will, Nicholas."

"No, Tom, strangely, I do not. I thought, as the tale was unfolding, that I *would* feel that, but it has not struck me that way. But I do worry that it will diminish, if not undermine, the soundness of the actions we are taking jointly. The problem is that once you have broken an egg, you can never put it back as it was before...! Never."

As he reflected on this new information he realised that, even if he had had the news a day previously, it would not have changed his course of action. They were, now, far too committed to back down.

There was another piece of news that puzzled him, too, and none of his friends had an explanation for it...

Originally, the Horncastle host had apparently been told they should go to Ancaster, well to the south of Lincoln, to muster there, alongside the men from Boston and South Lincolnshire. If that was the case it suggested someone had originally had in mind a quick move down to London with a significant-sized host.

But then the decision had been changed and the Horncastle men had been told to come to Lincoln after all. What was not clear, was actually *who* was taking these confusing strategic decisions, nor *why* the decisions had changed. It seemed fairly clear, however, that the decisions were made by gentry from Horncastle, but which gentlemen? It was also clear that there had been no discussion with Louth gentry, since Guy knew nothing of these decisions either.

Nicholas had a suspicion that there may be a move to sow confusion in the minds of the 'common rebels'. The trouble was, despite the tongue-in-cheek comment by Sir Edward Dymocke to Nicholas, that neither Nicholas, nor any of his friends, who started all this action, had enough experience of 'warfare' to seriously challenge the strategic decisions being recommended. So they had to take the advice of those in the know, like it or lump it!

These gentlemen, *'experienced in the arts of warfare'* included Sir William Ayscough and Sir Robert Tyrwhitt, both of whom had shown a distinct lack of enthusiasm for the overall action of the Lincolnshire commonwealth. They had to be dragged kicking to the table, which prompted a lack of confidence in the decision making at the top. All Nicholas and his comrades could do was to try and 'keep them honest' as much as possible!

It was rumoured that Ayscough and Tyrwhitt were, more or less, sworn mortal enemies, for some reason that only they knew, and had been for years! Yet, now, they seemed to be excellent working partners – so, perhaps the threat of the 'common rebels' brought them together? *'They may be working against the common interest of the ordinary folk?'*

These thoughts were all roiling around in Nicholas' mind, as he tried to process the information, and get his mind into a position to understand what decisions they might need to discuss, and make, at the meeting of the uprising's Great Council. Perhaps just as important was to decide what *questions* should be asked. Sometimes it was '*asking the right question*' that provided the impetus for a sound decision. That was a lesson he had learned as producer of the Corpus Christi plays, admittedly not quite the same as decisions on 'warfare' – but, surely, the principle was much the same?

Nicholas decided he did not have the luxury of time to *think*, and just spoke up...

"Now, we have to decide exactly who is going to this Great Council meeting in Lincoln. Sir Edward Dymocke said to keep the numbers down to one hundred of the commonwealth. That is probably a reasonable point. So, let us work on that basis, then."

"We need to decide on the size of the religious house representation first. My first thought was for about one third of the total. But, after hearing about what happened in Horncastle, I rather think we need to keep their numbers rather lower. We need to be able to outvote them, if they get too violent in their ideas. So, shall we say twenty five at most, then twenty five each from Louth and Horncastle area, leaving twenty five to represent all the other areas of Lincolnshire, from Grimsby and North Lincolnshire down to Boston and the southern villages? Guy and I will be there as captains, of course, as well as William Leach."

Kyme's voice interrupted Nicholas to remind him that he would be on his way to Sleaford, to fetch Lord Hussey, and, therefore, would *not* be at the meeting. And then, Father Kendall chipped in again at this point, to say that he would be firm with the religious groups, where he had some influence.

"I can guarantee at least five sound priests," he said, "who will accept they should be in this group of twenty five. Then, we are probably talking about ten monks from the closed houses, and another ten from the houses which are still open. I really do not think we have much sway over who is chosen there. And it will, I fear, undoubtedly include Monk Morland who has been so 'busy' with us for the last few days..."

"Busy as in busybody", Great James sneered quietly in the background! "There's one religious man I don't trust!"...then Kendall resumed...

"I think we need to get started in passing these decisions to everyone else, to act on quickly; since we need to be leaving here in less than two hours, and there are bound to be arguments about the details."

"At the moment we are in the saddle, but if we do not move quickly, our decisions will be pre-empted. Remember, the Leaches were present in that discussion about numbers, and I am sure they will have their own ideas they want to pursue – all favouring Horncastle interests no doubt! Since *we* started it off in Louth, however, and Louth is by far the largest town in the area, we have the upper hand for the time being. We must make sure it stays that way!"

Captain Cobbler smiled at the 'political' thinking apparent in his friend's speech. What a world it might be, if Father Kendall was able to represent them in Parliament! Surely the gentry cannot always have everything for themselves? *'I won't see it in my lifetime!'* he thought.

As they had been speaking, Jack Bawnus had managed to write the same numbers out several times on scraps of paper, which he had brought with him. This meant that the message would be consistent and, hopefully, therefore, authoritative. Nicholas was very conscious, that if the commonwealth seemed, always, to be argumentative about things, it would weaken them. Conversely, a little consistency, and common sense, would *strengthen* their hand, against the natural inclination of the gentry, to dismiss them as a rabble. So, now, messengers were sent quickly to leading individuals around the camp, with Bawnus's paper scraps in hand!

As the messengers returned, it became clear that this attempt at organisation seemed to have worked very well. Just the fact that someone had taken the trouble to think things through, made the message more acceptable to most of its recipients. The fact that the information also came to them as 'instructions' from the sheriff, their normal source of authority in such matters, helped it be seen in a positive light. Certainly, none took issue with the broad numbers Nicholas and his group had established, despite a little grumbling that *'not everyone would get to go'* into Lincoln!

Also it was apparent from some of the loud arguments they could hear, that there seemed to be some fairly serious 'bargaining' as to who should represent each of the areas, or categories. In fact, some of the loudest verbal battles, appeared to emanate from the groups of black-, or grey-robed, priests and monks dotted around the field!

Generally, though, it was apparent that many of the decisions had been quite easy to make, at least amongst the main gathering here at Grange de Lings. So, as they were to learn later, it had been quite easy for the Horncastle contingent to make their decisions on representation, for example. William Leach was on the Great Council as a captain anyway, so two Leach brothers, a Leach cousin *and* the ubiquitous Phillip Trotter, had been chosen easily to represent the area. It was the final few names which had been subject to wrangling – at least that was how it was reported back to Nicholas later.

Together with that practical information, the gossip came back that Phillip Trotter was now wearing a magnificent set of full armour, and as far as anyone knew he had never before possessed such a set. The tittle-tattle was that he had forced his way into one of the Horncastle churches, and 'borrowed' the armour which old Sir Robert Dymocke had donated to the church. It was a set of armour given to one of his ancestors as the King's Champion at a previous Coronation! Whether this was true or not, Nicholas had no way of knowing, but he smiled at the cheek of the man, if it was true. At least the armour was more useful protecting a living man instead of standing guard over a crypt!

Monk Morland was, as expected, one of the first chosen to be a representative of the religious brethren, along with his young, voluble, henchman Father Richardson. Also Bishop Matthew Mackrell, the abbot of Barlings Abbey, was included easily as a representative, despite what someone had called his 'mock-protestations' about having to be dragged out of the abbey to join the muster.

As an aside, John Baker had reported that Barlings Abbey had been a major source of their flock of edible livestock that was now contentedly eating grass in a nearby field, waiting patiently, if unwittingly, to be butchered. The abbey was also the source of quite a few barrels of the delicious ale, they produced there; *and* honey; *and* flour so the abbot's protestations rang a little false!

Whilst the discussions about representation were going on, it had been arranged by John Baker's 'catering corps' that those selected for commonwealth representation on the Great Council, along with the gentry, and the force going off to Sleaford after Lord Hussey, would get to eat the first batch of roasted meat from the revolving spits which Nicholas had passed earlier, on his way into the muster fields. Thus they would all be ready to set off in time to get to their destinations at the arranged hour, leaving the rest to eat after they left.

The whole of the remaining muster from Grange de Lings would then move the last few miles to camp just outside Newport Arch before dark, the Horncastle group staying where they were at Myle Cross. This decision, about moving closer to the city, followed the change of heart by the Mayor of Lincoln, once he realised that he had to bend a little with the prevailing wind or lose control of the city from the inside!

It was clear that the ordinary people of Lincoln had, by now, heard of his letter to the county gentry, which had caused such a stir earlier in the week and were more than a little brassed-off with him! They wanted to bring the muster nearer the city, so they could feel they were playing a part too.

And so it was, that in just over an hour, around one hundred and twenty 'common rebels' were streaming through Newport Gate into the City of Lincoln. One of the solutions to voting, for some of the most fiercely contested representative positions, was to allow a few extra for each area! Nobody was quite sure whose idea it was but it certainly stopped quite a few heated arguments.

One wag commented that "...*the gentry won't notice anyway, they can't count ...at least, they can never count how much I should get for my work! I am always short at the end of a week!*" As well as laughter all round, this seemed to resolve pretty well all of the arguments! And the Sheriff was minded to pretend not to notice a few extra bodies.

The mayor had instructed the city guards to open the gates and give everyone free passage – he clearly decided to bend with the wind! And from Newport Arch to either the castle or the cathedral was but a short walk. In fact it started to rain a little just before they reached the city walls so a quick decision was made to head for the chapter house of the cathedral; clearly the gentlemen of Lincolnshire did not want to get either their armour, or their furs, wet this afternoon. Certainly no-one thought the decision had been made to keep the common folk dry, anyway!

For many of them it was the first time they had been into the cathedral, or even in this close proximity to it, and there was a lot of peering-about as they got closer. The towers reached into the grey sky, and the spires, which were now slick with rain, looked as though they might puncture the lowering clouds.

The brown autumn leaves which, for the last couple of days, had been *rustling* underfoot, as they walked the country byways, were now wet and making the cobbles of the Cathedral Close quite slippery to unwary walkers. Two of the cathedral deacons were positioned at the top of the lane leading down to the main west door, and pointed the way to a small gate in a wall, just to their right, which served as a back way into the cloisters. The men then had to pass a couple of rather ramshackle store areas, full of bits of old stonework, which had apparently fallen off the magnificent structure, and were being repaired or renewed.

Ugly gargoyles seen up close, reminded someone of a neighbour, causing more hearty laughter, until one of the more sober souls called for a "...*bit of 'ush! We're entering God's house!*", whereupon the laughter turned to a quieter sniggering, until even that was stopped, by a sharp elbow, or two, to a few ribs!

Through a couple more doors, and they were in the north cloister, and everyone 'shushed' at this point. The atmosphere was clearly redolent of cloaked priests, slowly perambulating the square cloisters, deep in thought, or silent prayer. The central square was gravelled, and open to the rain, but even that could not prevent a few hardy souls stepping out to get a close-up view of the largest western tower and spire. It required one to bend far backwards to see the top, as if from a mouse's eye view. It was quite vertiginous for some!

Nicholas, and several others, who rode in from Grange de Lings, had been directed to the Bishop's Palace, just beyond the cathedral, where they left their mounts under the charge of the stable lad there. Then they had to walk across to the south door (actually, several of them jogged over as it was beginning to rain quite hard now!), entering the transept, under the wonderful, colourful, tracery of the Bishop's Eye window, rather dull and dark today, in the cloudy weather.

Thomas Kendall, Nicholas, and his brother-in-law, Tom Foster, were walking in together, when Nicholas and Tom started to say the same thing at the same time...

"...*do you remember...?*" and then laughed. They were both remembering the time, long ago in their lives, when they came with the Louth boys' choir to sing in the cathedral, for the newly elevated Cardinal Wolsey. Wolsey had only been appointed Bishop of Lincoln the year before, rising in the church hierarchy to Archbishop of York, and then Cardinal, almost before the quill was dry on that first promotion.

Tom was sixteen, and Nicholas fourteen, and both their voices had broken. Nicholas was singing tenor rather unsurely but Tom was already master of his richly sonorous voice, and had been picked out for special praise afterwards, by the gracious red presence of Wolsey himself. For some reason, the rotund Wolsey had spent a few minutes telling them of his special view of etiquette, that they...

"...should be delicate in manner of eating, chew liberally and wipe fingers and lips, copiously, on clean napkins, before taking a sip of wine from the glass. The glass, itself, should be held by the stem, if white wine, or firmly by the bowl if red wine..."

Quite how they all managed to keep straight faces for this advice, neither of them could now recall, although it seemed that there was a lot of biting of lips, before they were able to release their laughter on the long walk home. Most of them had never seen a napkin, let alone a clean one, and the only wine any of them could recall was the communion wine at church, which left a shrivelled mouth afterwards.

Many of them had never seen a glass, either! The only advice from the cardinal, which they referred back to with any frequency, was to chew their food "...*liberally*..." This seemed to require them to chew rather noisily, too, a habit that was frowned on by schoolmasters and parents alike. All of which ensured that the rather disgusting habit had a much longer life than if it had been quietly ignored!

Walking through the cathedral now, Nicholas, strangely, felt a similar nervousness to that which he had felt as a young lad, due to sing in front of a large and important gathering. He recalled his sense of awe upon entering the magnificent building. Now, his sense of awe was more to do with the size, and nature, of the task in hand. But the history of the building probably made the task more daunting, than otherwise. Nevertheless, he pulled his shoulders back, and pushed these feelings to the back of his mind.

Most of the gentlemen of the new 'Great Council' were already present in the Chapter House, as Captain Cobbler entered, just ahead of the rest of the common folk, who had walked through the cloisters. These men were now uncommonly silent, perhaps over-awed by their surroundings.

When he entered the Chapter House, Nicholas had a feeling that they had interrupted a conversation, one that did not resume in its previous track. He was curious as to what discussion had been interrupted, but since Guy Kyme was well on his way to Sleaford, along with quite a few others, to try and bring in Lord Hussey, there was no-one Nicholas could question in order to discover the topic of the discussion. This left him with an uneasy feeling, and doubts he could not readily identify.

Sheriff Dymocke was all smiles, and welcoming bonhomie, but still it did not feel quite right? It was certainly pretty crowded by the time everyone had squeezed through the door from the cloisters. The first part of the meeting was all practicality; dealing with mundane matters, of who was based where, and what food resources were to hand, to feed the large numbers of men present.

Plans were made about what arts of war would be practised, by whom, the next day. And quite a few of the 'common rebels' chipped in with ideas that seemed to be welcomed by the gentry running the meeting. So long as it was not too wet, there would be wrestling bouts, to help train strength, archery competitions to train accuracy, and speed; and riding competitions, to cover the cavalry strengths needed for combat. It all seemed quite a bit of fun, in fact, and the lads seemed in good humour about it.

Nicholas did not jump into the discussion straight away, and, indeed, chose to hold back several times on points he would have liked more information about, but it all seemed rather unreal, as if the meeting was being run, intentionally, to keep everyone in good humour, not wishing to let the genie out of the bag.

Many – in fact *most* – of the leading gentlemen of the county were there, (Lord Hussey, Lord Burgh, and the Duke of Suffolk excepted). And the common folk of Louth and Horncastle, Grimsby and Alford, and many more smaller villages were either there or represented by someone close by. And quite a large handful of priests and monks and former monks were there too...

And yet... and yet.....?

And yet, despite the high feelings that had been running, all summer, about the closure of the religious houses, everyone seemed so quiet and compliant. Perhaps Nicholas had made a tactical mistake choosing the chapter house as a venue. At one point, it all became *so* quiet, that there was even some shuffling, as if people were looking for an excuse to leave, and go home.

Sir Edward Dymocke even called Nicholas, by name – or at least his 'nom de guerre' – inviting him to put a view forward...

"Captain Cobbler – you have been strangely quiet so far, surely you have a view on the matters we are discussing? Would you like to share your thoughts with us all?"

Nicholas decided this was the critical moment.

He had perched, half sitting, on a corner of the stone bench which ran round the outside wall of the chapter house. He paused, not moving but looking the Sheriff directly in the eye. Dymocke had made the comment seem like a challenge – '*Now's your time...Now or never!*'

Carefully watching Dymocke's eyes, for any 'tell', which might indicate he was about to move on to someone else, Nicholas let the silence continue, until the tension in the room began to rise. Everyone was now expecting him to say something, and he moved, just enough, so that it was clear that he *would* speak, but kept his silence a little longer.

Then, taking his time, he rose and climbed onto the bench he had been perched on, giving him quite a commanding view of most of the chapter house. The central pillar blocked his view directly across the room, of course. More to the point just now, however, was the fact that by standing on the bench, everyone had a good view of *him* too!

"Yes..." he paused, letting the tension rise another notch... "I have some thoughts."

"It seems to me, that we have allowed ourselves to become distracted, by the *appearance* of action. The fact of the muster; the plans for wrestling matches; and archery contests; the horsemanship that will be tested: these things have all taken our concentration away from the central thrust of our concerns. All of these are important, of course, and will cement the host, now met together in very large numbers, outwith the City of Lincoln. They now represent a huge combined force in the county, so they should not be ignored, or overlooked. But we seem in grave danger of doing just that – ignoring them!"

"This whole thing started because Chancellor Cromwell, by devious means, managed to persuade the king's Privy Council to approve the closure of most of the religious houses, in our county, and counties to the north of Lincolnshire, all of these actions being to the detriment of the people, and our commonwealth. It is rumoured – and we believe these rumours, despite many attempts to persuade us that they *are* only rumours – that the next steps will involve the theft of our commonwealth treasures from our very churches."

"This is *why* we are acting. This is *why* we have gathered in such numbers. This is *why* we are braving the elements, and the possible wrath of our lord, the king. We want to *stop* the undoing of our community. We want to *stop* the plucking out of the heart of our commonwealth. We want to *stop* the ravishing of the mother church!"

"Instead of talking about wrestling matches, we should instead be talking of where we go from here. Instead of talking about cavalry training, we should be considering what options we have, to bring in other people; to bring in other counties; to bring in other gentlemen and other Lords."

"It is infinitely sad, that several men have lost their lives at the hands of some who have been involved with us. And those perpetrators of violence will have to pay for their sins, in due time, of course, to their Maker, if no-one else! There is no doubt, however, that it will make the tasks ahead more difficult for us, too, because we cannot justify murder, in the name of all that's Holy!"

Some of the religious brethren actually appeared to hang their heads at this point... *'and well they may...'*, Nicholas thought! He continued...

"We have now to consider what lies ahead, in terms of opportunities, and in terms of the dangers that we face. Since I am a simple shoe-maker, and not a warlike strategist, we must listen to the advice of those that are. Let it be known, however, that we are not under any obligation to *take* that advice, if it seemeth unsound! And this leads me to the first of a number of questions, which I believe need to be answered by those who know what the answers are!"

He looked the sheriff directly in the eye...

"My attention has been drawn to the fact that there was some confusion where the Horncastle host should muster. It was first mooted that they should meet at Ancaster, well to the south of Lincoln, but little different in distance measured from Horncastle. If the Horncastle host had been at Ancaster, instead of Myle Cross, just outside Lincoln city walls, they and the men from Boston and South Lincolnshire would have been at *least* a day's march nearer to London. Also, they would have been in a position to defend us from an advance, from any forces coming *up* from London, if that possibility had occurred whilst we were yet unready! My question, then, is this; and it falls into two parts:-

"Who first mooted the host going to Ancaster? And why was the decision changed for the host to come to Lincoln? Was it, perchance, a move to reduce the threat it would have posed to Cromwell and friends, being near the southern border of Lincolnshire?"

There was an undercurrent of a growl coming from sections of the 'common rebels' as they perceived the possibility of betrayal by gentlemen present... a possibility not many had considered before! This was accompanied by a nervous 'huffing and puffing' of some of those very gentlemen. Sir Edward Dymocke was all set to interrupt Nicholas at this point, but Nicholas put his hand firmly in the air, and stopped Dymocke from speaking...

"No, sir, you will hear me out. You asked me to speak and I AM speaking!" This flash of irritation brought more growls – but this time they were growls of approval!

Nicholas strengthened his voice, to establish his right to be speaking, and to be heard in full...

"My next question is about the articles we are intending to put before the king in his Privy Council"... he paused ... "– if we can."

"When we started this action, we were responding to a direct threat to our mother church, in two senses. Firstly, we were concerned our treasures would be stripped, and melted down, and put into the pockets of the Chancellor. Secondly, we were concerned that the Holy Saints were being bundled together as if they were sheaves of corn ready to be ripened."

"There were other worries about the direction of religious matters which I am not qualified to talk about – I am, after all, (he dragged the word out as '...awl...' to emphasise the pun, and was rewarded with a chuckle or two) a mere cobbler. So my question is a cobbler's question... Why have the articles been loaded with matters of high taxation, which have little bearing on how we common folk live ...and all to do with how the rich live? Can we not simplify them again? MUST we not simplify them again!?"

"My next question is also simple, so let it be the last – again it is in two parts. The first part is this... When shall we move on London?" A hearty cheer echoed around the chapter house, at this question, " ... and what plans are in place, or need to be put in place, to make sure we can move safely, soon, and in good order, towards the capital city?"

Captain Cobbler's pointed questions definitely livened-up the afternoon, and animated conversations sprang up all around the crowded space. People had clearly stopped *worrying* that they were in God's house, and should, therefore, be as quiet as lambs. They *were* in God's house and unfriendly people were threatening to steal God's family silverware! They must be stopped. The change of spirit in the meeting was quite remarkable… and it took just three sharply worded questions to puncture the sheriff's 'hail-fellow-well-met', feeling, of a few minutes previously.

Sir Edward Dymocke was clearly going to attempt to answer some of these questions, but he was beaten to the punch by Sir William Leach, who had divested himself of his armour, but was still wearing his chain mail and, therefore, rattled, rustled and clattered a little, as he spoke, and moved his arms about in emphasis.

"To answer one of your queries, Cobbler, it was *me* who suggested Ancaster as the muster point for the host from Horncastle, and surrounding villages, and the nearby towns of Alford and Spilsby – and you are quite right about it being closer to London; *that was exactly my point*. As to who changed the plan, and why, I do not actually know the answer, but I do have my suspicions, and I am pretty sure the person, or persons, is, or are, in this room".

There was no immediate admission forthcoming from anyone… so he went on…

"As for your last question, my view accords with yours; that we should now make haste to get on down to London, with the host, in its entirety. We should pick up the party in Sleaford, together with Lord Hussey, if possible, on the way. The cannon from Grimsby should be sent on their way *now*, with the host to follow tomorrow morning, after resting well tonight. Anyone wanting a wrestling match can have one tomorrow afternoon when we stop for the night in Ancaster."

"All the sheep and cattle, including the twenty head of sheep donated by myself and my brothers", he puffed his chest out at this remark, "should be sent on ahead, to make sure they are a little rested before we kill 'em to eat, otherwise the meat will be tough!"

"Never mind tough meat!" Sir Robert Tyrwhitt burst in to the discussion. But his voice was very weak, and squeaky, and sounded at odds with his large frame – he obviously ate well and regularly! – "Tough meat can be softened by hanging – which is what will happen to some of the tough meat in this room, if we rush down and threaten the king's peace, without giving him chance to answer our letters, which have already been sent!"

From the look on his face, he clearly thought this was an amusing aside and, indeed, a couple of young acolytes smirked in appreciation of his supposed wit, but the comment was greeted with scowls, and growls, from many in the room.

"Sir Robert makes a fine point!" Sir William Ayscough's gravelly voice contrasted distinctly with that of the object of his passing admiration. "We would be committing treason if we took an army up to London now, threatening the king's person, when we have just written a long letter pleading our case for humble consideration of our cause."

Somehow, paradoxically, the way he said *'our cause'*, cast doubt on his *ownership* of the cause in question, perhaps deliberately? It was Nicholas' view that Ayscough probably represented the toughest obstacle preventing any fair hearing of the views of the commonwealth thus far. As a result he needed very careful watching... so Nicholas was now rather regretting his hasty decision to send Guy Kyme off to Sleaford. It was good that he was there, but he was also needed *here*, as a watchdog, on the least trustworthy of the county gentlefolk!

Nevertheless, it was apparent that quite a few of the best-dressed people in the chapter house were in accord with the views Tyrwhitt and Ayscough presented. Several had pulled their shoulders back, and gave the appearance of becoming ready to physically defend their views, if necessary using their swords. At the same time, and for the same reason, many of the 'common rebels' present were taking a firmer grip of their blunter weaponry.

'Heaven forfend that an altercation should begin in God's own house!' ...thought Nicholas.

A more emollient voice joined the discussion at this point, and grips on weaponry were relaxed, as many recognised the voice of the abbot of Barlings Abbey, Bishop Mackrell. He was a renowned preacher, and had probably preached sermons in every church in Lincolnshire, at one time or another. It was almost certain he was universally 'loved' by the common folk of Lincolnshire. He had a folksy 'common touch' to his proselytising, and yet he was also appreciated for his keen mind and sharp wit around the finer dining tables in the county.

"This talk of violence – and the tension in the chapter house – makes

465

my soul weary, my friends." His arms opened wide to include everybody as his friends. "Captain Cobbler, here, is right to ask, with his second question, about the articles that are to be presented to the king."

"Questions of taxation are out of place, here and now. I say 'pif-paf' to questions of taxation! Jesus said quite clearly that we should *'render unto Caesar that which is Caesar's'*, and who am I to argue with our Lord Jesus about taxation."

"The central issue, about which we might argue, is Caesar's current policy of oppressing our mother church, and pillaging her silverware. I am here, of course, only as confessor, and advisor, since I have no quarrel with our Lord Chancellor Cromwell – Caesar's stand-in for this country of ours. This is no personal grudge on my part, either, since Barlings Abbey is safe and well from threat of closure, as far as I can tell."

No-one was quite sure whether the bishop's tongue was in his cheek at this point, because it was widely known that Bishop Mackrell had preached a consistent message against the closures of the religious houses around the country. He had visited Yorkshire several times, too, to preach the same message, so there were several quiet chuckles as he said this.

"I am only here as an advisor..." he reaffirmed his position, albeit with a slight smile on his face! "...and I might, therefore, advise you to tone down the articles about taxation, to a slight general grumble if you must, but to strengthen those articles which refer to the church, and the closure of religious houses. It is up to you, of course; as I say, I am only giving a little advice." And he waved his right hand gently as if waving away his right to speak. But the fact that he *had* spoken was duly noted, and his emollient voice had calmed the tension too, for the moment at least!

He had stood up quietly to make his remarks, and now the brethren on either side of him shuffled obligingly sideways for him to sit again. He gave a weary sigh as he sat, surely showing his weary soul! Either that or maybe it was just his age?

He wore a tonsure that was pure white, but his face was round, and unwrinkled, he was clearly a man at peace with himself, and had been so for many years. He never frowned, and no lines creased his forehead, though there were a few little smile wrinkles, at the corners of his eyes.

Bishop Mackrell's intervention certainly succeeded in calming the atmosphere, but it also refocused the discussion around the articles, rather than upon deciding whether or not to go to London. It was nearly another twenty minutes before anyone raised *that issue* again. Not surprisingly, perhaps, it was one of William Leach's brothers, Robert, this time with no clanking accompanying the voice, since the brother wore no chain mail. Much thinner than William, he nonetheless looked bulky in a new sheepskin coat. His voice lacked the power of William Leach's but the message was distinct, and raised considerable vocal support from the commoners in the chapter house.

This time, the sheriff did intervene before anyone else could speak, and he gave every impression of having heard all the arguments, and taken them under consideration fairly. His voice was calm and reflective.

"There have been strong points made by each speaker this afternoon, but we need to be fully agreed, so that when we *do* move, it is with the full-hearted commitment of all, otherwise we will convince no-one, let alone the Chancellor of England. It is mid-afternoon on Saturday so there is no chance of moving on this day. Tomorrow is Sunday and I believe Bishop Mackrell and his brethren will be pleased to lead the host in prayer so we can all ask our Maker for guidance. In spite of the hopes of Captain Cobbler and Sir William Leach, here, we all know that a major move takes organisation, and planning – even the good captain and Sir William know that too!"

"We can use the time tomorrow to make the necessary plans for moving on Monday, if that is what we decide to do. We can sharpen the wording of the articles which unite us all. The current list of articles was put together on horseback, and would benefit from calm re-consideration. Both the cobbler and the bishop have drawn our attention to weaknesses in them, not least, perhaps, that there are too many, and that they may be too general."

"You all know now, that there is sufficient money to pay the men twelve pence a day whilst the muster continues. This is something we proposed to start from Monday morning, so you all need to spread the word that this will happen. There is food enough, so that no-one will go hungry, and the men will need energy if they are to walk all the way to London!"

Even the suggestion that the sheriff now accepted the need to go to London, raised a sort of cheer in the chapter house, but the more perceptive souls there, knew that it was *only a suggestion* that it might happen, and not a decision. He was clearly appealing to the men's baser instincts, with food, and money, and hope. And Nicholas could sense that it had worked enough to ensure there would be no fervent demand for movement tomorrow, at least not for the moment.

Sir Edward continued...

"...and finally, by Monday morning, it is only reasonable to expect that there will be a response forthcoming from the king, so let me suggest that we adjourn this large meeting now, and reconvene it for Monday morning, when we shall be in a position to make more reasoned decisions than we are now. In the meantime we should go back to our fellows, and tell them of our discussions."

There were some voices raised in objection but it was all very hesitant, no strong emotions were being deployed, and it seemed that both Nicholas and Sir William Leach and their respective followers felt that, just at this point, some compromise may be needed now, in order to carry the day later.

When the meeting ended, Nicholas and his closest colleagues chose to go straight back to the Louth host, which had, by now, moved, as planned, to some vacant land just outside Newport Arch. On the way out of the gate, they passed a noisy crowd of men going in. Since they didn't recognise anyone, Nicholas thought it was probably part of the Horncastle host going in to meet up with the Leaches.

Nicholas also got the strong impression that they had, pretty liberally, been imbibing the free beer from Barlings Abbey! The noisy singing was, for example, well out of tune, and there was more than one song being attempted at the same time, always a sure sign of intoxication! He hoped there would be no trouble... but was not convinced that his hopes were realistic.

There were only about twenty men in the group, and although the guards on the Newport Arch challenged them for their names, there was no real attempt to stop them going into town. Three men in the group said they had family in town, and provided addresses which must have convinced the guards that they were simply going in for a boozy evening. Nicholas shouted over to them, too...

"Evening lads, have a good time in town, but don't cause any trouble will you!?"

"No, sir, Captain Cobbler, sir!", two of them managed in unison, doffing their caps to the group leaving town. They looked so much alike that they were clearly brothers, and may even have been twins.

The next morning, however, the gossip came back from town, that a crowd of men, none of whom were caught, had 'sacked' the Bishop's Palace. Apparently no-one was hurt. The bishop, and most of his closest staff, were out of town anyway, and it actually sounded as though the damage was minimal... a few broken windows and doors, and some small items of furniture hurled about in the Cathedral close, plus a lot of noise. It was, no doubt, worrying for the residents of the close, but perhaps somewhat exaggerated in the telling! Enough trouble, however, to cause Nicholas to sigh very heavily when he heard about it.

It had been cold overnight but the rain had held off. There had been a thunderstorm, somewhere in Nottinghamshire as far as they could tell. There was lightening, and distant rumbles of thunder, but it looked, and sounded, as though it was far enough away, to be on the other side of the river Trent.

છા છા છા છા છા

The Kingdom in Turmoil
Westminster Palace, early Sunday morning, 8th October 1536

Sir Edward Maddison was still alive...

In fact, after the first twenty four hours of being in permanent fear of being whisked off to the Tower of London for an appointment with the *axe-man* or, maybe worse still, the man in charge of the wrack, Maddison had, in fact, been treated quite handsomely, by the Lancaster Herald.

Instead of a cold cell in the Tower of London, Lancaster had lodged Maddison in a chamber at Westminster, with a couple of courtiers only a year or two younger than Maddison himself. They had been suitably over-awed by the tale of his swift ride down to London the other night.

He had been brought some fresh clothes while his had been taken to be washed. He had been fed well and told to 'stand by' for a return journey.

So, he had spent the next few days 'standing by', expecting at any minute to be given a roll of manuscript and told to hasten back to Lincolnshire. In fact, day had passed into night, and back into day, again more than once, and he was still there. Nevertheless there had been a lot of bustling about, with messengers going this way and that way. Indeed, the young men Maddison was lodging with had been brought into play as message-carriers, even though it was strictly below their normal level of personal dignity to have to actually '*do*' something useful.

Lancaster caught their feeling of dented dignity at one point, and roundly berated them for being '*...tardy and backward...*' when the kingdom was "*...in such a turmoil...*" Apart from that overheard comment Maddison was apparently being kept away from court discussions, since he was, perhaps, not entirely above suspicion, being a Lincolnshire lad himself.

He *had* overheard one other conversation, however, the previous evening (Saturday) whilst sitting quietly in the shadows next to a warm fire in a large chamber away from the main run of corridors in the palace. It was a discussion in hushed tones between two ladies of the court who, apparently, seemed to think themselves to be alone. At first he wasn't sure who it was but after a few sentences he realised that one of the women occasionally spoke an odd word with a foreign accent which revealed her to be of Spanish origin.

The second voice he recognised from social occasions in Lincolnshire to which he had been invited. It was none other than the young Duchess of Suffolk, and her mother Mary, Lady Willoughby, born in Spain as Maria de Salinas, and formerly chief Lady-in-waiting to Queen Catherine.

Once he had worked out exactly who it was he was listening to, he tried to listen even harder, and kept as quiet as the proverbial mouse...

"I really wanted to go back to Grimsthorpe this week, but the duke has put his foot down and told me very harshly that I have to stay here at court. I am so missing little Henry now that he is beginning to see the world around him and smile at everyone..."

"For once I have to agree with Suffolk – you will be much safer here in the protection of the court and with me here too..." Maddison could hear the smile in Maria's voice as she spoke to her daughter, "... and Henry will be fine, with that lovely girl looking after him – she's obviously very fond of the boy."

"You know very well that is not what I am worrying about!" said the younger woman.

"It seems the Lincolnshire rebels are set to move south at any time, and the duke is so concerned that he will not be able to stop them with the piecemeal force he has managed to pull together. He is on his way to Stamford now, with about three thousand men, and most of those unarmed. You should have heard him the other night just before he left – he was shouting at everyone. In fact I am surprised you didn't hear him – I know there were some who did."

"When that gentleman from Kent came up with just two hundred men, I thought the duke was going to strike his head off, there and then, in our chamber. 'Two *hundred*' he shouted, 'You should have brought two *thousand* men, and two hundred cavalry! And the men have no decent arms. As it is, I have had to send to the tower for all the

472

centrally held longbows, and harness. And even *that* won't be enough for an army of the size we need to crush the rebellion!"

"He was enraged at the man from Kent, about everything that was wrong, as if it was all Kent's fault – and I am sure it cannot be! Anyway, eventually, the Kent man apologised once too often, and said he was '... *sorry, but they were still picking the apples down there!'* Well, I thought the duke might burst, he looked so red in the face, and he started to take his sword out of its scabbard – I swear he was about to slice the Kent man's throat. I just quietly put my hand on his arm, and it seemed to calm him a little."

"And it wasn't just the man from Kent. Our chambers were full of messengers coming in, and going out, from, and to, all points of the compass. Most of them left the duke holding his head in his hands. The king has given him full responsibility for sorting out the rebellion, since it is in what Henry calls 'the duke's fiefdom', now that he owns so much of Lincolnshire, through my father's former possessions."

"The problem is that the duke is worried that he might fail for lack of an army – it seems to be really difficult to raise the men they need. Each messenger comes with a different excuse but the message is the same – '*You can only have a few men from here...'"*

Suddenly it went very quiet, and Maddison thought the women had slipped away, but they had simply stopped talking, as a servant walked past with a plate of food for someone down the corridor. When they started talking again it was Maria Salinas, Lady Willoughby who spoke first.

"Suffolk is going to be even less pleased, then, when he arrives in Stamford and he gets the next message from the king! I gather Henry is going to have to call on the Duke of Norfolk, to help them get a grip of the rebellion. For the life of me I cannot now recall why Norfolk was in disgrace in the first place but, today, the king said for all to hear, that Norfolk '...*is the only damned warrior the country possesses now, apart from me. I am going to have to let him take charge, if the rebels are serious.'"*

All of a sudden Maddison heard sobbing, and it was clear that the girl-duchess had had a fit of worry, about her son in Grimsthorpe. It must have been her mother's remark about the rebels being "...serious..."

"But, if they *are* serious," she wailed, "then Grimsthorpe is in danger as the rebels pass southwards towards the capital!!"

"Do not worry so, Catherine!" her mother said strongly. "Grimsthorpe is well defended. And, why would the rebels waste time attacking a little castle, when they could just walk past it, to get to the king, in London."

The sobbing sounds stopped, but Maddison did not think Maria Salinas was very convinced by her own argument in trying to comfort her daughter in her worried state. The women kept talking, but gradually walked out of Maddison's hearing, as mother and daughter went to find a comfortable place for Catherine to weep in private.

ଈ ଈ ଈ ଈ ଈ

A little further away, through several stone walls from where Maddison was listening, members of the Privy Council were meeting with the king. No-one was actually sobbing, yet, but the tension in the air was tangible.

The meeting had been going on for over an hour, and it was probably the tenth meeting they had had that day. Not every meeting included the king, but all had been necessitated by Henry's huge irritation over what had happened in Lincolnshire. Rumours were now coming in to the court that bonfires were burning on both banks of the Humber estuary, seemingly passing knowledge of the uprising from Lincolnshire to Yorkshire, and beyond.

The Duke of Norfolk had been summoned, and was expected to arrive before midnight. He was to be briefed as soon as he arrived, so this meeting was to ensure that the privy councillors were ready to brief the duke. And woe-betide them if they weren't – because, although the king was not present for this meeting, he made clear that he *would be* present for the meeting with the Duke of Norfolk.

And each meeting had been called to deal with a specific problem, each problem had been caused by an incoming negative message, telling them that '*this*' had not happened; or '*that*' could not be delivered where it was needed by the time it was needed; or '*something else*' would not be available before Tuesday at the earliest!

The biggest problem appeared to be manpower. Very few areas were able, or (*perhaps*?) willing to send men up towards Lincolnshire

474

right now, when they were needed to stop the Lincolnshire host from coming down to London.

ଔଔଔଔଔଔ

Chancellor Cromwell agreed with the Duke of Suffolk's suggestion, that at least ten thousand men were needed on the southern border of Lincolnshire, to be sure of preventing the rebels moving south with ease.

Cromwell had received messages from Lord Derby, and Lord Burgh, in Nottinghamshire, that they would be able to blockade the river crossing at Newark, on the River Trent, but that would only help if there was a threat from Yorkshire men coming south. The Lincolnshire host could move quickly south, through Grantham and Stamford, without hindrance. That was why Suffolk had been sent up to Stamford, of course, to stop them there.

The problem, however, was one of numbers. The Nottinghamshire contingent was not big enough to split between Newark and Stamford without risking the Trent crossing, and Suffolk would only have three thousand men at Stamford until, at the very least, Wednesday, and maybe several days beyond that.

Cromwell's spy network gave him varying estimates for the total combined Lincolnshire host as being somewhere between eleven thousand men and twenty thousand men. Even if he discounted the top figure as being fanciful, Cromwell knew that Suffolk would be overwhelmed by even eleven thousand men, if they moved straight away. They would simply walk over three thousand men, with hardly a scratch to show for it, especially if the armaments problem was not overcome.

He knew that they had less than two thousand longbows stored in the Tower of London and he was not sure, even now, whether each longbow had its own sheaf of arrows! The reply he had received from the armourer there was ambiguous to say the least. The man was presumably protecting his backside as much as he could! And there were only a few small cannon in store as well.

Nevertheless, he had ordered the bows and cannon to be dispatched straight away and they were all somewhere on the Great North Road, right now, trundling towards Stamford, presumably moving at a slower rate than the men were walking?

෧෧෧෧෧෧

A little while later...

Sir Richard Rich, having spent the last 12 months planning, and then overseeing, the closure and destruction of the monasteries as Chancellor for the Augmentation, had recently been invited onto the Privy Council (*a preferment he relished, nearly as much as he relished money itself*). He had been taking notes assiduously for the Privy Council meetings all day, and was still at that time in his life when he just loved to be busy. All the rest of the privy councillors were thoroughly tired of these meetings, but he was in his element.

He was a naturally devious person, and had been trained by Cromwell to hone his natural talents into an art form, so he had quickly taken responsibility for most of Cromwell's lesser spies, and added quite a few of his own, knowing that *knowledge itself* was power (or, at least, the primary *source* of power!).

Somewhat ascetic, he did not have Cromwell's expensive tastes and was, for the most part, miserly with his money and the many possessions he had acquired as Chancellor of the Augmentation. He just liked *having them* so that no-one else could! Also, he simply loved telling lies. He could lie to the Devil and get away with it, he was so good at it, and had no conscience whatsoever.

The king did not really like him as a person, but recognised a talent such as Rich possessed was very valuable, and let him get on with it, especially when it was in the king's own interests to do so.

And, so it was, that Sir Richard Rich was the first man to greet the Duke of Norfolk when he arrived, for what would now be the eleventh meeting of the Privy Council for this day. All the other councillors had found some excuse to arrive late at the meeting so they had time to swallow a bit of food, or imbibe a goblet, or more, of wine.

The servant showing the duke into the meeting room bowed low, and backed out of the room, as if in the king's presence, but the duke hardly noticed (and Rich made a mental note that the servant might be useful as a spy, because of his overweening obsequiousness!)

Now getting on in years, Norfolk was a very gruff speaker, and disliked Rich intensely. Looking round the room, as if for someone else to talk to (*frankly, anyone would have done, other than Rich*) he grunted, and then growled...

"Am I in the right place, Rich? I thought this was going to be a Privy Council meeting. What are you doing here?"

Completely unfazed by the insulting tone, Rich responded...

"Indeed you are Your Grace. And, indeed it is Your Grace ...and I am here because I have been collating all the information coming in to the Privy Council today, more or less acting as the Privy Secretary today , you might say," smiling a 'toady' smile for the duke's benefit, not that the duke himself felt much benefited by it.

"Everyone is expecting you, and will be here very shortly, I am sure. The king, too, indicated he would be present before the meeting ended. There is some wine over on the table there." His studied lack of willingness to get the duke a goblet of wine, as if he were a servant, was merely a small rebuke for the duke's refusal to accept that the man was fit to be a privy councillor.

Norfolk "hmmph"-ed, and went over to help himself to wine, gulping back a full goblet and refilling it in the space of a few seconds. His already red nose got a little redder. His presence must have been signalled quietly through the corridors of the palace, however, since the privy councillors quickly started rolling into the chamber, and taking their places around the large table in the centre of the room, before he could take a second mouthful.

As soon as Cromwell, richly clad in warm furs, came into the room, Sir Richard Rich retreated into the shadows, sitting at a table in the corner of the room – he could 'do' obsequiousness quite well, himself, when necessary! Cromwell felt no reason to delay starting the meeting...

"Welcome Your Grace; I see you have been given some wine..."

Norfolk did not see fit to correct him; he disliked Cromwell marginally less than Rich, but there was not much in it!

"...shall we get down to business?"

Rich, from the shadows, quickly ran through the major points the Privy Council had covered during the day; to whit, the delays, the problems, the excuses and the current position of the Duke of Suffolk and his "force". The rest of the privy councillors decided to keep quiet – at least if they said nothing, they could not then be blamed for all the things going wrong (so they hoped). Then Cromwell took over from Sir Richard Rich and summed up the situation as he perceived it…

"We seem to have a problem on our hands, as you can tell, Your Grace, and His Majesty would welcome your views and your experience of martial matters, at this critical time. He will join us shortly, as he is, at this moment, finishing his letter to the Lincolnshire gentry – I believe this will be his fourth version and each appears to be more strongly worded than its predecessor. So, what would Your Grace advise…?"

"*Bluff!*"

Norfolk's one-word answer was as brief as Cromwell's commentary, and question, had been wordy. Truth be told, they never saw eye to eye on anything anyway and the whole reason he had been more or less banished from court, was that he was always sniping at Cromwell. King Henry had tired of having to defend his chancellor against the old warrior. In particular, it was embarrassing, that Norfolk kept harking back to the "*old*" religion that "*…Cromwell was bent on destroying*".

Nevertheless an old warrior was exactly what the king needed right now.

Sir Richard Rich, noting that the duke could not possibly like him any less, whatever he said, decided he would probably, on balance, win the admiration of several *other* members of the Privy Council for asking the question they all, probably, wanted to have answered, but did not dare ask!

"I am not sure I follow your point, Your Grace, it is a little brief for my poorly informed mind."

Norfolk looked deep into the shadows, but could not really see the man who had uttered the question, so he chose to give his answer to the other members of the Privy Council directly. Adopting a tone of a patient parent, teaching slow offspring, he said…

"If you do not have the upper hand in a battle about to take place, you have to try and convince the other side that there are many reasons which *do* give you the upper hand. To start with, this means you have to keep all *real* strategic information from falling into the hands of the enemy – and then provide him with misleading strategic information which leads him to think that you are, actually, invincible."

"In short you have to BLUFF the enemy into believing you will win, whatever may happen. In that way, you might actually win the day or, better still, you might persuade your enemy that you WILL win, and he then decides to back down without a fight."

"The most likely option, however, is that you manage to persuade the enemy that he is at risk, which will delay him until you can rectify the weak strategic position, making sure that you then *do* have the upper hand, when the actual battle occurs!"

"In other words, as far as Lincolnshire is concerned, the rebels must be made to believe that they will be slaughtered if they attempt to move on London. This will then give us time to move men and materials into position to ensure the rebels *would* be slaughtered, if they tried to move on London. Simple... just bluff!"

Norfolk then paused, frowning a little...

"The problem is that, if they were to be led by someone with my strategic knowledge, their response is equally simple – they would call our bluff, and move anyway. Then *we* would get slaughtered. Who is leading them?"

Sir Richard Rich took great delight in answering the Duke...

"The sheriff, a shoemaker and a bishop – and we do not really think the sheriff is on their side, just that he is stuck with them!"

"That sounds like the start of a very bad joke..." someone blurted out before realising that it just might *become* a very bad joke indeed, and he would wish he had never said anything, so he went very quiet again. His quietness was just as well, because King Henry VIII chose that very moment to sweep into the chamber, his voluminous furs sweeping a draught of very cold autumnal air into the chamber with him!

Henry's first comment was directed clearly at the Duke of Norfolk...

"Well my Lord Duke, have you solved the problem for us? I have now finished my letter to the unworthy people of Lincolnshire, which I shall ask Rich here to read to you...!"

ଫ ଫ ଫ ଫ ଫ ଫ

The King's Letter
Lincoln Cathedral Chapter House,
Monday 9ᵗʰ October

There had been scattered showers on Sunday, and it had been cold again on Sunday night, with Monday morning starting cloudy and damp. So, the word had been circulated that the Great Council meeting of the host would be held in the chapter house again. The morning went from *'damp'* to *'wet'* when the rain started to pour, instead of drizzling, and everyone was greatly pleased to get in from the rain.

The atmosphere in the chapter house was getting steamy, as rainwater evaporated from the body warmth of close to two hundred bodies, packed in the circular space. For some reason it made Nicholas think of a barnful of steaming cattle, brought in for early morning milking. The sheriff had called everyone to order, but the meeting had barely started when the door from the cloisters opened, and a gentleman no one had seen before, walked in, soaked from head to toe, and accompanied by two sturdy yeomen.

He introduced himself as Sir John Thimbleby, from the village of Irnham, which very few men in the chapter house had ever heard of – situated at the very south of the County of Lincolnshire. Irnham was a long way from Lincoln, only just over a couple of miles from Grimsthorpe Castle, the Lincolnshire home of the Duke of Suffolk since his marriage to his ward Catherine, 11ᵗʰ Baroness Willoughby de Eresby, daughter of Maria de Salinas. It was a mere fifteen miles from Stamford.

Sir Edward Dymocke, realising that everyone was intrigued by the newcomer, asked how he came to be here.

Thimbleby firstly explained that two hundred of his tenants, and labouring men, and men from nearby villages, were, at this moment, walking through Newport Arch, and were making their way out to the muster fields, having walked all the way from the South Kesteven wapentake over the last two days.

"...the last part of the walk up the Steep Hill to get here to the cathedral, and Newport Arch, nearly did for us. Most of us were ready to collapse at the top! But it is a blessing to be here at last!"

For that he got a rousing cheer from most of those inside the chapter house.

"When we heard reports of the Duke of Suffolk not being far from Stamford, with a force from further south, I rang the common bell, to call people out, as I was duty-bound to do. But it was clear that everybody would rather come up here in friendship, than as part of an army to kill you all..." another huge cheer erupted "... so here we all are!"

Nicholas, still wearing his multi-coloured Coat of Motley, of course, bid them a most hearty welcome, and assured Thimbleby that his men would be fed an equally hearty breakfast once they arrived with the rest of the host outside the city. Thimbleby turned towards Nicholas and extended his hand...

"I am guessing you must be Captain Cobbler, perchance?" Both men, full of smiles, shook hands, and Sir Edward Dymocke, not to be outdone, bid the newcomers formally welcome to the meeting.

Sir William Leach also welcomed Thimbleby, and asked if they had much intelligence of the size of the army Suffolk was commanding...

"For, if the army is not large, we may be asking you and your men to march south with us again very soon!!"

"We do not have numbers with any exactitude," Sir John replied, the smile leaving his face "but one of my tenants, who had just been to Stamford market, had, in his words, '...*heard tell 'twas a large number of men*...' But I would put little credence on the remark, because he has been telling me for years he keeps a '...*large number of sheep*' but has never had above twenty to my certain knowledge!"

There was a certain amount of laughter in the chapter house at this remark, but it was of a 'nervous' kind, partly, at least, because few of the common folk could count above ten with any certainty. And some could not get above one, two, three, safely or, as Lincolnshire shepherds would say in their ancient local dialect... " *Yan, tan, tethera*..."

Despite the possibility of a large force awaiting them in Stamford, the talk now was of moving south, soon; and there was a weight of opinion building up to make the decision quickly. The discussion was picking up momentum when there was *another* interruption. This time, again, the interruption took the form of three very wet people coming into the chapter house.

These arrivals were from the north, rather than the south. It turned out that these three had started out very early this morning from the town of Beverley in Yorkshire, on the other side of the Humber estuary. They knew of the rising in Lincolnshire from the beacons burning on the south bank, and had responded with beacons of their own. This had set off a northward flow of fiery messages, across the Yorkshire hills and dales, but those messages were simply saying, '...*something is happening*', without detailing exactly what that '*something*' was.

The Beverley townspeople had been called out by the ringing of the common bell, as for a muster. It was clear that the activity had something to do with the subject that had been on everyone's lips during the summer – the closure of the religious houses – but no-one was quite sure what exactly was happening.

Indeed, there were so many questions, that it had been decided to send a deputation into Lincolnshire, to find out *exactly* what was happening, and to offer support from the town, and the surrounding area, if it was appropriate. Yet more cheering from the chapter house greeted this news, and the room was now buzzing with conversations, and questions, and a general clamour for action.

Sir Edward Dymocke, and Sir William Ayscough, and Sir Robert Tyrwhitt, were, each and all, trying to speak to generate a bit of calm over the proceedings, but there was too much excitement in the air, and too much noise for them to be heard. At one point, the monk Morland also stood on a bench and started to speak.

Since he had appeared at the meeting that morning accoutred with a half set of armour, and had been seen carrying a battle-axe (rather against his vows as a monk!), the rebels quietened down, expecting to hear fire and brimstone from him. But the message he was starting to convey, with his first couple of sentences, sounded like the message they expected to hear from the Sheriff about "...*trying to stay calm*..." They started shouting and jeering him until he was drowned out, and gave up trying.

Several of the lesser gentlemen who were there decided they had now had enough of the noise and over-excited clamour. So, they started to leave, but when it began to look as though all the gentry might be trying to excuse themselves, the rebels at the narrowest point of the chapter house closed ranks, and prevented a mass exodus of the gentlemen.

A few got through the crush before the blockage was complete, but it soon became clear to the common folk there, that there was no way the senior gentlemen of Lincolnshire could be trusted to go off by themselves into a huddle. They were, therefore, forced to stay until the meeting could be properly concluded.

And so the meeting went on noisily for another half an hour, before there was yet another interruption. This time it was again from the north. A deputation arrived from Halifax in West Yorkshire, bringing fraternal greetings, and a message, similar to that from Beverley,

"How can we help?"

The mood was now very buoyant and a decision was made, by acclamation, to send delegations from Lincoln, to both Beverley, and Halifax, to explain the background to the action in Lincolnshire. Guy Kyme – back from an unproductive trip to Sleaford to 'bring in' Lord Hussey, who had, however, remained elusive – was chosen to go to Beverley, with three others. And Thomas Mussenden, 'captured' at Caistor – but turned active by the time of his arrival in Louth – was deputed to go to Halifax, again with a couple of others.

Sir William Ayscough was '*prevailed upon*' to write a brief letter of introduction for each of the messengers, so that the briefing process would be seen as 'authoritative'. Frankly, since he was not in a position to leave the chapter house, he had little choice but to comply! The letters were sealed with Ayscough's private seal ...accompanied by a rousing cheer from the rebels. Ayscough, himself, looked rather uncomfortable.

ରେ ରେ ରେ ରେ ରେ

36 hours earlier in London...

The king's letter had been read, by Sir Richard Rich, to the assembled Privy Council, close to midnight on Saturday and, having been much-praised, of course, was then copied at least four times. Sir Edward Maddison was woken at four-thirty in the morning, and instructed to get ready to '*ride like the wind*' back to Lincolnshire with two copies of the letter. The first, he was to deliver to the Duke of Suffolk on the way through Stamford. The second, he was to deliver to Sir William Ayscough, who was now believed to be stopping somewhere in Cathedral Close in the City of Lincoln.

Another copy was strung onto Cromwell's file string, and yet another copy was to be sent by a different messenger to the Lords Derby and Burgh, in Nottingham.

Maddison was also to deliver two further letters to the Duke of Suffolk, one from Cromwell on behalf of the Privy Council, adding particulars of the strategy drawn up under the direction of the Duke of Norfolk. There was also a further, short, letter from Norfolk direct to Suffolk, emphasising certain stratagems he might use over the forthcoming days, to emphasise the '*bluff*'. Maddison was, of course, never to know what was in those letters, but he was to wait for the Duke of Suffolk to write his own letter, which he would then be required to deliver directly to the rebels in Lincoln.

The journey back to Lincoln would therefore be in two parts, and he would get to rest a little in Stamford at least. In fact, by the time the letters were ready, and his horse was made ready, too, it was close to seven of the clock on Sunday morning before he set off, retracing the steps by which he had arrived just a few days before.

One thing that slowed the whole process down even more, was that he was told he would be accompanied by Sir John Heneage, two other Lincolnshire gentlemen who had been at court for the last two weeks, and a quartet of the king's own guards. It was not that they did not trust him, of course! But, since it was a matter of national importance, nothing was to be left to chance.

ରଣରଣରଣରଣ

Heneage, after leaving Louth in some haste the previous Monday, a-feared of the devilish possession of men's souls in the town, had found his way down to London at a much slower pace than Maddison had achieved, stopping overnight in Stamford. Then when he arrived in London, at a late hour, he had gone straight to his brother's town residence and, pleading a headache, had taken to his bed straight away.

485

He had taken himself to court, after a late and light breakfast, to report his experiences to Chancellor Cromwell, only to find that the court was already in turmoil, following Maddison's unexpected entrance. At first Heneage was kept waiting for an audience, because one of Cromwell's under-secretaries had misheard his name, and not realised he was brother to Cromwell's subordinate, Thomas Heneage! And because Sir John told a rather garbled story of *'possession'*, the under-secretary thought he was in town to try and persuade the chancellor to set up a commission to look into exorcism!

It was only when the Lancaster Herald was going back into the meeting of the Privy Council, after escorting Maddison away, that he recognised Heneage sitting twiddling his thumbs in an ante-room. He said he was waiting for an audience with Cromwell, but Lancaster simply dragged him into the thick of the discussion. After *'humming and ha-ing'* for a few minutes, he eventually managed to speed his mind up, to provide a number of helpful, background, remarks from his own recent experience.

As it was, the presence of Sir John Heneage, the other gentlemen *and* the guards, on Maddison's journey back to his home county, slowed his progress on the road more than a little, compared with last Tuesday night/Wednesday morning.

The fearsome guards scared the life out of the innkeeper in Baldock, as well, when they all called there for new horses. However, by way of compensation, as it were, he made a fine profit from the food and drink he provided, and this time his servants got to keep the small tips they were given (the innkeeper's wife was out at the market, buying produce, which may have had something to do with that!)

When they reached their first port of call, Stamford, the interval of their stay there proved to be much longer than expected. Suffolk, of course, had to read the information; and then think; and then talk to Heneage (but not Maddison) about the Privy Council's wishes; and *then* he had to write his missive – so, all the horsemen (and the horses) had easily recovered physically from their journey before setting off again for Lincoln. The gentlemen, and guards, had been told clearly by Suffolk, not to ride, directly, all the way to Lincoln, in case they were captured. But they were to call on Lord Hussey in Sleaford, if he was still free, and find out "*how the land lay*" further into the County, before assessing what they should do.

෪෪෪෪෪

When they did arrive in Sleaford, Lord Hussey was back at his house again, having hidden away when Sir Christopher Ayscough, Guy Kyme and the others came looking for him. Hussey expressed himself as being "*...so pleased...*" to see a deputation from the king, but the sergeant of the guards said, out of the corner of his mouth, to one of his men

"...of course, he *would* say that wouldn't he!?"

Neither Heneage, nor Maddison, said anything at this point but Maddison was surprised to find that his own bailiff was currently residing at Lord Hussey's house. It had transpired that, after Maddison had left Louth the previous week with the letter for the king, his bailiff had been asked to take a copy of the same letter to Lord Hussey in Sleaford. He had been welcomed, by Hussey, to stay in safety ever since.

The bailiff, Tom Bailey by name, told Maddison and Heneage that, from what he had heard, it may be dangerous for the two gentlemen – and would "*...certainly be a death sentence for the guards*" – to risk going into the county town, but he believed he, himself, would be safe "*...not being a gentleman, and all!...*"

And, thus it was, that Bailey was riding alone, up the High Road of lower Lincoln town, just passing John o' Gaunt's Hall and the rather run-down cottages that flanked the High Road at this point, just as the delegation from Halifax had been walking into the chapter house of the cathedral, perched beautifully on the limestone cliff above him.

He decided he would head straight for the Cardinal's Hat Inn, hoping to find that one of the key gentlemen he had been directed to see, might be lodging there: Sir William Ayscough, Sir Robert Tyrwhitt, or Thomas Moigne. As he reached the High Bridge which crossed the River Witham as it coursed through the city, however, he was met – perhaps 'challenged' would be a better word – by a large group of rebels sheltering from the rain, under the canvas awnings normally used on market days.

He had been completely correct in his assumption that his master, and Sir John Heneage, would probably have been in danger. Indeed, at first, he did not feel particularly safe himself. However, his wife's cousin happened to be in this particular group of rebels, and recognised him, so the tension quickly drained away, and he was able to explain his business. He was told he should...

"Come with us, up to the cathedral, where the meeting is."

He wasn't sure, at first, quite what meeting he was being taken to, but decided it was impolitic to ask. His wife's cousin took the reins of his horse, and led the way through the Stonebow, the imposing new main gate of the entrance to the southern city. Sensing that the excitement would be considerable once they reached the cathedral – and would certainly be much better than standing in the rain near the river – pretty well everyone who was there followed on, too. Even though it was rather a rag-taggle mob, there was no problem getting through the city gate at the Stonebow.

When they reached the Cardinal's Hat, at the top of the Strait, Bailey dismounted and allowed a local lad to take the horse into the inn's yard. His wife's cousin had made it clear that the next stage of the journey was actually dangerous on horseback! The cobbles of Steep Hill had often proved too slippery for horses with metal shoes, and several complaints had been lodged with the mayor, since the cobbles had been laid. And, because the cobbles were twice as slippery when it rained, it was wisest for the party to walk the last couple of hundred yards on foot, otherwise broken limbs were highly likely!

Tom Bailey was a man of mature years, and had always eaten well, so walking up Steep Hill made him puff rather a lot. He was quite relieved, therefore, when they reached Exchequergate, leading through to Cathedral Close, and they were back on level ground. The gate itself was open, Mayor Sutton having decided the best policy for the safety of the city, was not to antagonise the many rebels temporarily based inside the city walls.

The guards were watchful, however, and when they saw so many men crowding round the corner into Exchequergate they had started to close the gate, and there were some harsh words spoken. Bailey's wife's cousin knew the sergeant of the gate guards, however, and was able to explain quickly that Bailey was carrying the king's response. The guards would soon find themselves in trouble, therefore, if the king's letter was delayed in getting to the gentlemen in the cathedral. The sergeant saw the sense in this comment, and ordered the gate to be opened again straight away – to much general cheering.

So, Bailey was swept through the gate into Cathedral Close, on a wave of enthusiastic, rain-soaked Lincolnshire men. Straight into the west entrance of the magnificent building, they went, through the nave to the choir, and then along the dark passageway that led to the cloisters and the chapter house.

Some of the lesser gentlemen, who had managed to slip out of the chapter house earlier, before the door was blocked, were still gossiping in the shelter of the cloisters, rather than braving the foul weather. Now, getting caught up in the excitement of the arrival of the king's reply, they looked to get back inside. Unfortunately for them, the incoming rebel group was even more anxious than they were to get inside, and the gentry were unceremoniously elbowed out of the way!

The chapter house already seemed full of people, but the pressure of nearly one hundred and fifty new bodies pushing their way in managed to fill the space to bursting. It surprised those inside that there was so much room for more, and disappointed the twenty or so people who just could not get through the doors, and had to try and listen from outside.

It took a little while for Tom Bailey to orientate himself amongst the crush, and then to search out one or more of his targets. The sheriff was probably the man with the most ostentatious clothes, and Captain Cobbler stood out from the crowd in his multi-coloured coat. Bailey, however, had been told to give the letters to Sir William Ayscough, Sir Robert Tyrwhitt or Thomas Moigne, and he kept searching the expensive furs, and faces, until he spied one of these three.

He first saw Tyrwhitt, but *he* was pinned in close to the central pillar of the chapter house and remained inaccessible. Then Moigne's face appeared, just to Bailey's right, and almost within reach, so it was Moigne who was favoured to receive the missives.

Moigne would, of course, have much preferred to take the letters and gather his group of gentlemen together, and read the letters in peace but that, clearly, was not going to happen, and there was much clamouring to hear the words of King Henry VIII directly.

Moigne was pushed, and pulled, and almost manhandled bodily, onto a corner of the stone bench that runs around the space, whereupon the Chapter of Deans would seat themselves in more peaceful times. As this was happening, he did manage to slip the scroll, with the seal of the Duke of Suffolk impressed upon a large splodge of dark red wax, into a deep pocket of his outer gown. All the while he kept the scroll displaying the king's seal up in front of him and highly visible all the time. That was the document everyone was watching.

The noise was overwhelming – even Nicholas was not able to make himself heard using his normal range of strength. There were simply too many different shouted comments coming from too many different places in the room.

He resorted to something he very rarely did. He shouted...

"*Oi*..!" ...it was more like a small explosion of gunpowder, than a normal human shout, and it stretched his throat to the limits. It did, however, just generate enough 'quiet' for him to be able to use his 'normal' voice projection to say...

"Let us have a bit of quiet, to *hear* what the king has said...we have been waiting long enough for the letter to arrive, so let us now hear it!"

There were several shouts of "...well said, Nicholas!" or "... good for you Captain Cobbler!" Gradually, the noise level subsided to loud grumbling rather than unbearable shouting... and then to a lot of "... shushing" as everybody shushed everybody else. Even the men who were "shushing" were shushed in their turn.

In this relative silence, Thomas Moigne broke the King's Seal with care and, almost, reverence. He seemed to be conscious that the scroll would actually have been handled personally by his prince and master. He began to unroll it carefully and started to read it – to himself! His lips were moving and he was clearly following the words along the lines but there was no sound coming out...

"Read it out loud!"

The imperative brought Moigne back to the present, and he realised he had not actually made any sounds, even though he had intended to. So he started again, this time using his lawyerly voice. Some in the room, though, felt as though they could hear the king's voice, tight with anger, as he penned the lines to the gentlemen of Lincolnshire.

Henry started with the point that had probably upset him the most (but, then, *many* points had upset him a lot!)

"'*When has it ever been heard that a prince's counsellors and bishops should be appointed by such ignorant common people...*'"

Moigne's voice trailed off as he read Henry's response, and he took a breath, and started the next sentence...

"...'*It is widely known that the suppression of religious houses...*'" but he got no further before he was interrupted again.

The parson of Snelland, a little village barely eight miles from Lincoln, was standing on the same stone bench as was Moigne and leaning over his shoulder, trying to read the king's words, as Moigne read them out to everybody. The parson, Thomas Radford, was a tall rangy man who looked very angular, even in his flowing parson's gown.

He appeared like a hawk over Moigne's left shoulder with his large thin nose (his choirboys called him 'Beaky', out of earshot!) Now he bellowed...

"*False read!*"

The parson's voice rang out in the crowded chapter house. Moigne flinched at the loud shout in his left ear, and was only prevented from falling off the bench by the crowds surrounding him! There was uproar following the parson's astonishing interruption, and it was several moments before Moigne could again be heard. He had been trying to be diplomatic...

He held a hand aloft by way of apology, and duly started Henry's letter once more... reading every single word this time!

"...'*When has it ever been heard that a prince's counsellors and bishops should be appointed by such ignorant common people...least of all by the rude commons of one of the most brute and beastly shires in the Country...*'"

...Complete uproar!

The noise of the protests against this damning comment by their prince was overwhelming. The stone walls shook with sound and Moigne could read no more for quite a while.

Outraged, a large number, perhaps as many as one hundred of the noisiest objectors, mostly the rabble who had walked with Maddison's bailiff up from the Stonebow, not part of the 'Great Council' anyway, pushed their way out of the chapter house. They spilled into the cloisters and the gravel quadrangle which the cloisters surrounded. Thus, many of them found themselves in the

491

rain again, albeit much reduced from earlier. It was now a steady, cold, autumn drizzle.

William Leach was *also* one of those now in the drizzle, together with a significant group of his Horncastle supporters, but the physical dampness made no impact upon his anger. There *was* no 'dampening' effect, and his voice was fiery, the drizzle almost sizzling off his hot head. Just those few words had been enough to light his short fuse...

"We must go ahead *now*, and march on London!" The rest of what he said was drowned in the cheering these words engendered amongst the men surrounding him.

ଔଔଔଔଔଔ

On the other hand, as Moigne's reading continued, for many of the gentlemen still present *inside* the chapter house, the king's anger at what had happened, was clear and justified. They felt ashamed that they had let the situation escalate, and, inwardly, many accepted his denial that he had been planning to raid the treasures of the community churches, as the rumours would have it.

But, for Nicholas, and the rest of the rebels present, the king's reply came as something of a shock, scathing as it was. The noise continued, but Nicholas and others, kept pressing Moigne to carry on reading, despite the fact that they disliked what they were hearing!

Their magnificent prince responded to every point that had been made in the original letter, on their behalf. And the tone of each response King Henry made, was the same, scathing and angry.

"The suppression of the religious houses was necessary as a reform of those who had been guilty of abominable living..."

This time the uproar came from the black-robed brethren present...

"Nooo!"...

"Shame!!"...

"Lies!"

The monk, Morland, who had so recently been anxious to restore quiet, was now red-faced, and about to burst with anger.

Henry's written 'voice' went on, now scathing, now sweetly reasonable...

"Many religious houses have been allowed to stand despite the Act of Suppression which would have dissolved them but, anyway, they have not relieved the poor, as was claimed."

"And the Act of Suppression was passed by the Whole Realm, represented in parliament, and was not the Act of any singular counsellor, nor yet the unconsidered Act of your prince..."

Some of the Gentlemen present were making the mistake of nodding their heads to Henry's words of reason, and there was yet another uproar as this 'head-nodding' was noticed. This time individual gentlemen were singled out, and shouts of disgust were directed personally, the tension in the air becoming palpable again.

The smell of fear began to pervade the air, as some individuals started to truly fear for their very lives. For some, it seemed that the chapter house had turned into a huge stone sarcophagus where they may end their days. And it was normally a place of such gentle contemplation of philosophical issues.

In moments of lesser noise *inside* the chapter house there was much noise heard from the rabble *outside* in the cloisters, as William Leach continued to wind everyone up to further action. Nevertheless Moigne was continually prompted to keep reading. He was now sweating with fear and trepidation over the difficulty of the task. He felt no authority in undertaking this role, and there was no protection afforded by the presence of the sheriff, nor of any of the other gentlemen. They were all proving to be powerless, in the face of so much intensity of hatred at the unfairness of it all.

"The Clergy's 'First Fruits' were granted to the Crown by the Whole Realm represented in Parliament..." King Henry's voice continued to berate his disloyal subjects, many of whom did not now feel part of that realm, nor fairly represented.

Then, more 'sweet reason' from King Henry...

"There were many complaints in past times, too, that England was '*in the hands of the church*', so why are you now complaining that, having freed you from the yoke of the overweening institution of the church in Rome, the crown should take a little taxation from these savings?"

And so the mix of anger and sweet reason continued, as did the noisy response! The anger of the rebels, at the stone wall of Henry's letter, now spilled over to be directed upon the gentlemen who had begun to show sympathy at some of the points he was making. And, now, particularly from the group *outside* in the cloisters, noisy claims were being made to "Kill the *'men of worship'*, who would gladly support the crown and the Privy Council – *now*, while we have them trapped in the chapter house."

William Leach's voice could be heard, literally, of course, in making some of these threats himself and also, symbolically, in the nature of the threats themselves, even when uttered by others.

Nicholas now found himself in difficulty, since he wanted none of this violence. He was sick to his soul of the violence that had already happened during the last week, and wanted no part in yet more killing. And, yet, many of those whose support had been so overwhelming for him and his leadership since the previous Sunday, were now amongst those baying for blood.

It was as if a blood-lust had taken control of the minds of otherwise reasonable men – as, indeed, perhaps it had! Nicholas had to say something – so he did...

"We are in God's house – call us not to commit murder!"

Others, too, spoke up with him for modesty, and moderation of behaviour, at this critical point. John Taylor argued for calm, as did Great James, the gentle giant, as always, stationed at Nicholas' right shoulder. The arguments and the discussions were ranging, hither and yon, between the chapter house and those in the cloisters. Gradually, more reasonable voices were encouraging people to ease out of the west door of the chapter house, to lessen the crowding and, perhaps, so that cooler heads might prevail.

ରେ ରେ ରେ ରେ ରେ

Whilst these debates were raging back and forth, no-one actually paid much attention to the main group of gentry, since it was apparent that they were at the mercy of the rebels anyway. So whether they were all slain this very afternoon, or whether they were left to come round to the rebel cause properly (and, if they refused, they could be slain in the morning, as some were now suggesting), mattered little. They were, anyway, in thrall to the rebels at this moment, were they not?

Or, so everyone thought! Therefore, no-one was taking much notice of them as a group...

Amongst themselves, however, the jittery, vulnerable, gentlemen had been quietly talking, and it was actually old Sir Robert Dymocke who turned out to be their saviour. As the King's Champion for all these years, he had always taken a keen interest in the *real* safety of his prince and master, as well as attending to the ceremonial duties. It had become, therefore, second nature to him, to carefully check out every space the king would enter, *before* the king ever actually entered that space. Even the king probably failed to realise he was always so well looked after whenever Dymocke was around.

Sir Robert would look for possible ambuscade situations: hidden corridors, curtained privy spaces, spiral stairs that appeared to go nowhere, large cupboards that could hide a man, or men! And he always looked for an escape route, to be ready if trouble should occur – a back entrance, or exit, a hidden corridor, or a window to a terrace. It was not a conscious process these days, but he was so used to doing it over the years that he automatically noted all of these things, and weighed up risks, and possible escape routes.

The chapter house of Lincoln Cathedral was a magnificent circular room with one entrance and exit – the large west door – which everybody used to get in, and to get out.

This had been the case today. And so, every member of the Great Council of the uprising had come in through those very doors, and then along the wide, but short, corridor into the large circular meeting area. There was no other corridor in or out, there was no opening window which led onto any terrace, and there were no hidden ambuscade opportunities. Dymocke had noted all of that.

But... there *was* a small door on the south side of the short corridor, covered with a fading red curtain; a door which hardly anyone even noticed. Normally, it was only ever used by the bishop, when there was a Dean's Chapter meeting in the chapter house, which he might, or might not, attend. Outside the door, there was a narrow gravel pathway which ran round the outside of the circular space, then split, right and left. The left pathway went to the chancery, and the right pathway slipped round the east end of the cathedral, to a side gate of the Bishop's Palace grounds.

Before the meeting had started that morning, Sir Robert had briefly looked behind the curtain, and opened the door as a matter of course, during his automatic checking process. So, he knew it to be unlocked and guessed, roughly, where it would lead. He had a quiet word with two of his tenants who were present with the rebels, but whom he felt sure he could trust. Without fully explaining why, he asked them if they would stand "*just so...*" with their shoulders together and their backs to the curtained door. Thus, no-one would easily see all the leading gentlemen of Lincolnshire, slipping sneakily out of the chapter house, without using the main west doors!!

He quietly passed the word to his son, the sheriff; and to Thomas Moigne (*who, by now was nearly losing his bladder control, he was so nervous after his ordeal, reading the king's letter out to a large, hostile, group of common folk*). They passed word to Sir Robert Tyrwhitt; and to Sir William Ayscough; and, through them, to other lesser gentlemen of the realm. Gentlemen who were, also no doubt, worried about their lives being at risk.

William Leach, in the cloisters, was just starting again to bluster about "*...slaying the gentry...*" – "*...NOW...*" – when one of his supporters, still inside the chapter house, noticed that a quiet '*exeunt*' of leading players in the drama had taken place! The chapter house now had many fewer people in it anyway, since most of the rebels were milling about in and around the cloisters, thankful that the rain had eventually stopped.

As the news of the escaping gentry became widely known, there was, suddenly, a crush of many common rebels trying to get back, quickly, inside the chapter house to cut off the escape of the miscreants. Too late, however, the gentry had all made their getaway. Several men tried to find, and follow, them but they had got clean away this time, unlike a week earlier in Caistor. So Leach's bluster was just that – bluster. Nothing further could be done at this moment.

The sense of anti-climax was dramatic in its effect. It knocked the wind out of everyone's sails. Suddenly, there seemed little to do but go back to their lodgings; or to their tents; or shelters, for the night. Find some food, and try and decide what should be done in the morning.

ରେ ରେ ରେ ରେ ରେ

"It's all downhill from now..."
The Rebellion unravels

☞   The straw wagon carrying the tower prisoners lurched on the London cobbles and roused Nicholas from his inner reflections. Several cobbles were missing from the roadway, which is why the wagon had bumped so much. Two of the condemned men had actually fallen over, and were now trying to scramble back to their feet. Several of the others were off-balance, including Nicholas, who was now hanging on to the side of the wagon. He was suddenly aware that he felt cold in his smock. Although the sun was shining on this last journey of his life, the air was still very cool on this spring morning.

He became aware of his surroundings, and realised there were people crowding either side of the road their wagon was on, peering to see who was going to be sliced up gorily this morning at the execution site. Some of the crowds were shouting, making what they thought might be clever, or cruel, remarks that would make their friends laugh. The sun had brought them out to watch the spectator sport of 'Execution', and the atmosphere on the street was generally rather excited, and full of anticipation of blood and gore.

Amidst all the noisy comments, the one which registered in Nicholas' mind had been rather quietly spoken, and probably referred to the physical characteristics of the road from this point on, but it was the double-meaning which grabbed at his attention...

"It is all downhill from here..."

Nicholas could not identify who had said the words, but it was a gentle voice, and the words were said with sympathy rather than scorn and, for that reason it caught at Nicholas' emotions. In particular, it brought to mind exactly the thought he had had all those months ago, in October last year, in the cloisters, at the meeting where the king's letter had been read to everyone, and then the gentlemen had sneaked away from the chapter house through the 'bishop's door' in the south wall.

Many people were incensed that they had got away so easily with their lives, and several gangs of rebels split away from the main group chasing shadows, thinking they knew where the miscreants would be; or where they may have slithered off to. But no-one came back to report that they had been found, or that help was needed to slay them on the spot. So, they were never slain.

Nicholas, himself, was thankful, at that point, that bloodshed had been avoided, but severely troubled that they had been duped in the way they had. And his thought had been, then, that it would "...*all be downhill from here!*" That is not to say that it would suddenly become easy! But, that it would inevitably be fast and furious, and probably totally out of control, from this point onwards! Like a runaway cart.

He had no idea how things would go in reality, but, for the first time since they had locked the doors of Louth church, barely a week before, he felt the pit in his stomach deepen, as if he would fall inwards into his own private purgatory – and he was normally such an optimist! Not that there was no optimism in the air around him – but he felt he could not share it this time. There were too many doubts and unknowns.

For example, they did *not* know how large was the force, commanded by the Duke of Suffolk, now believed to be in the Stamford area. Sir John Thimbleby had cast some doubt on the size of Suffolk's force, but really knew nothing for sure. Maddison's Bailiff, Tom Bailey, had reported his master's belief that Suffolk was having trouble raising a large force – but *that* view was apparently based upon hearsay of two women talking loosely in court... and just who the women were Bailey did not know, his master had not said.

If their identities *had been known*, and that the words had been spoken by the Duchess of Suffolk herself and Maria, Lady Willoughby, then maybe the course of history might be different...?

Nor did they have any support forthcoming from Lord Hussey. Much of the talk through the summer had been based upon an expectation that if, when the crops had been gathered in, some action were initiated in the county, then Lord Hussey would declare himself full square with the activists. But, now, he had shown himself to dither, and equivocate, when it really mattered, hiding himself away in Sleaford.

On the other hand, as pointed out many times by the most optimistic voices, solidarity and support was shown from afar. They had been told that there were over six thousand men from Boston, and South Lincolnshire, mustering at Ancaster this very day. They had had delegations from Beverley and Halifax, so, who was to say if further support might not be forthcoming from the northern reaches, as time went by. But would it be enough, and would it be timely?

And then, back to the negative side, the king's response had been as far from 'conciliatory' as might be imagined! Indeed, it was much less conciliatory than Nicholas had ever imagined it *could* have been! And their oath had always included support for the king as well as the church. This seemed ironic now!

Certainly, Henry had promised dire retribution for such base treason. He had not offered the least hint of any understanding of their true concerns. There was not the least positive slant that could be seen in any of his sentences! It was so unfair, and so unexpected.

This had incensed the hot-headed Leaches, and their supporters, and drove them to even greater anger and calls for a murderous response from the rebels.

Nevertheless, Nicholas knew he would not be able to carry, for much longer, the support of those who had earlier listened to his voice of reasoned action. Or those men, who, like him, had blanched at the bloodthirsty violence that had already sullied their hopes for rational argument, and persuasion.

ର ର ର ର ର ର

The large numbers gathered in the cloisters had gradually dispersed; some went off hunting the disappeared gentry, some to spread the message received from the king. Eventually, the rest, including Nicholas himself, simply headed back to the main camp, based in what were now rather muddy fields just outside Newport Arch, to the north of the cathedral.

Looking back, now, from his unsteady perch, on a straw wagon taking him to his death, and with the undoubted benefit of hindsight, he wondered if, perhaps, he should have been more strongly supportive of Leach's position. *Immediate action*!

It was a possible option but, even now, with his hindsight, he still considered that it would have required the leadership of one, or more, of the key figures from the top gentlemen of the county for it to have worked. And such leadership was certainly not forthcoming. On the contrary they had melted away so very effectively that the '*hunting parties*' could not find them. He did not believe it had been planned, simply that they had been lucky, and the hunting parties had not! Even now, Nicholas did not know where they got to.

In fact, the gentry had been extremely lucky – indeed, extraordinarily so! Many of the lesser gentlemen had split away from the group, and simply found their way back to whatever lodgings they had managed to arrange for themselves in Lincoln. Thus, in twos and threes, they had not attracted the attention of any common folk who had not been privy to the goings on in the cathedral itself.

The main group of leading gentlemen who had slipped away, including Ayscough, the Dymockes, Moigne, Tyrwhitt, and a few others, had first resolved to go into the Bishop's Palace, taking the right fork of the gravel path outside the chapter house. When they got inside the Bishop's Palace, however, several voices were raised, suggesting that it was so near the cathedral, that it would be one of the first places searched.

Whereupon, they all trooped downhill through the Bishop's Palace garden, to a small gate in the wall, which took them, by stages, to the Cardinal's Hat Inn. As it happened, the last of them was *just* closing that gate, when the first rebel search party burst through the main door of the Bishop's Palace, only to find the place empty.

That search party did not think to look into the garden, otherwise they might have noticed the gate being closed. So, they gave up there, and went back out into the Cathedral Close. Then they rushed off towards the castle, only to find those gates open, and the castle grounds empty and unguarded. So there were no gentlemen lurking there then. When that search party asked the mayor's guards, above Exchequergate, if they had seen them, the guards refused to say whether the gentry had come this way, or not, adding to the confusion.

By this time, Ayscough and the others had had a brief confabulation in the main bar of the inn. They knew, by now, that search parties had been established, and were, perhaps, close behind them, so they spoke loudly of going downhill to the Guildhall, which had been built over the Stonebow gate on the city's south wall.

Once outside the inn doors, however, they turned about and

retraced their steps *uphill*, back into the Bishop's Palace garden, and thence into the palace, where they chose a quiet back room to meet in. Word had already reached them that a search party had, by this time, looked in the palace, and given up that search!

It was a wonder, they were not seen as a group, since there were upwards of twenty men in the party and, thus, quite hard to miss. But their luck held, and the search party, which had visited the Cardinal's Hat, believed their 'bluff' and chased, hell-for-leather downhill, some men actually 'whooping' out loud as they ran down *'towards'* their quarry.

This excitement was short-lived, of course, since the quarry was not there.

The second large piece of luck for the gentry occurred as a misunderstanding between the first search party and the second, when they happened to meet, not far from the south wall of Lincoln. Somehow they *each* thought the other would search the palace again, and so *neither* did. Otherwise it is likely that blood would have been shed that afternoon, because, by then, the mood was turning very ugly in some quarters.

ᘏᘏᘏᘏᘏᘏ

In the Bishop's Palace...

Meanwhile, in the Bishop's Palace, a very nervous group of finely dressed gentlemen were discussing the situation in which they found themselves. They had posted a lookout at both the front gate, and at a window overlooking the garden gate, and had determined they would try and make a rush for the castle if need be. Or they might be able to order Mayor Sutton's guard troop to shut the Exchequergate gates, and defend the Cathedral Close if required, even though both possibilities ran serious risks of failure. At that point they had little idea just how lucky they had been thus far!

Very quickly, they had determined that the only course of action, that would save their necks from the king's executioner, was to cave in to the king's command, and make the best hand they could of containing the rebellion. The question was whether they could do this, and *still* save their necks from the rebels' home-made nooses. This conundrum was what was making them so nervous.

The king's letter had been most clear, not to say bloodthirsty, about the consequences of carrying on with the rebellion or, indeed, the consequences for the gentlemen themselves, of merely failing to turn the rebellion around. It promised severe retribution for this treason, with a little patriarchal concession, *if the rebellion were quelled quickly enough*. Just a hint of possible forgiveness, such as it was.

They were at least twenty minutes into their nervy discussion, before Moigne remembered the second letter he had managed to slip inside his cloak. Having to read the king's letter in front of a baying mob, had un-nerved him significantly, and he was only just beginning to compose himself again. He reached down inside his cloak, and extracted the small scroll from its deep hiding place, quickly breaking the Duke of Suffolk's seal, and unrolling the parchment.

It was not a long missive and it was in Latin, rather than plain English, which rather reduced the chances of it being easily read by eyes other than those for whom it was intended. Also there were many references to a simple card game that had only recently become popular at court, again reducing the likelihood of easy interpretation by the lower reaches of society. In short it was a risky strategy of being clear, but discrete, in order to pass on to the Lincolnshire gentlemen the advice to Suffolk from the 'Old Warrior' – the Duke of Norfolk.

Norfolk had stated his strategy very clearly, but much less discretely, for the benefit of the Privy Council in just the one word – BLUFF!

Suffolk knew they had a very small force at their disposal at Stamford, and poorly equipped at that! But he also knew that the rebels would probably *not* know the size or the state of his forces, at least not yet! He knew, too, that the king's letter was full of bluster about the condign punishment he was wont to serve out to "*...the rude Commons of one of the most brute and beastly shires in the Country...*"

If he could provoke even a little hinting by the gentry inside Lincoln of a really powerful force on its way to crush the rebellion he could create tension and terror in the minds of those '*rude Commons.*' The letter did not give away critical information as to the *actual size* of his forces – that would have been too dangerous. But he judged that if it reached the right eyes, the perceptive minds behind those eyes would know they should *over-emphasise* his strength, to persuade the rebels to back down.

Sadly, now, on his way to a gory death, Nicholas was able to perceive how well that simple strategy had worked. News had since reached them all, in their incarceration in the Tower, that there really *had been* very few troops with Suffolk in Stamford! If only they had held their ground! Goodness knows he tried to influence events in that way but they were caught by surprise by the tactics of the gentry the next morning.

 filler ornament

The morning after the night before...

After a rather damp and more or less sleepless night, with tensions running high, and rumours running higher (and faster!) around the muddy camp, Nicholas heard that William Leach had put the word about that the main captains and petty captains who were *in* the camp should meet, in the tented *'headquarters'* of the Horncastle contingent, at six of the clock in the morning.

It was still mostly dark, with the merest glimmers of light in the east, and Nicholas had broken his fast with some cold mutton, left from supper of the previous night, accompanied by the first of the morning's loaves cooked overnight by John Baker's team, washed down with some small beer. There were still showers of fine rain about, intermittently making everyone feel damp, and uncomfortable, all of the time.

When they had eaten, Nicholas took his son Robert to one side and tried, as quickly as possible, to sum up his current concerns that there was a significant danger that this day may see the beginning of an end to their hoped for venture. It might, therefore, be necessary for Robert to act quickly, and on his own initiative if that danger overtook them.

Robert had bridled at this expression of concern, and had started to make it clear to his father that he, and the others, retained full confidence in him and the plans they had all made. But Nicholas raised his right hand in a "Stop!" gesture, and shook his head slightly to arrest Robert in full flow. Robert recognised the gesture from many family discussions, and Nicholas was pleased to note that he responded quickly enough to his father's caution.

"It is good of you to be so loyal to my original ideas, lad, but I am being cautious rather than 'pessimistic' as you may have been about to say! But, you may need to act quickly to ensure your mother, and brother, are brought to safety at your cousin's house in the marsh lands north along the Humber bank. And once there, await better news from us all. I need to know you will be able and ready to act at a moment's notice – and to act without hesitation and, if necessary, on your own!

Robert was unsure exactly how to respond; he had not seen his father seeming so uncertain of himself before. Yet, at the same time, he knew that he had to listen to his father's caution, so tried hard to focus his mind, uncomfortable though it felt, even to consider the possibility of failure at this stage...

Nicholas was firm about what must happen if things did actually start to go wrong, but he was also anxious not to start a panic reaction amongst the men around him, so was keeping his voice low. Also, by his actions, he tried to give the impression to anyone watching him, that he was simply having a good heart-to-heart with his son. Every now and then he instructed Robert to "Relax a bit and smile, as if we are sharing a good family story!" Robert found this difficult to do, even though he tried hard to concur with his father's wishes!

Finally Nicholas arranged a few 'coded signals' with Robert, in case they did not have further opportunity to speak closely like this. Then he concluded, with a hearty slap on the back (which bore no relation to the words he spoke, but he hoped it might help to disguise the nature of the discussion.)

"So, Robert, if things look as though they are going to go from bad to worse, and you receive one of my unsubtle nods or winks, you know who to speak to and what to do... And you KNOW you need to do it all quietly and quickly, without hesitation?"

Robert pretended to smile, though he did not feel at all like smiling

...and pushed his father playfully on the shoulder, as if he had been given some unnecessary advice about his love life. And then the brief episode was over, and Nicholas went back to being full of bonhomie and good cheer, as far as the rest of the world was concerned.

"With no more ado..." he said aloud, and in general, to one and all round about... "let us go and hear what Goodman Leach has to say, about what happens next!"

In fact Goodman Leach was, himself, a little muted this morning, compared with his excitability the previous day. He was disillusioned, that the gentlemen of the county had, seemingly, vanished from sight the preceding afternoon, without being rediscovered. Indeed, Leach had even had several of his men scouting around during the night, and nothing had come to light of the movements of the main group of gentry.

There had been a couple of reports, that the Dymockes had been seen (or, strictly speaking, *MAY have been seen*) quietly being let in to one of the deacons' houses in Cathedral Close late in the evening. But, since the Cathedral Close had been secure behind the Exchequergate gate by then, and one report was second-hand anyway, (passed on by a cousin of one of Leach's men, who was part of the Mayor's guard troop) no immediate action ensued.

The other similar report had been from a girl who was a scullery maid at another of the houses in the Close. Her information was the first received, but had initially been discounted, as she was thought to be trying to impress her boyfriend. That was until the other, confirming, rumour had been received.

Quite a bit of time was spent this morning reviewing how their quarry had managed to stay so far out of sight. But finally Nicholas decided they were simply repeating themselves, and going round in ever-decreasing circles to no avail, and decided to say as much. For a moment or two William Leach looked daggers at him, then realised that what Captain Cobbler had said was, in fact, true. Leach rolled his eyes, raised his bushy eyebrows and then sighed, wafting a hand loosely, to acknowledge the decision to move on to new ground.

Nicholas was concerned, and not a little regretful, that in a spur-of-the-moment response to the good news brought from Yorkshire, they had decided to send Guy Kyme up to Beverley to explain events there. More than anything, he could have done with the sort of wise council

Kyme was wont to offer in such circumstances. Kyme had set off, more or less straight away after the Beverley delegation had arrived, and spoken their piece, on the grounds that, if they left sharply, they might get to Beverley before darkness fell, or at least be close by then.

Would it have made any difference to the outcome? Perhaps not, he thought, but his presence would have acted as an iron rod for Nicholas' backbone – something he certainly felt in need of this morning.

Nicholas was also missing Thomas Kendall, who had been called back to Louth to officiate at the funeral of Jack Long, one of the town's oldest residents.

"A matter of death and life!", Kendall had called it, smiling sadly – and Nicholas had to accept that life goes on – "even the dying part!"

However, their current venture seemed to many of them, to be the most important event of the year. Jack Long might normally have expected a big turnout at his passing, since he was so well-known, and had always been well-liked in Louth, but there would only be a handful of close family present for this, his last, visit to his church.

Nicholas was thus feeling the absence of two key people in this undertaking. They were people he could always rely on to have their *own* judgement about things, and be prepared to share their views equally with him, rather than simply relying on his word that "*this should happen*", or "*that should happen*".

Most of the other people here, whom he was close to, would support him all the way on whatever decision he might make. But they would never think to challenge such a decision if there were something he had overlooked. Eliza Jane's brother, Tom Foster, was really the only other person Nicholas could rely on to speak his mind, come-what-may. Even he had gone back to Louth for the funeral, however, since he was, of course, the main singing-man in the choir, much reduced though it would be today.

"One of the problems we have," Nicholas continued, as Leach had effectively conceded his point about going round in circles, "is that the foul weather has been draining the men's fortitude. We have been lucky, most of those of us here just now," he gestured towards the sailcloth cover over their heads, "with quite a bit of cover to keep us drier than most, or should I say, 'less wet than most'. But I know a lot of the men have been getting a good soaking for a couple of nights, and are feeling the cold."

"We Lincolnshire 'Yellowbellies' are a hardy breed, but I know we have been losing a few men, here and there, slipping away back home, simply because they have been so uncomfortable. We are going to have to provide some leadership, therefore, to keep everyone concentrating on the task in hand. That means we have to find a way to persuade the gentry to hold fast, and stay with us. My biggest worry is that yesterday's farce, losing track of them all, leaves us a lot of ground to catch up on, when, eventually, we do find them again!"

He was taking a breath, to launch into his next sentence, when their discussion was curtailed by noises of shouting coming from the southernmost part of the fields they were in. The attention of everyone was sharply drawn to the noises, which started with the shouting. They were, however, soon able to make out the heavy snorting, and snuffling, of horses which were being made to work hard. It was evident that there were many horses, too, not just an odd two or three.

On a dry day they would probably have heard a thundering of hooves, too, but the mud was too soft to make out the sound of any hooves 'thundering' today. There was, however, quite a bit of 'clanking' going on. It was the sound of a cavalry troop, in full armour, making fast progress!

The first feelings were ones of gladness, that the gentry had come to their senses, and were going to lead them all to victory. But those feelings were, sadly, very short-lived as they heard angry shouts.

"Make way there... get out of the road!"

"...move you dolt... or I will cut your head off!"

...as well as other angry expressions and expletives!

Several of the men close to the meeting of the commonwealth leaders, drew swords, or knives, or started to brandish their staffs, or whatever weapons were to hand, but they were in no sort of defensive shape, or order. The troop of horsed gentlemen cantering towards them through the myre of the rain-soaked field must have been nearly forty strong, mostly fully armoured, and with weapons drawn. The men on foot would have been cut to pieces in no time, if they had started a fight.

As it was, the main troop drew to a halt about fifteen yards from the covered area where Captain Cobbler, William Leach and the others were. It then split into three: the main party with Sheriff, Sir Edward Dymocke, and Moigne, facing the commonwealth leadership. Two smaller groups led by Sir Robert Tyrwhitt and Sir William Ayscough, respectively, moved to flank the unhorsed commonwealth group.

As they were doing this, a second troop of gentry on horseback – another twenty or so of them – trotted into the field, by the same southerly gate and, following in the tracks of the first group, spread themselves around. This time the horsemen faced outwards, to keep a gap between the first group of gentry, and the large, but undisciplined, 'rabble' in the fields, who were closing in to see what was happening or, perhaps, to defend their leaders against this intrusion.

The horses of this second group were restless, and their riders somewhat nervous, surrounded as they were by a large number of angry, and unpredictable, men with sticks, clubs, sickles and other assorted hand weaponry. But the troop was disciplined and well-armed, and armoured, and held the line, whilst Dymocke prepared to speak to Nicholas and Leach and the rest.

William Leach was almost apoplectic at this surprising turn of action, and had his sword drawn, with an equally angry brother, and cousin, either side of him. Nicholas laid a restraining hand on his shoulder and bade him keep calm...

"...until we hear what is to be said, at least!"

As he said this he looked around for his son, Robert, whom he knew would be nearby, but well-separated from, the main participants in the meeting that had been going on since they broke fast together, earlier. Catching Robert's eye, Nicholas gave him one of their pre-arranged signals; a slight nod, a flick of his eyes to the right, and pulling on his right ear, with his right hand, all of which meant...

"Be ready to go now, but wait until we hear what is said!"

Dymocke briefly looked around the field, as if to weigh up their chances of getting out of the field alive again after he had spoken, but there was no doubt, or fear, in his voice when he started to speak.

"You men..." even with his first two words, he had distanced himself from the action of the 'rebels', making Nicholas' heart sink...

"You men have planned, and carried out a series of actions which is clearly in rebellion against the King's Majesty, as we all heard from his considered reply yesterday to our letter about your, so-called, 'commonwealth action'. We appealed to his good counsel on your behalf. But he has rejected that appeal, not only with careful thought – but with anger too!"

"It is our view," here, he loosely waved his right hand to encompass the various gentlemen of the county, arrayed around him as he spoke, "...that this whole venture was misguided from the outset, and always destined to fail. It was only under dire threats to our persons and property, that we were persuaded to let it run its course."

Nicholas and many others could hardly credit these words, after the real involvement of several of these 'gentlemen' in the many acts of violence which had clouded the past week. Indeed, there were several shouts of "*Turncoat!*" as he spoke, and "*What about your oath!?*" Dymocke ignored such shouts and continued...

"It is now clear that the venture *has* run its course, and it must now be regarded as finished... and failed! The king has spoken, clearly, and he threatens condign punishment if the uprising were to continue. He has sent out a force of considerable puissance, now on its way north, to put the rebellion down. That force is now headed this way, woe-betide us all – all of *you*, indeed – if it arrives, and the Dukes of Suffolk and Norfolk find you have not listened to the king."

"Go home – give this foolishness up. The king commands it, and we commend it! You have stretched the credibility of the gentlemen of this county, by putting us in this position of trying to protect you, as fathers will try to protect their children. God has sent rain, to persuade you of the grave discomfort, of your actions. Now, we command you to give up this mischief, and take yourselves home. Get back to the work of the fields, and seeing to your everyday needs, and those of your wives, and children. We will not condone any further misbehaviour from any of you!"

Sir William Leach could contain himself no longer and brandished his sword in Dymocke's direction, shouting incoherently. Leach had not yet donned his armour today and now regretted it, otherwise he may well have launched himself at Dymocke and the other gentry, even though they be on horseback. The fact that he would soon be struck down, without his outer skin of metal, made him stick to words alone for the time being! After a few moments the words became intelligible.

"You are acting treacherously to the commonwealth, to whom you all pledged oaths, on the Good Book, in God's name. You know, full well, that we are not in rebellion against the crown. We have all pledged our loyalty to the king, and the church, and the commonalty, as have you

509

all! But now, you have the cowardly audacity to track backwards, and blame us for putting you in this position. You speak with the forked tongue of a serpent."

At this point, again, words now failed Leach, and he started spluttering once more. He was clearly so angry at the turn of events, and so cross with himself, for the rebels' lack of preparedness for allowing the gentry just to gallop into the field, without let or hindrance – '*we should have posted guards, and archers, to stop such a relatively small horsed troop, from getting so far into the centre of their camp!*'

He was also still feeling cross at their failure the day before in *not* finding out what the gentry were up to.

Since the previous afternoon, Nicholas had been more than half-expecting some kind of betrayal from the gentry, and, as a result, he felt unable to say anything constructive. Despite this sense, even *his* brain had not envisaged this eventuality – of the whole group of gentlemen just galloping into the camp unannounced.

What rather surprised everyone now, was that the voice that did emerge at this stage in the proceedings was, in fact, not a local one. It belonged to Sir John Thimbleby, who had only just joined them, from the southernmost point of Lincolnshire, yesterday.

"*This is an outrageous act of cowardice, and betrayal!*"

There were cheers for this short, but heartfelt, expression of the feelings of the majority of the men in the field. No doubt some felt a little aggrieved, that the thoughts had been expressed by a stranger amongst them. Indeed Nicholas wished the words had been his!

However, the truth probably was that Thimbleby was the only one here who knew the Dymockes *too little*, to know that they would always side with authority, which emanated from the crown. Such behaviour had been bred into them for generation upon generation. Indeed, it was probably only the loyalty Sir Robert Dymocke had felt towards the former queen, Catherine, that had tempted him, thus far, to allow his fealty towards Henry to be found wanting. Even that small quirk, however, had been eradicated by the strong words of Henry's letter of yesterday.

෫෫෫෫෫෫

As Thimbleby spoke, Nicholas took the opportunity to search out Robert in the crowd. Robert had been watching his father like a hawk, and it took the merest of nods for Nicholas to goad his son into his next pre-planned action.

Robert looked very nervous but held himself in check, until his father looked away again, back towards Dymocke and Moigne. Then, as quietly as he could, and without drawing any attention to himself, he slowly slipped away from the group, gradually making his way away from them, first of all to one of the tented areas, as if to fetch something from his tent. Then he went out of the north gate from the field, which took him behind a high thorn hedgerow and out of sight of the main centre of attention.

It has to be said that, even now, he was very reluctant to be walking away from the centre of the action, and felt as though he was, perhaps, letting his father down by going. The truth was, however, that he had been persuaded by his father's words, and now felt a very strong conviction, that this *was* the right thing for him to do, even though it seemed the opposite!

As soon as he was out of sight of the crowd he speeded up, but kept his eyes lowered, so as not to get into any kind of conversation, or confrontation, with anyone. Fairly quickly, he had gone beyond most of the men present who were, anyway, still moving in, *towards* the field he had just left.

A few moments later he was walking to where most of the horses were being cared for. He knew, well enough, the lad who was in charge of the string of ponies which included his own, as they were the same age and had grown up together in Louth. So, it was no problem to spin him some yarn, about running an errand for his father. Thinking about it as he left the field, though, it wasn't a yarn... it was simply the truth; just maybe not the *whole* truth.

So, within a few minutes of getting the 'go now' signal from his father, he was mounted and on the main track away from there, and trotting on his new pony towards Louth; and his mother; and Arthur, his younger brother. He tried not to 'race' his pony too much, because he did not yet know its limitations, and wanted to make sure he got to his destination in moderate time, rather than not at all!

He knew, too, that he must also take the news of what was

happening, to Thomas Kendall and Tom Foster, his priest and his uncle respectively. Both of them would know that speedy action would then be needed to ensure the safety of the families of those who had been most closely involved in the development of the uprising – or outright 'rebellion' as it would now, probably, be portrayed.

As he had been leaving the field, he heard Moigne's voice take over from Dymocke in speaking to the multitude. The tone was a little milder, and more lawyerly, as befitted the man who spoke, but nevertheless the message seemed to be the same...

"Go home! Your intent has been established, but it has been mistaken in the manner in which it was undertaken. You have challenged the legitimate authority of your prince, as he avowed in his communication with us all yesterday. And he has sent men of integrity, and men experienced in the arts of war, to put you to the sword, if you are found in a state of agitation, and open revolt, when the king's army arrives."

"Go home! Take your families, once more, under your wings, and ensure the harvests are secure for the winter. Attend to the ploughing of the fields, ready for planting in the spring. Mend your fishing nets, and brew your beers, and ales, and fruit wines, and be prepared for winter settling in. We will talk to the dukes when they arrive, and divert as much as we can, of the righteous anger of the king, and his army of loyal subjects. But, if you are still in flagrant breach of His Majesty's peace, woe-betide all of us."

At this, many conversations arose amongst the men in the field, creating a susurration, as if an autumn wind had suddenly started in the trees. Perhaps a little strangely, there was no-one making a hue and cry. Many of those present seemed to take for granted the natural authority of the speakers, and accepted their right to speak as they did! Moigne continued...

"We feel certain that the Duke of Suffolk, and the officers of his army, will wish to talk to your leaders amongst the commonwealth, but we cannot protect you from his wrath if you still pose a threat to his authority. Pack up this makeshift camp and go home to your families. Leave your leaders here to face the duke with us."

It almost sounded as if the gentry would speak up for the uprising, as it had originally been hoped. Almost – but not truly! Nicholas had half-expected that the troop on horseback might make an attempt to arrest the leaders using force; on Leach and himself most particularly. It was really, however, an ill-disguised move to *'divide and rule'*, using their inborn authority to quietly dismantle action that had taken months of diligent talking, and persuasion, by Nicholas and others, to build.

The trouble was, that most of the men would take the words at face value and, as long as the gentry did not 'tip their hand' by trying to use force, it was likely that the majority of the men in the field, would automatically accept the gentry's right to lead, as gentlemen of the county had always led them for generations, into battle, and out.

No doubt there might have been much blood spilled if either side had taken to arms at that point. However, although Sir William Ayscough, on the gentry side, and Sir William Leach, on the commonalty side, were clearly both itching for action to ensue, no-one actually raised a sword, or other dangerous weapon, in anger.

Great James had automatically placed himself just behind Nicholas' left shoulder, as soon as the troop of horses had entered the field. And he stood there now, ready to place himself between Nicholas and whatever threat might present itself. But it was as clear as a bell to Nicholas that it was over.

Without the real leadership of the gentry of the county, nothing of substance would come of their actions, and, all of a sudden, he felt deeply disillusioned. Not particularly fearful for his life, as perhaps he should be, but just so disappointed in the vagaries of human nature. No doubt there would still be more shouting and ruffling before it was all over and done in fact. But, for Nicholas, this moment was the defining moment of failure.

The gentry had acted, after all – but they had acted for the safety of their own skins, not for the betterment of the community; not for the protection of years of tradition; not for the safety of the ill, or those suffering misfortune, or, simply, the ravages of age and infirmity.

The gentry had acted, as so often they did, for their own sake; and their own families; and their own riches. So why, oh why, did he feel so let down and disappointed? Why had he let himself believe things might be different this time? Selflessness was not a trait commonly held, perhaps least of all amongst the higher echelons of society in the County of Lincolnshire. Not that he was ever part of it. Indeed, Nicholas had never even been *close* to being part of it!

And yet, still, there was a little spark of light in his mind, that, once the king's forces arrived they might yet talk to them, and have them listen... But, no, he was surely fooling himself? Eliza Jane always called him a *'true optimist'*, and insisted on calling herself, a *'realist'* – meaning, she thought he was *too optimistic* for his own good, and when it came down to *'real life'*, she was actually more likely to be right.

He had teased her back, saying that *she* was really a pessimist. He claimed it was better to be optimistic in life, and suffer an occasional disappointment, when things did not work out, than to worry all the time about things failing, and only feel good when something nice happens unexpectedly! Even then, he said, a pessimist would worry that the *'something nice'* was just disguising *'something terrible'*, lurking around the corner. Nicholas thought it must be terrible, to be worried all the time about things going wrong.

So, was this one of those times that things would not work out? He was beginning to think that maybe it was. But, of course, his optimism suggested there might still be a positive outcome – was it justified? Perhaps not, but, then...? He had to pinch himself, almost, to get back to the present.

His mind had wandered, and he had not heard the first part of Sir Edward Dymocke's most recent sentence ...something about "... staying here."

"...stay here. And in a situation like this, which is so far from everyone's normal day-to-day experience, we need to take some hostages, to ensure your debate is good and honest, and not led astray by hot-headedness. We will guarantee the safety of such hostages whilst-so-ever the host is law-abiding. But if there is more 'ruffling', then woe-betide us all."

"We have been instructed to take at least ten hostages: four from Louth, three from Horncastle, two from Alford and one from Grimsby and a hostage each representing the closed religious communities and those houses that are still intact. How you choose the hostages is up to you, but they must be recognisable leaders of their communities."

Nicholas realised immediately that the gentry were creating a 'divide and rule' option, again, to make sure that there was no sense of solidarity established in the host, as a single entity. Just the way everyone now started talking in little groups, meant there would be no robust rejection of the idea. Each group was likely to act on its own, rather than see the welfare of the whole as vital. Perhaps if he acted quickly – but what could he do?

There was just a chance they could, as a host, establish a sense of unity again. He thought William Leach's action-based leadership might now be more valuable to the host, than his own stance of being reasonable. He was also concerned that if the gentry insisted that William Leach became one of the hostages, then the whole situation may flare up immediately, and become a bloodbath. Certainly *some of the gentry* may lose their lives, but it was also certain that many, many, of his friends would lose theirs, too, and to what purpose?

Then he remembered something Bill Cole said many years ago, when he left him recovering from a broken leg in an abbey near Grantham. It was something which befitted his optimistic frame of mind. Bill's leg had been broken badly in two different places, falling from his horse in the badly swollen River Witham, and Nicholas had had to kill the horse, whose leg had also been broken. Cole had said, sadly...

"The horse, bless him, has gone to a better stable in the sky, but although badly damaged, I live on to fight another day!"

Nicholas then made another association in his mind with Guy Kyme who was now, almost certainly, in Beverley; and Tom Mussenden, who was now almost certainly, in Halifax, spreading the word of what was happening in Lincolnshire.

His inner thoughts were telling him that, '...*we have suffered setbacks here, some of which were of our own making; not defending the fields here, from a pre-emptive strike from a few mounted gentlemen*', being one sure example! So we are '...*damaged*', but we can '...*live on to fight another day*'. By which time, we may be able to receive help from further north.'

Suddenly, he had an idea, but there was no time, nor any opportunity, to *discuss* it with anyone else. Guy Kyme, Father Kendall and brother-in-law Tom Foster were all elsewhere, anyway. So he just took a deep breath, and trusted his own judgement. His 'inner' voice was being quite insistent '...*just DO IT, Nicholas...*!'

His 'outer' voice was penetrating, and insistent too, even over the multitude of conversations, going on all at once between members of the various groups Sir Edward Dymocke had referred to as the groups who should provide hostages. Captain Cobbler, now climbed and stood on a nearby bench, and was speaking again...

"Sir Edward... I have no desire to seem arrogant..."

In fact, he was relying on the expectation that Sir Edward would think *that very thing*, and be influenced in his thinking, by such an expectation!

"But I believe you do not *need* ten hostages for your purposes. You just need ONE hostage, recognisable by all the men here and this will guarantee everything you want, about the host being peaceful, and the men going about their business. That would be me!"

His theatrical declamation had been perfect. By the time he had reached the end of this sentence, there was virtual silence in the field. Indeed, he had to stop himself smiling as he thought back to another world, years before, when he was guest of the Van Planck family... The silence was just like that which sometimes accompanied the 'family saying' that "*Joop has spoken!*" Only, this time, it was *Nicholas* who had 'spoken', and pretty well everyone was now looking at him!

He caught the eye of Sir William Leach and, with the most minute of movements, shook his head to indicate that ... '*...once I have gone you need to be talking, not about peace, but about ACTION!*' But he was not at all certain Leach had received the message he was sending?

Nicholas was, indeed, hoping that by offering himself in this way, he would act as a unifying element for the host, and give them the opportunity to "...live on to fight another day!"

The Sheriff of Lincolnshire looked somewhat surprised at this strange intervention by the man in the multi-coloured Coat of Motley. And he gave every indication of mulling the idea in his mind, but the fact was that he had decided straight away to accept this offer by Captain Cobbler, because he was exactly the sort of hostage who would be valued by the host. He believed they would be influenced by their 'hero' being held, in order to guarantee appropriate behaviour.

So much so that, without any further discussion with his colleagues, he made to speak for them all. In fact, Sir William Ayscough would have advised him against accepting the Cobbler's proposal, on the basis that he was looking forward to a "...bit of a bloodbath ...to teach these peasants a lesson!" He probably would not have admitted as much, of course!

But the sheriff accepted Captain Cobbler's idea, in totality.

The giant of Louth, Great James, self-appointed protector of his Captain Cobbler, was horrified at Nicholas' proposal and took no time in saying so, directly to Nicholas' face. Nicholas took his friend by both upper arms, not the easiest of tasks given James's great height, and dug his thumbs hard into the man's bulging muscles to get his attention.

"James... JAMES! I will brook no argument. I am doing this for the good of all, and I am doing it knowing I am at risk... But the truth is that we are ALL at risk, if I *do not* do it. If I am to die, I would not wish to die knowing I could have done something to protect all my friends, but I did not do that thing! And we all may yet 'live to fight another day', if I *do* do this!"

There was no more time for a detailed argument with his protector, and it seemed that Sir William Leach had, perhaps, seen Nicholas' tiny shake of his head and was duly ready to act.

"What do say you, Sheriff Dymocke? Our Grand Captain, Captain Cobbler here, has made you an offer which should be impossible to refuse..."

The sheriff chose to interrupt Leach in mid-sentence.

"Indeed, Sir William, I was just about to accept Cobbler Melton's offer of acting as surety for the host you have gathered here. We expect to see the host broken-up, and its constituent parts sent back to where they belong! We know it was mooted that the men, forming the host, should be paid twelve pence per day, as from this Monday last. Since it is now Tuesday, and some organisation is required to disband the host safely, and surely, we propose that the gentlemen, here arrayed, will cover the cost of paying all the men present from Monday, until the end of tomorrow – Wednesday – in order to ensure a quick disbandment."

Judging by the look Sir Robert Tyrwhitt gave his colleague at this point, it was clear that Sheriff Dymocke had just made an *on-the-spot* decision which they had *not* had chance to discuss beforehand! And as one of the richer gentlemen present, he knew that a lot of those 'twelve pence' promises would come from *his* pocket! He judged, however, that it was something he should not challenge immediately. He might be able to twist Dymocke's arm, for the sheriff to accept a larger-than-normal share, since it had been Dymocke's own idea, but that argument would best be had behind closed doors!

There was no doubting that the mood of the men in the field had changed, and was continuing to change, as one man explained what had gone on to his neighbour – who then explained it to *his* neighbour, and so on, out towards the hedgerows, and into the other fields. Even so, the exchanges of information about hostages, and money, had been too quick for many present to grasp. It would take a great deal of further conversation, until everyone actually understood what had transpired here in the last few minutes.

So, Nicholas sent for his horse and said farewell, for the moment, to his many friends from Louth, and his new friends from Horncastle, and Alford, and Bardney, and Boston, and Grimsby... and, indeed, from Irnham, in South Kesteven wapentake. There were still, however, many men on the outer fringes of the fields, who were uncertain as to what was happening, and *'why is Captain Cobbler getting on his horse, and leaving with the armoured gentlemen...who seem to be threatening us all with King Henry's condign punishment?'*

In fact, Sir John Thimbleby, from Irnham, was the last to speak to Nicholas as he prepared to leave the field.

"I have known you for but a few hours Captain Cobbler, but it seems to me that your actions today have been very selfless, and courageous. I hope they are rewarded with a successful outcome now, but if not, I trust they will be rewarded in heaven. Godspeed, my new friend, and we will see you soon, I hope!"

Sadly, Thimbleby's hopes were not to be rewarded. Not in this world anyway.

ଔ ଔ ଔ ଔ ଔ

Condign Punishment...
10am: 29th March 1537

The last few yards of the journey to Tyburn, passed in a blur for Nicholas. Many faces turned, from amongst the crowd, to stare at the spectacle of 'rebels', about to suffer the condign punishment, that had been meted out to so many, over the last few months. These were the last of the rebels to be sent to their maker, having been incarcerated, and questioned, over the very cold winter. It was still cold today, though the sun was shining, and most of the prisoners were shivering in their white smocks.

They reached the square, which looked familiar to Nicholas but slightly odd at the same time. Then he realised he had been here before, in his teen years, when he was an apprenticed shoemaker in London. Indeed he had witnessed some executions himself, and the reason the place looked slightly odd, was that he was, of course, seeing it from a different perspective.

He and his fellow prisoners were now the centre of attention, whereas before he had been standing some way off, looking over the heads of others (strictly speaking it was probably *between* the heads of others). His, then, new acquaintance, Tom Butcher (a butcher's apprentice – "*Butcher by name, butcher by trade!*") had given his running commentary, from the raised platform of a stone plinth, that had probably once held a statue. It had, long since, been broken, and moved. But it was Tom Butcher who had been looking *over* the heads of people in front.

Nicholas now felt very concerned that he would end up embarrassing himself, in front of these baying crowds, a feeling he had not anticipated, but one which came to him, as he recalled the events of that day, many years ago.

He was in the first of the two carts being used, so would probably end up in the first group to be despatched. The guards with them started prodding at their prisoners, to get them to move off the carts. There were twelve prisoners, and only six gibbets, so there was certainly going to be a double show for the excited crowds of hags to gawk over.

Nicholas was the third man to be shuffled up onto the platform, and he was suddenly grabbed by both arms, by the man wearing the mask of the executioner. He was surprised when the man behind the mask addressed him by name.

"Cap'n Cobbler – Nicholas – I only have time to say this once, and quickly at that. 'Tis Tom Butcher, from that day, twenty years ago, when you saw your first execution."

"You was right about the acting then – and I was wrong! But I have since been granted my wish, and have been executioner here, on and off, for the last six years. It sometimes happens, as you guessed, that we do a bit of 'business', and theatre, for a fee, to ensure a quick ending for prisoners. But this time, it is personal, just for you!"

"Two reasons... I knew you years ago, and liked you from the first; lily-livered though you seem'd to be. Second reason is, that I followed what you was doing, in Lincolnshire, as Captain Cobbler. And I reckon you was right!"

"But I can never *say* so, apart from today, direct to you. Your ending will be quick as I can make it. Hold tight."

And with that, the strong hands of this butcher, with spatulate fingers from handling large slabs of meat for many years, took him firmly by the upper arms, and lifted him to a stool just six inches, or so, higher than the others around him. It took Nicholas a couple of minutes to grasp the words he had just heard through the executioner's mask; and, all the time, he was trying to concentrate on the prayers he was saying to his God.

He had said the Lord's Prayer several times, on the cart journey from the tower, and now said it again aloud, as the executioner's helper placed a rough rope over his head, and began to tighten it.

His old acquaintance, Tom, now to be his executioner, pushed his helper out of the way at this point, just as there was a scuffling in the nearby crowd. Nicholas could not make out what was being said or shouted, there was just too much noise going on. But suddenly Tom Butcher was by his side, and squeezed his arm just once.

He barely had time to utter his last heartfelt prayer to his Lord Jesus...

"Oh my good Lord Jesus, thank you for my life, and my boon

companion, and everlasting love, Eliza Jane, and our two fine sons, Robert and Arthur. May their lives be long and full of love..."

...when suddenly there was only air beneath his feet, and he heard the last sound he would ever hear, as one of the bones in his neck cracked...

He had been feeling the cold of late March, but now he could feel the warmth of the sun overhead, light suffusing his senses. And he could feel, rather than see, his mother's presence, and that of her father, his grandfather, whom he had not seen for many years. He had always been a lovely man, gentle, good humoured, always smiling...

Not far away, he could make out the voices of his father, and his older brother Robert talking quietly in the background. And old Johann Kirkkgarde seemed to be there too ...holding out a brand-new Coat of Motley, to replace the one he had had taken from him, in the Tower. Perhaps it wasn't going to be such a bad day after all?

The end...

Epilogue

Robert Melton, Captain Cobbler's eldest son, had reached Louth, just as the funeral of Jack Long was breaking up, and the family members and the few other mourners present, were making their way over to the rectory. Father Thomas Kendall's housekeeper had arranged a small cold-collation for them there, and a little fruit wine, before they all dispersed, homeward bound.

The priest, Father Kendall, was talking to the choir men, Robert's uncle; Tom Foster and Tom's father – Robert's grandfather – Thomas senior. So, although Robert really wanted to rush straight home and talk to his mother first, he decided it would be worth stopping and being able to talk to these three all together, rather than searching them all out separately later on!

In fact, it did not take very long to bring them up to date, and tell them about the dramatic entry of the gentry into the camp, and Dymocke's dire message of retribution, about the puissant force the Duke of Suffolk was bringing up from the south. The tale told, Robert now felt better for having listened to his father carefully, and for having carried out his wishes.

Kendall, in particular, strongly supported Robert's action, and said that he, and the Fosters, would ensure the word got around to those who needed to be told. There had been discussions of "...*what would happen if everything went wrong...?*"

These discussions had all been brief, in the light of the optimism which had accompanied all the earlier planning. Nevertheless, certain families, where the risk had been recognised as real, had all made some provision for '*disappearing*' for a while, if necessary, to relatives, or friends, in distant places, which the world may pass by without noticing.

So Robert felt relieved when Father Kendall sent him packing to his mother's house, and felt he had done his duty now, and all that remained was for them to look out for themselves. Eliza Jane gave her oldest son a big hug when he rushed through the door, and did her level best to keep her tears from flowing, though she felt a sense of deep loss, as if Nicholas was already dead and buried.

Although they had referred to the possibility of failure, just a few evenings previously, she had always felt such confidence in her husband, and his decisions, that she had not truly entertained the *actual* possibility of failure. And even now, she saw the next planned move as a precautionary one, and fully expected to be laughing about it with Nicholas, in just a few short days' time. Well, maybe not quite 'fully' expecting...?

She already had a bag, and two saddle bags, packed with as many essentials as they could carry between them. The lads were now old enough to take considerable burdens without complaint. She had packed all their money, as well (not a great lot, when it came down to it!) and a bag of Nicholas' best tools, as well as several items of value, in case they had to sell things, to get by, in the short term.

They had already spoken with Eliza Jane's cousin, in Barton-on-the-Humber, to establish the *principle* of them being able to stay indefinitely, should the need arise. So, really, the only issue of importance was how quickly they could get from Louth to the North Lincolnshire coast, and to the safety of her cousin's house, now that they had decided it must be done.

As a further precaution, none of the families who had been contemplating the '*escape to the wilds*' as an option, had ever told the other families where they had arranged to go. Eliza Jane had thought that this precaution was, perhaps, a bit extreme, but Nicholas had been adamant that, once disappeared, everyone could stay disappeared, without having to worry about being chased into their hiding-holes.

Now the moment had come, she saw the merit in such secrecy. So, only Tom Foster, Eliza Jane's brother, and their father, Tom Foster senior, in Louth, knew in detail where, exactly, she and her sons would be going. Nicholas did too, of course, and so she was hoping, desperately, that it was him she would see very soon, walking boldly through the door of her cousin's small cottage, telling her everything was well.

Normally, if they were going to her cousin's on the coast, they would have set out quite early in the morning, because it was a little way over twenty miles, altogether. But that was around the distance Robert had already travelled since mid-morning near Lincoln, so by the time Eliza Jane had got the message, and they had scurried around, finally getting things together, it was not going to be long before the light would fade.

But Nicholas had emphasised how important it would be to move "...*straight away*..." in this eventuality, so move they would!

Robert had fetched their second horse from the stables, just past 'Old Ma Foster's' big chicken-coop across the road. Quite why they still called it that, Eliza Jane could not think, because her grandmother had been dead these many years, and they had kept almost no chickens for a long time. But once something has a name like that, it tends to stick, she supposed? It was now dilapidated and full of rammel and hardly warranted the term 'chicken coop' since it would no longer have imprisoned a single hen – too many holes for chickens to get out, or foxes to get in!

Frankly, the old horse was in barely better shape than the chicken coop – she was a very ancient mare they occasionally used as a pack animal, if they had deliveries to make around the villages. '*Nicholas, of course, had their best mare with him in Lincoln...*' Eliza Jane sighed a huge sigh, as this thought crossed her mind, unbidden.

She was still thinking about this little conundrum, about the name of the tumble-down shed, when they were already two miles away, up the Grimsby road. She guessed this was partly to keep her mind off the real *reason* for the journey. For this family visit, they would normally go on the Grimsby road, nearly all the way into Grimsby, before turning off to Barton. But in their planning, they had thought it might be better to take the *lesser* route this time, taking the left fork in Ludborough.

It was much less-well-travelled than the Grimsby road, so the actual roadway was less-well-cared-for, but with fewer people on it too, of course. Indeed, there was virtually no-one, at this time of day, at this time of year!

Eliza Jane had insisted that Robert should continue to ride his new pony, while Arthur rode the old pack-horse, and she walked alongside the pair of them. Robert had grumbled in a 'manly' way, of course, but his mother had asserted her motherly authority, and she got her way, at least for the first part of the trip.

It was virtually dark by the time they reached Ludborough, but rather than stop in, or near, the village, they carried on, planning to camp in a convenient copse, some way past the village and set out again at first light. They had a goodly piece of sailcloth with them, to keep the rain off, if it should start. In fact, it seemed as if the rain might hold off this night. Also, they had brought water, and food, with them so they were self-reliant, at least, needing to bother no-one.

When they did stop, Robert saw to the horses, first, and made sure they were well-tied-up to a sturdy tree. His mother, and brother, set up the sail-cloth encampment, and broke out their supplies, for a comforting brief snap, before attempting to sleep for a few hours. As it was, Robert went out like a light – he was very tired physically – and his younger brother, Arthur, after a little tossing and turning, followed him into the *Land of Nod*, quite soon thereafter.

But sleep, of any kind, eluded Eliza Jane, and by morning she looked and felt like a rag-doll, and her anguish was tangible. She had almost dozed a couple of times, but the rustle of a small night creature, or the hoot of an owl, would bring her fully awake again. Her mind was full of nightmarish thoughts, about the welfare of her lovely husband and – apart from the fact that she was actually awake – she would have called them 'a nightmare' anyway!

After a quick gulp of water, and a little dry meat, to break their fast, they got off to a very early start; so much so, that they were at her cousin's by mid-morning anyway. And it turned out that it was a good job they had stopped when they did, to camp. Only a mile or so further on, they came across a stream, that would normally be quite easy to step over on the stepping stones, but the recent rains had swollen the stream, and the land thereabouts was soaked through.

It would have been a dangerous crossing in the dark and, even in the early morning light, they managed to get extremely wet, before getting back onto a sound, dry, pathway on the other side. Eliza Jane remembered, with a shudder, the tale Nicholas had told her, about his fateful journey down to London, when he was only sixteen and the struggles he had endured, to cope with a man and a horse, each with a badly broken leg!

Eliza Jane's cousin, John, welcomed them warmly, but with great concern, for he well-knew that the only reason they could be there was that things had gone badly wrong in Lincoln. They had managed to get a message to him, the week previously, explaining *why* he might be getting sudden visitors, and why they may have to be there for the long term.

He showed them to the room they would be calling theirs, and put more logs on the fire, so they could dry out. And he gave them all a tot of spirit (that he made at home on a regular basis) to "...*set their minds in better order!..*"

Actually, it did have that effect on Eliza Jane, but it just made Arthur choke and gasp. It seemed to grow on him, however, over the years, as the family became part of the little village of Barton on Humber, making a new home, and mourning the loss of a good husband and father.

The first few months were both the best, and the worst. In one way, the best for Eliza Jane, since she had finally heard, properly, that Nicholas was still alive, and whilst still alive, there was also hope. She certainly hoped he was staying optimistic!

But it was also the worst, because she did not know what condition his life took and the winter was terrible, so she knew not to expect him to be comfortable, and her imaginings were dire, though perhaps no more dire than his *actual* life!

They had to earn their keep too, of course, since her cousin was not a man of great means. Robert and Arthur found various kinds of manual work, through the winter months, which brought them in a few pennies, and Eliza Jane took in washing, which also contributed to the household income. The quality of the food they could buy, however, took quite a sharp drop from their usual eating habits. This bore down on the boys, since they were still growing madly, and they really needed feeding properly.

They heard all about the development of the subsequent Pilgrimage of Grace, too, in Yorkshire and further north, since Robert Aske, who became its Grand Captain, called in the village several times on his way across the great Humber by ferry. So, news was always quite up-to-date from at least someone in the village. Robert met Aske a couple of times, too, and thought of him as a bit of a pirate since he wore an eye-patch, having lost the sight of one eye in a childhood accident.

Robert was always very careful never to mention his surname of Melton, though, in case their identity, as the family of Captain Cobbler, was discovered. But he did talk to his mother about joining the Pilgrimage of Grace, as a way to rescue his father from prison.

It was the only time they had a serious argument, but his mother absolutely forbade him to have anything to do with it. Absolutely!

For his part, he thought it might lead to getting his father free, and he pushed the idea as far as he dare, but, in the end, his mother's wrath was enough to keep him sullenly at home. Sometime in the first week of April 1537, the news reached their little village, that Captain Cobbler had been *hung, drawn and quartered* in London, along with Father Thomas Kendall, Lord Hussey, and several others. Although they always expected this outcome, of course, once he had been captured, and sent down to the tower, there had always been *just a possibility* of reprieve.

Eliza Jane cried and sobbed inconsolably, railing at God's cruelty. Her sons, Robert and Arthur, felt helpless in the face of such deep grief, not knowing quite how to salve their mother's pain.

Two days later, Joseph Waterland, a distant cousin of Nicholas, but always a close and good family friend, visited them in their hiding place. It was his second visit. It had been on the basis of his earlier visit, of course, having been told of their whereabouts by Tom Foster, that he had been able to tell Nicholas of their safety, to set *his* mind at rest, in the tower.

Now, he was able to set *their* minds at rest, that Nicholas had known of their safety, and had made his peace with God before the fateful day. He was also able to tell them about the executioner's 'kindness', in giving Nicholas a quick death, rather than the gory, long-drawn-out affair they may have just heard of in the street.

Eliza Jane was an incredibly strong woman, but it took all of her extensive will-power, not to fall apart at all of this overwhelming news. Really the only thing that stopped her breaking down completely was the need to care for her younger son, Arthur. He had been very quiet, and withdrawn, since they had been in Barton-on-the-Humber, and she was extremely worried about him.

Robert had been much the stronger, in bearing the heavy news of his father's incarceration and death, but on the day Joseph Waterland came to see them, it had been Robert who had burst into floods of tears, and hugged his mother, as if his life depended upon it. Arthur was just very pale, and very quiet, keeping it all in his head. Not even a quiet sob – at least not just then.

Eliza Jane's cousin, John, had two cats, to keep control of the level of mice in the house, and it happened that a few weeks later, one of the cats had three kittens, the unlooked-for present of a visiting tom-cat. Arthur had befriended the cats in his quietude, and when one of the three little kittens fell under the wheel of John's pony-trap and was crushed, Arthur was devastated, and cried, and cried, all day.

Gradually, as time passed by, and the horror of it all faded a little, the boys began to take part in village life, perhaps helping to serve drinks at one of the church ales, or helping with the harvesting, as everybody did. And it was on May Day, a year later, just after his seventeenth birthday, that Robert rather shyly announced to his mother that he had taken "...something of a fancy..." for a girl called Mary, the butcher's daughter; and "...might he bring her home to tea on Sunday next?"

For the rest of her life, Eliza Jane told all and sundry that May 1st 1538 was the first time she had smiled in over eighteen months.

രുരുരുരുരു

About the Author – Keith Melton

Keith Melton was born and brought up in North Hykeham, near Lincoln, attending school at the North Kesteven Grammar School. He went on to university at UMIST in Manchester, reading mathematics and management sciences. On leaving university he became a media and marketing analyst for Lintas, a multinational advertising agency then owned by Unilever. He left there to undertake a research degree in marketing back at UMIST and, from there, went on to lecture in International Marketing at Nottingham Trent University.

Keith set up and became founding Director of the Institute for Sustainable Development in Business at Nottingham Trent in 1998, advising businesses on environmental issues. He retired in 2006 and has since been researching and writing this novel about his namesake, Nicholas Melton.

Although he has yet to uncover definite genealogical links to Nicholas Melton – who became famous around the country in 1536 as 'Captain Cobbler' – the author, Keith Melton, has 'adopted' him into his family, bringing insights as to how Captain Cobbler may have behaved and felt around five hundred years ago. So far, Keith's genealogy takes the Melton line back to about the 1680's to Barton-on-Humber in north Lincolnshire.

Keith and his brothers, their father, grandfather and great-grandfather Melton have all played a part as business and community leaders in different ways, both in Lincolnshire and more widely. A great-uncle played both the organ in chapel and the piano for the silent movies in Lincoln in the early part of the last century!

So Captain Cobbler's community links would have run deep and his commitment to the task he faced would be strong, intelligent and charismatic.

Keith married his Lincolnshire-born teen sweetheart, Tricia in 1971. Tricia died in 2008 and, the following year, Keith met his Brazilian-born lady, Fatima, who had also been widowed in 2008. They married in July 2011 and they now live partly in Brazil and partly in England.

Read more about the book and its author on Captain Cobbler's website:-

http://www.captaincobbler.com

Lightning Source UK Ltd.
Milton Keynes UK
UKOW05f1127050913

9 781475 9977